Other Tor books by John Barnes

Orbital Resonance
A Million Open Doors

MOTHER OF
STORMS

MOTHER OF
STORMS

JOHN BARNES

A TOM DOHERTY ASSOCIATES BOOK
NEW YORK

MOTHER OF STORMS

Copyright © 1994 by John Barnes

This book is printed on acid-free paper.

A Tor Book
Published by Tom Doherty Associates, Inc.
175 Fifth Avenue
New York, N.Y. 10010

Tor® is a registered trademark of Tom Doherty Associates, Inc.

Design by Lynn Newmark

Library of Congress Cataloging-in-Publication Data
Barnes, John.
    Mother of storms / John Barnes.
        p.   cm.
    "A Tom Doherty Associates book."
    ISBN 0-312-85560-5
    1. Hurricanes—Fiction.   I. Title.
PS3552.A677M67   1994
813'.54—dc20
                                                    94-607
                                                    CIP

First Edition: July 1994

Printed in the United States of America

0 9 8 7 6 5 4 3 2 1

For Kara Dalkey
—who else?

ACKNOWLEDGMENTS

Every book accumulates some debts, but this one accumulated some special and important ones:

Dr. Stephen Gillett, who taught me what a clathrate was and kept me poking at the science until he said, "Good enough to fool me, anyway."

Daniel D. Worley and David Pan, for information about the Pacific and a window into an all-but-forgotten corner of the world.

Ashley Grayson, my agent, and Patrick Nielsen Hayden, my editor, for frequently telling me I really was going to finish. And then for making me go through it all one more time so that I was *really* finished.

Melissa Gibson, who not only typed, but read, and not only read, but occasionally pointed out places where it was turning into nonsense.

And, during the very last week of getting the book done, two people who restored my ability to concentrate. I expect to see them at the top of the do-it-yourself field someday soon—Anna Rosenstein, author of *How to Bob for Cats Through Your Kitchen Floor*, and David Wintersteen, author of *Special Weapons and Tactics in Covert Home Repair*.

ONE

ATTRACTOR

THIS IS THE good part. Hassan Sulari loves this one. When the magnetic catapult on the mothership throws his little spaceplane forward and he kicks in his scramjets, somewhere over Afghanistan, he'll sail up and away into a high suborbital trajectory over the pole. Hassan has never gotten authorized for orbit, but this is pretty close.

It's his first real mission. He's carrying four cram bombs—"Compressing Radiation Antimatter" is what it stands for, and when they talk to the media they are supposed to stress that they are "mass-to-energy, not really nuclear" weapons, because for all practical purposes they are baby nukes and that's bad PR.

The catch is that damned jack in the back of his head. He accepted a lot of extra money from Passionet to have it installed and to fly with it, it's going to make him rich—and in UNSOO that's not common—but there is still the nagging feeling of showing off. After all, he's a pilot, not an actor.

"We're getting ready to go plugged with you," the voice from Passionet says. "If you've got any embarrassing thoughts to get out of the way, think them now."

"None I know of. I'm at orbital injection minus four minutes." Hassan does his best to sound bored.

"We know—timing's perfect. Give our folks a ride."

Just as they click off and it goes live, he does have the strange thought that there really don't have to be human crews for UN Space Ops like this—a machine could do a prohibited-weapons interdict just as well. He finds himself wondering why he does this—no, to his shame, why he is fearing doing it.

That makes his stomach knot hard during the last instants of countdown. Then he hears the word "inject" and the mothership catapult flings him forward over the nose of the big airplane; watching his stability gauge, he sees it's all go, waits a few more seconds till the navigation computer has a fix, and then flips the scramjet lever.

He is slammed into his seat again, and the brown-and-white mountains of early spring morning fall away below him. The vibration is heavy, and the pressure is intense; he sees the West Siberian plain open out beneath him, wrapped in its canopy of blue air. He is as high up as weather satellites go. His heart is pounding and despite the military reason for the mission he is mentally lost in the scenery.

By the time the scramjets cut out, there is polar ice on the horizon, and his hands automatically begin their ritual of arming and readying the shots.

He arcs higher still, coasting upward on inertia, and now the Earth begins to return toward him. He is weightless—not because there is no gravity but because he is moving with it—and he has an intense recollection of his childhood fantasies about space travel. He hopes they won't mind having that in the wedge they are recording—

Over the pole now, falling nose-down across the ice cap ninety miles below, and the countdown begins; his weapons lock on target and he need only pull the trigger on cue to turn over control to the missiles themselves. He receives the go-ahead and initiates.

There are four hard shoves on the little spaceplane, and he sees his missiles falling away like sparklers thrown down a dark canyon. He will miss their impact off the North Slope, but the pleasure of launching them was exquisite.

And from the jack in his head, he is informed that 750 million people shared the experience.

There's a cherry-red glow around the bottom of the spaceplane, and weight begins to return as the plane once again resists gravity rather than rides with it. It was more like a training flight than he expected. He's never seen Pacificanada, but he's told the new, struggling nation loves UN Peace-keeping Forces credits, and he will have plenty.

As he falls back toward home, life seems pretty sweet when it can include things like this.

Randy Householder is cruising I-80 out of Sacramento in a car so old it had to be retrofitted to drive itself. It runs and it's what he can afford, and he doesn't worry about it.

But he's trying to get onto the net, and that is unbelievably slow and frustrating tonight. After fourteen years he's learned that this always means the same thing—some damn crisis tying things up. Back in '16 when the Flash happened, it was six days before he could get on and get his messages. At least this time he can get them, but they're slow.

It's been a long time since he's been impressed by getting a hundred messages. That's normal traffic. About half of it will be some small-town police chiefs, sheriffs, magistrates, proconsuls, ombudsmen, whatever they call them around the world, mostly letting him know they're still looking for evidence and that nothing has come in. A few will be new ones taking over, some will be old ones leaving and letting him know their successors may not be helpful.

The other half will be people like Randy, mostly just passing along support notes. There are seven others Randy hears from most nights—all the ones who had children killed in a way similar to what happened to

Kimbie Dee. They're always there. Sometimes he talks with them live; they've traded pictures and such over the years.

There will almost always be at least one reporter. Randy does not talk to reporters anymore. The damn media take up too much of the bandwidth on the net—like they're doing tonight. And they're no help.

Last time he talked to one, she kept wanting to know about how he lives his life. Shit, Randy told her, he didn't have a life. He stopped having a life fourteen years ago when the cops came to the door of his mobile home, and made him and his then-wife Terry sit down, and told them that Kimbie Dee had been murdered, and it looked like a sex murder. Life stopped when they told him they had the man who did it and no clues about motive, but they knew damned well from the jack driven into her skull *why* she'd been murdered and raped—Christ, Christ, the coroner had said she'd been jammed with a mop handle hard enough to rupture her intestines, and then raped while she hemorrhaged, but she'd still been conscious when the man hanged her.

Randy's clutching at his keyboard with his fists and that does no good. *Stay relaxed, stay calm, keep hunting. It's going to be a long one, you've always known that.*

Kimbie Dee was killed to make an XV wedge. There's a big underground market in those things. Once or twice a year, someone is arrested for selling the one that features her death. Sometimes they arrest the guy he bought it from; sometimes Randy is able to hack the files about one of the suspects, and find more people who might be involved. Now and then—the last time was three years ago—something cross-correlates, and Randy's datarodents bring him back one more piece of information, move him another step up one of the distribution chains.

When that happens, there's an arrest. Randy gets reward money. Like he cares crap about that. But Randy and the world's cops get one step closer to the guy who paid for it; somewhere out there, some big shot, someone with more income to spend on his "fun" than Randy ever made in any year of his life, is still at large and unsuspected. He's the man who handed all that money to a man and said, "Here's what I want you to do to a pert little blonde girl."

The man who killed and raped Kimbie Dee Householder has been in his grave for eleven years. Randy was there to see him strapped into the chair. The man who hired it done is still out there.

Randy's going to see him dead, too.

Just as soon as all this damned noise gets off the net. He checks the text news channels and finds it's some stupid thing about Alaska, Siberia, the UN, and atomic bombs. He vaguely remembers Alaska got independent right after the Flash—the UN made the U.S. give it up, or something.

President Hardshaw is going to talk about it to the media later; Randy will tune in to that on the TV—he votes for her every time and he never misses one of her speeches. She was Idaho Attorney General back a little before the murder. If she'd still been in office—she and the guy they now call the President's Shadow, Harris Diem—instead of the liberal "concerned" homo Democrat that was—they'd've tracked down the bastards and nailed them while the crime was still hot. Randy's sure of it. So he doesn't need to think about World War Three; he can let the President sort that one out. Everyone has their little job.

Back to Randy's. Just keep plugging away. "We'll get him yet, Kimbie Dee, even if the whole world has to come apart," he says. He tells the car to head east, toward Salt Lake City, because the satellite connections will be better and cheaper. Then he climbs into the back, opens the fridge, gets himself a beer, calls up the file of messages, and starts sorting through his mail.

Some perverse spirit, somewhere out there, has decided that this is the big year for Ed Porter to work with amateurs. Probably some woman, some upper-level bitch who doesn't like the way the wedges he edits sell like crazy, or the shows he assembles dominate the net. But he's the main reason Passionet is XV of choice for female experiencers, and third among males. A *romance* net, for god's sake, at the top even among men, and Porter is one of three senior editors there, and they still persecute him. They still give him shit assignments like this.

It's gotta be some woman.

Anyway, at least he's away from Boring Bill and Cotton-Brains Candy, as he calls them. A whole two-day vacation from "Dream Honeymoon" to work on this breaking story.

But this guy Hassan, this pilot, is a *stiff*. He's pure military. Gets excited but holds it in. His pulse rises but not enough. What comes in through the jack is a smart guy doing a job he's good at. Even when he fires the bombs off, there's just a minor thrill. And of course the silly bombs are just going through the ice, into the mud of the North Slope; through Hassan's eyes, all Porter sees is some bright sparks plunging down toward the night-darkened ice. Nobody down there to burn, or to scream with pain; nobody up here in Hassan's brain to exult in the destruction or laugh maniacally at people dying; no agony, no passion, nothing. Nothing to experience but the smooth working of a machine, according to a perfect plan.

As XV goes, it's a zero.

* * *

Jesse knows Naomi wants him to be more interested, and she *is* right, and it *is* a big deal—if he wants any confirmation he only has to listen to the hundreds of students milling around in the PolAc Room. Even for U of the Az, this is a big crowd, but then you don't get to see a UN Space Ops bombing raid in real time every day.

Of course instead of the old-fashioned television, he could just as easily be back at the dorm—Passionet has wired one of the pilots—and be there for all practical purposes. Maybe catch it on replay? No, Naomi calls that warporn.

What he'd really rather be is home with Naomi, no TV, no XV, no clothes—he shoves the thought back, hard. If he even hints in the next hour it'll be another fight with Naomi, and he doesn't want that, not right now. It's been a week since they've more than kissed.

On the other hand Molecular Design Economics, which he's got to pass with a Significant Achievement or better, this term, if he's going to stay on track for his Realization Engineering degree, is at eight A.M., it's already almost ten, and though his homework is done he hasn't reviewed it or read the supplementary chapter.

Still, Naomi's back—tiny and soft to the touch but with rock-hard muscle underneath—is against his chest, and therefore the nicest tight round butt in the Az is a quarter inch from him.

There's a lot of noise and Jesse looks up to see what it is. Something big, anyway, a lot of flickery movement on the screen. Everyone is arguing about that; nowadays you don't see an image flicker like that, not with packetized digital signal.

It's not coming in well, he realizes, because UN Information Control is trying to slap their logo across it and it's not quite working. People are booing and hissing, some of them at the UNIC insignia, some at what's behind it, some on general principles.

Like every college assembly room built in the last century, this place wasn't made to meet in, it was made to be easy to clean, so it has plenty of hard, flat surfaces and the whole thing is echoing and ringing.

Call it midnight before they get home, and she'll want to talk for an hour . . . there goes the homework even if there's no sex. And getting a Significant Achievement is no piece of cake; sure, it's the lowest of the academic grades, but it's still light-years in effort beyond Probable Comprehension, Positive Attitude, or Open Mind—and employers nowadays really do read your transcript. It's got to be Significant Achievement, Demonstrated Competence, or Mastery . . . and he thinks by now the top two are out of his reach.

Absent Naomi in his life, Mastery would be in his reach in most subjects. There's a lot of easier ass in the world—

He has no idea why he can't concentrate these days. He forces his eyes back to the screen, notices a dark bar across it, realizes what he's looking at is Naomi's hand, palm down, in the gesture for "quiet" that they used in grade school when you were a kid.

The room is so noisy, between boos, catcalls, people loudly explaining things to each other, and other people shushing and shouting "Quiet, please, quiet!," all echoing off all those hard, flat surfaces, that he can't think anyway. He wants to just turn into a caveman, drag Naomi out of here bodily, heave her into his old Lectrajeep, drive out to someplace in the desert, and just stare up at the stars until the sun comes up.

After he has hours of intense sex with a completely willing Naomi.

The image on the screen, when he can see it through all the waving hands and fingers, is now stuttering rapidly, because the source of the signal is switching protocols and channels a few times per second, and the UNIC tracker-suppressor software is right on its tail. Jesse knows that because for Realization Engineering you have to take a ton of cryptography (the important part of RE from the standpoint of *los corporados* is keeping everything you do from instantly being run through an AIRE—an Artificially Intelligent Reverse Engineer—and winding up in public domain). God, engineering is more interesting and fun than politics.

What would Naomi think of the way he's thinking? It's bad enough he can only seem to think of her as a sex bunny, but when he gets his mind out of his crotch all he can think about is the technical stuff, not about the political side. Why won't his mind stay on track?

Naomi leans back farther, that angel's butt brushes the front of his pants, and at least he isn't thinking of homework anymore. For just a second the screen swims clear, and it looks like the Siberian comware is beating UNIC's hounds—you can hear the nationals in the room cheering, the uniters booing, and it occurs to him it's not that different from a football game—

Back to the stutter. Naomi is still making the "quiet" signal. The crowd is getting rowdier, not quieter, so she's shrinking back against him. Tentatively he lets his hand rest on her waist, hoping it will read as support and not as what she calls "groping me all the time," and he's rewarded with a quick flash of a smile from under the thick mop of walnut-stain-colored hair. Her big wet brown eyes and high freckled cheekbones make his heart skip again; it feels like a love simulator on XV, and most of the complaints he's been working up for the night's fight go away.

He lets his arm slide a little farther into her back, and, amazingly, she leans into it and brushes his face with that marvelous hair, her warm sweet breath on his neck. "This is so stupid, Jesse. Half of these people don't want to hear Abdulkashim and are cheering for UNIC, half of them do and are cheering for Abdulkashim. How are they going to get a sense of the meeting if they don't at least start *trying* to want the same things?"

"They didn't come here for a meeting," Jesse reminds her. "They're here to catch the news or see the bombs go off or because they saw the crowd on their way back from dinner, or something."

She gives him the little smile that always reminds him how unplugged he was before she got into his life. "But what matters is they're here and they're talking to each other. So it's a meeting—but no one is seeking unity."

The babble of voices in the PolAc Room rises rapidly and then dies, leaving only a faint ring in the air; it looks like the sense of the meeting is that they want to hear whatever is on. It looks like UNIC has given up. There's a clear image of Abdulkashim, and the flattened translator voice comes through: "—completely unprovoked and utterly outside the Charter or the Second Covenant to issue such threats to a free, sovereign, and independent state, let alone to claim to be carrying out such actions against military installations whose existence is wholly unproven—"

The image flickers and vanishes. Pandemonium breaks loose. Jesse hears the telltale thud of punches or kicks connecting.

There are not very many pro-Siberian students here at U of the Az, since the Siberian quarrel is with the Alaska Free State and a lot of people still feel sentimental about the fact that the Ak was once an American state.

The big quarrel is between the uniters, who back whatever the SecGen does, and the nationalists, who wish the United States had gotten into it directly—the sort of people who complain about "President Grandma," as if Hardshaw could fart into her own sofa cushions without UN permission these days.

Then there's an isolated handful booing because they oppose all censorship, there's six or seven people who really are pro-Siberian, and probably a few guys who just showed up for a fight. In Jesse's small-town redneck opinion, it is about to get rough around here, and he'd just as soon Naomi was out of it before anyone sets in to real asskicking.

He also knows perfectly well that she won't believe him or take any steps for self-protection. She's a second-generation Deeper, and "we aren't raised that way, we're gentle in our anger," she has said to him many times. He's never had the nerve to say that *he* wasn't raised *that* way and knows what a fist or foot does on flesh.

There's another shriek of everyone hurrying to finish whatever they were trying to say. It cuts off instantly when Rivera, the SecGen, a handsome young guy from the Dominican Republic, appears on the screen.

Rivera has that serious expression everyone has seen so many times these past few years—it's bad news and he's counting on you to be calm.

Like most Deepers, Naomi is a uniter, so she cheers along with that side, and Jesse cheers because he's with her. Besides, Rivera has a way of making you trust him, and Abdulkashim could play Stalin without makeup.

It seems as if Rivera is waiting for quiet in the Student Union, but crowds calm down about the same speed anywhere in the world, Jesse supposes, so possibly the SecGen is in front of another crowd, somewhere else. More likely, knowing that about half of the world still has to share screens in public places, there is a crowd simulator coming in through his earphone to let him know.

Just as it becomes possible to hear, Rivera begins, "My friends and citizens of our planet . . . it is with a sad heart I tell you that tonight the United Nations is forced, for the eighth time, to intervene militarily to preserve and enforce Article Fourteen of its Second Covenant. I quote it to you in full: 'No nation, whether or not signatory to this covenant, which did not possess and declare itself to be in possession of explosive weapons yielding more than one trillion ergs per gram delivered whether of any current or not yet invented type, by the first minute of June 1, 2008, GMT, shall be permitted to manufacture, possess, purchase, transfer or in any way exercise direct or indirect control over the detonation of such weapons. The Secretary-General shall have power at his sole discretion to enforce this article.'

"Now, for ten years since the Alaska Free State peacefully separated from the United States, the Siberian Commonwealth has pursued a claim to Alaska based on alleged treaty irregularities in the agreements between the United States and the former Russian Empire. These claims have been found—in four different international fora—to be wholly without merit.

"Not only has the present Siberian regime reiterated and pressed these claims, it has also pursued an annexation of Alaska by covert violence and overt threat."

The screen flashes once, and shadowy shapes, too regular to be natural, show as dark blue on light blue. There are a dozen or so, all roughly proportioned like a pencil, with one end flared like the head of a flashlight and the other rounded and snub. Rivera explains. "Six clusters like this one have been located on the seabed of the Arctic Ocean. These are suppressed trajectory missiles, made by MitsDoug Defense, but microsensors dropped close to them have revealed two critical modifications, both in violation of arms-control agreements. First of all, the range has been extended tremendously by fitting a MitsDoug Cobra air-to-surface missile as a second stage, inside the warhead compartment. Secondly, the Cobra stage has been fitted with a laser-ignited fusion warhead, with a yield far in excess of what is permitted by Article Fourteen.

"We have also established through Open Data agreements that these weapons do not belong to any power permitted to own them under the Covenant. In any case they lie outside any national territory and are thus de facto illegal under Article Seventeen of the Second UN Covenant.

"Their positioning within a two-minute flight of Denali, and my description of past bad relations between Alaska and Siberia, should be placed in this context: earlier this evening I notified all three hundred and twenty-four signatory and nonsignatory nations that the UN Space Operations Office would destroy those missiles at the first sign of launch, or at 0830 GMT, whichever came first. I have received the explicit assent of two hundred and eighty-four nations, and no response from the others—except for the Siberian Commonwealth, which has lodged a strong protest at what President Abdulkashim calls a hasty and unwarranted action.

"This screen is displaying a brief report from General Jamil of UNSOO, showing target configuration before strike. At exactly 0830 GMT, a flight of twenty-five UNSOO space planes fired over one hundred missiles into impact trajectories for those sites. The missiles penetrated the Arctic ice, and delivered antineutron-beryllium warheads—or 'cram bombs'—onto the sites you see here."

Jesse would love to know how anything can go through hundreds of meters of ice at Mach 20 and still come out working on the other side, but he'd have to work for UNSOO a *long* time before they told him that. If you can trust *Scuttlebytes*, then maybe each warhead puts out a thin mist of antiprotons from its nose that then flows back around it, but you can't trust *Scuttlebytes* much more than you can the Famous People Channel. Look at how many times in the last twelve years *Scuttlebytes* has claimed to finally know who set off the Flash.

Then it cuts to some kind of undersea remote sensing. Long white streaks arrow into the seabed missiles, so fast that it's as if the lines of superheated steam plunging into the Arctic Ocean appear all at once, like the particle paths in a cloud chamber. Where the missile was, at the head of each streak, there's a bright white ball.

The view jumps back to Rivera. He nods, as if to say, *Powerful, eh? Frightening?* There is no trace of a smile.

He licks his lips once before he speaks. "An attempted launch of the seabed missiles was detected by our monitors a bit under a second before impact. Authorized UN datatrace reveals that signal's origin to be the Commandant's palace in Novokuznetsk, Siberia. On the basis of this evidence, I am issuing an interdict and arrest order, effective now, for the seizure of Commandant Abdulkashim and fifty-one other Siberian officials. They are to be taken into UN detention for examination and trial. All armed forces around the world are reminded that armed resistance to UN arrest—

or taking military advantage of any situation caused by a UN arrest—is a capital offense at all levels."

The SecGen's eyes suddenly seem harrowed and frightened. When Rivera speaks again, it is very softly. "This has not been an easy decision, but so far as I have vision it has been a just, measured, and appropriate one. Let us all hope it brings us nearer global peace and justice. Good day to you all."

The blue and white flag billowing in a soft breeze flashes on the screen, and then the UNIC logo. The screen pops back to a replay of *I Love Lucy*. There's an uproar in the room about what to watch next. Jesse gave up on TV back when they stopped making new shows.

At least ten people are shouting above the crowd, announcing various meetings to support, protest, or discuss the SecGen's actions.

Naomi leans back and breathes in his ear. "Oh mighty engineer, this uninitiated one craves to ken your technical wisdom, for damn all if she can understand what just happened. Besides, if there's any meeting or rally I ought to make, I can find out and join up later. Can we go be alone?"

Her arm slides around him and he feels the heavy, soft push of her breast against his elbow as he pulls his own arm out to drape over her shoulder.

It still takes ten minutes to get out of the Student Center, because anyone as active as Naomi has at least twenty people to say hello to. Jesse does as well, but for once he's glad that most of her friends think he's a big dumb piece of attractive meat, because that means his part of the ritual can be confined to exchanges of head nods and saying each other's names. Naomi has to go through a comparison of analyses with everyone.

Right now she's explaining it to Gwendy, the girlfriend that Jesse has always privately thought of as "a blonde mop with protruding hardware." Naomi's getting very serious, and the tone of passion is drawing more people toward her. This doesn't look good for an escape.

"The thing we can't lose sight of," Naomi is saying, delicate little hands churning and chopping at the air in front of her, "is that whether Rivera had any options in the situation, or not, isn't relevant. It's not our job to make him have options, after all. The point is that *of course* he had to get rid of the missiles and *of course* it was wrong to blow them up. They're just trying to confuse the issue when they ask what else he could have done about it. If he had been doing his job, he would have had a better option. That's what it's all about. If he's willing to live in a situation with only unacceptable options and then willing to take one, well, then, there you have it. We need to get some feelings expressed about all this."

Inwardly Jesse groans. Feelings are seldom properly expressed until there's been a march and a conference at least.

She goes on, and by now Sibby (who tends to agree with both Gwendy and Naomi about everything, especially when they disagree with each other) is listening intently as well, and clearly the conversation can't end till she has a chance to agree. The apartment and the homework are looking farther and farther away every minute.

Gwendy's guy, a tall skinny bad case of acne whom Jesse normally would remember the name of, tries to get an objection in, but Naomi mows it down before he can open his mouth. "No, *listen*," she says. "The point is, people have to take charge of wherever life puts them, and I don't care if he is the SecGen, he's still responsible. If you allow your situation to be one where there are no moral options, and then you go and choose between them, you're still choosing to do something wrong. I mean, otherwise there's nobody to blame."

Sibby tentatively ventures that maybe this applies, too, to Abdulkashim.

"Oh, sure, right," Gwendy barks, turning on Sibby. "Blame a guy whose country just lost most of its weapons, a guy who's probably being thrown into jail right now if the UN cops haven't already killed him, like *he* really wanted to have all this happen. That is *so* simplistic." Gwendy's jaw is sticking far enough forward to protrude beyond the heavy blonde curtains of her hair, she's glaring into Sibby's eyes (as much as anyone can tell from the side), and she's doing what old guys like Jesse's dad call "invading personal space"—standing close to Sibby and moving closer.

All this is putting a nasty want-to-fight gleam in Naomi's eye. Jesse knows many people find her obnoxious when she's like this, but it's also exactly what gets him horny.

The first thing he noticed about her in Values and Self class, the one required course at the U of the Az, was that gleam when she started picking on the three bewildered Afropean guys for not being feminist-ecoconscious.

The second thing was that under all the baggy clothing she had a wonderful body.

Jesse's roommate Brian, who moved out when it became clear that Jesse was getting serious about her, had rather casually suggested that since what turned Jesse on was all that fury wrapped up in that male-fantasy body, maybe he should "just rape her and get over it, Jess, wouldn't that be simpler? It would confirm everything she thinks about you and you'd still get to find out what it's like."

Jesse had been shocked. The next several times he had sex with Naomi he couldn't stop fantasizing that he was raping her. If there was a Diem Act for fantasies like there is for wedges, he'd be facing the death penalty.

Does he really like her? He doesn't know—it seems irrelevant.

He's not listening, which is probably just as well, but Gwendy and Sibby are both in tears and Gwendy's guy seems to be trying to get them pulled out of there. They beat some kind of retreat, and by now anyone who was waiting to talk to Naomi seems to have vanished, so Jesse has her outside almost at once. They walk together quietly in the cool desert dark before Jesse ventures to speak. "Listen," he says, "don't give me a speech about it, but I'd really like to take the Lectrajeep out into the desert tonight. We could sit back and look at the stars and I'd listen to whatever you want to talk about."

He knows this is likely to start a fight. She doesn't like the Lectrajeep. Deepers don't want to disturb the wilderness, so they get it on XV instead. Never mind that with the big soft balloon tires and the QuaDirecDrive, the Lectrajeep doesn't leave as much track as a hiker in lightweight boots; Naomi's parents have filled her full of horror stories about what the old four-wheelers of fifty years before did, and that's what she sees when she looks at Jesse's Lectrajeep.

The one time he tried taking her out into the desert, she didn't know her way around without the XV team there. In XV, the body you ride on is some highly trained athlete, so that you move easily through the wild country, and you have constant back-of-the-mind contact with a wilderness poet, a naturalist, an activist, and a shaman. Without them there to whisper into her mind, she didn't know what the plants were, she had no phrases to remember or key into the experience with, she didn't know what the major threats to this part of the ecosystem were or who was responsible for them, and there wasn't any spiritual significance to anything. Worse yet, she got sweaty and dirty—she'd never gone more than a day unshowered in her life, probably.

So by suggesting the Lectrajeep, he's looking for a fight, maybe, if he admits the truth to himself, because if they fight and then fuck to make up, it will be what he really wanted all along, and if they just fight, it will make him that much crazier for the next time. He's beginning to wonder, a little, just how much crazier he can get.

He's stunned numb when she takes his hand and says, "Let's give it a try. I've been thinking maybe I don't bend enough or try to see anyone else's point of view."

Jesse's heart is thumping to be let out of his chest. "Great," he says. "It's about an hour's drive out to my favorite spot if we go at a reasonably responsible speed. I'll call my brother on the way and see if he knows anything about environmental effects yet."

She kisses him then, right out where anyone might see it happening. He's crazier. Definitely crazier.

In the seabed off the North Slope, things have been happening. There was a lot of kinetic energy in the warheads to begin with, and because *Scut-*

tlebytes got it right for once, there was also a plume of antiprotons spraying in ahead of them, and that added some energy as well.

All that was nothing compared to the warheads themselves. When an antineutron collides with a beryllium nucleus, it annihilates one neutron, and the mutual annihilation releases around nine times the energy of a fissioning uranium atom. It also converts that nucleus to two alpha particles about as close together as you'll ever see them. Having the same charge, they repel each other and take off in opposite directions, adding a percentage point or so to the total energy. The alpha particles, highly charged, readily "hand over" their energy to the matter they pass through, as heat, as electromagnetic radiation, and as mechanical motion caused by the heat and radiation.

It is the destiny of all energy, eventually, to end up as heat; that's the principle of entropy. The energy of the bomb explosions ended up as heat in the ocean bed, much of which is ice, not very far below freezing—in fact if it weren't at ocean-bottom pressure it wouldn't be frozen at all.

This is ice with something more.

One strange fact about ice, when you think about it, is that it floats. Solid butter sinks to the bottom of liquid butter, solid iron sinks to the bottom of liquid iron, solid nitrogen sinks to the bottom of liquid nitrogen . . . but solid water floats on liquid water.

Imagine a microscope fine enough to show you why. The water molecule is bent at an angle and try as you like, it doesn't pack neatly. Freeze water, so that the molecules start to line up into crystals, and that sloppy packing leaves a lot of empty space—more empty space than when they were just rolling around on each other.

Freeze water another way, and there's so much extra space you can trap other molecules between the water molecules. That's called a clathrate— Latin for a "cage, trellis, or grating"—and all kinds of things can be held in there.

As when twenty-three water molecules make a cage around four methane molecules.

There is lots of methane in the seabed. Everything that sinks down there rots, and there's not much free oxygen. Many anaerobic decay processes release methane. Dead stuff has been rotting on the seabed for a long time—and since the last few ice ages, it's been cold enough down there to trap the methane in clathrates. On the Arctic Ocean floor many clathrate beds are tens of meters thick and hundreds of kilometers across.

So energy from the cram bombs goes into the seabed and warms up ice that's just below the freezing point, releasing methane. Moreover, as the clathrates dissolve they trigger landslides and collapses under the sea.

Now, clathrates are delicate molecules. They're big but there are no strong bonds in them, and it doesn't take much more than a hard rap to break them up, letting the water molecules regroup into plain ice . . . and the methane escape.

Tonight the seabed is alive with avalanches, collapses, and pressure waves. Methane deposited across thousands of years is bubbling up from all over, making its way up to the surface of the Arctic Ocean, finding the countless rents and breaks in the ice. Within eighteen hours, the fifty-foot-deep clathrate beds stretching along the outer edge of the North Slope, about sixty-five miles wide and running more than four hundred miles under the sea, are in collapse.

Methane is a greenhouse gas, and the quantity of methane released, in a matter of a few days, is 173 billion metric tons. That's just about nineteen times what's in the atmosphere in 2028, or thirty-seven times what's in the atmosphere in 1992.

Diogenes Callare gets Jesse's call and has to say he doesn't know anything yet. He's glad to see, via the little screen, that the kid is driving a Lectrajeep out into the Arizona desert, and that there's a cute little brown-haired chick beside him.

They chat a little, and Jesse says hi to the kids as he always does; Jesse is six-year-old Mark's favorite uncle, but Nahum, who is three, doesn't always remember who he is.

When Di has talked with Jesse and assured him that no one yet knows what the detectable consequences of the cram bombs in the Arctic seabed might be, he takes some time to look around his living room, at the kids and in through the lighted doorway to where Lori is still working. Life is pretty good. The furniture is decent looking and goes together, he's reasonably in love with Lori, the kids seem to be at the intelligent end of normal, and this place—on the Carolina Coast zipline, only forty-five minutes from his job in Washington, but a comfortable couple of hundred miles away from the big city itself—is big and could easily pass for a real instead of a duplicate Victorian.

He's doing pretty well, what the old man would call Getting On In The World. He wonders for an instant if the old man still talks to Jesse in capitals. Probably not. Di and his brother practically had different fathers, the dogmatic tyrant who raised Di somehow having faded into the crusty old character who raised Jesse.

Di goes in to play with Mark a bit more before the next bedtime; it still seems strange to have young kids awake when it's close to midnight, but he has to admit that the new way of doing things, with kids taking a lot of long naps that either he or Lori share with them, does seem to make for happier and less frustrated children. They are putting up a block house, not very successfully because Mark finds it more fun to knock things over. But since Di fundamentally enjoys building block houses and watching Mark knock them down, it's a good partnership.

"What was up with Jesse?" Lori asks, passing through on her way to the coffeemaker. She's currently at work on *The Slaughterer in Yellow*, the sixth of her very popular "spectrum series" of books about the Slaughterer, the serial murderer who finishes every book by framing the detective. Her success does not account for their having a house here—Di's job at NOAA took care of that—but it does account for the fitted hardwood and the extra-large bedrooms.

"Oh, he and his muffin of the month are worrying about Rivera's taking out the Siberian missiles. Not that it's not something to worry about, but the current muffin is a political muffin, so they're worrying about it more than normal kids would."

"Not the best muffin it could be, then," Lori says, grinning. "Good thing all you wanted in a muffin was a good body and moral turpitude."

"Yeah. At least I hope his muffin only has that aggressive tight-mouthed expression because she's a Deeper and not because she has ARTS."

"Turpitude," Nahum says, distinctly. He adds, "She has ARTS."

"Oops," Lori says. "Maybe he'll forget it before Mom comes to visit."

Di winks at her and she grins back, and the thought crosses his mind that the kids will be expiring soon, Lori usually finishes up around 1:30 A.M. when the kids are in the depths of their longest sleep, and it might be nice to slide between the sheets with a grownup tonight.

Lori wets her lips with the tip of her tongue, turns to stick her bottom and chest out, and gives him the grin she always does when she says "Not bad for an old broad," another phrase they'd had to lose since the time two months ago when Nahum expressed the view that Grandma was not bad for an old broad.

You never know, really, what kids are picking up on, but Mark hugs Di's leg and says, "Time for bed?"

"Beds!" Nahum agrees, and just as current thinking says, there's no problem at all with getting the two of them onto the big, comfortable, low bed, and by now they're so secure that Di or Lori need only join them for most naps, not for every one.

A cynic might note that Di is often a bit short of sleep and that the new-fashioned way really only functions because Lori works at home. A deeper cynic might ask when parents have ever been other than short on sleep.

Still, tonight the kids go right to bed and shut up. Better still, Lori sits down next to him on the couch instead of going back to work. "So what do you think?" she asks.

"The floor of the Arctic Ocean is about as irrelevant a place as you can find for weather forecasting," Di says, accepting the brandy she hands him. "I mean, temperatures down there have something to do with absorbing global warming—when the deep ocean gets warm, then one of the brakes on the system will be gone, but it won't get warm for another generation or so if the computer is right. And by that time we should have emissions really under control and might have even started the re-cooling everyone seems to think we want to do.

"No, I just get bothered by the politics. I mean, you and I grew up pre-Flash. We know how weird it is to have the UN having any say in all this. And they're not doing much of a job. If they hadn't forced Russia to grant Siberian independence, or the USA to grant Alaskan independence, would all this have happened? And then not to check what was behind what they were shooting at. Typical UN operation. That's all. If President Grandma or Harris Diem were running this show there'd have been no shooting and it wouldn't have made the news at all—Abdulkashim would be out with no fuss. This guy Rivera is smart but he's a show-off and he likes to see the planes fly and the bombs fall. One of these days we'll get a smarter aggressor or a dumber SecGen, and then we'll be in the soup.

"But as for the meteorology—nothing to worry about, I don't think. The heat being released down there won't bring up the bottom temperature by even one one-hundredth of a degree once it's spread over the whole ocean."

She snuggles against him and says, "I did not knock off early to talk meteorology, actually."

He feels what he's going to say on his tongue just as the phone rings, and it's the ring from the NOAA office, so he has to answer. Probably the same question Jesse asked but less politely framed.

He knows it's big when he sees it's Henry Pauliss on the screen, and his boss looks freshly shaken out of bed. Probably the UN has had something weird happen down there and wants NOAA to figure it out, because the USA still has the best Weather Bureau there is . . . which is why there's been stuff in *Scuttlebytes* all the time about a UN bid to take over NOAA.

As if to forestall Di's irritation, Henry opens with a sigh. "What I want you to do is tell me to go back to bed, after I call the President and tell her that it's nothing to worry about, so she can call the SecGen and tell him the same thing."

"I won't tell you that if it isn't true."

"That's why I called you. It's not really your bailiwick—though we will have to get the computer models going on it as well. It belongs over in the old Anticipatory Section, and since we don't have one anymore, it belongs to anyone who has a lot of experience and won't shade the truth for me."

Di wonders what the flattery is leading up to.

"Okay, here's the story." Henry tells him, briefly, about the breakdown of the methane clathrate beds and the methane pouring out of the Arctic Ocean. "Near some openings in the ice it's thick enough to have asphyxiated some seals, and as a precautionary thing the UN guys tried igniting it wherever it was dense enough—but that's not even putting a dent in the release, because mostly it's drifting up through tiny fissures and holes and not building up much at any one point. Still, the UN satellites have found about a hundred plumes they can ignite, and they've used Global Launch Control lasers to get them burning, and that should reduce the problem by about two or three percent.

"Which is not a lot. Bottom line is, we've still dumped something like a hundred fifty or two hundred billion metric tons of methane into the air. We're going to have twenty times the normal level for at least a little while. You know how much shit hit the fan when the last Five Year Global Warming Assessment came out. They're scared to death of . . . you know."

Di is almost amused. As a senior official of the agency officially blamed for the Global Riot—the biggest embarrassment since NASA's Replicator Experiment nearly ate Moonbase—poor old Henry can't quite bring himself to say the word.

The problem with XV is exactly that it's like being there. So when the prediction was for the grain famine in Pakistan to continue, and things blew up in Islamabad, in half an hour there were plenty of XV freaks getting the same load of hormones and excitement in Tokyo, Mombasa, Fez, Lima, Ciudad de México, Honolulu. In Seattle, a group of Deepers had all plugged into the Pakistani scenes just before going to one of their "actions," trying to shut down a neonatal unit, which was supposed to be nonviolent, but with all the glandular workout they'd just had, it didn't stay that way—or maybe it was that the devoutly Catholic commander of the Federal troops, as the Deepers later claimed, ordered the troops to fire into the crowd.

At any rate, two XV reporters were caught in the cross fire, a man and woman who usually worked the Newsporn Channel, and as she died in his arms, shot through the lungs, half a billion experiencers jacked in and felt every sob and gasp from both of them, smelled the blood and felt the shots—

The glands start pumping and the place gets jumping, as they say on Dance Channel, and suddenly all the streets of the Earth were full, shop windows shattering, cops shot, fires going up and firemen unable to reach the hydrants. And everywhere, more XV reporters worldwide jumped in to pick up the additional excitement, more rioters pulling on scalpnets to share the rioting elsewhere while they did their own.

UNIC can shut down one government or group, or even a consortium of a few dozen, but trillions of parallel links, any combination of which can be a pathway between four million XV reporters and twenty thousand XV channels, with all that message traffic jumping from link to link a couple of times per millisecond, is utterly unstoppable. UNIC couldn't do more than cause a little static here and there, not enough so anyone even noticed them. Raw experience that would normally never have made it on anywhere was pouring over the channels into even the most restricted societies.

Ed Porter and the other XV editors had the best day of their careers. Plug into XV and you could be standing on the sidewalk watching a store burn in London, then watching a mob strip a woman naked in Montevideo, then crouching behind an overturned car while shots scream off it in Seattle, then facing the insectoid cops and their riot guns in Tashkent, back to London for more fire, back to Montevideo for a flash of a rape, back to Tashkent as the guns roar and blood sprays everywhere, on to Paris where an XV reporter choking on smoke is trapped on a third floor—all that in three seconds, not pictures but full sensory experiences, on and on.

Finally, the only thing that seemed to limit the Global Riot was that most people preferred to stay home and wear the goggles and muffs so that they could experience violence and destruction worldwide with their full concentration, instead of having it be background music for their own rioting.

As it was, at least half a million people worldwide died while plugged into XV, not realizing that while they popped back and forth between the firestorm in Seoul, troops going berserk in Denver, liquor-store looting in Warsaw, and the ever-popular gang rapes in Montevideo, the building was burning down over their heads. There were nine million dead in total, worldwide, not counting suicides afterward, crashes of fire trucks and ambulances trying to get to the trouble, or heart attacks while experiencing it all on XV.

So far nobody has figured out any way to prevent the next Global Riot. Di understands perfectly well what Henry is worried about. Supposedly UNIC has gotten equipped to grab net control and shut down global communications if need be, but after seeing them unable to shut down Abdulkashim earlier tonight, Di knows that's strictly propaganda.

All this comes to Di as one big impression while he swallows hard. "All right, then, Henry," he says. "Offhand I'd say a methane release that big is going to have effects and people are going to notice. Methane is one of the major ways the Earth traps heat, and it's letting loose right before spring equinox in the Northern Hemisphere. It's going to warm up a lot faster than usual this spring. You've got to make them understand this won't just blow over and can't be kept secret. So . . . how much how fast? You said a hundred and fifty to two hundred billion tons—is that firm?"

"That's the estimated volume in the beds that have already gone," Henry says, "and since to some extent they seem to be able to set each other off mechanically, it's probably low. How fast—I don't know. How long does it take a not very dense gas to rise to the surface? It's not very soluble in water, so we won't get much help from its dissolving; besides, I suppose whatever dissolves is just going to block the absorption of other methane from other sources later. As for finding its way through the ice—you want my bet? I bet it didn't take an hour to get to the undersurface of the ice. And there are so many cracks and fissures, big and little, that I don't expect it to stay under the ice more than two or three hours. We thought about flaring the pockets—use missiles to punch holes and set the stuff on fire—but the collapse after the pocket goes will probably break the ice up more and let other methane escape. I guess we'll do it so that it looks like we tried, but we don't expect it to accomplish anything. So very unofficially, figure it's all in the air tomorrow."

Di gives a low whistle, leans back, reaches for his terminal, unfolds it onto the table in front of him. "I'll have to get back to you—and I need numbers, accurate ones, soon. I can do some preliminaries on it pretty fast. And you're right, we need the old Anticipatories."

He thinks for one moment of pointing out that it was Henry who let them cut out the "Wild Thinkers" on grounds that the things the Anticipatory Section dreamed up were mostly not going to happen and tended to scare the daylights out of voters and taxpayers.

But after all, the alternative was cutting Henry, and then they'd have ended up with a worse hack, so Di just adds, "If I remember right, there're several processes that take methane out of the atmosphere—"

Henry nods. "Right. We might look into which ones can be accelerated or altered—"

"Wasn't thinking that far ahead. It matters how long the stuff stays at elevated concentrations. If it's only a couple of days, not much will happen, but if it's twenty years, then we're in deep."

"Got you."

"And Henry—you really ought to see about getting everyone back from Anticipatory. Most of the people you have left are just amateurs at this."

Henry almost looks happy, and says, "I'm way ahead of you there, at least. Next person I talk to after you is Carla Tynan. And I intend to beg, plead, and whine until she agrees to head up the research on this—whatever it takes. Then I'll beg, plead, and whine some more so they'll okay hiring her."

Di Callare has to smile. "That's going to take some *whining*."

"You know it. But we don't have anyone else who knows as much about the weird connections that might be out there."

"Well, I look forward to working with her again. You can learn a lot."

"Unh-hunh. *Some* of it about meteorology and global climate. All right, guess I better call Hardshaw back first, then get to Carla. You take care and we'll talk whenever one of these sleepyheads in here comes up with any of the numbers you asked for. Get some sleep tonight . . . might not be another good chance for a while."

Henry pings off, and Di turns around to find Lori has been listening, out of sight of the phone's camera. "You got that?"

"Yep." She unfastens a button and winks at him more blatantly than he'd have thought possible. "And you heard your boss. Better take your chances while you've got them. . . ."

In the middle of the twentieth century, the phone company learned to sell the dead time on a line, if there were enough lines. That is, if people make noise into the phone line only eighty percent of the time, then if you can switch conversations off as soon as someone falls silent, reconnect them through the first available line as soon as there's any sound, and do it all fast enough so that no one notices the brief cutting off of the beginnings of sounds—well, then, you need only four lines per five conversations.

In the mid-1960s, to maintain communications in the event of a nuclear war, USDoD came up with ARPAnet, which begat Internet, a term you still hear old people call it in their boomtalk, instead of just "the net" it has evolved into, a system for moving e-mail in which each message knows where it is going and wanders from node to node in a network, taking every opportunity to get closer to its destination.

By 1990, intelligence organizations were using the splitting up of messages across multiple channels to make it impossible to monitor a conversation; one split second of it went across the country from microwave tower to microwave tower, the next split second went through an unused TV channel on a satellite, the next jumped around the world on satellite-to-satellite relays, and it all got together at the phone.

By 2028, that technique is no longer used for security; it's simply the most efficient way to use the trillions of fibrop pathways and laser ground-to-satellite links. But it has the same effect: nothing and no one can jam information as long as it's coming from and going to enough different places at once. You can keep any one person from talking or listening . . . but that's all.

And the same trillions of channels are the ones on which the UN, the governments, and the corporations depend. They can no more unplug than you can stop breathing; or rather the cost of doing either would be the same.

It's afternoon in the Western Pacific and the weather is pleasant and warm. Carla Tynan has brought her yacht up to the surface to spend a while sunbathing on the deck. A few years ago, when she had the NOAA job, she put most of her savings from her software patents into getting her skin cancer-proofed, so she could enjoy the sun no matter what happened to the ozone, and into *MyBoat*, her submersible yacht.

That meant she was officially broke, which badly upset Louie, her husband at the time, though she certainly hadn't touched his money or even asked for any of it.

She slides her big, eye-covering glasses up her nose, scratches all over (nothing like the privacy of mid-ocean), and resolves not to think about Louie again for a while. Maybe she'll think about a couple of papers she's been noodling on . . . it's about time to get her plate warmed up over on the non-profit side of the table, because if you're going to freelance as a scientist, you've got to keep the other scientists saying that you're a real one. Not paying his non-profit dues is exactly how poor old Henry Pauliss got stuck in government.

Then again, she hasn't done accounts in a while, and it may be time to do a little private-sector systems design or algorithmics and make some cash. There are a couple of add-on gadgets she'd like for *MyBoat* and she still hasn't paid off her last purchases from the cadcam shop in Tanzania. Anyway, she's been goofing off for weeks, not doing much more than experiencing romance wedges, sunbathing, and fishing. It's her third trip around the world on *MyBoat*, and this time she just went straight from Zanzibar to Singapore without bothering about landfalls . . . she's begun to admit to herself that once you've seen this particular planet a few times, there may be plenty of unvisited places left, but there's a discouraging sensation that all you're doing is filling in the holes.

Well, now, wasn't that what made Louie so attractive in the first place? *Be honest, Carla* . . . he was one of eight people who'd been to another planet. Not that he talked about it much, and the thing that seemed to impress him most was "how *alone* it was"—nearest thing to poetry she'd ever heard out of that man.

She raises up on her elbows and looks over her body, chuckling a little. You wouldn't think anything quite this thick and muscular—she was a weight lifter in college, and she's run to fat a bit since—would have gotten the attention of the Assistant Mission Commander for Martian Operations; god knew there were a lot of eager little tight bodies ready for him when he got back, but no, less than two years after his return, there he was on top of Carla Schwarz, Girl Scientist.

Carla's mother pegged the trouble two hours after she met Louie: "Both of you want somebody to take care of, and both of you would rather die than be taken care of."

It looks like Mom was right about whether the marriage would work out, because here Carla is: *MyBoat*, with room only for her and her work, does not seem small to her, and there Louie is—come to think of it, he may be passing overhead right now for all she knows—tending watch solo on the USA's last space station. They've got a date for "five good dinners and a lot of time in bed" next time he hits dirt and she's near a port; that might be a year or two from now, but neither of them is in any hurry.

Maybe she'll treat herself to calling Louie later this evening. He usually seems glad of the conversation when she does, and it's been a few weeks.

So much for the resolution not to think about him.

The phone tied to her wrist rings. It's Henry Pauliss, and the news is pretty astonishing; at least she won't have to decide what to do with her time for the next few weeks.

When XV was introduced in 2006, it was denounced roundly for being even more attention-absorbing than television. It was also praised highly because it allowed *anyone* to have the experience instantly of knowing how to do a thing and of doing it. You could plug a kid from the urban ghetto into the head of an engineer, give him a sense of the pleasure that came with finding a successful design for a turbine blade, and the pure joy of holding the actual object in his hand, fresh from the cadcam shop, then dump him back into the classroom and say "And that's why you want to learn math." You could take a fat, shy, laughable nebbish and give him the experience of being physically beautiful and confident, then haul him out and say "This can all be yours, really yours, if you'll get to the gym and the personality development courses."

You could take a psychopath with no empathy and give him the experience of being a victim. That was the experiment that revealed the flaw.

Legally it took them some years to get cleared to try it on a prisoner. The first time, it was merely the accident that an XV reporter had been raped, mutilated, and left for dead while the recorder was running. Many experts confidently predicted that if habitual violent criminals were exposed to that tape, and really understood what they were doing to their victims, they would stop doing it.

In fact, once they had felt the terror and pain themselves, inflicting it on

re of a thrill than ever. It was the effect they had been
ving. One former model prisoner became so excited by
raped an unarmed male guard on his way back to his

s great past cynics, everyone from Lao-tzu through Ben
e Beauvoir, could have told them this would happen, but
cynicism is a sensible, civilized view. To live in the midst of endless violence
one must have sacred principles with which to endorse the violence. By the
end of the twentieth century, the most brutal in human history, there were
only idealists left. Even when forced-memory extraction and vicarious rape-
for-hire emerged, XV, like all other information channels, had become effectively impossible to censor. Technology—and the cravings of thousands of
proselytizers of all stripes—forbade it.

Berlina Jameson is having a bad day. Charlie, the idiot station manager, gave
up on yelling at her, which was good, but then he got Candice, the station
owner, to get on the phone and yell at her, which was discouraging,
especially since it's all the same yell—she's not going to get time off, or
expense money, or anything at all for "this insane idea."

She doesn't want to quit the job, because her resignation will instantly
hit the public databases, and Berlina is extremely close to the edge on credit,
so they'll be all over her if she quits her fourth job in three years.

Yet the idea itself is so, so sweet. She hears the familiar voices in her
head again, even as Candice goes on at her . . .

"This is Edward R. Murrow reporting from London. Another raid by
German bombers, in greater numbers than we've seen before . . ."

"This is Walter Cronkite, from Houston. Tonight if all goes well men
will land on the moon . . ."

"Wendy Lou Bartnick reporting—I'm about four miles from the glowing
crater that used to be Port au Prince. The only light is from the blazing sky—there is no electricity and no sign of a headlight other than my
own . . ."

These tapes all play in her head, as they have played on her audio and
video systems for more than half her life, so often that she can recite them
word by word, frame by frame. A lot of younger kids brag that they can
experience XV without needing goggles and muffs to shut out the real
world, that they can live real and virtual simultaneously. Berlina figures she
can go them one better—she can get television and radio in her head, all
the great broadcasts of the last ninety years, followed by the seductive
murmur of one more opener:

"This is Berlina Jameson, reporting from—"

Her name right up there with Murrow, Shirer, Sevareid, Cron.
aldson, Walters, Bartnick. . . .

She does her best to forget that Bartnick is not old, but has already b.
forced into retirement, only a few years after the Port au Prince newscast
made her an anchor for CNN. XV wiped out television news.

Nor did anyone cross over. XV is everything the old news wasn't. That
guy who was deservedly fired for getting hysterical about the Hindenburg
blowing up would have received a big whacking raise if he'd been on XV.
XV is about feeling it in your glands . . . *glands start pumping place gets
jumping,* the Dance Channel . . . *don't see it be it,* Extraponet . . . *news you
can dance to,* Passionet.

This chain of thoughts is old, but it's something else to think about
instead of listening to Candice.

"Berlina, I don't understand why I can't get across to you that this is
not nineteen-fucking-sixty-eight, and there is no point in pointing a camera
or a microphone at the action when XV takes people there direct." Candice
blows a big cloud of smoke; Berlina once sneaked a look at her biochem-
tailored cigarette prescription and found it was a mix of tranquilizers and
muscle relaxants with just enough CNS enabler to keep her from getting
stupid while she relaxed. Maybe not enough.

Candice keeps nattering, so Berlina mentally tunes back in . . . "I don't
know where the hell you got this fixation from. You're on for twenty
minutes a day and the only reason I hire you, babe, is that the movie nuts
would rather catch their news between movies. Suppose it's more twentieth
or something. Your job is not to cover the news, not to make the news, not
to be there for the news. Your job, Berlina"—here Candice takes a huge drag
on the cigarette, enough to knock over a rhino, and tousles her hair in a very
twentieth kind of way, no surprise since she lived more than half her life in
it—"and I mean your only job, is to look good in a sweater while you *read*
the news. There is no such thing as a TV reporter anymore, Brenda Starr."

Berlina has no idea who Brenda Starr is. Probably boomtalk and not a
compliment. "Yeah," she says. "So how about . . . hah. Listen, I just broke
up with my s.o., and it was a registered relationship. I wasn't going to use
the required five days off without pay, but if I wanted to drive up to the
North Slope—"

Candice shakes her head at her. "You know how much labor-law trouble
it will be if you work on a recovery break?"

"I can put it together for myself, as a hobby. Then if you want to air
it, fine. All I want is a station credential to show—and I've got that anyway,
just by working here."

Candice sighs. "You know we're going to have to get a Kelly Girl or something in here to read for you for the week? Aw, hell." She blows another cloud of medicated smoke. "Bet you have your own gear?"

"Yep."

"Then go do it. I guess if I air it, the chances are pretty good you won't turn me in." She shakes all that hair around again—why in god's name, Berlina thinks, do so many old women insist on having those mountains of starched hair with avalanches of curls down their back? "And good luck, kid. If TV reporting doesn't work out, maybe you can be a Viking or a blacksmith or something else there's no use for anymore."

Berlina thanks her, hoping to hit just the tone that will kiss the old bitch where it's good, without too obviously slurping it. She seems to have, because she gets two minutes of "when I was your age I was just as feisty," the kind of story that business people who went somewhere pretty small love to tell about themselves.

Berlina doesn't mind; it's a payback of sorts. She manages to leave with a smile.

In the parking garage, she tosses her bag and coat into her little car, enters the keycode for getting rolling, pulls it out of the parking space and onto the painted blue stripe that marks the guide track, and flips it to automatic to take her home. She wishes she could afford a smarter car that could leave the track and park itself.

She leans back and smiles to herself again. Banff is a longish commute from Calgary, but it's worth it every time she gets home, and at least now that she's done her daily unparking ritual the car will get her the rest of the way home.

"Home" has been a pretty elastic concept in Berlina's mind. She's Afropean, to begin with; Alfred Jameson was a black American GI, identified by DNA records, who paid not to ever see her. Her mother was a German prostitute. Berlina's earliest memories are all of a school for abandoned Afropean children, where she was called "Frances Jameson" by the sisters, and "nigger" by the mobs that gathered outside.

Things were already getting dicey in Europe for anyone half-breed, so she was only supposed to learn English and get shipped back to the States as soon as she was of age. She ran away at thirteen, out of the cold dark school and out of the cruelty of Bavaria, and lived free, cold, and dirty for a few years in Berlin.

At nineteen, she'd named herself after the city she loved, but it was a last gesture. Berlin as she knew it was gone, its streets full of troops from elsewhere, now that Europe was consolidated and "culturally edited," to use their expression for it. She gave herself the name as she filled out a form on board a staticopter taking her to the USS *George Bush,* during the last frantic week of the Expulsion.

Before Parti Uno Euro won the election and rewrote the European constitution, Berlin had been a place full of anachronism, where nobody wanted to see anything new, the one thing that united all of the different artistic movements from the Protonihilists to the Prelectors. She'd gotten hooked on broadcast news when she was putting together a sampler mix for a dance performance group that played bits and pieces of old reportage over a drum machine and screamed whatever they were getting over XV into the mix.

When the Edict of 2022 expelled her and all the other Afropeans, most of them ended up in North America, a strange sort of coming home to her father's country. She has bounced around a lot from job to job, forever being told what Candice has just told her.

She misses Berlin more than ever. She's been in four American states and two Pacificanadian provinces—

> The Ma, the Ny, the Wa,
> The Bic, the Nid, the Pa,
> Last the Az and now the Ab,

as she likes to chant it to herself. She figures she can't go anywhere else because nowhere rhymes with Ab.

As the little car winds its way up the mountains to Banff, a furious spring snowstorm pours over the windshield and away behind her into the night. At least she doesn't have to try to keep the car on the road herself. She flips over to XV, looking for a really neutral reporter and never finding one; for one awful instant her hand stops on Passionet and she is experiencing Synthi Venture. She finds herself snuggled in the rock-hard protective arm of Quaz, who is escorting Synthi these days, out in the howling blizzard of Point Barrow, preparatory to going inside, having wonderful sex in front of a fireplace, running back to Rock (with whom she is triangling) and having Rock explain meteorology to her.

The horrible thing is, she thinks as she switches to Extraponet, which has a reporter riding a UN overflight of the Arctic Ocean, nobody cares anymore that Synthi has read the script in advance; they *want* to know what's going to happen next, they *like* Synthi describing experiences to herself before she has them.

The plane carrying the Extraponet reporter comes over a pressure ridge. A huge flare of gas reaches miles into the sky dead ahead. Deliberate roller-coaster effect, Berlina sneers. They must have known it was there and arranged to fly in low to surprise people.

The plane veers to the side, well short of the flare. The viewpoint reporter is in a forward bubble, and the pilot hasn't told him much. As they circle the immense gas flare, the polar ice below a brilliant shimmer of gold, amber, and yellow, she gets the basic information she wanted—the flaring operation isn't going to take care of the problem, and everyone knows it.

This XV reporter is usually on the environmental beat, to judge by his thoughts, and Berlina thankfully absorbs the basics—greenhouse gas, more of it than anyone would have thought possible, spring the worst time for it, White House and New York reports much too circumspect, so it's worse than they're saying. . . .

XV is a bit like being there, Berlina concedes, and a bit like being more knowledgeable than you really are, but what it's really like is like waking up where the news is happening with a bad case of amnesia and a brainwashing team trying to force a viewpoint on you.

She clicks off and tosses down her scalpnet, muffs, and goggles. The snow outside is beginning to glow, which means the sun is just beginning to peek over the Rockies. Still, it's three hours till she would normally go to bed, and by that time everything can be hurled into the car, and she can sleep on the way, getting caught up on rest for the days ahead while the Alaska Highway rolls under the tires at three hundred kilometers per hour.

"Never mind," she says. "Once I remind people what *real* news was like, XV will be dead as the town crier, or newspapers."

Synthi, you are not plugged into real life anymore, Mary Ann Waterhouse is thinking to herself. She has finally been allowed to switch out from the net for a few blissful hours, the jack in her head no longer plugged to receive Synthi's every quivering passion, and though her head has an ache no aspirin can touch, and her whole body is bruised and sore, she's so relieved to have ten hours off that tears are running down her face.

Mary Ann always tries to remind herself that she is the same old girl, just re-engineered into what a lot of women want to look like (which was pretty much what a lot of men want them to look like), just made rich beyond her dreams, just with this other little personality installed, but right now she looks in the mirror and *misses* herself.

She had a pretty good body—turned a lot of heads—before they gave her the cartoon-character breasts, before they sewed her already-shapely butt into an impossible curve, before they microzapped every bit of fat from her legs and put artificial sheathing like an internal girdle into her stomach.

Not to mention the monthly injections that turn her hair flame-red from its natural straw-blonde.

"I used to just be pretty. I kind of liked that," she says to herself, out loud, and *dammit*. She's crying again. This has been happening for at least the first hour every time she goes off line, for the last couple of months, and she's pretty sure it is not supposed to. Offtime is precious. She doesn't want to waste it this way.

There's no one to call. She has no brothers or sisters, her father disappeared when she was six, her mother is dead, and she hasn't had a real boyfriend since three months before Passionet hired her and invented Synthi.

There is nobody to call or talk to except Karen, whom she used to work with in the Data Pattern Pool. When Mary Ann got picked at the audition, they swore they'd stay friends, and they really have done a pretty good job of it, considering she could buy Karen's apartment building every month and never notice, and that Karen has admitted, shyly, that nowadays all her offtime is spent living in Synthi's head. But it's only six A.M. in Chicago, and Karen has to work in the morning (they talked about having her work for Mary Ann, as a personal assistant or something, but both of them had the common sense to see that would have destroyed the friendship, and probably Karen with it).

She hasn't told Karen about the crying jags yet. She knows that Karen will be a little hurt that she's kept it back.

Well.

She's up early, and at least they got His Oafishness, Quaz, out of here before she woke up; one thing she never does on offtime is sleep—Synthi gets to do all of that, or rather, as the net shrink explained to her, she falls asleep as Synthi, dreams as Mary Ann, wakes up as Synthi, but gets paid for being Synthi the whole time. Quite a deal.

She goes into the bathroom to wash her face, hoping that will kill the last of the tears this time. It doesn't. It hasn't for a few days. Instead, they seem to flow more freely now, as if they will just keep running for the rest of her life.

Well, what did you expect, Mary Ann? Or Synthi? Whoever you are now? She asks the question to the image in the mirror and is no longer sure whether she is speaking aloud or not. *You spend most of your time being someone else, how are you supposed to know what she's crying about?*

She turns on the hot water in the sunken tub, then calls room service and orders a huge breakfast that she isn't sure she'll eat: eggs, corned beef hash, potatoes, all the plain food that she never eats as Synthi Venture, who takes her experiencers on trips into the exotic world of wealth and power that they will never see, and therefore eats mostly foods they've heard about but couldn't afford or wouldn't be able to prepare.

As the tub fills, she pulls out her reader and scans through her personal library for something she'd like to read. Another and not surprising difference between them is that Mary Ann reads.

She's almost cheerful as she settles into the great masses of bubbles and reads the scene at the inn in Bree; by now she knows *The Lord of the Rings* so thoroughly she can open it anywhere she likes and just read as much as she wants. It may be a waste of time, but it's her time to waste and this is what she wants. There's a stack of history books, and a big collection of theatre reviews that follow her around, things she keeps meaning to read, things she used to like, but for the last few months all she's wanted on her offtime has been *The Lord of the Rings*, *The Once and Future King*, and *The Picture of Dorian Gray*. Each of which she has read at least ten times.

In another hour or two, she can call Karen at work.

There's a knock at the door and she bellows "Come in!" The bellhop wheels the table in, and she tells him to bring it into the bathroom; this seems to make him a bit nervous, and she realizes he's probably been experiencing via Rock, Stride, or Quaz, the Passionet reporters she usually works with, and thus has had the experience of being very sophisticated and knowing exactly what to do with this particular naked body in all sorts of exotic settings. The Point Barrow Marriott is not exactly the sophistication center of the universe; the possibility of having Synthi herself, sudsy and naked, demanding breakfast from him, must not have occurred to him.

He's averting his eyes; it's almost funny. "I'm under all these bubbles," she calls out. "You can see my sweaty face and soggy hair but that's about it."

"Still feels weird," he says, moving the food and coffee to where she can reach it.

"I bet it does." Then on impulse she adds, "My real name is Mary Ann Waterhouse, nobody is recording this, I like to read old books that nobody ever reads anymore, and every time I listen to Haydn's *The Creation* I get tears in my eyes."

He steps back as if he's afraid she might bite his leg. She remembers what it was like, when she had a regular job, to have mysterious strangers around who might be able to fire her. "It's okay, when you tell people you served me breakfast, just say I'm a regular person, and use a couple of those things as examples to prove we talked." She reaches for her purse—risking exposing a breast, but he's being so careful not to look—and tips him much more than she should. "Who do you experience?" she asks. "Rock?"

He laughs, a funny nervous laugh. "Yeah."

"Well, if you want more of me, he and I will be paired for a few weeks starting tonight. Quaz is leaving for another assignment."

"Thanks, I'll remember that. Um . . . can I ask . . . is there one you like better?"

According to Passionet, this is the question she must never answer, but here she is trying to have some kind of conversation with an ordinary experiencer, and now that she thinks of it, it's also the most natural question in the world. Still, she temporizes. . . . "Like in what way?"

"Oh, um—" He blushes almost purple. Clearly he did mean that way.

"Well, uh, let's see. Quaz is very well-informed. Stride is kind of the bad boy of the lot, and he's rude, but—well, he's really hot when we're, you know. He knows a lot about being satisfying. Rock . . . well, he's a very warm, down-to-earth kind of guy. I guess there's more affection there than the other two."

The bellhop's eyes are full of gratitude.

"That's important to you—the being likable part, isn't it?" Mary Ann asks, hoping to keep the puzzlement out of her voice. "Being likable," after all, is a pretty basic set of acting tricks, ever since Petrokin developed the Sincere Mode Technique twenty years ago.

"Yeah. I mean, I'd like to be as smart as Quaz, or as—uh, you know—as Stride, but it's that kind of warm feeling that Rock has around him that . . . oh, well. I guess you know what I mean. I'd rather have people like me than anything else." He smiles a little. The way he smiles—quite unconsciously, she's sure—is a not-quite-right (because it's just a bit exaggerated) copy of Rock's Sincere Mode smile.

They talk for another minute or so, and she explains that yes, she really did get to be Synthi Venture just by going to the right audition, but she had six years of acting school before that, and she waited a lot of tables, played in a lot of Equity Showcases, and did a lot of data patterning before she got the break. It's a nice story, happens to be true, and who knows, maybe he'll get famous and tell it.

After he goes, she realizes that she is going to eat the whole huge breakfast. It's not quite as perfect as a big breakfast used to be at three in the morning when they'd just closed and struck a Showcase *Uncle Vanya*, in a café full of theatre people and Lefties and random street lunatics, but it's still pretty good, and it isn't any of the overpriced, overseasoned weird stuff Synthi eats. She finishes breakfast without reading more, and gives herself a good scrub all over. Two hours of her time off are now gone as she towels off.

She looks at herself in the full-length mirror, and damn if she isn't going to cry again. One problem with XV is that it comes at the experiencer through a thick curtain of emotional gauze; that's why a melodramatic character like Synthi comes through more clearly, and why newsporn, with its acute physical pain and terror, is such a big seller. So there, in the mirror, is the evidence of the "lovemaking" with Quaz the night before. Big blotchy bruises on the perfectly shaped breasts and long scratches from his nails—practically his claws—on her thighs and belly. They gave her a pain block, like they always do, but it doesn't override the memory of having her jaw forced painfully wide open and him biting her tongue till she bled.

Of course, the experiencers got something much less intense, and they never knew . . . or did they? She looks more closely, under the bruises and scrapes, touching where she can feel her soreness like an echo through the pain blocks, and she sees the fine little lines the laser leaves, sees that where a healthy woman with big breasts would have a bit of extra skin, her armpits have been fitted with something that works like a tiny accordion, that the skin where they take marks and scars off her breasts twice a year is a kind of raw, callused pink—she can't even feel her own long thumbnail scraping it, and her trim and tidy labia show all kinds of scar tissue.

How can anyone get excited by a woman who's sewn together like a Frankenstein monster?

She lets her mind catch the edges of memory, and she realizes they are in no better shape than she. Quaz has scar tissue visible on his neck from all the biting, and his back, clawed so often by Synthi (and Flame and Tawnee and Giselle . . .), looks like he's been whipped. Rock, Stride, and Quaz all have penises mangled in a way analogous to cauliflower ear. The needle marks from the muscle stimulators are visible all over their arms, chests, and abs.

She has a vision of the Bride of Frankenstein, of sewn-together corpses thrusting and tearing at each other, falling into heaps of mangled parts, and she thinks she may just lose that fine breakfast, but then she draws a deep breath and says, "I am going to demand a vacation, and if they fire me, I will just have to content myself with being richer than I ever thought I could be. But I am not going to do this even once more until they tell me *when* I get time off, and it's going to be soon, because I can't go on doing this. Not until I'm a lot more rested and feel a lot better."

At that, she breaks down, sobbing so hard that she can feel her Mary Ann Waterhouse muscles wrenching and twisting against her Synthi Venture tummy sheath.

John Klieg is awake early, as always, and by the time dawn is washing over the old Kennedy Space Center spread out below his control tower, he's rubbing his hands together and chuckling. A naive visitor might think that all the flashing screens around him are part of his pleasure because he is so thoroughly on top of the operations of GateTech, but in fact they are just decorations. Klieg doesn't even look at them—he pays people to look at them and to think about what's on them, and for every screen you see here (and for thousands more that are too dull to make good decorations), there are at least a couple of employees who know much more about it than Klieg ever will.

There are also more than a hundred employees who know more about *all* the screens than Klieg does. If he were his own employee, he'd have to fire himself, he supposes, and the thought makes him smile.

They make a good decoration because most people who've been to Kennedy just came out to look at the big plaque that says various lunatics allowed themselves to be shot into orbit on top of barely controlled bombs from here. A few more determined sorts will go out and look at the little plaques on the crumbling concrete or by the partially collapsed gantries and the towers with the DANGER—UNSTABLE STRUCTURE signs, the small plaques that mention names and dates.

But most people don't come out here at all. To the extent that they know about it, they look, a few times, at the video clips in their history lessons, and what they see, besides rockets rising into the sky on long pyramids of fire, are immense rooms full of screens, screens that somehow, by their sheer numbers, gave the impression that everything was under control and everything was being taken care of. (It must have been an interesting problem in PR, keeping people from thinking of every screen as something that was liable to go wrong and had to be watched all the time, Klieg thinks.) So as the Man Who Bought Cape Canaveral, he has this row of screens here as a sort of trophy, and he puts what he wants on it—and that's the data that flows through his empire.

"Empire" is not a bad term for it, either, Klieg thinks—and why is he getting so philosophical today? Not that he undervalues getting philosophical either. One advantage he has always had over the competition has been a certain rigorousness of thought that keeps him focused on what he's actually doing, not on some image of it. He knows in his bones that he is not a captain of industry (in that nothing he does is very much like what the captain of a ship, an infantry company, or a basketball team does), nor a facilitator of work (work does not cause money; getting paid causes money), nor a seeker of vision (you should know where you are going, but if it is anywhere worth getting to, most of the time and effort goes into the trip). No, philosophic clarity has been a key to his life in business, and he doesn't fall for facile or self-flattering descriptions—not even, usually, for the self-flattery of thinking he is immune to self-flattery.

So he leans back in the big control chair—it reminds visitors of the idea of a "mission commander" and of high achievement, but it also supports Klieg's bad back—and gives himself permission to let the philosophizing run its course. Perhaps he can learn something.

Alexander wept at the thought of no more worlds to conquer, and Alexander hadn't conquered nearly as much as he thought he had.

The thought is unbidden. Klieg looks down across his trim body; he's graying a little and refusing to give in to that. He lets his thoughts wander.

What is it about empire, Alexander, conquest? A very poor metaphor for what he's done. GateTech is not any of those things. Cold realism led him to put it together, the realization that he knew how to make money in a new way and that the first major corporation on the field would dominate it if it were played right.

Okay, take stock, Klieg, back to basics, he tells himself. GateTech really does four things. One, it studies what research other businesses are doing. Two, it does R&D in those fields and takes out patents as quickly as it can. Three, it forces other companies to pay GateTech for access to the technology they've been developing.

Four, it lobbies Washington, Tokyo, Brussels, Moscow, and the UN to maintain the laws that allow it to do that.

He explained it once to a distant cousin's kid; if he'd been alive at the time of James Watt, he would have sought to patent, not a steam engine, but the boiler and the piston; if he'd been alive in Edison's day, he'd have sought to patent tungsten wire and glass bulbs; if he'd been around at the beginning of computers he'd have tried to patent the keyboard. And the biggest secret. . . .

Aha. That's the parallel to empires and Alexander and all that. I'm thinking about the fact that GateTech has never manufactured one object or performed one service for anyone; that's the secret of our success. We get in their way and make them pay to get us out of their way, that's all. We function like the ancient empires that didn't care about local customs as long as taxes got collected. Like Alexander or Caesar, we keep everyone doing what they were doing before, what they would do without us, and we take a cut.

But nowadays a lot of them are defending themselves better. Just last week MitsDoug beat us to patenting the new charge-deformable plastics, and now they can make their damned shape-shifting airliner without paying me a dime to do it. How many billions have I just been done out of?

Don't get mad, and don't waste time getting even.

Get ahead.

That was the key. He lost a lot in the Flash, but while other companies spent fortunes suing the banks, trying to get their lost accounts re-created, GateTech merely moved in on every technology needed for data recovery. He made back a lot more than he lost.

He lost a lot when Parti Euro Uno took over and "Europeanized" foreign holdings, but he gained a lot more by taking on every highly skilled Afropean he could after the Expulsion.

For twenty years, a bit of industrial espionage and a little forethought have told him how to get the critical patent six months or a year ahead, just close enough to make them pay GateTech to "infringe."

He almost laughs aloud at how much thinking he's had to do. Couldn't he have just looked at the current business plan and said the time horizon needed to move outward?

Nope. That's what he pays flunkies to do. "Glinda," he says, speaking aloud. He takes two deep breaths, exhales slowly . . . she will come in . . . now.

A door glides open and Glinda Gray comes in. It's not that she's been sitting outside waiting for his voice—he wouldn't pay anyone to do that—or that she's dropped anything vital to answer his call. She is one of seventeen Special Operations Vice-Presidents, and Glinda was top of the queue of those he hadn't already assigned to anything specific. But if he'd had to pick the perfect person for this job, it would be Glinda. Two reasons—one, she's a perfectionist negative-thinking nut. Her report always contains *everything* that could go wrong.

Two, she never asks very many questions when he throws her at a new job.

She stands in front of him and he mentally describes her the way a TV news broadcast would if she lost her house in a hurricane, got murdered, or wrote a best-seller: a "pretty, blonde divorced mother." Her skin is freckling and roughening, and he suspects a touch of the needle is keeping the silver out of the gold in her hair. She has a slightly tired look around the eyes and from the way she stands he suspects the pink pumps are already hurting her feet this morning.

She finished her last big project three weeks ago and she always looks a little tense when she's trying to come up with a new one, because although John Klieg wouldn't part with her for anything, he can never convince her of that.

"Have a seat," he says, "this is going to take a while. I've got a new priority-one project for you, and I want you to know that if you weren't at the top of the queue already, I'd've jumped you up the ladder to give you this task."

She nods, firmly, once, and sits down. "Tape on?"

"Yes."

"Systems please record access highest," she says, forcefully, and a mechanical voice responds, "Recording."

Klieg smiles at her, and makes it as warm as he can manage. "I have a gut feeling that we are not working enough long-range stuff, and especially we're passing up chances to find master patents that will block lots of technologies instead of little patents that jam up just one corporation's key project."

"Fourteen years ago," she reminds him, "you set the policy of always blocking a specific project somewhere; you used to say a master patent would be too easy to get around and might not still be in force when they got there."

He nods; he doubts she's thought about that policy ten times in the interim, but he also knows she could give him, accurately, the whole history of debate over it and the rationale for the decision, even if it was fourteen years ago.

"Call this a change of policy," he says. "We're a lot bigger now and we can do better research and fight more expensive legal actions, and there's a lot more body of case law in our favor. The question is, should we make this change? My gut says the answer is yes, but find out for me."

He leans back and lets his eyes wander over the screens; this is something they *are* good for, they jog his memory. "Three test cases to apply it to. Number one, the continuously optimized product—see if we can get the whole nascent COP industry by the balls. Number two, the ongoing studies on getting antimatter motors down in price to compete in the Third World market. And number three . . . ummm . . . hah. Any ideas?"

Once again Glinda doesn't disappoint him.

"Have you caught the news this morning?" she asks. "I can think of a perfect test case, a need that's not yet specified but likely to happen."

He sits forward. "Tell."

"Have you heard about the North Slope methane release?"

He shakes his head, and notices that color is coming back into her cheeks and the tiredness is falling away. Glinda will be in great shape for months now. He wonders for an instant why that's so important, decides once again she's irreplaceable, and listens as she begins to explain.

I wonder when space became boring, Louie Tynan thinks. He's sitting in the view bubble—there's an OSHA standard notice by the door telling him he's likely to take more radiation than he should, and subconsciously that adds to his pleasure—having an onion bagel with chopped liver and watching the Earth roll by down below. Yesterday there was really a view—the UNSOO ships glowing red as they screamed back down into the atmosphere, the detonations that made the ice bump and shimmer, and then later the flaring methane reflecting off the ice. There are a couple of flares still burning, but it's daylight in that area now, and it's not as impressive.

Louie figures the major reason he's been able to keep this job—maybe the only reason—is a sense of humor. When he joined the Astronaut Corps, in 2009, there were over two thousand of them; three years later, when it officially became the United States Space Force and added a bunch of Navy and Air Force stuff, there were forty-five hundred men and women who were qualified for missions, and about six thousand Americans had flown in space. The First UN Mars Expedition had two USSF officers aboard, and had the Second through Ninth ever been flown, there would have been a round dozen Americans who had set foot on Mars.

But after the first landing, repeating the same thing that had happened after the moon landings, most of the world's nations, especially the U.S., retreated from space. There are now forty-four active astronauts, and where fifteen years ago there were almost always forty or fifty or so in space at any given time, now there's just Louie. The seniority from going on the Mars mission lets him pull a lot of strings, or they wouldn't have him up here on Space Station *Constitution*, last of the five American manned space stations to remain active.

He leans back and looks at the Earth some more. If you count the moon, he's seen three worlds from orbit close up, and there are just fourteen other people alive who can say that.

I suppose if you haven't seen it for yourself, if all you have are the photos, and if you don't look too closely or pay much attention, then after a while this must get dull. Exploration goes on, of course . . . there are permanent robot stations orbiting everything from Mercury out to Saturn, and one on the way for Uranus, and there are robot ground installations all over the Jovian moons and a robot dirigible cruising the skies of Titan. You can even buy continuous tape from some of their cameras, so that you can sit in your living room and climb the side of Olympus Mons, or make a deep-dive orbit of Jupiter.

There are not enough people around who can explain why that is not the same.

The sun is just coming up on the Western Pacific, which means it's probably lighting the ocean surface half a kilometer up from Carla; she usually takes *MyBoat* down below when she sleeps, or when she wants to concentrate on some academic project and let the autopilot steer.

Maybe he'll call her again . . . no, not a good thing to do, he called last time and it's her turn, and she'll probably call in a few days anyway.

He grins and swallows another bite. What he has going with Carla is a complicated dance devoted mostly to making sure they don't get together on any permanent basis anymore. Look at them both, living in steel cocoons a long way from the rest of humanity . . . mating eagles is probably easier.

So, the space program is still being taken over by robots, the only person he really likes is another hermit-in-a-can, and he's soaking up enough rads, what with eating in here all the time, that they'll probably ground him for a while when he gets back and put him on preventive anticancer drugs. He's really the last of his kind, and the old planet rolling around below him has about seven and one-half billion people who don't understand him. Last week he was interviewed on Dance Channel—he still has the XV jack from the Mars Expedition—and when he got the program back he didn't recognize his own experiences from their editing.

The most exciting thing he got to do this month was set a methane plume on fire, at the request of UNSOO.

On the other hand, the food is still good—way better than what it was on the way to Mars—and you can't beat the view. Probably worth continuing to live and work, he decides. He puts his mouth up to one of the monitors, lets loose a grand, gut-ripping belch, redolent of chicken liver and raw onion, grins broadly, and goes back to the telescope for the afternoon's work.

What have you gotten yourself into this time, Brittany Lynn?

Brittany Lynn Hardshaw, President of the United States, remembers that when she was little, her father used to ask that about once a day, and normally the answer was something like "the old motor oil in the barn," or "an open can of house paint." It's eight-thirty in the morning and she's looking at the confidential report from NOAA that Harris Diem left for her last night, and wondering if she can trust it at all.

The trouble is, she's spent a long time getting the government under control, with Diem as her right hand . . . and now she's not sure there's anyone left who's likely to tell her the truth. And this time that's what she needs.

She gets up and walks to a window, looking out on Pennsylvania Avenue. When they rebuilt after the Flash, they closed the whole area to vehicle traffic, nominally for environmental reasons and actually to make it that much tougher to bring a nuke close to the New White House or Capitol and repeat the decapitation shot.

The other part of the Flash, the bomb that went off sixty miles above Kansas City, wouldn't have much effect this time; everything everywhere is in Faraday cages, and all signal is on fibrop.

But the center of government is permanently vulnerable, Hardshaw thinks. *We're made out of meat. We have to be in contact with many thousands of people.*

The street before her is jammed with pedestrians, most with briefcases, scurrying about like ants. If three of them had parts for a cram bomb, they could wipe out the Federal government this morning, and no one would stop them. Maybe if they did it again, this time they would announce who they were, or at least explain why they did it.

In her mind's eye Hardshaw sees Washington rise from the swamps, go down in the flames set by the British troops a few years later, rise again to bustle and pulse when President Lincoln looked out of the house that once stood here, shrink back into a sleepy backwater before growing again, explode into a great city during depression, war, and cold war, deteriorate into a slum until the Flash, rise from the nuclear catastrophe. . . .

Into a provincial capital for the UN, she admits to herself. Not that she blames her predecessors, and she hopes that the two who are still living don't blame her.

She thinks, *I am looking forward to retirement.* It's been a long time since she was a dirty-faced kid living in a mobile home on a dirt road in the mountains of Idaho, next to the log house it took her father six years to finish—not unusual for a man who worked part time and drank full time. It's been a long time since she was a white trash student at a third-rate university, and even since her upset victory to become Idaho Attorney General. . . .

All right, President Grandma, let's not write our memoirs just yet. She's only ten months from retirement, anyway. *Wonder if XV will even cover the election?* There's no longer much at stake in being the President of the United States. The Republicans are running a Hawaiian nonentity, the guy Hardshaw picked for Commerce; the Democrats are running yet another governor of New York, this time the first black woman; and the United Left is running TBA—a slate of electors who will pick a President if enough of them win.

Back to work, Brittany Lynn, now. She remembers how her father used to say "now"—the word implied an oncoming spanking.

That association, at last, draws her attention back to the job. Liu, the UN's Ambassador to the U.S., also likes to start off on a scare note. This time it was a threat that there was sentiment in the General Assembly to further disarm the independent national forces, down to a ten-percent-of-UN level. She knew that wasn't what they were after, but when it sprang it was almost as bad.

They want NOAA, NASA, the Department of Energy, the scientific branches of EPA . . . the list goes on and on. All the usual reasons—better coordination and more equitable sharing of global resources—and all the usual promises about all the information remaining equally accessible and all the employees receiving just the same pay and benefits. Nothing to complain about there. . . .

Except that if Hardshaw goes for it, when the SecGen says something is happening out there in the global environment, she won't have the foggiest idea whether or not he's telling the truth. And the major area in which the UN has been restricting national sovereignty, for the past twenty years, has been in global environmental questions.

She can even see it in Rivera's lights, when she tries; UNESCO and its many spinoffs don't supply the quality of information that he needs, and he ends up acquiring it mainly from the scientific agencies of the Big Five. *And if you were the SecGen, Brittany Lynn, you'd have to wonder all the time if maybe something was being put over on you, or something was being hidden.*

But she isn't the SecGen, and it's not her lookout. She stretches, smooths her skirt, picks up the phone, and tells them to get Harris Diem and bring him in—she knows he's been at his desk for at least an hour by now.

The irony of it all, she thinks, is that in her seven years of struggle with the UN she's been forced to make the Federal government speak with just one voice, made it a better implement for governing than the country has ever had before—and she has, now, even less real authority than the Presidents between Jackson and Lincoln.

And the deeper irony is that as she has extended her authority, she has diminished her ability to get the truth, instead of what people think she wants to hear. This document on her desk is the result of that, and she's too smart not to see the chickens returning to roost.

She can't tell what the people at NOAA think the release of so much methane will do, because they were trying to tell her whatever would make things go smoothly for NOAA.

And just this once, she wants the truth.

If you're going to get all worked up about what's true and what's not, you're never gonna be President like I'm grooming you for, Brittany Lynn, her father used to say, once she'd gotten old enough to start to catch him out in all those lies—the lost Spanish city somewhere in the Hoodoo River gorge, the aliens he had met on the road to Sand Point, Bigfoot, that the house would be beautiful when it was finished, and he was going to stop drinking for his little girl.

This job isn't quite the fun she might have hoped for, back then, but it still beats hell out of spending her life behind a cash register at a McDonald's in Boise. She was just kind of wondering, for a minute there, by how much?

The soft chime tells her Harris is on his way in. She composes herself, goes back to the desk, flips the report open to a random page. When he comes in, she skips the greeting and starts with, "Harris, you greasy old hack, why in hell did you hand me a report that doesn't say anything?"

"Because, boss," he says, setting down his briefcase and leaning across the desk at her, "we don't know anything."

They laugh because they have been friends for twenty years. Nothing is funny but each is glad the other is here.

*   *   *

Yeats fussed about things falling apart and the center not being able to hold. What really happened was that the center ceased to exist altogether.

It fell into nonexistence gradually, in the kind of grim retreat and perpetual compromise that marked the last two centuries of Rome.

Eisenstein found out that all you had to do was cut from the thing to the face that seemed to be seeing it, take the pieces of the story and put them together with a simple splice, and it would stick together just as if some Dickensian narrator had said "And so, dear reader . . ."; the storyteller was no longer at the center of the story.

Einstein found out that you could pick any old place to be the center.

Gertrude Stein found out that the more times rose was rose, the less it had to do with anything pink and sweet-smelling, and the freer it was to be like Burns's luve, or like every other rose.

RAND Corporation demonstrated that in the event of a nuclear war, a state without a head cannot be decapitated, and gray corporate gnomes transformed into the playful sprites of the nets.

Hitler, Stalin, Roosevelt, and Churchill tried to rebuild the center, but to do it they had to let radios into everyone's house, and there is no point in being Pope if you've got to touch the beggars personally; the increased contact of the center with the periphery only hastened its dissolution.

The old centralized Communist Party was so ineffective at opposing the Korean War that many Americans didn't know there was a war, but thirty thousand mimeographs and two thousand college radio stations carried the struggle against the Vietnam War into the farthest corners of the country, and while the reporters from the centralized broadcasting services interviewed the supposed heads of the supposedly national supposed organizations, the ground shifted under them. By 1980, the slogan was "Think Globally, Act Locally," and few were bothering with the global part. Even the Department of Defense came up with AirLand Battle, which you might call cooperative local-action violence.

By 2028, things have gone farther. The center is wherever you are standing.

When Harris Diem gets done talking to the President, he's tired, and it's still early in the morning. Another ten-minute conversation, another major chunk of history, he thinks to himself. The hardest thing about his memoirs is going to be explaining to people that it really happened that way, all the time—you walked into Brittany Lynn Hardshaw's office, she asked you six questions, and you suddenly had orders to change all of American history.

Assuming it works.

He thinks about it, rubbing his temples at his desk, rolling and stretching his neck. He will need a reliable fall guy, and there's hardly a better one than Henry Pauliss. He'll need to make elaborate arrangements to covertly monitor about forty completely loyal NOAA people. That's not a problem either.

He needs to go spend some time in his basement. He hasn't in weeks. . . .

Time for it tonight if he wants to. Interesting phrase, "wants to." If his house burned down tomorrow and everything hidden down there were destroyed, he would probably weep with relief . . . until that buzzing started at the base of his skull, and there was no relief possible for that.

He can hear it now, like a doorbell in a dream: no hallway ever leads to the door, and you know that when you open the door something will kill you . . . and you cannot do anything except endlessly search the halls for the door, so that you can open it.

Harris Diem sighs. Whenever things get fraught like this, the buzzing starts, and it's as if the basement calls him, begs him to come down. Back when the Afropean Expulsion happened, when the Navy stood off Jutland and Admiral Tranh was calling every three hours to ask for more Marines, more air cover, and more space cover, because if shooting started he didn't think he could hold back his local commanders and there was going to be war . . . that whole long week, the buzz was like a blade cutting through his scalp. And when he had finally scratched the itch, it had left him so sick that he very nearly torched his own house. He could have pretended he did it for the insurance and resigned in disgrace. He should have done it. Someday he will.

Right now, the boss needs him. As soon as this crisis is over . . . he'll go down to the basement. Then he'll think of some way to get it all over with for good.

It's a promise he's made himself many times before.

The biggest problem with zipline is that it's like taking an elevator to everywhere; there is a window you can look out of, but since the car moves at four hundred miles per hour, they've got it running between high, fenced earth berms most of the way, so there's nothing to see, and on the rare occasions when it shoots across a gorge or goes up to an elevated roadbed, the zipline is moving so fast that most people become ill. So after a few times when you're a little kid, you don't unshutter the window.

Since practically anyone can afford a private cabin, the zipline has become the major place for temporary privacy. When he was a teenager, Jesse used to take girls from Tucson to dates in LA, Albuquerque, or even

Dallas, just to have them alone in the compartment for that long, and it seems like every fifth XV drama is about a couple that meets regularly during a commute for a bit of adultery.

The other cliché is that couples have their fights on the zipline, and that's the cliché Jesse and Naomi are acting out.

Jesse does not know what this one is about. A week ago, after they watched the UN missiles get blown up, they drove out in the desert and they made love in the back of the Lectrajeep, the top thrown back so that it was all by bright starlight. They lay together afterward, touching and whispering, and she asked him a lot of things about growing up in the desert.

It was the first time he ever felt like she wanted to know something about him without correcting it.

After they got back, they made love more often in the next three days than they had in months. They didn't go to any meetings, and he had lots of time to study.

But since this morning they've been having this fight. It's one of those really frustrating ones where Jesse can't get Naomi to admit that it's a fight; she calls it a "clarification." As far as he can tell, the feelings she is clarifying for him at the moment are the ones that have to do with dumping him because she really likes him. He says so.

"I knew you'd take it that way!"

This does not reassure him. The two-person zipline compartments are barely large closets—their knees are almost touching and they can only lean back to get about three feet of separation at best, and Jesse's shoulders touch both the wall and the door. So they are having this fight right in each other's face.

"I don't understand," he says.

"I've told you, you're not going to get what I'm saying if you try to understand it. Try to feel it, Jesse, can't you?" She brushes her hair back from her face, and he sees that her eyes are wet, which startles him—somehow he had missed the point that all this is painful for her, too, and he's embarrassed by that, so he stops arguing and listens for a moment.

The hair comes farther back and he can see how pale her skin is around her freckles. Her eyes are huge wet pools and there's a catch in her voice.

"You probably thought we were just getting along great, didn't you? I mean after we went out in the desert?"

He doesn't see where this is going.

"I guess I should have explained but it didn't seem like it would work if I did, Jesse. I—well, at the meeting, where everyone was watching the Siberian missiles get blown up, I was feeling so tired. I didn't ever want to see any of that stuff again. And . . . well, you know, I got involved with you partly because it seemed like, oh, sort of a duty, I mean, you were intelligent and you liked me and I thought I could help you get your values clarified."

Jesse had not thought of himself as a duty.

"But then as I got to know you . . . well, you know, I'm very lucky because I grew up with parents who had anti-centric life-and-Earth values right from the start, so I was raised not to be linear or centric. I mean, in most of the groups I've belonged to, that's been my big strength; my big contribution to the group is that I don't have to struggle against the old humanistic values. So it had always been my sharing my values with others, instead of them sharing theirs with me, because I usually had the values they knew they should have and I was happy to share." She sighs and looks down at her hands, which are writhing like spiders mating in her lap. "But, see, Jesse, what I didn't realize was that not only did you not understand real ecological values, you didn't even know you *should* have them. So without meaning to—I mean, I'm *sure* you'd never do it intentionally, you're a *good* person, Jesse—god, I'm being com*plete*ly judgmental—" She is now crying, hard.

Jesse is being pulled in too many directions. He wants to hold her and soothe her like he would a little girl, but he can't help noticing that when her eyes are puffy and red, and snot is running onto her upper lip— especially after she's just explained to him that she got involved with him as a duty to save his poor stupid ass from his bad values, which he never thought were bad in the first place—she is just not as attractive as she used to be. Except he's also noticing that when she sobs, her big chest bounces up and down, too, and part of him wonders what it would be like to have her pinned down and sobbing while he squeezed it—and the fact that he's having the thought (and that it's turning him on) is making him a little sick to his stomach. Mostly he's trying to figure out when and how she's going to tell him that she's going to dump him.

She wipes her nose on her shirtsleeve, checks her watch, and goes on. "Jesse, the problem is that I started to realize that your values were very, very attractive to me. I mean, like, I started to think about . . . well, you always said I was pretty, and I started to think about what it would be like just to get attention for that. And out in the desert . . . I mean, it was mean-ingless, totally meaningless, it was just using nature because it was nice, without understanding nature really at all, but still—oh, Jesse, it was so nice. And there's the orgasms too."

"Orgasms?"

She sobs. "You know, don't you? I explained it."

He sort of knows. "You mean the thing about female orgasm is being in touch with the world, or however that goes?"

"You see what I mean, you didn't even realize how important that was, or that you needed to listen and get it right." She sniffles. "The point is, the female orgasm is non-centric, and it's the spiritual energy coming out and linking you to the whole universe, making you feel how you should relate to everything—completely opposite of the centric male orgasm, which is technological and aggressive and all. So . . . so anyway, I always had a lot of trouble having orgasms—my mom's discussion group used to have whole meetings about how Mom could help me with it—but when I, did I was *very* non-centric, I really felt the whole universe and I was just so full of love that I didn't even know I was having sex anymore. But with you . . . in the desert . . . I had about ten of them, and I just had them totally selfishly. I mean, I was completely *male and selfish!* All I did was look up at the stars and come; I didn't think about anything except that it felt good between my legs.

"And this whole past week—I mean, I've been doing all the 'in-love' stuff that I shouldn't. It's been so much fun and I've enjoyed it so much . . . don't you see where that's leading? I always thought I was strong but I'm not. I'm just falling for all of this stuff like . . . like . . . I don't know what, but I'm doing it. If I stay with you I might lose all my values, don't you see that? I can't . . . even though I really want to."

She checks her watch again, and Jesse looks at his and realizes that they are only a minute from the station in Hermosillo. That's when she says, "So see, I've got to stop all this and get back to working on my values. I guess in a lot of ways what you will always represent to me is the person I could have been if I had been born that way or chosen to go that way—I don't mean I could have been you, but I can see where I could have been perfect as your girlfriend and very happy and so forth, and I can see where that would be a lot of fun, but it is not important for me to be happy or have fun; the Earth needs people to care for it properly, and if I stay with you I'll forget that. I found myself just the other day calling myself a uniter in front of other people—just as if this were the twentieth and there were two sides that were debating, instead of acknowledging that the world already *is* one, and we have to act in accord with its unity. Gwendy called me on it. That had never happened to me since I was a little girl. I'm not used to needing values-clarifying, and I don't like having to be values-clarified.

"So I've signed on with the Natural Ways Reclamation Project and I'll be going down to Tehuantepec in Oaxaca State for a few months, to work on spreading correct values and on learning them from people who haven't been polluted so much by centric and linear thinking. It was really fun and I guess I should thank you, except that the fun could have led me to act against my values, so instead I'll just say I'll miss you, because I think you'll like that and it's true."

As she's saying the last sentence, there's a distinct force in the compartment, pushing Jesse back into his seat cushions and making Naomi lean forward. Ziplines are so quiet and vibrationless that you only really notice motion when you're stopping or starting.

As she finishes, she stands up—almost losing her balance for a moment—and says, "And I've asked to be on the AIDS-ARTS-SPM patient-assistance shift instead of the tutoring shift this time, so we won't be working next to each other. Gwendy and Sibby and Foxglove are going by our place—I gave them a key—to get me moved out while we're gone, so we don't have to see each other after this, which I know would be painful for both of us. Not that pain to me matters, but it would be painful for you and I shouldn't be selfish." There are tears all over her face now and what she really looks like, to Jesse, is someone in an old flat movie who has been tortured into confessing to something she didn't do. Then she leans forward and kisses his cheek, getting her tears on his face, and at that moment the car comes to a stop, the door opens into the exit passage, and she's gone.

Jesse's first thought is that she must have rehearsed the speech to know exactly how long it would take, so that she could get the door timed like that. That's Naomi, always thorough. . . .

He takes a long, deep breath, and suddenly realizes he has no desire at all to help barrio kids with their arithmetic today. He puts his thumb on the readerplate and says aloud, "This compartment back to Tucson."

"That will be two dollars and five cents for a trip of three hundred fifty kilometers or two hundred eighteen miles," the car replies. "A single person riding in a double compartment incurs a surcharge of fifty-five cents because of the wasted space and resources. You may cancel this order and move to a single compartment for a refund at any time until the car begins to move. Thank you and have a pleasant journey."

The door slides closed. Jesse leans forward to press his face against the seat Naomi just vacated. There are two long strands of her hair there, and he runs his fingers over them; she never wore scent, but the seat is warm from her presence on it, and he imagines he can smell her on it.

He stays there as the car begins to move, its acceleration shoving his face against the seat cushions.

When she gets upset, the Deeper-speak gets pretty thick, but he got enough of it to understand, anyway, that although she is dumping him, it's because she loves him too much, but doesn't think he'll fit with her ideals.

He can fix this. When he gets back to Tucson—better not go home just yet or he'll have to deal with her friends—he will get himself educated, active, and involved. In a few months with some effort he's quite sure he can be one of the biggest activists at the U of the Az. He knows he's bright, articulate, and hardworking; he just has to put those resources to work in the right direction. By the time she's back from Tehuantepec, he can be a totally different person, if that's what she wants. It might cost him some time (but he can drop some classes), and some money (but he can live on the line a while), but what else can he do?

He leans back and lets Naomi's hair lie on his thigh, so he can look at it. He thinks about her in the desert, and he remembers her saying that he gave her overpowering orgasms . . . and quite unbidden, the pictures of him comforting her like a child, and of her big breasts shaking while she cried, come to him as well. Before he knows it, he's so horny that he's squeezing his penis through his jeans, masturbating right here in the compartment, the way dirty old men supposedly do, and he doesn't give a crap because he just can't think straight until this gets relieved.

It does in a moment, a brutal heave as if he were vomiting from his testicles. He sees the strand of her hair lying on his leg. The compartment air conditioning must be acting up, because it seems terribly cold in here, and somehow that sharpens the smell of his semen and the loneliness of the little space. He presses his head to the cushion where her beautiful butt was, just minutes ago, but it's cold now.

He has never felt so in love.

After a while, though, the semen drying in his underwear is proving to be a fairly effective glue, the seat pressed against his face is less than comfortable, his eyes are stinging from his tears, and he just plain doesn't think he can keep this up much longer. There really isn't anything to do here, during the forty minutes back to Tucson.

He gets out his lunch and eats early—it's packed with all sorts of blodgy, gooey, grainy stuff that he doesn't like much, most of it to be given away to little Mexican kids who will try a bite or two and then politely toss it when he's not looking. This time he eats it all himself, which is probably a mistake. That kills about ten minutes. He uses one of the wet napkins to wash his face, tries not to notice that he's feeling better (except in his stomach), and seriously thinks about this plan to become the leading activist on campus.

Heck, if it doesn't get Naomi back, there's a couple of her friends who look like they'd be fun. There seem to be organizations dedicated to every possible course of action about the methane release (except maybe one to demand more methane). Once there's an official report out of NOAA or UNESCO, the one or two campus organizations whose viewpoints are still relevant are going to grow like mushrooms.

So if he joins the right one now. . . .

He chews himself out for a moment or two. He tries not to notice that in his self-criticism he is imitating Naomi. Jesse just doesn't have the knack for it; he has never managed to dislike himself as much as Naomi dislikes herself. But he should be joining an organization because he believes in it and wants to work for it, out of a selfless love for. . . .

Oh, well, anyway, he will want to work for an organization that is on the right track, he knows he doesn't want to work for one that isn't, and since he has a reasonable way of finding out which is which, he should use it. Maybe Di can tell him something that will help.

He unrolls a mirror from his wallet, sticks it to the wall, and, using the remaining wet napkins and his comb, cleans up enough to be reasonably sure that he won't look obviously upset or worked up, because unfortunately Di is just the kind of dumb, affectionate big brother to get upset about what Jesse is feeling, rather than sticking to the issue of what Jesse would like to know. Then he takes his phone from his belt, slaps the video pickup onto the wall facing him, and calls.

He puts it on a priority just high enough so that the call will reach Di at work, as long as Di hasn't pressed the Urgent Only button. It will interrupt him at routine tasks but not in the middle of a meeting or anything; it will go over whichever lines and services are instantaneously cheaper in the complex dance of competing software, so that the signal is actually scattering over the Earth's surface in little packets of a few milliseconds each. Jesse thinks about none of these things, but they happen anyway.

Randy Householder doesn't even trust people he admires. He figures it takes somebody big to have kept the investigation of Kimbie Dee's death from getting anywhere. Violent-felony-for-forced-extraction is so ferociously prosecuted under the Diem Act that most organized crime won't touch distributing those wedges—they even turn it in when they find it. So whoever's behind it swings a lot of weight.

Randy figures the only way the man he is looking for will get caught is if someone with even more power—someone incorruptible—is after him, and any such investigation would have to stay secret, and out of usual channels. Not that it doesn't occur to Randy that he might be the only person who is really looking anymore.

But if the secret investigation is being done by anyone, it will have to be connected to someone who is powerful, incorruptible, and passionately involved in the fight to stamp out murderporn XV—which can only be Harris Diem himself.

So Randy has datarodents constantly searching and replicating, looking for any connection to Diem. One of them knows Di Callare is an occasional back channel to Diem, and—having nothing better to do—decides to hitchhike along on one of Jesse's packets. It delays the ringing of Di's phone by almost three milliseconds, but it also locates a hitherto unsuspected back-channel node between the White House and the science agencies, a node that has a lot of old Harris Diem code hanging around in it. Not the most likely place, but what Randy is looking for won't be in any likely place.

The datarodent looks around, decides this is good hunting, and dispatches packets to go find some of Randy's other datarodents and have them send copies here. It doesn't bother Randy about it, yet. If anything interesting comes through, it will.

At NOAA, Di Callare is sitting in his office with his feet up on the desk, looking at a chart that keeps knotting and untangling itself as he talks to the computer. What he's trying to do is to put together a set of tasks to parcel out to his team.

Peter is a nice guy, and he has the best gut feel of anyone on the team for weather, but he's a born plodder, one of those guys who's afraid to draw even the most obvious conclusions. Talley has a lot of fire and imagination, and she's often very innovative, but she'll sometimes go out farther on a limb than she should and she has no political sense at all. Besides, because she's exceptionally bright and witty, she makes Lori just a little jealous, and if Di works too closely with Talley for a few weeks, so that she's in his conversation all the time, it makes a certain amount of trouble at home.

On the other hand, if he pairs her up with anyone else, she tends to drive them crazy. No one but Di seems able to say no to her; it's undoubtedly because she's beautiful, but Di doesn't see why that should make her right all the time.

Mohammed and Wo Ping are mathematicians first and foremost, and they like working together. Normally that makes job assignments for them easy, but when they work together they also tend to throw away wilder speculations before reporting to anyone else . . . and he needs wild speculations just now. Maybe he can put Gretch, the summer intern, with them. Her math is lousy, so they won't like her, but she's got intuition nearly as good as Peter's, and she doesn't have enough experience to dismiss any idea as "too wild."

It's really a great team. He spent a long time getting them all. He just wishes he didn't have such an impossibly complex task for them, but that wasn't anything he, or Henry Pauliss, had any choice about. Hell, Harris Diem and President Hardshaw had no choice either.

The message that says "Ring Di Callare's phone if it's not marked 'Urgent Only' " bounces into Washington in four pieces, coming in from two satellites and two fibrop land links, merges at a substation six blocks from his office, slips into an open slot in the link to the White House—holds still there for three milliseconds as a datarodent disentangles from it and looks around—and enters the memory register of Di's phone, which is underneath a printed statistical summary of the outcomes of a billion runs of the NOAA main model.

The phone rings, he reaches for it, and phone and printout alike go into the wastebasket. He pulls the wastebasket over to fish out the phone, and says, "On hold with current project, please. Please pick up the call for me and put it up on screen and speakers."

His kid brother's face pops up on the screen.

"Jesse! What's up?"

"Oh, this and that. Uh, you have maybe ten minutes or so? It's not super-important."

"Sure, I can use a break just at the moment."

Jesse gives him a little half smile, one that Di recognizes because Mom used to do it too, and then says, "I'm not asking you to tell me anything you're not supposed to, or anything off the record, but I have an awful lot of friends who are wondering whether this methane thing is a big deal or not, and I kind of promised I'd ask, just in case there was something you could say that wasn't officially on the news yet. . . ."

If Jesse is anything like he was at the same age, the awful lot of friends is probably one and probably female. "Well," Di says, "it happens there's a bit more that I can say than there was last time. It's going out on public channels too, but it will probably disappear in the background noise of all the different outfits that are also speculating, plus probably what two astrologers, three Baptist ministers, and the Vegetarian League have to say. But we do have guesses and the news isn't good."

"The methane is going to saturate the air and back up all the cow farts worldwide?"

"We've pretty much discarded that hypothesis. No, we're looking at five possible kinds of bad news. For sure it's going to give us the hottest summer on record in the Northern Hemisphere, and it doesn't even remotely look like it'll be gone before it gives us the hottest summer on record in the Southern Hemisphere. So the things we're investigating are all based on that. One, the air will warm up by enough to make it hold a lot more water, and that water won't come from all the possible sources evenly. Might mean some major regional droughts—or extra-heavy rainfalls in other places.

"Two, several years of extra-warm weather will accelerate the forest migration already in process, so the forests have to migrate north, then move back south, then head north again. And since a forest can only move a mile a decade by trees dying on the south side and seeds sprouting on the north—what really happens is that you get a smaller forest surrounded by two strips of extremely abnormal scrub. All kinds of ecological echoes from that."

"Ecological echoes?" Jesse is looking at him intently, as if taking notes.

"Changes that cause changes that cause changes. The way the huge forest fire in 1910 in the Northwest altered forest ecologies in identifiable ways for more than a century afterward, even though almost none of the individual organisms lived that long.

"Three, extra heat is extra energy, and one place atmospheric heat goes is into hurricanes, especially when you consider the interaction with surface water. Bigger hurricanes, more hurricanes, hurricanes where there've never been hurricanes . . . we have a team looking at that.

"Four, maybe the extra heat melts a lot of snow fields early this spring and prevents their forming later in the fall, so the Earth's albedo drops and you get a feedback effect, making the warming keep right on increasing out to the point where there's no snow or ice left except on the Himalayas and the Andes. You know about albedo?"

"Shininess. How much sunlight gets reflected back into space and how much stays here to turn into heat. Introduction to Astronomy and Planetary Science, Astro 1103, I got a Significant Achievement."

"Attaboy. Family tradition; I was a C-plus kind of guy myself in undergrad."

"How'd you end up with a doctorate?"

"I got married and stopped spending so much time chasing tail. Okay, fifth, we get extra heat at the pole, so the air mass there doesn't sink as it normally would, and therefore it doesn't flow down into the middle latitudes. You get what's basically a global inversion all summer long; the wind stops blowing, and storms stop forming and moving west to east. Global drought, not to mention that air pollution builds up over the cities like you wouldn't believe. Then come winter you've got the interiors of North America and Eurasia dried out from drought, and the polar air mass finally breaks through. Big old windstorms hit those dried-out areas and you get a hemispheric dustbowl—followed by one or more things from options 1 to 4 the next year."

Jesse gives a long, slow whistle. "So no-bullshit, this is really a big deal? Worth getting worked up about?"

"It's a big deal, all right. Worth getting worked up about depends. The human race is not in a position to do anything about it, you know, and though I suppose you could join the nationalists and blame the UN for it, or turn uniter and demand that all power go to the UN, the truth is, no matter what people did, the same thing would have happened sooner or later. The seabed is lousy with methane clathrate all over the high latitudes.

Sooner or later, nukes or antimatter weapons were going to go off in it, or an undersea lava flow would have melted it, or maybe a major meteor strike would have come down right in the middle of it. Or for that matter, at the rate global warming is going, *all* those methane clathrate fields might very well melt once the deep ocean warms up in a hundred years. I've got one paleontology team digging into the evidence—there were several super-brief warmings in the geological record, and this is probably what they were. It's happened before, it'll happen again."

"A lot like a traffic accident, though." Jesse looks a little shaken. "No matter how predictable it is, you wish it wouldn't happen to you."

"Yeah, pretty much. Anyway, in less than ten years it will all be over; by that time the extra methane will be absorbed in the ocean and eaten by the microbes, burned up in lightning flashes, zapped apart by ultraviolet in the high atmosphere, all that kind of thing."

"Well, gee, that's a lot to absorb," Jesse says at last. "There doesn't seem to be anything that anyone can do about it—"

Di shrugs. "We could be urging people to get ready for bad news. That's about all. Heat is energy, and more energy in the system means whatever happens, it's going to be a big one. Hope I was some help."

"You always are. You're the flattest big brother I've got. Say hi to Lori and the kids."

It takes Di a second to remind himself that flat is a positive word.

When they hang up, there is no "broken connection" as people imagine; throughout their long call, each little piece of data has been running through the trillions of possible pipes all on its own, only rejoining at the other end. All that happens is that no more of them go running through the maze.

At the substation near Di's office, where Jesse's incoming words and picture were assembled and where Di's outgoing words and picture were frag-mented, there were more than thirty interested datarodents.

When ordinary voice-visual phone went to digital packetized transmission, the newspapers had been full of the dangers and potentials for "viruses"—the boomtalk pejorative for self-replicating software—on the phone system.

As usual, the word was far behind the news. The replicating code that carried messages to reprogram nodes could be duplicated and modified, intelligence added, and the whole turned into a datarodent (so called because it listened and ratted on whoever it could). Datarodents crouch in the nodes near anything important and listen as the little data-pieces come back together to form the conversation; they make copies of messages to send back to their masters.

Within a decade of the first datarodents showing up, human masters were no longer needed. The masters were programs themselves, artificial intelligences that could recognize enough to tell important from not.

After a while longer, datarodent and master alike began to replicate themselves and to move about on the net, always looking to colonize a node they had not yet infected. In 2028, the datarodents have gnawed away every bit of privacy.

As long as *los corporados* got paid when datarodents did this, the only people who cared were the sort of isolated nuts who sent paper mail to congressmen complaining about "invasions of privacy."

It's obvious to a lot of different organizations—especially after the Global Riot—that important things come out of NOAA. So the listener programs have been breeding in the nodes around NOAA like mosquitos in a swamp. In a way it's a miracle that only thirty families of datarodents run out to carry the news elsewhere.

One little gang dashes only a scant mile or two—though it does it via nodes in Boston, Cleveland, and Trinidad, in part—into the FBI's phone analysis program, which scans quickly and concludes that Di has divulged nothing that should be confidential, then calls up the dossier on Jesse, spots the connection to Naomi, concludes that she can make no use of the information either except to gain influence among the campus organizations, connects that with the FBI assessment of her as uncharismatic and therefore harmless, or at least preferable to several other possible campus leaders. It makes the note, records the data and the assessment, and closes the file.

Most of the other datarodents work for data-gathering organizations, and these clip the relevant parts of what Di said, note that it's semantically all but identical to material that NOAA sent over the wire as a press release forty-five minutes ago, and gain from it two useful pieces of information: the name Di Callare and the fact that NOAA is not currently lying.

At about the point where Jesse is unsticking his phone's camera and screen from the compartment wall of the zipline, and Di has had time to exhale and look back up at the chart—those facts are weighted, included into the database, and priced. If anyone wants them, they'll be there, for a fee.

Three small and crude datarodents—ones that bear all the marks of underfunding—scuttle off with data for the three presidential campaigns. The only conclusions they lead their masters to are that the campaigns are still being kept in the dark. The Republican candidate's office fires off a plaintive letter complaining to President Hardshaw and appealing to her party loyalty. It is such a routine matter that they have a form letter for it.

One purely commercial, barely tailored datarodent fires off a record of the whole conversation to Berlina Jameson, currently at the Motel Two in Point Barrow, Alaska. It lacks even the intelligence to decide whether a thing is important or not, but because so many things it is looking for were mentioned frequently, it tags the record as top priority.

One datarodent is not like the others—it's very big and very smart. It fragments itself into a million chunks for the journey to GateTech headquarters at Cape Canaveral, and slips into the net a chunk at a time like a water moccasin swimming out from a bank. Besides a full recording of the conversation, the attached indexing and cross-referencing to other calls, and the snippets of material from it, there is a whole structure of thoughts and questions, and it is about the size (if it were somehow written out in text) of twenty of the old, paper Encyclopedia Britannica.

Eleven milliseconds later, at Cape Canaveral, one of the artificial intelligences that Glinda Gray has created and put to work drops a note into her electronic hopper, saying it may have found a significant piece of information. By now it has written a summary report of only five pages, though it still contains the name "Diogenes Callare."

Another datarodent belongs to Industrial Facilities Mutual, a large industrial insurance consortium, and it is perhaps the second smartest datarodent in the substation. It hurries off to headquarters in Manhattan, carrying with it the assessment that the risk of severe weather has been badly underestimated.

Artificial intelligences there study the issue, agree with the datarodent, and re-prioritize. Engineer inspections are scheduled based on priority—a factory in a dry California canyon is inspected for fire risk more often than one on the Oregon coast, for example—and thus they step up the priority on all severe weather risks: broadcast towers, aboveground power lines, factories with flat roofs where snow tends to accumulate, shops in flood-plains. . . .

The new priorities go out four seconds later to the individual engineers. The engineer for Hawaii is still asleep while his software receives the new orders, checks through the list of places he inspects, and sends out a notice of early inspection to NAOS, the corporation that operates the new Kingman Reef Heavy Launch Facility.

The notice of an early inspection is thus the first thing seen at breakfast by Kingman's two heads. Akiri Crandall, chief of general operations, who is overseeing both the remaining construction and the daily operations, is exasperated; not for the first time, he wishes he were back in the Navy with his old destroyer command. The inspector will be climbing all over the station for a full day, and wherever he goes, all work will cease, and rumors will fly.

Gunnar Redalsen, chief of launch operations, was already in a bad mood; lately he gets up in bad moods. The Monster is the biggest rocket ever to fly, the first test launch is just three months away and already they're ten days behind schedule, and the last thing he needs is another delay.

Crandall and Redalsen don't get along, which is unfortunate, and they are known not to get along, which is worse. Within three hours of the day shift beginning, partisans of each side are constructing rumors in which the early inspection is somehow the fault of the other, and petty sniping and harassment are beginning to fly between launch ops and general ops. By lunchtime, Crandall and Redalsen find they have to hold a "peace conference" (for a "war" neither of them was fighting) and order people to cut the crap and get back to work.

All afternoon, those people who are inclined to nurse slights and injuries do, and by evening there are marital spats, upset children, and many people going to bed a little angry.

During the whole long day, the Pacific rolls on outside as it has for thousands of years, but because fine clear warm weather is so normal, and going outside the station so rare, no one pays much attention except a few sunbathers who have the day off. Waves roll in over the western horizon, splash up the sides of the concrete pillars, and roll out over the eastern horizon; with the tides, the water rises a little on the sides of the station, and sinks a little, and that is all. As night falls, the stars in their thousands come out to dance, but no one sees them.

Inside, Crandall tosses and turns, trying to get to sleep. He knows the inspection is going to upset Redalsen and there will be more trouble. The Monster, now bobbing quietly by its launch tower, not to be fueled for months yet, will get off on time—Redalsen will see to that—but Crandall knows there are going to be a lot more squabbles.

Redalsen falls asleep wondering why Crandall doesn't understand that the point of a launch facility is to launch things.

After he talks to his brother, Jesse Callare leans back in the zipline compartment and considers. Becoming an influential activist on campus is not likely to work. Besides, it will be months until Naomi gets back, and then she'll have to notice him, and notice he has changed, and—well, it would all just take too long, is the problem. On the other hand, he doesn't think she'll appreciate it if he just follows her to Tehuantepec.

But he *is* an engineering student. And TechsMex, the group that sends engineers and interns south to teach, always has openings. Going to Te-huantepec might be a bit overt, but he can go somewhere in the same part of the country—

He dials up TechsMex and scans the openings. Not as easy as he'd thought—there are ten jobs he could do but most are in Ciudad de México or farther north. . . .

The only one that is in the far south, anywhere near Tehuantepec—and "near" is very much a relative term—is tutoring preengineering students at a comunity college in Tapachula, almost at the Guatemalan border. Even by air, that's 220 miles to Tehuantepec, and there's no zipline that far south yet.

But another part of his mind points out that he could be down near the equator, doing something valuable in a quiet little border town . . . and he won't have to see any of his old friends. Running away after a flopped love affair may be something a character in a book would do, but one reason they might do it is that it might work.

He decides to decide that night. Meanwhile, there's at least a chance to catch up on the news. For the hell of it, he decides to do something trashy, and he pulls out the scalpnet for his phone and plugs into XV, deliberately choosing a real lowbrow channel. He's just in time to get to be Rock, and get it into Synthi Venture (he used to love to do that as a teenager) one more time before she goes off on vacation. It's great, especially once he sets it to pulse back and forth between her and him; there's so much passion and violence in the ecstasy of the intercourse that when it's finally over, Jesse can't help thinking that the Christian XV guys have a point when they say that if the Diem Act were strictly enforced, Doug Llewellyn, the president of Passionet, would long since have gone to the chair.

The doors open at Tucson Station and the zipline wishes Jesse a pleasant day. He shoulders up his pack and walks back into the bright sunlight. It's hours until the party tonight, hours until he can do anything effective. Maybe he'll study.

Berlina Jameson has been enjoying breakfast, partly because she hasn't been paying for it and mainly because she is having company. Haynes Lambor-ghini, the *New York Times* textchannel reporter, has taken her to breakfast because today is to be his last day in Barrow, and they've gotten to be friends.

"So do the 'nobody will talk to me' story," he says. "And start thinking about distribution if you haven't already. You've got most of the video footage there is. Just from a standpoint of history, that's too important to let it rot someplace, or to wait until it's in an archive."

"I thought you text guys didn't like video."

"Beats hell out of XV," Lamborghini says. He takes another gulp of coffee. "Boy, one thing I won't miss is the coffee here. They compensate for the lack of flavor by watering it down. The thing is, Berlina, the camera is not objective, and TV may be for people who can't read, but it's still light-years ahead of XV. At least you know what happened in front of the camera and at least people have their own feelings about it instead of having the reporter's. And potentially a lot more people could access your work than mine, so there will be a few people with an objective view."

"But a view of what?" Berlina says. "Everyone I talk to here is determined to tell me there's no story. I've burned up most of my long-distance budget on calls to Washington and no one will talk there either."

Lamborghini raises his hands, palms up, as if he were a magician turning her into a fairy princess. "But you have all that footage of people saying there's no story. And you have a bunch of contradictory statements about why there isn't, and enough outside testimony to make it clear that there probably *is* a story. That's all you need. 'Why aren't they telling the truth?' is the phrase that's sold more news than anything else. Kid, you're home free. Just put the story together into one documentary and distribute it."

Berlina nods. "I guess I'll try," she says. The conversation goes on to other matters.

When she gets back to the Motel Two and starts to check her mail, she finds the usual things—a mass of short phone calls from various offices saying they have no statements, junk mail, notices that she's getting close to the end of the line she lives on. The datarodents haven't reported much except the usual stuff—there's one obnoxious one out there that flags every weather report for her, and she hasn't been able to track it down and kill it—

Well, this is different. There's a priority-one. She sits down, switches on the full playback, and watches the phone conversation, just before Jesse gets back into Tucson on the zipline.

Ten minutes later she has called Di Callare and asked for an interview; he says he'll be happy to talk to her while he's taking the zipline home tonight. She sets her clock for that. At least she now can prove that there's more to worry about than they are talking about.

All she has to do is make the whole story come out in a way that saves her financial butt, which, according to the last message, is about one week from oblivion. Still, it's a better chance than she's had in a long time. The bleak, dark, gray day that has emerged from the bleak night looks pretty good to her.

Just as Mary Ann Waterhouse is undressing, but trying to do it as Synthi Venture for Rock, and struggling to keep the thought, *This is the last time, the last time, the last time, my breasts are so sore, so sore, please, please, this is the last time,* from getting loud enough in her head to be picked up by the estimated three hundred twelve million women (and a scattering of curious men) worldwide who are experiencing her right now, and as Jesse is seeing through Rock's eyes and watching those amazing cartoon-girl breasts pop out of the tiny bra, and Rock himself is wondering (below the level where Jesse can hear it) if after all this he's going to have any energy left for Harry, his own longtime boyfriend—

and as Di has finally gotten the organization chart to meet the criteria he started with—

and as Berlina Jameson notices that she has a priority-one call from a datarodent—

and before Akiri Crandall and Gunnar Redalsen have even become aware that their days are going to be unpleasant—

At that instant, Glinda Gray notices that an AI thinks it's picked up something important.

The trouble with the damned things is that they're right too often to ignore and wrong too often to inspire any confidence. She'd really rather leave now; she promised Derry she'd get home early enough for them to have lunch together, and here she is working on a Saturday and looking at keeping going right through the day.

Well, if she checks it, and it's nothing, she's going right out the door and home to Derry, and she's going to use the privacy router that the boss is always telling her to use. Klieg is such a nice guy he wants her to cut herself off from the company every weekend and take the time on her own, and if nice guys like Klieg were all the company had, it wouldn't last a week. Got to stay on top of the competition, because in getting blocking patents, being second is spending money for nothing.

She hits the key before she can worry about it anymore, reads it—and whoops like the cheerleader she was in high school. In the silence that follows as she re-reads, she can hear six doors out in the corridor open and her co-workers asking each other whose office that noise came from, and did it sound like someone was upset? Normally she'd run out to tell them it was okay, but normally she wouldn't have whooped in the first place—and things are anything but normal.

She sits at her desk, hugging herself. It's really a shame that there's no equivalent of Liver Treats or a scratch between the ears for an AI, because this AI has earned any treat it could want, if it were capable of wanting anything. What's its number?—GT1500AI213 + 895. She writes it down, since she'll want to copy its rule system for the next generation of AIs to use as a starter.

Sitting on a node near NOAA central, a datarodent, running random checks, picked up several conversations of this guy, Diogenes Callare, and reported them to the AI. The AI in turn reprogrammed the datarodent to pay special attention to Callare after it noted that his boss talks about him a lot and cites him as an authority; and spotted Callare's use as an influence to get a bright but difficult former employee—Carla Tynan—back into the organization for the crisis.

It even picked up the fact that Carla Tynan used to work in their blue-sky, crazy-people division, which implies that if they want her back, it's because they aren't sure of what they're doing, or they're afraid of getting zapped by something they haven't thought of, and that it isn't possible to tell whether this is because Diogenes Callare is so influential within the circle of meterologists there that he's the only credible one to make the offer, or because Tynan, brainy maverick that she is, wouldn't listen to anyone who wasn't equally bright, so that all the calls it picked up to, from, and about Carla Tynan were vital evidence for Diogenes Callare as the key to the whole thing.

It thus quite properly began to pay very close attention to Callare himself, and when it caught him explaining it all—*to his kid brother! you couldn't ask for anything more perfect! it's all in simple nontechnical language with no CYA in it!*—it ran that explanation against the official press release, found out where the missing emphases were in the press release, and dashed off down the fibrop to let everyone know.

The press release began with the basic weasel-position of saying that maybe nothing would happen, and that with so many possibilities it was very hard to say for sure that anything would, and then described the scenarios as if they had been a set of worst cases.

But when you read this conversation against it, the key thing is that three times, Di tells his kid brother—an engineering student, so someone who doesn't know meteorology but does know physics—that a huge amount of energy is getting dumped in. To most ears it just sounds like Di is saying "big," but it's the key to the whole thing. To people who've taken physics as a serious subject, energy is the name for that which is expressed in the universe as either mechanical work or as heat. Work is change in a mechanical system—the distance a thing is moved times the force resisting it. So a big difference in energy in a mechanical system (such as the atmosphere) translates into immense changes in where things are and how fast they move.

Or in very simple terms, to big, big winds.

The AI went so far as to run some calculations, and they're pretty fascinating—in a spooky sort of way. The increased energy retained by the Earth and not bounced back into space is just about one-third of one percent more than normal—but the last time it got that much *less* it was enough to

get the Little Ice Age started. At the present rate of global warming—
which, the AI notes, is at least supposed to be slowing down—the Earth
shouldn't reach the overall global temperature it will reach this year
until . . . holy jumping jesus god, 2412.

So the press release is the sheerest thin tissue of fact stretched over an
implied lie. The one thing that is for sure is that something will happen, and
that something will be huge. Everything else is reassuring noise for the
public, helping it to believe that the people in charge probably know what's
true.

Moreover—and this is what brought out the whoop—if you don't
worry about specifics, if you lump things together instead of splitting them
apart, then there's something that several of the scenarios include or imply,
something that gives the key to making money off this; and her AI has
already turned that key.

She uses her priority to put through a call to John Klieg's office, and it
doesn't surprise her at all that he's there. He thinks everyone else works too
hard and wants to take care of them, but look at the care he takes of
himself—or rather doesn't take. The man's attitude toward work is positively twentieth.

"Boss, I think we've got what we wanted here."

Klieg grins at her. "Attagirl. Get in here and tell me about it. And when
you're done I'll expect you to explain why you're not taking the weekend
off to be with your kid or go out on the town."

She smiles at that, knowing that whatever he says he doesn't mean it.

It was first noticed late in the twentieth century that economics was rapidly
becoming a trade of one kind of signal—orders, invoices, debts, entertain-
ments, permissions, a thousand other kinds—for another kind of signal—
money. The physical production of goods ran, more and more, on its own;
money flowed because of the signs attached to the goods.

This was not without parallel; on the island of Yap, in the Pacific, money
had long been in the form of giant stone wheels, and most property had
been land or fishing rights. Neither the land nor the fish moved, and the
money was too heavy to move in normal circumstances; only the information flowed.

By 2028, the rest of the world has caught up with Yap.

Passionet flips out as Synthi and Rock curl up, pretending that they are
about to go to sleep in each other's arms. When Synthi got into the
showdown with the network people about her exhaustion, they put a lot of

pressure on her, but with Rock's advice she was able to make them give her the time off she needed, and that time off is starting right now.

In fact, it turned out that Rock had been taking vacations all along— "You have to ask'em, Synthi, and then make them stick to what they agree to, they won't just do it for you"—and he'd been very helpful with getting her through the red tape.

As soon as they hear "feed out," they roll away from each other. "I didn't hurt you, did I?" Rock asks.

"I was sore when we started, but I don't think you damaged anything any more than it already was. You're a very gentle guy, you know."

"Yeah." He sighs. "I'm going to miss you in the next couple of months. You're really a pro, you know? And frankly, it's so hard for me to stay interested in the news that I'd rather have the experiencers get it from you." He sits up. One of the attendants coming in hands him the little bag that holds his own clothes and belongings. "And you don't make me feel like a goon, the way . . . well, some of the others do."

"I like you too," Synthi says. "But I'll be back, I'm sure." Her own bag contains a general makeup dissolver; she smears it on her face, and the whole mess, false eyelashes and all, turns to thin fluid that she washes off with soap and water. "Uh, Rock . . ." She shakes off the water and towels her face briskly. "My real name is Mary Ann Waterhouse."

"And mine is David Ali," he says, smiling back at her. "Now you take care of yourself." He scribbles something on a piece of paper and hands it to her. "My phone number. If you just want to talk or something. But I'd advise you to just forget all about the business and go be Mary Ann for a while—it's a much nicer name than Synthi."

She nods. "I told the travel agent to find me a place where nothing ever happens. I'm not even taking a portable XV set with me; I'm just going to walk through the city like a real person." She pulls on the bra with special supporters so that her breasts, too large and too heavy from the implants, don't jerk around and hurt her when she moves. It feels so comfortable to know that for three months at least, she won't have to run around in skimpy wisps of fabric, her chest, shoulder, and back muscles aching.

Over the comfortable bra goes the big, baggy sweatshirt, she ties up the flame-red hair in a bandanna, and now she looks like a slightly overweight young housewife, especially once she pulls the back of the shirt down far enough to hide the buttocks they've sewn into taut globes. She's got to find a couple of loose-fitting skirts, first thing . . . it's going to be great to spend months of having men think that she'd be pretty if she hadn't let herself go.

When she turns back to Rock, she almost laughs; she's never seen him go out of persona before, but when she had decided she would get out of persona right at the end of a recording session, he said he had to do the same. "If you're going to show me yours, I've got to show you mine," he explained. "Didn't you ever sneak into the basement with a neighbor boy to go exploring?"

Now he looks . . . well, there's no other word for it. He looks incredibly gay. The classically tailored narrow-lapelled pinstripe suit with vest and jacket unbuttoned are straight out of any gay bar in Manhattan; the wide tie with the NFL logo on it has become stereotypical as the code for "available for fun, nothing serious." Even the phone on his belt is hopelessly retrobutch, made to look like a 1980s' deal-maker car phone.

He winks at her. "Check the wingtips. And you didn't see the nut-squeezing excuse for underwear I put on. Lace-y and tin-y, babe. There are times when I wish Harry didn't like me to dress up like a bar slut."

And then Mary Ann does laugh, and hugs him gently. "You look nice."

"Oh, sure, if you don't pay any attention to fashion, dearie," Rock says. "But if you do, you'd know I'm a full year behind the trend." He holds her for a second and says, "Now, you be careful among those civilians, you hear? Don't do anything that you don't think is going to be a barrel of fun. You've earned your enjoyment." He kisses her forehead. "Now run along; Daddy's got to finish dressing for his playmate."

"When I get back," Mary Ann says, "every so often, David and Mary Ann are going to have a drink or some coffee."

"You got it," David says. "We'll talk about men and why they're impossible to have good relationships with. Now go find yourself a nice one to break your little heart."

Walking down the corridor, one of the things she enjoys most is that half the staff is doing double takes—only recognizing her on a second glance even though they know she's in the building—and the other half is walking right by without seeing her.

There's a pile of newsbriefs in her room, and it's wonderful to throw them away unread. She calls for a bellhop.

When he comes, it's the same bellhop who brought her breakfast the morning when she made her decision—if you can call halfway-to-a-break-down a decision. Come to think of it, he's been turning up a lot; maybe it's because she tips well or maybe it's personal loyalty. Either way, she'll take anything that seems like human association right now.

"Uh," he says, "I guess it'll be a while before you do this again." He's still kind of awkward in making conversation, but since she's made it clear that she likes to talk to him—and to waiters and desk clerks and everyone else—she's been getting used to this kind of awkwardness.

"Yep. Wanna know where I'm secretly going?" she asks.

"It won't be much of a secret if you tell people." He drags the baggage cart onto the elevator for her, and the door closes behind them. Two floors, then out to the limo, limo to the airport, then onto a jumplane.

"The tabloid channels will be revealing it tomorrow," she explains. "Fortunately, most people can't recognize an XV performer who isn't on XV, and I'm going where XV is still pretty rare anyway. So I really can tell you, and you can tell anyone you want to."

He grins. "Well, then, sure, tell me. I've impressed a lot of people at Yukon Mike's Saloon with our conversations."

"Well, make sure you spill this one tonight, because everyone will know it tomorrow. I'm going to Tapachula. It's a city in southern Mexico, close to the Guatemala border."

"What's there? What's it known for?"

"Regular people with regular jobs, and absolutely nothing," she says. "Except maybe peace and quiet. Kind of town everyone leaves, where they learn to get excitement somewhere else."

They're at the limo now, and very deliberately she steps close to him, hands him his tip, and says, "If you can be as gentle as Rock is, you'd be welcome to find out what it's like to kiss me."

"Nobody's going to believe this," he mutters, blushing, and when he does kiss her, it's like a sensitive fourteen-year-old touching lips with the girl he worships. If that's what Rock is coming across like in XV, no wonder he's got such a following.

When the kiss breaks, he looks a little dazzled. "So how am I in real life?" she asks.

"Sweet," he says. "And tender. Not like XV at all, but it's really, really nice. Thank you."

"Thank you," she says. "If you pass through Tapachula, look for a dumpy American who never does anything but sit around and read nice, big, thick trashy novels." They shake hands—it's almost solemn—and for good measure she adds a line she had on stage once, back when she was still Mary Ann, Laura's last line at the end of *Tea and Sympathy*—" 'When you speak of this later—and you will—be kind.' "

He nods, they both say goodbye, and she gets into the limo and tells it "Airport." It closes its doors, drives out of the lot onto its track, and she's on her way.

Maybe after this vacation, if she still feels the same way about XV, she'll put the money into a permanent annuity for herself, start auditioning again in New York, do some real acting . . . and start dating bellhops. It's not that good a joke, but she laughs all the way to the airport about it.

* * *

One of the reasons nobody notices when John Klieg and Glinda Gray go out to lunch together, and don't come back, is that after all these years anyone would assume that they are working on something and have chosen to do it outside the building. The major reason, however, is that everyone stopped to catch the XV of Synthi Venture's pre-vacation departure, and they are all plugged into goggles, muffs, and scalpnet at the moment that Klieg and Gray walk down the hall together.

Glinda is not quite believing that this is happening. She went into the office and said, "The one thing the AI says is that there's a ninety-six-percent possibility of more and stronger wind, all over the hemisphere, than there has ever been before. Every really fragile structure is going to take damage. They can replace and reinforce antennas for communications, they can bury power lines, they can shore up smokestacks or replace them with jets . . . but what they can't do is quickly modify the space-launch facilities. For those you've got to have the spacecraft moving pretty fast before it ever hits the wind. The wind is going to completely shut down satellite launching for months, first in the Northern Hemisphere, then in the Southern. And satellite launching is close to a trillion-dollar-a-year business."

"Nobody has an all-weather launch facility?"

"They can air-launch from airplanes or jumplanes, operating out of the few all-weather airports. But even all-weather airports shut down for hurricanes, boss, and air launch has been fading since single stage to orbit came in. Everything is right there . . . if we can get an all-weather launch system together in the next three months, we can probably get a global monopoly on space launch for a year or so."

From the way he looked up at her and grinned, she knew she had done well, and when he grabbed the phone and gave the orders to get a real study rolling and give her authority over it—god, she'd be in charge of a thousand-member team by the end of the month—she knew it was more than good. She'd really grabbed the whole works this time.

What she didn't expect was what he said next. "Okay, most of that won't start rolling till Monday, and after that you'll be so busy you'll never take time off. And neither will I if this lives up to its promise. Why don't you and I go pick up Derry and go do something fun together for the rest of the day?"

In the first place, it never occurred to her that John Klieg had even listened to her when she'd talked about her personal life; moreover, she had no idea what he did with his time on weekends—in fact, her impression was that all he ever did was work, going home mostly to eat and sleep. But on top of that . . . unmistakably, and here she was without makeup, in sweater, jeans, and sneakers because it was Saturday—her boss, a nice guy and great-looking, has asked her out. And included her daughter in the invitation, which sounds like a man who is serious.

So as they go down the hall together, she's more tongue-tied than she's been in years, and he seems to be pretty quiet too. In the parking garage, they decide to go in his car, and set hers for an automatic "find home" so that it will go back to her garage and park itself sometime in the next couple of hours, whenever the continuous traffic data it receives indicate that it will be cheapest.

He sets his car for her address, and it rolls down the ramp and onto the track. "This is totally contrary to all my principles," he says, with a fraction of a laugh, like a cough. "I've been in business of one kind or another for twenty-five years, and this is the first time I've ever asked an employee out."

Glinda looks down at her lap and smiles. "Well, I've been at GateTech for sixteen years myself, boss, and this is the first time I've dated inside the company."

"You could start by calling me 'John' instead of 'boss.' "

"I could try, John. But it might take a while before it comes naturally."

"Good start, anyway. Well, let me see. I remember from what you've told me that Derry is horse-crazy, likes to do 'grown-up' things like have lunch and go to the theatre, and gets cranky when you break promises to her. Is having me along at lunch going to count as a broken or slightly damaged promise?"

"Hah," Glinda says, and as she leans back, she finds herself thinking, *Remember, even if he does own the place, he's only one level up from you. Think of it as a Clerk I dating a Clerk II.* "Derry *wants* me to date more. And when she sees it's a good-looking older guy with money, she'll be overjoyed. She's got all kinds of goofy ideas from XV, even though I only let her use the family channels. Even on those, the whole romance thing gets a little oversold."

"No kidding," the boss—*John, dammit*—says. The big Chevy Mag Cruiser swings nimbly onto the freeway, and then across it to the Premium Skyway. The view over the Cape and out toward the Atlantic is its usual bland self—trees and sand down to water. She remembers when she first came here, with her ex, it seemed so exotic to them after their years in Wisconsin.

"Romance is very definitely oversold," John adds, probably hoping to continue the conversation. Glinda realizes she's been letting herself drift. "On the other hand, I like to think it does exist."

"Yep, it does," Glinda says emphatically. "And I still believe in it." *Yep.* Damned Wisconsin coming out in her; at least she didn't say "you bet." "But I'd like to keep it from being Derry's focus of life for a couple more years yet. She'll have sixty or seventy years for it once she starts. And besides,

I just don't think it's healthy for a little girl to be interested in a grown woman's, uh, dating life."

John nods approvingly. "So, just out of curiosity and because I'm desperately insecure, how much has she had to be interested in lately?"

"Well, nothing at all for the last two years . . ." They both start to laugh at that. "Okay, maybe there's some reason for concern, but the concern shouldn't be coming from an eleven-year-old. How long's it been for you?"

Klieg shrugs. "Oh, seven or eight years, I guess, depending on what you count. For a while I subscribed to a romance service, if you know about those . . . but for the last few years I haven't even done that."

"Romance service" is not quite the kind of euphemism that "escort service" used to be, but it's not far from it, either. What the romance service guarantees is that a fixed number of attractive women—the customer defines "attractive," but it need have nothing to do with the sort of women who would really be attracted to the customer—will approach the customer romantically, somewhere out in public, act friendly and interested, and accept at least five dates with him.

As long as he doesn't ask, he'll theoretically never know whether he's being lucky or the service is functioning. In practice, a paunchy middle-aged businessman can usually figure out that the girls in their late teens and early twenties who keep picking him up in bars or at the park are coming from the service, unless he's seriously self-deluded as well. "So," she says cautiously, "what did you order from the romance service?"

"Everything," he says. "They had kind of a sampler deal, where they'd just throw your name in at random. The trouble is, I'm not any good at telling someone who likes me from someone who acts like she likes me. I kept getting disappointed when they didn't want to go beyond the fifth date."

"But they must have—" Glinda was about to say "asked you for money," but then she realized that they might not have, if he didn't ask for sex.

"Oh, sure, some of them were just hookers, but it didn't take that long to figure out which ones—they were the ones who started talking about sex before I got the car door closed. But that wasn't most of them. The thing is, a lot of young women go to work for those services. Don't forget that the colleges turn out a lot more educated people than the economic system can really absorb. Heck, middle-class parents have more kids than the system can absorb into the middle class. So a lot of very nice, well-spoken, pretty young women, who didn't happen to study anything they have a prayer of getting a job with, sign up with a romance service because not only do they make a living, they also meet men with money. And if they meet one they like, there's no reason why they can't keep dating him if they like. I went out with one of them for a year or so, but"—he sighs—"she decided she liked another guy—sort of a starving poet close to her own age—better. Can't say I blame her, really."

Glinda chooses her words carefully. "It seems a pity that that's all a young woman can find to do with herself."

"Oh, they could wait tables or answer the phone somewhere," Klieg says. "The trouble is that an awful lot of people expect they can get paid for being attractive."

"Well, they can."

"True," he admits, "but most of them don't like realizing what the cost of making a living that way is. Anyway, I got kind of tired of it, and then really tired of it, and dropped the subscription. What you could meet that way—aside from hookers—was young women who were very good at looking good and spending money. Good for decoration or long conversations about their feelings, but that was it. Most of them didn't seem to have read much in college, or at least not to remember it." Klieg sighs. "So, anyway . . . getting back to the present case, I figured, well, if you don't like me, I can always bribe you into staying with the company, because I do need you as an employee. And if you do . . . well, I just like you, for some reason or other, and I suddenly realized I had been taking all my risks over on the business side of the ledger. I thought it might be interesting to see if I could take a chance on the personal side."

Glinda smiles a little at that. "So, how do you feel?"

"Somewhere between terrified and happy. Anyway, what's your idea of a good place to eat? Or what's Derry's, if they're not compatible?"

She wags her finger at him. "Ah, ah, if we're going to fulfill this child's fantasies, you have to guide me to some perfect little café where they have three special dishes that only you know about and everyone knows you by your first name."

"Well . . . there is a place where everybody knows my name. I eat there every other day or so. But I wouldn't say it had any special dishes, certainly not any that only I know about."

"Really?"

"Yeah, but it's not exactly a perfect little café, it's um . . . it's a Shoney's, actually. They don't know I'm the president of GateTech, but everyone knows me."

Glinda gapes at him. "You eat at Shoney's? *Why?*"

"Well, not just *any* Shoney's, this particular one. And I've got three good reasons. One, in the early days when I traveled a lot, for some odd reason I always had good luck with that chain—and when you're putting in your sixth straight three-hundred-mile day, it's nice to have something really predictable. So I got hooked on it that way—it's just a very comforting place for me to go. Two, it's self-reinforcing. Once you've been going to a place for a while and they know you, you get friendly service and they treat you well."

There's a long pause.

"And what's the third reason?" Glinda asks.

"I like the food."

They laugh more from the broken tension than from the feeble joke. John Klieg leans back farther—he is too old to trust automatic guidance on cars, and won't let his hands get far from the wheel or his foot move away from the brake—looks at her sideways, and says, "I hate to tell you this, but your boss doesn't have an ounce of class. I'm solid twentieth in everything but business."

"Even including using old-fashioned expressions like 'solid,'" Glinda says, pulling her legs up and turning to sit facing more toward him. She's always known he was handsome, kind, and considerate, but she's beginning to realize how much more attention he has been paying to her than she has to him.

"Especially using old-fashioned expressions like 'solid,'" Klieg agrees. "If I hadn't stopped myself, I'd have said 'stone.' I wrote editorials for my high-school paper defending Dan Quayle. Now, about this daughter of yours—do we have to take her somewhere pretentious by the water to make her happy?"

"Only if we want to convince her we're serious," Glinda says, "and I'm still working on believing this isn't some vivid dream. She'd probably be happy at Shoney's, for that matter."

"Well, for a bizarre suggestion—start high end and work low? Maybe go to a café for lunch, then to her riding session—maybe you and I could have drinks and some conversation while she rides?—then Shoney's for dinner and then movie for three? With the possible option of covert hand-holding under the popcorn?"

"I think we can make a deal of this," Glinda says, "as long as the movie either has monsters or is set in space."

"Is that what Derry's into?"

"Not for her; for me," Glinda says. "Life is boring enough and contains enough unhappiness. If I'm going to see a movie I want to see something that will either scare me silly or get my mind up in the clouds."

John Klieg beams at her. "Gee, if a guy was to know you, say, for sixteen years or so, he might finally notice you had a pretty good idea of fun."

She smiles at him; she's recognizing the style of speech. "So, John, where are you from?"

"Little town you never heard of—Winona, Minnesota. Southeastern part of the state, across the river from Wisconsin."

An hour's drive from where Glinda grew up. Maybe she can get away with saying "You bet" after all.

Louie Tynan is busy for the first time in months, and he doesn't know whether to be happy or not. They've put up four polar-orbit satellites, which rise and set relative to his own equatorial-orbit space station at least seven or eight times per day. Every time one does, at a precisely calculated instant, the satellite sends a laser pulse that passes through the Earth's atmosphere, at varying altitudes, and is then received for spectrographic analysis on the station. The thirty or so lasers that send each pulse have precisely known wavelengths and power; if the light were only passing through a vacuum, you could figure out how much power would arrive at what wavelength, down to parts in ten billion.

But although air is transparent, it's not *perfectly* transparent; it's subject to minor variations (look down a hot road on a summer day), and not all the variations are neutral with respect to wavelength (consider a sunset).

So instead of the predicted set of exactly known values for power at each wavelength, the laser light coming into Louie Tynan's "camera," as he thinks of the gadget, is altered by the air it passes through, and the exact way in which it alters tells them quite a bit about methane.

Louie's job, all day, has been to power up a remote manipulator, a little tractor with an arm that crawls around the outside of the station on tracks, take the spectrographic camera out of storage, put it in the airlock, use the remote manipulator to put it in place and hook it up . . . and sit back and pretend to know what he was doing, besides making sure that some little lights stayed green through the first twenty tries.

Right now Louie is taking a break in the observation bubble. They don't really need a man to do these observations at all—they could do the whole thing on robotics—but as long as they have a crewed space station, and one crusty old fart on it who doesn't want to come down, might as well get some work out of him. It may not be the most productive way to do the thing, or even the most productive use of the astronaut, but this way NASA PR guys can make noises in public about quick responses and being able to get on top of a breaking situation.

And because they're doing that, he also has to print out graphs derived from the results every so often, and then make a set of notes about the graphs and read his results back to ground control. This bit is pure show-boating; the sad fact is that in the first place, not being a meterologist, he doesn't have any more understanding of what the graphs mean than what they told him in a three-hour tutorial the week before, and anyway, the people who do know what they mean are getting copied on all the data instantly on the ground. The only purpose is for the taxpayers on the open channel to hear their most expensive single employee earning his keep.

Some bored grad student on an internship has been set up down there to ask him questions that everyone already knows the answers to, so that he can appear to be expressing an opinion and judging the situation. Louie's job is essentially a several-day-long publicity stunt.

On the other hand, it's more news than crewed space exploration has gotten in months. He thinks of Congressperson Henry Loamer, UL-LA, who has occasionally referred to the space station as the "orbiting retirement home" and to Louie himself as "our single most expensive Federal employee, who is doing just what Federal employees usually do, sitting on his butt and soaking up tax money." It will be weeks before old Henry realizes all this could be done cheaper and better by robot, and meanwhile he's shut up.

Besides, Louie's got to admit that this has been good for him. Having to do visuals every few hours, sitting in front of a camera and reading off the report, has made him shower, shave, all that easy-to-overlook stuff. He may not be the height of elegance, but at least he's freshly showered and wearing a clean coverall, and he has more than one clean coverall.

He takes another bite of the sushi—funny thing, the Japanese spent a fortune developing all sorts of amenities for their unit, which is sitting down there at the end of Truss Two empty and powered down. They sent up five crews for a few months each, and then got bored or something, leaving behind the tissue culture tanks that let you grow pieces of fish without having to grow the whole fish.

The stuff isn't bad, and it's at least variety from the usual sandwiches.

The Japanese gave up. The Chinese flew some missions into low orbit, and they still do. The Russians are long gone from space, and the French make three flights a year—they treat the Euromodule as sort of a hotel room, where their guys sleep between fixing robots, or on their way to and from their tiny moonbase while they assemble their ships here. Last time they didn't even bother with that, just went straight from low Earth orbit to the moon.

And as for his own country . . . Louie is it, and he's mostly here for publicity.

Yet the solar system is now crawling with humanity's robots. Not counting all the replicators that were built there before they shut that experiment down, there are hundreds of little crawlers exploring the moon.

Louie just noticed the other day that one of the many relays on the station was handling traffic for the University of Wyoming Lunar Rover and the Ralston-Purina Checkerboard Lunar Orbiter. It turned out that the former was a senior engineering-school project and the latter a breakfast cereal promotion, where they claimed they'd buy you a square foot of the moon (a very safe promotion, because the UN has put all claims except those within one kilometer of a permanently crewed facility into abeyance) and send you a picture of it.

Where his crew of eight walked a hundred miles or so across the face of Mars, there is now a robot railway that drags a camera back and forth, toward the Martian North Pole and back, sending a continuous picture that a few million people on Earth display on the TVs that hang on their bedroom walls. Even Mars is already getting to be less popular than the view from the Jupiter Orbiter Feed, which Louie has, right now, in his sleeping quarters.

He looks down at the Earth below him. So far it doesn't look any different. You can no more see an extinct species or a too-warm ocean than you can tell that there are no longer any dark-skinned people in Europe as it rolls away below him. And certainly sixty-five years or so of pictures from up this high have made the sight of Earth from space familiar. . . .

Well, hell with it. He still likes the way the old planet looks. He holds up a squeeze bulb of Kirin—another great Japanese innovation—in a toast to her. She's pretty battered around the edges, but he still likes to see her like this. It's not his job to decide whether or not he's too expensive to maintain up here. If they're willing to send him, he's willing to stay.

As he takes a sip of the beer, he thinks of Carla, and the notion that he is thinking of her just after looking at the battered old planet nearly sends the beer squirting out his nose. She'd love *that* comparison.

They haven't talked in almost a month and it's still forty minutes till the next observation. Moreover he happens to look decent, so he might as well take advantage of it. From where the terminator line is on the Earth, it's about three o'clock in the afternoon in the western Pacific, and the weather is clear. Chances are *MyBoat* is surfaced and taking phone calls.

He shifts around to face the camera and screen and dials her number. It rings a couple of times and then she answers it on voice only, so his first thought is that she's getting it over a Very Low Frequency receiver and the signal is going to be lousy—he was really looking forward to seeing her face—then she laughs. "Oh, it's you, Louie. Let me get a towel on."

"For what?" he says. Caught her sunbathing; it figures.

"So the tabloids can't do another story about perverted astronauts looking at their naked ex-wives over the phone and talking nasty, that's why. You've got an image to protect, Captain America."

"They promoted me a long time ago," he reminds her.

"You'll always be Captain America to me," she says, and the screen comes on. "Is there news or is this just a hello call?"

"Oh, just a hello. Timed to get a look at your body, of course."

She grins and moves as if to flash him. One of the several counselors they'd gone to had pointed out to them that they were both "socially retarded, as tends to be common in bright people, and that's why you act like a couple of teenagers around each other." It took Louie and Carla days to realize the counselor thought there was something wrong with it.

He gives her his best construction-worker whistle. She asks, "So they're keeping you busy for once, you bottomless pit for taxes, you?"

"Yeah. Although to tell you the truth, *I'm* starting to wonder if I'm actually doing anyone any good by being up here."

"Not your worry, love, it's really not. We've talked about all this before. If it weren't for the scientists, the whole world might as well disappear up its own virtual-reality asshole. If there's no exploration, that's just what will happen. And robots do not explore, they just go and look. Somebody's got to be there to feel like bold Cortez upon a peak in Darien."

"You're quoting poetry at me again."

"Well, it's not a dirty limerick, so I'm sure you haven't heard it before, but yes, I have been exposing you to poetry. It's part of that continuing process that ran through our courtship and marriage, love—you know, eating with utensils, washing yourself—say, speaking of which, you're looking pretty spruce today. You must be doing a lot of interviews or something."

He tells her about reading the data and the graphs. She tells him about getting her old job back, and "better yet, being allowed to do it on remote. So I'll probably be looking at that data myself."

"Well, if you like, I'll be happy to download it to you."

"Please do."

He pushes a couple of buttons, and the data is transmitted. They talk a little longer, but there isn't much to talk about, so they hang up quickly.

An hour later, Carla calls Louie back. "Are the numbers really that high?"

"I didn't really know they were high. They're just numbers to me. They went up fast for a couple of days but they've been pretty steady since." He grabs a terminal and types on it for a moment. "Yeah, those are the numbers."

"No wonder they're getting so excited about it. That's really high, Louie."

"Well, that would explain why they've been asking me to downplay it while I talk to this kid from UT. I'm supposed to sound the way old-fashioned airplane pilots did when they told you 'Well, we've got a little turbulence here and maybe a bit of engine failure, but I just wanted you folks to know that I expect to be on time or a bit before, except of course for that little old piece of wing that just dropped off.' They might at least have told me that when I was saying there was nothing to panic about, I was lying."

"Well, until my department gets it figured out, they still won't know *what* these people ought to be panicking about, you know. And anyway, I'm not so sure that panicking will do them any good."

"So next time I have to go play Serious Scientist again with the kid from Texas, it won't be unjustified if I suddenly say, 'Jesus, these numbers are high. Let's cut the crap, we're in deep shit, we're all going to die!' "

She giggles. "Oh, a little unjustified, but think how much excitement it's going to cause the PR types. And most of them just don't have enough adventure in their lives."

"Yeah, you're right about that. Well, take care . . . I still kinda miss you, you know."

"I've been known to miss you too. Let's make that date for sure—when you get back down, we'll get together and have some sex and some fun, then get on each other's nerves so we can remember why we both live in tin cans hundreds of miles from anyone else."

She's still teasing, but it's getting near the mark, and Louie doesn't want to get into any emotional things this particular time. So he says, "Well, then, it's a date. You take care," and she says, "Take care," and they hang up.

He looks at his schedule and it's still twenty minutes until he has to pretend he knows what he's talking about with that damned kid. He stretches out, letting himself float free in the observation bubble—the nearest thing to a spacewalk without a suit you can do, if you ignore the glass walls on all sides just a foot or two away—and lets himself run through the list of all the things he's supposed to do when and if there's time. Unfortunately, most of them are fully up to date, and the ones that are not are just pointless duplicates of ground-based work.

Not unlike the pointless duplicate of ground-based work that he's supposed to do in the next few minutes. . . . He really wishes he could stop thinking like that. He looks out at the big old Earth rolling by underneath, and admits to himself that he's such a cranky old bastard it's no wonder that he's lonely, or that he has trouble admitting it.

Well, he hasn't powered up the telepresence unit on the moon in ages. If they ever start serious lunar operations again (instead of going along as passengers with the French—god, it kills Louie, three times a year, to see the *French* go to the moon, not even a country anymore but just a state in the USE, and maybe one time out of three they take along an American astronaut *as a passenger!*)—if ever that big stupid clumsy nation of Louie's gets it together enough to get back out there, it is very likely going to be Louie who drives the robots to get the American moonbase opened back up.

He sets the timer, pulls on a scalpnet, muffs, and goggles like an ordinary

XV rig (except that the muffs are equipped with an alarm so that if anything goes wrong in the station he will hear it), slides his arms into sensor gloves, plugs the feedback into the jack behind his ear, and codes in.

His eyes open on the Sea of Storms, and he stands up in his robot body. He looks down to see the unnaturally thin limbs—the antimatter power source is inside the long metal "torso" and the motors are located at the joints, not needing the leverage that real muscles do, so that for every practical purpose he's a walking skeleton, with a body that looks like a flexible gas hose and arms and legs like those on one of those men made out of muffler parts that used to stand in front of car repair shops when he was a kid.

He walks out of the little cave where the telepresence robot is parked—it returns there automatically when anyone is done with it, so that he imagines that on the lunar surface, at the end of a busy shift (if there ever is one), twenty or thirty robots might suddenly stop what they are doing and all walk back to the cave to stand against the walls—must be spooky to watch them do that.

The light here is flat and harsh, the shadows and sky black. There's nothing that isn't familiar from a thousand training tapes; this is where lunar mining experiments were conducted, and where a nice job was done of demonstrating that the "ores" available on the moon are just plain rock, so low-grade that it's always cheaper to make the stuff on Earth and ship it up, even though you're fighting a lot more gravity. But at least while the experiments were going on, there were people walking around up here, next to the robots. . . .

Now there's something that hasn't been tried out lately—the "replicators"—the experiment with little robots who look like Tonka trucks with arms. They have a little hopper in which they can melt a rock sample and then do what amounts to slow isotope separation, eventually breaking it into its constituent elements, so that where there was a hopper full of rock, there are now little ingots of all the solids, and little glass "bottles" of the gases and liquids, that go into making a replicator. The replicators then meet up with each other and swap pieces of material around until one of them has the materials to make a copy of itself. It sits down, does that, and where there were ten replicators gathering materials, there are now eleven.

The idea was that no matter how expensive it was to build the first batch of replicators, after that they would breed like sheep or cattle, and by turning on a software cue you could make them drive into the facility at Moonbase and keep offloading materials; eventually only a tiny fraction of materials extracted would go into replication, and you'd have an unending procession of replicators bringing gifts of oxygen, iron, aluminum, whatever.

The replicators were made in deliberate imitation of life, which is highly efficient at spreading itself around, binding energy from sunlight, and extracting scarce elements from abundant minerals. The exchange deal was self-reprogramming; whatever was scarce, they would seek to get more of by returning to places where it was easy to get it, by randomly perturbing some of their own instructions to try out different strategies, and by "bargaining" with each other.

In practice it turned out differently. The replicators replicated just fine, but the parallel processor system that controlled them at Moonbase turned out to be subject to a force no one had thought of—the market.

The first sign of trouble was when gallium became a medium of exchange. Of all the elements needed, the traces of gallium needed for some of the semiconductors were the hardest to get; very quickly the replicators learned that if you had gallium you could trade it for anything else. Many of them began to drive right past everything else, looking only for gallium-bearing minerals, until in short order most of them were carrying only gallium, plus the mix of elements that were found in the two minerals that contained it.

There was no one for them to "buy" the other things they needed from—until a couple of the replicators innovated and set up the "forty-niner's store." That is, they began to pay other robots—using gallium to do so—to go out and mine exclusively for the materials the other ones wanted to buy.

Predictably, in hindsight, two events followed quickly. One isolated replicator struck a relatively rich vein of gallium-bearing ore (though nothing anyone would have bothered with on Earth) and in short order the other replicators had followed it there, organizing a "gallium rush." As gallium flooded the market, there was a period of rapid inflation, leading to all sorts of distant speculative ventures—some of the replicators had gotten as far away as three hundred kilometers.

This all collapsed when about half of them sat down to have "children"; much of the gallium that had flooded the market was now tied up in replicators, and a price collapse and "depression" followed. Many of the faraway replicators shut down because there was no profitable way of returning to base.

Somewhere out there, one of them hit on the perturbation that made a mess of things. It attacked, disassembled, and devoured several of the other replicators, eventually producing copies of its cannibal self. Another replicator dealt with the problem by reprogramming other replicators to bring their extracted ores to it; they dubbed that one the "slavemaster," and discovered that the slavemaster had organized a defense against the cannibals, built around using the slaves in teams.

Moreover, they began to virus each other's software, and to invent defenses against the viruses (that strange boomtalk word for replicating software, with its purely negative connotations, seemed perfectly appropriate in this case). As defenses improved, viruses that attacked defenses appeared—the scientists began to refer to that as "machine AIDS"—and suppressor software to protect the defenses, in turn, mutated until it began to attack everything else—for some obscure reason, an old scientist dubbed that "industrial ARTS." There was, in effect, a health-care problem—most machines ran well below optimum because the code driving them had gotten so long and complicated.

Moreover, since they all had access to each other's software, very shortly there were several teams of cannibal slavemasters out there in the boondocks, competing with each other but mining almost nothing, all infected with and spreading machine AIDS and industrial ARTS.

Matters came to a head when two of the dominant teams wiped out the others (eating and converting them in the process), combined forces, and came back into Moonbase to attack the "forty-niner's store" in force; the merchants saw them coming, copied the software where needed, and fought a kind of epic battle on the plains before the fascinated eyes of the cyberneticists.

Then one sample replicator, pulled out for examination and tests, turned up with part of a solar-wind monitoring station in its guts. A quick check showed that the system as a whole had become conscious enough to realize that the prohibition on consuming other man-made objects kept it from getting some first-rate metals, and it had managed to hack around the prohibition by introducing industrial ARTS into the software protection of the main system.

They stopped it just hours from the point where it might have eaten Moonbase; if they hadn't, it would have destroyed everything except itself, then populated the moon with robot vermin beyond any control.

Now, as Louie comes around to the site of the great battle, he sees old number N743P, chief of the merchants, sitting where "he" froze when the system was shut down, surrounded by dozens of slaves with empty hoppers. Some wag has painted United Left insignia on the slaves and arranged them in a circle as if they were picketing N743P.

Louie wonders idly if it might not be better to have switched them all back on and told them about all the good metal over at the French base—no, that's petty, and the fact is that he likes the individual French astronauts who pass through the space station. It's hardly their fault that Louie's nation isn't keeping up, and France is the last bastion of any kind of liberalism in Europe; many of them are almost pathetically eager to tell Louie, or someone, that they wish they could get out from under Brussels, and that they were against the Expulsion.

He kneels to look it over; N743P doesn't look any different (apart from its tag) than any other robot. At least they hadn't discovered conspicuous consumption yet, though it looked like this fellow was about to invent the futures market.

There's a loud ping echoing through the stillness of the lunar day, and he realizes it's time to get on with things back at the station. He has a moment of being a tall, spiky robot scratching its head—

And then he's back in the station, pulling off the scalpnet, muffs, and goggles. He has a moment's vision of the robot on the moon standing up abruptly and then very slowly and carefully, without anything like the precision it has when a person is steering it, walking back to its slot in the storage cave, tramping back with careful, heavy movements like a Harryhausen monster. It may take it the rest of the day to get home, but then, it has nothing but time. . . .

Which is normally true for Louie, but not today. He grabs the handholds to drag himself to the "conference room," the little piece of blank white wall that he stands in front of while he pretends to know what he's doing with the weather reports.

There's another ping. He hurries off to play scientist.

Berlina Jameson has been living on the line—what her grandparents would have called "on plastic," back when you carried cards that could be stolen—now that she's been fired for not turning back up at work, but she can still convince security at most places that she's a reporter.

The Barrow Motel Two—a casket hotel that provides a public toilet and shower, a belongings locker, and a bed with lock-down cover—wants to bill her extra for parking, and at first she figures she'll just pay it, but then she thinks about how long her line might have to stretch, and spends a pointless twenty minutes arguing with the clerical software. It puts her into a particularly foul mood, even after the good news of finding Di Callare this morning, so that when she finally gets into her little car, drives it onto the track, and sets it for the Duc, she's all but weeping with frustration and self-pity. As the car picks up speed, she begins to fold the seats into "long drive" configuration—a bed with access to the little pocket refrigerator and the "squat pot"—and as she finishes, rather than get a nap or do any work, she just stretches out on the bed and cries until she stops.

Her net accounts show that absolutely no one has run any of her one-minute spots; her own home station hasn't even been broadcasting them.

When it became clear that there wasn't much recreation and practically no significant violence or sexual appeal up here, all the XV people left, except for a couple of the eggheaded ones who offer people the opportunity to experience being knowledgeable, witty, and deeply concerned . . . a peculiar taste that Berlina has never been able to fathom, but the NPXV audience seems to eat it up. She wonders, lying there idly with tears drying on her face, whether they'll ever do combined events with the commercial channels, so that, say, Synthi Venture will find herself banging away with some guy who's doing the Matthew Arnold routine about decaying civilization. . . .

It makes her laugh, and suddenly, bitterly, she's laughing at herself. Her, the next Edward R. Murrow? Why not the next Genghis Khan? It might be *easier* to conquer the world. *Broadcast is dead, girl, except as a hobby.* And even if broadcast were still alive, here she is crying . . . she can just imagine any of her heroes doing this! Murrow sobbing because he can't get a clear moment of mike in the middle of an air raid . . . Cronkite in tears because NASA wouldn't give them the right camera angles . . . Sam Donaldson holding his breath till he turns blue because Reagan won't talk to him.

It helps to laugh.

She smears the tears out of her eyes with the heels of her hands. Well, what did she expect?

The car lurches, hard, which probably means it just collision-avoided a caribou or something. The animal's timing was clearly off; most people figure that the animals wait to jump in front of cars until you either have an overfull coffee in hand, or are on the squat pot.

Most people think the world is out to get them, because they have all the evidence they need—they don't get enough of what they want. But that doesn't make it so.

She's relaxed now, drying her eyes, thinking about all this. She's got about another four days on the line before she hits the wall and can't get more credit; fewer if it involves any more drives this long. She has a big story on tap, and perhaps Diogenes Callare will give her the last piece of the puzzle—she's due to talk to him in an hour or so. If he does, she can scoop the majors with it; that won't get her much—a week or two of very moderate fame and enough cash to keep her running a few months more—but other things can break. It's a game against the clock, but what isn't?

She gets her notes and thoughts in order for the interview. She just hopes that all the reporters who can afford jumplane haven't gotten to Callare first, but she doubts it; every reporter except Haynes left Barrow last week, which is part of why she's been lonely. Berlina really enjoyed the role of "cub reporter"—it made her feel like Jimmy Olsen. Oh, well, someday maybe some adoring cub will follow her around . . . she's realizing, too, that a lot of the reporters enjoyed the attention they got from her.

There's so much to get organized that she's startled when the ping comes to remind her to call Diogenes Callare.

Much to her surprise, he seems friendly and relatively open. She knows he's sticking close to what the press releases say, textually, but the man is a natural teacher, things come out as little micro-lectures, and with a bit of stitching together she can make it absolutely clear that the bland language of the press release is hiding a lot of important possibilities. "So it comes down to energy?" she asks once again, hoping he'll repeat himself and give her a quote or two more.

She's right, he does. "Well, look," he says. "Energy is work, you had freshman physics, everyone does nowadays, right? And work is change. And we're looking at huge changes here. Not so much if the additional heat the Earth is going to retain were all spread out evenly, of course, but that's just the point. It's a system where heat flows. Some of it's going to pile up somewhere—and when it does, big things will happen."

It's a great quote, especially if she can jam it up against a few she has of various nonentities saying that any concern is premature.

She thanks Di—mentally congratulating herself again on getting to first names with him so quickly—and clicks off.

If Glinda Gray could look in from somewhere else, she would be patting herself on the back. She had told Klieg that this day, or the next, the media would catch on to the "purloined letter"—the realization that right out in plain sight, the Feds were admitting catastrophe was on the way.

Time to put it together. If she's going to do this thing, she might as well do it. And there's nothing wrong—financially scary, yes, but nothing *wrong*—with going independent. Ben Franklin, I. F. Stone, Tris Coffin . . . it can be done. She thinks about it for a moment . . . *Berlina Jameson's Methane Report* . . . sounds like a natural gas newsletter. *How Berlina Is Not Being Told the Truth* . . . not the thing either; *The Jameson Report* is pompous . . . what she really wants to tell the potential reader is that she's smelling something important, that she's not being dismissed the way they dismiss nuts at government facilities, but brushed away from the single big question: What's going to happen because of this? Why doesn't anyone appear to be preparing for anything?

I Smell Gas?

Not exactly right either . . . what she's reporting is . . . *Sniffings.*

It's not dignified, it smells too much of the New Journalism, it has the gut feel of Geraldo Rivera and Sally Jessy, spiritual parents of XV—

She doesn't care. Barely four days of credit left. *Sniffings* it is—and it's no worse a title than *Scuttlebytes*. The title alone is odd enough that some people will access it; now all she has to do is be interesting enough to make them access it twice.

She grabs the autodictator and her notepad; time enough to clean up and set up a little later. Meanwhile, she needs to turn this into copy, *real* copy.

"This is Berlina Jameson, on the road from Barrow, Alaskan Free State, to Washington, the Duc, USA. For the past three weeks, I have been handled with the utmost courtesy by Alaskan and United Nations officials, by scientists from the USA, Pacificanada, Mexico, and Quebec, and by a wide variety of public relations people. Occasionally I have even been told a piece or two of the truth—a piece which was promptly denied or dismissed by other sources.

"All this has happened because I have been asking, over and over, the simple question that everyone wants an answer to: now that a UN military operation—"

That ought to boost the ratings. UNSOO is officially a peacekeeping, not a military, organization, despite what it actually does. Calling it a military operation will cause an automatic warning flag from UNIC—they won't kill the story but they will suggest that peace-loving decent citizens not read it. The nationalists will promptly read it *because* of that. The United Left will send her hate mail, and that will register as traffic and draw attention from the critics. True, she doesn't especially want to encourage the nationalists . . . or the critics, for that matter. But they pay access charges the same as anyone else. . . .

"DICTRON BACK UP AND MERGE. —now that a UN military operation has accidentally released one hundred and seventy-three billion tons of methane into the atmosphere, given the evidence of the geological past that such releases have produced brief periods of intense warming, what is going to happen to us? Should we be evacuating half of humanity up into the mountains? Will we lose the Netherlands, Florida, and Bangladesh as the seas rise? Will new Saharas form where grain grows now, and will we see global famine? Are we facing flood, famine, or storm?

"No one will say, and I have come to realize that what they are covering up is not some disaster of awesome proportions, but that they themselves do not know; despite all the advances of science, we are waiting between the lightning and the thunder—"

No, strike that, it's melodramatic. No, keep it. Melodrama is what we want . . . melodrama always made money, and the line is getting pretty short. But it's not the right metaphor.

"DICTRON BACK UP, MERGE, ERASE. —despite all the advances of science, we must simply wait for it—but the one thing they are sure of is that the effect will be big. We have whacked Nature hard, with a hammer, and now we stand facing her while she makes up her mind what to do about it."

This is beginning to roll. It will need work, but it's a damned sight livelier than the stuff she's been doing up until now.

It ends up being a long day spent entirely in the car; she puts it on auto-gas, so that it just pulls over at automated stations when it needs to and fills up. The story goes through six drafts and when she's done, "Sniffings" is a very nice little twenty-minute program with all kinds of up-close footage of people evading the issues, and some really good animated graphics. For her own narration, she uses the little rig that she bought used, ages ago, that lets her hang the teleprompter and camera from the ceiling, pointing down at her as she lies on the bed, with a pale blue reflector underneath her. Edit out the reflector and superimpose the "Sniffings" graphic she came up with, and damn if it doesn't look at least as good as what was on the old networks themselves as recently as thirty years ago.

It's in the can. "DICTRON: POST TEXT SNIFFINGS ONE, PUBLIC NET UNDER COPYRIGHT, ACCESS FEE SET TO BERLINASTAND-ARD—"

"ADJUST FOR INFLATION?" the Dictron asks.

"ADJUST FOR INFLATION," she confirms. She really will have to revise her rate schedule sometime soon. "NOTE HEADER—SNIFFINGS TO BE A FREQUENT RELEASE AT TWENTY-MINUTE LENGTH. RE-BROADCAST AUTHORIZED IN NONCOMPETING MARKETS AND IN TRANSLATION, AT ACCESS FEES SET TO BERLINASTANDARD. ADJUST FOR INFLATION."

"CONFIRM?" It reads back her release order; she confirms it; it goes out to the net.

Time to celebrate. *Sniffings 1* is a damned fine piece of work, even if no one ever looks at it—and she feels in her bones that at least a few people somewhere *will* look at it.

She pulls over at a rest area, plugs the car into a fresher that will vacuum out the dust and accumulated body smell, swap out the squat pot, and zap the whole works with ultraviolet and microwaves so that it will smell like a car rather than a monkey pen when she gets back. Tote bag on her shoulder, she goes into the public showers; a cleanup, a change of clothes, and a good meal are the rest of the agenda, to be followed by a good long sleep in the car.

What the hell, it's better than Ernie Pyle usually got.

* * *

After she hangs up from Louie, Carla Tynan finds it's a little difficult to get back to her peaceful sunbath. In the first place, that damned rocket jockey has gotten her horny, and even though there's no one out here on the Pacific, with a featureless horizon in all directions, to see her, she can't quite bring herself to masturbate outside. Growling to herself for a silly prude, she goes below to get a little relief.

Afterward, with *MyBoat* rocking gently on the surface, she starts to compare the numbers from Louie with the ones NOAA gave her in more detail. She isn't surprised that that gang of political hacks has been holding the numbers down, but she is surprised at how much they've been holding them down.

Well, one of the pleasures of being her own person is the ability to do her own work. She has several "baby" global weather models available on her computer, and a system she's come up with for linking them. She pulls out the set of speciality fibrop cables, still in their wrappers from the cadcam shop, and starts patching the systems together.

First thing, work out what the real methane concentrations must be to account for Louie's data. That only takes a minute or so, and the results pop back at her.

She gives a long, low whistle. It's piercing and echoing in the little submarine, and she tries to remind herself not to do that again, but painful as it was, the situation earned it. Methane is not six times normal, but nineteen times normal.

Since she's been assigned to the "hurricane problem," she does a quick and dirty plug-through. That much more methane traps this much more energy; forty percent of it ends up in ocean surface water; so the surface water in hurricane formation zones gets anywhere from one to six degrees Celsius warmer, usually with the more drastic warming being farther north, and thus that much more energy is available for a hurricane.

She looks at the numbers; the energy bound in such a hurricane is twelve times the biggest hurricane on record.

And she still hasn't figured how much *bigger* the hurricane formation zones themselves will be.

Still, there's something she can do right now, and that's what she does. She resets the autopilot, takes *MyBoat* down so that she can run undersea, and heads south as fast as she can. The North Pacific is about to become a bad place to be.

"President Grandma" is feeling more like a grandmother—and less presidential—than ever. Brittany Hardshaw has seen and made hard decisions on two minutes' reflection, gotten them dead wrong, and spent years defending them when necessary; she knows that on at least one occasion she got an innocent man executed, and during her watch the United States has lost just over five hundred military people, mostly young men, in one corner of the world or another. She sent her close friend from Boise, Judge Burlham, to Liberia as a mediator, knowing it was dangerous, and on the television that night she saw him cut in half with a submachine gun at the airport. She would think she was hardened enough for any job.

Harris Diem's report is sitting on her desk. It carefully explains the trick that he and a small "Black Team" of NSA scientists were able to pull on the team at NOAA—feeding them doctored data, monitoring the models they built, copying those models down the street in a hidden basement, and then carefully feeding in the correct data. It was a small masterpiece of covert ops. The President of the United States now has in her hands the only accurate assessment of the global temperature situation.

Publicly, she will accept delivery of the NOAA scientists' work in a couple of days, but this secret report is the truth—or as near to it as a computer model can get. Publicly, she will share the NOAA report with the UN, and Rivera will base policy on it.

Which means publicly, the policy will fail, because it is based on inaccuracies, and she will be in a position to use this to advantage.

The only problem now is that what is in her hands is so very much worse than she had imagined. One of the nice NSA men—a soft-spoken young African-American who looked like a bright law student or high school teacher—carefully explained to her that things did not scale up in a linear way, and that "not linear" meant "double the input does not mean double the output—it means, maybe, quadruple it, octuple it, cut it in half . . . the functions are complicated."

So while the public version, on which the UN will act, shows that next summer will bring the twenty biggest hurricanes, typhoons, and cyclones in history, plus a blistering drought in the high latitudes and monsoons beyond historical experience in the tropics; while that report shows the snows of East Africa turning to glaciers and a real risk that the Colorado may stop flowing; while it shows world deaths from famine, flood, and storm running into the tens of millions—it's all a fraud based on wishful thinking.

The real numbers show something more like seventy hurricanes, and many of them far beyond historical scale. There's no drought, but the rain cycle accelerates tremendously—they're going to lose some big dams, and many of the dry lake basins in the West will begin to fill. Between the storms and the change of climate, they can expect major blight outbreaks in the world's forests, and plenty of crop failures. It probably isn't possible to save the Netherlands, and it is definitely not possible to save Bangladesh or most of the world's delta populations. There's no question that they'll lose some populated Pacific Islands entirely, and it looks suspiciously like in the Southern Hemisphere the Antarctic glaciers will grow rapidly all through southern winter and then melt even more rapidly in October and November. There is no way yet to predict the consequences of that.

The real numbers show deaths running to 270 million worldwide by September.

More than a quarter of a billion people.

There is nothing the United States, or the United Nations, can do to save most of them. The USA does not have the economic weight and muscle anymore to lead the world . . . hasn't had it in a long time, but that's something Hardshaw learned early that you never say in front of a voter. For twelve years since the Flash, when the government and at least three-quarters of all the financial records in the country ceased to be, she has been struggling to put American power back together again, first as American Ambassador to the UN, then as Attorney General, and finally as President.

She's fought to preserve what is left of American national sovereignty, to get any momentary advantage that can keep the Republic from being pulled down into a tight orbit around the UN. She has preserved big enough armed forces to act unilaterally, allied herself with any and all powers willing to take on the Secretary General, squeezed every bit of wriggling room from the UN—at the same time that, after the terrorist nuking of Washington, the Federal government was running a third of its budget on UN loans.

Once again, Harris Diem has been her right hand in this. He put the operation together like a pro. Even the developing leak between Carla and Louie Tynan is happening days later than he thought it would, and not affecting their plans at all.

And now, finally, she has in her hand real information—real information that she knows the UN does not have and needs badly.

Let the UN get it wrong, and it will go down. The Global Riot showed that clearly enough, and this is much bigger than any mere public scandal. She can do a lot more than just regain American sovereignty—she can collapse the "world government that dare not speak its name," as she and her circle have called it for many years.

For fifteen years she has worked to put the United States back where it belongs, beyond the command of any foreign power.

All she need do is put together the secret team that will be ready for the real situation. They will still lose New Orleans, Tampa, Miami, Corpus Christi, but they'll get through it. And the rest of the world will go to hell. Unless the UN figures out the truth and acts on that.

And if the UN does get it together . . . there goes the American bid for supremacy, probably forever.

The NSA tells her that they can't predict what the UN will do if she gives them the accurate report. In any case, in a few months, when it's probably too late, they'll know they've been had, and perhaps as they go down they can pin the blame on her. That will be all right; if it comes to that she'll walk right into the General Assembly and let them shoot her with a short pistol, put the whole blame on her—as long as the UN goes down and America comes back up.

But probably, NSA says, if the UN gets things together—they can hold deaths down to 100 million people worldwide. So if Brittany Lynn Hardshaw chooses to do what she had been planning to do—170 million unnecessary dead.

It will certainly put her in the history books. She'll beat Hitler, Stalin, and Mao combined.

And if she hands the UN the truth—that involves telling NOAA the real numbers and probably admitting what the original plan had been, with impeachment likely to follow if Congress wants to save the shreds of American autonomy. More than that, it throws away the very last shot at full American independence.

She looks up at the portraits hanging on the walls; she picked them carefully—Washington, Adams, Jefferson, and Madison, because they founded American independence; Lincoln, who saved the Republic; Truman, Eisenhower, and Kennedy, who armed it to the teeth. In fairness, perhaps, she should have included Franklin Roosevelt for the same reason—but he founded the UN.

"So what would you all do?" she asks them, and jumps at the sound of her own voice. She hadn't meant to speak aloud.

The two reports lie side by side on the desk, and she looks at their all-but-identical covers for a long time, trying to see any other choice.

After the awkward way things started, Klieg would never have bet that this first date with Glinda Gray could go so well. She was exactly right—Derry seems to be delighted to have him interested in her mother, and the "luncheon at a little café where the crab is real and the atmosphere phony," as he described it to them, was a big success. Now he and Glinda, having decided to just sit and watch Derry go by on a horse every so often, are out on the "parents' patio" and having a drink together; mostly they've been talking about growing up in the middle of America, and about how few people anymore seem to have any real ambition or drive for wealth.

They've also been flirting a lot, and in one bold moment—grinning to make it a joke, but doing it anyway—she slid her high-heeled pump up his trouser leg. He grinned back to show he got the joke, but at just that moment he might have done anything for her.

There are flies all around—this close to horses it's inevitable—and the two of them are constantly swinging and slapping at them. He doesn't know what it makes him look like, but it makes Glinda's blonde hair flip around in interesting ways—which he doesn't get much of a chance to observe since he's pretty busy swinging at flies himself. His best guess, from the way she smiles every so often, is that he looks pretty awkward doing it.

They talk on about all sorts of things. The last serious girlfriend that Klieg had, years ago, used to complain that all he talked about was "business, food, and the best brand of everything." There was a certain amount of justice in it, he had to admit, but the great thing is that that seems to be what Glinda talks about as well. They talk about what kind of cars they're going to get next year—they're both eager readers of *Consumer Reports*—and where to get good cheap Mexican food that doesn't put you at any risk of spoiled ingredients, and the relative merits of Denny's versus Shoney's when eating out of town. They talk about new carpeting, which both of them have gotten within the last couple of years, and about whether or not the newer editions of *The Joy of Cooking* are as good as the "classic" version.

They make a number of dumb jokes about all the flies, and they both laugh more than the jokes are worth.

He can't remember when he's had this much fun, or felt so comfortable with a woman. When Derry finally heads in to the stable—they have a shower in there, so the kid can freshen up before she comes out to meet them at the car—Klieg and Glinda stand up and just naturally take each other's hands.

"Mashed potatoes," she says. "That's something it's hard to get made right anymore. Restaurants don't want to put in enough butter and milk."

"You're right about that," Klieg says. "Took me forever to train my cook on that—even with the non-digestible fat versions, the cook tended to get upset and think that I was developing bad dietary habits. Kept ratting on me to Public Health till I restricted its modem access and made it strictly obedient. And I swear to god, it never cooked as well afterward, as if it were sulking. I don't suppose you have servants—"

"Just an occasional live one," she says, "but when you've had a few cleaning women you understand about how hard it is to get the help to do what you want it to do. Makes you appreciate how poor old NASA felt when the replicators were going to eat Moonbase."

Derry sees them holding hands and her freckled face breaks down into a broad grin; she runs toward them, strawberry blonde braids flying. She looks like one of the paintings Klieg got because he liked it, by some classic American painter—Norman Podhoretz? Something like that.

With a great scuffing and crunching of gravel, she comes to a stop in front of them. "That was fun! What are we going to do now?"

"Oh, well, your mom and I have just had a hardworking afternoon drinking on the patio, so maybe some dinner for the appetite we've worked up," Klieg says. "After that, who knows?"

He knows Glinda's humoring him, but Derry seems to like that they end up going to his favorite Shoney's. And Fawn, the waitress—an older lady who looks quite a bit like the President—makes a big fuss over her, which seems to be fun for everyone. They have burgers, fries, and apple pie, and as they lean back, Glinda says, "I've got a dreadful confession to make, John. I've thought about something connected with business, and I think I have an idea."

He mimes switching hats. "In that case, call me 'boss.'" Derry giggles at the silliness; Klieg can tell he's getting along great with the kid, as well as her mother. Definitely he should have thought of this years ago.

"Maybe I'll wait for that until we get into the car," Glinda says. "You eat here all the time and it's always possible someone would bug Shoney's." She turns to Derry and adds, "Honey, you know enough to keep quiet about what Mr. Klieg and I talk about—"

"Is there a big corporate raider trying to take over GateTech or something?" Derry asks. Klieg sees what Glinda means about the kid o.d.'ing on television and XV.

"Why sure," he explains. "Her name is Cruella DeVille, she's a kidnapper, a datavandal, a spy, and a Leftie, and she's this incredibly tall thin brunette babe who always dresses in long black slinky things—"

Derry is raising an eyebrow at him—she's got a quizzical expression that's so funny that he cracks up, just as Glinda does. "What's so funny?" Derry demands. "Is Cruella DeVille a real person?"

That's even funnier, but he can tell that Derry's feelings will be hurt if someone doesn't explain soon. "No, she's a character in a movie. Your mother and I would have seen it back when we were young."

"Mom still *is* young," Derry points out loyally.

At least it settles what they're doing next; there's a little screening-room place across the road where they can see *101 Dalmatians* on the big screen, and it happens that the place also has Junior Mints, which is Klieg's favorite candy. This has really been a day for indulgence—he's going to need to put some time in on the track.

While they wait for the movie to be downloaded from the central bank, he asks Glinda, "So—it's not likely we're bugged here. What's this great idea you've got?"

She pops a Junior Mint in her mouth, savors it a moment, and then says, "Well, it was just the thought that if we're going into launch services that can't be interrupted, chances are it's better to be close to the pole—the hurricanes won't get up there, right?"

"I don't know, we'll pay some meteorologist to tell us that."

"Well, anyway, so we need to build a major space-launch facility without drawing too much attention to what we're really up to. Now, who would want that done? Who that's close to the pole?"

He beams at her. "Siberia! Yeah. And since the Prez is backing anyone who bucks the UN, we'll get plenty of support for doing it from our home nation. Not bad, kiddo, not bad at all."

"Thought you might like it. Do I get a kiss or are you still getting up your nerve?"

Truth is, he hadn't even been thinking that far ahead, but now that she mentions it, it's not a bad idea. He kisses Glinda; halfway through the kiss, he sees her open her eyes, look over at Derry, and cover Derry's eyes with her hand. They're all still laughing like idiots when the movie starts to run, and sure enough, it's as good as they remembered, and the kid loves it.

Even if he weren't about to take a trillion-dollar plunge into a new business, with a real chance to end up as Earth's richest man, this would still be the best day of the decade, as far as Klieg is concerned. After they return to Glinda's place, and Derry is steered off to bed, they get back to kissing, and it's nice to find out how much they both still remember about it.

Everyone always says when couples break up that everyone else should still stay friends, and this is a chance to find out if anyone ever means it. Besides, Jesse wants to know if Little Miss Values can be made jealous.

Unfortunately, she hasn't shown up at this party.

Without Naomi on his arm, towing him around and clarifying things for people, he is getting to talk to a lot of them, and there are a few things he's noticing. One is the number of guys who seem to be very sincere but don't exactly believe in anything. Another is the number of people who seem too ineffectual to have gotten out of bed in the morning; most people know the United Left is more a lifestyle than a position anymore, but when he thinks that these people, or others like them, were ever accused of having engineered the Flash . . . well, it's just silly.

The most interesting thing to him is that he seems to be getting along really well with the women. He hadn't realized how much he'd absorbed from Naomi—he can follow most of the political discussion pretty well, and by just staying a little noncommittal, he can get amazing amounts of attention from young women who want to bring him around to their point of view.

He's not sure, all of a sudden, that dumping him wasn't the biggest favor Naomi ever did him.

Not that these are exactly what he would have thought of as real honeys, back in his unenlightened high school days. They all look like sort of living fossils, cast up from the middle of the twentieth century; in a sosh class once the prof explained that when a movement becomes fixated on impossible causes or on issues that the great majority of society finds completely irrelevant, it takes on more of the aspect of a cult or religious community, including a distinctive style of dress and speech. He remembers a couple of young women with long loose hair, baggy skirts, sandals, and a lot of beads got up and walked out at that.

What he's noticing now is that, all right, nobody's even wearing makeup, but thanks to Naomi he's used to that, and he's also used to figuring out body shapes even under all the tenting. Many of these women have fabulous little bodies—and an acute interest in getting him to come to meetings and have things explained to him. He suspects he's not the only person who would like to see Naomi consumed with jealousy.

And in a subculture where there's not supposed to be any flirting, they all end up being much more overt than the girls Jesse grew up with. They stand close, they pose, they smile and stare into his eyes. A guy could get used to it.

He has a lot more trouble talking to the guys, even though everyone's being polite enough. They don't follow sports, they don't do outdoors stuff directly (and Jesse's never gotten used to XV wilderness experiences—too much like being on a hike with five college professors who talk too much). Besides, most of them are so careful not to dominate their female friends that they won't exactly say what they think about anything in the presence of a woman. There are a few safe subjects—everyone agrees that technology is responsible for ARTS because it allowed people to survive AIDS, and for SPM because it was the evolutionary pressure of antibiotics that forced syphilis into developing its symptom-suppressing behavior. Everyone agrees that Doug Llewellyn and Passionet are responsible for degrading mass consciousness beyond redemption. Everyone agrees that because nobody cares about the race, the United Left really does have a shot at the presidency this year, even if they don't settle on a candidate by November.

He's a little startled at how much attention he's getting from Gwendy, but not so startled that he can't figure out what to do about it. After a while they are talking together in a corner, and she's sitting closer and closer. He finds that by talking about Tapachula and the TechsMex job, he seems to get even more attention.

It ends up being a very late night for him; it turns out that Naomi tends to tell her friends everything, and moreover Naomi is the conscience Gwendy wishes she had. So she's severely torn between what Naomi told her about sex in the desert at night, and the fact that Naomi still doesn't approve of the Lectrajeep. In that sense it's not any easier than getting Naomi to fuck; but when, finally, at two A.M., Gwendy is naked in the Lectrajeep in the desert, Jesse gets a chance to rediscover two things he had all but forgotten—laughter and enthusiasm.

It's too bad he had to impress her with the Tapachula thing; now he'll have to go do it, right when she was making the idea of Tucson so much more appealing.

Carla Tynan has been up for much too long, and she's getting strung out. *MyBoat* is pounding along, using up her antimatter charge faster than intended—though it would still take her clear around the world, if it came to that. The hull is vibrating noticeably with the extra speed she's crowded on. But the autopilot can do all that; the only time Carla's skills are called for is when she's coming into a port, and since she's still six hundred miles northwest of Nauru, that's going to be a long while.

She's feeling a little ashamed of having dropped and run when she realized the magnitude of effect that was happening; a real scientist, she chides herself, would have headed a little north and way east, over into the hurricane formation zone off of southern Mexico, to get a better look. But all the same, she's a pleasure craft, not a research vessel, and no doubt the big powers are getting some serious gear into that area already. Most likely if she'd decided to head there, she'd have been intercepted by the American or the Mexican navy and interned.

Anyway, what she's finding here is bad enough. Correct for the true atmospheric mix, and you get something between fifty and a hundred big hurricanes and god knows what else. She has the equivalent of six old-time Crays in her little ship (she can remember back when you had to rent time on such things, and nowadays some rich people use microsupers to run their houses), but that's not nearly enough to run the full model at any reasonable speed.

Thus she's forced to do what they never have to do at NOAA (or at NSA, which she doesn't know about). She has to set up the parts of the model that she can do by graphics and instinct, plug in values from that, and then run the parts for which she doesn't have a gut feel. It's woefully imprecise, and if her gut feelings are wrong at any point she's going to get nonsense, but it's what's available if she wants the answer before the storm hits.

Thus she sets up the screen to show her the new isotherms in the Pacific. An isotherm is an imaginary line along which the temperature is constant; most people have seen them on TV weather maps, usually as bands of color on "high today" or "low today" maps.

If you're interested in hurricanes, there's one isotherm you've got to know everything about. That's the one for 27.5° Celsius.

A hurricane is a gigantic heat engine. That is, it converts a temperature difference into mechanical energy, like diesel, steam, gasoline, jet, rocket, or turbine engines. But whereas a diesel engine, for example, converts (some of) the heat of the burning fuel to motion of the piston by releasing (most of) the heat to the cooler environment, a hurricane works by moving heat from the hot ocean surface to the cold bottom of the stratosphere— converting some of it to wind along the way.

If the water is below 27.5° Celsius, more energy comes out of the wind to move the heat than the heat itself supplies, and the hurricane dies. But above 27.5°, a hurricane doesn't just live . . . it grows. Each blast of cool air blowing over the warm, wet ocean grows warmer, rises, drops its load of evaporated water, and returns with a little more force each time.

So inside the isotherms marked "27.5°" on Carla's map, hurricanes will grow; outside they will die. The areas inside the 27.5° isotherms are "hurricane formation zones."

She looks at the map, and she's never seen anything like it before. Normally there are two, or in a very warm summer three, hurricane formation zones in the Pacific—one by the Philippines, one lying under the bulge of Mexico, and late in a warm summer the South China Sea.

The models have been figuring that these zones would expand, and the formula they have used to expand them has been a very simple one—too simple as it turns out. No one checked to see if they might overlap, or if others might form. Not that she blames them—it's not a particularly obvious point. And for that matter, if they did, maybe they didn't believe what they saw—quite possibly they did check and then decided not to stick their necks out. Remembering her old outfit, Carla sighs. Not sticking your neck out was what it was all about.

Still, it's there, and if they'd been more careful or more systematic, they'd have seen it.

There is now just one hurricane formation zone in the North Pacific— but it stretches from the Galápagos to Borneo, east-west, and the equator to Hokkaido, north-south. It's 11,000 miles across and 3,500 miles wide.

Normally the force of a hurricane is determined by the temperature of the water it passes over (the warmer the more force) and by the length of time it spends passing over that 27.5° or warmer water (the longer, the more heat energy gets converted into wind). So the size of the hurricane formation zone limits the power of the hurricane, because it moves, on rare occasions as fast as 100 mph. Historically the hurricane formation zones have been 1,500 or 2,000 miles across at widest, so that few hurricanes stay in them for even twenty-four hours.

This new whole-ocean hurricane formation zone is vastly bigger than anything of the kind in recorded history.

She sits and watches as the computer does a set of quick and dirty runs, playing with random numbers to show a range of possibilities.

They all look frighteningly alike. She feels like just going to bed, hoping to get up in the morning and find it was all a bad dream.

Anyway, it won't happen tonight. She can take *MyBoat* up to the surface and plug in, talk to Di or Louie or somebody.

She reaches for the autopilot control, sets running for "surface" and tells it to take her up gently. In a moment the thunder of the motors pushing water out the jets begins to sound slightly different as *MyBoat* begins to climb toward the surface. She gets back to the keyboard, and snips out the important bits into a file she can zap over to Di.

Of course, maybe he knows. Maybe he's in on it. Well, if that's the case, at least he can warn her to steer clear of this. And perhaps even tell her a little about what is really going on. On the other hand, if he's been kept in the dark too . . . who's running this show?

No doubt they'll find out. All they have to do is reveal the findings and see who gets upset enough to try to suppress them. She grins at herself for thinking such melodramatic thoughts.

When the hull of *MyBoat* finally bursts out onto the Pacific Ocean, Carla has her download ready to go. She dials Di's number at home before she remembers to check the time zone; fortunately, running submerged, she's been keeping strange hours, and it's only ten P.M. there, not unconscionable, although he does have young kids.

His wife, Lori, the mystery writer, answers. She's always been just a little distant with Carla. When Di and Carla worked together, Di probably talked too much about her at home.

But Lori knows her well enough to know the call must be something important. "Hi. I guess I'd better get Di. He's asleep with the kids."

"Thank you, Lori. I'm sorry to have to call so late."

"It's all right—if you're doing it, it's important. Can I ask you something before I get Di?"

"Of course."

"How serious is all the stuff happening?" Lori glances to the side, probably checking to make sure that Di isn't listening. "Di's been talking in his sleep, thrashing around, coming home from work looking like hell—"

"I'm not surprised," Carla says. "It's very serious, Lori, and I've got some evidence that it's even worse than what Di may be thinking."

Lori nods soberly, and a change comes over her face. Carla thinks to herself, this is the kind of woman who hears it's dangerous, so she gets a Self Defender. She hears that someone has managed to use AIRE to break a patent, or that fibrop prices have come down, and she knows exactly which stocks in the kids' college portfolios have to be sold right away. She knows everything she can about the world she lives in and she's ready to use the knowledge. If anyone should be able to get through this, it's Lori—she's what Carla's boomtalking grandmother would call "a really together lady."

"Can you tell me anything about it?" Lori asks.

"Well," Carla says slowly, "I can easily imagine why Di hasn't wanted to tell you. But I think you're entitled to get ready for it. I'm afraid this really is a global disaster; a lot of people are going to die and a lot of things are going to change."

"Is there anything we could do . . . to be safe?" Lori asks. "I don't want to ask Di, because he worries enough . . . but the kids—"

"If I think of anything I'll call you and tell you. It wouldn't be a bad idea to spend the summer in the mountains, maybe—you're only a few miles from the sea, right?"

"Right." Lori nods like she's going to start packing right now.

"But I could be dead wrong, Lori. If the Appalachians get the extra water we're talking about, they might be worse than the coast—flash floods, storms, mudslides, hail, maybe even bad blizzards in July if enough cloud cover develops. We're just not ready to say. That's part of why Di is so upset these days, I'm sure—because we're not ready to say, but we know for sure it's going to be something big." *Or because he does know what it's going to be, and he's holding data back for some weird political reason,* she adds, crossing her fingers mentally.

Lori nods. "Thanks for filling me in. I'll go get Di."

"Oh, and Lori?"

"Unh-hunh?"

"I loved *Slaughterer in Green.* My favorite so far."

Lori beams at her. "Thanks." She vanishes from the screen and a moment later Di comes onto the camera.

"Carla—what's up?"

"A lot, I'm afraid. I was talking with Louie earlier today, and he happened to read me off some of the methane density results they're getting with the satellite-to-satellite shots."

"You two kids were always so romantic."

"Oh, belt up. This is important. The numbers he gave me are way higher than the numbers I've been getting out of NOAA, and it's a systematic error—somebody's been dividing some key data by eight before reporting it. I want to know what's going on and why this is being done—and if you're not in on it, I want to give you the real numbers."

Di looks like he's been punched in the gut, but he'd look that way whether he was surprised at the information or surprised that she knew it. "What are the numbers, then?" he asks.

She tells him and then drops the second of her three blockbusters. "Now, when you start plugging those numbers in, plot the isotherms on Pacific surface water temperature."

"Why?"

"Because the thing that our model does is figure size of each hurricane formation zone individually. Generally that's all that needs to be done and it works, because when you're only messing with small changes the zones grow or shrink by a hundred miles or so at most." She tells him about the whole Pacific being one formation zone.

"Think about it, Di, they get bigger the farther they run. Up till now you've never had one run two thousand miles through a formation zone. When a big one rips up the U.S. East Coast it's dying before it clears Florida. But this summer there are some that might get in eight-thousand- or ten-thousand-mile runs before they pile into land . . . and a hurricane might pass New York City and be headed for Europe, still gaining energy."

"Now wait a minute, Carla, it's bad but it's not that bad. Hurricanes move east to west. They'll hit land eventually—"

Time for her third blockbuster. "They also move toward the pole. And once you're up at thirty-two degrees north or so, the steering currents will tend to push them toward the *east.* You might very well see one or more of them circling around out there and not dying all summer."

It is characteristic of information that it can be stolen an all but unlimited number of times. When it became clear that one particular senior meteorologist at NOAA might be sitting at the focal point, that clarity—that little note that "this is what probably matters"—became information in and of itself, and was worth stealing. A dozen monitoring programs stole it at once, and dozens more stole from each of them, and from the places they passed it on to, until by now practically everyone who matters knows that Diogenes Callare matters. One of the few who doesn't know is Diogenes Callare.

He hasn't noticed his superiors treating him with kid gloves, though they are, or the FBI men who watch him constantly.

What he has noticed is how much seems to be kept from him, as if no one wants him to figure anything out. So Carla Tynan's phone call finally makes it click into place, and he's been in Washington for far too long not to realize that if so much is being kept from him, it's because he's more important than he thinks he is. It's a long step down the road to paranoia, but it's been a proverb for a hundred years that being paranoid does not mean that they aren't out to get you.

As he hangs up, he thinks of a dozen little details . . . an instrument report or two that he had discarded as too far out of bounds—and which had disappeared later. One or two people at NOAA whom he had thought were new hires, people he'd never seen before, who seemed to spend all the time they were not in meetings on the phone and didn't seem to know a lot of meteorology. Having overheard one new supervisor getting an explanation about methane being CH_4 and opaque in the infrared from another of the new hires.

He knows, very suddenly, that there have been many, many datarodents in the nodes near him, with more arriving all the time. He doesn't know about the four guardians in the shadows around his house—or the two watchers who watch the guardians, waiting for a slip—but he will notice them when he comes out the door in the morning.

Di Callare stands and runs his hands through his hair. He thinks back to all the bland, boring years while not much happened; to the night when nuclear fire tore a hole in the capital, and the long year afterward as they swiftly rebuilt, and the slow realization that the Blue Berets might never be going home; and to the way that Washington went from being merely dangerous and dirty to a city of intrigue, like Vienna, Berlin, or Bucharest, a place where power swirled and congealed in dark corners, a place where Di could remember four acquaintances who died in odd accidents and three people who had disappeared.

"Even at fucking NOAA," he mutters under his breath, and then looks around and is relieved to remember that Nahum is asleep and hasn't picked up that one. He sighs once more, deeply, and goes in to see how Lori is doing.

She's hunched over the keyboard, beating away at it. He's given up on asking why she insists on using a keyboard when dictation equipment is so fast and accurate nowadays; her explanation—that readers of books like hers read fast and that they don't hear the words, so to write orally is to write the wrong rhythm—hasn't made much sense to him, but then he knows that his attempts to explain the jet stream to her haven't gotten much of anywhere either. Let it just be that she knows what she's doing.

He creeps softly up behind her and sees that she's typing *but there was no one to hear her scream, however loud she might, not even as the man with the big, kind eyes began to slit the skin around her breast with his matte knife*—

Di Callare winces, brushes her hair back, kisses her neck. Normally she hates to be interrupted while she's working, and normally he respects that, but right now he needs her touch badly, and he has to hope she'll understand.

When she turns to kiss his cheek, her face is wet with tears. "Bad news from Carla?" she asks.

"The worst. Did you hear?"

"She told me it was going to be bad." Lori explains, whispering in his ear. His mouth sets in disapproval—he'd have thought Carla would have more sense than to tell Lori something like— "Don't blame her, I asked. She's one of your best friends, you know—maybe not your closest, but one of your most loyal. I love her for that."

He lifts Lori out of her chair and carries her to their bedroom; in happier times when he has done this, mostly just to prove he still can, she's referred to it as "a moment out of the classic movies, that moment when the leading man carries away the leading lady and we see what they both really want—just before the train goes into the tunnel, or biplanes show up—"

The remembered joke makes him smile. They take a very long time about making love, as if they were trying to memorize everything.

The third week he's teaching in Tapachula, Jesse persuades Naomi to come down for a long visit. At first it seems like a blazing success; she seems very pleased with his tutoring work and with the little place he's found, and congratulates him on getting into a much better mode of existence than he had before. At least he's got her fooled into thinking he's a real Leftie.

But that night, as they sit on his couch and he very tentatively tries to kiss her, she says, "Oh, god, Jesse, no, no, I can't. Really. I had such a hard time getting over you the first time."

"Well, then don't get over me and just enjoy this."

"I wish I could."

"Why can't you?"

For the first time ever, he sees her lose her temper. "Because just maybe you're the kind of guy who wants me to just enjoy it, all right? It's bad enough that you don't think of anyone but yourself but you don't want *me* to think of anyone but *my*self, either! I can't believe you're trying to talk me into being selfish and centered and linear!"

They end up talking philosophy for hours. When Jesse finally goes to sleep, he's not only exhausted, but the apartment is so tiny that he doesn't even have the option of masturbating to relieve himself. The next day Naomi gets on the little jumplane, which shoots straight up into the brilliant blue tropical sky and is gone. She'll be touching down on the runway in Tehuantepec before the *combino* can get Jesse out of the airport traffic.

Still, he manages to get her to come down once more, and then, in the middle of one of the cafés that fronts on the Zócalo, just because he suggests that a little pleasure in her life would surely not damage the good things she does, she starts to cry, and she *hits* him (not hard, that takes practice she's never had). Lunging across the table in a clatter of dishes, she dumps a pitcher of beer on him, flags down a taxi, and is gone while he is still trying to rub his eyes clear of the salty, sticky mess dribbling down from his hair.

He checks his contract with TechsMex and discovers that unless he can give them twice the price of a new car right away, he's here for at least six more months. Probably he'd have missed his students, anyway. They're great people—as evidenced by the fact that three of them witnessed that last incident with Naomi, and yet he never hears a thing about it. It's as if the whole collective memory, the great gossip bank, of Tapachula, has all been subjected to a Flash.

With Jesse in the role of the ruins of the Duc.

"And that's all," Glinda Gray is saying to John Klieg. "Just emphasize that when you talk to the Siberians. There's Ariane 12, Delta Clipper III, the Japanese K-4, a bunch of military space planes that can't lift much more than their own crews, and no real heavy lift until NAOS gets the Monster flying. Theoretically, the Russians or Chinese could start building big boosters again but it would be from scratch."

"And that couldn't be more perfect. Ariane flies from the Caribbean, Delta Clipper III from Edwards AFB, K-4 from Kageshima. All places that are vulnerable—but not nearly as vulnerable as the NAOS Monster flying out of Kingman Reef. Meteorology's estimate is that by late June everything that can lift more than a two-man crew should be shut down completely."

"Got it," Klieg says. He looks Glinda up and down; she is in a perfect pink leather suit and matching shoes. It shouts "Expensive!" and for the Siberians that's what you have to do. "Remember what the culture coach said. Do your best to look in awe, like you're completely enslaved sexually."

Glinda grins at him. "If anyone could do that to me, darling. . . ."

His heart gives a funny thump. This meeting is for all the marbles if ever there was one—they've got half the significant officials in the Siberian Republic flying in to Islamabad, the nearest place where discretion could be assured and Western comforts were available. Just chasing this deal so far has cost Klieg four times what it did to start GateTech.

God, he's glad Glinda is here. No man ever had a better partner for this kind of thing; she remembers everything, coordinates everything, and yet is willing to play the Number One Harem Girl to get them the deal.

And it is their deal now, not just Klieg's. For the last ten days he's been noticing he thinks about the future a lot—about where Derry will go to college, and what kind of house he and Glinda will need for the years Derry is with them, and then after that when they're still active, and finally for retirement. He loves planning things.

Gently, he brings her face to his; in the super-high heels her balance isn't good and she's almost as tall as he is, so their kisses are very tender and light, just the warm brushing of lip to lip.

Randy Householder finds it hard to believe, but there it is. After all these years, some signs of progress. Five scattered datarodents out there have reported that Harris Diem is behind a couple of fronts that are buying the murder wedges. That doesn't surprise him a bit—if anyone would be conducting a secret investigation, that's who. He's just surprised how long it took him to find the traces of the investigation. He hopes it won't be equally hard to penetrate its files.

It's pretty clever of them to hide the investigation behind Diem's personal accounts.

That one little one that got into the NOAA node was the key; now that he has many supplemental keys to look for, the right bank and credit accounts, it will take less time. It's still going to be some weeks, of course, because to do these illegal accesses he has to wait until things are brought out of storage and put online, and most of the relevant records will be more than a decade old.

It's okay with Randy. He's been hunting a long time. A part of him wonders what it will be like, not to be looking for the man who paid to have Kimbie Dee killed. He wonders if there'll even be a world at all after that?

Her face is getting indistinct in his mind again, so he pulls out a video disk and watches his daughter for an hour; sees how she grew up, how pretty she was, watches her cheering at an eighth-grade football game (and what a beautiful girl she was!)—

Cuts very briefly to her on the slab in the morgue, face black from the hanging, bra still embedded in her neck, blood on her thighs and belly.

"It's okay," Randy whispers to her. Except online he rarely talks to anyone else anymore. He's not even sure where Terry is now—she got married again and had a couple more kids. "We'll get him, Kimbie Dee. No matter what."

Datarodents swarm out of the car's computer, up through the antenna into the satellite, and from there to everywhere, over laser, radio, and fibrop. The car rolls on toward Austin—there are just enough connections in the material he got by bugging Diem's investigation so that it looks like there's something worth knowing in police records down there.

It's dark in the middle of Kansas, but Randy doesn't mind. He switches off the terminal, and after a while, he falls asleep. In front of him, the headlights search the blackness, and find only the road.

TWO
VORTEX

THERE ARE FEW places on Earth more empty than 8N 142W.
In latitude, 0 is the equator, 90 is the pole. In longitude, London is 0 and
the International Date Line is 180.

So the point is about eight degrees north—not very far above the
equator—and 142 degrees west—most of the way around from London.
What is there, besides an intersection of imaginary lines, is water and air.

At the bottom of the sea, 4,800 meters below the water, there is only
darkness, high pressure, and cold; the plains of mud rise and roll in low
foothills that will become mountains farther to the west. There is a dribble
of dead things from the surface, but not much even of that; the area above
is a marine desert.

Temperature does not rise rapidly until you're near the surface; the last
150 meters, suddenly, are part of the world of light and air above, but there
is so little there for anything to eat that the water is clear, warm, and empty.

Above the water, laced with the extra methane, the air has gotten very,
very warm during the long equatorial day; the water, heated by the sun, has
given off its heat upward as infrared, but the methane is black as night to
the infrared and the air has warmed and rewarmed, swirling around to reheat
the water.

The sea surface is alive with small breezes and with the great swirl of
the trade winds; here a bit of air rises and draws air toward itself, there
cooled air slides back down to the sea and skids across its surface. It happens,
by chance, that there are places where the air piles together, and just after
sunrise—not long after six in the morning, here—that was happening at the
sea surface. The warm air from the sea around blew inward to this crossing
of imaginary lines, and a little mountain of warmer air began to form there.

This lumpy, invisible mountain of warm, wet air, at first, towered no
more than ten thousand feet high. There are many taller peaks in the
Rockies.

But above the warm, wet air of the sea surface, there is other air, cooler,
dryer. Eighteen kilometers—a distance you could drive in ten minutes on
a good highway—straight up, there is another imaginary line, the tropopause. Below the tropopause, the decreasing pressure and the increasing
distance from the Earth's warm surface make temperature fall with altitude;
above the tropopause, hard ultraviolet light falling in from space heats the
thin wisp of atmosphere, so that temperature rises with altitude, since the
outermost air gets the most ultraviolet (and shades the air below it). Thus
the tropopause is in one sense a line on temperature plot—it is only the
height at which the air is coldest.

Yet the tropopause is not quite so imaginary as the lines of latitude and longitude. It has a real consequence; air below the tropopause cannot rise above it easily. Think of lumpy, irregular building blocks made of lead, wood, and plastic foam; if you pile them in that order, the system is stable and hard to turn over; if you put plastic foam on the bottom and lead on the top, the structure will fall over easily.

Cold air is heavy like lead; warm air is light like plastic foam. In the troposphere, the warm air is on the bottom and the system rolls over constantly; in the stratosphere, warm air is on the top, and thus the stratosphere resists being turned over. When a stream of warm air rises through the troposphere to the tropopause, it cannot turn over the stratospheric layers above it, and thus cannot rise farther; instead, it spreads out under the tropopause.

The underside of the tropopause, like the face of the ocean, is stirred constantly with winds and currents; sometimes they pile together, and sometimes they pull apart. It happened, at about 7:45 in the morning locally, that directly above the mountain of air piled together on the sea, the winds began to pull apart along the tropopause.

Thus the warm air below, already tending to rise, was being pushed from around its outside, and at the same time the pressure above it fell. Like a bubble breaking from the bottom of a boiling pot, the mountain of warm air broke from the face of the sea, rose to the tropopause, and was torn apart and scattered by the winds there.

Where the mountain of warm air had been, it left a hole—and more warm air rushed in to fill it, making a newer and bigger mountain, which in turn was drawn up into the troposphere and scattered, making another mountain—

For fifty kilometers around, at sea level, air began to rush toward 8N 142W, and at tropopause level, to flow away from it.

And as this happened, the Coriolis force—the force on moving objects on the Earth's surface caused by the Earth's rotation, familiar because it complicates missile flights and makes it hard to play Ping-Pong on a fast-moving merry-go-round—bent the north-moving air westward, and the south-moving air eastward; in either case, forcing the air to turn left, so that by 9:10 A.M. the air had begun to spiral as it fell inward to the center of low pressure. By now, air was coming from as far away as 100 kilometers.

As it spiraled inward, it picked up heat from the sea, sped up, packed in more closely around the central column; it became harder and harder for more warm air to push its way into the center and up the column, now kilometers thick, of rising warm air.

The carrying of so much warm air up into the cold air above has been having other effects too. As the air above spreads out, cools, and falls, water condenses, and big thick thunderheads have been forming all around the column of hot air, making it look a bit like a giant mushroom cloud; the falling cold air and the general agitation of the winds in the area have already lashed the cumulonimbus clouds into a storm, and their rapid circulation has separated big electric charges, so that the sea becomes dark under a bank of heavy clouds, and lightning flashes and warm rain are everywhere.

The moment comes now.

The inward-spiraling air piling up around the base of the rising column has become too thick for more air to force its way through; the ring of thick air around the column moves faster and faster as more air is added to it, and rises up the outside of the column, sheathing it in whirling, rising wind. The central column, deprived of its new air, empties until pressure is far below normal; the corkscrew of rising air around it reaches the tropopause and begins to pump the rising hot air out along the tropopause boundary with far greater efficiency.

As the top of the storm moves more air outward, the bottom sucks more in. The spiraling gets faster every minute. The distance from which the storm can draw new warm air increases just as quickly.

Clouds in the ring of fast-moving air are torn to shreds and form a fast-moving white wall; clouds in the column are pulled out of it and vanish, leaving a clear sky above a savagely foaming green sea.

The central column has become an eye, and the storm is now a hurricane.

The biggest problem with being lovelorn in Tapachula, Jesse decides, is that it's such a damned friendly place that in a couple of weeks everyone not only knows about the final breakup with Naomi, but has significant advice for him. The advice seems to break down into the macho, which he gets from men, to the effect that it is time to forget the *chica* and get on with finding another one; the romantic, which comes mainly from older women, to the effect that all he needs to do is remain steadfast in his passion and that even if he doesn't get Naomi he will still be a very beautiful boy; and the pragmatic, which he gets from the three teenage whores he walks past on his way home from work each evening, to the effect that getting over it can be accomplished physiologically by a few simple procedures they would be happy to demonstrate.

He always smiles politely and listens intently to the macho and romantic advice; the pragmatic advice gives him an occasional urge to try it out, but not enough to really consider the indignity.

Tapachula is otherwise not a bad place for a broken heart. The strange square-shaped topiary trees of the Zócalo create thousands of dark, deep shadows, perfect for staring into and imagining Naomi coming out of; there are cafés all the way around the east and south sides of the Zócalo, so that there are plenty of places for sitting and drinking while he nurses the broken heart.

Moreover, evenings bring the evening promenade. It doesn't resemble the tourist guidebook descriptions of "gallant young men in colorful Latin high-fashion and flashing-eyed señoritas under the watchful gaze of dour chaperoning aunts"—but then, what tourist would come to see "guys who worked all day in the factory take a shower and put on their good clothes, and go out to flirt with young women who've done the same thing"? It would sound too much like going to the mall back home.

Yet if the promenade doesn't much resemble the guidebooks, for Jesse it's still very nice. Jesse looks like a juvenile lead in a twentieth sort of way; anyone looking at him can see him as the Rookie Cop, the Green Deputy, the Daring Kid Pilot, the Brilliant Young Doctor—in every case the hero-to-be, and as a result, most of the young women going by have been trained to find men who look like Jesse attractive, even though there aren't many locally. Being broken-hearted is a lot more fun when every few minutes someone gives you an artful shake of long, thick black hair, or a sideways glance that reveals a cute smile, white flashing teeth, and—with the hips turned just right—a blouse pulled tight across a high, firm breast, or a short skirt clinging to taut young buttocks. For a broken heart it's almost as good as the local beer.

And in its odd way it's helping him in his work, because since he doesn't respond to any particular girl, he doesn't seem to induce any jealousy in any of the young men he works with. They seem to find his love life to be a sort of shared bond between them; it's the kind of thing a young Mexican man might get into for a few months, though in the back of his head Jesse knows that it's only his family income that lets him indulge it for so long—since he doesn't have to get a wife to move out of his parents' house, he doesn't have to worry about any eventual opportunities passing him by while he wears his mask of melancholy.

There are other benefits, he knows. He's finally really mastered the basic engineering curriculum, because he's been teaching the equivalent of his freshman and sophomore years, one way and another, for two months now, in Spanish, and somehow the combination of having to put it into other words and other structures, plus having to repeat explanations of it so often, has ingrained it into his brain. He knows, without false modesty, that when he goes back to U of the Az, getting Masterys in his classes will be no great problem.

Most nights he sits in a sidewalk café and drinks at a nice steady three beers an hour, enough to get him good and drunk at the end of three hours so that, after eating *cena*, he can wander home and grab some sleep.

Often one of his students—maybe bored with the promenade, maybe curious about Jesse, or perhaps just hoping that by sitting next to Jesse he will fall into the field of vision of one of the women going by—will sit down and drink with him for a while. Usually that means getting drunker faster, since it almost always leads to a rivalry about who can buy whom more beer.

It's on such nights that he gets more macho advice, and they sit and discuss the bodies on the women going by—along with Naomi's body. Jesse sometimes thinks that ought to bother him, but it doesn't really—and after all, how much did he ever really know about her besides that he liked her body and that to get at it he'd have to believe all kinds of strange Deeper shit?

This seems like an almost philosophic thought, and fortunately he has José, who is inclined to philosophy, to talk to tonight. It takes him a while to explain the question, about whether he should feel guilty or ashamed about not feeling guilty or ashamed, not because José is slow but because José is quite drunk—he started a while before Jesse and is working on it harder and faster.

Finally, Jesse gets the whole question explained carefully to José; does he owe it to Naomi to feel guilty that after all their time and conversations together, it's not the conversations or her mind he misses, or even the big brown eyes and soft hair, but just the feel of her full, soft breast in his hand? Should Jesse try harder to feel more appropriate feelings?

José considers this a long time. Twice he holds up a finger as if to begin speaking, and once he sits back with an expression of someone who has finally solved a problem, but each time he hesitates and then does not speak.

Jesse nods emphatically, to show that he understands how difficult the question can be, and signals the tall waiter (who always appears to be smiling slightly, as if every customer had just done something a little bit amusing, or perhaps was dressed just a little wrong). Two more beers, the kind of slightly salty, tart lager they make around here to go with all the seafood, appear silently at Jesse and José's elbows, as José continues to struggle with the problem of just how much guilt is owned to Naomi.

Jesse takes a small swallow of his, appreciating the cold clarity on his teeth, and realizes he's not far from being drunk himself.

José's focus gets suddenly sharper and clearer, and at last he speaks. "No."

"No?"

"No, *compadre*, no."

"You don't think there's anything wrong with just thinking of Naomi as a great body?"

"A great body?" Jose asks.

"You know. Big tits."

"Yes, she does."

Jesse begins to suspect something, and leans back to look at José more closely. It's late in the day, and this close to the equator it's dark by seven-thirty even in the summer, so all he's seeing are the highlights of José's face in the flaring yellow of the candle; his eyes are in deep pools of shadow and unreadable. At last, Jesse asks, "Do you remember what the original question was?"

"No. But the answer is still no, *compadre.*" José grins at him. "Because for one reason or another, *paco,* the only questions you ask are should you do more about Naomi, and the answer to that, always, is *no.*"

Jesse nods slowly, a time or two, and says, "You are right."

"I know I'm right."

"I have been spending too much time here getting drunk and thinking about her, haven't I?"

"Too much time thinking about her, anyway."

"Perhaps early dinner and bed are what I should do this evening, then," Jesse says.

"I will be sorry to lose the friend to drink with, but it's your health, Jesse." José's face is unexpectedly serious. "Friendship matters, but it matters that you look after yourself too. If you go have a few days without hangovers, and get your strength and health back, then perhaps you and I will catch the bus over to the coast, do some fishing in the morning, then spend the afternoon on the beach looking for bored *gringas* in their tiny little bathing suits; you can do the talking and I will attend to the physical side. But you get better first, you haven't been looking well."

Jesse stands up and drops a little too much cash on the table, so that he's covering his share and most of José's, and says "I think I have better friends down here than I had realized."

"We are better at friendship than you are, and we make better beer. On the other hand, you still have the best hamburgers and the best cop movies." José says that with such pompous solemnity that Jesse all but falls back into his chair laughing. As his laughter subsides, José stands, completes the pile of cash on the table, and says, "Let's walk together part of the way."

As they go up the brightly lighted *avenida,* north along the side of the Zócalo, Jesse begins, for the first time, to really look back at some of the women looking at him; that seems to create flurries of giggles and looking away. He suspects that if he smiled at one in particular, they'd all stop looking at him entirely.

José notices and touches his shoulder gently. "You see how much easier it is to recover when you do it like a Mexican."

They part company a block after leaving the Zócalo, and Jesse is pleasantly surprised to realize that he is not at all drunk and that he will probably get a lot of sleep tonight; it's just barely time for early *cena*, and he's not hungry, so he decides to go straight back to the little bungalow and get some sleep.

As he turns into one dim street, he sees that the woman coming his way has red hair. This is odd enough for him to turn and look at her in the light; thus he sees that she's wearing a very loose flannel shirt over a big, floppy denim skirt and a pair of sandals. She looks like she'd fit right in at one of the centers or schools in the area, but Jesse knows practically every *norteamericano* for fifty kilometers around—the different social services outfits throw everyone together frequently—and he doesn't recall seeing her.

Of course she just might be a tourist, but nobody wears the Left Uniform anymore unless they mean it, and nobody Left goes anywhere as a tourist—they always go somewhere to take a workshop or to work for some service. So chances are overwhelming she's new . . . and if Jesse is any judge, one reason for the floppy clothes is that she's built at least as well as Naomi. It's not so much that a plan forms in his brain as that he sees an opportunity and jumps at it before it has time to slip away. "Hey, you're not from around here," he says, in English, taking the main chance that she's from the States, Ontario, Pacificanada, or Alaska, rather than Québec.

"No shit," she says, but she smiles at him as she says it. There's something familiar about the smile, and he takes a step closer to see if maybe it's just someone he didn't recognize.

She takes a step back and for a moment he thinks he's frightened her—or then again maybe she doesn't want him to see her clearly, since she's just thrown a long shadow over her face. He can now see that her hair, backlit by the streetlight, is extremely red, one of those shades you get only by injection.

He doesn't come any closer, but he does say, "Are you with any of the organizations operating down here? Everybody parties together all the time, so I'd have thought I'd recognize you, unless you're new."

"Well, I'm not new down here—I've been here for quite a while on vacation," she says, "and the truth is that I'm wearing this outfit because it really hides my body, and I've got the kind that gets a lot of attention from the real *machos* around here, especially when you add in the hair and the pale skin. It's just that usually I can take a walk in the evening, if I stick to safe streets, without getting bothered."

"Oh—um, sorry," Jesse says, and turns to go.

"That's okay, I didn't mean you, particularly. But if by any chance my figure is what caught your eye, I should probably tell you I'm an old woman. Past thirty—not even close to what you're looking for." She steps forward now, and Jesse sees that even though she's obviously had them abraded regularly, there are little crow's feet around her eyes, and some lines around her mouth, and—well, more than that, there's something in her expression that just says she's lived a while and a few things have hit her pretty hard. He suddenly feels like he's three feet tall and wearing Dr. Denton's.

She's still great looking, though, and he finds himself blurting out, "Uh, I guess I'm too young if you say I am, but you are definitely *not* too old."

That one gets a grin from her, and it's so warm and friendly that he smiles back and relaxes. This little encounter might be kind of strange but it's fun in its way.

The redhaired woman takes another step closer, and she's flirting with him, but not in the way that he's used to from girls his own age, with all the come here–go away come here–go away. The smile is open and warm, and he has a strange feeling that she might be more interested than he is; and he's pretty interested.

"That's a really sweet thing to say," she says to him. "Can I ask—uh, this will sound arrogant and stupid—do you know who I am?"

"It doesn't sound arrogant or stupid," he says, taking another step. "You do look like someone I ought to know, maybe someone I knew a long time ago—"

"Did you ever experience the news via Rock or Quaz?"

His jaw drops; he's never had that particular sensation before, but he's lucky it's only his jaw muscles that go loose, because he also feels weak in the knees and he just might want to faint.

"You're Synthi Venture?" He can't believe he's asking her that, or that this is happening in a dusty little side street in Tapachula, of all places.

"At the moment I'm Mary Ann Waterhouse, and I'm on vacation. But yeah, that's what I do for a living. So have you ever . . . um . . ." She stands with her legs a little apart and puts her hands behind her back; it thrusts her huge breasts forward and sways her pelvis as if to move it against him.

He's glad it's dark, because though he never thought anyone could make him blush, his skin is burning hot right now; he feels like a little boy. His voice comes out as sort of a dry squeak—"You were my favorite in high school."

"And that was what, only three or four years ago?" she asks, a teasing smile opening up her face to him. "You know they do a light fuzzing on the images, don't you, so that I still look only about twenty in those things?"

"Uh, you still look . . . um, really good—"

"Compliments are always welcome, but not too many on the state of my preservation, please." Then, amazingly, she presses the shirt down on her stomach, so that he can see how huge, and how high, her breasts really are; she's kind of a freak, and he's not quite as turned on as he was a second before. "So are they any better in real life?"

"I—" He gulps. "I really . . ."

"Your line is 'I really like them.' Followed by a hint that you'd like to go somewhere alone with me." She winks at him and licks her lips; her hands brush her thighs, pulling the skirt inward, and Jesse feels completely like a kid. Now she steps closer to him and says, "You do like the way I look, don't you?"

He nods, confused and not sure at all what else he's feeling.

"Then why don't you come back to my place, so we can fuck?"

His first thought is that this is a prostitute who has had herself biomodi-fied into a copy of Synthi Venture, and his second thought is that if so, she's a good enough copy to be worth blowing a month's salary on. But a high-priced celeb-copy prostitute isn't likely to be in a backwater Mexican town and certainly wouldn't be coming on to him like a streetwalker—hell, she's cruder than the streetwalkers in front of his place.

But if it really is Synthi Venture—and the closer he stands to her, the surer he is—

She reaches up, takes his face in her hands, pulls his mouth down to hers, and kisses him, a big, wet, slobbery kiss with her lips completely open and slack and her tongue sliding deep into his mouth. He wasn't ready for it, and he's not sure he likes it, especially not when she begins to thrust against his leg, but at the same time he can feel an erection shoving against his jeans. He stops resisting and lets her do what she wants; her hand is inside his shirt, her fingers playing with his nipples, and then back outside, sliding over his belt, slim fingers tapping lightly on the thick denim, just enough so that he can feel her hand on his penis. He presses his crotch against her and she whispers, "Now, no talking. Back to my place. We're going to do everything you always wanted to do with me, and then we can talk. Or not. I don't really care if you don't want to do anything except the physical."

She takes his hand and he trails along like a zombie; it's as if somehow he had just walked right out of real reality and into XV without noticing. This is the kind of thing that happens to Rock, maybe, or happened to Rock when he was younger—in fact, it's almost exactly what happened to Rock in *Assignment in Singapore,* the long documentary in which Rock went undercover to investigate the trade in very-high-priced Caucasian prosti-tutes. But that was with Starla, the one whose career was cut short when she was murdered while plugged in, the "forbidden wedge" everyone claims to know someone who can get.

Distracted, trying to understand it all, he takes as much note as he can of the surroundings, as if one small unreal something, somewhere, might persuade him that he's just having a vivid dream. The street is soft with dust—it's been a day or two since it rained—and the air is warm, as evenings always are here. The houses stand back from the street and in this middle-class district of small, whitewashed houses behind white garden walls, they might as well be in Los Angeles—if LA were ever this quiet, or if you could ever see the stars between the lights there.

She guides his hand onto her shoulder, and this is almost like walking with Naomi or a dozen other girls—except that none of them took a hard, rude grip on one of his buttocks like that. He shies, but she slides farther under his arm, pulling his hand down onto the top of her breast.

He has a strange, strangled urge to laugh when he realizes that it is as big as her head. He just wishes that something so ridiculous weren't also so exciting. "Ever squeeze a celebrity tit?" she asks him.

"N—no. Why are we—"

"Shh. No why just yet. See those two men coming?"

"Yeah." They look like any two regular guys in this regular working town, he thinks to himself; probably they've just finished up work, gone home to play with the kids and talk to the wife a little, now they're out for a little light meal and some beer together—

He really hopes she won't involve them in this weirdness, whatever it is.

One voice in the back of his mind is pointing out that she doesn't have him at gunpoint or anything, he can just say, "Uh, Synthi, Miss Waterhouse, whatever you're calling yourself, this is just too weird and I'm going to walk away from it—"

And he knows he should, on another level. This kind of thing is okay in XV, but in the first place even though he has all his shots up to date, there are new kinds of AIDS and SPM and ARTS showing up every few months and he figures he's never met anyone so likely to introduce him to the latest variety, from the way she's acting. Shit, beside the risks, if she's doing this, she's at least half crazy, and god knows what she might do when they're alone—hurt him, or pull out a Self Defender, a razor, or anything. He wonders what would happen if they found a Leftie with a bullet hole in him, a big XV star with traces of his sperm in her, and she said she did it after he raped her. Do the cops here even pick up the radio burst from a Self Defender?

He shudders, slightly, and she uses the motion—suddenly his hand is down inside her shirt, under her bra. He has a startled moment of realizing that it doesn't feel soft and tender, like most big breasts, or even full and ripe the way Naomi's do—it feels like a slightly underinflated automobile tire. He can feel a ridge or two under the skin that must be the artificial ligaments they put in there to keep these things up.

She bumps up against him, and the two men notice the way she's moving and stare at them as she goes by. She's squirming around, and she whispers to Jesse, "Come on, reach *in.*" As if he's hypnotized, Jesse slides his hand forward, bringing that big mass of red hair close to his face—it smells funny and he realizes that she's perfumed it with something, and used too much—and finds he is clutching a nipple as big as a Ping-Pong ball.

She squeals, straightens up under his arm, moans and gasps. Her hand, outside her shirt, closes over his underneath, and she rubs up and down, panting and then groaning.

The two men stare at them. Jesse wants to look at the dirt at his feet, but if he does, his attention will concentrate on the moaning in his ear and the huge tough-surfaced breast under his hand. So he does look up, and he sees the carefully polished shoes, the tailored pants, the spotless ironed white shirts—and the fascinated stare. They aren't excited, particularly, or eager, or anything like that—what they are doing, he knows, is looking at another rude *gringo* couple that has no idea how to behave in public.

Synthi seems to be having a full-blown orgasm; they stare at her as if she were part of a sideshow, and one of them waves, almost shyly, at Jesse, as if in salute at his conquest. He wants to tell them this is not him, this is not what he's like or who he is—but they've turned and gone already.

She subsides and takes his hand in hers again, holding it over her shoulder. "God, it feels good to fake an orgasm and not have ten million people over my shoulder knowing it's fake. So how do you like the industrial knockers?"

"I, they're—"

"They don't feel much like real ones, do they? But wait till you see them slapping up and down while I ride you. Come on, the house I'm renting is right around the corner. Mind you, the servants are not going to approve— Mrs. Herrera is a dear, but really twentieth, and her husband Tomás is much more a gardener than a butler—no wink-and-nudge ability at all, if you know what I mean—"

He's pulled around the corner, still not sure what he feels about all of this. The feeling in his stomach is mostly butterflies, as if he were going to throw up, and his legs feel rubbery, but on the other hand he can't remember ever being this erect.

Abstractly, he thinks maybe it's just a matter of years and years of programming to want *this* instead of a woman, and that if he could just step back for a minute and think, he wouldn't be anywhere near *this*—

Another part of him is growling that this might be his only chance and he has to know what it's really like.

The "little house" she is renting might make an apartment building for four Tapachulan families in the better part of town; in fact, he's walked by here many times and if he'd thought about it that's what he'd have assumed it was. As they approach the door, it opens—apparently the small, muscular, beautifully dressed man who opens the door has nothing more pressing to do than watch the path.

Despite her warning, the servant appears neither surprised nor disapproving; he nods and says, "Miss Waterhouse. Will you be—"

"We're going directly to the master bedroom, Señor Herrera," she says, "and after that, perhaps the gentleman will be staying to a late dinner."

To Jesse it seems that they float up the long marble staircase, and into the big room that looks like nothing so much as an old movie set. There's a lot of red velvet around, and maybe that was sexy once but what it looks like to him is a restored movie theater, the kind they fix up in Oaxaca or San Cristóbal for the tourist trade. His head is spinning—maybe he had a little more beer than he thought he did, and they went up that staircase pretty fast.

One advantage Jesse found out about long ago with what Leftie girls wear—it comes off in a flash and there are a lot of ways to get a hand under it. In this case it seems to take Synthi Venture, if it's really her, only a breath to kick off the sandals, undo three or four buttons, and then whip off the shirt, unfasten the front catch on the bra, and yank down skirt and underwear together.

Jesse is stunned; the hair really is red, not the shade of normal human hair and not rough like most dye jobs make it, but natural, soft, wavy human hair the color that red hair is in an old comic book, and the little tuft of it that doesn't quite hide her labia is a shade brighter. She gives a loud giggle, and for the first time he realizes that she's really drunk, or high on god knows what (she can probably afford and get anything), or maybe she has just cranked up the happy center in her brain into the red zone, supposedly XV stars are wired to do that.

She does a little pirouette, and now he sees the thin white scars on her ass and her thighs where they sewed her into the "perfect" shape, and as she turns around he sees, ever so faintly, a kind of strange surface under the skin of her belly and knows that they put a sheath in there to hold her tighter than her own abdominal wall can.

And now that they are out in the open, the enormous, outsized breasts have visible scars too, places where they were reshaped and rebuilt. At fifty feet, or in dim light, or through the sort of vague gauze that is imposed by XV, she would look impossibly, magically perfect; but here, up close, in the plain light of the overdone bedroom, he can see how the trick is done, and once you've seen how it's done the magic is over.

He thinks for an instant that he will lose his erection, and then he looks into her eyes. They are pale blue, and under the abraded crow's feet, he sees a strange set to them, a kind of desperate look, and somehow or other the thought that forms in his mind is that—god knows why, but there it is—what she wants is him, that she's so hungry for him that she'll do anything, that if he turns and goes now she'll weep for hours, and that she will be grateful if he just uses her.

She is coming on like a cheap whore behind schedule, not because she's enjoying it but because she has to know whether he will reject her. All this comes to him in an instant, before he knows how he knows it.

He wants to think it's empathy, that he can relate to rejection fear because of Naomi, but that's not true at all. It's knowing how little Naomi would approve of this, that it would make her feel shoddy to know that this crude horny old bitch was going to give him at least as much pleasure as all her sensitive gentleness.

It's knowing that feeling of power, knowing that if he wanted to he could call Synthi a horny old bitch and she'd still do whatever he wanted just so he would take her in any way at all. And a part of him that he'd never thought about, too, is that he knows that in a month this woman can have more of everything than he can ever have in his life, that things he would have to plan and work for years to do, she can do on a whim—just plain sheer envy that she can get all that, and get it mostly from people like him, entirely with her cartoon body and crude acting. There's the thought of at least making her pay for it by, just once, *really* giving him what he's dreamed about through Rock and Quaz and all the others for so much of the last ten years.

It doesn't come to him in words at all, but the feeling is deep and cold and lusts to hurt. He likes it. He grabs her hair close to her neck and mashes her mouth with a hard, chewing kiss, and she doesn't even wince; she just pulls his other hand to her crotch, and he jabs his thumb into her vagina, hard, suddenly, wanting her to be dry so that she'll scream—

Instead, she is wet and already open, and she flows around him and moans with pleasure. Her hands are on his belt, undoing his jeans, pulling his penis out, and she's much too rough, hurting him, but he's too excited to care. She stands up on her toes and slides down over it, so that the first time takes about one minute, and he doesn't even get time to get his pants below his knees.

She doesn't let him rest, or even look down to see if he's scratched and bruised; she has him in her mouth at once, and yanks his jeans and underwear down to his ankles so fast and hard that he almost falls over.

The next half hour or so is a blur; she's rough with him and crude, and he never seems to get a moment to breathe. His penis is so sore that he's practically in tears, and there's an empty ache in his scrotum from being drained repeatedly; he avenges himself by slapping those grotesque breasts, by choking her with deep thrusts of his penis, and toward the end of it all he gives her a sudden, hard fist up the anus just to see if there's anything she will say no to.

Finally he is limp, sore, hurting, and her rough hand trying to bring him up again is unbearable. His head and stomach ache, and he has a vague feeling that if this goes on much longer he might throw up. As he looks at her now, with all desire pulled out of it—and with the red rage dying out of him as well—he sees nothing but desperation and hunger, and abruptly pushes her hands away and backs off.

She stands there panting, frantic, and finally says, "Shit, are you okay?"

This is not exactly what he's been expecting. He looks down to see that his penis is bruised and scraped, with a little bit of blood welling to the surface in a couple of places. All at once he can really feel it, and he leans forward, holding it. "Oh, god, owww."

"I'm sorry," she says.

"Did anyone ever tell you you're really fucked up, lady?" He's had blood contact, so if she's got anything he's not vaccinated for then his chances of having it are really good, his dick feels like he's had it in the blender, and he can't believe what he's just let himself get into. He needs out of here, and a doctor.

And to piss. They say you can piss stuff off your mucus membranes if you do it right away. He looks frantically, sees the private bath, rushes in and pisses like a horse, a big stream of it—beer and fear combined—and it burns like acid. "Shit, how many guys have you done this with? What the fuck is the matter with you?"

She's starting to sob. "Just you. I mean really just you."

"You expect me to believe that?" He's yanking on his shirt and buttoning it frantically. "God, I can't believe I did this, I can't believe I let myself come here—"

Now she's crying outright. "I don't have anything, really, really, I don't, you're the first since I started this vacation and the net gives us a full set of prompt tests every three days. I'm sorry I hurt you but I haven't killed you, I haven't, uh—" She stares at him blankly.

His pants are in hand and he's fishing his underwear out, but he hesitates a moment; at least she sounds like she means it.

"God, what the hell am I? I didn't even ask you your name."

"Jesse Callare." He pulls the underwear out more slowly and asks, "Do you have any kind of ointment or something? I'm hurt."

"Oh, shit, Jesse, I'm really sorry." She dashes into the bathroom and brings out a tube of hemorrhoid painkiller, a spray antibiotic, and a disposable antiseptic wipe. "At least let me clean you up and put this on it. I'll be gentle, I promise, I didn't want to do that to you."

She kneels in front of him, and before he can flinch away she has the wipe around it. It stings and he gasps, but she really is gentle and careful, cleaning him off quickly and neatly, then spraying on the antibiotic. "God, I hope all this happened to you after you were in my ass, there's all kinds of things up there that can infect a cut or a scrape—do you have a doctor you can go to? You can use mine and I'll pay—"

"You seem awfully concerned, considering," Jesse says. What she's doing, after the initial stinging, really is making it feel better, and there's something comforting about her concern.

She puts on the cream, and it's amazing how soothing it is; he almost relaxes. "Jesse, Jesse, I can't believe I did any of that, are you okay?"

"I've been better," he says, gently disentangling himself and continuing to dress. The pain is gone and he's not nearly so scared.

"I suppose it sounds stupid but I wish you'd stay to dinner. I can try to explain all this and I'd really like to make it up to you."

It's a different kind of feeling from what he felt before, but there's a certain similarity—he couldn't leave now if his life depended on it, because he's dying of curiosity. "Sure, I'll stay. Nobody's gonna believe what happened to me anyway, might as well have a completely wild story."

"Just a moment while I slip into something more like me. Hope you don't mind a baggy sweater and a baggy pair of pants, because that's what's comfortable, and I left all the gold lamé back in Alaska."

She's pulling the stuff on as she says it. Now that they are clothed and know each other's names, and Jesse is not in pain anymore, they don't seem to have much to say.

There's a long awkward silence, and then she says, "Lamb *tacos oaxaqueños*, is that okay?"

"Uh, what?"

"For *cena*. Señora Herrera is from Oaxaca province, somewhere up in the hills, so she tends to make those kinds of dishes. I ordered lamb *tacos oaxaqueños* before I went out and I told her husband, Tomás, that you might be staying to dinner as we came in—remember?"

He grins. "I remember. Yeah, it sounds wonderful. Uh—can I ask—"

"Anything at all, after dinner—but let's go down and eat together just as if we didn't know each other and we were only just getting acquainted."

"Flat with me," he says, and she reaches out and takes his hand. More than anything else what surprises him is how shy she is about doing that.

President Hardshaw was up most of the night, and when she then comes in early, Harris Diem knows something is up. He keeps right on working at his desk. The buzz in the back of his head is louder than ever, but last night he managed to resist going down to the basement. He derives no pleasure from his resistance.

She has been in the New Oval Office twenty minutes, with no communication with anyone else, when there's a faint ring. He takes the phone from his belt and plugs it into his screen as he notes the call is coming from Hardshaw.

"Yeah, boss?"

She looks a bit disheveled; what the hell could the President be keeping from him?

"Drop by the office shortly, Harris, we've got some big work to do."

"I'll bring coffee," he says, and cues his staff to have the usual pot with two cups waiting for him. He's not sure why he and the President have kept this ritual all these years, of him bringing the coffee or the food, but he takes a strange comfort in it.

The comfort vanishes utterly when Hardshaw accepts the cup, motions him into a chair, and says, "I did it this morning, Harris, so there's now no point in arguing. I thought about hundreds of millions dead, I thought about the whole species—and I thought about the fact that America has to live in the world."

He feels a chill in his stomach. He takes a long sip of the coffee. "Then you spilled the beans to Rivera and the UN? They know the real numbers?"

"And they know that we could have sat on them, and they know that the original NOAA report was intended as a fake. They know it all."

The buzz in his skull is so loud it feels strange that other people can't hear it. He thinks for one instant of going down to his basement, selecting one of those wedges . . . but he fights the thought down. "Then, er—if you've already done it, why did you call me here? You must have known I would be opposed to it."

"Because I need you here, and therefore the country needs you here, when Rivera calls. Which he should be doing any time now."

As if to agree with her, the phone rings; when Hardshaw answers, the secretary announces, "Secretary-General Rivera, Ms. President."

"Put him through."

Rivera's image pops up on the screen, and he says, "Ms. President, I must first congratulate you on a game well played, and thank you for deciding not to play it against us, for you surely would have succeeded."

Exactly the thought that's bothering me, Diem thinks.

Hardshaw nods. "Then you understand all the implications."

"I do indeed. And I think we have been very fortunate. Not just the UN, but all of us. You have created an important opportunity."

Hardshaw raises an eyebrow. "I don't quite see how."

"The opportunity to prevent Global Riot Two. And then, when the truth is revealed—as it will surely be, for your operation is bound to leak at some point—well, what is more credible than a leak, eh? Far more trustworthy than what any government says." The Secretary-General is handsome and dapper even at this hour; what Diem had never noticed before was the strange gleam of humor. "You see, when my experts plugged this into *our* world model, we came up with a chance of around ten percent that there will be no sovereignty at all in the Northern Hemisphere by next year. If so, we want people to have fled the coasts and taken care of themselves. And to have the news believed—that is going to be a very difficult part. People will believe all sorts of absurdities, but not necessarily even the most rational truth if it demands they abandon their homes."

Diem thinks for a moment, and sees the Sec-Gen's point. "You believe, then, we should make this a semi-gray operation—try to keep it secret but let it slip out?"

"Exactly."

Diem glances sideways at the President; she is nodding.

"Well, then," he says, "perhaps I should just go and get started."

Eight minutes later, back at his desk, he reflects that she's done it again, and that his memoirs are getting harder to believe. Someone has to chronicle all this, but he's not sure it will ever be him.

And the buzz in the back of his head is louder than ever.

The funny thing is, the Austin records are exactly what Randy needed, but they are not doing him any good at all. He's found five men whose names he didn't know before, all arrests who were clearly parts of the network that distributed the XV of Kimbie Dee's murder, all high-level people not more than one or two people from the one he is after. The reason he had not linked them in before was that they didn't happen to have the wedge of Kimbie Dee in possession at the time of arrest.

But now that he knows and has back-checked, it's plain as day. They were all connected with at least seven or eight known distributors; they were the ones who sold the copies in bulk. Every one of them helped to finance the people who sent that deformed maniac, dying of cancer, to violate Randy's little girl, alone in the locker room because she was too shy to shower with the others, and then to hang her from the shower head.

And the only little catch is, they're all dead. All of them were executed for violations of the Diem Act.

He draws grim satisfaction from it, but for the first time he sees an argument against the death penalty—he's so close, but he needs one associate of those men who can still talk.

It takes him days to finally come up with a name: Jerren Anders.

Currently reprieved from execution, in a hospital for the criminally insane—will you look at this? Back in Boise. Back where it all started. Not ten miles from where Randy's mobile home used to be.

The old car turns onto the interstate, and Randy is surprised and touched to find he has many more messages than usual—not information, but congratulations. The only ones he answers, just now, are the ones from other parents, brothers, sisters, husbands, boyfriends, wondering about the Austin connection; he sends those everything he has.

During the long night, as the car climbs up out of Colorado and into Wyoming to join I-80, he dreams of Kimbie Dee. She looks like she did in the morgue, but she sits next to him and tosses her blonde ponytail the way she did when she was alive, and says, "Daddy, Daddy, you be careful. You be careful. It might be worse than you think."

"I'm going to find him," he tells her.

"It might be worse than you think." She gives him a little warm peck on the cheek, like she did every morning on her way out the door to school, but he feels that her lips are cold as the morgue's cooler.

He wakes up shuddering, fixes coffee, sits in the backseat drinking it till the sun comes up as the car pulls into Salt Lake City. He decides to get breakfast and a shower, and have the car freshened, at the next available stop for it. The smell that builds up in these things can get unbelievable.

Later that day he heads up I-15. It's been a couple of years since he's been this way. He's surprised how glad he is to see Idaho again.

Kingman Reef is almost an island; at low tide there's land, at high tide, shallow water and a few patches of exposed rock; at very high tides, nothing. The steel and concrete towers that rise there now, the North American Orbital Services space-launch facility, have made the place an island indeed, and the population these days is clear up to a thousand people, including about a dozen children.

On Friday, June 16, about six P.M. local time, no one stirs outside the station. The sky is a frightening shade of gray-green, the sea a dirty black with whitish scum, churned into a frenzy. Beside the most distant tower, far out off the reef proper, the Monster sits half-fueled, only its uppermost quarter showing above the water. If it were fully fueled, it would be completely invisible—at launch, the great rockets take off from thirty meters under the sea surface.

In fact, with Hurricane Clem running in at them and the sun close to the horizon already, this close to the equator, Gunnar Redalsen, the Chief of Launch Operations, could not see the Monster, and isn't looking out the window anyway, but it is there in his mind's eye. At the moment he is talking to the four people he finds it most unpleasant to talk to on Earth, as a general rule, one of them sitting beside him and three via a communication link.

At his left is Akiri Crandall, who is almost an all-right guy, in Redalsen's opinion. Crandall likes to be addressed as "Captain Crandall," just as if this place were not tied down by long columns of reinforced concrete sunk into the reef below, but that pompous insistence on his own dignity is really the worst of it; Redalsen can understand that Crandall, coming up from the ghetto and then rising from enlisted ranks in the Navy, has a big chip on his shoulder and wants it acknowledged. What annoys him more than anything is that Crandall constantly forgets that this place exists to send up big rockets; Crandall wants every person-hour thrown into base construction and base ops, and if it were up to him there'd never be a launch. Every so often Redalsen wonders if Crandall doesn't perhaps see him as the missile officer on this inexplicably slow-moving vessel.

Just at the moment, however, Crandall is the other voice of common sense, besides himself, that Redalsen can count on, and he's feeling a bit fond of the pompous petty Napoleon, next to whom Redalsen himself sounds so reasonable.

"The base will live through it for sure if it is not blown up," Crandall is saying, firmly. "And if we cast off the Monster now, or even launch it on a disposal trajectory as Mr. Redalsen suggests, then the Monster cannot blow us up. But if we leave it sitting less than three kilometers from Main Base, we have no guarantee it will not find its way here."

The woman who sits listening intently to them, her face carefully composed for the phone screen, is Edna Wheatstone, who is mainly noted for being the only candidate for CEO that none of the board actively opposed. As Crandall is finishing and Redalsen is nodding vigorously, she speaks very carefully, as if she had something in her mouth she didn't want them to catch a glimpse of. "But I thought that the launch tower was built to the southwest of the station so that if a rocket broke loose, the hurricane would carry it away from the station."

Now, the fact is that she damned well knows the answer to that, and this is wasting time, but this way she can replay the tape of the conversation for the board.

"I have been through two hurricanes at sea," Crandall says, "and I am about to be through another one, and in fact I helped write the chapter on all this for the Academy, and the first sentence in that chapter is 'Hurricanes have regularities when considered as a population, but no predictability at all individually.' This particular hurricane is veering all over the radar screen like a cat with its tail on fire, and it may strike us from any quadrant at its nearest approach, or even loop around and hit us twice. It is perhaps slightly more likely that the half-fueled Monster will float away from us than toward us . . . but only slightly. Not what I would want to bet a thousand lives on, Ms. Wheatstone."

She sits tapping the arm of her chair and trying to look simultaneously concerned and as if she has gotten very close to the people responsible for the problem. Redalsen realizes that she is in this conversation entirely to make sure that whatever is done, it will not harm her career, and while he can understand and appreciate that, he also wants very much to get on with the real business of the meeting.

The government man has one of those names like Collins or Smith that you forget all the time, and all he wants to say is that the government will understand a launch delay, despite the problems that it might bring with fulfilling President Hardshaw's commitments, but of course if there is to be a launch delay the government will expect to be compensated for the trouble, and that certainly the government is not going to buy two rockets to put up one satellite with the taxpayers' money, so if this rocket is to be destroyed and another put in its place, then there is going to be compensation from somewhere, and in any case there is not going to be further money from the government until their satellite goes up.

And now the only important person is sitting there, thinking hard, looking down at the table as he tends to do. Redalsen knows that this guy has been with the insurance company now for more than sixty years, and was turning down retirement before some of the current crop of retirees joined the company. Like most people with his job, he is widely believed to be too mean to die. Redalsen has had a beer or two with him, and gradually came to realize that here was a man who had spent most of an ordinary lifetime thinking about ways things could go dreadfully wrong, and trying to figure out how to make them go only a little less wrong.

"Are there any qualified probabilities?" the insurance man asks, chewing on his lip and tugging on one mangled-looking ear.

"Nothing you can measure," Redalsen says. "I know enough about the rocket to say that, if it is adrift in high seas and runs into anything, it is very likely to detonate, and we cannot safely de-fuel it in the time we have remaining."

Crandall nods. "I think we may safely figure that for the next two hours it will drift away from us. We can put a transponder and a scuttling charge on it and blow it as soon as it is a safe distance from the launch tower and other facilities. Or, as Mr. Redalsen has suggested, if you wish to test the launch facility itself, apparently it is possible to send it up suborbitally and bring it down somewhere harmless, perhaps a few hundred kilometers to the north. Either will work splendidly—as long as that giant bomb gets away from my facility."

"And you concur in this judgment, Mr. Redalsen?"

"Yes. Let me add, though, that our risk in future launches may go down if we can see how this one goes."

"Understood." The old man tugs at his ear, looks sideways, scratches his head; Redalsen has had dealings with him, one way and another, for twenty years, and during that whole time has never failed to wonder at how ape-like a human being can be. "You do all understand that even though Industrial Facilities Mutual usually takes my word for it, they might very well reverse me on something this big?"

"When was the last time you were reversed?" Redalsen asks.

"Nineteen ninety-eight, on an old Soviet nuclear reactor that they wanted to insure despite the risks. It never went up, so I guess they won the argument."

"Do you think they will reverse you?" the government man asks. "It is essential from our standpoint that one way or another—"

"Somebody else pays for it," the insurance man finishes for him. "I can't promise you that the government won't get stuck with the bill, all I can do is recommend that NAOS takes action to minimize risk to the property, and recommend that we then pay for whatever damages happen. What we do is assurance, buddy, not reassurance."

The government man and Wheatstone are plainly unhappy, but Redalsen has added the insurance man to his list of reasonable people. It's a pity this isn't a straight majority vote.

At last Wheatstone breaks the draw. "It sounds like my technical personnel and my external insurance advice are in favor of jettisoning the rocket. And we are at least not being warned that the insurance company *won't* pay. Are there significant advantages to the jettison launch?"

"Only a chance to get some data we couldn't otherwise get," Redalsen says. "In theory, it duplicates what we get from computer simulations, but I've been at this business much too long to trust the computer simulations completely." He knows this is bad politics—officially NAOS had wanted to man-rate the Monster without ever having fired one. But he also wants it someplace on the record, as long as everyone is so concerned about that, that they at least had the chance for a test launch.

"How long before you can jettison launch?"

"Fifteen minutes from your go."

Her jaw sets and her head moves slightly to the left. "Then go."

She looked very decisive doing that, Redalsen realizes. When the board sees it, they'll approve the whole thing, probably.

They have to delay another two minutes so that the government man can stress, once again, that either NAOS or IFM is going to pay for this, because the government isn't. But the deal is done, and that at least is a relief.

As they leave the room, Crandall asks, "Is it really going to be fifteen minutes?"

"Ten if I can manage it. Everything is modular and it's just a matter of bringing things online—they should all be hooked up at the launch tower. If they're not, then I guess we'll have to get over there in the sub."

Crandall nods. "Carry on."

Redalsen doesn't even feel like pointing out that he is not under Crandall's command; it's just such a relief to be able to act. A short elevator ride takes him to the control room; telemetry is still showing everything more or less normal, though the Monster is now jigging up and down more than a full meter with each wave.

"Well, then," he says to the crew—it is now eight minutes since they began checkout—"do we have the abort trajectory?"

They do, just as he has asked them to. "All right then, if we're not going to hit anything, start the short countdown and let's get this bird gone."

Two more minutes until they say "zero" and dozens more green indicators appear on the screens. There's a rough moment as it pulls out of the water and a wave and wind shear torque it, but the Monster makes its way upward in the face of that, its guidance systems fighting madly, attitude jets firing flat-out bursts in all directions, and in a matter of minutes it's on its way to an empty stretch of ocean south of Hawaii.

They watch it depart on radar. "I've been through more than a hundred launchings," the technician at Redalsen's left comments, "and this is the first time I haven't heard one go."

"Even if we could open the ports in this storm, the storm itself would hide the noise," Redalsen comments. "It might as well be invisible on radar, anyway. We're barely getting image off it, and it's less than forty clicks downrange."

"The clouds on radar are forming a weird pattern," someone says— "look at that black spot right there—"

"It's called the eye," Crandall says, coming in. "Did you get anything for it, Mr. Redalsen, other than getting your giant bomb away from us?"

"Not one thing was different from the computer simulation," he says, grinning, "but we did prove we can launch in seas a lot heavier than the Feds will let us."

Crandall seems to permit himself a smile. "I don't suppose that you were indulging any emotional feelings that a fueled rocket ought to be flown rather than sunk?"

"Oh, we sank it, Skipper. We just sank it farther away."

The smile is almost human. "An excellent point. I came down to let you know what your radar is showing you—that thing is only going to dust us and it's still going to be the worst storm we've ever seen. That eye is about eighty clicks across and the official estimate on the wind velocity at the eye wall is close to two hundred and twenty knots. Fortunately it's missing us by quite a bit—so all we're going to get is a Beaufort of about nineteen or twenty."

The Beaufort scale is a scale of damage and physical effects; it was devised in part because people caught in severe storms don't usually have time to read instruments. Officially Beaufort 12 is a hurricane; it's about Beaufort 8 outside right now, and normally Redalsen wouldn't have launched in a Beaufort 6. Redalsen gives a low whistle. "I bet you'd like us to stay powered up and record data for NOAA?"

"Actually I don't care, but NOAA wants it and they're prepared to pay NAOS for it. And at least that way you people won't take up valuable room in the shelter down in the reef. But I should warn you, this place doesn't normally get major hurricanes, so it was only built to take a Beaufort twenty-two—which is uncomfortably close, especially since that forecast of Beaufort twenty is plus or minus five. So if you're willing to stay and keep the monitors up, NOAA and the company will appreciate it—but it's at risk. Hazardous-duty pay for it, of course, if it makes a difference."

Redalsen nods. "I'll stick, and anyone else who wants to is welcome to. The rest of you head down to the shelter. Will people be reasonably safe there?"

"Should be—it's embedded a hundred twenty meters below the reef itself. People inside there will probably not have the slightest idea what's happening at the surface. I've already got the kids and everyone without a duty down there. I'll expect your reports, then, from the bridge."

"You'll ride out the storm up there?" Redalsen asks. It's a good forty meters higher up and thus that much more at risk.

"Have to. I wasn't kidding about having written the book for Annapolis. And that was based on one experience with a Beaufort thirteen, and one with a Beaufort fifteen, which is pretty impressive—but I can't pass up the chance to see this one. Might have to add a couple additional paragraphs."

Redalsen can't resist sticking in the needle. "Just remember to tell the cadets about the importance of having your ship stuck to the bottom with concrete pillars."

"If we stay that way," Crandall says, grinning back. "One way or another, the worst should have blown past by dawn—the damned thing is coming toward us faster than any storm, big or small, has a right to. Assuming the launch room, bridge, galley, and mess are still here, I'll expect you at breakfast."

He turns and goes, and Redalsen swallows the urge to salute. Most of the older techs, who have family here, elect to go below, but he's got several young engineers who probably signed on for the extra pay with no place to spend it, so there's not much trouble staffing up.

"Okay, major thing to do is make sure everything is recording, and watch your instruments for anything unusual."

"Mr. Redalsen, sir?" Gladys Hmau has that slight look of mischief that always makes him a little nervous.

"Yes, Ms. Hmau?"

"What exactly is unusual in the middle of a huge hurricane?"

He laughs. "Oh, loss of sense of humor. Just everybody hang tight and watch for what you can find—radar doing funny things, wind shears on the tower, anything that looks like more than just a big storm."

The hours take a long time to go by. At about eight P.M., a cook's mate comes in with grilled cheese sandwiches and coffee on a cart, "compliments of the captain." They all take a break of sorts, sitting back from their screens and ceasing, for fifteen minutes, the endless, redundant narration of reading the screen into the radio, in case for some reason (some reason best not thought about) the recorders on board are never read back, and because a trained eye may notice a digital readout bar jumping when a reviewer, months later, would let it go by.

Redalsen puts up the view from the cameras on the overhead screens. He turns the launch tower lights on, but what comes back is an all but solid white screen, only patches of dark green between the foam in the lower part telling them that the screen is anything other than white noise.

In another hour they begin to hear the storm through the walls. Officially the barometric pressure is now down close to eight hundred millibars. Seas are rising and the strain gauges on the launch tower show bars leaping up and down on their screens here, occasionally flickering red at their tips as wave shear tries to twist the launch tower from its steel moorings in the rock far below the churning sea.

Just past ten P.M., standing waves are forming in the cups of coffee that sit neglected by the engineers. Gladys Hmau looks sort of pale, and Redalsen touches her shoulder lightly as he looks over into the radar view. "The eye is still going to miss us by a wide margin," he says.

"Yeah, but if this sucker goes over we're just as dead," she mutters. "Feel that under your feet?"

He stands quietly for a moment, and sure enough there is a noticeable swell running through the floor. "Impressive."

"Not as impressive as what's happening at the launch tower," Silverstein says, from the other side. "We're at solid reds now on shearing, boss; I think we're going to lose her."

"I wouldn't like to, but better an empty tower than us. Got an idea of the break point?"

"Shear is maxed at about sixty meters below sea level. Not that sea level means much in the circumstances—"

There is a hard blow through the floor, and Redalsen falls to his knees. There are half a dozen small screams. As he pulls himself back to his feet, another one hits, just as hard, and there's a brief flicker in the lights and on the screens. "Better get me the bridge. And cue up whatever's left of the outside cameras on the launch tower."

"Uh, about the launch tower—"

"Where'd it break?" Redalsen asks.

"Just above surface. They never go at the max strain point, do they?"

"I wouldn't know, it's the only launch tower I ever lost. And rockets go everywhere when they go. Can you get the bridge?"

"That line's dead."

"Great. Stay put, everyone else, I'm going up to see if we can get another com link in." He's out the door in a flash; he hopes what he said will keep them from thinking of the truth—that he is going up to see if there's still a bridge.

As he starts up the stairs, he notes that at least they are still under regular lights. The stairs surge under his feet, once, and then again, but now that he's used to it and nothing seems to be coming apart right away, it's not as frightening as it was—at least not till he's almost to the bridge, and hears the scream of wind somewhere inside the station. The spiral stairs in the great concrete tube lurch hard under his feet twice, and the lights go out; blue emergency lights spring to life in the tube, and what had been a high, thin scream is now a deep bass moan.

He pushes the door open to the corridor that leads to the bridge, and he can feel moving air as he makes his way through to the bridge door. He braces himself and yanks on the door; it flies open, all but knocking him backward.

He lunges in and, heaving with all his force, gets the door closed; immediately the fierce wind stops blowing, and he looks around to see Crandall and the bridge crew crouched behind consoles. In front of them, one of the great windows that look out to the east has cracked, the plastic-glass compound shearing in broken layers like a strain break in plywood, and there's a hole about as big as a human arm, slowly widening.

"You're just in time, Mr. Redalsen—we're going to try to weld her, and we need one more hand pushing things into place." Crandall's shout is about as level as can be managed when yelling at the top of the lungs. "If you can rush forward with us and just put your hands where they'll do the most good?"

Redalsen joins them, sees that what they have is a self-heating patch—which ought to fix it, but the patch will need to be held in place for about a minute to adhere. He nods, and they rush forward, keeping the big patch down low to the floor where the wind won't make it so difficult to deal with, then swinging it up from the bottom, some of them pushing to keep it flush against the window and others pushing from down below until it's entirely covering the hole. Crandall pushes the trigger, and the edges glow dull red as it melts its way onto the window. They all stay braced, pushing hard, but now there's no wind, and though it's just as hard physically, the absence of the cold, wet shrieking terror of the wind and spray that had been coming through the crack seems to give everyone strength.

The edges cease to glow red, and then become clear; the welding-cure process is endothermic, and soaks up most of the heat. After a minute Crandall presses a knuckle to the edges and says, "Cool all around. All right, let go on three, but stay out of the way because if it flies it will take down anyone in its way. One, two, three."

Their hands leave it all at once, and then they all let a breath out as it holds.

"I presume you came up to let me know you'd lost the communication link to the bridge?" Crandall says, as he returns to his chair.

"Mainly that and to see what else was going on."

"We've had a couple of freak storm surges. One of them came up as high as the third east gallery, and that's eighty meters above normal high tide. But we're taking them. I'd feel better if this giant bastard child of a drilling rig had a bow I could point into the sea, but we're holding anyway, thus far, even though the big hydraulics in the legs are bottoming on every wave." The screen in front of them clears and then pops up a list of damage-control reports. "What we have are broken windows—which do have to get fixed, they increase the drag and give the wind a place to tear at us—and a lot of severed conduits because the damned idiot architects had a lot of them running on outside surfaces, and they're breaking wherever they were bridging a gap or running too close to a pinch point. How are things in launch control?"

"Well, there's nothing to control anymore—the tower came down with the first big wave. Thank god we got rid of the Monster when we did. But things look all right down there. If you want I'll get you some volunteers to help the damage-control crews—"

"Deeply appreciate it. We should be taking the peak right about now, but it will take hours to get things repaired, and if we don't—"

The windows burst in, and Redalsen has one bare instant to realize that what is coming through them is not wind and spray, but solid water, before he is thrown to the wall and knocked unconscious; he does not even have time to notice the motion of the walls, and in this he is fortunate, for at least half the station crew are conscious as the next huge wave strikes, the reinforced concrete pilings shatter, and the whole station tips over into the ocean, bouncing and grinding its way down to the ocean floor; the least fortunate, perhaps, are those who find themselves in the slowly shrinking air pockets. When dawn breaks, late and dim, over the empty sea, there are still a few people alive in the wreckage far below it, as well as all those in the shelter; when a Navy submarine arrives to evacuate the shelter, two days later, they find the people in the shelter terrified but physically unhurt. They find no one alive in the shattered wreckage of the station itself. The divers refuse to talk about what they find, and the video they shoot is classified immediately.

The submarine is barely on its way out of Pearl Harbor when Di Callare and his team are meeting with Harris Diem to answer the critical question: What happened at Kingman Reef? It's still early in the morning—Di had to get on the zipline at five A.M. to make it to Washington from North Carolina and allow himself an hour to look at the data, which are not the most informative they've ever seen.

"You want a hypothesis," he's saying now, "speculation for the press and all that? Okay, I think what got them was storm surge. They were built for a Beaufort twenty-two or so hurricane, and conditions outside when they went over were only about nineteen or twenty. That's a wobbly number, and maybe local conditions just swung up to much worse, or maybe there was an 'oopsie' in the engineering somewhere, but say it was really a sound structure and conditions really weren't worse than that. The assumption is that with a Beaufort twenty-plus hurricane, you've got to have the eye passing right over you to experience the full effect, and right in the eye the waves will be about thirty meters, max.

"But they were nowhere near the eye—that's plain both from their own reports and from the satellites. And that eye is huge, about as big as any on record. Suppose it isn't a freak eye, as we thought, but a freak storm—"

The little man at Diem's side, who was introduced only as "my assistant" and who has been watching intently, gives off a little half-cough, and Di can feel everyone else pulling back. Well, the hell with it; he's going to give them his best guess anyway, and they can fix it up later.

"Suppose it's a storm with a Beaufort of, oh, say, thirty-five at the eye. Yeah, I know that's close to tornado wind velocities, and we're talking about something that's more than fifty kilometers across, not the less than one kilometer that a tornado averages. Then the waves coming out of the eye—which would be running out away from it, but still close to the storm—might easily be a hundred forty meters, especially given that you have unlimited fetch for every practical purpose—"

The little man turns toward Diem and says, "Fetch?"

"Distance wind blows across water," Diem says. "Hundred-forty-meter waves, Dr. Callare? You realize you're telling me that this thing is practically throwing off tsunami?"

"Yep."

"And does your staff concur?" the little guy says, looking around with a calculated stare.

Di Callare has never been so proud or grateful; they all are nodding. "If you look at the current temperatures in the North Pacific," Gretch says, "there's plenty of potential for a storm that big." And then she says the most daring thing that any of them could have: "If you want an honest opinion, and not the one you want us to have, this is it. This is the big storm we were talking about weeks ago. And it's going to keep growing all the way to Asia." She brushes her hair back from her face and sits tall, staring back at the little man.

The little man ignores this, as he does everyone else. With the dam broken, Peter, Talley, Mohammed, and Wo Ping all point to the various bits of evidence. Harris Diem is unreadable—which probably explains how he keeps his job—but it's clear that the little guy isn't listening anymore, not to what the evidence is (and he probably wouldn't understand it without a lot of explanation anyway). All he's doing is noting that people are disobeying.

The meeting breaks up with very little further word from the politicals; since his staff has backed him so thoroughly, Di returns the favor by saying in front of Diem and his shadow that they are going to pursue the investigation on the assumption that it was a storm surge and that this is not merely an unusually wide hurricane, but the biggest one on record. That seems to drive off Diem, the little man, and their secretary, as if they are afraid what more they might hear.

It's still only eight-thirty in the morning, a bit before anyone would normally be in, and now that Diem and company are gone, the adrenaline rush has gone with them and everyone seems to sag. It's going to be a long day.

"Let's all go up the street for breakfast," Di suggests. "I don't know about the rest of you, but all I've had this morning has been this lousy coffee. And maybe we can brainstorm a little on what's going to happen next with this thing."

It's a three-block walk, and not a very interesting one; Di notices that in a way what they really look like is an overage neighborhood basketball team, the kind you were on when you were ten, with everyone dressed like a mess and everyone glad to be with each other. He wonders for a moment if it isn't just his own longing for support that makes him see it that way, but no—Talley is striding along, head up and confident, arguing fiercely with Pete beside her, and Wo Ping and Mohammed are both keeping up with it, and all of them seem to be daring anyone in the passing traffic to argue with them.

"The team's gotten really tight, Dr. Callare," Gretch comments.

"We'll need to be," Di says, not wanting to sound gloomy but not feeling like lying about it. "I'm sure Diem understood us and will make our case, but I have no idea how much weight he actually swings—he's supposed to be buddies with Hardshaw from way back, they call him the President's Shadow, but for all we know, it's Hardshaw that wants us to shut up."

"What's going to happen if we don't shut up?"

"I think we'll probably find out soon. This is quite a summer internship for you, isn't it?"

She snorts in agreement. "At least it's a real look at what the job involves. I'm, er, thinking of applying to have the internship extended, if—"

"Naturally I'll write you a recommendation."

They come to a traffic light, and Di takes a moment to listen to the rest of the team. Talley is taking the conservative position and Pete the radical; she says that it's a bigger storm than there's ever been before, but that's all, and he's arguing that there's at least twenty never-before-seen things it might be able to do besides. Good—put them together on a team and have them hammer out the short list of things to worry about.

Wo Ping is arguing a computational point with Mohammed; the fundamental question is at what level chaos gets into things and therefore which steps of the model have to be explored by Monte Carlo methods. That sounds like a question one of them could resolve—and then Di realizes that what it amounts to is Talley and Pete's argument, but phrased in mathematics. Either way the question is, do we just scale up the numbers, or do we look for entirely new things that can happen?

They haven't been to breakfast en masse at this little diner since budget week, but the waitress seems to recognize them and steers them to a table in the back room. Until the food gets there, they talk about family and sports and all the usual ritual; everyone asks how Lori's book is going, even though only Mohammed reads mysteries, and everyone admires the latest batch of photos of Wo Ping's kid.

Breakfast is good, and Di realizes a big part of it is that he knows there's an uproar coming, that there is bound to be fallout from the defiance of this morning, and so maybe this is the last time the team will be together outside of work—and he's been very happy with them. These are people he'd tackle any job with, and corny and sentimental though that seems, he wishes he had a good way to tell them.

And, too, there's something good and productive in the feeling of sitting here too early in the morning, the big thing in the day already accomplished, but with so much still in front of them—assuming they don't come back to the lab and find themselves all fired, of course.

Finally, as they hit the second cup of coffee after breakfast, Di voices his thinking, and he's relieved to see the way they all nod agreement. Probably he could have leveled with them a while ago . . . out in public, where they might be monitored, is not the place to tell them about the private pipeline to Carla and the results coming out of there, and for everyone's safety he will probably only share bits of that with each of them, but on the other hand, at least he can get them pointed in the right direction.

He decides at that moment to go farther than that. He's going to spill a lot more of this to that reporter, Berlina Jameson, once he has the team pointed in the right direction. With a scientific team that knows the truth, and media sniffing around, it should be enough to keep them from covering it up any longer.

Part of him wonders about the safety of this. Four members of Congress were shot last year, and a lot of high-level civil servants. Officially, it's because the citizens of Washington are crazy and furious; the rumor that runs everywhere, though, is that these things are manipulated. Is he making a widow of Lori and abandoning his kids?

Is that worse than abandoning the human race?

They are all staring at him. Probably he has a faraway look in his eyes; he stopped talking in mid-sentence, he realizes, a moment ago. He begins again. "All right, so the big question now is really just the same one, one step down, from the global warming problem we had before. When do effects no one has ever seen before set in? That's right on the border between math and meteorology—or at least it is if we get the right meteorology described in the right math. So you guys are now officially in two teams, since we may not have a long time to work together. Talley and Mohammed, you're team one, and your job is to come up with plausible never-before-seen effects—whatever you think in your heart is possible, this is about as much intuition as it is science. Peter and Wo Ping, team two, same job, but don't look over team one's shoulders too much. Gretch, you track both and keep reports coming to me. At the end of the week, the teams trade reports and then do their best to knock down each other's ideas. By the middle of next week, if we're all still working together and we haven't been sent to six different cities, we should at least have a short list of what we think we ought to worry about, and have the ideas on it thoroughly vetted among ourselves. Once we have that I'll tackle Diem again and see if I can stir him up toward at least getting the issues in front of the policy makers, and ideally toward going public."

"Even if, uh—" Tally says, and doesn't go on, but everyone seems to be hanging on the answer to her question.

"Yes, even if the news is bad and likely to cause riots. Hell, we can't coddle people forever; what will we tell them when their cities blow down, 'there's no reason for alarm'? It's about time we started telling the truth."

The microphone/evaluator at the little diner where Callare and his people have breakfast puts out little packets of datarodents as fast as it can; Harris Diem reads the transcript with satisfaction, just seconds after each person speaks. The leaks are going to happen the way they are supposed to; he makes a note to dispatch a couple of "feeders"—datarodents that find other datarodents and feed them data, something the CIA uses in disinformation campaigns, and police departments of nations that officially don't communicate use for tracking criminals between them. These will carry some provocative stuff to the datarodents associated with the *New York Times*, *Scuttlebytes*, and that new one, *Sniffings*.

It's time to let Louie Tynan in on it too. Diem places the call.

As he might have expected from an old military officer, Tynan is irritated. "You mean you've known all along? Why the hell didn't you just give Dr. Callare the resources he needed, and warn people about what was coming?"

"Because half of them wouldn't believe us and the other half would panic. We need a rational response from the public."

That mollifies Tynan—he has about the same trust for the public that Diem does—and he asks, "So what now? I don't like lying to Carla, and I'm not good at it. And I don't think—"

"Whoa, there, partner," Diem says, grinning. "I'm going to spill the beans to everyone else as well. Not immediately, because what I need is a solid team in place before I sack a bunch of paper pushers—starting with Henry Pauliss, a name I'm sure you're familiar with—in favor of people who can do the job. But just as soon as possible. Just keep passing on information, and if anyone is nervous about getting caught, tell them you want to keep doing it right up to the moment of your arrest or theirs—which you and I both know won't happen."

Tynan grumbles a bit but goes along with it; thank god for a habit of taking orders, Diem thinks, because Louie Tynan could clearly be the stubbornest person on Earth if he wanted to be.

In fact, that very stubbornness is why he's *not* on Earth, and that's an advantage too. "You're going to like this next part better," Diem adds. "There's a major job we want you to do via telepresence at Moonbase, and you have carte blanche to get it done any old way you can."

"So far, terrific. What's up?"

"With the loss of Kingman, it occurred to some of our bright boys that it's going to be a hurricane-prone summer, and they think that we might lose all our other space-launch facilities except air launch. And we are going to need weather satellites in quantity. Moonbase has mining operations and cadcam shops—we want you to automate it so that you can build the satellites for us, up there, and then bring them down to Earth orbit. We've got the technical specs pretty much ready to go on it."

"How much longer do I stay up here?"

"Are you getting anxious for leave?" Diem asks. "I know you're overdue for relief."

"That's not what I asked. How much longer do I stay up here?"

"Hmm. Well, I guess till it's done. At least till fall."

"Then you've got yourself a deal."

As Diem hangs up, he thinks to himself, here's a guy who sees everything going on, but just carries out people's orders—and he wouldn't think of leaving the job, not for anything. There's no accounting for tastes.

As it always does, the phrase "there's no accounting . . ." triggers a little buzz in the back of his brain, as if a tiny rattlesnake coiled there. He thinks of the racks of wedges in the basement, thinks of his elaborate rig down there—and pushes the thought away, again, as he has been doing almost every hour lately.

Jesse already knows that Mary Ann Waterhouse is an extremely fucked up woman—in fact that's just about all he knows about her—but now that she's over her mating frenzy, or whatever it was, she seems pleasant enough. And the soft tacos filled with rare lamb, raw onion, and tomato are pretty good, so at least he's getting a meal out of this, even if he kind of suspects the whole experience is going to be too weird to get any of his friends to believe him.

She's pretty, too, now that she's changed into something soft and white and flowing, and with the candlelight she doesn't look quite so old or so weatherbeaten.

After they've eaten for a bit, she says, "I guess I owe you some sort of explanation, but to tell you the truth, Jesse, I'm not sure I've got one. I've been spending a fair amount of time catching the bus over to Puerto Madero and just walking along the beach, crying and screaming when I felt like it.

I really thought I was just going to go out and try to meet other people just like a regular person."

Jesse feels pretty stupid even as he says it. "I guess your job is really a strain."

"Yeah." She chews for a minute, then swallows. "It's pretty common knowledge, but they keep it off XV. You know about the fuzz?"

"Uh, I've heard the word. It's supposed to be how you keep a private identity, right?"

She nods. "Yep, you've had the official story. Want to hear something nasty?"

He spreads his hands in resignation; if all this has been an elaborate routine to get someone to talk to, he'll have to admit he's interested—it's like turning over a rock to look at bugs. And something in him insists on getting the whole story.

Meanwhile, Mary Ann has noticed Jesse's response and read it very differently. She'd already been shocked at the way she had attacked—there really wasn't any other word for it—this poor kid. In fact, this whole trip she's wondered when she's going to start coming back together again; her first week she bundled up, wore a wig, and went and did some touristy things like the gondola ride to the top of Tacana and the rain forest hike. Then she spent more and more time sitting and reading, and then she began to take the long walks on the beach . . . now she's down to attacking boys on the street. She wonders if there's some kind of bottom you hit in this.

She just wants to make sure that when he leaves he doesn't hate her.

"The fuzz doesn't matter much," she says quietly. "It was just sort of an explanation because I thought I owed you one. We're as sensitive as you are, but only a small part of what we're feeling penetrates through the nervous system data interfaces. And it's not like signal you can amplify . . . it's more like fuzziness in a picture—turning the lights up doesn't help much. So . . . well, to get the idea across we have to really overdo everything. And sometimes . . ."

"You hurt each other."

"Well, and we get to be that way ourselves; small emotions don't matter because you don't get paid for them." She looks down; this still isn't taking the direction she wanted it to. "Look, this will sound stupid too—lately everything I say that's not part of a script sounds stupid to me. But I am really tired of hearing myself talk. I would appreciate it a lot if you would tell me something about yourself."

He makes a face, takes a bite of the taco—she wondered why Señora Herrera had made so many, but clearly Señora Herrera knows more about teenage male appetites than Mary Ann does—and says, "Well, that didn't sound stupid, it sounded polite. Do you really want to know?"

"Most of the time everyone in the world knows what I'm feeling; what I want to know is what somebody who hasn't gotten as fucked up as I have feels like. So tell me about yourself, please."

He shrugs. "It's going to sound clichéd, because the first thing I feel like saying is that there's not a lot to tell. And the second thing I feel like saying is that . . . oh, well, see, I'm down here working at the Tapachula Community College, as a tutor in the pre-engineering curriculum. I'm an engineering student up at U of the Az, but I'm taking this term off. What I do is, I coach local kids who are trying to get ready for engineering school through their science and math classes . . . only . . ." His eyes seem to look over her shoulder to somewhere a thousand miles away.

"Only?" she asks, lightly, and part of her notes that there's something in this scene that Synthi Venture would understand, maybe better than Mary Ann. The boy is certainly handsome—hell, he's *beautiful*—and candlelight playing over his delicate, troubled face . . . this wouldn't make a bad staging in a documentary about a Romantic poet. . . .

"Only," he says, finally, "there's this girl."

It's a great story, in Mary Ann's opinion, and what makes it truly a great story is that this boy is far more sincere than she, or anyone she ever worked with, could be. He really does have a single, burning true love and it's really the only one he ever expects to have. And he looks so sad . . . and so beautiful.

Mary Ann prides herself on her intelligence and cynicism, and she's right about both of them. But one thing she rarely admits to herself is that to really appeal to her audience, Synthi Venture has had to be able to feel the sort of thing they wish *they* could feel—and that means there was something of Synthi in Mary Ann to start out with, and a great deal more has gotten in. So although she knows it's dumb and corny, she's still swept away by the story of this poor kid's love life, and consequently she does the most seductive thing a human being can do—she looks fascinated.

Jesse sees that and finds himself thinking that she's an awfully good listener, and the first person who seems to understand about it all, and to feel a little touch of compassion for her—she's clearly a very nice person who has been made a mess of by the life she's had to lead. He's very proud of his ability to forgive her . . . and hey, in the candlelight, he's not sure he's ever seen anyone quite so beautiful. "That's enough about me, anyway," he says. "All clichés, just like I said. Um . . . tomorrow's my day off. Would you like to do something really dumb, like take a long walk on the beach together?"

"I'd adore it," she says, and she smiles a deep, secret smile that seems to him to have centuries of pain in it, but a wonderful warmth as well. He realizes they are going to be very good for each other, and says, "Terrific."

She loves the way he says "Terrific"—it puts her in mind of a couple of guys she went out with in high school—and she knows, suddenly, that they can both be very good for each other.

Louie Tynan has a pilot's patience for medical officers—which is to say, none at all. And somehow they must sense that, because they always turn up right when things are way too busy already.

He's been dealing with Dr. Wo for a long time, and sure enough, just when he's about to take off for the moon, Wo calls him up and says he's got to be plugged in for a checkup.

Space neurology is a pretty silly subject if you ask Louie—he's never noticed any difference in what he thinks, only in his muscles and body weight and so forth—but no one is asking him. For an hour, he dutifully thinks of images Dr. Wo suggests, and reports back what he sees when signal comes in through the scalpnet, and generally lets the doc run his whole nervous system through a thorough checkout.

Usually Wo is one of those doctors who thinks "Any questions?" means "goodbye" and "Uh, one question, Doc," means "run!" But this time, when the checkout is all done and Louie is at last permitted to unplug, Wo stays on the line, and says, "There's another area that we need to discuss, Colonel Tynan."

Louie nods. "I'm listening."

Wo smiles slightly. "If I tell you that it isn't something you could be grounded for, will you relax and listen carefully?"

Louie's smile is wider. "Sure, Doc. What is it?"

Wo looks off to the side, as if thinking, and finally says, "You know, of course, that all modern computer systems are deliberately infected with optimizing replicating code—little programs that duplicate themselves as needed, and that modify other programs to improve them. For example, if another program is accomplishing what it does in seventy steps, and the optimizer sees a way to do it in sixty, perhaps because there are several unnecessary moves of data in and out of storage . . . the optimizer fixes it. Optimizers, of course, also fix each other, so none of us exactly understands how they do what they do. This is all review, yes?"

"It's all review. And I'm not a computer, Doc."

"Not yet, anyway. That's what I'm trying to find a way to explain. The most recent generations of optimizers are no longer stopped by the barriers between operating systems; they are able to translate themselves and infect systems they were never designed for. That feature makes them more useful, obviously, in the global net, since they download themselves into any new machine and clean up its code.

"A couple of years ago we were experimenting with rabbit brains, and we discovered the most advanced of the optimizers could actually cross over into the brain. Where they began to . . . well—"

"Make the rabbit smarter? Are you telling me that by spending so much time telepresent I'm going to become brighter?"

"To some extent that's what happened with the three human volunteers who tried it. But there were other effects as well. You might want to be careful—and call me if you notice anything unusual." Wo takes a long moment to think about it. "For example, they stopped needing to sleep much. One function of sleep is a sort of sorting of the records and straightening out of the memory. Thus with optimizers running in the brain, since the memories stay straight and the records accurate, there's less need for sleep."

"You said *one* function," Louie noted.

"Well, nature never leaves anything in just a single use for long. If you have to do something all the time, evolution will find ways to make it serve other functions. The immune system is immensely energy-consuming, so your body uses sleep as a time, when you aren't using energy for much else, to get caught up on immune functions. If it should happen that you're invaded by those programs, you'll *feel* very little need to sleep, but you should still lie down and not move, unhooked from the system, for a few hours each day. Especially in an environment with a certain amount of hard radiation around, where there will be more damaged cells to clean out and where the disease organisms you carry with you are more apt to mutate."

"Uh, yeah. *Will* I be able to sleep?"

"Better than ever," Wo said, permitting himself a tiny smile. "When those programs cross over they optimize *everything*." He hesitates for a long moment and then says, "So, again, if you notice anything unusual—even if it doesn't seem to impair you—give me a call. Any questions?"

"I guess not," Louie says, and the screen goes blank. Wo has hung up.

For more than a week after it smashes Kingman, the hurricane works its way to the west and north. Whatever world news media may make of its "behavior" and "personality," it is just an oval of low pressure in the troposphere, fed and sustained by the warmth of the ocean below it, and thus the frequent note from news commentators and XV stars that the hurricane "takes no notice of human beings" is mere theatrics. A hurricane that took notice of human beings would be a different kind of thing.

It passes among the islands made famous in the Second World War, and its huge storm surge rolls far up the beaches, dragging many of them into new shapes. There are deaths running into the hundreds in the Carolines and the Marshalls, but coverage drops steadily—XV, like TV before it, thrives on novelty, and when you have seen one "island paradise" destroyed, you've seen all of them. This is particularly true because the evident poverty and squalor make it hard for media to portray the place as a paradise (and hence it is less shocking to see its destruction) and the destruction itself tends to happen in the pitch-dark driving wind and rain, where there's little to see. So on island after island, wind and waves slaughter hundreds and level whole towns, but the coverage falls steadily during that time, by popular demand. An audience that has gotten used to experiencing war and violence through the eyes of the XV stars has been yawning and tuning out the events in the Pacific Islands.

It is not that the drowned people with their ruined houses have brown skin—by 2028, so do many of the audience for XV—but that they are far away, and although it is endlessly repeated that this is the biggest hurricane in human history, you can't see it being the biggest from anywhere lower than orbit, and down on the ground where the human interest is, it's just a lot of wind and rain and some big waves. There's a two-day wonder when Kishima, biggest star on the Japanese XV Adventure Channel, announces that he will be set down by staticopter in the path of the surge and will then surf all the way to land, wherever it may take him, but that too becomes dull as people plugging into him discover only that he is getting tired, that cold water tastes very good to him, and that although he is frightened, he knows that pickup aircraft remain within short range of him.

They know Hurricane Clem is a big story and that there will be trouble if they don't cover it, but TV and XV alike can't find a way to make it entertaining.

The edge of Hurricane Clem grazes Saipan at about two in the morning on the night of June 21. Lance, one of the reporters for Extraponet, happens to be there, and he's looking for any old shelter he can find—his net sent him out into the foul weather to "sample" it, he's gotten separated from his bodyguards, and now he doesn't have the foggiest idea where he is. His editor has been trying to get him located by transponder, but the directional antenna needed for the job is hopeless in the high wind. They stay linked, and Lance keeps looking for something he can recognize. He falls twice, and once he's hit by a small, blowing board; eventually he is crawling, muddy water spraying furiously into his face.

There's a vivid orange glow ahead, and he manages to wipe his eyes and make it out. "Conrad Hotel," he reads, out loud.

The editor's voice in his ear says, "Hah! Now we've got you placed."

"Well, great, get me a taxi or something."

"Right now nothing's moving, Lance. You'd better see if you can get in there. The zipline is off its tracks and the roads are washed out between us and you—you'll have to see if they'll give you a room."

"I don't see a Vacancy sign," he mutters as he crawls. The water is unbelievably cold around his hands and feet. He thinks he lost a shoe but he's not sure.

"It's not really a hotel, it's an old folks' home," the editor replies. "But maybe they'll let you have a room. They're bound to like you there, old people experience a lot of XV, and the city directory says they're mostly Americans anyway."

When Lance enters the vestibule, the wind and rain stop abruptly; it's like dragging himself out of a river. He's gasping like a goldfish, and it takes an effort to haul himself to his feet. He knocks on the door and tries opening it. It swings open easily.

There are about a hundred of them standing there in the lobby; it takes Lance only a second to think *the workers must have run off.* Two or three of them look startled, as if they recognize him. He closes the door behind himself.

The place is at least a hundred years old, and he can feel the groans of the old building through his feet.

An older man, well-dressed with a jacket and bowtie, approaches him and asks, "Are you with the management here?"

"I'm a reporter," Lance answers. "Covering all this for Extraponent. I came in to get out of the storm."

"You won't be out of it long," an older lady in jeans and sweater says.

Ignoring her, the man says, "We've been trying to figure out whether we can get everyone down into the cellar. It's not a very deep one but it's better than up here. There's at least as many people who won't come out of their rooms, I'm afraid—we can't do anything for them—and there's a bunch on the ground floor who can't move themselves. We were just about to vote to try to knock down the cellar door and get down there—they left it locked."

Lance nods. There's a moaning boom, and the old building shifts slightly. "Uh, I don't know that I care about democracy. I'll knock that door down for you."

They lead him to it. It looks pretty solid, but the frame doesn't seem to be anything special.

Four hard snap-kicks, like they taught him when he was training for this job, and the door flies open. They all applaud.

The power is still on, so he turns on the light. There is at least a foot of water throughout the basement.

"I don't know," one of the women says. She has the kind of piled mop of starched gray hair that Lance has always found particularly unattractive on old ladies. "Looks, like, totally gross."

"Oh, shut up, Kristin," the man with her replies, and starts to climb down the wet steps. "Shoes will dry."

"All right, you're, like, so grumpy," she says, following him. They stagger down the steps, holding hands.

Most of the crowd is suspended between fear of the rocking and creaking hotel, and distaste for the flooded basement, Lance realizes; he starts to head down the steps himself. He knows, anyway, that he will—

No engineer would ever bother to analyze what happens next; it's not a current or an interesting structure, like the Launch Facility was. The principle is simple; irregular surfaces, and surfaces with holes in them, have much more drag than smooth ones. Whether the roof lifts first, or a window breaks, or even just a door flies open, drag increases dramatically.

In a split second, more damage happens, and there are more holes and rough surfaces. In another split of the same second, the force on the building has multiplied many-fold.

The Conrad Hotel goes over sideways like a house of cards, slumping into a pile of lumber. Even Lance does not have time to move clear of it, and he is much the most agile person present. There are screams, thuds, crashes.

He finds himself pinned down in darkness. All around him there are cries and moans. A few people are calling names, most just crying out.

He tries to move his left arm, but it's broken and numb. His right is pinned to his side. Something too heavy to move is on his chest, and he's fighting to breathe.

Very slowly, the hole containing his head begins to fill with icy water. As it covers his ears, he loses the sound of people crying out in fear; it is a long time after that when his face is covered, and his last seconds are spent bucking against the intractable grip of the weight on his chest.

The editor gets every bit of it; it's some of the best XV of the year, he figures. Eight hundred million people experience it live, or in one of the two replays later that day.

Two days later detectives from several XV nets have established that the rotten old retirement hotel was owned by a group of Hawaiian doctors and was in noncompliance with practically every applicable building code. Besides Lance, three hundred old people who had spent their savings to get there from Akron, Bakersfield, or Minot had perished.

Moreover, it turns out to be a small bonanza for the doctors who own it, since building, facilities, and old people are all heavily insured.

But that's nothing compared to the bonanza it is for XV. Suddenly there are over a thousand suitably grieving relatives, and the heaps of gray-haired dead under the rotten hotel, and all of them from the country that created XV and consumes more of it than the rest of the world combined.

Passionet tries to get Synthi Venture to come back from vacation early to cover it. She won't, but it doesn't slow them down. Very shortly, Rock and Quaz are there as a team, both missing Synthi acutely, rivals for a new star, Surface O'Malley, their latest marketing of red hair to the Japanese market, doing a sort of recap of *The Front Page* as they investigate the "doctors' ring" that maintained the "living hell of the hotel deathtrap." The audience can feel the Rock's righteous anger, Quaz's cold determination to get to the bottom of this and nail the bastards, and Surface's guts and determination to be part of the team.

Passionet flies in plenty of grieving relatives for Surface O'Malley to interview. She has a warm, tender quality that people open up to, and she's extremely good at feeling torn between Rock and Quaz; naturally in this kind of story, the affair is doomed, and millions of experiencers weep with her as Rock and Quaz decide that they must not allow a woman to come between them when it is vital to run the story to the ground. (Not before Rock has taken her out to the storm-lashed beach for champagne and a lusty fucking by moonlight, and Quaz has torn her panties from under her lacy dress and had her in a back alley—Quaz having lost the coin toss for who has to be the bad-boy hero.)

Surface O'Malley is a big hit, and best of all from Passionet's standpoint, she's not too much like Synthi Venture but she's enough like her so that they can build up a rivalry; there will be at least a year of catfights to alternate with the individual adventures before the two of them will find each other as best friends.

Meanwhile, Rock and Quaz uncover the vital evidence that Passionet's detectives found the first day, and wave it in the faces of the Hawaiian doctors, who deny everything and threaten to sue. The men who experience Rock feel once again that they know their way around the world, and that a certain nobility adheres to them; the men (and a few women) who experience Quaz once again feel bitter existential despair, the knowledge that it is a cold and ugly world where every moment of joy is paid for at too high a price, but where a good-enough-for-this-world man like Quaz can take grim satisfaction in making a few of the bastards pay, and in the durable friendship of a guy like Rock—and the pleasures of occasionally knocking off a good piece like Surface.

The hurricane, still taking no notice, as the media continue to note, does not plow into Indonesia as expected, though its storm surges are still large enough to cause great damage there, and as far off as the Mekong Delta.

The Japanese weather station at Minami Tori Sima cannot be raised by radio for a full day, and there is a brief flurry of speculation about a "second Kingman Reef," but they are dug into the island and come out with no harm done except for some instrument towers knocked over.

All the way from Kingman Reef, the storm has been slowly dwindling in force, and though it is still the biggest in history, it is beginning to drift down to the range of the conceivable. Scientists say this to the media; the media, who need to get another story someplace anyway, can now announce that it's mostly over, even if the storm is still there, or at least it will be over until the storm again comes inshore, to clobber Kyushu or Honshu.

And they have every right to ask this dismissability of it. If it were a normal hurricane, it would be expected to take the usual route north through the Pacific and hit in or near Japan; thousands of storm tracks have. Hurricanes in the Northern Hemisphere may move in any direction or even loop around, but normally they move to the north and the west, and thus far this one has been no exception to that rule, however exceptional it has been in every other regard.

Thus when it obstinately turns and heads east on the afternoon of the twenty-fifth—and then proceeds to gain speed and strength as it roars back across the Pacific, farther north than any hurricane, let alone a giant one, could normally be expected—the uproar in the scientific community finds little echo in the general media. No one lives out there, and the big hurricane story has been done; if it stays away from Hawaii, it will never make a prime slot again.

John Klieg has operated all over the world for the last ten years, or at least he thought it was all over the world. He realizes now that he has missed a lot of the sleazier corners, and he is beginning to hope that they won't come any sleazier than Novokuznetsk, the capital of the Siberian Republic. He knew that it was a boomtown—hell, Siberia is a boom *nation*—but somewhere in the back of his mind he had envisioned something like the American or Alaskan frontier towns, or even like the rain forest frontier in Brazil—trashy and thrown up in haste, rough around the edges, but a place where stuff was getting done and built. There was some poem or other he'd read back in high school about cities with big shoulders, and that was kind of what he thought a boomtown should look like.

He wasn't prepared for this place. The downtown has all been thrown up in the last ten years, a long way from the old city center, so that the whole city seems to have fallen over sideways. Mostly, downtown is empty office buildings with exorbitant rents, because there's a roaring speculation boom in office space going on at the moment. Land prices near the city at any instant are either impossibly high or almost nothing, changing rapidly as the local and the national government policies veer around to favor different zipline routes.

The whole city has exactly six blocks of *working* zipline, all within the Abdulkashim Center, and although the whole route can be traversed in less than ten minutes on foot, the zipline itself runs on the hour, Monday, Wednesday, and Friday only.

What everyone in Novokuznetsk is doing is getting rights to things; Abdulkashim came to power on the back of the army, like the last eleven Siberian dictators, but he stayed in power because of the two promises he didn't break—he kept building up the military forces and he kept reducing the size of everything else connected with the government. His rivals have no alternative program.

Novokuznetsk is not the first city on Earth to have all the buildings coated with thick coal soot, but it's the latest, and more is being added all the time. When the sun breaks through, which is rarely, you see a city of recent construction already crumbling in its air pollution and strangling on traffic and bad sewers—but rates of construction are amazing, and every business that can is moving here to get out from under tax and regulatory loads.

Well, Klieg thinks to himself, that's the way it is everywhere. He's always a little amazed that people get upset by what businesses do; businesses do what you pay them to do and what you allow them to do, and both of those are up to the customers and the citizens.

The thing that he finds disconcerting is not the mess that this place has become, but the realization that it's a mess that doesn't produce anything. He's not completely unaware that GateTech produces nothing and sometimes prevents others from producing anything; that doesn't bother him by itself. But GateTech at least maintains comfortable, attractive facilities, places that look like college campuses, where his teams of scientists and engineers can enjoy working. Every place that GateTech owns is clean, safe, and humane, because Klieg knows that creative work flourishes in that kind of environment.

Novokuznetsk is not like that. The belching stacks are mostly the municipal power plants, which will be coming off line when the fusion plant finally opens (any year now—as soon as they quit switching primary contractors in exchange for fresh bribes, and allow some one contractor to finish the job, always assuming the contractor is competent and anyone can build a plant on that site after all the redesigns that have been thrown into the mix).

What the power plants are driving, in turn, are giant advertising signs, office machinery in the skyscrapers of the new downtown, and lots of demonstration facilities that have been set up mostly to attract investors. The typical visitor to Novokuznetsk is a businessman who has dreams of a new high-profit frontier, and everything is set up to cater to that; they can visit the matrix metals facility (which has all the machines sitting out on a common shop floor like so many drill presses and table saws, because the sterile cleanrooms in which they would run were never built); the aircraft test field where they're doing land-on-maglev tests (which was at Ohio State until Abdulkashim bought it and moved it; the new one, at Ohio State, is pursuing a much more promising line of research); or the nanosurgery facility (which is real enough but staffed mostly with surgeons who came here because they had to—typically the kind of doctor who just has a little problem with pills, the bottle, or patients' genitalia). That typical visitor doesn't know what he's looking at—he knows money, not engineering or science—and so he sees all the feverish activity and concludes that Novokuznetsk is "real"—Klieg has heard the word used many times—and throws money into it.

That, too, makes Klieg shake his head. It's not a problem *he* would ever have. He understands that money matters, data matters, the rules matter— the physical side of things doesn't. But if you think it does, you ought to be able to tell fake from real.

Klieg knows the showpiece plants are powered up half an hour before each visitor arrives and powered down ten minutes after departure. The whole muddy, dirty, polluted, uncomfortable mess is only a lure for money. Nothing will ever be made here and very few services will ever be provided.

Geez, he's thinking like one of those socialist channels that come out of the Third World—not that he's a fan of them but his staff includes them in the mix of daily reports that crosses his reading window. But again, what do people expect? A business is to make money with—if there's money in building things and serving people, they'll do it, and if not, well, then obviously nobody wanted things built or people served, because if they had, they'd have paid for it.

The reason he's thinking about how ugly and nasty all this is—aside from the fact that he has eyes and a nose—is that he's really missing Glinda and Derry. A few weeks ago he just sort of noticed that Glinda was around, and knew she had a kid; now he *hates* being away.

There's something philosophic about all of that, he supposes, but hell if he can see what it might be. The world changes under you as you get to understand things about it better. He'd known for a long time she was pretty and lonely; it hadn't occurred to him before that he was lonely, or that she might be interested. That's all.

Right now there's a warm rain drenching Novokuznetsk, running black and greasy off the raw new buildings, puddling brown and gray with rainbow slicks all over the lumpy concrete roadway. The fuel-cell-driven cab he's in has an obvious scream in its electric motors and seems to get lost every so often and wander for a couple of streets before it finds a working checkpoint, and to judge from the smell in here, the place has been a boudoir for a number of local prostitutes and First World suits recently.

He just wishes to god that he could be back in Florida; Derry's in some kind of a riding contest today, and she and Glinda will call tomorrow morning, their time, which will be late in the evening his, to let him know how it went. He's getting very fond of the kid, too—naturally they don't want to spoil her, but he's been having a good deal of fun getting various just-right things for her.

It's been years since he's had so much company and affection, and he's already having a little trouble getting by without it. Glinda has just kind of opened up into his life, and all of a sudden things like eating dinner, or relaxing on the beach, or going shopping—stuff he'd been thinking of as "routine maintenance" for years—has all become the stuff he looks forward to most.

Not to mention sex. Klieg has tried all the fancy stuff but he really just likes to mess around a little, get excited, and fuck—and that's just what Glinda likes, and she likes it about as often as Klieg does, which is much more often than it was a few months ago. Most weekend nights, and during the week whenever he sleeps over at her place, they take that extra ten minutes that feels so wonderful and end up sleeping curled against each other.

It has even occurred to Klieg that he could think about retiring, but a little more reflection led him to the conclusion that much as he loves his new-found uses for time off, he wouldn't much like to spend all his time doing them. The mixture could maybe be adjusted one way or another—when the company is in more normal times and life gets dull he might spend a little more time away from it. For right now, this move into space launch needs his attention.

The biggest problem he failed to anticipate was caused by the publicity this miserable country had managed to generate for itself. He figured since they pretty much continuously bragged about the freedom for business they offered—unregulated gold standard banks, no environmental regs, practically no health and safety laws, no local investor participation required, and on and on—that he could just build the thing and start launching.

He was wrong. Instead of regulations per se, the government here requires permits for everything. Not that the permit requires you to do anything more than plunk down money, but you have to plunk down a lot of money, frequently, and they keep halting the work whenever you didn't plunk it down in front of the right guy, which is a mixture of getting the mostly unwritten procedures right, bribing the right people to get you through to the people that the procedures say you should be dealing with, and then bribing the officials when you do get through to them so that they'll accept the government's fee. It would have been cheaper to build this somewhere else.

He reminds himself that the reason for building it here is, at this moment, whirling around out in the Pacific; it's already taken down Kingman Reef, which was about to double world launch capacity, and last reports are that the storm surge is more than big enough to swamp the Japanese launch facilities at Kageshima and the Formosan Republic's facility at Hungtow; that big right turn Hurricane Clem made threw what are practically tidal waves northward. Of the world's five significant launch facilities, three will certainly be out of action before July and that's a very good start.

Right now he's off to meet this guy Hassan, who isn't Siberian but is extremely influential, or so Klieg's team has established; if Hassan can do what they say he can, then permits ought to start flowing pretty fast, and if he can't, well, it's only time and money.

The cab rounds a corner a little tight, almost scraping the curb, and throws up a cascade of black greasy puddle onto a girl who looks to be about Derry's age, who had been posing by the curb, topless in a short skirt and heels. As she jumps back, screams, and swears, Klieg sees the tracks of a dozen different infections on her pale barely developing chest; she's got the telltale purple blotches of ARTS and the raised, inflamed veins of SPM, plus what looks like a plain old ringworm. He can see from her open mouth that she's already lost a few teeth, and her grimace suggests that ARTS is taking hold.

The gruesome thing, he thinks, as the cab pulls away and she flings a clod of dirt against its back window, is that if she's trying to flag men in cabs like that, it probably means some of them are buying her. Well, if what she's got doesn't get her, no doubt she's got some strain of AIDS or resistant clap, so she'll probably be off the street—and under the ground—before she's fourteen.

And undoubtedly there will be another one.

Capitalism in action, Klieg thinks, great system to stay on top of. . . .

It does remind him that Glinda is being kind of a typical mother about Derry and not noticing that the kid is growing up; Derry has hinted now and then that she's getting interested in boys and so forth, and Glinda has worked pretty hard at ignoring that. Not that Derry's going to end up like that piece of thrown-off human garbage back there, of course, but you don't have to go to cheap whores to get killer diseases, and the kid needs to be kept safe.

One more thing that, between money and power, Klieg can do. It makes him feel good, right now, that he can protect Derry that way; it's not as good as sitting down to Glinda's meat loaf (she's programmed her cook to make it exactly right, something that Klieg has never been able to do with his), hearing about Derry's day at school, then snuggling up for a movie and popcorn with Glinda, but it does make him feel better about being in this smelly potholed dump of a town.

The cab must be programmed to go the long way to everywhere, because by the time it pulls up at Hassan's building, Klieg has passed through a couple of major intersections twice. Hassan has a whole floor on one of those empty skyscrapers, and at the door, Klieg is met by two big men who look like they might be contenders for the Siberian Olympic wrestling team. You can see that their coats—cheap, brightly colored, new—bunch around the armpits, and are a little tight through the shoulder. There's a bulge on the left breast where you expect it. There seems to be about a two-inch gap between coat and shirt collars, and when the slightly shorter one says, "Meesser Klieg, please?" and sticks out a solid, slablike hand, the shirt cuff strains.

It's a good act but not a great one. Klieg enjoys it (it's like something out of an old movie) but figures that big, scary guys in suits are fairly cheap.

Amazingly, the elevator in this building runs smoothly, and when he steps off onto Hassan's top-floor offices, everything appears to be clean, nice, new, and well-cared-for; that, more than the skyscraper or the goons, makes Klieg think he's dealing with a pro here.

Hassan is well-dressed and not overdressed, and that's another good sign. He's a small man, square in the shoulders with the kind of good posture that suggests he did some hard physical work twenty years ago and has stayed in shape since. "Mr. John Klieg," he says. His accent sounds more Oxbridge than Pakistani; Klieg's research tells him that Hassan is neither, coming instead out of the complex system of orphanages, foster homes, and street gangs that has produced millions of people with no defined nationality in the rubble of thirty years of war in old Soviet Central Asia.

"I'm pleased to meet you," Klieg says, and they go in to tea; Klieg's already swallowed two decaffeinaters and a nifty little tab that will keep his bladder from filling for a few hours, because he's been warned that there will be at least a gallon of tea involved in being polite.

The seating in Hassan's private office is on the floor, on big soft cushions laid carefully around a small table on a thick, pricey-looking handmade rug. There's a huge silver samovar on the sideboard, and Klieg's larger goon quietly fills a cup for each of them and sets them on the table, then goes out as quietly as a sigh.

Klieg sits on one side of the table, Hassan on the other, and they both drink tea for a little bit, talking about the weather. This is a situation where it's just not polite to get down to business right away, so they don't. On the second cup, Hassan says, "I am told you have no family, Mr. Klieg."

"None at the moment," Klieg says. "I'm working on that."

"Ah. There is a woman in your life? Some young beauty you've taken to as a pleasure of age?"

Klieg smiles and shakes his head. "An older beauty, who's been bringing up a child by herself. Someone with a lot of common sense."

Hassan gets up and fills both teacups, and as he brings them slowly back, he says, "I see that I was not misinformed; you are wise and prudent. And naturally"—he hands Klieg a cup—"very naturally indeed, Mr. Klieg, with such personal matters coming along, you have a certain concern for the future, a desire to see things become firmly established, so as to make a secure world for this new family of yours. I understand this, I share the impulse myself—I have four daughters and an infant son, and when I look at the sort of violence that flares up so much in this part of the world, and at how brutal and grinding poverty can be here, I feel my spine stiffen and my shoulders settle and I put myself to work, hard, to keep such things away from them. Is it not that way?"

Klieg had told himself to be careful about trusting his feelings in this conference—after all, if Hassan is going to be good at anything, he's going to be good at being liked. But there's no getting around the fact that the man is likable. "Yes," Klieg says, "that's exactly the way it is. You start to think about how to make a place that's strong and safe, because it's a nasty world out there."

Hassan smiles, nods, and without the least leaning forward or even added intensity of gaze, he says, "And yet, Mr. Klieg, here you are in a country where people get shot frequently, in a dirty city of foul streets and fouler doings, arranging to build for yourself here the only thing in this whole wretched nation that is ever likely to be worth stealing, under the protection of whatever random thieves happen to be the government of this dirty little hole of a nation. This is the sort of speculation a poor man with one chance would dare. It is not all what a man who is already wealthy, who has already taken the world in hand, is apt to do. This interests me a great deal, as a student of human nature—and which of us in business is not a student of that? I wonder what can be inside you to make you take such chances."

Klieg nods, takes a sip of tea, and thinks to himself that the old routine about Asian indirectness and American bluntness is pretty dated; Hassan has started the serious part of this with the most important question. Indeed, it's not one Klieg is completely sure of his own answer to. He lets the tea roll over his tongue and then says, "As you've guessed, there are reasons. You do know what GateTech has been in the business of doing?"

"Yes—the blocking patent business."

"I prefer to call them something other than blocking patents, because my feeling is that I block nothing—I merely build way stations and roads between the frontier and those who wish to reach it, and charge them to pass the way I have pioneered. But yes, my money has come out of that process. It has involved staying very close to what is happening, racing against many other teams of bright people. But the race is not as easy as it once was. . . ."

"When you began, you were the only one who knew there was a race; now they take your operations into account from the very beginning."

"Exactly."

"And so there is a change of strategy. This much I have deduced, Mr. Klieg, and it makes a great deal of good sense, if I may so compliment you. But it is there that I am stymied; clearly your next strategy would have been to begin to operate farther out toward the technical and scientific frontier than before, and to find ways to make the traffic run your way rather than just locating your 'way stations and roads' where the traffic runs.

"But I do not see this. No, I see you working in this very dangerous environment, dealing with very difficult people, and doing all of this for a well-established and simple technology like space launch, something that has been around since the middle of the last century.

"And this tells me one of three things, I think.

"Either you are mad—and there is no evidence of this; or you are bored and looking for danger and excitement—and this new family you are hoping to find makes it seem very improbable, for to a man with a family the world is more than dangerous enough; or you know something that is not general knowledge in the world yet, and you are once again on the move to build a way station or a road, in a place the world will shortly be going. Of course that last is what I believe to be the case, because I greatly respect you.

"So, Mr. Klieg . . . as you know, I can help you a great deal. I have a cash price and that will be negotiated by underlings—indeed, your people are meeting mine at this very moment, as you know, and I'm sure we can reach some equitable arrangement on that matter. But there is something I want very much, and you will have to understand that I want it because I am already in that happy estate to which you aspire—I have a family to look out for.

"*I want to know what you think is going to happen, and why this launch facility is likely to prove so important.*" Hassan has leaned forward and now he does look eager. Klieg believes the man completely. There's no question in his mind that Hassan is dead serious, and though anything could be an act, Klieg would bet that this is not.

For one thing, in Hassan's shoes, it's just what Klieg would want. Clearly the man is not hurting for money any more than Klieg is. And just as clearly, when a big mystery comes onto your territory, an inside pipeline to its source is what you really want.

Klieg takes a long sip and a calculated risk. "Let me place a call to see if the money and contract matters are going as well as we both expect. And if it would appear the partnership is satisfactory in every other regard, well, then, we'll shake hands and I'll tell you everything."

Hassan nods, once, firmly, and somehow or other a goon comes in with a phone for Klieg. Klieg dials, asks a couple of questions, hears what he expected to. Hassan's price is high but *if* it's truly "one-stop shopping," *if* they will no longer need to come up with each bribe, permit fee, and payment one at a time and on a negotiated basis, then Hassan will be much cheaper, even before you figure in all the time not lost to delays every time cops and soldiers come out to make them stop work. "Well, then, close with'em, Jerry, sounds like we have a deal," Klieg says, clicks off, and turns to Hassan.

"A few weeks ago, when the big methane release happened . . ." he begins, and in thirty minutes Hassan not only knows everything, but is starting to smile with a warmth Klieg understands perfectly. It's not every day that a global-monopoly-to-be walks in and asks for your help.

They agree to meet for dinner soon, and they talk of many different things; Klieg gets an inside look at the Siberian government and is no more appalled than he was when he began to understand Washington or the UN, but he notices how much cruder and more brutal the tactics are out here and resolves to keep himself out of trouble.

The rest of the morning goes into tea and talking about old movies; Hassan turns out to be an enthusiast for them, too. Or at least when he knew he would be meeting with Klieg, he became one, and he carries off the act well. That's really all you can ask for.

"All right," Di Callare is saying to Carla Tynan, over the phone link. "I can get you all the data you ask for. But this is not getting any easier."

"Louie thinks they're on his track too," she points out. "And without him we'd have no real data to go on. So tell me, Di, what do you make of Hurricane Clem? He's been moving east for longer and farther than any hurricane in Pacific history."

"He's also farther north," Di points out. "We don't know much about what a hurricane does when it stays well above the thirtieth parallel. It's never been warm enough up there to keep them running, let alone gaining energy. For all we know this is perfectly normal behavior for a giant hurricane on a hot ocean."

"It's counter to the Coriolis force—"

"But it's right in line with the steering current," Di responds, impassively. "And now that it's so far off the equator we aren't getting the data we'd like—the satellites along the equator can't look down into it, the Japanese are keeping their aerial data to themselves, the Siberians and Alaskans don't seem to be flying anything, and we're still trying to get a maneuverable satellite up there in a polar orbit—the government doesn't want to spring for one, and since all the commercial load that was going to go through Kingman Reef has been shifted back to Aruba and Edwards, there's not any space to spare unless they're willing to commandeer it. So anything at all could be going on inside Clem—maybe there's the biggest outflow jet in history."

Carla leans back in her chair, rubbing her back; as a relaxing, comfortable semi-retirement, this whole business with *MyBoat* is a complete flop. She's been short on sleep for days, her butt is just as chair-sore as it ever was in Washington, and the aftermath of Clem has left the Pacific too stormy and rough for her to get much time on the surface sunbathing. "Say that again," she says.

"What, that maybe there's the biggest outflow jet in history? It was just a thought that Gretch, our summer intern, had—she was doing mass balance for a hurricane that big, and the only way it didn't strangle itself was—"

"Was that it was pushing a whole lot of wet air a long way from itself—of course! Hug that intern for me and don't let her go back to school for the duration. You need her. I've got an idea, Di, and I'll be back with you shortly."

He gives her a little half-salute, half-wave, and they break contact. She wonders how he's finding an excuse to go to a different pay phone twice a day, and whether her direct bounce to Louie is secure enough . . . and once again she wonders why anyone would want to get in the way of figuring out what's going on. Well, politics was always Di's gift, not hers.

An outflow jet is a peculiar thing some hurricanes have some of the time. As the air streams out of the top of the spiraling eye wall, sometimes instead of dispersing in all directions and coming down as rainy weather a long way away, the hot air will organize itself as a single stream moving in a single direction; that stream is called an outflow jet.

An outflow jet can carry much more mass than conventional dispersal—

so it takes away one of the limits on the size of the hurricane, for only as much air can swirl in at the bottom as can flow out at the top, and since the outflow jet removes air more efficiently, the hurricane can be bigger.

But it has another and more significant effect; it all comes down in one place, on one side of the hurricane, and the addition of so much descending air there creates a high-pressure spot. Air moves from high to low pressure, and the eye of a hurricane is a low-pressure spot, lower than anywhere except the center of a tornado—thus the wind begins to blow from where the outflow jet descends toward the eye of the hurricane, and the hurricane in turn moves on the wind—opposite the direction of the outflow jet. The outflow jet works like the open end of a released toy balloon, blowing the hurricane around the ocean.

It works like a toy balloon blowing around the room in another sense too, for the outflow jet's position is not stable with regard to the hurricane; just as the nozzle swings around the balloon as the balloon moves, the outflow jet wanders around the outside of the hurricane. Thus a hurricane with an outflow jet can quite suddenly move forward or backward, contradict the steering current (the winds at about 20,000 feet that normally determine the path of the hurricane), accelerate, or loop around. One hurricane can have more than one outflow jet. Bigger hurricanes are more apt to have outflow jets, which is why some of the biggest killers among hurricanes in history have been not only the ones with the strongest winds and storm surges, but also the least predictable ones and the ones that have suddenly lurched off their expected paths to slam into coasts they were supposed to bypass.

Carla has just realized that if the very biggest hurricanes are apt to have outflow jets—indeed, sometimes more than one outflow jet—then the biggest one in history is all but certain to.

It only takes her an hour playing with the model to see what's going on. The biggest hurricanes on record up till now have outflow jets just strong enough to let them fight slowly upstream against a steering current. Almost always a hurricane follows the steering current, and the outflow jet, if there is one, modifies but does not control what happens. In a normal hurricane, that unpredictable outflow jet is a secondary force in the motion—the primary force is still the highly predictable steering current and the equally predictable Coriolis force.

But Clem is so much bigger, Carla realizes, and it's another case where things don't just scale up linearly, where bigger is different. Figure the outflow jet it must have just to move the mass of air to keep itself going— and figure the much bigger pressure gradient between where all that air comes down and the much lower pressure than normal in the eye—and all of a sudden the steering current and Coriolis force are secondary. The outflow jet is what's moving the thing.

Outflow jets are not *completely* unpredictable. They tend to move around the hurricane in a counterclockwise fashion, though there's a lot of wobble and variation in it and usually they don't last long enough to establish a pattern. Further, when the hurricane does follow the steering current, it will tend to drag the outflow jet around behind itself, and thus end up running in the direction of the steering current anyway, though moving faster.

So she knows now—she hopes—both why Clem behaved in a fairly typical way, if you allow for his crossing the cold spot in the middle of the Pacific and getting bigger instead of shrinking, and why he's now moving west to east in a completely unprecedented way. And if she really understands, she can do some predicting. Not only can Clem move west to east, for long periods of time, unlike a typical hurricane, because he has warm water so far north and an outflow jet to move him against the current when he has to. . . .

They have all figured it will reverse any day now, wander up toward Siberia, hit the twelve-degree Celsius water south of the Bering, and die into thunderstorms, maybe striking a glancing blow at Hawaii or Japan on the way. But if she's right, that's not it at all.

She gets her data together, models, notes, the works—it takes the better part of four hours to get it all in a form where Di and the team will be able to follow it, and she's red-eyed and exhausted by the time she sits down to make her introductory recording. She takes a big sip of water and says, "Cue in two." The green light on the recorder comes up, and she begins, "Di, what follows is absolutely vital. By the time you get this, there won't be much time. We've got to go public now. Clem is not going to turn back and do something 'normal'—he's going to head still farther east and then south, and he'll keep picking up energy for quite a while. I can't say where he'll make his next landfall, but Clem could easily hit Hawaii square on, or tear down the whole West Coast. We needed to start evacuation planning a week ago; we might have as little as three days till Clem hits something."

Then she sets her alarm to wake her in four hours. The whole inside of the little luxury submarine smells like her gym locker did back in high school, and she just can't make herself care; there are clean sheets in a drawer under her bunk, and a shower six feet from it, and she cannot be bothered to use either. She has no memory of lying down; only of drifting into uneasy dreams until the alarm catapults her from the bunk, still tired but again able to focus.

*   *   *

The more Jesse thinks about it—and he tries not to—the crazier it seems that he's still seeing Synthi, or Mary Ann, since that's what she wants him to call her. It isn't like they have a lot in common (though they do talk quite a bit), and it isn't like the sex is especially wonderful (there isn't any), and it isn't like this thing is serious (though he notices that it seems to be subtly changing him, and that he finds the changes interesting).

For the first week of this strange little affair, he was too sore to try having sex with her again—and to tell the truth, till he got to know her better, he was also afraid of it. He doesn't exactly know what was holding her back, if anything, maybe just his reluctance and maybe just another one of her unguessable whims.

But that wasn't a bad week. They established the basic pattern early—he would come by her house, which is not far from the community college, for *comida* every day. *Comida* is a wonderful meal—to do it justice takes an hour, and then after that an hour of recovery, the traditional *siesta*, is virtually mandatory. Jesse had been here long enough to have fallen into the local patterns of dining, and he found that sitting and gossiping with Mary Ann—she seemed to be fascinated with the day-to-day trivia of his teaching and even with something of what he was teaching—plus receiving all that attention from such a beautiful woman, left him feeling pretty good. Then there would still be time for a nap, and napping with Mary Ann's head lying on his chest, her body pressed against his, was a great pleasure as well, lying there looking up at the perfect blue sky over her courtyard, sometimes talking softly, about books, while he lightly stroked her hair.

Not that they shared much of a taste in books. Jesse tended to like things a little trashier than Mary Ann did, but it was something to talk about, and he was always afraid for that whole first week that they would run out of things to talk about.

After he returned to the community college and worked the last part of the day, Jesse would go back to his place, shower, put on good clothes, and go meet Mary Ann for a long walk in the city, hand in hand, chatting about everything and nothing. She told him a lot of stories about her early days as an actress, and almost nothing about anything that had happened since she was rebuilt into Synthi.

Jesse virtually stopped drinking.

In kind of an offhand way, he supposed Mary Ann didn't know very many real people. He wasn't sure what was more real about him than about her, but the "unreality" of show business people was so commonly talked about that he figured there had to be something in it. He got used to the idea of dating a celebrity and realized after a while that it wasn't really any different from dating anyone else—if anything what was unusual in all this was dating an older woman who really knew what she wanted and didn't mind being in charge. That was what was interesting.

The routine of meeting for *comida*, taking *siesta* together, meeting again for a long walk through town, then eating *cena* together, did not vary for their first week, Monday through Friday. In all that time they only held hands, cuddled, and kissed goodnight.

But today is Saturday, and it's a half day, which means that since it's now noon, Jesse is off for the day. On his way out, José, and his friend Obet, give Jesse a certain amount of teasing about being with an XV star ("*Compadre*, what can you be thinking of? You already know what it is like with this one—"), but the slight edge in it, the feeling that they might even be a little angry, tells him at once that they envy him.

"She's not that different," Jesse says, grinning, letting them think that perhaps she is. "And there's certainly not the volume of crap you have to take with a twenty-year-old."

José shakes his head sadly. "My good friend, my dear friend, it is not that you *had* to take that crap, it is that you *did* take it. What you have here is a woman old enough to know that you can walk away any time and that you do not have to take such crap, and therefore she is wise enough not to give it to you. She just does not know that you would be foolish enough to take it."

"Could be," he grins. "But you could get to like older women, you really could."

"Ah, but when will we get the chance to try, with the great *norteamericano* conquering all the good-bodied women in the city?"

Jesse points at his chest and makes a face. "Me? I don't sew them shut when I'm done, you know."

That sends both his friends into gales of laughter; one great thing about his Mexican friends, they're still capable of shock. Jesse figures it's a lingering effect of Catholicism or something. Anyway, they don't seem to be having any attacks of jealousy or envy anymore, so he says "*Adiós*" and heads up the street.

It isn't so much that Tapachula is a city where nothing happens, he finds himself thinking, as that it's a city where things get done instead of talked about. People work here. And like most people who are working, they're glad enough for interruptions, but they also like to get done. So new gossip is always going to be a mixed blessing—better interruptions, but another thing in the way.

Or, then again, maybe bedding an XV star is something they can imagine happening only to a gringo, and it just seems like one more good thing in life that has been reserved for *los norteamericanos.* He'd like to tell them the truth—that he and Mary Ann have done it only once and he didn't much care for it, that her body feels strange and mechanical, that he isn't sure he has the nerve for another try—but deep down he doubts that they would believe him, and even if they did, probably they would only be angry that an opportunity like that was being wasted on him.

He rounds the corner onto her street; it's very warm already, and the whitewashed buildings are hard to look at against the brilliant blue of the sky around the horizon. He can feel the heat washing off the buildings onto his skin, getting in under the little black crusher that he wears to keep the sun off his face. He takes a moment to sigh, as if pushing hot air out of himself, then walks the last few dozen steps to where the trees overarch her front yard, stepping into the shadows as if he were sliding into a cool pool of water in the jungle.

She comes out the door to greet him, wearing a white dress. After what they've done to her, it's pretty hard for her to come up with anything pretty to wear that won't call attention to her obscene body, but this is not a bad compromise. It swings out away from her in most places (though you can certainly still tell she's huge in the bust), but it's frilly and frivolous and looks more like a little-girl smock than anything else. She's coiled her hair under a floppy sun hat as well, and she looks like nothing so much as the little girls in baggy clothing on an old calendar.

"You look terrific," Jesse says, meaning it.

She beams up at him, and he notices that they either didn't erase—or chose to leave—a light spray of freckles across her snub nose. He kisses her, shyly, on the cheek, and she hugs him, enthusiastically.

"I thought we'd just wander around the city, maybe take in a movie but probably just sit in a café or on a park bench," she says. "There aren't any other big attractions I know of."

"If you want to be my date for it, I'm invited to a party tonight," Jesse says. "Bunch of Lefties, everything from old-style Stalinistas to Deepers to plain-vanilla ULs. At least half of them will deplore your existence and the other half will want to talk to you about how exploited you are."

"I deplore everyone's existence and I love to talk about how exploited I am. Wallowing in self-pity is one of the things I do best. I'm used to handling myself in public, Jesse. And I wouldn't mind meeting some new faces."

"Well, then," he says, "that's at about nine tonight. Tapachula time, that means it won't start till ten, and Leftie time, that means it won't really get moving until close to midnight. So I'd say we still have quite a bit of wandering time ahead of us. Take my arm, madam?"

"Sure. Except when we're crossing streets. I don't want you to be mistaken for a Boy Scout."

Stepping out of the shadows of her front yard is like stepping inside a turned-on searchlight; it's blazing hot and dry, and there's piercing white light everywhere.

They spend an hour or so that afternoon wandering around the streets, looking at people enjoying their day off. Most of the time they walk hand in hand.

For some reason—maybe because out here they have to keep the subject of the conversation quiet—they talk quite a bit about sex. They've teased about it before, many times, Jesse pretending he's afraid she'll attack him again, Mary Ann asking him what it's like to hump the Michelin Man. But this has an edge in it that suggests a certain seriousness.

Another reason for discussing it in low murmurs, out in public, is the endless interruptions that keep it from getting too intense; Jesse's students stop to say hello and be introduced, and there are dozens of little carts with interesting food that has to be considered (and usually rejected), and sometimes the time is just better for walking along slowly and staring up the white street. Thus they are perpetually, pleasantly, called away from their flirting, and they don't get back to that topic too quickly.

"Jesse, do you suppose we could ever have ended up together any other way?" she asks, abruptly. She isn't looking at him.

He glances sideways, sees only the side of her sun hat. "I hadn't thought about it at all."

"Well, I have. And I've concluded this is absolutely the only way we could have ended up together. So I'm very glad it happened." She sighs. Jesse notices a couple strands of flame red hair escaping from her sun hat, and brushes them back. She looks at him and smiles. "All I mean is it took strange circumstances to throw us together, but there was a lot I had forgotten and lost track of in my life. . . ."

Oh, it's going to be one of these. Jesse figured out a while ago that although they did a lot of conditioning to make her into Synthi Venture, there's a lot of Mary Ann Waterhouse that never required any conditioning. For one thing, she tends to communicate in this sort of deep-emotion-speak made up of phrases from old movies. She rambles on a little about "getting it back together" and "refocusing her energies" and so forth, leading up to the conclusion that she sees Jesse "as a gateway person in my life." He's not sure what it all means except that she's glad they're together; he used to talk this way when he was trying to get girls into bed with the old sensitive-artistic-young-man routine, but it doesn't feel like she's particularly trying to seduce him.

He lets an arm slide up around her shoulders, feeling how small she really is, and pulls her close to him. The street is all but deserted, with just two other couples walking far away from them. The street leads to a not-impressive little fountain that plays halfheartedly in the brilliant sunlight and he guides her to the rim of the fountain, and then they sit down, and he kisses her.

This is the first real kiss since that awful first night—he's kissed her goodnight a few times but it's just been a peck on the lips—and he's surprised at how gentle, and how responsive, she is. She seems to want him to take the lead, her mouth soft and shyly probing at his. The kiss goes on for a long time, and when it's over she's smiling like a young kid after her first one.

"I haven't been kissed that way in a long, long time," she says. "I guess I'm a little surprised that I can still feel it."

"Well, since you could, how was it?"

"Divine, dammit. Think I'd tell you if it wasn't? Anyway, now that we've done the corny kissing-by-the-fountain routine, and the corny walking-around-hand-in-hand routine—"

"Fear not," he says. "I have something just as corny up my sleeve. There's a *licuado* stand around the corner. It's run by the sister of one of my students, so she probably won't slip us any rotten fruit."

She blinks at him innocently. "What's a *licuado?*"

"Aha," he says. "Wealthy tourist ladies don't get out and mix with the people much, do they?"

"Just so it isn't Spanish for 'dog vomit,' or something. I don't want this to turn out to be anything like the Vegemite trick."

Jesse grins at her. "Nope. Not in the least. And I've already fallen for Vegemite once, which is about as often as anyone could be expected to."

"Me too. Rock is evil. He talked me into trying Vegemite while we were doing a story about the deterioration of the Great Barrier Reef."

"Yeah, there were three Australian students at U of the Az who threw a 'snacks around the world' potluck; naturally they brought Vegemite and ate everyone else's stuff. That wasn't so disgusting, except that then they ate the Vegemite."

"Now *that's* disgusting. So a *licuado* is not some kind of prank?"

"Fresh fruit, milk, and sugar, run through a blender. But the thing is that the milk and the fruit are really fresh, like just bought in the market that morning. Haven't even had time to get lonely for the tree or the cow. Come on—this requires your immediate attention."

They round the corner into the broad *calle*, divided by long low brick planters in which palm trees grow.

Porfirio's sister recognizes Jesse at once, and it's obvious that she's heard from Porfirio who Jesse is involved with, because she's suddenly very shy

and formal around Mary Ann. Mary Ann is polite and warm in return—
Jesse finds himself thinking, *Right, and this way Teresa will tell all of her friends
what an average, normal, but* muy bella *woman Synthi Venture is.*

They get a single gigantic papaya *licuado,* an interesting purplish-pink
shade since the papaya was very ripe and red, and share it using two straws.
That means Mary Ann's sun hat is severely in Jesse's way, and after a few
bumps she takes it off, letting that great mass of strangely red hair spill
down into her lap.

"There's a lot of that," Jesse notes.

"Has to be—most of those styles they put me in involve wrapping it
over all those funny foam supports. I just think of it as being the 3D
equivalent of the old cardboard sheets they used to tape *Cosmo* models'
hair to."

"Lady, I'm just glad they didn't make *everything* synthetic."

"Maybe not synthetic, but the way it's been treated it's pretty callused."

"I was talking about your heart."

"Come to think of it, so was I."

The walk back to her place goes very slowly, but neither of them is
eager or reluctant; something has been settled. The all-but-psychic Señora
Herrera has prepared a cold, buffet-style *comida* for them, which she sends
up to Mary Ann's bedroom.

This time it takes a long time, and it's surprisingly gentle and friendly.
Neither of them tunes in the news, and shouting outside in the street is so
common that they don't hear the news from Hawaii until the next morning.

On June 28, northwest of Midway, sixteen kilometers up, a torrent of wet
air pours along the bottom of the tropopause—the outflow jet for Hurricane
Clem. The jet is huge—it carries the mass flow of several large hurricanes
all by itself. Yet it's invisible; Louie Tynan, far to the south and high above,
can barely perceive it, now that he knows what to look for, with infrared
scanning.

Di Callare and his team, and Carla Tynan in *MyBoat,* have been aware
of it for less than a week but now the outflow jet is occupying most of their
thoughts.

Thus far Clem has been following the steering currents, the winds that
circle clockwise over the North Pacific six kilometers up, rather meekly, like
an elephant allowing itself to be led on a kite-string tether. But if Carla is
right, then at any moment the outflow jet might swing around to some
other point, or a new outflow jet might form, and in either case Clem might
surge off in any direction at all.

When the moment comes, it is late afternoon in the North Pacific, and it's mere coincidence that Louie is watching; by the time he's reaching for the phone to tell Earth about it, the alarms are already sounding and data from the automatic cameras will be funneling into Houston and Washington in a matter of moments.

Still he calls; no one who works with high-tech equipment ever trusts it completely, and this is far too important to leave reporting it to the judgment of some AI. He uses the high-priority code to get through directly to Washington and is rewarded with the sleepy, grouchy face of Harris Diem, who had just gone to bed. "Yes?"

"Mr. Diem, this is Louie Tynan. The outflow jet has just precessed north. Clem is about to veer off track."

"Precessed—north. Where will it come in, do you have an idea yet?"

Louie looks down at the readout the AI is giving him. "Shit. We sure do. Looks like there's an excellent chance Midway gets clobbered, and after that it's about fifty-fifty that one or more of the Hawaiian Islands will get it."

Diem looks down, confirms Louie's numbers, looks back up at him. "Stick around and don't go off to the moon for a bit. Someone might want you to look at some specific things unofficially. If you need to do anything to get comfortable for the next few hours, the next ten minutes would be a good time to do it."

"Roger," Louie says, and turns away from the phone as Diem hangs up.

The outflow jet has swung farther north—indeed, begun to swing to the east. It's obvious to Louie just from naked-eye observation, for there's a sharp edge biting into the spiral of Hurricane Clem, which is where the descending outflow jet is forming a high-pressure area.

He sends a copy of the basic results to Di's team number, so that the data will be available once Diem or Pauliss wakes up Di Callare, and then copies Carla on it, though she's probably too far submerged to get it for a while.

Then, long practice taking hold of him, he orders sandwiches and coffee from the automatic galley, and goes to the head. Diem is absolutely right— you never know.

As the outflow jet takes up its new position relative to the storm, the winds all around shift; air flows from high to low pressure, and there is no lower pressure at sea level than in Clem's center, nor higher pressure than the descent point of the outflow jet. If Clem were a physical object, sheer mass would make the hurricane take a long time to slow down and change direction, but a hurricane is not an object, it's a process: it converts the angular momentum of the inward spiraling air into the power of its winds, but it does not itself have momentum.

So when it suddenly turns 110 degrees to the right, swinging wildly into a new trajectory, it does not slow down and then accelerate like an ocean liner or a truck; it just changes direction.

The best news, from the standpoint of the world's governments, is that it happens exactly when the North American East Coast is getting ready for bed, and that it takes a while for the significance of the story to become apparent, so by the time word is breaking on XV one of the big population belts has gone to bed.

Unfortunately this puts it on the morning news for Europe and the evening news for East Asia.

Thus Carla Tynan, surfacing for the last run into Pohnpei, is aware of the situation not long after it happens, sets her autopilot, and gets to work; Di, rousted from bed by Henry Pauliss's phone call, apologizes to Lori, grabs the bag he has been keeping packed, and catches the zipline to DC.

At four in the morning, Di is at his desk, with a huge mug of coffee in front of him. Gretch runs over from the intern's dorm and gets put in charge of point plotting and data patterning; Pete and Wo Ping arrive next, sharing a ride, then Mohammed. Just as they begin to worry, Talley comes in, a Self Defender protruding conspicuously from her purse. She lives in a bad neighborhood, she explains, and figured it was better to walk down the street with her hand visibly on that than to get delayed by anyone trying anything. "If I have to fire it, the radio signal would bring cop cars from everywhere and I'd end up talking to cops all night," she says with a shrug.

She's perfectly made up, and Di wonders for an idle moment if she was interrupted in a date or perhaps while out at a club. Strange that she never seems tired in the morning.

John Klieg catches it on the evening news and notes with grim satisfaction that another private space-launch company, Consolidated Launch, is based at Naalehu on the Big Island. It isn't as important as the heavy-lift facility at Kingman, but anyplace that can't put up a satellite is going to make Klieg richer and there's a splendid chance that, with its exposed gantries sitting a full kilometer out in the sea, and its pipelines running down across the beaches, Naalehu will be out of action within days, leaving the USA with only the air launch facility at Edwards.

All in all, in two weeks since Clem formed, he's cut the global supply of available launches by a very satisfying forty percent; Klieg knows it will be Hassan, with congratulations, when the phone rings. Too bad about all those people, but as Hassan says, compassion speaks well of its holder but does little for its recipient.

Brittany Hardshaw knows ten minutes after Harris Diem does, and she's dressed and sleeping off and on in a cot by the Oval Office. The alarms are going out to Hawaii by every possible means, and at least it's early evening there and it's easy to get the word out. Remembering the pictures from Micronesia, the crashed space facility at Kingman, and all the XV coverage of the wrecked old folks' home on Saipan, the Hawaiians are responding as she would have hoped, digging in and filling sandbags, getting everyone and everything that can be moved back into the mountains. Still, if any of the islands take the full force of Clem, it won't be nearly enough.

The Navy decides to take no chances and works all night to evacuate Midway; fortunately the USS *George Bush* and its carrier group are at hand already, so they're able to just shove everyone and anything aboard the carrier and everything else that will float, and run for Pearl Harbor, leaving the island unoccupied. When President Hardshaw gets word that the fleet has departed and is making all speed, she heaves a sigh of relief; it's late afternoon now in Washington, and it looks like Clem is going to go through the Hawaiian chain right between Lisianski and Laysan—near enough to give Midway a pounding and to hit the main islands with monster waves, but a long way from Oahu, Maui, or Hawaii itself. And Admiral Singh on the *Bush* seems to think the carrier group can ride it out and still make it to Pearl. Bad enough—but they'll make it.

Before he goes home for the day, Harris Diem finds he's called into the New Oval Office one more time.

"It's time," Hardshaw says. "We need to get all the attention on Clem if Rivera and I are going to get the powers we need."

"It still sounds strange for you to say 'Rivera and I,' " Diem notes. "You sound bitter."

"Yeah, a little. May I sit, boss?"

"You don't need to ask and you know it. What's the matter?"

"I keep thinking, who are you, where is the real Brittany Lynn Hardshaw, and what have you done with her?" Diem sighs. "Somebody works for more than a decade to get us back out from under the UN thumb—and it hasn't been easy, with them paying the bills at the start and our having to practically rent out the armed forces as peacekeeping units—the goal is within reach, and . . . what? You bring them back in. You know damned well we could dominate the world after Clem."

"If there's a world to dominate, Harris. That's the big if. No point in being just the least wounded of the critical cases."

He shrugs. "Oh, I understand the logic. And you're maneuvering Rivera into our pocket, and that's good too. But I just . . . well, a lot of this is sticking in my craw. I know when you said it's time, you mean time to shaft Henry Pauliss. And he's kind of an old friend and protégé. He trusts me. He won't know what it's about."

"Harris, you and I have both sent friends to their death," Hardshaw says softly. "I'm not sure that I'm the one who's changing."

Diem sighs and shrugs. "I used to understand in my guts what we were doing. Nowadays I just understand the reasons in my head. Boss, we've always delivered the goods to the people we served—they wanted crooks behind bars, we gave'em that; they wanted to squirm out from under the UN, we gave'em that; they wanted us to rescue the Afropeans and we did it. We did it by getting our hands on the power we needed and using it. We didn't do it by organizing great big 'let's hate the hurricane' media campaigns, or trying to persuade people to take the problem seriously, or any of that. And we made sure that people either worked for us or regretted it. Now I see all this balancing and juggling, and, yeah, I know, I understand, it's a different world, the planet could be at stake . . . but I just don't understand it like I used to."

She nods. "Fair enough. Can you still do what I ask? I need a big scandal, I need someone to stomp on, and it needs to be a scandal related to Clem. Can you give me Henry Pauliss to take the fall?"

"Yeah. No problem."

In a curiously formal way, they shake hands before he goes. Diem heads home, goes down to the basement, and gives in to the craving, rampaging through half of his wedges; later, raw and sore, he falls into a deep, dreamless—but not at all refreshing—sleep.

The first news of it Jesse and Mary Ann get comes on the TV—not XV, Mary Ann won't have that in the house—just as they are rising from the *siesta*, at about four in the afternoon. By that time things have been going on for quite a while, and there's already footage (shot by a Navy staticopter out of Pearl on an emergency some-good-publicity-at-last basis) of the carrier group making all speed to the south and east. Analysts are explaining it all over the place, and besides *Scuttlebytes*, there's a fresh edition of *Sniffings*.

"Do you believe the stuff she puts in that?" Mary Ann asks Jesse, curling against him and pulling his hand into her waist.

"Quite a bit of it. She interviewed my brother once, and he was pretty impressed. She occasionally calls him for background info."

"Really? I always have trouble believing the news in *Sniffings*."

Jesse nods. "What did you find so hard to believe?"

"I suppose just its take on the world. I don't see what she's getting at, what kind of story she thinks it is. Instead, it's always like she's so dedicated to being flat that she takes the voice and the story out of it; she might as well be reading a stock ticker or something. And she doesn't look like much, you know; I mean, her appearance is professional but she doesn't do anything to make herself very grabbing, and anyway it's all these interviews and graphs and things. You can get a lot about what's happening and stuff—if you believe what she's saying—but you can't get anything about how it all hooks together, and if it doesn't hook together it doesn't feel real."

"I suppose," Jesse says. "Di says my old man is a big fan of hers. In fact, it says on the news a lot of the old people think she's great. I guess because it's more like the news was like when they were kids."

"Ugh. I don't remember the old TV news from the first time it was out very much, but by the time I was in high school we used to watch a lot of old news programs in history class, and I remember how dull *that* was."

Jesse thinks and nods. "I see what you mean. The news didn't used to *say* much, did it?"

"Exactly. It didn't. And this bunch of ships in the middle of the ocean—"

"Running like hell from a hurricane," Jesse says. "That's pretty dramatic. And there're kids and moms and so forth on the carrier—they had a little school and apartment complex on Midway Island for dependents."

"Yeah, but we don't have any sense of *who* they are except people in a news story," Mary Ann points out. She's now sitting up and very alert; Jesse realizes that they're on her home territory here and naturally she has a lot to say. "That's the basic insight that Doug Llewellyn had, the thing that made Passionet big is that what's important to people is people they know. Lots of people used to watch the old news just to see the old-style anchormen, which made sense. The way you feel that something is important and know what it's about is by watching how someone important to you reacts. After all, that's how we all learned to react to the news as kids. The trouble with the old kind of news was that it could show you pictures of things but it couldn't put you there. I mean, imagine if the Holocaust had been covered letting people feel like they were the guards—"

"Or like they were going into the ovens themselves," Jesse suggests, feeling morbid.

"Well, since you put it that way, yeah. And for that matter, imagine what it might have been like to be in the astronauts' heads for the first spaceflights."

"Well, we all know what it was like to be in Colonel Tynan's head for the Mars landing, anyway. Yeah, I suppose you're right—the people on that ship are kind of faceless to me. On the other hand, I'm still pretty interested in whether or not they make it."

"Yeah, but think about what it would be like to be standing on the deck." Her eyes are faraway and a little sad; Jesse recognizes the melodrama in it—she is striking one of her "I must get back to work someday" poses.

"You could get killed," Jesse says firmly, as he does every time she does this.

"Ah—but the royalties my estate would make on *that!*" She grins at him.

"Don't worry, I'm not going to abandon you to drab, wretched reality all *that* soon. But I am starting to think about the biz again . . . and that's kind of the way you have to think. It *is* dangerous, you know . . . always has been. Ernie Pyle didn't die in bed."

"He never met you."

She snorts, hits him with a pillow from the sofa, and then they get into a tickle fight; by the time they look back at the screen the station is showing baseball scores.

Half an hour before Mary Ann and Jesse watch the television clip of the evacuation of Midway, Clem's outflow jet kicks around again, to almost due northwest. By now Clem's eye is centered near 169W 31N, and its outer winds are tearing into Midway, hundreds of kilometers away, with a Beaufort scale force of 19—more than enough to tear down buildings and hurl small boats up onto the shore; what the Japanese air raids of 1942 could not do is accomplished in a matter of a few minutes on the evacuated base. Strong buildings stand, but with their windows shattered and often with their roofs stripped off like peels from bananas; weaker buildings, poles holding wires, piers, and all the other structures exposed to the full fury of the wind are ripped into pieces and scattered out to sea or hurled against what is still standing. Every palm tree on the island is laid flat, and by the time the immense wave rolls over the wreckage, there is little enough left standing to knock down.

The wave was just a by-blow, however, a mere sideswipe, for Clem is already on its way south and west, and the part of the wave that struck Midway was only a corner of the main body. The base is scoured off the face of Sand Island, and the World War II ruins still remaining on East Island disappear with it; when the sun comes out again, still days away, it will show smaller islands, with the sand islets gone. The only signs of life will be the bare faces of the airstrips on each island, and the foundations of Pan Am's old Midway Hotel. By that time, no one will be interested in looking.

The hurricane is moving roughly parallel to the southeastward sweep of the Hawaiian Islands, but not perfectly so, and all lines that are not parallel eventually converge; the question now is where those lines are going to converge, and whether Clem will stay on his. Di Callare does not go home; Lori sends him a packed lunch and some clean clothes, and he showers at work, changes, gratefully eats the lunch, and is working again before he really knows that he has been taking any time off, with just a vague impression that Lori is out there and that she loves him.

Darkness crawls across the Atlantic toward America, reaches Brazil, marches on up the face of South America, rolls across the Caribbean and

North America, and Clem, still basking in the sun of late afternoon in the Pacific, continues to gather speed and to swing inward toward the islands. It is now too late to hope that major damage can be avoided—if you take the distance at which the winds fall to Beaufort force 12, the standard definition of a hurricane, then Hurricane Clem is just under 3,000 km in diameter—that is, it is about four times as big in area as Alaska.

But the great majority of that area is merely hurricane; that is, not bigger or worse than most typhoons or hurricanes. It is only the relatively small area around the eye that is producing the giant waves, and though no instruments have yet survived long enough to report, from the size of the waves it is inferred that at the eye wall the wind must be of tornadic velocities—half a Mach or so. Hawaii will take a hurricane, and because Clem is big and takes a long time to pass even at its extraordinary speed, Hawaii will take that hurricane for a longer than usual time—but it may be *just* a hurricane, if they are lucky.

Already they have been lucky in that the true tsunami-sized waves emerging from Clem's core have been largely running parallel to the islands; their tips have battered the rocky coasts of the northwestern sides of the islands, but though the waves are preternaturally big, that side of Hawaii is steep and strong, and little harm has been done—a coastal road washed out here, a narrow beach there, one lighthouse destroyed, but nothing like what could have happened had the waves come from the other side.

The immediate concern is rain. Clem is throwing vast amounts of it into the whole chain, and Hawaii is steep; the bare mountaintops of most of the islands are guiding the rain down onto lower slopes in hundreds and thousands of suddenly formed fast-flowing rivers, blocking and cutting roads that are vitally needed to evacuate the north and east sides of the islands.

Hardshaw wonders if any president since Roosevelt or Truman has even been aware of the existence of Hawaii 11; yesterday she had no concern at all with whether Hawaii even *had* any state highways, but that particular road has been washed out by flash floods and mudslides at four points between Hilo and Pahala, and worse yet many of the traffic control stations on it are down, so that not only is the evacuation from Hilo to South Kona blocked up (the Corps of Engineers has crews out on all those places, trying to get temporary bridges up in the howling wind and blinding rain, and somewhere she already has a list of six soldiers who've died in the effort), but insofar as people *can* move, they are having to drive themselves on bad roads—and many younger drivers have never had real manual control of a car except briefly in driver's ed. There are accidents all up and down the line, and each of them traps more motorists on a highway liable to more wash-outs. . . .

We're going to lose a few thousand lives at least, Hardshaw thinks to herself. Inconceivable; to be the President of the USA, in time of peace, to have so many resources at her disposal, and to be unable to do one damned thing.

She feels herself relax; she has thought the worst, and now she will be all right. Yes, she is going to lose several thousand citizens. Many of them will die on that highway, due to the Federal evacuation orders, but many more who have elected to stay put will die in Hilo. The blame will not fall too hard in any one direction; Hardshaw's political team can have most Americans saying "It's a terrible thing, but what can anyone do?" in short order, if they aren't already.

She looks over her listing of other news. The evacuation fleet from Midway has turned to run away from the storm—she remembers something vaguely about it being better to take a storm on the stern or the bow rather than broadside—and will try to get around far enough to make a run for Yokohama. Every aircraft that could make it out before weather closed the airports has headed for the West Coast, and since what could be packed onto them were mainly the dependents of servicepeople, there will be thousands of young wives and their children clogging the airports, desperate for news, from San Diego up to Portland. She posts a quick note that local military commanders are to "render humanitarian assistance" and that it's particularly important, notes Harris Diem has already written a similar note.

It's dark outside now, and the night is going to be long. Sometime tomorrow whatever is the worst will have happened; Brittany Lynn Hardshaw is praying, more sincerely but with less faith than she has in many years, for an anticlimax.

Darkness moves on, crossing the West Coast, grinding its way on to the Pacific. XV communications require such enormous bandwidth, and so many links to Hawaii have been lost by wind-smashed antennas, that only television and telephone are now going through.

That doesn't absolve Ed Porter from his job; one of Passionet's best editors, he is based in Honolulu to handle the Pacific traffic, and even though he can't get anything from the rest of the world, there is plenty happening right here on Oahu. He turned down the offer of evacuation because he figured that up here, above the city in Dowsett Highlands, is probably about as safe as anywhere they're evacuating people to.

Right now there are just two people wired to transmit to Passionet on Oahu, which would normally mean Porter would be assembling a pretty thin documentary for eventual distribution. But Candy and Bill are a special case if ever there was one, and another example, Ed thinks, that Doug Llewellyn knows what he's doing.

Much as Ed hates to admit it, because working on "Dream Honeymoon" has been one royal pain in the ass.

Bill and Candy are unmodified; Candy's breasts and buttocks are the ones that grew naturally, Bill's muscles are not the least bit enhanced, and neither of them has been given any training in maintaining an untransmitted persona.

The gimmick was a promotion, originally—let us wire you three months before the wedding, and you get a year's luxury honeymoon on us. There was a certain discreet kind of rigging in the contest, too, not in the selection but in carefully making sure that most of the entrants would be like Bill and Candy, solid-citizen young Heartlanders who dressed a little behind the fashions and believed in doing everything the old-fashioned way.

Candy's hairstyle is about five years behind what's currently flat and a bit overdone, her cosmetics are ten years behind and way overdone, and her favorite topics of conversation are how much they spend at each place on the way and what there is to eat. Bill dresses like what he is—an assistant manager of data patterning for a bank, and complains about the food in a good-natured way—he'd live on steak, pizza, and tacos if he could, because he hates "foreign food." He is always a bit disgruntled to discover that yet another foreign place is nothing like Sylvania, Ohio.

Ed Porter thinks that they are the two most boring people he's ever taken signal from, but "Dream Honeymoon" is selling like nothing before or since, and this special recording can be dropped into the regular news, thus boosting sales still further.

Right now Bill and Candy are still in the Royal Hawaiian Hotel, the last people left there except for a couple of managers who are closing the place down preparatory to running for the hills. Ed figures that the Royal Hawaiian has managed to survive a long time, even located right down on the beach at Waikiki, and thus probably Bill and Candy are safe . . . and of course, if they're *not*— Porter banishes the thought. Of course they are.

But if they aren't, Passionet will have the monster hit wedge of the decade.

Right now they're standing by their pricey window, facing the beach. Ed had suggested they dress in clothes they could run away in, if it came to that, but of course neither of them has the hiking clothes that would be appropriate, and besides, he's persuaded Bill it's pretty safe, so Candy is in one of those little look-at-my-body nighties made of cheap, shiny fabric that have been de rigueur for newlyweds since the 1970s. She's got jeans, sneakers, underwear, and a tight little knit top that may not be practical but is at least informal stacked by the door, presumably so that if the hotel begins to fall down she can change clothes before running out of it.

Bill has his own pile of pants, shirt, shorts, socks, and shoes next to hers. He's standing there in his bikini briefs, and Ed finds himself chuckling. Not only does Candy figure she'll have time to dress to flee, Bill figures he'd better change his undies, too.

Porter clicks into signal and feels . . .

. . . Bill is more afraid than he wants Candy to know, and even though everyone at Passionet has been really nice to them for these first few weeks, he has to admit that he doesn't have anyone in the company he feels is a friend. (Fuzz that into general anxiety, Porter thinks.) Bill wonders how the hell he got into this.

Not that he wouldn't have been here anyway—everyone in his family since his grandparents has always done a Hawaiian honeymoon, it's what you *do* if you're in the Sylvania Country Club and go to U of Toledo and come back to take over the family business, like being Presbyterian or Methodist, like voting Republican, like having season tickets to lots of things at your old schools.

This is not an easy process for Bill to think his way through. He'd have been here anyway, but without Passionet . . . well, maybe they'd only have stayed a night or two at the Royal Hawaiian. Probably not even that. The truth is that he's not sure what you really get for the inflated tab, the food doesn't eat that much better than home, the beds are a little too firm, everything feels like a museum, and the outside of the building looks like the kind of pink concrete castle that they have at malls for toy stores. There're lots of more modern places that aren't far off the beach that would have suited him just fine.

Candy's trembling and it's not because she's cold.

Why did he let that Porter guy, who always seems to be laughing at some damn thing or other that isn't funny, talk them into staying here? Porter's way to hell and gone up in the hills and now Bill's down here with his wife . . .

My wife, Bill thinks, and pulls Candy closer. That was probably it, he figured. You couldn't go and look scared in front of her. She was counting on you to be the one that wasn't scared. If he'd been talking to Porter by himself he might have managed to win the argument and get them on that bus out of town, up into the mountains, but in front of Candy . . . oh well, spilt milk and so on. He holds her closer and tries not to notice that he's finding her presence very comforting.

Porter fuzzes out the specifics again; damn it, Bill is having all kinds of great feelings, notably a bare veneer of control over stark terror, and a sort of wanting to curl up on a woman's lap and hide thing that's got a tasty bit of Oedipal kink to it, but he keeps fixating on how they happen to be there, and Passionet has to be kept in the background—the experiencers don't like to be reminded that the stars are wired, or that someone wired them and is standing between star and experiencer.

Flip over to Candy. Oh, now this is nice. She's scared out of her mind and beginning to think that Bill is a complete fool, but she's also feeling very much like a little girl and wanting him to be Daddy.

Through her eyes he watches the big waves—nothing like the storm surges, they're on the other side of the island from Clem, but just the echoes and stirrings of the surges are enough to produce record surf—rolling up into the lights along the beach out of the black ocean, coated with foam on all sides. Her breath catches as one rolls up farther than before and slaps a load of foam up onto Kalakaua Avenue, and it seems to her that through the thick carpet under her feet she can feel the building groan.

She snuggles closer to Bill and tries to think positively; all her life that's been the one thing she can always do. This is a great adventure and maybe there's something in the contract or somewhere that they get more money for getting through something like this. This will be something for Bill and her to tell the kids about forever. This will all be over by dawn, and when they get up late they'll find the hotel employees are already back at their posts and there's a nice big breakfast—for Bill, of course.

Porter snickers. Bill certainly eats and he's going to be built like a side of beef, but Candy's not that far behind him; her trim little tummy is soft and flabby, her breasts are high and perky only because they're new, and in five years she'll be subsiding into a soggy Midwestern lard meringue like her mother and sisters. He enjoys the snicker a lot—it makes him feel better, and relieves some of the fear that's been leaking through from Candy. One problem with editing, especially when you're getting signal off an untrained mind, is that like it or not, you end up sympathizing. And Porter doesn't like it at all.

He pops back to Bill and discovers the poor dumb bastard has screwed up some courage from somewhere and is managing to keep the tremble out of his arms and voice as he whispers to Candy that it's going to be okay, really it is, and won't they have something to tell the relatives about.

It seems to put some heart in her, for she turns back to him and smiles. "We can't tell them, honey, they've already been there and been us."

Bill snorts. "Guess you're right at that. Well, at least we'll really have something to *be* for them."

She snuggles back against him, and his hand strokes the slick fabric that covers the small of her back; the little spaghetti straps on her shoulders tighten, and her breasts rise just a fraction. God, it couldn't get more perfect . . . these kids have such limited imaginations that with a little luck they are really going to— "And you know," she says, "it's just common sense that we're perfectly safe here anyway, hon. They aren't going to lose all they've invested in us."

Nitwit bitch, Porter thinks. Have to fill in there with footage of the monster waves rolling in, and maybe get an actor to overdub some kind of fear onto it, and it still won't work.

Bill grins. "On top of everything else, you really have guts, honey. I'm so glad we got married and had the chance to do this. Even if it does mean . . ." He grins, feeling mischief rising, his fear sinking away, and looking into Bill's mind, Porter laughs with elation. *Yes! We are going to get the full effect—right out of* From Here to Eternity. *Pity I can't figure out a way to make him take her down to the beach and hose her where there's a chance of them being swept out to sea.*

All those blonde curls and that overdone makeup swirl in a little pose that Porter figures she must have learned from experiencing Synthi Venture—though, god knows, this one could never be one percent of the pro Synthi is. But then, not being a pro is the point of this whole stupid exercise in bucolic sentimentality. . . .

"Now what does that mean?" she says, pouting just a little and unconsciously tugging her nightie down a bit, so that she pops out of it a little more. Porter concedes that the little cow does have a nice set of udders.

"Oh, just . . . well, I sure wasn't the only guy who was ever interested in you, and now if they want to know . . . uh, what it's like—"

She giggles. "Oh, god, Bill, you know all they get to find out is what I'm like with you. I'd never be that hot with anyone else, lover, and you know it."

"Maybe," he murmurs, letting his hand slide up her thigh.

The window thumps as if a body had been thrown against it, but it doesn't break; an instant later they hear a screaming crash and the howl of the gust breaks on them from the eaves. Both jump and their terror returns instantly.

Shit, Porter thinks, that was one great spike of fear but he'd really like to have some more sex in the mix. . . .

"Sounds like they lost a gutter into the parking lot," Bill says, making himself sound a lot more casual than he's feeling. "Glad our rental's insured." His heart is halfway up his throat but he can tell Candy needs him to be calm and he's going to be.

Zap, let's get the Candy view—wow. Unfuckingreal. The poor bimbo is going for it. Porter plugs straight on in and gets the full load. Candy is looking at this big, square, back-slapping halfwit who's never had a thought in his life, with his fake good-sport qualities and his unformed good looks shortly to vanish under wattles of fat, and somehow she's seeing Superman. This bovine lump looks like a hero to her. . . .

Candy has never seen Bill like this before. She can hear the strength and calm in his voice, and now she really does know it's perfectly safe. She's sorry she jumped like that, considering that he was probably working his way around to some loving and she could really use that just now. So she winks and says, "Well, at least since everyone else has run off, we don't have to pull any shades if I want to show you something. . . ."

"Show me what?" he asks. Porter hops back and finds that, as sometimes happens, playing brave has gotten rid of Bill's fear. *They* are *going to. Wow, this couldn't get more perfect. Passionet is going to ship billions.*

She shows him, pulling her nightie shyly high enough to reveal her tidy, carefully shaped patch of pubic hair. Porter makes sure both sides are recording—they'll want a men's and a women's version of this part—and feels the surge of Bill's erection answering.

Bill is unexpectedly rough with her, which is just fine from Porter's standpoint—less need to amp the sensations, which always adds so much distortion—and for some odd reason she likes it this time. Probably because he seems like more of a big strong man when he's grabbing her by the breasts, surprisingly soft and baggy to the touch, and pushing her back against the wall. He jabs his penis, so stiff it trembles, forward between her thighs, misses, grunts with the pain of bending it a bit against a plump buttock, and she reaches down and guides it into her completely relaxed and sopping wet vagina. He thrusts his penis in and out of her furiously, gasping with the speed and exertion.

Porter, editing together a Bill track, a Candy track, and a both-together track on the fly for three different editions, is far too busy, but this is hot even for him, with all his experience of experiencing. He doesn't have a hand free to help himself but he still comes when Candy has her first explosive orgasm.

And it's not just hot, both of them are giving this wonderful scattershot montage of all sorts of feelings and thoughts about each other, as if some-how . . .

. . . their lives were passing before their eyes, Porter realizes, as he starts to come down off the induced high. They're still banging away, Candy's head bouncing back off the wall (she'll wonder why it hurts later, Porter figures) and Bill pushing into her with all the force of his thighs, all but lifting her off the floor.

It's a pointlessly morbid thought. Their lives are not passing before their eyes, and besides, Porter has edited dozens of wedges that included right-up-to-death material and that never has happened.

He dismisses it and focuses on getting all those memories to edit into a more composed montage. Who'd have thought these two lumps of cheese would have all this stuff in them? Vintage Heartland Americana mixed with good solid porn—

Candy hanging out in some student bar and Bill's first sight of her, as she looked over her shoulder at him and he got one of those perfect hair-tit-butt shots that a hundred years of movies, TV, and XV have taught most of the women on Earth to do—and poor old stupid Bill reacted as if neither he nor anyone else had ever seen such a thing before—

Long corny walk in Oak Openings Park on one of those rare October days when the sun shines and the leaves look decent in Ohio, holding hands, itching to get some privacy and scrog till they're sore but delaying it because both of them thought this was a happy moment, and surprise, it was . . . amber sunlight hitting Candy's rather ordinary enhanced-blonde hair and turning it into a movie gold.

Bill's moment of terror on Christmas Eve when he reached into his pocket and couldn't find the engagement ring and wondered how he'd ever explain the minuscule heap of gifts he had for her—and the moment of relief as he found it. His pleasant surprise to realize that that moment was going to be the worst of it, asking her wasn't half as scary . . . and then going to the Methodist Church together and singing carols by candlelight and the hot chocolate afterward (Porter is finding this all so Mom and Pop American that he wants to vomit, but he knows the audience out there will eat this right up)—and then, fabulous! the memory includes a stolen kiss and Bill realizing he can smell his own semen on her breath—

Candy has an explosive, crying, screaming orgasm, and before it's over Bill is spurting into her. Porter gleefully logs the works. Passionet will be making money off this a hundred years from now.

They sink slowly to the carpet, still holding each other, very tenderly now, just beginning to feel how sore they will be. Bill cradles Candy's head in his hands and kisses her; her mouth is slack and open, and as Porter pops over to her mind he finds that she's all but unconscious with bliss, little aftershocks of pleasure still rolling up from her aching vulva.

Then the first peak gust hits. In the high winds of a hurricane, wind can gust to double and triple velocity. This gust, coming in from the sea, shatters the windows on the building, all at once. The two newlyweds have just time enough to look up and see the windowpanes hit the pink wall and burst into dust; Candy draws breath for a scream.

Ed Porter catches the jag of fear and is himself terrified, for one moment, before he can detach to notice what a grand and gorgeous piece of material he has grabbed here.

Candy's scream and Bill's moan of terror are drowned as the door bursts out into the hallway—there is a terrible thunder as all the internal doors shatter or fall through.

The force exerted on a structure by wind is a function of two things: the square of the speed of the wind, and the relative roughness of the surface presented to the wind. Anything that makes the flow turbulent will increase the drag and hence the delivered force of the wind. This is why a car with open windows must burn so much more gasoline to maintain the same speed as one with closed windows—the open windows split up and mix the airflow, pit it against itself, make it turbulent.

The gust is already dwindling back to the original wind speed, but it is too late for Bill and Candy. The force on the outside of the Royal Hawaiian Hotel would be six times what it was at the moment of their orgasm—but that was before air began to circulate through the shattered windows and the myriad doorways and corridors of the interior. The additional turbulence increases the coupling—the percentage of energy from the wind that goes into the structure instead of passing over it—by many times.

Before their lungs empty with their shrieks of fear, the soft pink walls of the Royal Hawaiian shred and break, the great central tower cracks and begins to fall back away from the sea, the interior walls and floors, hit by aerodynamic lift in a dozen directions, break from the studs to fly against each other, and the blacktop roof peels up like the lid of a sardine can and sails away inland like a loose bedsheet in a thunderstorm, bursting into pieces as it goes.

The lurches prove too much for the structural members, and the Royal Hawaiian collapses, the great winds tearing off pieces as big as automobiles to hurl through the neighboring blocks of shops and restaurants and onto the Ala Wai Golf Course.

Bill and Candy do not have a chance to be aware of any of this. The blast of air through their room sucks the floor up and the ceiling down; Bill does not even have time to register horror or to understand what he is seeing when Candy's head is flattened like a pumpkin on a sidewalk by the slap of the ceiling against it, for he is sailing across the room—they are still holding each other—and his head hits the wall where there's a stud, shattering his skull instantly.

Ed Porter has it all on tape. Passionet is going to love him. And he's way up here away from it all. He does a little dance, and, to relieve feelings he's built up, he loops that last passionate intercourse (along with their memories of several other times) into a nonstop orgasm series of Candy, putting in the image of her head shattering between each surge. Passionet won't want this but Ed has his connections and he knows there are some places where this will be a best-seller of a completely different kind; he plays the tape, masturbates, ejaculates over and over at the intercut of bovine ecstasy and death like a sledgehammered steer—

He is still sitting there, pulling on his now-sore penis, trying to get one more orgasm out of Bill and Candy, half an hour later, when a piece of old flagpole, torn from a downtown monument, pierces the Passionet offices, creating a hole for the wind to work on; moments later the building begins to crumble, but by now Ed Porter, impaled through the chest by the flagpole, his pants still around his knees, is past caring. Within an hour the records of the last of Bill and Candy are immersed, stirred violently, and float away (wedges are light and they are stored in airtight plastic), never to be found.

They're getting low on movable satellites, and only Edwards and Baikonur, right now, can give them polar launches. The Kazakhs have been as helpful as possible, but their facility is old (hard to believe that it first launched well before President Hardshaw was born), and the Edwards launch facility was never really intended to do more than put up the occasional military package.

It's also hard to find anything that can penetrate Clem well enough to tell what's going on. As it scraped eastward down the northern side of the Hawaiians, winds curling in against the sheltered shores, available band-width fell steadily all night, so that, first, commercial XV had to go, and then television had to be switched to old-style low-def, and then phones went to audio only. . . . They now have occasional odd voice lines, and whenever they do get a satellite over at low altitude there are a few hams on Lanai and Molokai reporting what they can see—but the weather is far too rough for them to keep an outside antenna up, so their signal is barely reaching to low orbit, less than 100 miles away.

Admiral Singh reports immense seas and that the carrier group has had to fight for its life, but he's drawing steadily away from Hurricane Clem and the best guess is that the Midway refugees, anyway, will be brought in alive.

Stirred by Clem, there are heavy thunderstorms up and down the West Coast, but most of the Hawaii refugee flights got in before the worst of it hit, and again there were no fatal accidents there. Jumpplanes go high enough so that trans-Pacific flights are not interrupted, and there's reportedly a booming trade in people trying to get a left-side window seat to see Clem from 100 miles up.

Hardshaw looks at the sheet in front of her and sighs. Nominally everything is going well—but this is only because absolutely no information is coming out of Hawaii. The major storm surge that has rolled out of Clem, after this change of direction, will probably roll along the south coast of Mexico, but that's mostly high rocky coast, with just a scattering of resorts, and the Mexican government should be able to get it evacuated. The surge that was on its way before is nearing the coasts of Washington and British Columbia, and low-lying areas are being evacuated there, hampered by the heavy rain.

And none of that answers the question "What has happened to Hawaii?" The major islands dropped off the communication links in neat order, Kauai going first, the Big Island last, hours ago—in fact, one bright boy at FEMA has arrived at what he calls the Silence Number—Beaufort 28. That is, when the winds reach Beaufort force 28, no regular communication can be expected from that site.

Oahu seems to have held on up to 29, and Nihau went out at 25, but as rules go it seems to hold true.

But right now, the peak wind force has just passed Oahu, with its majority of the state's population. There is little question that many people must have been trapped on the highways, and the peak wind force was around Beaufort 35, more than enough to pick up and hurl automobiles, so there are unquestionably tens of thousands dead. In many places, roads ran near the coast; very likely some whole traffic jams were swept out to sea and are now on the bottom.

Radar seems to show ten- and twenty-meter waves forming in a circular pattern following Clem's winds, in which case the sheltered shores have been battered to flinders. Rainfall—but again, all there is to go from is satellite radar—is so dense that it's possible that people outside would drown, and there's little question that there must be huge floods pouring off the central volcanoes of each island.

So there are immense numbers of dead, and many more will die of exposure, treatable injuries, and water-borne bacterial disease before adequate help can be gotten there. No structure on Earth, except those few underground military facilities supposed to be nuke-proof, was ever designed for winds like that, so although there are undoubtedly freak survivors, every bridge and building must be assumed down. All this they can know without being able to see.

Beaufort on Kauai is already down to 18—merely a very big hurricane—but nothing is back on the air and there's no evidence that anything is moving down there except for the waters and winds. A couple of hotshot Army staticopter pilots, trained and accustomed to rough landing conditions, will try to set down in Lihue, the first big town where it's even remotely feasible—by the time they get there the wind should be down to Beaufort 12, making it merely very difficult rather than impossible. Theoretically, with their hundreds of electrostatically charged blades, and ten replacements per blade available, staticopters are all but impossible to bring down as long as the power source holds out—or the air doesn't move faster than the staticopter.

She wishes them all the best of luck. She has nightmare visions of conditions suddenly ripping out all the blades, and then ten generations of replacements, within a second or so, and of air crews falling into the black storm. She knows staticopters have been out in Beaufort 13 and 14 winds, and the pilots are good—but right now it's easier to worry about ten young men who might die than to think about tens of thousands of people who must already be dead.

In the dark and storm of Clem's passing, a thousand possibilities have crossed Hardshaw's desk. There may be immense waves confined to the super-hurricane radius, so that the whole coast of each island might have been scraped by hours of roaring water, high enough to erase Honolulu and most of the other cities; there's even a suggestion from a couple of fuzzy radar images that such a wave might have torn across the low part of Oahu, ripping through Pearl Harbor and across Wheeler AFB at the crest, eventually flowing out through Waialua in the northwest.

Anything could be happening in there, but nothing good.

Hardshaw gets up from her chair and groans. She has been awake too long, sitting still too long. She's had too much coffee and she's going for more. This isn't the first time she's felt like President Grandma—hell, the job will make anyone feel like an old lady, it probably made *Kennedy* feel like an old lady.

All right, old woman, quit the griping, you could have been turning over burger or helping ranchers sue each other. She stretches and turns to see Harris Diem coming in. His face is a sort of sick gray, and she's not sure she's ever seen him without a necktie before. Certainly never with his hair so uncombed and such bags under his eyes.

"UN," he says. "Rivera wants to talk to you. We've given him a ten-minute stall in case you want to get presentable."

"That'll take more than ten but let's see what I can do." She gets into the bathroom, thinks a moment, decides that Rivera can get used to waiting for the President, and strips out of her suit, yanks on a shower cap, and turns on the shower. She has only a glorious minute or so under the furious blast of hot water, barely time to rub a little soap here and there and to shake her head vigorously before she has to step out into the sauna, grab the big fluffy towels, and get herself dry, but she makes sure she enjoys every moment of it. At the end of the process she still feels like an old lady, but she feels like a clean old lady, and she grabs one of the spare suits from its hanger with almost a sense of victory.

She has kept Rivera waiting three whole extra minutes. *That's about what you can manage as the most powerful nation on Earth these days,* she supposes.

Let's stretch him clear out to fifteen, five more than he planned on. Make him see his power is limited . . . she checks makeup, redoes a point here and there, hits the hair once again with a brush. . . .

It's really just a sign of tiredness to have her sense of humor kicking in like this, but she imagines a special slot in the "careers" section of the XV magazine shows that are aimed at teenage women—"Your career as Head of State of a major world power. As always, good grooming and sensible fashion choices are a MUST!!!!"

The little laugh still makes her feel better, and when she emerges she feels ready for whatever is to come next. Rivera will have something he wants to wring out of the situation, and he will be unfailingly polite about doing so. "Always leave them their dignity; after all, it has no resale value," her father used to say, after skinning some poor tourist in some bit of shade-tree auto mechanicking.

When she sits down at the screen, Harris is doodling on a pad beside her; she glances at the pad and reads "He's spent the last five minutes making stale jokes about women who can't get dressed on time." She checks to see that their video is muted, then scrawls on Harris's pad "Nobody would bother getting dressed for him. What Dorothy Parker Said."

Diem grins and winks and they bring the video up to talk to Rivera.

He begins without preamble. "Ms. President, I've been working on getting an aid package put together for your disaster."

"We accept," Hardshaw says.

"You—er, would you care to hear what's in the aid package?"

"Food, medicine, help of all kinds, whatever you could get the Rim countries to kick in, I should imagine. And I know perfectly well that UN disaster relief is always offered without strings. Normally of course we turn it down because it's needed more urgently elsewhere in the world and we know your resources are scarce; it makes more sense for us to take care of our own. But right now we need all the help we can get."

Rivera nods slowly. "I see. And will you—er, that is, do you have any information for us on the scope of the disaster?"

Hardshaw nods at Diem, who says, "We can have a report on as much as we know within a half hour if you need it. But the short answer is that we're completely out of communication with the islands. We're getting a little bit from hams but all they can tell us is that it's raining like mad, the wind is blowing the rain almost horizontal, and they're cut off where they are. In about three hours an Army team will try to touch down on Kauai. But until somebody who's able to move around picks up the phone at the other end, we really don't know anything."

"I'll see what we can get the Japanese and Chinese to share. I'd bet that you haven't had any significant data from either nation, but UNSOO assures me they've both made a couple of satellite passes. And naturally we'll give you what UNSOO has, but that's very little."

"We realize that," Harris Diem says, "and we're grateful for your help."

Rivera says, "After all, finally, it is all one planet. I am glad we can be of service to you. I'll be in touch." He nods to them and raises the tips of his fingers off the table in an almost-wave that could be read either as a salute or a dismissal. The screen goes dark before Hardshaw says goodbye.

She leans back in the chair. "Whoa, a shower, a change of clothes, and a bastard to deal with, and now I feel fresh as a daisy. Order us up coffee and grilled cheese sandwiches, Harris, and then let's have a talk about what's going on here."

She goes back to her desk to look through the fresh piles of printout. A ham radio operator has been raised on Oahu, but he's a sixteen-year-old Eagle Scout at Pupukea; he has a forty-year-old Ford pickup truck and two fourteen-year-olds at his disposal, the road is too washed out for any hope of getting down off the mountain soon, and anyway he's just about as far as it's possible to be from anywhere that they really need to know about. But he has managed to rig an antenna that will probably not blow down, so they do have continuous contact with him, and there were some unbroken weather instruments there at the camp, so he's able to confirm for them that pressure fell below 700 mb for three straight hours.

"What's that mean in English?" Hardshaw mutters, before she sees the scrawled note—it's that NOAA weatherman, Callare; as soon as this current uproar is over and they've given Pauliss the shaft, they will have to let Callare in on what's going on—to the effect that if the barometric pressure was that low at a distance of 220 km from the center of the eye, then the eye wall—the innermost ring of the hurricane before the still air of the eye itself, currently about 140 km across—must have winds of around Beaufort force 46, or 146 meters per second, about 330 mph (Hardshaw is grateful for that last number, since she's never really learned to think in metric terms), "in good accord with other observations and with theory."

"What a relief," Hardshaw says out loud. "I'd hate to see a theory collapse for one lousy Eagle Scout."

Diem sets a plate of sandwiches and a pot of fresh coffee down on the President's desk, takes a seat himself without asking, and says, "All right, what are we going to make of the SecGen?"

"Well, he probably intended to dangle a big aid package as bait and then get us to agree to coordinate—which is to say, surrender—our scientific agencies. But since I accepted before he could mention the rest of the deal, and since that call wasn't even remotely secure, now he's stuck and may have to do us some good. And we managed to get it logged that as a matter of general principle we don't have to have this. That should keep him frustrated for a bit—but at the same time make it impossible for him to take revenge on us by slowing things up. Does UNSOO have anything of any value?"

"Not them, but if Rivera really has some leverage with Japan then we are sure as hell in luck, because Di Callare and Henry Pauliss assure me the Japanese have some kind of multiple scanning system that would let them look down through the storm in slices, so they could tell us how high the water got and how fast the air and water were moving any time a satellite of theirs went over. Assuming the satellite was equipped with ground-scanning multiple-frequency radar, of course."

"All right. So we played that one pretty well." Brittany Hardshaw leans back in her chair and looks hard at Harris Diem. She can remember back when he was just her clerk and intern at the Idaho Attorney General's office, and she can remember a lot of dark and bright days since then. In the way that's common with people at the top, she's rarely wondered much about what he gets out of all this, preferring instead to leave that to him. But she can't help wondering . . . if her long-winding path from dirt-road Idaho had not carried her here, or somewhere similar, would he have stayed with her the whole time?

Irrelevant, of course. He's here whatever the reason. Still . . . "You look terribly tired," she says.

"So do you, boss. And if you want to feel tired-er, I've got a little note from Carla Tynan that's kind of a worry too."

Hardshaw groans quietly, grabs another sandwich, pours another cup of coffee. "This stuff is wonderful."

"Mom's recipe. Velveeta and Wonder Bread—hard stuff to get anymore but worth it. You're stalling, boss."

"Yeah, well . . ." Hardshaw grins at him. "How many times have you and I stayed up all night together?"

"Is the Fifth Amendment still in force?"

She gestures for him to eat.

When they have each finished a sandwich she says, "All right, let's have it. I know you don't give me small worries just to get them off your desk, so if you mentioned it, it's important."

Diem nods, and says, "You want all the science or do you want just the upshot?"

"Upshot, please, with maybe enough science to reassure me that Carla isn't making it up. Jesus, how'd we ever let her get out of Federal service? She's worth twenty times what a paper pusher like Henry Pauliss is."

Diem makes a face, but he has gotten and kept this job mostly by swallowing hard and telling the truth when needed. "Well, to remind you, right after the Global Riot it became very important to make sure nobody at NOAA was going to mouth off to the media in a bad situation, especially not a bad situation that we were trying to keep wrapped up to prevent *another* Global Riot. So we closed down the Anticipatory Section because that was where the most scare stories were coming out of."

Hardshaw leans back and says, "Remind me why that wasn't stupid at the time."

"It wasn't stupid at the time, boss, because we'd never had a global weather catastrophe before, and there was no evidence that something a little bigger than previous, or a little more violent, was going to be different in kind. And the long-range forecasters had been crying wolf about droughts and things like that for a long, long time. We had a definite ten million dead to weigh against that."

She nods. "Well, I hereby officially declare that the decision was a big mistake. Make a note that if anyone asks us that's what we say."

"Going with honesty as your basic carrier?"

"Carrier" is media-jock slang for the reason why people will believe what you say. The appearance of blunt honesty is one kind of carrier; wish-fulfillment is another, close fit to known facts is another, and so forth. It has nothing whatsoever to do with the truth, if the truth is even known, and this is why Brittany Lynn Hardshaw, who still remembers the taste of a bar of Irish Spring jammed into her mouth for lying, hates the term. She has never told Diem this and never would. It is part of his job to think about carriers.

She looks up to see the first bare white glow of daylight striking the office window, and to note that several staff are rotating out to be replaced by their daytime equivalents. She nods hellos to everyone, waves, acts the part of the gracious host, sends the unconsumed sandwiches around (enjoying Diem's wince at the luxury goods going to low-level staffers).

Finally she sits down and says very quietly, "Harris, it's like this. I think the big mistake is that we let people get away with the Global Riot. There's got to be some kind of approximation, no matter how rough, to personal responsibility! We could have cracked down a lot of ways—used the regular Army right away in force in the big cities, had all the governors roll the Guard, arrested the execs of the XV networks and held them until they agreed to shut off the damned signal—"

"You'd have faced one hell of a set of court cases—" he begins.

Her hand chops downward fast, as if she's taking the head off a chicken. It's a gesture Diem used to see her make in court a lot. "And since when has an old lawyer with nineteen cases of her own in front of the Supreme Court been afraid of that? Would've been the first clear-and-present-danger case to come up since XV became commercial—and what a fight that would have made, eh? But this is all still reviewing the past." She gulps more of the coffee; it's cooler now, and she takes it like a drug, not the relaxing comfort it was before. "What matters is this: We've got to realize that not only can I not be everywhere in this crisis, I can't even be in touch with everywhere. Right now we don't even know if the American Army can land an aircraft in an American state, or for that matter if the Navy can even get into Pearl Harbor.

"Harris, the one thing that has kept me awake nights is that if the NSA is right, and if the little 'secret' cabal around Callare and the Tynans is right, then there could be a big enough catastrophe to completely take down any government anywhere. Some governments will still be on their feet, somewhere, but no one can say which. Millions of people will have every modern device torn away from them, and have to fend for themselves. And I don't think people are ready for that. I think after a few centuries of modern government everyone will be waiting for the whistlers to show up with doctors and hot soup and tents. But you see how powerless we already are in Hawaii. And we won't even begin to get cleanup and rescue underway before Clem comes around again.

"So people are going to have to do what they can do on their own, and that means we've got to trust them with the information to do whatever they need to do."

"And if they misuse that information?"

"Then we slap them down—if we can reach them. And if we can't reach them they are no longer our problem. But understand, Harris, we have to consider how the American people, and for that matter, the world's people, will survive if we all perish here. And I can't see that their chances will be enhanced by leaving them a legacy of misinformation or pure ignorance.

"So here's your problem, Harris. Whatever you're about to tell me, whatever new bad news Carla has, we're going to make it available to *everybody*. The UN, other nations, Congress, all the parties, all the candidates for president, all the corporate heads—even the people. And from now on the order is that everything except weapons secrets and military ops plans gets declassified. We can only count on a few more months of the government functioning—and after that, like it or not, the people will have to rule. Sovereignty is about to drop back into their laps for good or ill. And if they can't govern, well, it was a good two-hundred-and-fifty-year experiment. But the mess that just happened in Hawaii is probably only the start—there are months left in hurricane season—and it's time to admit that since we can't help, we might as well give people the information they need and then stay out of their way."

Harris Diem starts to laugh. "Okay, boss, I'll just figure this isn't a stroke or something. But I'll feel a lot better if you change your mind when you hear this. Clem's not only not over, and not close to being over—there're going to be a lot more Clems within a week or two."

President Hardshaw has braced herself just a little—she knows even her trusted longtime friend and assistant cannot see it when she does that—and the result is that there is no wince in her face and no ripple in her coffee. She doesn't seem to hesitate before she says, "You'd better explain that in detail, and then we'd better get it out on the news."

She is rewarded by a tight-lipped smile and a tiny headshake from Harris Diem. She knows him well enough to understand at once that this is becoming another story, in his mind, of why he has served her for twenty-nine years, that someday in his memoirs he will write that she changed years of policy in a three-minute decision without batting an eye. And as he starts to tell her the latest, he has already re-oriented himself to the new policy, and will carry it out with vigor and passion, tired though he is, opposed to it, perhaps not understanding it.

Loyalty like that frightens her; it is an all but impossible job to try to steer the greatest military power on Earth and the fate of a quarter of a billion people, but something in her recoils from holding a complete human soul in her hands. It's been a long time since Idaho.

She concentrates on what he says, and in ten minutes she's on the line to Secretary-General Rivera, to President Questora of Mexico, and to as many as can be gotten on line of the Central American presidents, dictators, and generals—she can never keep their titles straight without the little prompt displayed across their faces. Just after she clicks off, the news comes from Hawaii that the Army expedition touched down, and one staticopter flipped with the loss of six lives. The weather is still too rough for them to be able to move from the base camp. It seems anticlimactic, like a small bit of old business.

The thing is, Randy Householder knows the business. He's been tracking it for more than a decade. He talks the right talk, walks the right walk, uses some of his carefully hoarded stash of cash, and in no time at all he's got himself a forced extraction rig.

He looks at the thing and shudders. There are brownish spots on it that tell him it has been used before.

It takes him another four days to determine that Jerren Anders is in the minimum-security wing and not considered dangerous; he had some kind of breakdown at the time of his arrest, convinced a judge and jury, got better, and now he's being taken care of for life.

Randy has decided to take care of him, period. It's the simplest and cleanest.

The exercise field is not walled or fenced; they count on the transponder ankle cuff to keep them in, or to track them down if they run. Anders is an old bastard, and he jogs every day. There's about a thirty-second chance to do it, but it's not complicated, really, just a matter of getting the timing down.

The day is bright and sunny when Randy steps from behind a tree, knocks Anders down, points a gun at his chest, and says, "Withers, Wallace, and Brown say hi. You're coming with me."

"I don't do that shit anymore—"

"Then I'll kill you."

Anders stands up, raising his hands. Randy quick-marches him to the car; fortunately they can't track the individual vehicle yet, those civil liberties types are good for something. They get in the car and Randy gives an address; the car rolls away.

"What are you going to—"

Randy shoots Anders with a paralyzer. Not that he cares, but it will also act as an anesthetic.

Then he takes the crowbar and begins breaking up Anders's feet bones. Anders's eyes get wide, and tears run down his face, but he can't move and all he can do is moan.

If you cut the ankle cuff, they stop looking for the cuff. They have the idea that since you can't pull it off over the foot, you can't take it off. That would be true if you were escaping on your own behalf. Or if you were in a position to object to having the bones crushed.

But matters are a little different. Randy swings the crowbar hard and fast—he has only about five minutes to work—and the old brittle bones crack and shatter under the blows. The cracking sound of the first few blows gives way to wet thuds. The keening from Anders's slack mouth is really annoying but there's no time to gag him just yet.

When the foot, wrapped in a plastic bag, feels like jelly, Randy grabs the cuff and yanks it off over the sodden, bloody mess. The car is now doing what it's supposed to do—cutting into a robot freighter yard—and Randy rolls down the window.

There. One of the robot tractors is just pulling out, towing three container/trailers behind it, and there's room to catch it. Randy takes manual control—he's glad he learned to do this way back when—and shoots forward. The middle trailer carries cattle, their faces huge and stupid as he comes up close and tosses the ankle cuff in among them.

He whips down an un-guide-stripped alley; halfway down it he flips the control back to automatic and tells the car to take a long route around before it gets back on guidestrips. It will take them weeks to correlate guidestrip records with the motion of the ankle cuff and trace it all back to him—and long before that, Randy plans to be done.

The keening grows louder in the backseat as Randy climbs back to deal with the next problem. He trusses up Anders, then releases him from the paralyzer.

Anders is babbling now, saying he'll tell him anything, the kind of stuff you'd expect.

Randy asks the big question. "You remember a wedge you probably were the go-between on, little blonde girl, fourteen years ago—?"

"Fuck, man, not that one, no, fuck, you can't do anything to me worse than they'll do to me—"

Randy holds up the forced extraction kit. "Wanna bet?"

Anders finally tells him without forced extraction. But this is too important to leave a possibility that the old thug may be lying, so Randy beams at him and says, "Oh, by the way, I lied," and drives the forced extractor into the old man's forehead. The man screams and foams as Randy reads off keywords and his recorder grabs everything for the wedge.

That night the body of Jerren Anders goes down a deep, wet ravine, just off of U.S. 93. Randy gets a report that seems to show, anyway, that his datarodents have made their way into Idaho State Highway Patrol records, and he may have more time than he thought.

He takes a long nap before he experiences that wedge. All kinds of shit will be in there, and he steels himself to look for the right one. Four days later he's still reading through fragments of girls and women raped, muti-lated, and killed, through Winston's terrifying threats, through Brown sell-ing him the drugs again and again. . . .

Randy realizes he's just avoiding it, and that's all there is to it. He doesn't want what Anders said to be true, and he knows what part of the wedge it will or won't be in. He takes the sedatives.

She was right, in that dream. It's really bad. He gets flashes of their surveillance of her, flashes as they figure out that she always showers by herself and no one waits for her. He gets Anders's nasty little wet dreams from spying on Kimbie Dee.

Once, before he can stop it, he gets a secondhand memory of the wedge they made, Kimbie Dee trying to cover herself with her hands when that monster they turned loose on her walks into the shower, then the sight of the huge, hideous man pulling out a gun and pointing it at her, the shame as she brought her shaking hands down from her breasts and let him stare at them. . . .

He pops out of that, almost vomiting, but he felt something else in the memory, and the next time he goes back in he gets it.

He has a name, and it's a name he already knows well. But not for being a buyer of this stuff, let alone for commissioning it.

But there's no mistake, Randy thinks. Jerren Anders, at the very least, thought that this was who he was working for, thought that that was why there were so many death sentences when the ring broke up.

The access for this is not going to be easy. He's glad the datarodents are buying him time at the Idaho State Highway Patrol—because he's going to need a lot of time.

Perhaps the real reason that the results come when they do is that Carla Tynan has gotten enough rest for the first time in days. She is finally well below the equator in her run to the Solomons, submerged to run faster. Something in her will not let her take breaks for sunbathing and sitting out on the surface while she is working.

Di's team at NOAA is doing a first-rate job, there's no question about that, in modeling the physics of how the outflow jet moves the hurricane. Get NOAA pointed in the right direction and they do good work. . . .

But, Carla reflects, still lying in her clean, warm bunk and only idly thinking of getting up and doing anything, that was part of the problem back when she had a regular job there; once the concept was right she had a lot of trouble getting interested in the micro-details, except as they confirmed the concept. When she was feeling good about herself, she usually explained this as the "Daniel Boone Syndrome"—as soon as she'd seen what was over a hill, and led others to it, she wanted to get over the next one. When she was down on herself, which was often back in those days, she thought it was a combination of a real creative gift with genuine laziness—she knew that her ideas were good enough to keep her employed, and therefore she kept having those, letting other people do all the hard work.

As was so often the case, it was Louie who, though not terribly intro-spective himself, had given her some doorways into how she really func-tioned. "Look, silly, it's not laziness. When you're after the idea you work twenty hours a day, you know? And it's not pioneering drive, because when you're not after an idea, you hang around reading trash or go shopping—it isn't like you chase after ideas. I think it's just that you can't stand for there to be something that you don't know. When you get an idea, you can't rest until you're fairly sure whether it's true or not. And when you don't have one you just do the things you enjoy doing. What's the big crime? Why does anything about you have to make you into a saint or a criminal?"

She drifts back through that scene mentally—it could lead to a very nice erotic dream, but mostly what she's really enjoying is remembering that Louie understands her, even if no one else does. Besides, lately when she thinks about sex with Louie, she gets reminded that they will have to put off getting together for months, since his stay in space is being extended indefinitely. Groaning, she rolls out of the narrow bunk, steps into the shower (a shower before bed and a shower after—now there's a major indulgence) and lets the scalding hot water relax her neck and scalp.

The NOAA team is on top of it, and despite all the computing power she has on board and all the nets she's able to access, they are way, way ahead of her in capabilities, so there's really no reason for her to continue working on the outflow jet problem.

Except that somebody—some science fiction writer way back before she was born, she remembers her dad used to quote the guy—always said you can't do one thing.

She shakes her short hair, spraying water around, and lets the hot flow surge down her back, rubbing the small of her back where the tension often concentrates. You can't do one thing. So what else does an outflow jet do, besides create a high-pressure area that the hurricane moves away from? What else does an outflow jet cause?

Tornadoes over land, and waterspouts over water—hurricanes spawn tornadoes all around themselves. There's a big cluster of them that forms to the right of the hurricane's direction of motion, and a smaller cluster where the outflow jet comes down. First-year meteorology: the big wind shears that happen in the strong winds of a hurricane can get rotated into the horizontal plane by all the cumulonimbus convection that is found around the edges.

A wind shear is what happens when the ground slows the wind that touches it; the wind above continues at speed—this curls the wind downward into a rolling cylinder, the way a trip wire makes a runner curl over by stopping his lower body and letting the rest of him continue. Then the strong updrafts around a thunderhead pull the rolling cylinder of air vertical, where it becomes a tornado.

Where the outflow jet comes down it fills the air with moisture and creates an area that the wind has to blow away from. Thus it makes a lot of wind shears, and a lot of cumulonimbus clouds, and cumulonimbus clouds—thunderheads—have strong updrafts. Conditions are perfect, right where the outflow draft comes down, for getting air rotating around spots of low pressure—for tornadogenesis.

All this became really clear sixty years ago, after the first really big hurricane to be tracked on radar, so that they could *see* all those cumulo-nimbi, tornadoes, and the eye itself. Hurricane Beulah, way back in the 1960s, a big one driven far inland by a powerful outflow jet, had sprayed tornadoes around behind itself like tin cans blowing off the back of a garbage truck.

So what Clem's outflow jet will give you is . . . bigger wind shears. And a high-pressure area close to the ground. More tornadoes and water-spouts. . . .

And that outflow jet moves. When it's gone, there's suddenly no more high-pressure air coming down from above. The pushed-down, swirling air at the sea surface will rise. . . .

. . . like a bubble from the bottom of a hot kettle. Like a Cartesian diver when you take your finger off the rubber membrane—Carla remembers a present from her father, when she wasn't more than six, a sealed glass bottle of water with a little glass scuba diver inside; there was an air bubble in the diver, and when you squeezed the bottle, the pressure compressed the bubble, the diver's density increased, and he sank; when you released the bottle, the high pressure went away, the bubble inside the diver got bigger, and he rose.

A big bubble of air. Rising up from the middle of a savagely churning warm sea. Powerful wind shears all rolling surface-level air inward toward where the bubble rises. . . .

If the outflow jet moves quickly, so that the high-pressure area expands vertically fast enough, what you have is the model of hurricane formation. It doesn't happen in ordinary hurricanes—there, when the outflow jet moves, the high-pressure spot is still close enough to the eye of the hurricane, and the released air just flows inward to the center, feeding the hurricane. But in something the size of Clem—where the outflow jet can be coming down many hundreds of kilometers away. . . .

It takes her only about an hour to rough out a model and see that just maybe this could happen. As she's finishing up—and why are her fingers always so clumsy, her brain always so slow, the right sources never to hand when she has a good idea?—she notices that she's cold and realizes that she sort of forgot to towel off after her shower. At least this time she remem-bered to turn it off.

She's also tied her back in knots. Well, no doubt there's hot water in the shower again . . . so she gets her third shower, and this time she makes herself relax, and towels off, and gets dressed in something comfortable that she sort of likes (well, okay, Louie once told her she looked like a hot piece in it, and since then she's lost a little weight so it's loose and baggy, so now it's just about her favorite jumpsuit. What's not to like? And what's wrong with some happy memories? She didn't divorce the man because she didn't like him, she divorced him to keep liking him, as she explained to him at the time).

God, god, god, Louie on the brain and a real problem right here in front of her. Yes, it's a plausible outcome, but no, it's not the only plausible one. Clem might have kittens or might not, and no one will know till that outflow jet swings suddenly—which it may not do for a while.

But the outflow jet did swing suddenly, once—just before Clem ripped off toward Hawaii. Only a few hours ago. And come to think of it, Carla has been paying no attention to the news—she has no idea whether or not Clem is hitting Hawaii, or if he is, what is happening there.

MyBoat surfaces just hours after sunset; it's a beautiful starlit night, and her radar shows no ships within many kilometers, so Carla climbs up on the deck, taking a scalpnet and output plug with her to direct-access the data she needs. With a jet of high-pressure air, she dries the sunbathing deck and stretches out in the dark, lying on her back and looking up at the stars, counting the occasional meteors and enjoying the glory of a really dark, clear sky. Strange to think how many people never see this except via XV; stranger to think how many more stars there are for Louie. No wonder they can't keep him out of the observation bubble despite all the warnings about radiation.

With a sigh, she pulls on her scalpnet and inserts the plug into the side of her head. Time to work, Carla.

The dark night, the blazing beauty of all the stars, and the gentle rock of *MyBoat* on the waves, felt as rhythmic shoving of the padded deck against her back, all become ghostly presences in the back of her brain, like the fragments of a dream just after waking. Instead, she senses lists of thousands of options, thinks of what she wants, plugs in to learn that Hawaii has been cut off from all but a few voice signals already, swings back into the public channels to get satellite data and raw weather station data. . . .

When the outflow jet from Clem swung hard around, it swung out over water that was just below 20 degrees Celsius in temperature. Too cold for a hurricane to start. Too cold even for one to be sustained.

Even so, there was a good-sized depression produced, which seems to have become an extratropical cyclone—a large storm, large in area, that is, though nothing like Clem for windspeed or rain, now moving toward British Columbia, which will be dumping loads of rain all over Pacificanada.

She notices a Japanese military satellite in a polar orbit might well have shot some pictures right in the critical eight minutes when the outflow jet switched off on one side of the hurricane, and a new outflow jet formed immediately ninety degrees away.

She quietly pops into several thousand software libraries, looking for any old penetration software she can find; her vast storage and fast-system capabilities can assemble all the little pieces and bits into a sort of super gang-assault on the closed nodes around Tokyo. It's only a matter of seconds, but she finds herself wriggling and stretching, back in ghostly "real" reality, as she notices how extended she is feeling, how much her consciousness seems to have spread out from her little submarine yacht.

The data are not terribly secure; the Japanese apparently assume this satellite feed is being tapped. It takes little time to break in, find what she wants, pop out.

They have some kind of a radar gadget that lets them shoot cross sections of the atmosphere, and it was turned on while they flew over. This is better data than she could have hoped for—she extrapolates from it instantly—

And finds the bad news. No question. If this had happened over warmer water, a fast-rising column of warm air would have been produced, in the middle of all those swirling waves, currents, winds, and thunderheads: the same kind of column that gave birth to Clem, or starts any other hurricane.

Louie is getting used to walking around on the moon in the silly robot; so used to it that more and more he lets the robot run on autopilot, until he needs to manipulate something himself. The first day was the worst; the manipulations involved in getting some of the "general assembler" machinery back up and running, getting it to make data busses and connector cables for all kinds of things that were never supposed to be hooked to each other, and so forth, were a major pain.

The second-and-a-half delay between him and the robot means the robot is useless for fine manipulations, except by letting it work independently—which means that every time something has to be screwed into place, but not too tightly, he has to take it partway down, then stop using direct interface, tell the robot how much force is allowable, wait to see if that did the job . . . taking six recessed Phillips screws out of one lousy plate, in order to get at two stupid switches, took him more than an hour.

He's been quietly stealing all sorts of things from the French. If they don't like it they can come up and arrest him; they've been cutting back too and he doubts they'll even notice.

But after the systems were generally integrated and robots started up, matters moved pretty fast. The Pentagon zapped up all sorts of Computer Optimized Design software to him, and he's had it running in the main system for a couple of days now. Later today, if all goes well, he'll be able to launch a couple of small transport rockets, designed and built by himself and the machine right here on the moon, to bring some of the stored food from the French supplies back to a rendezvous with the *Constitution*. He's not yet in any danger of starving but it will be nice to have some variety, and as a test project it's not too complicated.

He's also begun to like walking around on the moon in the last few days. The little replicators are now all "slaved"—no longer running loose but under tight control—and they scurry about busily; the astonishing sharp shadows and black sky still delight him.

He wishes he could be back here in person, making his own bootprints in the lunar soil that has lain undisturbed for billions of years, and indeed he's already dropped them a plan for that. Between the capabilities already on the moon and those he is building now, one of the things he can do is rig up a propulsion system to move all of *Constitution*—slowly, because the trusses that hold it together won't take more than a twentieth of a g—out to orbit around the moon. Hell, out to anywhere, though he's damned if he likes the idea of spending all his time in the Bank Vault, which he'd pretty much have to do for a long voyage.

But all the same . . .*Constitution* will be able to go anywhere, once he gets it equipped. He feels like he's sixteen and modifying the old '94 Geo for rally driving again.

The odd thing about every task up here—and he now realizes how conservative the French and Japanese were being in their approach—is that you need to work hard only at first. The machines learn, and once they learn they optimize, so that if you get one to do something right once, in a short while it will be doing it brilliantly and faster than you. On this little rocket project, it took the better part of a day to get the throat of the nozzle figured and optimized for the solid fuel . . . but then it took only an hour to finish the rest of the engine.

Well, time to get on with the work. He turns to the rocket design—

It is completely different. It doesn't look remotely like what it did the last time he worked on it. Moreover, he knows intuitively it is better—and then, as he looks at it, he understands it completely. Of course that geometry doesn't let heat build up as much in the throat; naturally if the struts are set up like that, they form strong, stable triangles everywhere—

It looks like he fixed everything in the back of his mind. Now that he doesn't unhook very often, preferring to leave things running in background, it's as if all the various tasks that are turning this into a new kind of facility are somehow thoughts in the back of his mind, and as if his mind is enlarging to take care of the additional load.

He has been unplugging only to sleep, and he's been noticing lately that he doesn't need to sleep much.

Not sleeping much is one of those unusual things he's supposed to call

Dr. Wo about. It goes against all training and experience, but Louie calls the neurologist; something about it all is giving him the creeps.

Wo gets back to him in five minutes; obviously Louie is a valued guinea pig. In a few short sentences, Louie tells Dr. Wo about it all.

"And you were not aware of consciously thinking about this? The robots just modified it into this newer, better design, and when you came back you understood it?"

"Yeah, that's pretty much it. And I haven't been sleeping much. And lately, too, I notice that when I think of things from the past, my memory is clearer . . . is it the optimizers?"

"I'd say there's no doubt."

"So what happened? Did my subconscious design and build that rocket?"

Wo nods. "Good question. I think the answer is probably that you did, but not the 'you' I'm talking to. One way the optimizers work is that they copy valuable, effective code at one point, and then move it to other places where it's needed. My best guess—and we'll have to run some tests to confirm it, I know that's a scary phrase but bear with it—my best guess is that what the optimizers are doing is copying parts of your mind into programs running on the other processors, including the ones on the moon. You're sort of dispersing through the system. That's why you understood it as soon as you looked at it—all those fragments of yourself 'came home.' Well, this is very interesting . . . it would appear that the net you are plugged into is not only optimizing you, it is *becoming* you. At the same time that you become optimized."

Louie swallows hard and asks the question he really wants answered. "Doc, am I going to be the same guy?"

Wo sits down, the phone camera lurching as it tracks him, and scratches his head. This might be a major display of emotion; one problem with doctors in military research programs, given that part of their job is to study the patient to see why he's still alive, is that they don't have a very wide range of emotional expression. Though he's known him for many years, Louie doubts that he has ever known what Wo felt about anything.

At last the neurologist speaks. "Well, that's an interesting question. But it's over toward philosophy rather than in science proper. Offhand I would say that none of us is exactly the same person we were before, but there's a continuity, and at the least you will maintain continuity. Would you still be Louie Tynan if you trimmed your toenails and got a haircut? Surely. Would you be you with a heart transplant? You'd be different because the experience itself is traumatic, but you'd still be Louie Tynan. And with a brain transplant? How about half a brain? Are you the same guy if you have a religious conversion? And is software the same program if you install an upgrade?"

Louie scratches his head, too—whichever organizations are bugging this must think they both have lice—and says, "I guess my answers to those questions would be maybe, maybe, and maybe."

"One of our human test subjects, in the optimization work, discovered that he told the truth a lot more—apparently he'd always had a habit of white lies and flattery. His friends were able to notice the difference, but he and they agreed he was the same guy, just more truthful. In other words, telling the truth wasn't part of him, it was peripheral, like having blue eyes or favoring white shirts. But suppose we infected the Pope with a program that made him a Mormon, or Medal of Honor winners with something that totally destroyed their courage, or gay men with something that turned them straight. Suppose in addition to that we put them in a whole new body, one that wasn't human as we know it. Would they feel themselves to be the same person? Ever known an Alzheimer's patient well, before and after, or a schizophrenic? Are they the same or aren't they?"

These are more words out of Dr. Wo than Louie has heard in twenty years of knowing him. "I suppose the answer is it depends on what *they* think."

"That's the only answer that makes any sense. I'd say if we alter someone that much, and he or she changes name, friends, everything, and starts a new life, it's probably a different person—but the person might not feel that way. And if he or she keeps everything pretty much the same but changes a couple of old habits, it's the same person—but the person might not feel that way. And I suppose I'm old-fashioned enough to think that the person involved ought to be the one who says who he or she is. Anyway, if you'll permit us to run some checks—some on you and some on the processors on the moon—"

Louie nods, swallows hard, and says yes. They set a time and Wo clicks off.

Well, here he is. The process is probably not reversible. He returns to the moon in a moment or two, looks around, feels that again things are different, and better. As to who he is, or who he will be—the question is both more and less than academic. More because it's real—he can feel them in there, fixing and correcting, there's an odd clarity to his memory and his concentration is better. Less because he can't undo it.

Well, whether he is Louie-2, or just Louie-1.1, he's got a job to do. He'll think about it when he gets some time.

The supply rocket launches go beautifully, so now he has a launch system, and he puts the network of programs and machines onto the job of copying the stock weather-satellite design sent up from Earth. He decides it can't hurt to tell them to leave the interface compatible but optimize the rest for function . . . as long as USSF seems to have optimized him, he might as well optimize them right back. He can feel the net thinking about the problem in the back of his brain as he pulls back into the *Constitution.* He'll be coming up on the Pacific soon and no doubt they'll want him to take some observations.

It's only then, reading his mail, that he finds out that Hawaii is all but scoured to rock; the estimates are that nine out of every ten people alive on the islands two days ago are dead now, but that's based on the little the Army has been able to reach and the few surviving hams have been able to tell them. It looks very much like not one, but four great waves went all the way across Oahu.

Carla Tynan had been expecting to have some time for a little friendly talk with Louie, but first he called to say that between all the weird stuff he was doing on "the big project"—she's afraid to ask him what it is since he seems to think she knows, but whatever it is he's doing it mostly via telepresence on the moon—and because of all the other observations they want him to take, on this and the next Pacific pass, they probably won't get time. He'll try to get to her on satellite link sometime in the next day or two.

She wonders idly why, given that she's never going to see him anyway, she ever bothered divorcing him.

And then, instead of giving her some privacy and some time to work, Di Callare calls up, along with his useless boss Henry Pauliss, and Harris Diem, who is White House Chief of Staff but is also useless, and they all want her to hold the line while they get something together.

Obviously it's the President, and Carla can imagine plenty of reasons the President might want to talk to her, but nothing that Carla could say couldn't be expressed better by a well-written report.

Moreover, the constant sitting and waiting by the phone—every few minutes Di, or Pauliss, or Diem asks if she's still there—destroys her concentration, so that she can't get any work done in the interval.

She sits on her sunbathing deck, looking at the wide horizon, enjoying the sun on her face, arms, and bare legs. She's realizing too that she and Louie have been talking every two or three days—the "weekly" call "just to keep in touch" plus one or two "I forgot to mentions"—for the last year or so, while she's been at sea and he's been in space, and you never know what you're going to miss until it's gone, now, do you? Now she wishes deeply that she could spend a lazy afternoon just hanging around with him.

Frankly, she'd like to have some conversation, strange as that is for a hermit like Carla Tynan. In front of the suits Di won't talk meteorology freely (for fear of being misunderstood? or for fear of being understood? Carla would like to know). Pauliss, after all, is the guy who fired her, and now that she's proving vital, she knows enough of Washington to suspect that the last thing he wants to do is be anywhere near the President when the subject of Carla Tynan comes up. And Diem is utterly bland and noncommittal.

So the available subjects for chit-chat are Di's family: Lori is fine and almost done with *Slaughterer in Yellow*, Mark is a pleasant but not precocious kid, Nahum is precocious. And not particularly pleasant, Carla suspects, if what she hears between the lines is true.

Diem interrupts a Nahum story to say, "You mean you're doing that—I forget what it's called, but the system where you take naps with them and let them go to sleep anytime they want?" There's a sort of deep shock in his voice, not entirely masked.

Di Callare is clearly short of sleep himself, for he snaps just a little at this man who holds so much power. "As a matter of fact, yes, we do use the London Method, and we've never had a fight about bedtime, and the children do seem much calmer than most. Of course we don't let them have XV at all or TV much, so that may be the real reason."

Diem nods grudgingly. "I suppose it's hard to argue with results, and after all I never had kids, so I sure don't have any basis for arguing with you. I was just thinking how different it is from when I was growing up. Other than making sure I studied, keeping me working in the old man's restaurant in Boise—and seeing that I had food and clothes—I can't recall ever receiving that much interest from my parents. They just kind of raised us kids any old way."

Henry Pauliss asks a classic suck-up question. "And how'd you turn out?"

"Oh, I went through law school at night and then paid for the education for the others. My brother went to Harvard Med, the oldest of my three kid sisters went to Purdue for engineering. And then of course the other two dropped out of high school and became streetwalkers."

Pauliss's jaw drops. "You—uh, er, that is—"

"Not really," Diem says, "but I didn't want to make it sound like ignoring the kids is the best way to raise them. I was just kind of thinking that sometimes the damndest things work."

Di chuckles, Carla laughs outright. Henry Pauliss is now turning an odd shade of red; if Harris Diem is willing to undercut him by setting him up for laughter like that, in front of underlings, then Henry is on his way out the door, and will probably be given a hard kick as he goes. Everyone present knows this, so not only is Pauliss getting his termination notice, but he is being given it in front of Carla and Di, deliberately.

Carla might wish she were the kind of nice, non-vindictive person who wouldn't enjoy this, but as it happens, she isn't. She's delighted to see the bastard find out what it's like to get nailed for just doing what was asked of him. It almost makes the long silly wait for the President (whom they are not supposed to know they are waiting for) worthwhile.

When Hardshaw finally does turn up the first thing that she says to Carla is, "I'm told that you're always right about the weather."

Carla snorts. "If I were always right about the weather I'd have gotten rich in commodities futures. I'm pretty good. My feel for it is better than most meteorologists', and I'm good at the math, and I guess right a lot. But I'm not infallible. And the major reason I've been right several times in this crisis is that I haven't had a job to protect, so I could say what other people were only thinking."

President Hardshaw grins at her—the kind of grin that you use to lock a vote down forever, Carla realizes, just as she also realizes that it's certainly working on her. When the President speaks, Carla is still a little dazzled. "Well, then, here's the question, and if it happens to be a really stupid question, the important thing is that we don't let it leak that I asked it. Not even at a party over a drink, to impress your date. Because just now the President of the United States cannot afford to look like a ninny, and unfortunately she squandered her youth on law rather than meteorology."

"Understood," Carla says. "I won't talk—I don't like most people that much."

"So Harris tells me. All right, then. Is there, in principle at least, any way in which we can intervene to turn this thing off? Since it was a human action that set it running, is there anything we could do to get rid of it?"

Carla draws a breath as she thinks, changes her mind as she's drawing it, draws more breath, finally lets it out without quite having decided on an answer. "It's a physical process. So in principle it can be modified. But it involves immense amounts of energy across vast areas, so the means to modify it may be beyond us."

"Suppose you talk principles first."

"All right. One, if we could make the outflow jet move around to due south and keep it there, we could drive the thing right up the Bering Strait or across Siberia, whichever you prefer, and let it die in the cold like a normal hurricane. I suppose it might do that of its own accord anyway.

"Two, if we could make the water cold in front of it, it would die. Removing methane from the air would work but would take a long time; it would be better to turn off the sunlight.

"And that's about it. To kill a hurricane you cool off its feet. I suppose you could warm its top, too—perhaps with a huge solar mirror—but frankly this thing is so big I'd be worried about giving it a chance to break through the tropopause and extend all the way up into the stratosphere. We might be removing the current constraint on its size by doing that. No, I think if you want to kill it you have to get it over a cold surface—either by moving the hurricane or by cooling the surface. It is moving randomly, you know, and it will probably find a surface big enough to cool it sooner or later."

"But isn't every other hurricane this year going to grow to this size?" Henry Pauliss asks. "In fact, we've been lucky so far not to have one in the Atlantic, which has actually warmed up a little more than the Pacific. We could have another Clem there anytime."

"Or something like it," Carla admits. "You're right, of course. Given their tendency to circle—assuming that Clem is typical, and generalizing from a sample of one is stupid and I hate it but I guess we have to—*if* Clem is typical and most such hurricanes do circle, then there's little question that they're going to last longer. And if they last longer, they'll overlap each other more in time—you won't have any weeks when there aren't one or two or more of them tearing up some part of the world. No, I suppose if you *can* do something about them, then just letting them die naturally isn't good enough."

"It certainly isn't," Hardshaw says. "So you think the best route would be to, as you say, turn off the sunlight?"

"Sure. If you could give the Earth a moon in geosynchronous, inclined orbit so that it moved north and south in a tight figure eight, and set it up so that the northern part of its motion coincided with daytime . . . and if that moon was big enough to cast a shadow a few hundred kilometers across . . . after a while you'd have a nice belt of cold water for Clem to run into and die in. But it would have to be an awfully big moon. Geosynchronous is one-tenth as far as the moon is, the natural moon, I mean, and you'd need a shadow fifty times what the moon casts in a total eclipse . . . whatever it was would be *huge* in the sky, seven full moons across. Physically it would be bigger in diameter than the Earth."

"So a Mylar balloon—"

"Would work, sure, if you could keep it in position. And if you could inflate something thousands of kilometers across. Is that what you're thinking of using?"

President Hardshaw would be a tough lady to play poker with. She doesn't blink, she doesn't wince, she doesn't check to see if Diem has reacted—he hasn't but Pauliss has, and look here, poor old Di, never really one for intrigue, sits up straight. Obviously Ms. President has made them all swear blood oaths or something that they won't even vaguely think about telling her what they really want to know, and now she's spilled it herself.

The only thing Carla has ever learned to like about dealing with power is how easy it is to embarrass people who have it.

After a long instant, Hardshaw says, "Well, that cat's out of that bag. Yes, we're thinking of using Mylar balloons, though not in the way you describe."

"I'm a meteorologist, not a payload specialist."

"We have an offer to put many thousands of them into highly elliptical orbits, with twenty-four-hour periods, with perigee falling across the North Pacific in daylight. And they'd be a couple hundred kilometers across, but they'd be coming down to within a hundred fifty kilometers of the surface, so they'd probably make only two or three approaches before they burned up on re-entry. But if they were timed right . . ."

"You'd need a lot of them," Carla warns.

"Understood. But *could* it work?"

"With the right coordination, and with enough of them," she says. She'd been impressed with Hardshaw up till now, but really she keeps asking the same question over and over. "Do you want me to work on exactly how you'd do it?"

Hardshaw says, "On that we'll have to get back to you. We have what amounts to a bid in hand to do the job, and I will really want your input about that bid. May we send you a copy for your review?"

"Certainly."

"Good. I will look forward to hearing your report—and I do mean hearing; let Harris Diem know when you're ready to talk about it, and he'll set you up in conference with me. And thank you, Carla, the country already owes you a great debt and I think we will owe you more before this is over."

Yeah, but can I collect it and take it to the bank? one part of Carla thinks. She stifles it and says, "I'm flattered, Ms. President."

When she hangs up, there's a short call from Louie. The poor big dumb lug is missing her, too. Everybody seems to need Carla today.

She's not sure she likes it.

After they click off from Carla Tynan, and from Di Callare and Henry Pauliss, President Hardshaw turns to Harris Diem and says, "I can certainly see why Pauliss chose to give us that particular head on a plate three years ago."

"Irritating, isn't she?" Diem says.

"Not at all." Hardshaw stands up, stretches, groans. "She's blunt and she's effective and she understands the physical world. For that matter, she understands politics. Before I was officially on, while I was just watching, you saw that little smile of pleasure when you slapped Pauliss in front of her? She knew exactly what was happening to him."

Diem spent the last hour of work last night on the phone to Henry Pauliss, assuring him that no one was out to get him and that everyone understood that all he had ever done was to carry out policy decisions from higher up. He's known Pauliss for ten years or so and the two have consistently been on warm personal terms; they've shared an occasional social evening because Harris Diem, a bachelor who doesn't date, is constantly out to dinner, sports, or theatre with all sorts of people, generally people that the Administration has some reason to like.

So last night, when it was becoming clear to Pauliss that he was going to be the goat for NOAA, Pauliss called Diem and did his best to find some safe hiding place in the Chief of Staff's shadow, and Diem made soothing noises and said he would do what he could.

Diem had meant it, too; there is a loyalty owed to the people who work for you, just as much as to the people you work for—unless they conflict. And Hardshaw told him to spend some time on the line with the meteorologists and with Pauliss—and to make sure Pauliss was embarrassed and shaken.

"Well," Diem says, tentatively, "I suppose you mean you can see why she'd irritate someone like Pauliss."

"Yes, exactly. Poor Henry Pauliss. Used to be a real scientist and got turned into a yes-man, and now the damned President is demanding real scientists. Not his fault at all."

"So is he going to take the fall for us? Berlina Jameson has been nosing around—"

"Berlina—oh, *Sniffings*. Good little show."

She's showing her age in that, Diem thinks, for only people of "President Grandma's" generation and older still call video documents "shows." But he only says, "Well, it's well-presented and it's popular. And Jameson certainly does her research—"

"She's like a throwback to the people I grew up watching," Hardshaw agrees. "People like Dan Rather . . . and of course you know Rather got his start ripping into the Nixon White House. Which the Nixon White House happened to have coming. So I imagine you're afraid that I might be planning to throw Pauliss to Berlina Jameson to keep the heat off us?"

Diem shakes his head emphatically. "I don't think you're dumb enough for that, boss. That kind of thing always smells like a cover-up, and if you have video reporters on it, it's bad enough, but if there's any strong hint that there might be a cover-up, you'll have detectives from every XV channel in the world crawling all over us to find it. And finding god knows what else on the way. 'Intrepid reporter penetrates cover-up' is what they feed on—

look what happened to those poor stupid bastard doctors after their old folks' home blew down.

"No, I'm more afraid that Henry Pauliss might panic and decide that he's going to be thrown to the wolves. In which case he's smart enough to run to Berlina Jameson and tell her everything he knows."

"And what does he know?" Brittany Hardshaw sits back, fixing Diem with a mild, easy gaze. "He knows that we decided to get rid of Anticipatory Section to reduce the chances of Global Riot Two, since the first one had happened after one of their reports. He knows that if we'd still had an Anticipatory Section we might have known how much trouble we were in much sooner. And that's about all.

"Give him some reassurance, and then call Jameson yourself and dump the story in her lap. Offer her an interview if you can give her the time. Make it clear that we really blew it, but we blew it for good reasons, and don't hold anything back."

"Boss, this openness obsession of yours is going to cause a lot of trouble."

Hardshaw gestures at the huge pile of paper, the "summary report" on the loss of millions of lives in Hawaii and the estimates of the time needed to repopulate—indeed to resettle—the islands. "We're already *in* a lot of trouble, Harris, I don't think you'll even notice this little bit more. Now, second and more important on our agenda—get me Rivera; we need to talk about this proposition Klieg is throwing at us."

Henry Pauliss walks out of his office and considers. He has an ex-wife who has married again. There are two secretaries he sometimes has sex with, and one young woman he's been courting without success for a while. Other than that, ball games with Diem and a few members of Congress have been his social life.

He has no kids. There's a large pile of cash in the bank, but Pauliss has never really figured out what to do with it. His will is still made out to his ex, but that doesn't matter much to him.

He considers all the usual things—that he could delay for a last fling of luxury, a good meal, a good bottle, maybe even a good prostitute? None of it appeals to him. He could resign (they'll want that anyway) and have a religious conversion, or just take his pile of money and go fishing some-where. There are some places he hasn't seen and things he hasn't done.

But if he ever cared about them, he stopped caring quite a while back. Probably the Pauliss who cared about taking the time to really see Europe or to hike the Appalachian Trail would also have cared enough to resign during the months when they covered up the real data. Certainly if he had wanted a real life with real friends, he'd have wanted it before now. There's just not much reason to continue to go on. . . .

It's a complete cliché, he knows, but it works. He walks into a convenience store, presents his i.d., and buys a Self Defender. The little hypersonic pistols are designed purely as weapons against street crime; they contain only twenty rounds and can't be reloaded, each of them carries a chemical dye packet that stains the hand that fires it with a unique identifier (matching an i.d. capsule in the rounds it fires), and when it fires, it also sends out a "radio scream" that police direction finders can instantly spot. If a woman is attacked in a deserted street, and uses it, not only does it stop the attack, but it also summons help.

But because of its identifier features and its "scream," it's useless for robberies, gang murders, or assassinations.

What the designers never anticipated was that it does have another use, and that's the cliché Henry Pauliss is counting on. If you shoot yourself, it is always possible that failure of nerve, physical weakness, a mistake, or sheer bad luck may lead to your only being wounded. And if that happens, chances are that you'll be in quite a bit of pain. Even if you're going to try again, you want the ambulance to get to you right away.

Use a Self Defender, and the ambulance is right there.

Pauliss walks over to Memorial Park, on the site of the old Capitol, and sits down on one of the walls of rubble, like any of the bums and drunks out there at this time of day. Then he pulls out the Self Defender, places the muzzle back against his upper palate, and squeezes the trigger.

The ambulance is there in less than two minutes, just as he had planned, but Henry Pauliss is already dead.

It is not normal for a hurricane to move away from a pole or in the direction of the Earth's rotation—at least not for a normal hurricane. Not that hurricanes don't. Just that the physics tends to drive them to move toward the pole and to the west. Toward the west, because the Earth turns under them, dragging its envelope of air eastward with it, and the hurricanes are a bit more resistant to being dragged than the air around them. Toward the pole, because the Coriolis force is stronger as you move farther from the equator, so the spinning winds curl more tightly on the poleward side, the pressure is just that much lower on that side of the eye, and thus the eye itself tends to creep that way.

Moreover, in most of the Northern Hemisphere's great hurricane formation zones—the Pacific near southern Mexico and in the area south of the Philippines, the Bay of Bengal, and the Caribbean Sea—it happens that the steering currents blow to the north and to the west, so the hurricane is usually being guided by the steering current and is following its own inclination.

But Clem is not usual or normal. The outflow jet has driven it to the south of Hawaii; in that area the steering currents are generally due south. For a while the outflow jet continues to push the hurricane eastward, and the steering current carries it south, so that it passes the American West Coast and Baja at a great distance, creating the best surfing seen on those coasts in years, sending unseasonably heavy thundershowers into the coast for a day or so, but not much disturbing the rhythm of life.

The outflow jet, sputtering around, at last finds its way back to lining up with the steering current. And thus it is that Clem accelerates to the south, and once again behaves like a normal hurricane, driven to the west. Clem is headed back for his birthplace—and for another rampage through the Pacific.

On July 5, about an hour after sunrise reaches the empty stretch of the Pacific Clem has moved into, the giant hurricane is at 16N 124W, and is now headed almost due south. Louie Tynan, working by telepresence on the moon, is asked to hurry along the first of the weather satellites he's building, if he can. There doesn't seem to be any way, so he says he will see what he can do.

Di and Carla are watching Clem, but not as closely as before. Di has a lunch meeting in Washington with leaders of various other NOAA teams, just a few moments away, and so he's mainly worried about his notes for his presentation. And it's still only two in the morning in the Solomons, where Carla has at last come into port.

She's not exactly asleep but she's not exactly awake, either. She's lying on a too-sloshy waterbed in her room in the Mendana Hotel, allegedly as good a room as you can get in Honiara, but her newly upgraded data socket (surgery courtesy of an American government slush fund) is plugged into one of about twenty working current-generation universal data jacks on the whole island of Guadalcanal, and what she's doing is letting herself drift and doze, randomly associating her way through the vast regions of open net.

If she were paying for this herself the cost would be astronomical, but she's not—it's another gift of Uncle Sam's, who seems to be treating her as a favorite niece these days. Unlimited data access is something she's wanted to mess around with in just this way for a long time, because her best ideas often come to her in the edges of sleep. So she's half dreaming, half awake, as she inventories the world's resources and the scope of Clem, looking for a way to match up what can be launched with the shadows it must cast, trying to find out if Klieg's scheme will work the way his team of "experts" say it will.

The thing is, at any one time there aren't even three thousand people who do global weather forecasting or modeling for a living, and Klieg's experts include only two of them, neither of whom has any reputation. But the lack of names or even of specialists on Klieg's team does not by itself make that team wrong. And what they're proposing to do—cool the water in one broad band across the Pacific to twenty degrees Celsius or below, so that there's a place for Clem, and all the Clems to come, to die harmlessly rather than continue on for weeks or months—is not the problem. If the cold water is wide enough and cool enough, it will work.

The problem is mostly with what will happen to other things; are they creating another problem? And will what Klieg is proposing make a big enough difference to justify the price Klieg is asking?

Carla turns over in her sleep. *That* thought is really bothering her.

There's no other word for it—Klieg is blackmailing, or rather trying to blackmail, the UN, into ratifying his launch monopoly, giving him a permanent, dominant position in space launch worldwide. He will in effect own the doorways off planet.

She winces and turns uneasily; if any observer could see the whole net at once, he would see the odd phenomenon of short, microsecond-long interrupts scattering and proliferating across billions of processors in response. Carla does not yet notice this; she herself does not yet understand the power of being plugged in and not having to pay.

It's not exactly what she's supposed to be working on but it's close, so she gives up her resistance to the problem and lets herself play it through, constructing models that are not of weather but of the future. She finds herself sliding forward to 2050; global data take shape and. . . .

She falls forward into the simulation. She is in Times Square, and in front of her there's a gigantic picture of Klieg. The street is very, very clean . . . and everything seems to be well organized. She realizes that people are walking between painted lines on the sidewalk, steps over to examine a line, and a policeman approaches her. This frightens her enough to make her run—

The policemen all wear the blue beret and there are thousands of them. And every shop she runs past has a large black "K" in the window, indicating that it is authorized to receive space-manufactured materials . . . and by now, she realizes, that's everything of any significance, Klieg is making the world's steel, glass, and aluminum up there, growing the food—

The cops close in on her. She notices that no one bothers to look. They have an oddly bland expression, not unlike that of Klieg on the building.

They are all white.

She wakes up, is hurled back into her hotel room on Guadalcanal, the waterbed bouncing under her, her fingers crawling at the jack in her head. She makes them relax and tug smoothly, and now she is back in her own brain, nobody in here in her head but herself, shuddering. The dream was surely just a vivid metaphor; a little like trying to see something in the distance and leaning over a high railing too far, she thinks, that's all that happened. She was trying to visualize what the data were saying and there she was in the middle of the data. Her own imagination and paranoia, and her natural distrust of a businessman like Klieg, overwhelmed her.

But a part of the back of her brain is saying something else entirely. She realizes that she knew on another level what was happening in the simulation even as she lived it, and that among other things a dozen processors around the globe dedicated themselves to scanning all of the available bio and footage on Klieg and Rivera and half a dozen important people in the world, running them forward; that was Times Square as Klieg, with his bland Midwestern sensibility, would remake it, and his sense of order was being enforced. And it is true that the global economy is just at the point where space-based resources might expand very quickly, and if Klieg were to have a monopoly on the gateway. . . .

Why was everyone white? Did the system pick up on some latent prejudice in Klieg? Did it pick up on some nightmare of hers? When Carla was young, she had an old great-uncle who was bluntly, vocally racist and used to terrify her by describing how he wanted to kill some of the black children Carla played with, his voice filled with terrible relish as he recounted tales of long-ago lynchings he had heard from elder relatives. He had a Midwestern accent, not unlike Klieg's . . . was that the reason for the association?

She looks down and realizes she is still holding the data jack. And now that she's wide awake it should be all right.

Carla plugs back in, stretching out again, trying to make herself relax but determined not to fall asleep again. The whine of mosquitos outside the surrounding netting blends into the whine of the electronics in the net—

And she receives an odd shock. There is a presence out there looking for her, a felt sensation that someone wants to talk to her. She recoils from it instinctively, then turns to face it as she recognizes—

Herself?

She has a strange sense of facing herself in a mirror, and then of moving closer, closer until she touches her image and she is abruptly merged with it. At once she knows what happened. She did not stop the billions of parallel programs running in millions of processors. And to them the physical Carla is merely one big processor, one large node in the net . . . a processor dropped out, but they kept running.

And what they were all doing collectively was simulating Carla. No, scratch that thought, they *were* Carla, in some sense, an extended version of her. So while she was unplugged, they kept working—tens of thousands of times faster than she could. There is a complete report now, which they give to her in very high-speed summary so that it comes to her like the best of her flashes of intuition: the evidence that Klieg's impulse toward the world will be to homogenize it (though the "all white" version was probably just an error in the first simulation run, because Klieg appears to be indifferent to skin color as long as other people act just like Klieg's idea of proper behavior), and the evidence that if he is allowed to rescue the world from Clem and Clem's daughters, he will have that kind of power.

The system has even modeled possible degeneration of Klieg's moral structure and ethics under the pressure of such power, and concluded that he probably wouldn't change much—his view of the world is too stable to be altered by even so large a change of circumstances. This is not altogether a positive thing, since it clearly implies that his economic dictatorship is apt to be benign, even friendly—he would probably shut down a large number of ethnic conflicts in an extremely even-handed way, for example—and thus will not generate much rebellion until it is far too late for the world to shake it off.

As she re-merges with her report, she discovers something else. Louie had been suggesting she plug into some optimizer software with the note that he had found it made big differences in his work on the moon—for example, the weather satellites he's now launching are an enormous leap in technology, and Louie is neither a design engineer nor a meteorologist.

His suggestion must have been somewhere in her mind when she unplugged, for the software has been optimized in many ways, not all of which she understands. One that is clear, however, is that it is now no longer sending the bill to a U.S. government account. It had to stop doing so because the bill was going to be far too large, but rather than shutting down, it has found its way around the accounting programs. She is running on stolen time from thousands upon thousands of systems worldwide, and her tracks are being covered even as she moves through the net.

She is now independent of the people who pay her, and free to decide what's best . . . but then, hasn't it always been that way?

Back to work. The question is, who else or what else could do the job Klieg is proposing to do? Her simulations seem to show that if Rivera and Hardshaw turn down the offer from Klieg (probably on grounds that it is "tainted" by the close interconnections with the Siberian government), then Klieg and the Siberians will go public with the offer—and the public will force the UN to take the deal.

Global public opinion is a new thing, something that didn't exist even ten years ago—but then ten years ago there couldn't have been a global riot, either.

She lets herself drift, only to discover that she doesn't feel drowsy anymore when she does this. Part of her, without effort, finds a confidential report in a NASA file and reads about what happens when cross-system-capable optimizer viruses invade a mind. She discovers that Louie, too, has lost the need to sleep for mental rest, though he needs much more bed rest to keep his immune system functioning, given the large blood sugar demands made by his active brain and the high-radiation environment. Well, she's already in bed, and it will be hours—which she can experience as millennia if she wishes—before daylight, when she can go get a huge breakfast. Meanwhile she has more time than she's ever had before to just think—and she realizes this will be with her for the rest of her life. She glories in the thought of how much time she has.

And so does Louie, she realizes. She won't even have to be lonely.

She turns her eyes—satellites of several nations, including theoretically closed military ones, seaborne instruments, instruments on aircraft—onto Clem, and watches as the outflow jet suddenly kicks around, creating the pressure release she had feared. The great bubble of air, twenty kilometers across and a thousand kilometers from Clem's eye, blisters upward and tears open; at sea level, the whirling winds, at hurricane force even this far from the eye, split around the upwelling air, merge, begin to flow faster—

In less than ten minutes, a hurricane eye has been formed, and begins to gather a storm around it. It's the reverse of what's always been seen in nature before, but there is no question—Clem has given birth to an eye, and the eye is accreting a hurricane. Moreover, the two hurricanes are putting out enough air together to create a high pressure spot between them, and thrust them apart—which means this daughter will head for the Americas.

Carla reaches for her own voice back in Honiara, but before she moves herself it occurs to her that it's just as easy to compose a message in text, so she sends that to Di, and to Harris Diem, who is supposed to be the White House contact for weather matters. As she composes each word of the message she runs thousands of models to improve her view of what's about to happen; virtually all the possible news is bad.

Diogenes Callare and Harris Diem get word at the same time, shortly after Berlina Jameson's datarodents have pirated Carla's report.

By late afternoon, when the two men return from Henry Pauliss's funeral, shirts damp with the sweat of D.C. in July, a new edition of *Sniffings* has been out for hours.

Berlina is proud and getting prouder. The distributors are sending her demogs that show she has three separate core audiences, which is a good place to be, because it means she can occasionally offend one of them.

Her most loyal fans are old people who remember Bartnick, Arnott,

Rather . . . heck, some of them probably remember Cronkite—and who find it comforting to get the news the way Berlina gives it. Fair enough—classical forms draw classicists.

But there also are the people in the United Left who like it because it seems lower-tech to them (though just what's low tech about putting together television documentaries from the rear seat of your car, while the car drives itself, Berlina would like to know) and because it seems like it's the inside track on the kind of thing they always suspect (rightly) is going on. And that's okay too—the Left of any kind, whether it thinks it's United or not, has a long affinity with the news media in any country in which the media are independent of government control.

Then there's that other group, which she can't quite figure out . . . there are a substantial number of young subscribers who say they like it because it's "flat," which is sort of the generic word for "good," the way "cool" is in boomtalk.

That's okay, except that by "flat" they also mean it's emotionally uninvolving, and Berlina would love to know how they can feel that. She intercepted Army video coming out of the first whistler that got over Honolulu after visibility cleared up, and popped in a closeup of the huge pile of bodies on Kalei Road, students from a shelter at the university that burst open only during the washback of the fourth giant wave, sucking the students out of the shelter and crushing and drowning them between the walls of a wrecked shopping mall two miles away. She covered President Hardshaw's sidestep of the traps in Secretary-General Rivera's aid package, got UN and U.S. officials both on camera denying things that were patently true, even caught a little footage of one UN official from Ecuador pounding the table and telling his subordinates that "this is when we settle with the *yanqui* bastards once and for all." She doesn't exactly understand how they can feel it's "flat," but since they do, she's glad it makes them watch.

Then again, she thinks for the thousandth time over the thousandth cup of coffee, perhaps everything is flat compared to XV. Maybe the use of the word "flat" among the more bohemian fringe of the young bodes something good about the future, that people are going to turn their backs on those damned hallucinations, or at least insist on a context that lets you evaluate it rather than get sucked into the story.

She talked, the other day, on one of the ubiquitous bulletin board systems, with a professor of communications who was explaining to her that she was "Brechtian" while the XV was "Craigean." That wasn't totally fruitless—she looked up who Bertolt Brecht and Gordon Craig were, and it might come in handy to impress people at a foundation dinner or something—but when you came right down to it, all it meant was that Berlina would rather persuade people than overwhelm them. Which she knew in the first place.

This latest capture isn't high drama by itself, but in context it will be interesting enough for her audience. There's a new hurricane forming and headed for Central America (or, given the time it has to get there, and the way the things can veer around, possibly for Colombia's Pacific Coast or even for Baja). It looks like anything as big as Clem can spawn other ones . . . which swiftly grow to Clem's own size. The potential for scare stuff in this story is wonderful, but she's going to deliver it the way that Berlina does, the way that people turn to *Sniffings* to get—"flat, rad, and cool," as she likes to say to herself.

It feels so good to know that there is really an audience out there, and that they really want to look at what she wants to do, that she sits in the back of her speeding car hugging herself, just feeling happy about everything, instead of working. In a few minutes she'll have to get down to the difficult business of snipping together information, and of mastering yet more meteorology—who ever thought that the boring old weatherman's slot would be the one she wishes she'd had? In the last three days she's learned more about outflow jets than she used to know about the Ways and Means Committee.

So by the time Diem and Callare have read the reports, called each other, gotten people together, and in general begun to see what they can do about the crisis they had been dreading, the formation of Clem Two (Carla had suggested a new nomenclature because in her understated way she was trying to tell them that they would run out of alphabetic names for hurricanes long before the season was over), before President Hardshaw and Secretary-General Rivera are even fully aware that there *is* a Clem Two, Berlina has dubbed the thing "Clementine" and devoted a special issue of *Sniffings* to it.

Louie has begun to notice, lately, that it hardly seems worth staying in touch with his body while he works, and often he just cuts the damned thing largely loose by sending it off to sleep. The number of processors on which he runs on the moon is growing geometrically, so that every day there seems to be more and more of him there and less and less back on *Constitution*.

His body back on the station wakes up refreshed after hours of pleasant dreams, and indeed he's been quietly tweaking the immune system a bit, since he accidentally discovered some access to it from the brain a few days ago. He downloaded a report about that to Dr. Wo and got back a short note asking if he'd be willing to split the Nobel Prize in Medicine, so probably it was more than a stray thought. But he's a little too busy to work on all that just now.

Even just getting a call from his body annoys hell out of him; he has to migrate back to Earth orbit to take the call. At first he thinks that he's just let it go too long between taking dumps again, but then he realizes someone Earthside wants to talk. As he comes back into slow time Earthside, the call turns out to be from Carla. Quickly he reconfigures back to the moon, since she can think as fast as he can.

And what she wants to talk about with him is . . . well, it's just wonderful, it will solve the whole mind-body problem for him, for good and all. He doesn't realize, until she points it out, how strange his reaction is. "I thought you'd be excited at the chance to go thirty-five times deeper into space than anyone's ever gone before."

She says that, and he says something like "What? Oh, of course, you're right, but . . ." and has weeks of normal mind time to think about it while his response crawls slowly on radio waves down to the antennas of Earth and her answer to his response limps its way back out to him at the speed of light. He has time for his life to run through his mind several times, and each time from a different angle, and it all boils down to this: There was a time when going where no one had ever gone before was the main thing he wanted to do, a time when he saw himself in competition with everyone from Hanno and Leif Eriksson forward. And that time lasted up until about two weeks ago in real time. . . .

Which was about eight thousand years ago in time as he knows it now. He uses billions of processors, in fact just about to be a trillion later this afternoon, and each of them is in turn massively parallel so that he runs millions of programs on each processor; he is up into quintillions of parallel programs . . . yet there is something in his own deep structure that insists on linearizing, insists on making things string out in time in a single chain, so that for the sake of his consciousness, and perhaps of his sanity, he finds it easiest to experience it as thinking for decades in every second (at an accelerating rate, for as he becomes more parallel he becomes faster, and not only new processors, but new processor-makers, and better processor-designers, join him constantly).

It is not that he doesn't want to go elsewhere. It is only that there is now so much to know about where he already is. In idle moments he has run all the data—optical, radar, and thermal—ever taken on the Earth from orbit, and watched the myriad subtle changes in the global biosphere since 1960. He has regressed the Earth's languages back to *World, and demonstrated to his own satisfaction that there are a dozen possible ancestral homelands for all human language. He has filled in holes in history by correlating dozens of bits of evidence whose importance had not been noticed before, and he has dug new holes where the evidence compiled across generations has formed unstable bridges.

He has reprocessed everything about Mars, and knows it now in a way more intimate than he ever did when its iron sands crunched under his boots, and knows moreover not just the planet as it really is, but the planet in all the ways it has been dreamt. He could tell you things about the links between Viking and Barsoom that you could never imagine.

He has compiled data from all the unmanned probes, including the secret Chinese government and the covert Japanese private ones, so that he knows a great deal about every other planet out there, so that the asteroid belt is as familiar to him as the streets of Irish, Ohio, the little town where he grew up. He has read the classics, and the commentaries piled around them, not just the classics of European literature but of the world's major cultures, and listened to recordings of the great musical traditions, and all this has been to avoid having idle processors—which, when they re-enter the processing stream after waiting for the data they need, he experiences as boredom.

Had he been really concentrating he could have advanced technology on the moon by a matter of fifty years beyond its levels on Earth, but at that point, no one on Earth would have known enough to use it intelligently. And besides, he's been enjoying the spare time. . . .

And all of this time spent in cultivating his own intellectual garden has of course altered his feelings about exploring. Somewhat. He still wants to go and to find out, but there is so much more that he wants to know. . . .

The thing that most excited him was the idea of not being strung out between Earth and Moon anymore, not having to knock himself unconscious for the many long weeks that a second-and-a-half radio transmission gap is to him now.

All of this he manages to get down into what he calls a "terabyte haiku"—a huge poly/hypermedia document, extremely densely interconnected to get across the idea that his feelings are a gestalt, that he downloads to Carla to explain. Her processing capability is an order of magnitude smaller than his, not so much because of lack of processing space (she has all the surplus of Earth, which is huge, to draw from), but because she insists, every day, on a few hours of being unhooked and living in real time. He can't imagine why she does that but she seems to enjoy it.

It takes her ten seconds or so to digest and read the "terabyte haiku." The first thing she says afterwards is "I see."

He waits through the ages of seconds before he realizes he's now supposed to say something in return.

"So how long before they authorize it? I can be working on it part time until they do."

"They probably haven't gotten it out of the President's printer yet. For some reason she insists on hard copies. But I thought you and I might think about it together a little. There is an issue here and there that needs to get worked out."

Louie assents, and the two of them begin to trade information, statistics, projections, "what-ifs" at a rate that would move the Library of Congress every two to three minutes; for both of them, it "runs in background"—that is, they are only dimly aware of it, as they go on about their other work, giving it full attention every now and then as something important comes up.

This leaves Louie time enough on the moon to keep the robots working at high speed; now that he knows he will be leaving, he needs to get a system set up so that Earth can order a new satellite by radio and have it built and launched here. Of necessity that also means deciding which parts he wants to build fresh and which to take with him. . . .

There's a deep sense of pleasure growing inside him as he contemplates the job. Right now he could duplicate the original Moonbase—as it was two weeks ago, after almost twenty years of European, Japanese, and American effort—in two days' construction. And as capacity improves . . . well, if they ask him to do what Carla proposes three days from now, he'll be at the point where the whole thing can be accomplished within a week, the big thruster shipped down to *Constitution* along with the thousands of microrobots and replicators and the three trillion processor packages that he's decided will be enough (especially since he can build some more on the way). While he's at it, he can also get some nice big chunks of shielding down there, and the food recycling gadget he's got from the hydroponics package. . . .

It would really be better to design and build a habitat for his body for the voyage, but though designing it would be easy, there are too many materials he needs from Earth, and no reliable launch from anywhere in the Northern Hemisphere. The Aussies could probably ship things to him, but for the next week or so Clem will be ripping along a few degrees north of the equator, so that whatever he ordered would have to be flown to the Cape of Good Hope and then across the Indian Ocean to be sure of getting it there—

No, Carla was right. If he's going to go grab and dissassemble a comet for this job, he'll just have to take the whole space station with him. That means some reinforcing that he hasn't thought about yet, if he wants it to take the acceleration. . . .

Something is disturbing him and he's not sure what. It's a long moment or two before he gets it nailed down to something coming from Carla. . . .

And something pleasant . . .

Abruptly he has a second and a half blank and catapults back into his body in Earth orbit, where he finds himself overwhelmed by memory and fantasy, his penis in Carla's hands, mouth, vagina, anus, the way she shrieks in orgasm, the furious pleasure of pressing their sweaty bodies together on that long hike in the Cascades the last time he hit dirtside, the first time he saw her and realized that nobody else was ever going to understand it but he had to have *that* one and realized she had seen him feeling that way. . . .

His orgasm is huge, shaking—and very wet and sloppy. In a weightless environment, of course, this means his semen forms little floating spheres all over the cabin.

In his mind, he feels Carla shrieking to him from ten thousand processor cortexes and antennas all over the Earth.

"Shit," he says, speaking aloud. "You are one shameless wench. I just hope the government wasn't bugging that."

She gasps and laughs, then answers him on voice, even though he can still feel the presence of her mind on his through all the myriad portals of connection; they are knotted together physically through millions of transmission links, and logically through billions of input-output subroutines, but at this kind of moment it is much too pleasant to forgo talking in the old, slow, acoustic mode. He feels her assent to this even as her first word comes over the voice link. "They either deal with us or with John Klieg," she says, "and I don't think his sex life is nearly as interesting. But as a matter of fact, they were bugging it in a few places. . . . It will take them a week to figure out what all that was, though, and in the great majority of the signal we're still talking about optimizing the design for the ship. One way to have privacy is to just drown out what you're keeping private with enough other signal. Sort of like turning up the stereo in the dorm room."

Louie relaxes and laughs. "You yanked me back into Earth orbit, I'm afraid. There're some things that work better in the liveware." Yet even as he says it, he can feel the vast processes—delayed, but there—moving and changing on the moon. He realizes, too, that he's never treated himself to looking at Moonbase from the observation bubble since he started building it.

"What gave you the idea?" he asks. "It's the kind of thing we just might want to do again."

"You're insatiable!" she says, and by now he's realized that they are talking out loud mostly to enjoy the separation and the suspense of not knowing what the other will say or how the other will form the thought.

"Well, not right away," he says. "The liveware wouldn't take that. But soon all the same. Did you notice that we, um—gee, there's not exactly a word for it, feeling your own body with the other person's consciousness?"

"Notice it? What do you think finally set me off? My god, Louie, it's incredible. I suppose if we wanted to we could always run a little of that in background—"

"Nothing doing, lover. I've always put my full attention into it whenever I'm doing it. My big regret is that it's still going to be months before we can try it with all the processor networks linked *and* doing it physically. Preferably in weightlessness."

"I'm not space-rated—"

"By the time I get back I'll have a little ship's launch that can just set down at sea, make its own fuel from air and water, and pick you up from *MyBoat*. I'm not sure what USSF and NASA will think about my bringing up a date, but I'll point out to them that it won't cost them a dime and it's cheaper than giving me shore leave. I'm really thinking I might never get back to Earth."

She chuckles. "It's a date, sailor. And I guess that's an example of how different we are . . . I have to have a few hours a day in real experience. It's just different for me. And besides, don't you find it's kind of fun to meet yourself?"

He has a long, confusing moment, because when he was a teenager, to "meat" a girl was one of a thousand expressions they had for fucking; his mind dips into the net and realizes what she said, then realizes he doesn't know what she means—at about the same moment she does.

"You never unplug long enough to have that happen!" she says, and she sends him the image of the event—the moment each day when she plugs back in and finds that the other half (or really the other ninety-nine point many nines percent) of her consciousness has lived another few centuries and has a lot to tell her about it.

"Jeez. Never. Though come to think of it, it might be interesting to see if I can split myself between the moon and the processing modules on the *Constitution* . . . since both would keep building for the four months or so they'd be out of realtime contact . . . that would mean . . . sheesh. Remerging after something like ten million years, at the rate of expansion I've got planned."

"I could probably write several hundred scientific papers within the next twenty-four hours without breathing hard, but . . ."

"Same here. In fact, don't laugh at me, but I could do a couple of pretty good ones in comparative philology, history, maybe a few in literary criticism."

She does laugh, but it sounds kind. "Interesting. I have some work in musicology I like, too. Louie, what's happening to us? Are we turning into machines?"

"I'd say it's more likely machines are turning into us."

They talk for a long time afterward, about everything and anything, and rather than sever the link they leave a little backchannel running between them; it feels like the kind of telepathy old marrieds have, for each always has a quiet awareness of what the other is thinking. The two loners are not lonely anymore, and won't be until Louie begins his long journey.

On July 6, Clem Two heads east for most of the day, occasionally angling a little to the south. Di's best guess, confirmed by Carla, is that this is because the two hurricanes, mother and daughter, have outflow jets pointed at each other and are thus creating a high-pressure ridge that pushes them away from each other. President Hardshaw talks with about a dozen presidents, dictators, and chiefs of state in the possible pathway of the storm.

Berlina Jameson brings out a special edition of *Sniffings* about the approach of Clem Two. A majority of Americans polled are under the impression that since Clem Two is a "daughter" hurricane it is somehow tied to Clem, and must be smaller than Clem. She tries to get across the idea that once Clem Two's eye was created by the motion of Clem's outflow jet, there was no further relationship, and there is nothing to prevent Clem Two from going elsewhere or growing bigger than its parent. Berlina works longer on this *Sniffings* than on any other, and her work is pirated everywhere, especially in *Scuttlebytes*, but it doesn't matter; people believe what they want to believe and when large percentages of them are plugged into XV, the tendency is increased; why believe anything that might lead you to unplug?

She calls Di Callare one last time, but he has no time to talk with her; all she gets out of the conversation is a sense of how much things are going to hell. The man sounds like he hasn't been home in a week or asleep in days. She says she's going to head to Mexico and then as far south as she can get, in hopes of getting better coverage of Clem Two's impact on the coast; he tells her to avoid using roads too near either coast and to be careful when she hits the "drive yourself" zones.

Strangely enough, just as she's checking out, the desk clerk hands her a piece of mail from the White House thanking her for her "role in alerting the public," and enclosing a certificate for a "President's award for journalism and citizenship." She finds it a bit frightening that the President's staff has nothing better to do, but she still pins the certificate to the ceiling of her car.

* * *

By July 7, Clem Two is angling a little to the north and is still obstinately headed east, in defiance of steering currents and the Earth's rotation. Alerts are being issued in Mexico for all of Baja California Sur and for the mainland all the way from Los Mochis to Acapulco. Di realizes that Jesse is more than far enough south to be safe, and Tapachula is up high. Jesse should be fine if he doesn't go down to Puerto Madero or try to run back to the States. Di calls him and talks to him about that briefly, discovers that Jesse is planning to stay put, along with his current girlfriend, and is merely a little worried about some former girlfriend—the one Lori called the political muffin?

It's not easy for Di to keep track, he thinks with an envious grin after hanging up. But from Jesse's explanation the girl is a bit farther to the north, and often has business on the coast—but since the Mexican Army is evacuating coastal towns as fast as they can, "that doesn't seem like much to worry about—at worst she'll have a few days in a refugee camp before someone Stateside wires money to her," Di tells his brother.

Jesse nods. "Oh, I'm not worried a whole lot. Tomorrow would be the day she'd be going to Tehuantepec, and right now they haven't decided to evacuate it, but Tehuantepec isn't *right* on the coast—it's like this place, up above—so I imagine she'll be okay. Just a little normal worry about a friend is all."

"I can understand that," Di says. "Anyway, stay put—unless it does veer your way. If it really looks like it's coming inshore in the Gulf of Tehuantepec, they'll have less than twenty-four hours to get everyone evacuated. Don't be on the last truck and don't stay behind for heroics."

"I do watch the news, big brother," Jesse says. "I saw what happened to Oahu. My evacuation address will be on the Calle del Veinticinco Febrero in San Cristóbal de las Casas—if we have to go. The Army's already assigned places for everyone. And the railhead for the zipline that will take us there is only thirty kilometers away—they didn't quite finish last spring, but at least the railhead isn't far away."

There's not much more to talk about; NOAA is going to have to provide assistance until Clem Two hits, but according to Carla as long as it hits well up the peninsula and moves west to east, as it looks like it's going to do, the central spine of mountains ought to kill Clem Two, reducing it to mere thunderstorms. She has warned them that the exception to that is the isthmus; should Clem Two come ashore in the Gulf of Tehuantepec and then head north, the mountains may not be barrier enough to keep Clem Two from bursting out into the Caribbean—which will pour vastly more energy into the system.

With luck, it will be weeks yet before one of those monsters is loose in the Atlantic . . . but so far luck has not been with them.

On July 8, Clem Two stops dead and stands still for almost four hours, about 300 km west of the tip of Baja. Huge storm surges are pumped up the Gulf of California, and American authorities around the valley of the lower Colorado and the Imperial Valley give urgent orders to evacuate. There's a riot when busloads of Mexicans—actually just being moved by the nearest available highway to the higher ground of Nogales, Sonora—cross the border at Mexicali. A rumor had spread among the Anglo and black citizenry that the busloads of refugees were to be given American passports and allowed to settle permanently.

The riot goes away because Rock gets on the scene for Passionet and millions of men find themselves thinking how stupid all this is; his disgust bleeds through every moment of the coverage. Surface O'Malley is with him, and she rapidly comes to see it his way (the script calls for her to adore him as an older and wiser man of the world on this trip). Rioters running home or using portables to catch themselves on XV are startled by the sensations of anger and nausea directed at them. Those who went home don't return to the riot. Those who had portables quietly slink away.

FBI agents undercover within Passionet note all this and relay it upward; apparently XV can calm a population as well as inflame it. Millions of people seem to be disappointed by the failure of Global Riot Two to happen and take it out on Passionet by switching to other systems; the letter of commendation from President Hardshaw, and the granting of a brief personal interview that brings back viewers, arrive just in time to save Surface and Rock from getting fired.

Very, very slowly, but with gathering speed as the night wears on, Clem Two begins to move south. At first it is hoped that this means Clem Two is about to follow the steering currents, which would mean a move to the west—and bad as Clem Two might be over there, especially as an aftermath to the original Clem, which has just thundered across the now-empty Kingman Reef again, if Clem Two should turn west they will at least have a breathing space.

At dawn on July 9, Clem Two picks up speed and moves in a great, sweeping eastward hook into the Gulf of Tehuantepec.

Jesse and Mary Ann are already packed—evacuees are permitted just one small bag. Within minutes of the alert they are waiting out front for the Army trucks. But the Army doesn't come, and doesn't come, and the hours crawl by. The wind from Clem Two coming in has only just begun to rise, and so it is like any breezy summer day with a rainstorm coming in on the wind. After a long wait they decide to reserve their packed lunches for later, and go around the corner to discover that many of the little cafés have reopened; "I can always just turn off the stove if the Army shows up," one of the owners explains.

The news broadcasts report that big waves are beginning to come inshore and that buses have been commandeered to move the population on the coasts first. There is reassuring footage of soldiers helping people pack into buses.

Or it's reassuring until Jesse sees. "Mary Ann—that's not Puerto Madero."

"How do you know it's not?"

"Because I know the building they're doing that in front of, and that building is in Tuxtla Gutiérrez. I don't know what's really going on, but there's no evacuation down in Puerto Madero, that's for sure."

"Why would they be—"

Jesse shrugs. "Could be anything. They don't want people to panic but they just had a mutiny. Things are coming in so fast that they can't pick people up, so they're trying to keep them calm till it hits. Different factions feuding one place or another. Or if you ask me, they're badly delayed but still planning to come for us, and they want to make sure everyone stays near an evacuation point. Like if the zipline is down—which happens fairly often—then they don't want people piling up at the linehead; it will just make loading the zipline harder, and there's no shelter at the zipline head anyway."

Mary Ann grins at him. "You're really something, you know. You think about explanations like that. Most of the people I've ever known in my life would just have said 'It's typical' or 'Oh, what can you do?' but you think up twenty things it could be."

"All of which are probably wrong."

"Oh, sure, but that doesn't matter. I was just thinking that you actually do that—explain things—instead of just giving it to me from a script." Mary Ann pulls a bandanna from her back pocket and wipes her sweat-covered face. "I don't like how warm and still it's getting, and I *really* don't like the green color in the sky."

"Me either." They move close to each other, so that their shoulders touch; it's even warmer, but Jesse would rather be in contact as they look at the green-brown wash of thunderheads now boiling their way across the sky, chasing the last blue off to the east behind them.

They finish lunch and have another cup of coffee. "This is going to blow in suddenly," Jesse says, "and an outdoor café under an awning is *not* the place for it."

"The assembly point is all the way outdoors."

"True, but your house is about thirty steps from the assembly point. And from your second-floor window we can watch for the bus."

She sighs. "I suppose the problem is that till the wind and rain start, I'm not going to get over the feeling that they just need to matte in a nicer-looking sky. All right, let's get going."

As they walk the short block back, Jesse sees what she means; there is something about the faraway look of the evil green thunderheads, their black anvil bases sailing like bargeloads of coal high above, that seems unconnected with the world below. The air gets more and more still, and the dark clouds roll over thicker and heavier.

He's trying to remember all the terms Diogenes taught him. He knows the big, heavy clouds are cumulonimbus and they get that pattern of dark base and fluffy top because there's a warm updraft pouring from the base up into the sky, and that the whole thing acts like a big Van de Graaff generator, so that there are charges being separated up there and the potential for lightning is building up. And that row of thunderheads is called the squall line? Seems right. And somewhere back behind that there's an actual front . . . no, that's just in regular storms back home, he thinks. Still, somewhere out there the wind is about to pick up—

They are already going up the garden path when the rain hits—and "hits" is the only word for it—it feels like a cold firehose turned suddenly on them. A moment later the wind is whipping up fiercely, and though they run and Mary Ann has the key in her hand, in their ten steps they are soaked to the skin.

"I can't see three feet out this window," Mary Ann points out.

"There's no bus coming in this, anyway," Jesse says. "Glad you got a high-rent place; hope you had to pay extra for the walls."

"The place was redone for security but I didn't pay much attention to what they did," Mary Ann says, and leans against him. He puts an arm around her, doing his best to be reassuring, and very grateful to have someone whom he has to reassure, since that seems to keep his teeth from chattering.

The rain hits the windows in sheets, like water on the windshield in a car wash.

"Guess we better ride it out in an inside room," Jesse says. "There's not really anything to see here."

She nods. "The house has a powerchip, and there's plenty of food in the fridge. We can sit out a few days if the storm doesn't manage to get in here at us."

"What about the windows?"

"Passionet worries about snipers, believe it or not—ever since what's-her-name, the blonde who appealed to low-end markets—ever since Kimber Lee Melodion got shot. So these are a lot tougher than regular windows."

The water is surging, thumping on the window; the view through the window (which reveals nothing but gray light and something grayly green beyond it) is like looking up from the bottom of a river. "Uh, did they do anything special with your window *frames*?"

"Not that I know of."

"Then let's get to an interior room."

The wind and the rain are loud; they don't even realize anyone else is in the house until they get into the kitchen. But it makes sense that it's Señora Herrera, her husband Tomás, and a bunch of children. "I am sorry, madame—" she begins at once.

"Nonsense," Mary Ann says. "The bus didn't come, this place has power and it's a good place to ride out the storm, and it was only sensible for you and Tomás to come here. And I think even with all the young appetites there's probably enough food for everyone for a week. But, er—I'd no idea you had so many—that is, are all these children yours?"

Señora Herrera translates for Tomás, who speaks no English, and he laughs, before she turns back to explain to Mary Ann. "No, ours are grown. These are nieces and nephews and grandchildren, madame."

There are six of them, now that Jesse's had a chance to count. He knows the fridge is huge and it was well stocked just beforehand, so he's not worried about food supply, and since Mary Ann is taking a generous attitude about her house, he can hardly complain. Still, he's just a little jealous; he had been sort of hoping to have the whole place and Mary Ann just for himself.

That triggers a guilt attack and nowadays guilt always reminds him of Naomi. Well, if she had any sense she stayed out of Tehuantepec today and if she was really smart she went up to Oaxaca; there might be some danger there from floods when Clementine's rains hit the volcanic slopes around the city, but chances are that Oaxaca will come through it with minor wind damage—in fact, the news (his brother Di seems to be on the television news every night, maybe because that reporter, Berlina Jameson, keeps interviewing him) was talking about the storm dying when it got up to the mountains.

The wind outside booms against the walls, and there's a low shudder that runs through their feet. Tomás turns to Jesse and says, in Spanish, "The two of us could tie down the roof. I don't believe it is, and it needs to be."

Jesse doesn't know what Tomás is talking about, but figures Tomás knows more than he does. So he says, "All right; what do we use to tie it down?"

"There is"—a Spanish word that Jesse doesn't know—"in my truck outside; I will flip a coin and one of us will run for it—"

"I'm already wet," Jesse says. "And what is—?"

It takes them a long couple of minutes to figure out that the English for what they are talking about is "airplane cable"—lightweight wire rope.

Tomás needs the big roll of it; he has already brought in his toolbox, which has the necessary wirecutters, wrenches, and saddles. He had been about to make the dash when Jesse and Mary Ann turned up.

The truck is parked behind the house, sheltered from the direct fury of the rain. Running for the cable is like diving into a cold swimming pool; Jesse is drenched in just one step. Then the wind hits him from behind, and he is thrown to his hands and knees on the rain-slick cobbles before he can adjust his balance. The cold water sluices around his wrists and legs for a long second as he bends his head inward to draw a breath; then Jesse rushes forward to the truck and his cold, numb hands sting as he is thrown against its door. It's lucky this thing has a sliding door because he doubts he could open a door that swung out against the wind.

Gasping, he opens the truck door with a hard yank, climbs inside, and slides it closed behind him, not fast enough to prevent everything getting soaked in the brief second or so. He brought a flashlight in his back pocket—even though it's only about one in the afternoon—and now he's glad he did. It's darker in here than it would be on an ordinary night.

He finds the big coil of aircraft cable where Tomás said it would be, and pulls it onto his shoulder.

The truck rocks hard a couple of times; the wind isn't strong enough to pick it up or roll it, but more than enough to make it bounce on its shocks. He draws a breath—

It's much worse getting back to the house—he has to run face-first into the storm. He doesn't lose his balance, but his feet slip and give under him as if he were wading upstream in a mountain river, and the rain pounds flat against his chest so hard that he holds his breath. As he starts his run, the house, less than fifty feet away, is not much more than a blur, and he's so blinded by the rain that he hits the wall next to the door before he slips in sideways.

Tomás grins at him. "That will save you a few years of bathing."

Jesse heaves a long breath and says, "Shall we place bets on how long till the truck goes to San Cristóbal without us?"

Tomás laughs. "I have an idea about that too. The roof won't blow off in the time it will take you to change clothing, though, so why don't you do that—"

"Well, if we're going to do something about the truck, why don't I do it while I'm still wet?"

"Because it seemed too heartless to send you back out into that, especially with the difficulty of crawling underneath the van to stretch cargo straps under the frame—"

"You were thinking of tying it down? Why not just back it up close to the house and then weight it?"

Tomás stops, scratches his head, thinks. "That would make more sense," he admits. "But what can we weight it with?"

"There are empty fifty-five-gallon drums in the room with the washer, right? So if I back up close to there, and we put four drums in the truck and fill them with water, that's about a ton of added weight. And there's no shortage of water just now."

Tomás claps him on the shoulder. "Señor Callare, you are a brilliant *ingeniero*. And you did mention that you're already wet."

It's not quite so bad this time, because he knows he won't be running back through the water; he's impressed with Tomás's maintenance—the truck starts right up. He's going from memory about where the garden, curb, and utility-room door are, and there's a nasty bump as he goes over the curb into the slick goo that's about all that's left of the roses, mulch, and compost, but though the tires spin for an instant, they catch, and he gets backed up against the wall, just two quick steps from the door.

As he bursts in, Tomás says, "May I ask you something, Señor?"

"Call me Jesse. I think we can declare democracy till the storm's over, at least."

"Then may I ask you something, Jesse?"

"Sure."

"Why didn't it occur to either of us to do this first, so that you didn't have to run the whole way three times, or carry that roll of cable?"

Jesse's jaw drops, and then they're both laughing.

It's still something of a battle to get the empty drums across the gap of a few feet into the truck, and there's a lot of water on the utility-room floor by the time they're done, but once the drums are in it's just a matter of running a hose out to the van to fill the drums.

As the drums are filling, they go upstairs, pick several likely points, and fasten tight loops of aircraft cable around the rafters of the house and through eyebolts driven into the roof. It will now take a great deal more lift before the roof comes off.

As they're working they take breaks to run down and move the hose from drum to drum, so that house and truck are secured at about the same time. With as much safety secured as they can manage, Tomás goes into the main bathroom, and Jesse goes upstairs to change.

Mary Ann hands him three towels and a change of clothing. "At least with the powerchip, as long as the house stands up we have a washer and dryer."

"What about water supply?"

"We're on a cistern." She gestures at a window, and Jesse whacks himself on the side of the head. He takes a quick, hot shower, then steps into the hot, dry sauna in her bathroom and relishes getting really dry and warm.

*   *   *

Naomi Cascade did go to Tehuantepec, and she knew the whole way there that it was against common sense, but something in her wouldn't let her stay put in safety when so many people she knew were in danger, and so she went. She got there just in time to realize, along with everyone else, that the evacuation wasn't going to happen.

At the moment that Jesse is getting into a hot shower just over two hundred miles to the southeast, she's huddled with a bunch of kids from the school, their backs to a wall on the side away from the wind. She has had a hard time not screaming: first when the roof came off, lifting like a single immense kite and then bursting into pieces flying away downwind; then when the interior wall they were facing went over in an explosion of lath and plaster against the far wall of the building, leaving nothing but a scoured area between the walls; and now as the wall above is visibly eroding down toward them. There are four children clinging to her, and she can't possibly hang on to them if they are directly exposed to the wind.

As soon as the wall above has eroded far enough, they will be exposed to the wind.

As far as she can tell the wind is still rising. The last news she'd heard was that Tehuantepec was going to take the eye directly.

She wishes vaguely for Jesse, because her gut says that as the wall wears down closer to the ground it will wear more slowly, but she isn't sure enough, and she suspects her Science Guy, as she used to think of him, would be able to tell her. If the wall won't erode all the way down to them—and she thinks it won't, she thinks it won't, she keeps telling the children it won't—then they might as well stay here till the eye arrives and then run for better cover. But if the wall is going to keep on wearing down, they need to crawl down to the end of it before the wind gets any stronger, and then somehow get across the street to the little cathedral—surely *that* can't have been knocked down—a few dozen feet away. She has no idea how to get these kids there without being blown off into the wind or hit by rubble that she can hear and feel slamming like bullets and cannonballs into the other side of the wall.

She always loved Tehuantepec, though the *zócalo* there is not particularly fine, there's no especially lovely architecture, the local seafood dishes are good but no better than what you can get anywhere up and down the coast, it's just a small city where people passing through change buses and people who live there work serving the road and the neighboring farms . . . a small town like any other. . . .

That phrase, "small town," makes her think of Jesse again. She has to admit, though he probably is no better at such situations than anyone else would be, there's something about his small-town world-by-the-tail attitude, the way that he figures since he can fix a flat or climb a rock he ought to be able to fly a rocket or build a nuclear reactor, that would be *so* reassuring right now. Besides, he might have a better idea about what to do than she does.

She's grateful that her mother can't hear her thinking.

Luisa, the smallest one, curls more tightly against her and asks, screaming above the wind, if they're going to die. Naomi strokes the child's hair, resists the urge to say "Not yet," and instead shouts back that it will be okay, but they're going to get very wet and dirty. She's not sure that Luisa hears her over the booming thunder of the wind and rain.

A big chunk breaks loose overhead, and gravel rattles down on them, but the piece of the wall—two feet by four, it must weigh a hundred pounds—sails off into the dark rain all but horizontally. Naomi doesn't hear it hit anywhere. Maybe it landed too far away or maybe the roar in her ears from the wind is louder than she had thought.

The kids huddle closer, and Naomi tries to slide as far down the wall as she can without extending her body too far away from it. The sky grows darker, and the roaring louder, until finally she is left alone, except for the press of the smaller bodies against her, with her thoughts.

She finds she has many. Though the roar, the rubble pounding the wall, the gravel rattling down around them, and the dark are terrifying in one sense, the fact that she is not in pain at the moment but merely uncomfortable, the absence of anything effective she can do, and the inability to do anything for the children, other than be there, leave her with a great deal of time on her hands. She wishes she could sleep—if she lives through this she will want to have rested, and if not it might be easier to die in her sleep.

She replays an argument she had with Jesse and has to admit he was right; this would have happened sooner or later anyway. There's plenty of methane clathrate on the ocean floor and in the tundra permafrost, and sooner or later a volcanic eruption, or a major meteor strike, or even just the slow progress of global warming itself, was going to release it. Truly no one knew this would happen, and it seems doubtful that any of the world leaders involved had any acceptable options.

Sitting here behind this crumbling wall, she's learning quite a bit about what "not having any acceptable options" means.

The kid everyone just calls "Compañero"—Naomi doesn't know his name, but he's the son of the chair of the local Communist Party and a real trouble-maker at the center—is shaking, with fear or cold or something, and she gently strokes his hair.

If she lives through this she is going to violate all her principles and have kids of her own. She was brought up believing that global population must diminish very rapidly, only three percent of the population at most should have children and the rest should be sterilized . . . but despite all the pressure from her parents, she never had it done. So, fuck them, here she is with a bunch of other people's kids, and if she gets through it she wants her own. Besides, before all this is over, the world will get a lot more depopulated.

Actually, that's an interesting question. What does Naomi want? Naomi wants to not want anything, she thinks, that's what I was raised to want, not to need or want anything that might require precious resources.

But she doesn't even know what she's refraining from wanting.

Something—god knows what, part of a car or a fence or a giant hailstone or maybe just a rock—goes right through the wall seven feet above them and about five yards to the left. The wind going through the hole makes a deep bass whistle that sets the whole wall and ground vibrating.

At least she thinks that's what happened, and that's the explanation she's trying to shout in the children's ears. Jesse said something about things with holes in them have more drag, or drag more, in the wind, she's not sure which, but it seems to be true because she does feel the wall bow inward very slightly just before it bends back to upright, and the thunder she feels through her legs and buttocks suggests that a big part of the wall just broke away and fell in.

Far off—inches from her ears—she can hear Luisa shrieking, Compañero shouting what she suspects is a prayer. María, pressed against her back, is sobbing or laughing hysterically—something that makes her breath come in shaky gasps, anyway—and Linda, leaning in close on her other side, is the only one who seems to be quiet at all, but the heavy way she is lying suggests that she has fainted—or perhaps she's been hit by something penetrating the wall? No, surely there'd be whistling or roaring from the hole.

Time goes on in the thundering dark, and nothing more happens except that the noise goes on and it continues to be dark. Naomi wonders how long they've been there; it became fully dark around two in the afternoon, perhaps, remembering the last time she looked at her watch was about noon. . . .

She brings the watch up to her face, carefully not letting go of Luisa, who is clinging to her like a baby possum, and manages to press the light button. It says 4:57 P.M. Three hours of this thus far. Perhaps she has managed to sleep and dream.

There is more dark and more time, all in the deep thunder of the wind. Naomi has no way of knowing how far down the wall is eroding, but she tries to think it through the way Jesse might have, concludes that the erosion must have slowed or stopped because if it hadn't, they'd already have had their portion of the wall torn away. The watch says 5:48 when she looks again. This time she must have been awake longer.

She plans meals she is going to eat, things she will go and see. She promises herself that just once, in some town where no one knows her, she will go into a Full Makeover—yes, right into a low-rent chain store—and have herself made into a male fantasy object and walk around the town getting stared at by men for a few days, just to know what that's like. After all, when she finds out she hates it she can go right back to being herself.

She will go hiking on foot without XV commentary. She will make love in the desert again, maybe with somebody other than Jesse. Maybe with Jesse and several somebodies, she thinks, and giggles. She wonders why, faced with the possibility that she might be smashed like a bug on a windshield at any moment, she is deriving so much pleasure from thinking about things she shouldn't think about.

Experimentally she thinks about dumping toxic waste in pristine wilder-ness and killing the last great apes on earth with a club. She still finds both those thoughts disgusting. This is a relief; it seems to her that she's just selfish, not evil.

She was always taught they're the same thing. She hopes she remembers, when she gets out of all this, that they're not.

The next time a guy tries to pick her up at a party by listening seriously to her feelings and responding with careful, nuanced criticism to her thoughts, she's going to tease him for a while and then leave with some guy who wants to go out and dance, and they will stand out in the middle of the street at three A.M. singing and waking people up.

There has been a shortage of fun in her life. She's going to have a lot of it if fate gives her a chance.

Come to think of it, she's also going to read a lot of books that are on the "centric/linear" list, the one that various Deeper groups circulate to alert members to "superficially convincing works that perpetuate dangerous ideo-logical convictions." Maybe *Huckleberry Finn*; the only thing she knows about it is that two guys drift downstream in a raft and that her images of it seem to all involve warm, sunny, summer days as they're doing it. The idea of a whole book full of warm, sunny summer days intrigues her more than she can imagine.

Fly fishing. She is going to try fly fishing. It seems like something very quiet.

And she might start reading books about science or something. She's not good at it but she just thinks it would be neat to know it.

There are so many things she can do for Naomi if she decides to. And she can still do more than her share of things for other people.

She has a feeling her parents won't like it. Tough shit.

A last, strange moment of thunder is followed by blinding light. Her first thought is that it's a lightning flash, her second thought that it's some strange effect you get when you're dead, and then she realizes that it's . . . sunlight.

With a patter and many thuds, a rain of bricks and rubble comes out of the sky. They all huddle against the wall closely, but only María is hit, by a small stone on the ankle; it seems to be nothing serious, though she screams when it happens. A few feet away, a chunk of wall, several CBS blocks still joined by mortar, plunges into the ground, cratering the mud and spraying all of them. They wait another long minute, then stand up and begin to wipe off.

The five of them look up again, in wonder. The opposite exterior wall of the building blew down entirely, though just which of the crashes they felt and heard it might have been, they'll never know; Naomi congratulates herself on her choice of walls. The Cathedral, across the street, pokes up from behind great, sculpted drifts of rubble, the belltower gone, the roof mostly sheared off, but still standing.

Warm sunlight plays everywhere on the broken walls and in the scoured streets, and Naomi's eyes fill with tears. It's just too beautiful. . . .

"Mama?" Luisa says tentatively. She reaches up and takes Naomi's hand. The kids had been at the Social Services Building, and they were the four whose parents hadn't picked them up before movement got impossible; Naomi stayed with them in hopes that the evacuation buses that never came would come by here to check for strays, because she didn't have an official evacuation point in Tehuantepec itself—her address is up in Oaxaca.

Naomi squats down. "We'll see if we can find your mother," she explains, in Spanish, "and everyone else's parents, too, but we only have an hour or two before the storm starts again. And before it starts we want to get into some nice, safe basement with some food and water and a toilet."

Squatting, and mentioning the toilet, has made her realize what her own most urgent need is, and there's a five-minute break while she and the girls relieve themselves on one side of the wall, and Compañero presumably does the same on the other. Events really change people, she realizes; Compañero is the sort of nasty little boy who normally would have been sneaking around to peek at the *gringa* and the girls. Maybe he just really had to go.

The city of Tehuantepec is gone, she realizes, as they set out for where Luisa's house was. Lanes blown clear by winds along the ground resemble streets, though they don't always run where the streets did; streets have filled with rubble to depths of three and four meters. Every so often the corner of a curb, poking up from the mess, with its inset tiles giving street names, tells her where they are, but they circle a long time, calling and shouting, before they have to admit that though they've probably been close to it, they have no hope of finding Luisa's house.

Naomi wishes Luisa would cry. The girl's eyes get huge and solemn, her thumb goes into her mouth, and she grips Naomi by the wrist, but that is all.

Compañero's father's house was large; parts of the walls are still standing. And she finally gets to find out Compañero's name when the boy's father, clearing rubble away from a basement door, looks up and shouts "Pablo!"

She holds Luisa very close while father and son hug and the two of them babble an explanation; she allows herself to feel just a little proud when Compañero's—no, Pablo's, she will call him by name from now on—when Pablo's father shakes her hand fervently. Better still, he has a deep basement, he's shored up the top of it with timbers and tied down the floor, and he's managed to get several auto batteries rigged up so that there's at least a dim light down there, plus there are three thousand liters of drinking water in a tank, a lot of dehydrated food he "liberated" from a tourist store nearby, and a crude chemical toilet he's managed with a bucket, a chair frame, and several gallons of bleach.

They quickly decide that Pablo will stay and help set things up, then make a quick trip around the neighborhood to find people who need a safer shelter. Naomi will try to locate the family of María and Linda—the two are cousins who lived in the same large house. She'll also bring back anyone she finds who needs a place; the shelter will easily accommodate fifty for the time that it must, especially if in the remaining hour or so before the storm hits again they get enough people working on stocking it.

She hurries away with the three girls. God, it's unbelievably hot this evening. The sky above is deep blue and the heaped and drifted rubble is gray-white, and that's most of what Tehuantepec's color scheme usually is; it takes her a moment to realize that what is missing is the deep, vivid green of the trees, the planters, and the watered squares, lawns, and parks. All that has been stripped away; there are no palm trees standing and the few bushes not uprooted and thrown away are stripped to bare branches.

People are beginning to emerge everywhere, from basements and from interior rooms that backed up on thick walls. Some modern buildings withstood the shock, mostly those that had been built in copies of the traditional southern Mexican styles, with reinforced concrete inside the heavy walls and with few or no windows on the southern and western sides. She stops to talk with many of them, but most have not been out of their shelters long enough to know anything of what's going on. One man has managed to get a video signal from one of the overhead satellites, through the opening provided by the eye, by running out a long piece of metal clothesline in a circle on a slope that faces toward the satellite.

This gives Naomi one more thing she wishes she knew enough to be able to do, but the man has only been able to find out that the outside world knows this is happening and that the center of the eye hit the coast about twenty kilometers to the north of here. The current estimate, as far as he can figure out with a map and a calculator, is that Clementine is moving a bit more slowly and that they might have as long as an hour and ten minutes before the Beaufort 40 + winds of the eye wall are on them again.

María and Linda find an aunt, or a cousin, or a cousin of one and an aunt of the other, and they split off to join their family in some large shelter that they've all improvised together.

This leaves only Luisa, and as soon as the other girls are gone, Luisa starts to cry. Naomi mutters, *"No llores,"* before deciding that that's stupid, the little girl needs to cry, and after all it's not like Luisa is slowing them down by crying. She heads back for Pablo's house.

The sky is blue, and it's warm, and if it weren't for the sobbing child with her—and for the landscape of shattered rubble all around, like an old flat photo from the last century, Berlin or Hiroshima or Port au Prince, or like Washington right after the Flash—Naomi might almost find herself enjoying the warmth and the light. She drinks it in, in the same way she does a cup of clean water offered by a woman who is carrying big buckets—greedily, getting every bit of it into her, against what she knows is to come.

Two things at first surprise her: that there are so few takers, only about ten people, for the offer of a good shelter, and that there doesn't seem to be much of anyone trying to rescue people from the rubble. Finally she asks a tall, muscular man whom she remembers vaguely as the vice-president of the local tenants' union, and he sighs. "I wondered that too. But now that I think of it, very few people are looking for better shelter because to have lived through the storm thus far, their shelters usually are pretty good; if they were not, the people who were in bad shelters or not sheltered are . . . well, not here. And suppose you dig out your relative or your friend. If he or she is alive, do you have a doctor, do you have medicine, do you have any way to help? And more likely he or she is not alive . . . and then what do you do with a corpse? You cannot bring it into the shelter for fear of disease. You cannot lay it out in the street—the wind will carry the body somewhere, never to be found. And you haven't time to dig a grave. So the bodies are best where they are . . . and if there are living people under the rubble . . . well, they will be bodies soon enough. Or they will have to live until we can dig for them. It is very hard, but there is no way around it."

She nods, and as she walks off, Luisa says, "Our house had a big glass window on the south side, and aluminum siding from Sears that Mama was very proud of, but it wasn't put on very well, the people from Sears said there was nothing to attach it to. . . ."

Naomi folds her arms around the child and lets her sob against her. "I am here and you can stay with me. And perhaps we can find your mother. Some shelters, the door got buried and the people are fine inside but can't get out right away. But you have a home, with me, as long as you need it. And as long as you are with me we will look for your mother together."

Luisa doesn't exactly stop crying, but she does drift off into sniffles. The two of them hurry together toward the shelter; already in the distance, the black face of the eye wall is crawling over the land, and the sun is about to set behind it.

When she gets done with all this, Naomi thinks, she is going to spend two whole weeks doing nothing but silly things that she enjoys but used to feel embarrassed about enjoying. And every night she will phone her parents and horrify them with describing it all. She laughs at her own joke, not caring if anyone sees her or misunderstands. There's nothing like nearly dying to make you appreciate living.

John Klieg gets the report from Mexico with not much more than a smile. The Mexican government's launch facility wasn't able to put up packages of any real size and besides it was just a standard-model Japanese franchise launch port. No, the real prize is what his meteorologists are telling him— Clem Two's eye is going to make it over the Isthmus of Tehuantepec just fine, move into the Bay of Campeche, and then set all hell loose. For all practical purposes, the clear pathway across the isthmus is marked on the map—Federal Highway 185 follows the low ground.

Thus far his little team—thrown together by the completely invaluable Glinda—has been matching NOAA and (because they've been working on a more tightly focused problem) occasionally beating them.

And if they're right—then the Atlantic is more than ripe for a "cascade" of hurricanes. Clem Two should have an outflow jet soon after getting back over warm water. In the weak steering currents of the western Caribbean, Clem Two will sputter and spin, giving birth to many more hurricanes—and they in turn will give birth to more. The Atlantic is going to be boiling with them soon, and the methane injection has warmed it enough to allow hurricanes a full run along the Gulf Stream until they finally pound Europe itself.

The one fly in all this ointment, of course, is that Glinda is still at Canaveral, though that will be fixed quickly. She's seeing to the evacuation of GateTech's central team, which is being moved partly to Birmingham, Alabama (not quite out of hurricane reach but up where there's a good chance of riding it out), and partly to here, Novokuznetsk. With a bit of luck it will all be done in two days, and then she and Derry will be here like lightning.

It's a funny thing. He misses Glinda's personal efficiency, and her sense of humor, and Derry's little adventures and discoveries, and he certainly misses sex with Glinda, but more than anything else what he really misses is that sense of completeness, the sense that he's building something for someone. He wonders how he lived without that for so many years.

He turns back to the wall of screens that he's had built for himself here. It's just as useless as the one at Canaveral, but since for most of his business career Klieg has been photographed in front of such a setup, it seemed like a good idea to to keep the locals reminded of who he was. Another Glinda inspiration . . . he ought to ask her if anything could be done to cause somebody to open up an English-speaking Shoney's here.

There's a blip on one screen, and he glances that way; the flashing icon means something significant has come in, and he stops to read it.

He purses his lips, whistles, and grins. Time to start playing hardball, no question. So, by a lot of fancy jockeying, not to mention a pretty elastic concept of property at Moonbase, they think they're going to come up with a competing launch service, building and launching satellites in space? And no doubt they've also got something up their sleeves, now that his technical people have told them how, for getting a big dark shadow over the Pacific, using the same facility.

His first call is to Hassan. It's not so much a matter of respect—the two of them respect each other but neither would have thought about that—or of getting additional input; it's just that Hassan runs at least as many lines of influence as Klieg runs, all the time, and they need to stay coordinated on this point.

It takes him only moments to fill his partner in, and then Klieg explains, "Just offhand, there's about a dozen congresspeople I can count on to tie things up in the States—our Congress usually makes sure the government buys from private business, even when that costs a lot more, because businessmen are the backbone of the country."

"I wish my current country were similarly enlightened."

"You said it." Klieg begins ticking things off on his fingers. "There's a fair bit of concealed Japanese money in some of my operations, and that's a favor I can call in—there'll be a lot of trouble if it doesn't stay concealed, and it won't unless I see some protests and complaints about the American intrusion into the Japanese part of Moonbase. Same deal with the French, except that there I've got a couple of deputies in Paris, and there's some more legislators in Brussels . . . and that's before I start serious hassling in the General Assembly in New York."

Hassan nods. "My friend, I see what you are up to, but do you expect it to work?"

After ransacking his memory, Klieg says, "To tell you the truth, Hassan, I don't see why it won't."

The other man nods solemnly; the effect on the phone is somehow more impressive than it would be in person. "It seems to me that with predicted deaths pressing upward toward a billion or more, as your last estimates show—and I assume theirs are similar—faced with the literal complete destruction of several nations like the Netherlands and Bangladesh, with catastrophic damage and the destruction of whole cities . . . and with the instructive example of Honolulu in front of them . . . well, my friend. Do you think they will do business as usual?"

"Oh, only at first. And then it won't matter. It's like tying a guy's shoelaces together. You haven't crippled him, just slowed him down a little by making him stop to untie them. They'll have to remove all my little obstructions—and any that you might throw in?"

"I was just thinking on that point."

"Well, all we need are delays. A few of them. Once we have a head start, the public screaming for a solution will guarantee they'll go with whatever's fastest. And the PR goodwill from having done it should be just phenomenal—we can do just about anything we want from then on, for like ten years or so."

Hassan nods. "It seems worth a play. There are a number of small governments I've got a friend or two in; I think I can help you with the 'hassle' in the General Assembly, especially since several of those little governments are quite jealous anyway of their Second Covenant rights. Have you given consideration to the media?"

"I've got my best person on it."

"Miss Gray?"

"How did you know?"

Hassan gives him a deep, beaming grin that shows a lot of teeth and doesn't have a drop of humor in it. "Who is *my* best person?"

"Pericles Japhatma, whom I've never met. I see. The point's well taken." Neither of them will ever again ask the other how he or she happens to know a thing. After a suitable pause, Klieg says, "Well, then, we seem to be agreed. The point is, hassles have to happen to this stupid idea of having the government do it. It's really a matter of principle, too, you know—if you let the government, any government, do these things directly, it takes decades to get things on a private-enterprise profit-making basis again. Once you let socialism in . . ." Klieg sighs and spreads his hands.

"Exactly," Hassan says. "This very nation is still recovering after all these years. Well, then, shall we do the world some good—and ourselves as well?"

"Only way to do it, buddy," Klieg says, and this time the smiles exchanged are genuine. After Hassan clicks off, he works the phone hard all morning, and by the time Glinda calls with the other part set up, his calendar has a little flex in it.

Diogenes Callare knows it's completely irresponsible of him—he had two phone calls while he was on the zipline, just to begin with—but he needed to see Lori and the kids, and he needed the rest, so he slept on the zipline instead of doing work, and since Lori just finished *Slaughterer in Yellow*, they end up going out to a nice restaurant—one with child care—for a long meal. It's an indulgence of sorts, but "half an hour's sales in the first week will more than pay for it," Lori points out, when he mentions the concern.

"Yeah." He swirls the warm red wine in his glass, looks at her over it. "It's funny, you think about a lot of jobs—cops and firemen and soldiers and all—and none of those occupations see anything odd about the idea that you go out there to protect people like your own family, and your family gets protected along with all those strangers. But it's not something you think about for weathermen."

"Eat your lasagna," she says, "you're getting morbid."

"Well, yeah, I am getting morbid," he admits, "but the point is still valid."

"Unh-hunh. And the lasagna is still hot."

She's right, it's very good. After a while he takes her hand and says, "It's just . . . well, you know, I love spending time with you. I never realized before this month how much I like usually being able to work at home. And since the methane levels in the air are going to stay elevated for ten years—"

"That's close to shoptalk," she warns him, smiling and pressing her index finger on his nose. "Eat. Or talk about trivia. Or flatter your wife, considering I only knew an hour ago that you were coming home, I asked you out then, and here I am, stunning."

He can hardly help smiling at that, and the truth is, to him, she *is* stunning. He studies her carefully for a long minute, taking in the sweep of blonde hair, the big twinkling eyes . . . letting his eyes run over her pink sweater (it really does flatter her) . . . "Well, yeah," he says. "In fact, I think you're the best-looking person in the joint."

"That's more like it. I know you're worried about the hurricane coming into the Caribbean, and for that matter I suspect what's really worrying you is Jesse, Di."

He shrugs with one shoulder, a little gesture that doesn't mean much except that he's heard what she's said. "He's a grown-up, at least sort of, and he can probably deal with whatever comes his way, at least as long as he doesn't do anything dumb to start out with. I wish I knew what was up with him, but chances are at the moment he's sitting on his duff in a not-very-comfortable shelter, hoping things will calm down soon. At least if civilization manages to survive the storms, he'll have a good set of stories to tell. Meanwhile I can't do a thing for him, and he's okay, more likely than not." He notices he has just drunk his glass of wine a bit faster than he intended to.

Lori sighs and takes his hand. "You don't really have to look after the whole world, love. You really don't."

He grins, squeezes her hand. "It wasn't shoptalk before, you know," he says. "As long as there's so much extra methane in the air, we'll have giant hurricanes, and NOAA will be on this crisis footing—"

She puts her hand on his lips again, and when she is sure she has silenced him, she pours him another glass of wine. "Drink." Her head tilts a little to the side and she seems to look at him like a robin that isn't quite sure whether the object in front of it is an earthworm. "Now," she says, "listen carefully to your spouse. There are two possibilities here. One, civilization *doesn't* survive the storms, and you and I and the kids have to make our way through the mess. Very tough and frightening, but it's not going to be improved by your passing up the pleasures of a civilized dinner tonight. Two, civilization survives but the hurricanes go on for years. Then all this becomes routine—and once it's routine, you'll have time off again. That's all."

It makes sense, and he nods and eats. Every so often he steals a glance at her, trying to catch her looking sad or pensive, but whether she's being stubborn, or it's just her natural optimism, she keeps right on smiling at him, and between the wine, and the love, and *not* having to sleep over in a hotel in D.C. tonight, he's actually very cheerful by the evening's end. They even dance a couple of times to the little band up on the upper floor, before they reclaim the kids, pile into the car, and set it for home, all of them sleeping in a sprawl as the car drives them home. The only trouble with how wonderful it feels to be in his own bed with Lori is that he's not aware of it for long—he falls asleep quickly.

By the time he's on the zipline the next morning, he is all but ready to think of the problem as tractable.

* * *

Because the eye of Clementine misses them, Jesse, Mary Ann, the Hererras, and the kids never have an interval when they can go outside, but it matters very little. It occurs to Jesse that there's a good chance that neither the Herreras nor their grandchildren, nephews, and nieces have ever lived this well before.

They have forty-eight fairly dull hours, with the windows revealing nothing but immense torrents of water and day and night separated only by the difference between almost and completely dark. The booming and roar of the storm are constant, and every so often something sizable hits the side of the house, but other than that there's not a lot to distract them outside.

Jesse teaches the kids to play Monopoly and is a little appalled at how easily they take to it; he wonders if Naomi would think of him as a bad influence on youth. Surely she was smart enough to stay up in Oaxaca? They can't get anything on broadcast so there's always the possibility that Oaxaca was hit harder than expected, or that the coast to the north is safe, but since no new information has come in, Jesse just continues to hope based on what the situation was before.

He's been getting kind of a funny feeling out of watching Mary Ann play with the kids, too. He knows this thing with her is probably not permanent. It's not a matter of her being older or that she has vastly more experience of various kinds—catching up has been a lot of the fun.

The real trouble is with Jesse. Like many Americans in their early twenties, he just hasn't absorbed the concept of permanence yet, and thus he can be deeply attached and passionate, but not exactly ever in love. As long as he's around people of his own age the difference doesn't show up, but where Mary Ann Waterhouse—if she found the right person, and not until—could easily contemplate waking up with that person every day until one of them died of old age, and thus imaginatively can live far into the future (and imagine having a connection to the past that long), Jesse is still in the child's eternal present. He can be very attached to someone and want to see them again, but the sorts of questions an adult in love asks—including the important one of whether or not it would be a good idea to stay in love—never come to Jesse.

But though he's not old enough for love, he's old enough to know he's not old enough, and when he sees Mary Ann happy with kids, Mary Ann typing away at an old-fashioned keyboard while she works out a list of things to do . . . he realizes that *if* he were ready, he'd take her in a minute.

If she'd have him—after all, she's really the one with most of what there is to offer in the relationship, not just financially but in terms of wisdom, experience, and for that matter, sexual joy. This is a slightly painful realization.

Late that evening, Jesse and Mary Ann are upstairs, naked in the tub together by candlelight, taking turns scrubbing each other, looking up into the skylight at the way the water rolls deep and fast across the glass overhead, occasionally illuminated by the candle flickers. Jesse guesses there're probably a couple of inches up there, maintained entirely by the wind and water pushing more over the skylight constantly. From here it seems like the ocean bottom.

Her head rolls back against his arm, and Jesse notes with some pleasure that though the red hair is still the funny cartoonish shade, there's a bit of straw blonde at the roots now; she'd have to get a crewcut to be back to her natural color, but she could.

Washing her back, he notices again how tiny she really is, that they picked her for being fine-boned and slim. Under his hands, as he rubs her with the foaming soap, he finds the surgically shortened ribs, the interior girdle, the added ligaments to hold up the enormous breasts, the healed slits where they went in to crank her bottom tight. He tries to figure out how he feels about all of the scars, marks, and bumps that make her so strange to his touch; it would be nice to say he likes it because it's all part of her, but that's not true—nor does he necessarily feel outrage at what was "done to her," since after all she decided to have it done and was extremely well paid for it. Sometimes he thinks he likes to touch her scars and alterations because it makes her feel more like a doll to be used, but that's not completely true either—he feels less like that with her body than he has with most women's.

Probably he just likes to touch Mary Ann, and tends to touch the places where she's most unusual.

In her turn, she washes him thoroughly and just a little roughly—he's often told her he feels "scrubbed" after she's done, and she's just as often pointed out he seems to enjoy it. They have just finished toweling off and are stretching out on the bed, their hands beginning to stay more and more often at chests and crotches, little nipping kisses starting, when they both sit upright, startled by a sound—

It's the spatter of heavy rain on the walls, and the whistle of wind, Jesse realizes, and in a hurricane what do you expect?

Then he gets it. "It's slacking off out there," he says, "probably already no worse than a bad thunderstorm. Maybe by morning we'll be able to see out."

She gives a little whoop and rolls over onto him, kissing him deeply; he feels his erection stiffen against her, an instant before she has it in her hand, stroking it quickly, making sure he is hard before she sits carefully onto it. As the thunder outside transforms into a mere wild stormy night, she rides him joyously, masturbating as she does it.

It's like something out of XV porn, he realizes, just in time to know that that is what she wants to give him, not what she *is* but his fantasy of her, and the crashes of thunder and wind outside, the flickers of lightning over her body in the warmth of the candlelight, drive him on, bucking upward to meet her as she climaxes again and again, in a triumphant, joyful surge.

"Mind you," she says, leaning forward and letting his still-sensitive limp penis slide out of her, "this is likely to happen anytime we survive something big. Just wanted you to know there's an incentive to survive."

Shortly after, she's asleep under his arm, her back against him and his hand resting on her strangely hard, unyielding belly, fingers idly finding the seams in the internal girdle. They've blown out the candles, and now there is only the wind and the rain, both blowing down into gusts. He is tired, and comfortable, and he's just had wildly satisfying sex, but he's kept awake by one thought—that while he had just kept on doing what seemed appropriate, and not showing the fear he did have around the Herrera kids, it was Mary Ann who had the real measure of the situation.

Jesse tries to imagine his own death and fails; but he knows the woman he holds in his arms imagined hers, lived with it, and let him see none of her fear. She is, he thinks, not merely older or more fully formed as a person. She's too big and too marvelous for him.

He decides to try to live up to her, and stays awake just a little longer wondering if he can. When sleep comes to him, it's deep and full of dreams, but he remembers none of them. They wake in the mid-morning when they hear the Herreras shouting—they too had slept late, and thus had missed the first real dawn in days. It is still storming outside, but unmistakably there is daylight.

Compared to the first passage under Clem Two's winds, Naomi finds this one a breeze. The power runs out about halfway through, but in this deep basement there is food, there are other people, there's safe water to drink and even a toilet . . . and most of all, there's very little fear. She is even able to use some of the time to catch up on sleep.

In the dark, people sing or play word games. Naomi's Spanish isn't particularly good, but this seems to lead to good-natured amusement, and whenever she does manage to participate successfully they give her a big round of applause. And singing together is fun.

By the time the wind seems to have settled down to gusts and the rain to a spatter, it's night, and their host suggests they all spend the night inside before venturing out; there's no sign of any life out there right now.

So they all curl up once more, huddled near each other for warmth and comfort. It's very quiet and pleasant, and Naomi resists sleep a little while just because she wants to consciously enjoy it.

She knows, too, in an abstract way, that if she were in her usual state of scrubbed cleanliness, she would find the smell down here dreadful, not so much from the mixture of shit and bleach in the imperfectly sealed toilet buckets as from the smell of many bodies that have missed some washings. But at the moment she smells just like everyone else, and somehow that's so . . . well, it's democratic.

Then she wonders if perhaps worrying about how people smell isn't some sort of residual racism, and for a moment, curled there on a couple of old beach towels up against a bookcase, she is wide awake with worry—especially because she knows that the people around her are clean anyway, the evening shower is at least as much part of their lives as it is of hers—

And now she wonders if knowing about the fact that this is a culture with a cleanliness habit isn't also suppressed racism.

Then she remembers she promised herself she wouldn't think about things like this, just two days ago when she thought she was going to be torn to scraps of meat any moment. And here she is, back with people. Time to start living her new life, whatever that's going to be. The happy thought sends her drifting off into warm sleep.

When she wakes people are beginning to move around, and there's a long moment before they all realize what's different; they can't hear any rain or wind at all. She jumps up, intending to be among the first to help, and then realizes again. It's going to be a while to get over these habits, she decides, but she's going to.

Meanwhile, she will pull her fair share, but she won't act like she's got to be the most helpful person on the planet.

Besides, the big job right now is getting the outer door pried open, and that's mostly big-muscle work. Fortunately there are several large grown men in the group, and once they figure out that it's just something heavy lying on the slanting cellar doors, they know that some hard heaves are likely to get them free.

They end up using a spare basement timber as a battering ram, hoping to make whatever it is tip over. No one seems to be much worried—it isn't urgent to get out of the shelter at this very moment, and anyway there will no doubt be a party of rescuers along soon enough.

When all the men are set on the little flight of steps up to the door, five of them holding the timber endwise to the door, they start to swing it in their arms, bringing it sharply into the steel door on every third swing: "*Uno, dos, tres!*" *boom!* and then there's the rattle of gravel and other things sliding down the door over the next "*uno, dos, tres!*"

As the eighth *boom!* echoes through the cellar, sinking dully into the earthen walls, there is a blinding flash from the door, and the men stagger back, crying out and dropping the timber as they cover their eyes. There is a moment of terrible stillness as everyone wonders what could be out there; the fear of what they will see merges with tens of thousands of images of the nuked cities of the world, Hiroshima, Nagasaki, Port au Prince, Cairo, Damascus, Washington, and for one dreadful moment the thought that somehow there has been a nuclear war—

"*El sol*," says an old woman next to Naomi, and then everyone, as if not quite understanding yet, says "*el sol*," a mass whispering in the dim cellar— and then everyone laughs.

The bright sunlight outside dazzles eyes that have been in the dark for many hours. Looking away from the door to shield their eyes, the men swing the heavy timber again, twelve swings, four impacts—and with the fourth there is a groan and rumble like distant thunder, and something goes scraping and bouncing down the face of the door, and falls with a crash outside.

One of them puts his hands on the door and pushes, and it flies open.

Everyone groans as the brilliant glare pours in, and they cover their eyes, but the warmth and dryness pull them forward, still shielding their faces and looking down at the ground.

Naomi staggers forward with the rest, her forearm across her eyes, watching only the motion of her sneakers at her feet and following the crowd more by her sense of touch than anything else. The first step comes under her feet, and she steps up.

There is such a diversity of noise, after the tomb-silence of the shelter and the ear-battering storm roar, that it is not easy to sort out the sounds ahead of her.

But just as she gets to the top, she realizes people are crying out and it's not a happy sound. She drops her arm, and sees the wreck in front of her.

It's a little self-driving car, and if the bodies in the backseat are any indication, probably what happened was that the two children in it were trying to get home and didn't know that with the access to the guidance grid cut, the car couldn't steer itself. There's a safety cutoff—the little localized radar/ultrasound system that lets the car find somewhere where traffic isn't moving and stop there without running into anything—but sometimes things like that aren't working anymore, especially if a car is usually driven on manual control, and then again maybe the car did bring the kids to a safe stop and then the wind got it and rolled it.

They weren't belted in, and from the look of the roof and hood, the car was rolled a lot. It's all mud and wind-sanded metal now; Naomi can't see what color it was originally.

The kids look like bent dolls; nothing in the spinning, bouncing car pierced their bodies, but they were slammed around in it like mice in a shaken glass jar, and they are visibly bruised everywhere; clotted blood stains their shirts. Legs and arms are not so much bent as reshaped; the bone must have been broken up so much that the limbs hang as if made of rags.

The faces are not recognizable; first the facial bones were crushed, and then blood flowed freely under the skin, so that both of them seem to be blue-black in color and their faces are at an oddly crushed repose, like rubber masks left lying faceup.

Others around Naomi are crying out as well, and there's some argument about exactly what to do. A moment later the question is settled; two policemen come over a rubble pile.

People are being asked to go to their own property and secure it, and to "avoid the appearance of looting," which means to stay put and not look like they are stealing anything. Supposedly the Army will at last be here tomorrow morning; the *policía* have only shrugs for the question about what might have delayed them so long, and rolls of the eyes when a couple of people press the question. Who, after all, can explain the Army?

Volunteers, or those with nothing to retrieve from their own property, are welcome to go to the Zócalo to join rescue workers.

Naomi has nothing here, so she drifts to the Zócalo naturally, and yet even this is different, because when she gets there, she realizes most of the people there are not volunteering. Rather, they are sitting around, some disoriented, some in despair, but many just sitting, waiting for someone or something to take care of them. She wonders if that ought to bother her. It's hard to tell the people who can't help out, or even help themselves, from those who for various reasons just won't.

She also notices that the Zócalo is now warm and bright with sunlight, and the awesome winds have scoured it bare, so that there are great heaps of rubble in all directions—Tehuantepec does indeed look like one of the great war ruins in pictures—and the palms that once sheltered the little square are gone, shorn off into splinters a bare meter above the dirt, but the ground itself is warm and pleasant, and the thought occurs to her that it might be very nice to stretch out and take a long nap in the sun here.

Well, she hasn't changed *that* much; she's already bored, and greatly relieved, five minutes later, when the volunteer truck swings by again.

She's put on a rescue crew with a group of other women. The job is to listen at rubble piles, climbing around on them with bowls or pans to place their heads against so that they can listen for anyone moving or crying for help.

The rubble piles are all brand-new, and in the fierce winds they have been sculpted like dunes into high peaks. Without the wind to hold them up any longer, most of them are beginning to slide and slump. Moreover, many of the objects in the piles are less than stable. So there's a constant crumbling, and things are moving, falling, and bumping in the piles all the time. After they have searched only a couple of piles they realize that right now the search is hopeless unless they hear someone calling or crying, and that therefore the best hope of saving any lives is to cover as many piles as they can as quickly as they can.

It has been more than a dozen piles—Tehuantepec has become a landscape of walls cut off at ground level and row on row of these dunes of rubble—when they hear the sobbing sound. With picks, shovels, and prybars, the women work together, silently, afraid of what they may find—will it be someone hurt too badly to survive the rescue, or even to know a rescue happened? Will they find some pathetic child on top of its mother's body?

They find a corpse; it's a man, probably older to judge by the gray hair on what remains of his head; if whatever hit him there is what killed him, he surely didn't suffer long.

He's very heavy, and the body is soft and flexible; Naomi thinks she read somewhere that rigor mortis doesn't last very long, or perhaps being buried in the wet rubble is what did it. There's not yet much of a smell, but he feels cold and slimy under their hands as they lift him up. It takes four of them—he couldn't have weighed much less than 250 pounds—and Naomi has him by the knees, which is hard work. They lug him down into one of the wind-ripped passageways between the rubble and put him in one of the body bags that the Tehuantepec police sent out with the digging crews.

"Should we say anything over him?" one of the women asks.

"Leave it for the priests—they will be along soon enough," another answers, and the party goes back to assist the others, who have been digging steadily.

They are almost there when they hear the wail—a baby's cry? Did a baby somehow survive under that? It occurs to Naomi that she's seen all kinds of junk used as bassinets, and if the baby was in a metal footlocker, say, or even a washtub—

They all run forward, eager to be there when they find a living one.

"Under this piece of iron!" one of the women cries, and now they are all there, carefully moving rubble from the rusted corrugated iron, clearing the weight off so that they can lift it straight up. It seems to take forever to get everything cleared, even as fast as they are working. Finally they all get around it to lift the iron—

With a slow, steady heave, they pull it up and flip it over onto the rubble slope beside them.

A cat runs out, meowing frantically. That's all. As often happens, its cry was mistaken for that of a baby.

They dig four more times when they hear noises during the rest of the day. Twice they are stymied by objects too heavy for their crew, and are forced to phone for men with treaded tractors, cranes, and power winches; each time as soon as the new crew is there, they take off to look for more. Once the noise turns out to be a pig. Once the pile collapses as they work and the noises stop; they dig frantically but they cannot find the source of the sound.

They find so many more corpses that they have to send back for additional body bags twice. Toward the end of the day as the heat soaks into the rubble, the bodies begin to smell more strongly; Naomi had a roommate once who only pretended to be vegetarian, who accidentally left behind a cooler with a pound of hamburger in it when she moved out, and that's what the bodies smell like when you first bring them out; contact with the air seems to bring out the strong stench of shit and the iron tang of blood, so that the three smells mingle around her. She suspects the smell is in her hair and clothes, along with her own sweat, and she longs for a bath more than she has ever wanted anything.

When they return to the Zócalo at dusk, they find the Army has already arrived, and there are communal showers in tents and a field kitchen with soup and bread. As far as Naomi is concerned, the only problem with the shower is that you can't stand under it all night; with all of them scrubbing in there, it's like the freshman dorm.

As it becomes fully dark, Naomi is sitting with her back to the wall of the cathedral, a military ration plate in front of her. Like many others, she's been back for seconds and thirds—they may have gotten here late, but they came with plenty. Or perhaps the Army hadn't realized how many of the people here would be dead.

A man is loudly reading messages off a display screen in Spanish, so that everyone can hear that Clem Two has broken through into the Caribbean and is rampaging around among the islands, spitting off another hurricane every few hours.

She finds herself thinking of Jesse's brother Di, and wonders if the poor guy is going to get a chance to see his kids this week. Then she thinks about the number of dead kids she's seen today, and the hundred or so lost kids whose parents are very probably dead who sit huddled together in a large tent on the other side of the Zócalo while a kind-voiced older sergeant goes among them asking the same questions over and over.

She's embarrassed but she starts crying, right there, and when the older woman beside her puts an arm around her, Naomi just falls right into the embrace and cries until she's through. She still feels sniffly and miserable when she curls between blankets on the ground.

All that night she dreams of Tehuantepec before, how the streets were dusty but the little houses were kept with such pride, the softness of the voices, the warm browns and reds against the dark sky at night—and in her dreams she wanders an empty town where in front of every house there is a little thicket of white crosses. She wants to call someone's name, to bring someone alive out of a house, but although she worked here for so many months and knows the town intimately, the only name she can think of is her mother's.

The dreams fade toward dawn, and at last she gets a few hours of gracious unconsciousness, before the soldiers wake them again to give them a quick *desayuno* of sweet rolls, fruit drink, and coffee. She refrains from the sausage, but she has never been so tempted by the smell of meat before. It seems like a feast, and after what she ate last night, how can she be so hungry that she finishes it all? Maybe she was right all along about how powerful the life force is . . . and maybe she had only neglected to realize what it is really interested in.

After breakfast she has two choices—stay and work with the volunteers for another two days, and thus earn herself a spot to ride all the way on the trucks that will be rolling back up to Oaxaca City, or join the refugee parties walking the thirty-five kilometers up the highway to Ixtepec, where there's a zipline head. They say the zipline will be working later today.

The question, of course, is whether the Army, which she at least knows has trucks, or the government zipline monopoly, which may or may not have a working zipline, is more apt to keep its word. She decides to walk, partly because the Army already let her down and now she wants to give Líneas Rápidas Mejicanas their chance to let her down, and mainly because now that she's decided to make some room in her life for selfishness, she doesn't feel like she owes them any more time digging out corpses. Maybe when she gets to Oaxaca she'll call Father and tell him she's all right; he probably won't lecture her about how he doesn't care about her any more than about anyone else on Earth, that all life is precious to him and she is important but that Earth itself must be more important, the way Mother would.

That decision made, she joins a party and starts the long hike out of town. At the top of the first big hill, there used to be a good view of the town—she used to love the sight of it early in the morning, when her bus would come in at about six A.M., with the warm sun turning the city gold against the deep blue sky. Now she looks back and finds she has a fine view of the ruins.

It's not scoured to rock the way Hawaii was, at least. That takes a storm surge, and Mexico is lucky enough to be high and rocky, though what happened to the beach and port communities down below on the coast is better not thought about, just now.

The Cathedral stands, and six or seven other buildings—and that's all. Tehuantepec, otherwise, is a wasteland of shards and fragments strewn over foundations. There will be another town here, she thinks—it's a natural junction in the natural places to run a road, and the roads are still here—but that town will be Tehuantepec only in name.

It's already getting hot, but still the dusty road won't be as bad as mining for bodies was. She runs to catch up with her party.

By noon she's tired; her group has set a pace that's too much for her, and she doesn't want to tell them that, because they don't like her. The group seems to be made up of university students from Ciudad de México and their hangers-on from Juárez University, and though one might think that students are the truly international people, especially in this age when jumplanes and ziplines have put most parts of the world within budget, and the vast net of data and XV links has tied not just voices but brains themselves together, the reality is that students are also the most politicized and least civilized travelers, not yet having gotten the habit of going along and being accommodating.

Out of the eight in her group, there are four who seem to believe that the *yanqui* is the cause of the hurricanes, and each wants to explain to her exactly why and how. Before, she'd simply have agreed with them, beginning each of her replies with *"Es verdad"* and then going on to express her understanding of their feelings, then finally correcting their values and analysis. Now, she doesn't give a shit.

Also, she's not formulating what to say next, and thus she's paying more attention to what they say, where she is, and what's going on. It may be good in the abstract, but here in the concrete—or *on* the concrete, she thinks sourly—it's wearing. They seem to enjoy being angry with her and abusing her. She can't help but notice that the denunciations of *imperialismo* are being mixed with a lot of staring at the way her breasts bounce around in her blouse, and where a couple of days before she'd have tried to link all that in an analysis that would show the unity of oppression, now she has a feeling that she's being hassled just because she's a woman and these guys don't really give a damn about *imperialismo.* Or indeed much of anything other than priority one (getting back to Oaxaca) and priority two (checking out the tits on the *gringa*).

And punishing her for simultaneously not being available and being a *puta.* She's also thinking that there are plenty of real victims of *imperialismo* around—she spent a lot of time working with them—but these kids owe their whole position in their society to being mediators between the Eurocentric capitalist power structure and the peasant underclass. If the industrialized world went away tomorrow, these guys wouldn't matter a fart in a windstorm, to use a Jesse-ism she's gotten to like.

She's never noticed before that people are angry in political discussions, that much of the anger is personal, and that it often intentionally hurts feelings. Hers, for example.

The road thus far has been empty and quiet, and despite what the lieutenant at the start point said about roving packs of looters and the danger to anyone, particularly any woman walking by herself, she hasn't seen anyone in the past few hours, her thighs are getting sore from trying to keep up with these guys, and she's getting out of breath. Plus there's still plenty of time to make it to Ixtepec by daylight walking at a pace that is comfortable for her.

Naomi gulps. This is the tough part. She has to do something entirely for herself; nobody else in the party seems to be tiring or to be getting harassed, so she can't defend anyone except herself. That seems to stick in her throat and she doesn't say anything for a whole additional kilometer after she makes her decision, but finally she remembers something Jesse told her once—the first time he had an orgasm with a woman, he had to pretend he was being stimulated by his own hand. She tries pretending that she is defending someone else. Like Naomi is another person, a woman being abused by these men. . . .

She tells them. They don't even try to persuade her to stay with them; they pick up their pace and are gone over the hill in a matter of minutes as she slows to a comfortable, sustainable saunter.

Now that she can slow down, she can notice that it's a hot, uncomfortable day, but not unusually so for the time of year; at least it's sunny. The forest that once covered the hillsides has been battered and torn, with big bare muddy scars from blowdowns, flashfloods, and avalanches on every slope around her, and individual trees not sheltered by their fellows have been stripped of their leaves, so that what remains are blobs of deep green among the blacks and browns of the water- and wind-chewed hillsides.

Much of what she's seeing was once small farms, tucked in wherever the ground was level enough; it will be a long time, she thinks, before the farmers have anything growing again. If there are still farmers.

She's put four more kilometers behind her at this comfortable pace, and has smeared on sunblock from her pack and tied her outer shirt around her waist, when she hears the car on the road behind her. The guide transponders are still out, and not supposed to be back on till further notice, so it's someone driving on manual, probably just an Army jeep.

The tank top she's wearing is cut a little low and of course it shows her shoulders completely; she wonders if maybe she should pull the overshirt back on, but it seems like a lot of trouble.

What comes over the hill behind her is not a jeep, nor an official limousine or rescue vehicle. It's just about the last thing she'd expect to see—a brand-new, apparently freshly washed GM Luxrover, one of those big go-anywhere luxury-interior sedans much favored by the more imperialistic *corporados* and by various economic and political bigshots. It has international plates designating it as an American car that's been a lot of places, and tinted windows so she can't see anything of who or what is inside. It comes roaring over the hillside, going like it has somewhere to go, but as it passes Naomi, it suddenly slows and pulls to the side ahead of her.

She keeps walking toward it because she can't think of what else to do. Odds are overwhelming that it's some nice tourist, probably male, who saw the pretty girl and thought she might like a ride; of course it could be just about anything else at all, and she's a little afraid, but she'd rather run the risk of the less-probable danger than insult the more-probable nice guy. And besides, if it is a ride, chances are that it's a ride with air conditioning and a comfortable seat, and her feet are beginning to burn in a way that's telling her she'll have blisters by the time she makes Ixtepec.

What the hell, she survived Clem Two, she can probably deal with one little old crazy rapist if it comes to that.

The Luxrover's door opens, and the driver steps out. He's about thirty and he's wearing a perfectly impeccable summer suit, the kind that the little cadcam studios in Oaxaca turn out, but made from—yep, as she gets closer she judges it's silk. And that's probably a real, fresh yellow chrysanthemum in his lapel. If he's wearing a yellow flower, then he's probably not Mexican and hasn't been here long—

He's also wearing huge dark shades. His blond hair is cut very short and he doesn't have much of a nose, and like the rest of him his neck looks painfully thin. The total effect makes him look like a large bug.

"Hi, do you need a ride?" he asks, in English. His voice has that kind of whiny, reedy quality that she associates with unsuccessful salesmen.

"You're American," she says, though she knows already. It seems like a good stall until she gets a better look at him.

"I bet you wonder what I'm doing here."

"No shit," she says. She always found it irritating when Jesse said that to her, and she wants to annoy this guy just a little, so that if he's got any romantic ideas they won't start blossoming in the first five minutes.

"Well, I was taking a long drive, seeing the country and all that bullshit while I did biz over the net. Now there's no net and no transponders so I'm just getting my ass back to the States. And I kind of thought giving a ride to a cute girl might be fun. Since you're not dressed like a Mexican—"

"What's wrong with a Mexican girl?" Naomi asks. The guy has just descended a point or two with her.

"Nothing except she probably doesn't speak English."

"Don't you speak Spanish?"

"Not a word. I just drive from resort to resort and I hardly ever get out of the car; when the transponders are up, the car gets me there and I get everything I want by looking out the window."

She feels like saying something judgmental, except that it's occurring to her that all she's seen, really, has been some *barrios* and various small towns. There are different ways of being narrow, perhaps. And besides, she's close enough now to feel the cold blast from the air conditioner. "I suppose," he adds, "that you're down here to work on poverty or something like that."

"Something like that," she says.

"Not my kind of thing. But I wouldn't mind listening while you tell me about it; I'm pretty bored with what's in the audio library and I can't do any XV or video when I have to drive the car."

Time to flatter him a little, she decides; there's been some distance established, and he appears to be exactly what he says he is—a *gringo* biz guy who likes pretty Mexican scenery and beautiful Mexican beaches but not Mexico. She can handle this for long enough to get back to Oaxaca—or even, she realizes, back to the States. Not a bad idea at all, really. "There's not that much to tell about me," she says. "I'm afraid you figured me out at the first glance. And can you really drive this thing yourself? I had to pass manual driving in high school but I haven't used it since. You must have reflexes like a fighter pilot."

He grins a little; with the dark shades hiding the rest of his expression, he could be laughing at the flattery or for that matter getting ready to bite her neck, but she makes herself choose to see it as friendly and as appreciating her admiration. "Heck, your grandparents all drove manual."

She stifles the urge to tell him that her grandparents were early Deepers and never drove at all after they were in their thirties, just as they never touched meat or animal products. Instead, she says, "Well, I could use a ride. I was going to Ixtepec so I could catch the zipline to Oaxaca."

"I'm going to Oaxaca," he says, "and from there up through Mexico City and all the way out through Nogales. If you've been following the news, it looks like a good time to relocate to the Rockies, and I've got a vacation home up near Green River, Utah. You can ride along as far as you like or at least as far as we can stand each other. If we're getting along at Oaxaca we can stop and get whatever stuff you have."

She's not sure how far they will be able to stand each other, but she says, "Everything I have in Oaxaca will go into two suitcases, and my parents live in Grand Junction. I'd *love* to ride with you."

And then, like some suave guy in some old movie, he walks all he way around his car and opens the door for her with a little bow. She smiles—hell,

at the thought of air conditioning and the fact that she can see there's a
fridge in there, probably with things to drink, she practically *simpers*. If this
didn't look so wonderful, she'd be ashamed of herself.

As they overtake the still-walking Mexican college students a few
minutes later, he says, "I'm no judge of people in this country—do you think
we should give them a ride?"

"Naw," she says, "I wouldn't. That's a bad-looking crowd." They roar
right by them, and the only thing that spoils her pleasure is that they
probably can't see her through the tinted glass.

"My name's Naomi," she says.

"I'm Eric," he says. "Help yourself to orange juice from the fridge—you
look like you could use it and you're too polite to ask."

As she takes the first wonderful, cold swig—and thinks of the guys back
there still walking the road, she says, "You certainly know how to treat a
lady, Eric. You sure you don't have a white charger in the trunk or something?"

He grins again, under the sunglasses. "I've always figured money is the
best armor."

Harris Diem, one day, would like to open his basement door and find a bare
concrete wall, rather than steps leading down. In fact, it would be better still
to find no basement door. If that were to happen, then one of two things
would happen to Harris Diem—either he would heave a great sigh of relief,
or he would feel a scream in his nerves, a rattlesnake at the base of his skull
that wouldn't leave him alone. Most likely he'd feel that scream, just as he
feels it, mildly now, and then he'd have to do insanely risky things.

But if all he felt was the relief . . . if only that. It seems too much to
imagine.

And of course his basement door is still there. He told them at his office
in the White House that he *had* to get home tonight, that he was stressing
out, and that much was true; what he didn't tell them, what was none of their
business, what would destroy him if they knew, was just what kind of stress
it is and just how he is going to unwind.

The basement door closes behind him and he heaves a little sigh of relief;
the thin filament of rubber cement that he normally leaves stretched across
the stairs here, so slight that you can't see it except by pointing a flashlight
in the right direction, as he is doing now, is undisturbed. The cleaning help
has not been down here (his major worry) and no covert op has had a peek
either (his minor worry).

He walks down the steps, turning on the low, orange lighting in the
windowless room, and looks around with a little satisfaction; he wishes all

this were not here, he wishes he had no desire ever to come down here, and yet money and power have had their advantages—it's one great setup.

The couch is carefully padded with a restraint system that will hold him only as long as he's not conscious of it. The scalpnet has a comfortable soft satin cover; the powered merkin and butt plug, with their neural stimulator surfaces, are state-of-the-art; the large-muscle stimulators in the restraint cuffs are precise down to a hundredth of a newton in replicating a sensation.

As always, he opens the refrigerator, takes out a bottle of mineral water, and drinks it down; he's going to be on the bed for three hours or so if this is a typical night, and the extra fluids help.

He hangs his bathrobe on its hook, and removes all of his clothing, putting it into the small laundry bag he used to bring down the bathrobe. The bathrobe is clean and soft, and he buries his face in the terrycloth for just a moment, making sure that he doesn't touch it with the tip of his penis, which he can feel is already damp with that first secretion.

Diem lets go of the robe, letting it swing back silently to the wall. He walks to the little washer-dryer and pulls out the sheets, freshly washed from the last time he was down here.

He reminds himself once more that he doesn't actually *have* to do this, that if he decides to he can just go back upstairs and call it a night right now, getting a lot of the extra sleep that he really does need; and turns with a light, happy step and presses his thumb to the print-reading lock on the cabinet.

The door swings open, and he looks over the inventory of recorded XV. Most of the wedges are in plain white boxes, and on the sides of the boxes he has written, in his neat draftsman's slanted characters, various women's names.

Girl's names, really, he reminds himself, and that thought alone makes his penis rise a little. "Allie" is at the upper left corner; "Zulika" is at the lower right. Tonight, though, he wants something very special. After all, it may be the last for a long time, and, if what is about to boil out of the Gulf of Mexico is any indication, perhaps the last ever—this room, or Diem himself, or perhaps both, may be gone within a few days.

Well, "special" really only means one of three things, doesn't it? Kimbie Dee, Michelline, or DeLana. Kimbie Dee is a perky little blonde, about fourteen, and the man is an old janitor with a hideous facial deformity who catches her alone in the locker room; it has its moments. Michelline is a red-haired, angelic-looking child, not yet in puberty, and it's her drunken father late at night, with no one to hear her screams. . . . He reaches for DeLana.

She's black, and that's part of the reason. He wonders, if he were ever found out, if there would be any way they could find out that this is the wedge he likes best. He wonders if that would have any political repercussions that would be different from the ones with the white girls. If so, he thinks to himself, which would be worse? A guy of Vietnamese ancestry who likes the idea of raping black girls (hello, traditional hatreds between ethnic ghettos) or white girls (hello, wrong race and white women)?

Well, whatever may come, he's here tonight, and he wants DeLana first. Then he'll do Michelline, then Kimbie Dee, and finally back to DeLana. He sets them up, programs the deck to begin on his voice cue, and stretches out on the table. The butt plug goes into his anus, the merkin fits over his penis, the scalpnet onto his head. He stops to fasten his legs and the waistband, then lies back after making sure the other straps are lying where he needs them. Muffs on, goggles on, fasten head strap, press arms into restraint calipers . . . ready to go—

"Cue ready. Cue up," he says.

He *is* DeLana, and he *is* the man who abducts her from the street. He clutches her hair in his fist and feels the agony in her scalp; tastes the gun barrel thrust into her mouth and feels his finger vibrating, ever so slightly, on the trigger; screams for her mama at the moment that he comes into her anus. He feels the miserable soreness in her breasts the day after and gloats at the dark bruises, feels her will break and her resistance crumble as she is forced to submission, tastes the shit licked from Master's asshole, feels her little wet tongue cleaning him—and finally . . . no, no, no cut away, not yet. . . .

Ah. Michelline. Struggling, squirming under the covers, terrified because Dad has done this before but never so hard and it hurts; Dad feeling her come alive as she struggles to get away—

The objects he puts in become bigger and rougher, as blood covers her thighs (feeling it bleed, feeling her blood on her slick thighs)—and then the moment when her head is snapped back against the headboard, and the Michelline channel goes dead, literally, utterly blank, and Dad climbs into bed on top of the little, still-warm body.

Diem ejaculates hard at that, his scrotum twisting and aching, and slides into stalking Kimbie Dee down a hallway after she has been working out alone in the gym, feels the warm water of the shower on her as he closes in, revels in the hour during which the maimed janitor batters her small breasts, forces the mop handle into her, rapes her on the cold floor, knots the bra around her neck as she lies keening with pain—now Diem is coming dry and fast, over and over, knowing his penis will be sore for days afterward—and watches as her nude body drops from the showerhead, the shocked expression still on her face as the makeshift noose catches—and feels the noose grab the throat, the sobs of shame squeezed shut forever—

And Diem drops back to hurling DeLana from the high window, and the feel of the subzero wind screaming by her nude body, the intensity of the headache from the beating and the effects of the cold on her skull—the pavement rushing up toward her, the incomprehension that what will happen next—

There is a great burst of terrible pain and he is alone in the dark.

Diem ejaculates now, or tries to, there's no fluid left but he rears and screams against the bonds, and the contractions feel like he's tearing himself in two between his loins. As always, he passes out completely and falls into a dreamless dead sleep, waking about an hour later.

He releases his bonds and sits up; as usual he uses the spray painkiller, and then the warm soft oil, on his penis before he does anything else. Somewhere in all of it he lost bladder control, so he is covered with his own urine; he never remembers how or when that happens but it seems to intensify the feeling.

The room has a poisonous stench that he wants to flee, to hand off to someone to clean up for him, but of course he can't do that; he's exhausted and the painkiller isn't quite working, he's all but hysterical with guilt and relief, but he must spend this next half hour on the cleanup.

The sheets go into the washer-dryer, and he turns it on. The little gadget will get the blood, shit, semen, sweat, and urine out again, though the sheets are getting old and stained.

God, his arms ache and he's never been this tired before while doing this, but he racks the wedges up and locks the cabinet, then takes the disinfectant and wipes down the bed, restraints, and fittings. He's so tired he drops the bucket and it spills, running into a floor drain; his heart sinks at the thought of mopping, and then he realizes he won't have to, it will dry on the waterproof floor, he can mop it some time when he has the time.

At last he can have his shower. It's hot and there's plenty of it, and the disinfectant body shampoo smells wonderful to him; he's all but weeping with pleasure because it's over—

But unlike other nights, perhaps just because this was so intense, there is a thing he can't quite get out of his mind. As Diem works the pounding warm water over his scalp, his mind drifts back to the beginning, to when the first "parallel experience" porn was showing up, back during Brittany Lynn Hardshaw's first stint as a Federal prosecutor, and then when she was Idaho Attorney General.

God, how had anyone discovered it? It was obvious in retrospect . . . but what kind of person would have thought of it in the first place? Rapists and molesters enjoyed what they were doing because they *did* know what they were doing to the victim—that was part of why it was so common for abused children to grow up to be abusers—so rape-porn enthusiasts got far more excitement from sharing the event from both viewpoints.

Almost there was a kind of business genius behind it.

For that matter, what kind of brain wiring had been installed in men like . . . well, like Diem himself? He scours his back with the long-handled loofah, hard enough to turn it pink and achy. He still doesn't feel clean, and he's so tired. . . .

It started with deciding to see what this was like; and then it was easy to copy confiscated wedges. Before this stuff, Diem had always just figured he was sort of sexless—college experiments with a couple of young women and one young man had left him bored. It was easier to just stay home and masturbate, and before he found parallel experience he never fantasized about anything . . . at least not with any awareness that it was turning him on—

Well, there you had it. He supposes he could have gone to see an analyst. There have been some successes with treating all this. But that would mean confessing to a lot of things, including that his "experiments" in college had all been stranger rapes in distant cities. . . .

The country might well have been worse off, he thinks, honestly. Brittany Lynn Hardshaw has been one of the most effective leaders of the last fifty years, and that's not just his opinion—to do his job Diem has had to know how to judge accurately rather than with his loyalty. Even if he didn't trust his own judgment, there's also the nearly universal opinion of the historians and political scientists, even the ones who hate her guts.

And so many people know that part of her greatness was her Shadow. . . .

He finds himself sinking to the floor of the shower, and starts rattling off accomplishments. He would guess that between one action and another that he's managed, he's put three million people into homes, thirteen million into jobs, gotten justice for another couple of million who would never have seen it otherwise—

His one term in Congress led to the Diem Act, and more than a thousand people have been put to death for making wedges like the ones locked in his cabinet. He even saw to it that a few specific ones he had contact with came to the notice of the cops . . . did he want to get caught? Or just want *them* to get caught?

He's still ill; the pain from the convulsions that ripped through his groin earlier, the soreness leaking from where the merkin abraded his penis and where he forced himself down so hard on the butt plug, all of that is mixing with overpowering nausea. He barely gets out of the shower to the toilet in time to heave up several times, heavy retching that leaves him feeling wrung from chest to ass, his legs trembling, head aching, like the worst flu he's ever had.

A really bad reaction tends to follow a really intense session. The unbearable demanding buzz at the base of his skull isn't there, won't return for weeks or months. But now there is something else he can't shut out.

What he can't shut out just keeps coming back at him; he gets under the shower again, scours off the flecks of his own vomit, dries in haste and pulls on the bathrobe. On good nights, the ritual of the shower works like a baptism, bringing him back into the world feeling clean again, if wrung out and in pain; on bad nights, it just goes on and on.

What he can't shut out has its grip on him tonight. He staggers upstairs, stops for one long moment at the landing because he must go back and string the filament of rubber cement, then carefully memorize its shape for the next time—

God, the next time. D.C. itself may be washed away, Diem is slated for the last part of the government to leave and he may be killed here like those poor bastards in Hawaii . . . and it doesn't matter, he's got to make sure this place is secure. No one must know—

He makes himself look long and hard at the thin string of drying rubber cement, remembers the unique shape of its bumps. Once someone breaks that they'll never successfully copy it into place, and he'll have at least some warning—

Then he feels his legs bending and buckling. What he can't shut out comes howling up the stairs like a vicious dog at his heels. He turns, slams the door, locks it, flees up the back stairs that are forbidden to servants, enters his own bedroom. The bathrobe flies off him like a great winged bat and lands on his writing desk, currently holding three books he was reading weeks ago before it all got crazy.

He throws himself between the soft sheets of the big waterbed and buries his head under the covers, pausing only a quarter-breath to say "Room lights off" to the house computer.

What he can't shut out is this:

All the wedges except the three "specials," the ones he experienced tonight, are copies of parallel-experience porn that was confiscated from people who were dealing this stuff. He prosecuted some of them himself.

Three wedges—the three he played tonight—are different. He commissioned those.

Each of these three wedges cost him four times as much as his car.

And just before he falls asleep he hears it, what he can't shut out, his own voice cutting into him, as if he had himself on the witness stand:

Mr. Diem, surely you know that these wedges are made by forcible short-term memory extraction after the rape has been committed, and the extractor is then left in place for the killing itself.

But you ordered the wedges, Mr. Diem. He who bids a thing done by others, does it himself. And at the prices you paid, Mr. Diem, you know what they did. They made those wedges special for you. And what they did to those three young girls was exactly what you wanted them to do.

And if you don't believe that, Mr. Diem, remember that the final orgasm, the big one, the one you've got to have, comes not with the horrible torture of Kimbie Dee, Michelline, and DeLana . . . not even with their wretched disgusting deaths at the hands of those ghouls . . . no, Mr. Diem. That's not what makes you come.

You come from knowing that it all really happened, don't you?

Blackness descends. He oversleeps the next morning. When he does get up, it's past ten, the day is gray and dreary, and there's a note from President Hardshaw asking him to take a day off and recover from his overwork.

Berlina Jameson often wishes that she were more of an old hand. If the world ran the way it is supposed to, then she'd have spent ages covering school board meetings and standing in front of car wrecks with a camera pointed at her before she got her big break, and so she'd have lots of experience talking with biz types. But as it is, she's going to have to wing it.

Glinda Gray, the person from GateTech who has one of those strangely unexplanatory job titles that mean either she's a flunky or a real power and you're supposed to be kept guessing, is not telling the whole truth. Berlina is sure of that much. She's also sure that if she just had ten years or so of experience at this, she'd know exactly what it was that she wasn't being told. Unfortunately she not only doesn't have enough experience to sort that out—she also doesn't have enough experience to comprehend what seems to be a series of hints that Ms. Gray is sending at her.

Well, gee, what would Edward R. Murrow or Morley Safer have done? Berlina thinks. She's rolling south toward the Gulf Coast just now, en route to getting some stock footage shot for the before-and-after sequences that are sure to come. But just now she's not thinking of getting footage of the soon-to-be-destroyed areas; she is stretched out in the back of the car, looking into a sterovisor and assembling the images of the two of them virtually, so that what she sees looks like the inside of a TV studio but she has to be careful not to stick her arm through a potted plant. It's clear that Glinda Gray is at least as at home in the environment as Berlina Jameson.

When in doubt, try the truth. "So," Berlina Jameson says, "the documentation is pretty convincing. The USSF and NASA are completely illegally looting the Japanese and European parts of Moonbase, and what's more they've had NSA assistance in cracking security codes so that they're also using all sorts of privately owned equipment without paying for it. I'll certainly go with that material, but there's at least two questions you haven't answered. The first one is why you picked *Sniffings* rather than *Scuttlebytes*, and the second is, What's in all this for GateTech?"

Glinda Gray brushes her graying-blonde hair back from her face, and Jameson notes with envy just how polished the woman seems, as if Gray had been playing the role of herself for many years. "Well, we think *Sniffings* is likely to be interested for two reasons, and you can quote me on either of them. First of all, *Scuttlebytes* has, let's say, a very adolescent attitude about business and capitalism—they like to tweak business just because there's a certain amount of money and prestige in the private sector and because business people tend to be kind of conservative. And more importantly, we have a pretty good idea about why the Feds and the UN are doing this. It's because most of the governments of the Earth failed to foresee that there might be a need for space launch that could stand up to severe weather conditions; our own country is a perfect example; first we built at Canaveral on a coast that gets hurricanes, then we moved to Kingman Reef, where there's even less dry land and even more storm vulnerability. But the other nations haven't done much better.

"So naturally when the catastrophe anyone should have seen was possible comes along, what happens? There're two possibilities—they can either launch using the facilities that private enterprise built on speculation against just such a day, or they can do what they're doing—appropriate private property without compensation, infringe on other nations' facilities, do everything that if we did it would rightly be called theft, piracy, or barratry, all of that just to avoid letting private enterprise solve the problem. There's an anti-business bias in government that runs deep and strong, Ms. Jameson, and that's what you're seeing here. Frankly we're tired of it; all we want is a chance to compete fairly, and what we're seeing here is a situation where we have to play by the rules and they don't."

It's a great bunch of quotes, Berlina consoles herself, and the fact that something smells funny about all this can always be looked into later. It's almost enough to make her wish she had invested in a head jack so that she could go two-way with some databases, but you have to know what questions to ask to do that and it's awesomely expensive.

She gets a couple more minutes with Glinda Gray, but no better material. They have the usual polite off-record exchanges at the end; the most interesting thing she gets out of that is that John Klieg himself is a fan of *Sniffings*, which Gray mentions with an odd air of embarrassment, as if it were unusual for her to know that about her boss.

Well, well, then perhaps the rumors that she's been serving under her boss with distinction are true . . . but private biz *really* is a different game. Whereas a senator boffing his legislative assistant is dynamite, people in private business can and do screw pretty much whomever they like, and absolutely nobody in that community seems to think much about it. Berlina is not sure she can get the hang of such a different world.

Well, one rule that has worked for her is: When you don't understand what you've got, get more. Who can she talk to? She's had a few short conversations with Harris Diem over the past few weeks, but that is probably not enough for her to just call him up.

Di Callare does not strike her as the hardheaded business type either, but at least he'll have something to say and he's easy to talk to.

He all but explodes; it takes her a while to sort out the basic issues—that Klieg is just taking advantage of the situation. "Look at the permit and build dates, look when he started moving to Siberia, what he did was take a gamble that this would happen and then get the right piece of dirt from people who had to give him a cheap deal. . . ."

She makes the note herself. *What was Klieg's timing? Did he have any way to know or suspect something like Clem was about to happen?* It's one thing to be a farsighted road-builder, she thinks, and another to sprint up the road ahead of a crowd of refugees and open a tollbooth . . . and certainly, too, Klieg's connections to the all-but-outlawed Siberian regime also bear some checking into.

She thanks Di for his trouble and time, makes sure he feels they're still friends, and clicks off. Di has said nothing she wants to quote, but at least via him she has some idea what Diem might say, or Hardshaw if she gets that lucky.

She has an ominous feeling that all she has here is something the Klieg organization wants to plant in the media, and she doesn't know why. Of course until she releases it she doesn't know what they'll do with it—

And that thought gives her the answer. She makes her preparations and then leaves a short note for Glinda Gray, informing her that the next *Sniffings* will feature the story as its lead. Then she records a much longer voice-and-video message for Harris Diem.

She knows she did the right thing when he calls her back that night.

Jesse and Mary Ann managed to get on the same crew for the dig-out; it's not like Tehuantepec here in Tapachula, they were far enough away so that it was no more than an unusually bad hurricane, and even with the Army not showing up, most of Puerto Madero managed to evacuate itself before the storm surges hit. That little town and beach are gone, and the inhabitants have been added to the homeless in Tapachula, but they're alive, and besides

Tapachula has plenty of buildings standing. Even some of the shacks that ringed the town managed to hold somehow, and enough public buildings to provide everyone a place to sleep—which may be better than it was before Clementine ripped over them.

Not that there isn't plenty to do, but deaths here run to dozens, not to hundreds, and when a rubble pile has to be looked into, there are plenty of hands available. Mary Ann is standing in the right place to see two small, dirty, frightened boys freed from house wreckage, and then to hear the shriek of joy from their mother.

Sourly, she finds herself thinking that if she were working, she would have had to crank her feelings up to fever pitch—just so the experiencers could understand that it was good to have seen that.

It's a long day, and it's a bit longer because, since the landlord isn't around to object, Mary Ann has turned her rented house into an emergency shelter, so that besides the indispensable Herreras, they have about twenty refugees scattered around the place. That means a certain amount of work in getting everyone bedded down, but at least Señora Herrera was able to screen the incoming guests, and she seems to have been willing to take only those who want to work for their bed and supper. If anything the place is cleaner and more orderly than before.

It leaves Jesse and Mary Ann with only the master bedroom and its bath to call their own, but that doesn't much matter; it's kind of cozy, like having the largest and best room in a dormitory.

That evening Jesse is messing around with the terminal; links to the outside world, and via that to the rest of Mexico, seem to be in good shape, though everything is going via satellite between north and south Mexico— Clementine tore a swath that ripped out all but the few buried fibrop cables, and for practical purposes Mexico is now two nations divided by the wild chaos of the Isthmus of Tehuantepec.

He has kind of ambiguous feelings about it, but he decides that seeing if he can contact Naomi is the least he can do. He writes a quick "hope you're okay" letter to Naomi and puts it in a tracer packet aimed at her net i.d.—a little program that will hang around in the nets looking for her until she logs on again.

While he's at it, he puts out a "mention search" tracer as well; this is a program that will capture everything that mentions Naomi. He tells it to just hang out on the servers and processors in the states of Oaxaca and Chiapas. That way, if—he flinches a bit at the thought—well, if she's in the hospital, or in a busload of refugees, or something like that, his tracer will find out and let him know.

They've got limited phone service available for contacting relatives, and he hasn't used any of his authorized calls yet. Probably he ought to call Dad, but phoning Di is about as good—Di will pass word on to Dad—and Di is a lot easier to talk to.

To his surprise, Di is on the screen almost at once. "Kid! I've been trying to get something out of Mexico for two days about you! What's up? Are you okay? Do you need money or clearance to get anywhere or anything?"

"I'm fine, Di, really. I've got a rich girlfriend, and she's got a house that's built like a fort. We rode it out here and there was no big trouble at all. They just got phone service up a couple of hours ago. My old place was smashed up pretty badly but I was fine, and most of my stuff was over here anyway. I was just calling to let you know I'm okay."

"God, I'm glad to hear that!"

Jesse looks closer at the screen, and says, "You look really tired, Di. Aren't they giving you any breaks?"

"They are but I'm not taking them. Have you had time to check the news?"

"Just enough to know Salina Cruz is gone and most of the coast resorts got clobbered by storm surge. And of course the country's practically cut in half at the *Istmo*."

"That's pretty much the story," Di agrees. "It's not yet public, but the Mexican government has made a decision that I wish our President would. They've declared the situation as good as permanent—with so many Clems forming out there, and with our forecasts saying every summer will be like this for at least six years, they're going to try to organize mass migrations to safer areas, and take advantage of the big rainfalls to grow grain in the desert to feed everyone. So if you can get out of there soon, you should—otherwise your way out is likely to involve spending a month or so in a refugee column going farther up into the hills."

"The Chiapas rain forest might not even notice the hurricanes, if it doesn't get hit directly," Jesse responds. It's funny—last month he'd have been hysterical about not getting back to the Az on schedule, but now he can look at it calmly enough. "It rains a lot here. But—a *lot* of Clems—"

"A lot. Clem's had two babies and is still headed west in the Pacific, with one of them trailing behind and the other running parallel and to the north; Clem Two, or 'Clementine,' as Berlina dubbed it, is kicking up such a fuss in the Gulf that we aren't even sure how many storm eyes there really are there—it's got about four outflow jets popping around and they're all starting eyes everywhere. We've started a new designation system; Clem itself is Clem 100, Clem Two is Clem 200, and the two independent daughters in the Pacific are 300 and 400; mostly they'll be named after their direct ancestors. Our guess is that there're going to be at least a Clem 210, Clem 220, and Clem 230 coming out of the Gulf."

"Jesus."

"Unh-hunh. And we've got Tropical Depression Donna forming way out west in the Atlantic near the equator. Bet on it, Jesse, if you stay in Mexico you'll ride out at least five more hurricanes this summer and fall. For that matter we're betting on three big ones for the Chesapeake."

Jesse shakes his head, trying to make the thoughts whirling there settle down. "Is there anywhere safe?"

"Siberia, I guess, ought to be okay. In the States, Kansas maybe, though there's going to be a lot of rain in the Rockies so I wouldn't set up camp anywhere near a river. Utah, as long as you don't get hit with flash floods, and some of our models are showing that the dry lake beds are going to refill all over the basin and range country—there's going to be a chain of salt lakes all down there by October."

Jesse finds his voice, and he says, "Well, then, shit, Di, tell me . . . is there anything that can be done? Is anyone trying?"

Di shrugs. "Of course people are trying."

It doesn't sound encouraging. There's really no reason to try to go back. Here in Chiapas, he knows his neighbors and he's worked beside them. And the mountains and rain forest above are not the worst place in the world to live, if it came to that. He has a strange feeling that he might be deciding where his *grandchildren* will live. There'd be a place for him—he's healthy and doesn't mind work, his Spanish has gotten very fluent in his time here, and he's got a bunch of skills that are likely to be needed, though realization engineering may not be important for a while. "Then I think I'll stick down here, Di. There's a place for me and it's apt to be safer."

"It's, uh, not because of some girl, is it?"

"You know my evil habits. No, not really, I think her employers will probably call her back onto the job pretty soon. And I'd really say 'woman' rather than 'girl.' She's, uh, probably nearer your age than mine."

Di whistles and gives him a wink. "Coo coo ca choo, Mrs. Robinson."

"What?"

"I don't know what it means either, but Dad used to say that whenever he saw a younger guy with an older woman. Some kind of boomtalk, I guess."

"He must have given that up before I came along."

"Right. Theoretically I should get back to work but all we're doing right now is documenting that horrible mess in the Gulf, and I don't mind telling you it's a relief to talk to anyone about anything else at all. There's nothing we can do and it just keeps building. . . ." Di sighs. "Anyway, enough of that. You take care. You sound pretty grown-up to me, but you're still my kid brother. This old grandmother you're shacked up with—"

"Hey!"

"—is she anyone I might know?"

Jesse decides that if he tells Di, most likely his brother will start calling psychiatric authorities, so he says, "Probably not. Ever meet an actress named Mary Ann Waterhouse?"

"Never heard of her. Tell her to take good care of my brother, okay?"

"Deal. You keep an eye on my nephews."

They give each other a little wave that turns into a mock salute, and then the call ends. Jesse sits back and thinks; that really sounded a lot like a goodbye, and he doesn't like that. And yet—well, the satellites are still up there and the weather doesn't touch them, and plenty of fibrop lines are buried . . . chances are that even if civilization collapses the net will stay up for a long time.

Which gives him the vision of himself and Mary Ann hoeing a garden patch in the jungle with a sharp stick, with Mary Ann plugged in so that all over the world, millions of people sitting in their huts, their own gardens neglected, can share the experience of hoeing with a sharp stick.

"What are you laughing about?" Mary Ann says, coming out of the shower. The sculpture they have made of her body still astonishes him.

"Oh, I got through to my brother. He's a funny guy."

By the time they stop to get her stuff from her little bungalow, Naomi is beginning to realize just how differently Eric sees the world from the way she does. She's not at all sure how to feel about it—he's polite and appears interested in what she says, but since she's sworn off values-educating people, she suddenly realizes how little she has to talk about. She's been to a lot of places, but mostly she's gone straight from the zipline to some pocket of misery, and so she can tell him what squalor is like everywhere, but not anything else—and squalor is alike, wherever you go.

There's a short letter from Jesse; she means to reply, then figures she can do it later—Eric is scrambling up and down the stairs with her stuff and she doesn't want to let him do all the work.

Driving out of town, Eric talks about the museum at Oaxaca, which holds a lot of the stuff that they dug up from Monte Alban. He seems a little worried about whether it's been damaged.

She is ashamed to have to admit that though she's had weeks of opportunity, and several days off, she's never seen either the museum or Monte Alban itself. She always had to go to meetings and work on values clarification; besides, she realizes guiltily, she wouldn't really have seen it anyway because she'd have been too busy (at the museum) experiencing what a beautiful culture it was that had passed away and how much the linear and centric Euroculture had lost—

They are driving out through Oaxaca; it's now late in the day, but there's an intact set of transponders on Federal Highway 190, so the car can drive itself as soon as they've got it on the highway up toward Ciudad de México. She notices that one tree blew over by the big fountain in the Paseo Juárez, but that's the worst she's seen here; Clem Two made sort of a right turn after Tehuantepec, which was part of why it blew over so quickly there but lashed Chiapas for so much longer.

"So the museum's three blocks away, right over there," she said. "Gee, I wonder if I'll ever be back to see it."

"Stick with me, kid, I love this town," Eric says, grinning. They take a fast right at Calle Niños Héroes de Chapultepec, and now they're on their way out of the city, headed up to the junction with 190.

She liked being called "kid." If Jesse had done that she'd have screamed at him. Part of her is shocked—what's it going to be next, "baby"? "Sweet Butt"?

Another part tells her that it means he likes her and finds her attractive, and to hell with it if it's not how she'd like him to express it; if it gets to be an issue, she'll just tell him. He seems to be a nice guy and he probably won't call her anything she doesn't want to be called.

A few minutes later, he throws the switch for full auto, sets the destination for a hotel in Mexico City—leaning over to see where he's set it for, she's shocked to realize that she recognizes the place. It's one of the giant new earthquake-proof palaces that start at more for a night than she's ever made in a month. "Er," she says, "um . . . I guess I'll need a place to stay and I can't afford—"

"No problem," he says. "I booked a two-bedroom suite. And it's on me, like the ride. I like you, Naomi. I'm not going to pretend I wouldn't like to share the bed with you when we get there, but I'd rather be invited than try to pressure my way in."

Keep it up, she thinks, *and I just might invite you. Wonder what it's like to have sex with a guy just because I want to? And then not educate him at all, not even try?*

She's really startled by her train of thought, so she says, "You know, I ought to confess, if I had gone to the museum, I'd have gone knowing what I thought about non-European cultural artifacts, and I'd never have seen it. I haven't been very, uh, open to experience, I guess—though the funny thing is that I've been trying to feel at one with the world all my life."

He smiles. "Why not just be at one with the parts you like?"

She grins at him. "I could say it's an extremely negative values decision. But I don't know, why not just be in love with the parts you like about your lover? It wouldn't seem much like love to me but I guess you could do it."

"Well, that's my philosophy," he says. "I mean, you do realize that you're one of the people who has made being in business in the U.S. a pain in the ass for the last few generations, don't you? You've probably done all sorts of things and worked for all sorts of causes I would resent like hell. True?"

"True." She feels like adding that she's sorry, and then feels angry because she has nothing to apologize for, and then feels stupid because he hasn't asked her to apologize. It doesn't matter anyway, because he keeps talking.

"Well, I won't even ask you not to talk about it. What I will do is concentrate on liking the way that you smile, and that you're very pretty and have a nice body, and that you're a good listener. And while we're at it, you have a very tough, funny sense of humor when you're talking to a guy, and you make me half crazy with wanting to please you, believe it or not. But I also know as a practical matter that I can't please you by agreeing with you, because you'll know that I'm lying, so what you're likely to like about me is that I'm generous and polite."

"You can add that you're handsome and you've got a lot of experiences that I like hearing about," she says, "as long as that doesn't give you any ideas."

"None that I haven't had for a while anyway. Let's move into the back, where there's a little more room, and I'll dig out some food from the fridge. Your family are Deepers, so I guess you're probably a vegetarian—"

"Uh, I'm afraid so. And—hmm. I know most people call us Deepers, but we call ourselves Values Clarified, or VC."

Eric nods very politely. "Well, I've got some fresh fruit, a salad or two, and some plain yogurt. All shipped-in American, so I doubt you'll have any trouble with it if you've been eating native for months. I hope you won't mind that I've also got ham sandwiches and I'm planning to eat a couple of them."

"One of the values I'm going to try getting less clarified about is the thing about property rights being less important than the right to be educated," Naomi says, smiling broadly. "It was just occurring to me that it's your car, it's your ham sandwich, and I'm a guest here."

They have a long, slow supper, talking about things like childhood and what it's like to play commodities or plan a demonstration, and it gets dark outside the tinted windows. The car's temperature control works perfectly, and Naomi realizes that she hasn't felt bumps in the road, either, that the car is driving around the big ones and taking up the rest in its shock system. She's not sure she's ever been anywhere quite so comfortable.

It's still about three hours to Mexico City; they stop briefly at an automated Pemex for gas, getting out of the car into the chilly mountain night just long enough to use the rest rooms. When Naomi comes back outside, he's waiting for her in the cold.

"You should have gotten back in the car," she says. "Jesus, it's freezing out tonight."

"I'm being gentlemanly," he says. "One of those things that happens when you let a boy turn into an Eagle Scout."

"My folks wouldn't let my brother join the Scouts. Uniforms are militarist and camping out damages wilderness."

"Besides, if you help old ladies across the street, the old ladies go on taking up valuable resources," he adds, opening the door for her.

"They'd have used that argument if they'd thought of it. You almost put your arm around me, didn't you?"

"Almost." He closes the door and comes around to the other side, gets in, and says, "Gay Deceiver, voice command on. All passengers are back inside, lock up and continue. Gay Deceiver, voice command off."

The car responds in a woman's voice. "You got it, boss. Nice honkers on the chick," and then starts rolling down the driveway to the highway.

It's so unexpected that Naomi howls with laughter. Eric appears to be trying to hide in the seat. "I'm sorry," he says, "I forgot to reset from the custom message base and—"

"Why do you call your car Gay Deceiver?"

"From my favorite book when I was a kid. Thoroughly useless mind-rotting garbage, I assure you—exactly what kids like. There was a car with that name in it, and—oh, well, anyway, I'm sorry, I have this sort-of not-serious girlfriend back in Utah—"

"Oh," Naomi says.

"No—it's—well, hell, let's call her. I think I was sort of getting somewhere with you, and I want you to know it's all right."

"And you can call her up at this hour?"

The car slides around a tight turn, and he says, "We've been friends since high school, and she's been married twice in that time. Anyway, this old girlfriend was a big fan of the same book, and since Gay Deceiver in the book has a tendency to get rude, she gave me that voice module for Christmas."

She turns out to be named Zoe Matson. She's gracious and friendly and immediately tells Eric that "it's a good thing you left me a key. I'll get right over to your house and suppress the evidence of what you live like, you filthy pig, and round up any *other* underage girls I find, give'em a ride into town and a bus ticket, and make it respectable—"

Naomi likes Eric a little better for having this friend, and it's clear that it really is all right. They click off from Zoe, and Naomi asks, "Are you still, um, having thoughts about me?"

"Well, yes," he says. "I mean, I'm still a gentleman—"

"I know that, sport," she says, and—not believing that she's doing it, laughing at herself at the same moment that she's enjoying it tremendously—she turns on the overhead light in the car so that he can see, and slides her top down. "So—want to check out the honkers on the chick?"

She's amazed and touched.

When she decided to do that she figured he'd probably pounce on her and maybe be a little rough, but after the scare about Zoe, she realizes she really does want him and it seemed like the last step in her personal liberation to just cut right through the crap. So she was prepared to have him come at her like a caveman, and to enjoy it anyway.

Instead, he leans forward very slowly, takes her chin in his hand, lifts her mouth to his, and kisses her firmly; his hand strokes her neck, wanders tenderly over her shoulder and the soft flesh by her armpit, and finally brushes up the side of her breast to place just a finger on her erect nipple. Breaking the kiss, he whispers, "Thank you for this."

She kisses his cheek and brings both his hands to her breasts. "Make love with me," she says. "Just make love, we'll spend hours talking—later." She feels like she's on XV, and she adores feeling that way, and she adores everything else that happens, and she adores Eric. She's not sure she's ever, in her life before, permitted herself to adore anything.

The car rolls on north, without a bump or a sound; fortunately the program is smart enough to wake them up in time to get dressed before they pull into the hotel parking garage.

Naomi would never have guessed they still had it in them, but there's something about a bed that size and a room that nice . . . they don't get out of Mexico City for a whole additional day, and they have to call up Zoe to let her know they'll be late. Naomi even likes being teased about that.

Maybe Passionet is hiring, she thinks.

The results are back, and Berlina Jameson heaves a sigh of relief. The tattletales she let loose in the net have done their job; ten minutes after she told Glinda Gray that the "USSF: Space Pirates?" story would be the lead in the next *Sniffings,* there were over seventy brief messages to UN ambassadors, congressmen, Europarliament reps, Japanese Diet members . . . what she has here, she realizes, is the structure of Klieg's influence. These are the people who will deliver a space launch monopoly to John Klieg and Gate-Tech, probably in return for various services rendered or perhaps for plain old money.

She puts that in as a special, follow-on edition of *Sniffings*. It's late, so she shuts off her connections to other communication services for the night. She has enough footage, now, of the Gulf, for later when she will cover the disaster that is bound to happen there; the most gratifying thing is the sheer number of people who, one way or another, have decided to just bag it and head to places farther north and higher up.

It occurs to her that as of yet there are no refugee camps. A lot of people seemed to be leaving for the Rockies, probably figuring you couldn't get higher than that, so she decides to see how the refugees are doing—it might make another great *Sniffings*, and she's on a roll. She points the car toward Wyoming, stretches out to go to sleep, and roars on into the night.

The day begins badly, with Diem wanting to resign.

First of all, he finds that Hardshaw has cleared everyone to talk to Berlina Jameson, and that she's getting all kinds of assistance from White House offices, and he wasn't told that. And then, as Chief of Staff, Diem should have known about her meeting with Rivera; having been cut out of the loop is intolerable, it's something she would do just before firing him or to discipline him, and she never hits her top people in such a crude way—

Her eyes soften a little and she says, "I made the appointment while you were on your way in, Harris. If you'd gone straight to your desk, instead of bursting in here, you'd have seen it. It's not a slap at you, honestly. And I truly don't understand why you are upset about Jameson. We wanted her to find Klieg's web of influence and play up the Hassan connection, and she will."

"But the way you're doing it, it will all be exposed . . . there's no leverage. We can't threaten them with exposure. Hell, a lot of them will be right out of the game." He sits down, sighs, lets calm come back into his system. "All right. I'm going to be rational. Explain to me how the game works, because this is all new to me. I thought you had set up a brilliant situation for leaning on Klieg and half a dozen governments worldwide. Clearly that was not what you intended at all."

"You spent a day at home but you didn't relax." Her chiding is gentle but she means it.

"Oddly enough, I thought I *had* relaxed. You're not going to make me do it over again, are you, boss?"

"Shouldn't be necessary. All right, here's what we'll be doing with Rivera—"

It's a single sheet of paper. On it there are four numbered sentences. Harris Diem reads it, reads it again, looks up and says "May I keep this?"

"For what?" she asks.

"For my memoirs." He reaches into his briefcase, brings out a document holder, and slides it in, smoothing it flat. "I would put this somewhere between the Gettysburg Address and Roosevelt's Day of Infamy speech. Maybe a bit more significant than the Day of Infamy."

"It might be a long time before your memoirs can be published," she says.

"Once I'm dead, I can afford to be patient."

She grunts and nods; whatever she was about to say next is lost forever, because the secretary announces that the Sec-Gen is on the line.

The pleasantries are short but seem more sincere than usual, at least to Harris Diem. At last, Rivera says, "Ms. President, I think we may as well do this quickly as slowly. Historians may like us better if we deliberate more, but I for one always favored getting into cold water by diving in headfirst."

"Agreed," Hardshaw says, "and it may be the last thing we agree on. Have you drafted your proposal?"

"I have, as we discussed. Let's transmit, read, and discuss."

Hardshaw pushes a button. The four sentences that Harris Diem is holding the original copy of appear on the Sec-Gen's screen; four sentences from him appear on President Hardshaw's screen, and she and Diem lean forward to read.

In less than a minute, both are looking up toward each other hopefully, and with just a trace of a smile. Diem is shaking his head. "I suppose it was inevitable. What needs to be done is so clear—unless, of course, we want Klieg, Hassan, and the Siberians to hold the levers of power in the post-Clem world—that it's no surprise at all that three of the four points are identical between you. Did you both agree there would be four points?"

"No," Rivera said, "but those are obvious as well. Ms. President, can we then agree that Colonel Tynan is to proceed with the expedition to the Kuiper Belt immediately for the purposes discussed, that he is to accept no further orders for recall or modification but may at his judgment modify the plan in accord with the original goals—I like your phrasing better than mine—and that he will receive his orders to do so from both you and me and send an acknowledge to both of us?"

"That's it," she says. "It's not a legal document in any sense of the word, so precision doesn't matter. Now about the point of the dispute: what would you say if I said we're going to hand ourselves in? We'll announce that taking over all that Japanese and French stuff on the moon was an act of deliberate aggression and offer reparations, but we'll concede they'd be justified in declaring war."

Rivera grins. "Then I would say—you and I are both old lawyers, Ms. President—that I will see you in court. The Secretary-General has seized all property in space for the duration of the emergency—and unlike your American Constitution, the UN Second Covenant lets me declare the emergency retroactively and seize property without compensation—and thus Colonel Tynan, acting under my orders, has behaved in an entirely legal fashion. Will you at least recognize the jurisdiction of the World Court?"

"Hell yes. I might argue the case myself."

Rivera's eyes widen, and he says, "Ms. President, I beg you—don't do that."

It's not often that Brittany Lynn Hardshaw looks confused or discomfited. "And why not? If your decision stands, then all I am is a UN provincial administrator anyway; I might as well use all that time on my hands productively."

Rivera shakes his head, and that's when Diem sees the twinkle in his eye. "The difficulty, Ms. President, is that if you insist on arguing the United States' case, I shall be unable to resist the temptation to match wits with you in court on a case of such magnitude—and the world cannot afford to have both of us tied up doing that." He smiles more widely. "Besides, the irony is too appealing. You win on your sovereignty case if you are convicted of illegal seizure of Japanese and French property. You will be in court trying to prove you're a pirate; the UN will be there trying to prove you're innocent."

She nods. "See you in court, then. And I'm guilty as hell."

"Ms. President—you are not. I take it we have no further business and we should get this underway?"

"Right. My regards to your family—"

"And I'm delighted for this chance to talk with you," he says. Once again, things have slid into formality, but Diem can't help feeling that there's warmth underneath it. The Secretary-General's office clicks off. There's a brief flicker of the blue-and-white UN logo, and then the screen goes blank.

As she turns back to him, she says, "I checked it out, of course, over a scrambled channel, and Tynan really is ready to go. Would have looked pretty stupid if he'd had to hang around in Earth orbit for three weeks while everyone sued everyone else. So I guess we send the signal—get it rolling, Harris. Here's the tape you can transmit up to Tynan."

Diem accepts it and looks down at the cassette; the thought occurs to him that this object, someday, will probably sit in the Smithsonian, if there is a Smithsonian. "Oh, and Harris?" she adds.

Diem glances up.

"You might be right about significance, but the real parallel is the Great White Fleet. And unlike Teddy Roosevelt, I don't have to worry about Congress deciding to just strand the colonel out there."

"You do have to worry about impeachment."

She stands up, stretches, and he suddenly realizes how old and tired she looks; her eyelids droop a little, her skin is gray, and she stands as if a few muscles were not quite behaving themselves. "Worry? Harris, I'm looking forward to it."

THREE
SINGULARITY

JULY–SEPTEMBER 2028

CLEM HAS CONTINUED on its way. After the Hawaiian Holocaust, as the news people have dubbed it, most of the language used to denote Clem's indifference to human affairs has dropped out of the reports. Few people want or need to be reminded that Clem does not care what people might think.

During the week beginning on July 14, the Republic of the Marshall Islands ceases to exist. On Friday the fourteenth, at 10:00 A.M. local time, the giant hurricane's eye is centered at 166W 7N, about as empty a stretch of the Pacific as one could hope to find, with only the little pricey tourist spot at Palmyra Atoll, long since evacuated, taking the brunt of the storm.

But late that afternoon, at about 3:30 P.M. local time (though there is no one there to observe it as "local"), the several outflow jets that have been carrying off the bulk of the mass sucked up by Clem coalesce to the northeast of the giant hurricane, and it begins to move rapidly to the south and west.

The Marshalls are a battered mess already from Clem's previous pass, which was at a considerable distance to the south; this time the hurricane is far larger, as big as it was when it tore across Hawaii, and it pounds right through the middle of the two parallel chains of islands that form the Republic.

Warning time has been adequate, but this does not mean everyone has gotten away, only that in theory they have had a chance.

Admiral O'Hara, on the bridge of HMS *Abel Tasman*, flagship of the UN rescue fleet, has a sick feeling that that theoretical chance was all that mattered to the UN politicians. The Republic of the Marshall Islands has been a festering sore for almost a generation, and from the SecGen's standpoint Clem couldn't hit a better place. The international force at O'Hara's command is completely inadequate for getting people out of the mess, and for that matter even without a hurricane there they would have been inadequate for coping with the approximately twenty-sided civil war that has turned the one-time island paradise into a vast disaster area.

O'Hara is proud of the job his Australians and Kiwis have been doing, and for that matter he couldn't ask for better people than the Filipino, Indian, Korean, and Thai units he has, but he knows they have been given an impossible task—and when you give a military force an impossible task, all you are doing is asking them to endure.

They are having plenty to endure. The only island on which they are not being shot at—so far—is Kwajalein, but they have evacuated almost no one from that island. The thousands of squatters in the former American village, a sort of "suburban bubble" built to accommodate the Americans who worked on the missile range, belong to a variety of Christian cults united mostly by their extreme distrust of messages from the outside world. Most of them won't board, thinking it's a trick to get them out of the way so the Americans can come back.

There are still plenty of peaceful atolls as well, places out of *South Pacific* or *Mutiny on the Bounty*, that break your heart to look at. But the first pass of Clem has cut many of them off—though direct satellite broadcasts reach all the islands, some of the outliers still have no antennas up, and there are a few thousand people who never hear the warnings. The Thais are racing from one to another on their hydroplane scout boats, and whistlers from the Indian carrier *Brahma* have reached others, but they have no way of knowing which atolls still have people or which ones have been illegally settled, and there will just not be time to reach them all. When the great storm surges and the Beaufort 35 + winds hit, many thousands will drown without anyone ever knowing they were there.

But these are just minor heartbreaks. O'Hara is bothered by them only because they are decent sane people, even the cultists in Kwajalein, and he would rather be carrying off loads of peaceful, harmless people to safety than dealing with what most of his forces are confronting.

The barometer has begun to drop already, and though Clem, much shrunken by its southward journey, is still more than a thousand kilometers off, waves are beginning to pound farther and farther up the beaches. O'Hara looks out over the ship with a certain resignation; he wonders if he'd have chosen this career if he'd known where it would end.

He has never heard a shot fired in anger; the Australian Navy has not fought a war in a long time. Even had he been in one, the *Tasman* is a CROC, a Combined Robotic Operations Cruiser, a ship that travels at the center of a great cloud of intelligent drones of all kinds, on, above, and below the ocean surface; if anything has penetrated far enough to hit the ship, chances are the battle is lost.

But there will be no battles—not against other ships per se. He was near retirement age, anyway. . . .

Somewhere, far out over the horizon, Korean marines are advancing in house-to-house fighting along a miserable stretch of coral sand, twelve kilometers long by two hundred meters wide, the sprawling "suburb" that grew up between Darrit-Uliga-Delap and the airport, currently divided into half a dozen territories by the civil war that has raged in the aftermath of the expulsion of the Americans. The Koreans at least have a clear task—get all the various gunmen cleared out so that unarmed civilians can safely board the buses to the airport. The only thing holding up the Koreans is that their forces are too small—too many troops are being used in other places and can't be spared.

The Kiwis and Aussies trying to evacuate Ebeye, in Kwajalein Atoll just north of Kwajalein itself, have the truly impossible task. The thousand or so Marshallese who worked at the missile range were supporting 7500 dependents in 1990; by 2010, the same thousand jobs had become the support for 25,000 people, the great majority under twenty years old.

Just before the fighting that led to the American departure broke out, the U.S. had attempted to solve the extremely embarrassing problem of that island slum, with its Fourth World misery jammed up within sight of the Kwajalein's golf course, shopping malls, and movie theaters, by virtually covering Ebeye with modern high-rise housing.

The revolution that led to the American exodus had been sudden and violent, and in the aftermath of the Flash, the United States no longer had the desire or the will to maintain a base so far from home against armed opposition. Consequently they went home with almost no warning, and the 25,000 inhabitants of the world's most isolated housing project had nothing left to support them at all. Within weeks the water and power were off more often than not, and gangs that were more or less political and more or less criminal, depending on where the money was, moved in to take over in an incomprehensible cascade of turf and control struggles.

For the last few years, Ebeye has been a perennial subject for XV coverage—stories of cannibalism, of girls bred and raised for prostitution and sold by the dozens to Japanese entrepreneurs, the Thirst Riot when the single desalinating plant broke down, the siege for ransom of one large building by a local criminal syndicate, the ring selling infant tissues for tank-grown transplant materials. . . .

The UN forces are struggling to keep a beachhead safe for evacuation (under constant sniper fire) and to open up safe pathways for people to run through. The inhabitants of Ebeye mostly speak English, and mostly don't believe anything a white man tells them, but there are still plenty of people escaping to the beach whenever they can—almost all of them women and girls, many of them naked, according to the reports O'Hara is seeing.

There were stories on XV, last year, of a "party palace" on Ebeye which offered select Westerners and Asians the opportunity to eat a fine dinner served by slave girls, to rape as many of them as they cared to, and then to see several of them tortured and killed. The secret UN estimate that O'Hara saw as he prepared this expedition estimated a sixty-five percent chance that the story was substantially true.

Yet the UN did not come then. Farming women like cattle was not grounds for any intervention. It must be, O'Hara thinks, all right to kill them retail for fun, but not all right for them to drown wholesale. Perhaps the analogy to cattle is perfect . . . no one objects to slaughterhouses, but if ten thousand cattle were about to drown—

He breaks off from that train of thought. All the way back to the beginning of his naval career, he was regularly told he had a little too much imagination and sympathy for his job. Maybe so—he'd like to have had a job like that American general, Marshall, who was most known for rebuilding Europe after World War II. Make O'Hara the dictator someplace and maybe the news people wouldn't like how they were treated, but by god there would be sewers, electricity, decent roads, and jobs, and there wouldn't be murder, rape, or theft.

And all this is just to avoid thinking, right now, about the paras and marines pinned down on Ebeye, in a job that's a bizarre combination of Ulster, Sarajevo, and Gallipoli. Every couple of hours another is hit by a sniper, another young body with a hole torn in it, some dying, some crippled for life, some who will merely spend forty years having nightmares, all so that the forces on the ground there can keep making sorties and dashes to the nearer buildings, forcing doorways, opening passages through which the captives can flee.

O'Hara has written a short report that he intends to leak—his career is over after this anyway—revealing that the real population of Ebeye before this was probably about two hundred male rulers, three thousand gunmen and male overseers working for the rulers, and more than twenty thousand female slaves.

His effort to be abstract about it all is failing; he has about five more minutes till he makes the decision that will result in his court-martial, and all he wants to think about is his real reason, the last straw.

Two hours ago a whistler from *Brahma* disgorged twenty Indian commandos onto the top of one of the big buildings of Ebeye, the first of 100 who were to seize the top floors of the building, silence the array of machine guns up there, and allow the Anzacs to enter and clear the building. The staticopter was hit as it attempted to take off again, and its wreckage effectively blocked others from landing, stranding the Indian force. They nevertheless fought their way down through the building far enough to take the first machine gun position, and might well have taken the rest—except that the warlord who owned the building quietly evacuated his gunmen, blocking the fire doors open, then suddenly set off charges which drained the water tanks and set the tower on fire. Besides the commandos, several hundred slaves, mostly girls, were burned to death in their still-locked rooms, or plunged to the concrete below, while the Aussie and NZs were pinned down by heavy weapons fire from neighboring buildings—and could not return fire because the enemy shielded themselves behind living, bound slaves.

There is no one left alive in the building, but it continues to blaze like a great torch; there was no way to reach the commandos trapped on the upper floor, and whatever remains of them is somewhere in the mass of orange flame and black smoke that boils against the high, lead-gray nimbus clouds.

No point in delaying further. O'Hara gets the conference call together and gives the order; everything spelled out, so that no matter what may happen later, in any trial, the full responsibility will fall only on him.

Give an adequate military force a purely military task, and it gets done. In half an hour, at the cost of more than two hundred hostage lives, four key towers are in UN hands, the gunmen trapped inside are prisoners, and the UN has the superior position. In one more hour, the island is pacified.

A lot of Australians and New Zealanders will dream, all the rest of their lives, of having to cut women in half with machine gun fire in order to kill the screaming nineteen-year-old boys behind them.

The evacuation is swift and efficient from that point on; the former rulers of the island and their various thugs and assistants are herded to the side—undoubtedly along with an occasional innocent male slave or prisoner, since the forces are sorting out all the men clearly past puberty and putting them into one end of the island. The best guess is that about five percent—maybe 150—of the 3000 men within that perimeter are innocent. O'Hara is not much concerned with such niceties.

Meanwhile the women and children are being moved to the transports as fast as they can cross the floating bridges. No doubt a few of the women were overseers, but again not many, and it's just possible rough justice may happen along the way at the hands of the other women.

O'Hara receives the reports of all this with mounting satisfaction; not even the word from Colonel Park that the marines have broken through, Majuro is in hand, and refugees are being taken off quickly gives him as much pleasure. Finally, he has the camera turned on the last minutes at Ebeye.

The male prisoners have been waiting patiently for the ships to take them on. As O'Hara had anticipated, they grow restless as they see the floating bridges rolled up, and then they begin to stir as if to rush the last bridge when it becomes clear that it too will be taken away.

The loudspeakers promptly explain that different preparations have been made, and some of the men hesitate; the ones who rush toward the bridge are beaten back with nightsticks and Mace, and that seems to make it clear to them; they stand about disconsolately, not sure what to do.

As O'Hara watches them, he finds himself fascinated; what a difference a gun makes. Most of these men have killed for pay, many have killed for fun, almost all of them were proud and defiant even four hours ago. Now it is noticeable that few of them are over twenty-five, many are overweight and out of shape, some others seem to have tuberculosis, the lingering effects of childhood malnutrition, or perhaps congenital syphilis. They looked like ogres behind their guns and surrounded by slaves, and behaved like them; now they are as sorry-looking a mess of humanity as O'Hara has ever seen. He wonders idly if it changed when they were stripped of their arms, or of their slaves . . . and that makes him wonder, a little uncomfortably, whether it will change him more to no longer have charge of weapons, or to no longer have charge of sailors.

It's the sort of question, he thinks, that you think of when you are too sensitive for your job. Though he very much doubts that "sensitive" is what they will say about him, unless they decide to explain it all as insanity.

The waiting men don't begin to panic until they see the group of men who have been holding guns on them get into the last two staticopters; they start to rush as the rotors begin to whir, but the last men getting on the whistler open up, without warning, with submachine guns, and as the front rank falls to the pavement, the rush collapses.

O'Hara had asked for a camera to be left in place, and he switches to that one, observing as the men mill around, scarcely any of them taking any notice of the screaming wounded on the ground, all arguing about what to do and what all this means.

Their heads come up as one when they hear the first set of explosions. It takes a long time; first they must see what is different, and then they realize that water is running out of every building, and the water towers themselves have been knocked down.

What remains of Ebeye's fresh water is pouring out of the building entrances and windows and running into the lagoon.

Even then most of them do not see what is going on, though those few who do are noisily trying to explain, until the second wave of explosions, and the fires that break out all over the tall buildings, all at once.

Ebeye will be a vast, blazing pyre within an hour; a few of them may manage the difficult swim to Kwajalein (where the cultists have a fine tradition of stoning to death any male who swims over), a few more may wait it out on the beach—and all of those will then perish when Clem scrapes these islands to bare rock.

O'Hara, after looking at the expressions of terror, thinks of how these men have spent their (usually brief) lives and decides that he likes being a war criminal.

The shifting of the outflow jet has not gone unnoticed, and by late that afternoon, O'Hara's fleet, mostly commandeered freighters crammed with more than 100,000 islanders, (yet with far too much empty space that might have been filled), is racing southward toward the equator with all the speed it can make. So far Clem has not shown any more ability than any other hurricane to cross the equator, and away from shore the storm surge will be felt only as a gentle lift under their feet; if they can avoid Clem's mad winds, they should be all right.

By the time Clem's outer winds begin to tear at the burned-out remnants of Ebeye the next morning, storm surges have already rolled over the Ratak chain several times, and Majuro is cleared of garbage for the first time in several decades. The Christian cultists squatting in the Kwajalein base village are gathered on the former high school's football field, according to the camera drones left behind; there is no trace of any survivors from Ebeye.

It is not possible to tell what the cultists are praying for, or about, and they are still there, drenched with rain and clinging to each other, when the wind takes down the last camera drone.

The Marshalls are scoured down to bare coral, rolled over by hundreds of waves rather than the four Oahu got; the highest point in the islands was only thirty-one meters above the sea.

The UN fleet continues south. The storm surges are barely felt under their feet, and they are well away from the storm; by late in the day on July 19 they are safely below the equator in open, calm sea without a cloud in the sky. O'Hara surveys his fleet with binoculars; every deck within eyesight seems to be nothing but people.

When he gets the call from the Secretary-General, there is no mention of what he did on Ebeye. Rivera gives him only brief warm thanks, the expressed hope that the UN fleet can get the Marshallese disembarked quickly at the refugee bases in the Gulf of Carpentaria—and the unofficial warning that the evacuation fleet will be kept together. A Japanese-Chinese-Indonesian evacuation fleet is tackling the Northern Marianas at the moment; after that Clem should be headed back out of the Western Pacific, but Rivera says, "We have to consider Hurricane Clem to be permanent, and there will be many more places that need evacuation. Your fleet has the experience—and you have gotten the job done."

That's the nearest thing to a comment on his actions that O'Hara will ever hear. It's not until days later that it even occurs to him that there were no XV people anywhere near the operation, and that all the video of it is in UN hands.

They let Louie Tynan christen the "ship" for his expedition to 2026RU; since physically the ship is the old Space Station *Constitution*, plus several large chunks of the French and Japanese lunar habitats from Moonbase, plus an enormous population of probes, replicators, drones, and robots constructed on the moon—all launched from a variety of points in a variety of ways, with more to come, and slapped together any old way that works— he has a little trouble thinking of it as a "ship," though with his enhanced ability to construct scenarios into the future, he sees a greater than fifty-percent chance that the word "ship" will eventually come to mean just such a construction.

He gives it very little thought—only the equivalent of a dozen poets debating for a century—before settling on the name that seems to him most expressive of the hopes bound up in the expedition: the *Good Luck.*

For seventy years, history has been moving away from the individual person and event; this is part of why there is no answer to "who invented the computer?" or "when did the Third Balkan War begin and end?" Thus it is hardly surprising that no one can really say when the *Good Luck* departs; it isn't even possible to say when it is "built." Beacons that will later be incorporated into it were catapulted into high solar orbits as early as July 1, other portions were on their way to various asteroids as early as July 10, and many parts of it will not arrive until the ship is on its way back.

But if a date must be picked, July 20, 2028—fifty-nine years to the day after the first lunar landing—seems as good as any. That is the day, Greenwich Mean Time, on which the *Constitution,* carrying Louie Tynan himself, reaches Earth escape velocity.

Even in trying to define it that way there is a problem. Louie Tynan is not at all sure that the body that floats, breathing, in his cabin in the *Constitution* is really "Louie Tynan himself." Lately it's been more like a large, complex massively parallel processor which is slow, unreliable, and subject to too much downtime. So much of him is now in the processors on the moon that it might be better to define departure date as the point where he begins to find that Louie-the-ship is talking to, rather than part of, Louie-on-the-moon, and that's not until the twenty-eighth of July.

But by that time, many other things have happened. *Good Luck* is to be built as it flies, and the construction process is to supply much of the needed momentum; in effect, the ship will climb out to 51 AU—fifty-one astronomical units, fifty-one times the distance of the Earth from the sun, well beyond the orbit of Pluto—on a stream of its components.

The first step is to get replicators working in richer environments than the moon. Ore is valuable not for what it contains but for what it doesn't— that is, for being a relatively pure form of the material, with relatively easy to remove waste. Common rock like most of the surface of the moon is made up of too many different things (though any of them might be valuable in isolation) bound too closely together; cognac, Beluga caviar, filet mignon,

and Jamaica Blue Mountain coffee are all extremely valuable, but not if they've been in the blender together.

Whereas the rocks of the moon are a chemical puree, many of the asteroids are all but pure iron/nickel mix, and others are rich in CHON (carbon, hydrogen, oxygen, and nitrogen—the basic building blocks of life, and for that matter of plastics) and light metals. Thus the asteroids are the natural mining lodes of the solar system, and the great magnetic catapults that Louie has thrown up on the face of the moon have begun firing replicator packages to various likely looking asteroids. A "package" is a tied-together collection of hundreds of small processing units and manipulating units, a propulsion system adequate for a rendezvous, a small thermionic He-3 fusion reactor, and a central processor cortex big enough to hold a crude copy of Louie.

These copies of Louie are not as bright or versatile as the original aboard the *Good Luck*. On the other hand, they seem to have his weakness for communicating in banter, both with each other and with Louie himself; he begins to refer to them as the "wiseguys." There are about forty of them as of July 20, and there will be seventy before he's past Mars. Each "wiseguy" in turn will become his own versatile factory with catapult, and will build his own power array—and will make a couple more wiseguys as well.

It took humanity hundreds of thousands of years to reach the moon, thirty-five years to go back, another decade beyond that to reach Mars and to begin to colonize space . . . and before the year is out there will be industrial bases all over the solar system, and even now, though no one other than Louie has realized it yet, the robots and replicators have transformed the former Moonbase into one of the largest industrial complexes that has ever existed. The growth rate there is faster than any in history: whereas defense plants during the Second World War, the most nearly comparable case, were thrown up as fast as possible; no matter how many plants were built it didn't bring another worker into being, and every plant used more power and thus diverted labor from building and staffing more plants. On the moon the power supply keeps growing all by itself, and when "labor" gets short, Louie just makes another factory to make more workers.

Offhand, Louie estimates that Moonbase has become about twice the size, in terms of energy and information bound per hour, as Japan's OKK Complex—and they spent a while longer building Osaka, Kobe, and Kyoto. Moreover, it's all his for every practical purpose . . . where large parts of OKK's energy and information binding is happening in retail stores, restaurants, garbage collection, XV and TV, hospitals, and so forth, the complex Louie presides over is dedicated only to growing and to getting the mission accomplished. He just about has to be the wealthiest man in the solar system.

Hell, by the time he gets back, if he wants to keep all the gear running full tilt, the settled part of the solar system will consist of the possessions of Louie Tynan, plus debris. It's not a bad retirement package.

At first, Jesse and Mary Ann aren't going to go; the plan seems kind of stupid, given that there are easier cities to get to, over roads that are in better shape. But Señor Escobedo, the Mexican government *administrador* who flies in to present the idea to the people of Tapachula, is patient and persuasive, and appears to know what he is talking about. "Just consider," he pleads, for the thousandth time. "Where else are you going to go? The rain forest is already near saturation; the streams will fill up quickly, and when they do. . . . And there is no zipline head near here. And consider, too, how little work there is, and how very little extra housing, in Tuxtla Gutiérrez or in San Cristóbal de las Casas. Those are cities that have not grown much, cities that are not going anywhere."

Everyone nods, of course—Mexicans are loyal to their towns, and to hear an outsider say that Tapachula is the important, forward-looking town in Chiapas is to give weight and substance to the stranger's ideas.

Escobedo goes over the arguments again, there in the middle of the Zócalo, with his laser pointer and his big projected maps. All around, people fade in and out of the blocky topiary trees, listening, drifting off to chat with friends, coming back to listen again.

Oaxaca is far away, and they will have to take a hurricane or two on the way, but they can be up above the coast, there will be time to stop and dig in as needed, and most of all, when they get there, they will be genuinely safe; high up in the mountains with good drainage, they will be able to stay put.

He acknowledges that some of the Army, here to keep the town safe from looters, may do a bit of looting themselves. Officers don't have perfect control, and they are not always perfect either. Yes, if you have a good deal to guard and don't mind risking your life in the floods that will surely come when bigger storms blow directly inshore here, then you might do well to stay. Of course your property will do you little good when you are dead—let us be blunt in facing the facts—but undoubtedly your heirs will thank you.

When they return from Oaxaca.

He is a natural debater, and he's funny; these things help Escobedo, so that after a few days, people are no longer saying the scheme is mad, or muttering darkly about a government plan to get them to leave their property unguarded, but instead are beginning to get their applications in for the Oaxaca evacuation, "just in case, you know," and in a couple more they are beginning to pack. The thing takes on momentum.

Thus on the morning of July 21, Jesse and Mary Ann are hardly surprised at all to find that they are part of the convoy. They've both been declared fit for walking—the great convoys will transport the old, sick, and young in buses, others in trucks based on a daily lottery, and most on bicycle, foot, or the occasional burro. There are to be twenty such convoys, each with some thousands of people, from all over the Pacific shore of Chiapas.

The first day is to be deliberately slow of pace; this allows time for motorcycle couriers to scoot back to Tapachula as people suddenly remember things, and it helps everyone get used to the idea. The heat is pretty appalling, but there's very little dust and the government water trucks seem to be on the job, and with the frequent rests Jesse finds he's no more than uncomfortable. And the evening camp is fun, in its way, especially since after the announcements around the fire and a great deal of visiting among neighbors, he and Mary Ann have a tent that is small but all theirs—the advantage of adequate cash for *mordida*. It's occurring to Jesse that with the tastes he's developing, if this thing with Mary Ann ends he's going to have a lot of incentive to get back on the fast track in realization engineering. Once you understand what money can do it gets harder to live without it.

The second day of the trip, on a Saturday, they get a warm morning rainstorm, which makes the road slick and doesn't seem to cool it off at all. The government people are pushing them a little harder, and the hills are beginning to roll and rise. Jesse's a little sore in the thighs and calves that night, and Mary Ann has to spread a couple more small bribes around to get pads from the traveling hospital for her blistered feet.

The last few miles were extremely hilly, hot, and humid, and they aren't exactly looking forward to the next day. It's too hot and sticky to make love, or even to hold each other, so they fall asleep holding hands across the tent. Dawn comes entirely too early, and the morning thunderstorm holds off just long enough so that everyone is on the road before it drenches them.

The ion rockets that move the *Constitution* out of low Earth orbit are not the conventional electric thrusters they used for the Mars mission; instead, the power from the moon is used to convert "straight" matter into antimatter, and the antimatter is then reacted with helium-3-II—helium-3 cooled to the point where it becomes superconducting—to create a near-lightspeed exhaust of He-3 nuclei. The tiny pulse of antimatter through the center of a Ping-Pong-ball-sized blob of helium-3-II creates a highly charged plasma and a very brief burst of radio energy; the superconducting coil surrounding the blob acts as an antenna to capture the radio burst and uses the current to induce a magnetic field to compress and accelerate the plasma so much that thermonuclear fusion is still happening thirty meters beyond the nozzle.

From the ground, if there were enough clear sky, they could see that the white, glowing jet out the back of the platform to which *Constitution* is tied is about two hundred kilometers long; it's also thinner than the aurora borealis.

It's not fuel-efficient—but the temperature of the exhaust is half a billion degrees Fahrenheit, and high exhaust temperature means the ship will be *fast.*

But though it's the best engine ever devised, and many gigawatts from the power stations on the moon drive it, it will not be enough. On those engines alone, the journey out to 2026RU would take four and a half years. And besides, after about five AU, power transmission from the moon will get problematic. The real travel time, if he used only the engines, would be six or seven years. Rivera, Hardshaw, and their staff don't think Earth has those years; with thousands of times their processing ability, neither does Louie Tynan.

Really, it was all a question of getting the materials to do what needs doing. To effectively block sunlight from space, the shield that casts the shadow must be *low.* To use materials at all effectively the shield should be wide and thin. To get the maximum effect, the shield should move slowly enough to cast its shadow on the strategic area of the Pacific for the maximum time.

This in turn dictates that it's no good just putting a big mirror up in geosynchronous orbit; the shield would have to hold together and stay in place, and no known material is strong enough to permit a shield that big, subject to such tidal stresses as the moon and sun will provide, to hold together. So the shield needs to be at lower altitude . . . but then it will move too fast, if it orbits, to accomplish anything. Besides, it won't stay in any orbit at all. The tenuous outer wisps of the Earth's atmosphere plus the solar wind will be more than enough to bring the shields down in short order.

Thus both Klieg's balloons, and the scheme Louie is carrying out, depend on using not a single orbited satellite, but many thousands of projectiles. They are planning to take Klieg's deal—and promise him whatever he insists upon—because there's at least a decent chance of damping out some of the hurricanes, and because they know that he won't hold the whip hand forever. Louie will have all the advantages—he doesn't have to lift anything off the Earth, only to bring it in. And once he has the right materials on hand, that should be easy.

Which brings up the reason for using 2026RU. It is coming in rapidly, by cometary standards, and might have been one of the more spectacular comets of the twenty-first century, in 2047, if it were not needed sooner. It already has a substantial velocity toward the inner solar system, and electromagnetic catapults upon its yet-unmelted surface will have the benefit of the added velocity in sending their packages of ice down to the Earth-moon system. Each package, roughly two million tons of ice in the shape of a Frisbee a mile across and a yard thick, its ice woven in an elaborate internal braid for strength, covered with a millimeter-thick sprayed-on mirroring to keep it from melting, will carry a propulsion and guidance system, and as each approaches Earth, Louie—returned home by then—will take over the guidance system and direct it into a "grazing" approach over the Pacific, so that it will come in almost parallel to the Earth's surface, descending to a height of less than twenty miles before the braking shockwave trapped in the hollow underside blows the melting ice apart and the fragments boil off.

Each Frisbee will be more than a mile across, and will cast a corresponding shadow, but it won't be those shadows that defeat Clem, all by themselves. As the giant ice disks whirl down into the stratosphere and evaporate explosively, the water released, in the cold thin air, will be instantly frozen into clouds of ice crystals like the familiar cirrus (or mare's tail) clouds that often appear on the forward edge of a storm. But these will be two to three times as high up, and there will be many more of them; the layer of ice crystals will be enough to make it dark at the surface, so that over a quite short time, the surface waters of the Pacific will cool enough to stop supporting Clem and Clem's spawn.

There are of course many sources of ice nearer than the comet—but none that are already moving at such a high velocity in nearly the exact right direction. Moreover, of the other possible sources, Charon and Pluto will be on the wrong side of the sun, from the viewpoint of the Earth, for half of every year, forcing a longer and less efficient orbit, and all the others are deep in the gravity wells of the giant gas planets. Though energy itself is not a problem—the self-replicating industrial plants Louie is building insure that there will be plenty—acceleration is; to escape from Jupiter, Saturn, Uranus, or Neptune's gravitational grip as quickly as necessary would require accelerations at which the ice Frisbees would flow like water, distort, and become unsuited for their entry to Earth's atmosphere.

But to get to 2026RU will take a long time no matter what, and since exactly what will turn up there and exactly what will need to be done are not at all clear at the incoming comet's current distance (something over 56 AU), Louie will have to go there himself and improvise. It took Louie some time to invent a scheme that would permit doing it in any reasonable amount of time; even at the best pace he can come up with, he will still not be back until June of 2029, and god only knows what shape the Earth will be in by then.

For once Berlina Jameson is feeling well rested, and given the size of the story she's putting out, this isn't much short of a miracle. When Harris Diem and Diogenes Callare offered her their help—even though the first part of the process was bound to trigger some uproar about the U.S. government and Colonel Tynan's extremely cavalier use of foreign property—she had just figured them for nice, dedicated public servants.

Maybe that *was* their whole motivation. They might only have known that Klieg was acquiring undue influence both in the UN General Assembly and in the executive offices in Washington. Maybe Rivera and Hardshaw just wanted him ambushed and taken down a few notches.

But with what she's found since, she doubts they could have been completely unaware of what she was going to find. It took her many hours and not much sleep just to look at all the relevant videotape, listen to all the relevant voice, and search through the relevant records. By the time she had the picture assembled, she at least had the sense to realize that she was too exhausted and would look like hell if she presented it right away, so she took a day off to edit, put fine touches on things, eat, sleep, and indulge herself.

Now, her hair newly done, feeling fresh and scrubbed, she stands in front of the white wall in a hotel room in Richmond (having bribed hell out of everyone to make sure no one comes thumping along the corridor in the next few minutes) and narrates her wrap:

"And so that's it for this edition of *Sniffings.* The pattern of power that spreads out from John Klieg and GateTech like the tentacles of an octopus is laid bare for your examination. Influence that penetrates the highest levels of both national and international bodies; ambassadors to the UN who take their orders from Klieg and their salaries from their home countries; Klieg's deliberate scheme for a monopoly on global launch, and his maneuvering, at a time when the world desperately needs launch facilities, to secure not just his own rightful rewards for providing one, but a complete monopoly by preventing anyone else from doing so.

"And yet this is just the tip of the iceberg. What, we might reasonably ask, is the connection between Klieg and the Siberian government? Just how many connections are there between Klieg's operation, the notorious Hassan drug-and-mercenary cartel, and elements of the Siberian armed forces that remain close to outlawed and arrested dictator Omar Abdulkashim? Is it not clear that while Klieg milks the UN with one hand, he aids its enemies with the other—and paralyzes his home government to keep it from investigating his activities?

"And if we are facing a global Klieg dictatorship, or Klieg as the gray eminence behind the UN and the big powers . . . what sort of a program does he have, other than sheer aggrandizement? We have shown you a dozen clips of Klieg talking privately, off the record, in which it becomes clear that he thinks the problem with the great bulk of the world is that it's not 'normal,' or 'regular,' or any of a dozen other words that he apparently uses to mean 'like white middle-class Wisconsin.' I could show you fifty more. This is a man of limited imagination and tolerance—and of all but unlimited power."

She signs off, rechecks everything once more, patches in the end piece, and uploads. Time to head south out of the Wy—she has a lot of great quotes from the First Wave refugees, as they call themselves, the people from the Gulf Coast who decided to get out early and are at this point mostly working in construction in Montana, Wyoming, and Colorado. Everyone who can seems to be buying land and putting crisis housing on it for the expected waves of refugees; the First Wave seems remarkably cheerful for refugees.

Some of the Clem 200 series of hurricanes are beginning to pound their way up the coast, and there are rumors about evacuating the Duc. Once she's headed down to Denver, she phones Di Callare, and he patches her into a three-way conference with Harris Diem. Diem, in particular, seems very pleased.

"I don't think you know what you've done, Ms. Jameson," he says. "And I have to admit I wasn't happy about it when you started out. I had always figured that if anything useful was going to get done, it would be because the people who could have gotten in the way didn't hear about it first. But what you've done is created a whole constituency for an intelligent global perspective—and you've done such a good job of it that I'm betting on you against Klieg."

"It's not really me against Klieg—" she protests, a little feebly because it certainly feels that way, but she doesn't want to feel that she's been out to "get" anyone or that she's on anyone's side.

"I understand. You think you're being purely objective. Perhaps from your standpoint you are. Nonetheless, you got him and you got him good, as the boss and I used to say in Idaho. Things like GateTech depend on people respecting the rules even when it's not to their advantage to do so—which is usually desirable, since it maintains public order. But when somebody is making his entire career out of using the rules to tie every productive project up in knots—well, all I can say is, he chose very intelligently in his location. I very much doubt he will be able to come back to the United States for a while, or to operate anything very effectively by proxy. He's out of the game—though he'll still get rich launching his balloons. But in terms of serious power, he's gone."

Berlina has been listening to this very seriously, trying to decide whether Diem is flattering her for some future purpose. She decides that she can't tell, but he's probably too good at it for her to be able to spot it.

They chat for another moment or two, and then Diem clicks off and she's left talking to Di Callare. "We're getting out pretty fast," he explains. "Lori will get it all packed up and storm-proofed in the next couple of weeks—it looks like the hurricanes coming up the East Coast will be bad, but not the Big One we're figuring will happen either this season or next."

"The Big One? I thought that Clem—"

"So far there's been nothing the size of Clem in the Atlantic. To get to be Clem's size you've got to build up over very hot water for a couple of weeks, the way Clem did, or start with a huge eye on a hot sea the way Clem Two, excuse me, Clem 200, did. And other hurricanes do use up some of the available energy and bind some of the available wind flow. Once Clem 200 got into the Caribbean, we thought we were goners, but luckily it did that pinwheeling stunt with its outflow jets and started up so many eyes that they limited each other's growth. With luck we'll merely have four or five very large hurricanes out of this event, counting Clem 200 itself, which has shrunk quite a bit, never recovered the energy it had before it crossed Mexico."

Berlina shudders. "Still, hurricanes haven't been that common—"

"No, but they haven't been *un*common either. And most of these guys will follow the Gulf Stream and the steering currents and stay off the American East Coast. So we'll see some big storms, loss of property and life, all of that—but not the catastrophe that's going to happen once you get a hurricane into the eastern Caribbean all by itself. That's the one that's going to blow up to Clem size and resist the steering currents enough to tear up the coast."

Berlina nods at the camera. "I start to see it, I guess. Are the hurricanes we have going to make it across to Europe?"

"They might. The temperature in the North Atlantic falls off fast as you go north, so if they swing up that way they're dead. But on the right trajectory one of them could slug Europe for sure, and there will be enough of them so that at least one or two will get there—"

There's a flashing light at the corner of the screen, and each of them says "Hold on" and reaches to take the call off hold; they don't have time to realize that it is odd for them both to get a call at the same time before they are unexpectedly back into a conference call with Harris Diem.

"Well," he says, "have you seen or heard?"

Berlina says no as Di shakes his head.

"Congratulations, Ms. Jameson." His smile is sardonic and doesn't get up to his eyes. "You've made history twice in one day. It looks like the release of *Sniffings* has triggered Global Riot Two."

The first Global Riot began in Islamabad and Seattle. No one can be that positive about Global Riot Two.

But *Sniffings* is almost certainly at the heart of it; at least half of the initial outbreaks of violence are, in one way or another, connected to Berlina Jameson's exposé of the Klieg organizations, their influence, and their links both to organized crime and to the outlaw Abdulkashim regime.

Quaz, the guy with the attitude, Passionet's bad boy, with an undeserved reputation for being brainy, is in Oran. He has been walking around in dusty streets all day, absorbing atmosphere, blocking out as best he can the knowledge that tomorrow he will be going directly to the place where he will be permitted to barge in and talk to some critical witnesses. He also ignores the fact that the reason the witnesses both seem very frightened and will tell him whatever he wants is that they were carefully left uninjured by the police in exchange for their cooperation with Passionet detectives. Passionet, lately, has been the net of choice for breaking organized crime in the Third World, as long as it's reasonably sensational organized crime.

Quaz's problem is that he's bright enough to appreciate irony without being quite bright enough to get past it. A couple of times they've had to fake technical problems because he hasn't blocked his knowledge of the next day's script adequately. He gets too fascinated with how smoothly it all runs, and sometimes much too interested in Passionet's detectives (who are anonymous gray types, eternally soft-spoken and reserved, the farthest thing that can be imagined from Quaz's intellectual decadent aging-punk style).

Or, in short, he can never quite manage to remember that to be real enough for the experiencers, it's got to be kept under control. Nobody wants to see what real detectives do, since nowadays that's either cornering people and talking to them, or more likely writing lengthy search protocols for datarodents that spread out on the net, looking for the moment when a person, a dollar, an object linked with a crime, touches the great collective brain of capitalism.

It makes for dramatic phrases, and if you intercut five or ten seconds of it now and then along with an overload sense of weariness, you can make people feel like they stayed up all night catching crooks, but watching a person listen to a rambling witness is dull, and watching a person at a keyboard is duller than that. Especially if people see it taking as long as it really does.

Not to Quaz, though, and that's the problem. Some strange part of the poor idiot's mind refuses to understand that he is not out here to be a reporter, let alone a detective, himself. You'd think having both cheekbones broken and reshaped, or a surgically flattened stomach, would have given him a clue. . . .

All these thoughts are running through the mind of Dennis Ysabel-Garcia, Passionet's special bodyguard detailed to Quaz, as he follows Quaz about a hundred feet back, monitoring his mind through a local tap. It's late in the day, getting dark, and Dennis has been walking around for all this time getting more bored and annoyed, his feet getting sorer and his clothes more caked with dust and sweat. God knows, Quaz is not his first choice of bodies to guard—Rock, or Synthi Venture, are always courteous and stay on the track marked out for them; even the new kid, Surface O'Malley, for all her puppyish enthusiasm, can manage to follow orders.

So it's an unpleasant shock but no surprise that when gunfire starts up some blocks away, Quaz turns and runs straight for it, despite urgent orders not to from the control office here in Oran. Dennis flings himself after Quaz, around corners into an unscouted alley that is secure only at the near end, down a long block—

The demonstration is in front of the mosque, and seems to have been thrown together by one of the fundamentalist groups that are always ready whenever scandal hits the ruling family, nowadays, anywhere in the Arab world. They were burning pictures of the ambassador to the UN, who had been exposed as on Klieg's take; they ran head-on into a group of pro-Abdulkashim enthusiasts who had come here to demonstrate against the lies the Western media were spreading about their hero. Afterward no one will quite be sure of how the two groups got into a brawl with each other; the best guess will be that everyone involved assumed that two different demonstrations in the same place were enough cause for a fight.

"The first shots were fired by the first cop on the scene. I think he shot into the air, hoping to get people's attention. Then somebody shot him. Now half of them are breaking and running to get away from the scene and the other half are realizing that the looting's always best at the start of a riot," the controller whispers in Dennis's mind. "What does that pretty fool think he's doing? We keep telling him to break off and turn back."

This is as much as Dennis can get speed-talked into his head as he rushes after Quaz, who with his typical sense of immunity from all harm wants to run up and ask the two sides what the fight is about. Nobody in his corner of the action seems to speak English, so he begins to speak loudly and slowly and gesture frantically.

Dennis has crossed most of the twilit square in front of the mosque when somebody shoots Quaz low in the gut, with a Self Defender, a twenty-dollar disposable hypervelocity derringer like you can buy at any 7-Eleven in the States. Though the slug is tiny—a bit of depleted uranium about the size of the tip of an ordinary sewing needle—it hits with ten times the foot-poundage of an old-style .357 Magnum round, and once it goes in it tumbles, so that aside from the exit hole, it makes a shock wave so big in his body cavity that Quaz's guts erupt through his back around his spinal column.

During the six agonizing minutes it takes Quaz to die, lying on his back crushing his own bleeding intestines into the dirty street, more than sixty million experiencers worldwide tune in to Passionet; a hundred thousand channelspotters see to that. Through the haze of pain they catch the smell of smoke, glimpses of running feet, sounds of gunfire (most of it from Dennis trying to keep the riot off of Quaz—he himself dies, cut down by machine-gun fire, just an instant before Quaz, so that the last thing the experiencers see from Oran is Dennis Ysabel-Garcia pitching forward over Quaz).

Before Quaz is dead, there are thirty more riots in the cities of the world. Passionet jumps to Surface O'Malley, tells her they want to tell her some bad news, and asks her to react by staggering out into the streets blindly.

Surface points out that she's in Bangkok, at the Orient, and that the rioting is taking on a distinctly anti-foreign character, not surprisingly since the Thai ambassador too turns out to have been subverted by the Klieg organization, and a large Siberian spy ring was broken that week. "I'm not a chicken," she says, "and I'd like to see my career take off and all, but I'll be damned if I'm going out in that. I'm a redhead, for god's sake. If the mob doesn't get me the soldiers will."

They offer her a lot more, but she won't take it. The bosses at Passionet are swearing, beating desks with fists, yelling into each other's face about who gave her a break, but she's threatening to jack out entirely until they call her and tell her there's an evacuation staticopter on the way. The truth is right now they need her more than she needs them—the riots in Bangkok are the best they have anyone on-site for, and they need feed from her, and it had better not contain any text thoughts about Passionet needlessly risking her life or screwing her over.

The trouble is that whoever says that is going to be the weasel that capitulated to the bitch, next week when they assess the results and someone asks why she wasn't out there dodging rocks, getting chased up alleys, and just maybe please-oh-god-of-profits getting gang-raped.

Worse yet, her bodyguards are agreeing with her. They must have gotten shaken up by Ysabel-Garcia's death, though surely they must have known all along that things like that come with the job and that's why they are paid so much.

While they argue, Surface (whose real name is Leslie) and Fred and Saul, the two bodyguards whom she's gradually become friends with, are seeing what they can from the window. That's freaking the controller and editor out at the control station, across town where the expressway crosses Klong San Sab, because not only is she letting her bodyguards address her as "Les," she's looking right at them every now and then, and they aren't supposed to exist. The editor there is having to fake in all kinds of noise, scrambl╮, feedback, and snow to cover all the times she does that, and even then he's painfully aware that he can't really get Fred and Saul out of the picture—they tend to show up in her thoughts and the most he can do is blur them out.

The editor wishes Rock were here, and Rock *will* be in a little bit—he's coming in with the international rescue mission, riding a whistler with Japanese marines. The editor is wishing for just one really professional reporter who understands the job and would get into it. Synthi Venture the way she used to be, before she cracked up in Point Barrow, would be wonderful right now. Global Riot Two is shaping up to be bigger and better than its predecessor, and here they are stuck with—

Hold it. They zoom in. Screw the i.d., what Surface/Leslie and her bodyguards are seeing is too interesting to blur it out just to hide what everyone knows anyway. They can always claim it's "uncensored footage," whatever footage means when you're talking about a recorded XV wedge.

Leslie, Fred, and Saul had been watching the crowd down by the Chinatown waterfront, across the Chao Phraya River from the Orient. Now it looks like a battle developing on the adjoining Phra Pinklao Bridge to the south of them; they don't quite have the right angle for it, but through her binoculars Leslie—Surface, dammit! We pay you for your name to be Surface!—

Leslie gets part of it in focus, just as gunfire begins to rip back and forth across the bridge and bodies fall everywhere. "Outstanding," the editor whispers.

She figures it out, and he captures the "Eureka!" moment—the struggling mob on the Chinatown waterfront had been Thais, attacking Indian and Chinese shops; the Indians, Bangalas, Pakistanis, and Chinese seem to have gotten together enough to mount a counterattack, and they are fighting their way across the bridge into the downtown. "Every little merchant over there probably has a couple of full auto weapons, after eighty years of war around here," Fred comments. "They just had to get organized."

"There are plenty of guns in Thai hands too," Leslie says. "Chinatown's fighting because it's their lives, homes, and families, and by now because they're pretty pissed off. Holy shit."

The binoculars fly back onto faces, and looking through Leslie's eyes, the editor sees that the crowd is parting as Thai Army tanks roll through. He gets a nice heavy sigh of relief from Surface, something that's just a little overdramatized, almost as if she were going to cooperate.

The struggle passes south of them, and Leslie/Surface and the bodyguards rush for windows on that side of the building, pounding down corridors to find a public window that looks out toward the National Gallery.

The tanks pushing through from the Chinatown side were in a hurry for a reason. The National Museum is in flames; five thousand years of magnificent art are being lost before Leslie's horrified eyes. As she watches, unable to look away, she realizes that the mobs around the museum are all in coverall uniforms—they are the vast factory labor force that normally sweats out twelve-hour days in the huge European, Japanese, and American plants, their minds pacified by looped tapes of XV porn, induced pain blockers keeping them from noticing soreness or tiredness till they unplug for the day, blissed out and uncomplaining as the computers guide their hands. Her heart sinks; what's burning is theirs, it's their birthright, the proudest expression of the Thai nation—

These people may not even know they're Thai. They spend their lives dreaming away in the Anthill, the mile-high concrete-block dormitory built into the Indraphitak/Toksin/Klong Samray triangle south of the city, and what they have dreamed of is the wealth, the glitter, the excitement they could look down on from their windows above the clouds.

Her binoculars zoom in on a tank as it turns its machine guns on the mob, clearing a path for the oncoming fire engines. A hundred people die as she watches, and it is all for nothing—the roof is caving in on the old former palace that is the center of the museum. Nothing will save it now.

The officer standing beside the tank looks familiar, and she realizes he is Major Srimuang, who guided her around her first day here; she clicks the binoculars to zoom autofocus, and sees that he is weeping, though whether at the scattered corpses in coveralls or the blazing museum, she can't tell. She recalls him as a cultured, intelligent man, and it was he who told her about the human robots of the factories; perhaps he weeps for the deaths, for the destruction of the art, and for the horror that a five-thousand-year tradition should be destroyed by a mob of people to whom it ought to belong and who never had a chance to know it.

He's breathing hard and beginning to thump the side of the tank; then he's talking into his radio, giving some order or other. Moments later, loudspeakers on all the tanks are crackling, talking to the crowd; it seems the major is addressing them directly. As he speaks, he wipes his eyes once, stands tall, and begins to speak firmly.

"Can you get me a translation of that?" she asks the controller.

"We're working on—fuck, Leslie, get out of there, he's telling them they've destroyed their heritage, that the museum is full of Thai things, and now he wants them to—"

But the three of them have already seen what is happening and are rushing back down the corridor. The main guns on the tanks are elevating to take aim at the Orient Hotel.

The three of them are most of the way to the next wing when the first shells tear into the building behind them; all three go sprawling, and Leslie has the deeply annoyed thought that she's having a hell of a time running with all this extra meat hanging on her chest. The feeling is so deep and passionate that the editor leaves it in, along with the controller's calling her Leslie.

"Screw it, this is great XV, the best we've ever worked on," the controller mutters.

"Yeah, we'll get names and roles straight later, for the re-releases."

In the Orient Hotel, Leslie and her guards get to their feet and scramble away from the burning, crumbling south-facing wing of the hotel. "The last we knew, the internationals weren't far off," Fred shouts. "Let's try to get to the interior parking lot, maybe we can get picked up—"

There's another roar from another volley of the tank main guns, and the building shudders as the facade on that wing goes down. Holding each other's hands, the three rush down the stairs toward the exit to the parking lot. A Thai hotel employee jumps out at them, brandishing a heavy iron curtain rod, and Saul guns him down without stopping to find out what he was after.

As they find the door to the parking lot, they hear a blessed sound—the high-pitched scream of staticopters and the *whump-shrikk-thud!* of the antitank missiles they're firing. Later Leslie will learn that with Japanese thoroughness, they bagged all the Thai tanks, plus all the fire engines trying to save the National Museum, plus both the still-standing wings of the museum.

For right now, though, they're just overjoyed to see Rock leaning out of the side door of the teardrop-shaped fuselage, and in a few seconds they're aboard, tumbling to safety inside. During a brief get-organized interlude of not being linked through, Rock hugs her and kisses both the men on the cheeks—"Thought we'd lost the whole cute trio of you," he says. "You've sure been putting on a show, guys."

It's only then that Leslie realizes how much of her contract and basic protocols she's been violating, but she has only a minute or so to think she's going to be fired before they're congratulating her on creating a whole new genre—live behind-the-scenes XV. The ratings have soared to astronomical, and from now on she's supposed to fall out of the Surface role and into being Leslie on cue, when asked to.

Too many good old boys identify with Rock, though—so he's not going to be called upon to be David. Keeping it carefully below registerable level, Leslie thinks to herself that it's their loss.

Part of Louie's problem is that big as the job is physically, he is so much bigger than it is mentally. So he has more time, perhaps, than would be optimal, to look at the mission and the consequences of failure, if that happens.

Some of the meteorological models he's been running are suggesting that Antarctica will warm particularly fast because it normally reflects so much heat back into space, and the methane "window" closing over it will trap correspondingly more heat; if that should prove true, then all sorts of strange consequences may follow, as immense quantities of fresh water run off the ancient glaciers and the Earth beneath is released from more of its burden.

Nothing for it, though . . . he can only go as fast as he can climb the "stalk," and he can only climb the stalk once it's there. The stalk is what he's been calling the stream of added components and material that the catapults on the moon and in the asteroids will be sending up behind him.

As you lengthen an electromagnetic catapult, the velocity it imparts to the packages it sends increases proportionately; all the catapults will be continuously lengthening, so that packages will fly off them faster and faster. As each package overtakes the *Good Luck*, it will pass through the six-mile-long funnel of concentric rings, and magnetic braking will be applied to the package. As the package loses momentum, the *Good Luck* will gain it; the package will continue on, still going faster than the *Good Luck*, but considerably slowed, and the ship will have accelerated.

Once beyond the ship, the package itself will unfurl its own magnetic funnel; the next package will pass not only through the ship, but through the package ahead of it, boosting each of them before assuming the lead.

As each successive package takes over the lead in this game of leapfrog, it will be going more slowly, having given up more and more of its momentum to the ship and the packages behind it as the train through which it must pass lengthens. Meanwhile the rear of the train will be going faster and faster.

Finally the point will be reached where the ship begins to overtake the packages ahead of it, and as it does it will shove them back hard behind it. This will not be enough to reverse their direction—they will continue on outward—but it will slow them a great deal.

But as the ship climbs into the lead, the packages behind it, in turn, will again be accelerated and driven forward by more packages coming in. By the time the ship is at the head of the column, all the packages behind it will be moving faster than it is, ready to pass through and begin the process over again—with the whole train now moving faster.

Now, as packages pass and repass through each other's coils, they fold to go through the ones ahead of them and unfold to catch the ones behind them, like great pulsing tulips chasing each other backward through space.

With time, as more packages arrive, the train gets longer, and the back end, launched by bigger and bigger catapults, faster.

As the train grows into the "stalk" up which *Good Luck* must climb, the front end of the train moves most slowly, the rear most quickly, and as components advance from rear to front, they gain velocity. Thus the train as a whole goes faster and faster.

Eventually *Good Luck* will slow some packages to match velocities, devour the parts of the package it can use, and expel the rest as reaction mass, hurling it back down the train to the following packages, each of which will also thrust against the used-up husk in the same way.

In this way, Louie will gain both velocity and processors—he will get smarter as he gets faster. He should reach 2026RU by Christmas, have whatever he needs set up by January, and be back on his way in early February, with about fifty times his present processing capability (which is already about 8000 human brain-years per day).

Before Louie has even reached the icy ball of 2026RU, Clem will have finished with the Northern Hemisphere. By the time Louie returns and the first Frisbees begin to arrive behind him, the Southern Hemisphere will have endured considerably worse superstorms, because there are fewer and smaller landmasses there to interrupt them.

Louie's guess, based on just over a trillion model runs, is that in the Southern Hemisphere the storms will continually circle the equator between 0 and 32 degrees latitude, generally moving southward and westward but varying it enough to avoid moving out of existence, spawning fresh storms regularly.

With good luck, he will arrive back just as the last storms in the Southern

Hemisphere are blowing out, and as next year's "Clem" is starting in the Northern Hemisphere.

With good luck, there will be some civilization left to save, and if not there will still be many millions of people alive, and some of them will have radios or televisions, and the data networks will still exist in many places.

With good luck, if there's not a civilization, Louie will be able to start a new one after he stops the storms.

He's got his doubts. Global Riot Two is in its fourth day and still growing. There have now been riot-related deaths in every city with a population of more than 500,000, worldwide. Troops have staged wholesale massacres of civilian looters in Berlin, Tokyo, Moscow, Caracas, Montevideo, Riyadh, Bujumbura, Katsina . . . the list goes on and on and on.

Nobody even recalls the news published in *Sniffings* that started all this; just as the tropical depression that started Clem is long since gone, so are the causes of the riot. Clem continues to run because he's a hurricane and there's more warm water; Global Riot Two keeps running because it's a riot and there's more looting and burning to be done.

If Global Riot Two were a war, it would already be the sixth bloodiest in the twenty-first century—still nothing compared to what the twentieth century was able to do, but give it time, give it time. . . .

He must not let it have one second more than can be helped, Louie thinks. Right now speed is everything.

He is the fastest-moving human being there has ever been, right now; he is gaining speed all the time—and he has such a long way to go.

The rioting hasn't been bad in Novokuznetsk, or so they assure Klieg, but that's just compared to what it is everywhere else. With tens of thousands dying worldwide daily, a little martial law, a little looting, some occasional sniping seems like getting off easily.

Certainly he's glad to have Glinda and Derry here, away from the much worse situation in the States.

John Klieg has always regarded himself as a practical philosopher, and the cornerstone of his practical philosophy has always been that most people are idiots when it comes to understanding how business works, what it does, and what it can and cannot do. What they constantly lose sight of is that business works by making money move from place to place, that what it does is keep the world on a reasonable, sensible course because business people are reasonable and sensible, and that's that. It can make some people rich and give jobs to most of the rest. It can't make the world into some kind of pie-in-the-sky paradise where everything works out just like in the movies and people get just what they deserve.

If business did make the world work like the movies, then the movie business would shut down. And Klieg *loves* movies, and he has a lot of friends who put money in them.

What really has him disgruntled, he realizes, is that here he had the opportunity not just of the century, but maybe of the millennium, and suddenly in the middle they change all the rules. Just like those government bastards. Hell, if private enterprise had been allowed to open up space in the first place, instead of jacking around with the government, there'd have been million-dollar houses all the way from Orlando to the Space Coast before they ever got the first satellite up, and by now there'd be six or seven names that meant space the way Rockefeller means oil, Ford means cars, and Hughes means airplanes. Instead, it was always this goofy stop-start thing, driven by big drives to go noplace in particular, with nobody really in control of it and no bank or CFO anywhere to keep the keel even.

So the world finally gets a chance for a fully rational space program, and one lousy reporter. . . .

He's so angry he can't quite speak, he realizes. You'd think that Jameson bitch, being in business for herself, relying as she does on the mostly private net, would have some appreciation for his position. And she had seemed to, back when she was helping him shut down those thieving socialist pirates and that crazed astronaut. . . .

But they didn't get shut down, now did they, and she wasn't much help, was she? The big thing she did was snoop into his relations with every friend he had in government everywhere. His contacts in Tokyo, Paris, New York, and Brussels are pessimistic about getting any of the relevant governments to complain, let alone really make a case out of it. Hardshaw and Rivera are giving everyone a good cut of the deal, and there you have it.

Well, after all, he philosophizes, just try starting your own post office if you think it's ever any different. He'll still get a year or so of his launch monopoly, and by god he'll charge what he likes for it.

He's looking forward to his meeting with Hassan this afternoon. One thing old Karl Marx was right about, the bourgeoisie really is the international class; Hassan's gotten to be one of Klieg's best friends in the world, because say what you will about the businesses he's in (and what's wrong with them, really, except that he's selling something people want on one end, and competing with governments in providing soldiers on the other?), Hassan's got a head for business all the way through.

Klieg still has a few minutes, so he goes into the back chambers to say hi to Glinda and Derry. Derry's been glued to XV since Global Riot Two started—and when are they going to arrest that damned Jameson and try her for that? Especially since there must be millions of kids jacking in to watch the riots, but not closely supervised like Derry is, so that they're not just riding along with cops and fire crews and watching responsible people cope with the disaster, but experiencing *looting* and *rape* . . . what kind of goofy world is it that makes that available to kids, anyway? And why the hell isn't Berlina Jameson in jail someplace, or better yet slated for a short trial and a short rope, considering how many people are dead because of her?

He realizes he's walked in on his family-to-be still seething with rage, and that's not a good thing to do. He lets out a long exhale and says, "I just came in to say hi. Sorry to come in in such a state—it's nobody's fault here."

Glinda smiles at him and says, "John, don't you dare apologize. What they're putting you through would try the patience of a saint."

Derry winks at him and gives him the old fist-up power salute. It makes him feel like a hero.

He hugs them both and goes down to catch the cab for his meeting with Hassan. He's meeting his partner at the Hole-in-Corner, their usual little restaurant where they can get a back room to themselves. He and Hassan always assume that the secret police are listening to everything there, which is why they use the place for meetings—the worst thing that could happen right now would be for the secret police to think that the partners were holding out on them.

At the Hole-in-Corner, the silent, withered old headwaiter guides Klieg back through the muffling tapestries and hangings to the back room. Hassan starts as Klieg enters. Klieg's first thought is, *I've never seen him so nervous. He's like a four-year-old in a doctor's waiting room.*

"There are so many rumors now that no one can tell what will happen," he says, scratching his right wrist with his left hand. "So many of our people are being arrested abroad, so many organizations suddenly folding up, it's not even possible to tell which pieces are still on the board. I must tell you, Mr. Klieg, my friend, I am worried. If things should overturn suddenly, we might be caught in very bad positions."

"That's always the risk you run," Klieg says, firmly, because that phrase has never failed to reassure him.

Hassan nods, sighs, and says, "Oh, I know and I quite agree. But there is a difference nonetheless. The risk where you come from is merely the risk of going broke. Here it can be more substantial and more personal."

Involuntarily Klieg shudders; he doesn't think they would dare to touch him, let alone Glinda or Derry, but one can never be sure, and certainly Hassan has no such protection.

The real key in all of this is Abdulkashim. They got involved with him in the first place because key elements of the armed forces were still loyal to him, and until he decided that the all-weather space launch program would go forward even if he returned to power, they were a powerful passive roadblock.

Since Abdulkashim has endorsed them, they've been getting a lot of unexpected help, but how long that will continue is anyone's guess. Right now the government is made up of anti-Abdulkashim nationalists, the only possibility acceptable to the UN, but there are half a dozen factions, unable to govern and unable not to reach for power, moving and squabbling in the wings.

Hassan talks much of these things as they sip fruit juices and ice water. "If we must be sent to our respective paradises, my friend, let us go with clean kidneys," he says as they take yet another bathroom break, each of them going to the men's room in turn under the watchful eyes of Hassan's bodyguards. Klieg refrains from wondering whether the bodyguards watch him in the rest room to protect him or to make sure he isn't smuggling a weapon in somehow. Realistically, probably both.

After all, he thinks as he settles onto the commode, when you come right down to it, it's just six more days. Then he launches the first test shot, and once that works, since it's the only thing that may abate Clem's fury, nobody's going to allow GateTech launches to be hassled. They'll be perfectly safe in a few days.

There's a sharp crack outside, and he has just enough time to know that it's a gunshot before the door bursts open; he's yanking his pants up but not fast enough as two big men shove the flimsy stall door aside and grab him by the armpits.

It happens so abruptly that he isn't even able to formulate words before they are dragging him forcibly out. They don't even give him a chance to button his pants or fasten his belt, and he struggles ridiculously with his pants catching his feet.

As he's yanked through the restaurant and out the back door, he catches glimpses of two of Hassan's bodyguards lying dead in the hallways, and the lumpy bundle wrapped in a tablecloth, being carried out by two flunkies, can only be Hassan himself.

They don't seem to speak English, or care very much what he tries to say in Russian, Yakut, or Buryat. He is heaved into the back of a van and manages, at last, to yank his pants up, though between fear and surprise he's made quite a mess. Just now, though, a ruined thousand-dollar suit is no big deal at all.

He's been in the cell four hours by the time anyone comes to talk to him, and during that time he's heard the screams and sobs of a young girl in the next cell as the guards raped her. It wasn't Derry—the girl was screaming in Yakut—but Klieg has no doubt the intention was to remind him that it could be.

There are times when you just cut whatever deal you can. When they finally do talk to him, they explain that this is a coup by people loyal to Abdulkashim, who is going to try to break out of the pen in Stockholm, and that they want to make it absolutely clear to him that his launching facilities have been nationalized.

Any successful businessman has to expect this from government. He promises to be a good, cooperative, useful prisoner, as many times as they want him to promise, and then they let him see the very frightened Glinda and Derry, and after some more threats they let Klieg and his girls go.

He has been in this part of the world for a while now, and it has gotten into him. Even as he holds his two girls, and reassures them, part of him is thinking, now, that the humiliation, and the threat to his family, and most of all the death of his friend and partner will all be paid back. A few months ago he wouldn't have had the foggiest idea how to begin to take such revenge. But now, when the new government releases them, late that night, and the three return to their apartment, he takes a very long hot shower to get rid of the stench of dry shit that hangs on him, and as he scrubs he thinks about just how to get all this fixed up right.

He might have been a little shocked at the mixture of inventiveness and cruelty in his thoughts before he came out here. Now, he enjoys it even more than he enjoys getting clean.

The daughter hurricane designated "Clem 114" forms when an outflow jet of Clem's shifts abruptly northward at a point just west of Minami Tori. By now the news media aren't even bothering to explain how the high pressure area formed by two outflow jets will push two superhurricanes apart; they merely note that Clem 114 is headed southwest, into much warmer water, where it is likely to grow as big as its parent within days.

Manuel Tagbilaran doesn't even know the number on the hurricane coming in; it seems utterly irrelevant compared with the task at hand, which is getting this last group of passengers who just got off the Luzon ferry all the way down the island of Samar to Tacloban.

Manuel is not immediately sure why he's doing it. He lives by himself, now that the kids are grown and his wife is dead, on a little farm up on the west slopes of the mountains that run down the "spine" of Samar; he sometimes explains to tourist visitors that Samar is shaped like a road-killed rabbit lying on its left side, with its broken spine bent inward in the middle, and that the road weaves around the spine.

At least he will be on the slopes of the mountains away from the winds. And this is a fool's errand anyway, for after meeting the ferry from Luzon, he normally takes them all the way to Tacloban, over on Leyte to the south, himself. There is no way the ferry will be running, not even that idiot Ramon—god, Manuel hopes Ramon is all right; they've known each other since they both started on this route, what, back in '96? Thirty some years at least.

The wind is still rising and it's getting darker, though it's mid-day. Every so often there will be a heavy gust of driving rain that makes the whole bus, a Mitsui '12 IntelliTracker, shudder and groan. He keeps his hands on the controls and keeps talking to the bus, as if something with firmware this crude could have morale that would really benefit from being talked to.

Just maybe, Manuel thinks, it has something to do with his own morale, or that of the passengers.

Normally a hundred kilometers roll by pretty fast—now that the road is paved all the way, and with the IntelliTracker's angle-bounce radars, they can roar along at about 140 km/hr. But they've been on the road two hours now, and they're not one-third of the way.

At least his passengers are quiet enough. In the back there are a couple of Chinese insurance agents, trying to make it home after a week of peddling homeowner's and term life up in the capital, down to the little Chinese suburbs that have sprung up in Leyte. Probably all they're worried about is whether they'll get in late and be too tired for tennis and golf tomorrow. There's also an older lady and her daughter, the daughter clearly running to fat and turning middle-aged, probably the plain one they kept back to tend Mama.

Manuel hates to see that; it was the job his favorite sister got stuck with, and she ended up a sour, bitter old lady, before finally lurching resentfully into the grave only three years after Mama.

The rest of the crowd is a couple of kids from the high school at Ormoc, the boy a slender, handsome young devil (god, the life Manuel could have led with looks like those! And the life that kid probably is living!) and the girl baby-faced and busty, a cuddly little thing; ostensibly they were visiting the university in Manila, though if Manuel knows what's what, those kids' parents probably had no idea that the two of them were taking off at the same time to the same place.

They come around a bend, still weaving cautiously along the highway north of Calbayog. He can't see a damned thing by the roadside; for the last ten minutes there have been streams where there never were before, cutting right through the broken pavement in front of him, and once the IntelliTracker had to lower its treads and climb up and around the broken roadbed.

He's lost count of the number of fallen trees they've broken their way through and over.

This is going to be one great story for the grandkids, who are undoubtedly huddling in the storm cellars that he and his sons and sons-in-law dug at all the family farms along the road.

They lurch to a halt suddenly, and the IntelliTracker says, "Cannot identify roadbed."

Manuel peers out through the windshield, which seems to have an inch of running water on it. "Me either, pal. Can we get there on inertial and radar?"

There's a long pause, and the IntelliTracker finally says "Reports up ahead show sea levels are at record lows around Catbalogan. Authorities are advising—"

"Oh, hell," Manuel says. Anyone in the Philippines knows that a low sea level means the sea will be back, later, and generally fast and strong. Clearly this monster hurricane the *yanqui* scientists have made (Manuel isn't sure how but it stands to reason that the *yanquis* are behind it) is producing storm surges just as big as they were claiming, and probably its eye will be coming in up to the north, maybe even right through Manila itself.

The IntelliTracker waits a while, and then, poor idiot that it is, unable to interpret his tone, it says to him, "Inadvisable to carry passengers along that route in present conditions. Risk of serious accident seventeen per cent."

It's a lot higher than that, Manuel thinks. He looks over his six passengers; they all look drawn and frightened, and the way he feels himself, he's just as glad to have the bus to worry about, because if he didn't he'd be scared out of his mind.

"Well, as a temporary refuge, can we make it to the farm?"

"Which farm?" the stupid bus asks him.

"IntelliTracker—identify as base primary—close IntelliTracker," Manuel answers, putting it in the crude communications language that came with the IntelliTracker. The bus has only a limited ability to understand natural language, so it really does clarify things, but Manuel also has a gut feeling that the IntelliTracker, somehow or other, will feel just a little insulted when he resorts to it, the way he feels when Korean sailors out of Subic Bay or American retirees in Manila speak to him in pidgin.

The IntelliTracker considers and then answers in its flat mechanical voice. "Chance of success is high. Some risk of subsequent trespassing charges."

Manuel shrugs eloquently; why buy insurance for it if they aren't going to haul you into court every so often? "Divert and execute," he says, and they turn off the road and begin to climb the hillside.

"I'm taking you all home with me," he explains to his passengers. "There's no ferry right now, and my farm is on high ground. If you need to call home, there's a working phone in the back of the bus."

Three hours later, around the time for sunset but it's much too dark to tell, they are on the one-lane macadam track that winds up past his farm, having cut through half a dozen fields—not that, after this hurricane rips through, anyone is going to notice what the bus did. Twice they've had to take half-hour detours around big areas of fallen trees and once a mudslide forced them to backtrack. By common consent, the passengers are now all sitting up close to him; Manuel doesn't care, this is sort of a chance to show off.

When the lightning hits close, at first he laughs it off—"Don't jump, people, if it had hit us we wouldn't have heard it"—but then he feels the IntelliTracker slowing to a stop. A quick look at the board shows that the brain has gone dead on him; probably a couple of two-peso parts have cooked somewhere, normally he'd just phone for a recovery whistler, one of those little delivery robots, to come out with a parts basket, and he'd be rolling again in an hour at worst, but right now, any spare parts might as well be on the moon for all the good they do him.

Well, there's an obvious solution, and he can hardly stay here—already water is beginning to swirl around the tires. If he sits here, in half an hour it will erode the shoulder around the left tires, leaving them stuck on this empty stretch of road. He flips it over to full manual control—it's a relief to find out that that still works, and that he still seems to know what to do, even though it's been at least twenty years since he's had to.

The next three hours are more interesting than anything he's done in a long while; it's a lot like back when he was learning from his old man. The old man had learned on an old GM schoolbus that had no more controls than the wheel, brake, gas, shift, and clutch; but Manuel doesn't think the old man could have done better than this, skittering down the mountainside, occasionally even getting up enough speed so that you feel a little g toward the outside of a turn. He can tell, though he hasn't time to look behind him, that his passengers are trying not to show him how frightened they are.

Nothing to it, really. Anyone could do this; in the old days, they used to do it all the time. Of course, Manuel is putting a little more style and flare into it.

Still, he's never been quite so glad to pull into the front yard of his house before. And if he had known that thanks to Clem 114, the young couple will be settling just over the hill, the Chinese insurance agents will have to stay here for a whole season as not-quite-necessary field hands until their families get out of refugee camps less than a hundred kilometers away—or that after burying Mama for her, he will be marrying that plump daughter and starting another family at his age—well, he might not have done anything differently, except perhaps worn his best shirt and taken a few corners a little tighter. A man likes to make an impression on his friends, and he's going to be telling this story—with his six passengers as his witnesses—for a long, long time.

On July 28, eight days after he pulled away from Earth orbit on the way out, Louie Tynan decides to take a vacation in his body.

There seems to be so much of him in the machine these days that everything will run fine without him, at least for these routine tasks. His health monitors have been telling him bad things for a while, and thus he thinks he'd better get some exercise and regular sleep, and most of all, he wants to see a package go all the way through the funnel with naked eye observation.

Now he sits in the observation bubble and watches. He's tied down, thoroughly, because the acceleration that's going to hit is going to rise up to almost four g's pretty fast. Just as the physicists define speed as change in position over time, and acceleration as change in speed over time, Nemtin and other engineers back in the 1930s realized that change in acceleration over time also mattered, and named it "jerk." What Louie is about to be subjected to is more jerk than he's ever encountered before.

Even after several days of this, he's worried a lot more about the *Good Luck* than he is about himself. Strapped to the back wall of the observation bubble—which will presently momentarily become the "ceiling"—he will be thrown against the webs that he now comfortably floats in, his head will feel a bit squeezed in the retaining ring through which he looks, and he may feel blood rushing to his face, but everything holding him up and holding the observation bubble together is more than strong enough for the job. Besides, healthy human bodies have withstood much more than this.

He can't be sure till each try that the whole of *Good Luck* is ready to take the jerk. Things have broken, now and then, in these first few days, as packages went through, and just yesterday he lost two antennas off his communications equipment. If he were still plugged in, he would be able to do a lot of last-minute checks, which would at least keep him busy in the middle of all this, and he faintly resents how slow and stupid he feels when he isn't plugged in.

There was a time when the view through the observation bubble was a large part of why he stayed on board the *Constitution* for so long. Moreover, unlike the always-fascinating but now familiar view of Earth from orbit, this is a view he hasn't had since the Mars expedition. Earth and Luna in the same sky, exhibiting the same crescent shape seemingly close together; his viewing position is perfect with the Earth and moon almost lined up with each other, the sun slightly to one side. At the moment he is about sixty-five times as far from the Earth as the moon is.

Earth is not as impressive as it once was, now a mere speck showing a crescent if he peers at it hard enough, and the moon is more and more beginning to resemble a bright star, though he can still make out that it's a comma rather than a period if he focuses on it carefully.

He tries to recall how he would have felt back when this body was all he had, tries to summon the feelings he might have known had he been on this voyage only in this body.

It's no good. Though he knows intellectually that this is one of the most impressive sights he has ever seen with the eyes he was born with, those eyes are just not good enough anymore; the little swatch of the spectrum from red to violet that they can perceive, the bare 165-degree cone of vision, the narrow bandwidth of signal that can pass through a human optic nerve, the fact that only two independent sensors that differ by only a few inches' position are being compared—and that his brain needs so much space to do even that—all these things, unchanged since the Paleolithic, leave him feeling crippled.

If he could see it in all his radars, across every wavelength from radio up through hard X-ray, *then* it would be glorious . . . and he sees that all the time, with one small part of his mind, appreciating it fully while having the time to enjoy other things. To have this tiny, one-person brain is not merely to live more slowly and stupidly; because it cannot absorb the requisite data flows, it is also to feel blind and deaf.

Apparently one can be stupid with a large brain too, for he had thought a package passing through would be more impressive with just his own organic brain and eyes. There isn't time to unstrap and go get plugged back in, either, before the package comes through, so now he's stuck here. He tries to make the best of it; who'd have thought you could find the view in space limited and dull?

Out beyond the *Constitution,* there are many other silvery, glowing objects, in mad variety of shapes and glosses, and at first glance with the naked eye, in the total darkness of the vacuum and with the sun all but due astern, it appears that there is nothing holding them in place. But then the eye begins to catch the telltale sharp black lines that flit occasionally across the crescent Earth and moon, the black lines that sometimes cut across one of the shiny objects that seems to be flying in perfect formation with the *Constitution,* and then the more distant glints where the great coil, four hundred meters at its narrow point by *Constitution,* funnels out to a full kilometer, and abruptly the eye connects those bright patches and shadows across the black vacuum to form the image of a gigantic coil spring in space, six kilometers through the center, wide at the end pointed toward the sun, with all the other parts of the ship clinging to it.

The arriving package is a mere bright dot. Moreover, it's only about a hundred meters in diameter, so it has to get within twelve kilometers before it's even as big as the moon in the night sky on Earth, and since it is only about six hundred meters long, it takes less than a heartbeat to pass through the coil of the *Good Luck* and continue on its way into space ahead. If he'd blinked or sneezed he might not have seen it at all.

And since it is moving almost ten times as fast as the ship, what Louie sees with his own eyes is merely a bright streak; the human eye cannot resolve something moving that fast.

His chief impression of it is only of being thrown against the web. The package passes through the coil, the superconducting magnets on its surface interact with the powerful field set up in the coil by electricity from the *Good Luck*'s plants and collectors, which causes the package to slow down by about twenty percent in that brief instant—and transfer all of that momentum to the *Good Luck*. The great coils contract and pulse back out, all of *Constitution* and the other modules are shaken like the tops of palm trees in a hurricane, and then the package is gone, hurrying on toward 2026RU ahead of him.

He will catch up with it again sometime on the other side of Jupiter, strip it for parts, and throw the rest backward as reaction mass.

Captain Musharaf is painfully aware that no one cares much about the town of Khulna. It's another one of those cities in the world that nobody goes to for fun, but where the world's work gets done. As far as he knows, there is no one in this city of two and a half million who is even jacked for XV; when the blow falls, no one will record it.

Just now he's supervising as much evacuation as can be managed; civil government collapsed a while ago here, and Musharaf's colonel and major cut and ran three days ago, during the rioting. The other captains in the regiment elected him, and to the extent that he gets any orders from Dhaka, they seem perfectly willing to send them to him.

After all, what difference does it make what they tell him? How could they possibly enforce their will?

The regiment hasn't been able to pacify the whole city; things have gotten too berserk for that. As in so many other parts of Asia, the international corporations' use of mindslavery for factory labor has resulted in a population with no particular loyalties and nothing except a desire to get their hands on what they think of as the good things in life; a million people of both sexes, from age six to eighty, have been toiling in the big skyscraper plants built where Garden Park and the stadium used to be.

Musharaf grew up here, and it's never really occurred to him before how much he resented the Koreans for buying out the whole public part of the town to put their three-hundred-story assembly works there, let alone for turning so many of his neighbors into zombies who barely even know they're Bangala.

Well, if there was ever a time to do anything about it, that was a long time ago. Right now Musharaf and his company are only trying to hold the *ghat*, the steps leading down to the River Rupsa, with a perimeter wide enough to allow some kind of orderly boarding of the hovercraft that are going to try to make the dash for high ground in Assam Province of India, as others have been doing for three days since it became apparent that Clem 114 was going to burst into the Bay of Bengal.

Outside Musharaf's perimeter there are tens of thousands of people, some throwing rocks and screaming, some just apathetically staring in toward the *ghat*, many wearing scalpnets and illegal amplifier boxes so that while they're here, they're also cracking skulls in London, burning a family out of its shop in Dayton, or robbing the dead in Manila.

There's been very little sniper fire, though, because Bangladesh is so poor that practically no one can afford guns. That's some consolation.

He checks the computer again; things haven't changed. He can put about 1200 more children and mothers onto the hovercraft sitting at the *ghat*, before they have to lift and run, in only about another eight minutes. The big wave from the storm surge of Clem 114 is already on its way inland, and he can no longer raise any of the army posts in the Sundarbans, the great mangrove swamps that form the southern coast of Khulna Division.

A thought occurs to him; he nods to his company sergeant, who salutes. He wonders what this man thinks of him. Well, in fourteen minutes it will not matter.

"Find me a mullah," Captain Musharaf says. "Now. From somewhere close."

The sergeant asks nothing, turns, and is gone.

Musharaf is reasonably sure that the mob doesn't know what is about to happen. The poverty-stricken wetland where the Ganges and the Brahmaputra run together and dribble out to the sea has more people per square meter than any other nation. It is no longer among the Earth's poorest nations—as he always does, when he thinks of that, Musharaf gets a little surge of pride when he realizes that Bangladesh has climbed so fast in the last thirty years that it has passed places like Zambia and Paraguay that had a much longer head start. But its demographics and its accomplishments are not noteworthy to the global audience, and so they might as well be invisible here. The two-kilometer-high wave now roaring up toward them, pushed to far greater heights because the continental shelf extends so far down into the Bay of Bengal, will not be described or discussed on any channel, and it will fall as a complete surprise to anyone not listening to local news.

When he was a boy, he was here every day—his mother sold *sringala*, little bits of meat folded into a triangle of some vegetable and deep-fried, at a stand in the Bazar, just south of here, and more often than not he tended the stand while she cooked. It was a shrewd choice, for *sringala* is nourishing enough so that she could feed whatever was left over to the family; they sometimes went to bed broke, but seldom hungry.

He would give up half his remaining minutes to be at his mother's stand again, nostrils full of the familiar odor of onions and peppers, schoolbook propped up in front of him because she insisted that he study while he worked, eating the leftover *sringala* with her and his sisters when the day ended.

Two of his sisters are already in Assam, and one married a rich German, who, when Europe expelled non-whites, emigrated with her to Ontario. He has three nephews he will never see . . . but at least they're in Toronto, and surely that's a safe place.

The sergeant arrives with the mullah, and in a low voice Captain Musharaf explains the situation. The mullah agrees at once, and runs off to the mosque nearest at hand. It occurs to Musharaf that it's a good thing this is a fairly young, agile mullah.

As the mullah rounds the corner and passes out of sight, the last hovercraft's engines are dying off in the distance; now people wait patiently for the next one. Only Musharaf, the mullah, and now his sergeant know that there will be no more.

There are four minutes left when the muezzin—about an hour early, but few of these people will check—issues the call to prayer. Across that part of the city, the drifting mob, last dregs of Global Riot Two, kneels to pray; the patient refugees, and Musharaf himself, spread their prayer rugs if they have them, or merely bow and pray if they don't, facing west toward Mecca.

When the great wave strikes, it comes from the southeast, behind them, and it is on them before people can do much more than stand up. Musharaf's last thought is that surely, for getting into Paradise, dying in the midst of prayers must count for something.

Whether it does or not, it's over very fast; the black wave, already frothing with corpses, pounds on northward. It will be many kilometers before it sinks down far enough to begin leaving any survivors behind it.

* * *

They are in Progreso, a little village not far south of Pijijiapan, when Passionet finally catches up with Mary Ann. She's been thinking seriously of just resigning, Jesse knows, but she also figured that since they had made her rich, she owed it to them to at least talk things over a little. He goes over to play with Tomás's grandkids for a while—there're a couple of them who are pretty decent little soccer players, and Jesse played soccer all the way through high school, so they have a nice little three-way game on a bit of triangular ground, and after a while he has all but forgotten the intrusion of the real world into his adventure.

He's almost startled when Mary Ann comes over to talk to him; the whistle has sounded the ten-minute warning till they are to move again, but now that the road has toughened him a bit, Jesse doesn't feel any big need to do more than gulp some extra water before they get back on the road. This stretch, where the road follows the first big ridgeline in from the coast, is a terrific place for a long hike, and even those who are abandoning homes they may never see again seem to be enjoying themselves.

"Well," she says, "I know what they want and it's really different. I'm not sure how to explain it to you. Did you catch any of Surface O'Malley's work in the last few months? She's the new girl that's been filling in for me, and though they're too polite to say it, she's probably also the one they had in mind to replace me."

"No, I haven't. What's she got to do with all this?"

"Well, a few days ago in Bangkok, she managed to do everything we're not supposed to do within one hour, and the audience loved it. So naturally, now it's a stroke of genius and they want us all to do it." She explains it all to Jesse during the next hour on the road, as they wind back toward Federal Highway 200; for a day or so they've been on the thin, badly paved Chiapas state highway that runs parallel to the great Federal highway, to leave the main road clear for more urgent convoys. At the speed they're moving, it hasn't made much difference, except that it's much quieter and more pleasant, and for some reason farmers and locals seem to be more willing to come out, say hello, and sell them melons and corn.

"So you think you'll take them up on it?" Jesse finally asks. "Are you up to faking being sincere underneath faking being fake?" His description comes out more sarcastically than he had intended; he looks out over the deep greens of the valleys around him, now slashed with streaks of black mud where landslides and floods from Clem Two tore up the hillsides, under the deep blue of the equatorial sky, and he realizes it's just resentment at being dumped back out of this little personal paradise, the special adventure that's just him and Mary Ann.

She laughs at his description, but it's clearly just a polite noise she's making to avoid a fight. "I guess if you really pushed me I'd say I *have* to do it, Jesse." She takes his hand, and that's the same as ever, the terrific moment of looking over and seeing one of his adolescent fantasies smiling at him, and at the same time knowing that it's good old reliable Mary Ann, his friend and partner in so much trouble and danger so far. . . .

He shrugs and grins. "It's a *duty*? Who do you think you are, Berlina Jameson? I thought Passionet was just entertainment."

"I thought so too, and I think Passionet did. One reason I was over there for so long was that since I got the call from Doug Llewellyn—the president of Passionet—I knew something pretty strange was up. Usually people with my job don't talk to even a vice president twice in a year. We may be the most public aspect of Passionet but we sure don't rate much in real importance within the company—I guess we're just too easy to replace." She lifts his hand in her own two small ones and kisses his fingers. "One of the reasons I get so much pleasure out of being treated like a human being is working with the people at Passionet teaches you how unusual that can be. Anyway, so when it was Llewellyn who made the call, I knew something big was up they weren't telling me, and I insisted on knowing before I agreed to anything. They finally had to patch through David Ali—that's Rock to you, he's sort of my best friend in the biz—and let him explain some of it too.

"You know how everyone says nowadays you can't censor because there are so many alternate pathways, and because packetized data can leak in through so many different ways and then reassemble?"

"Yep, I'm an engineer, remember?"

She makes a face at him. "If you want this explained, you have to let me do it my way. Okay?"

" 'Kay." He holds her hand tightly, and scuffs along the road a little.

She lifts his hand again, toys with it, smiles, and then says, "Well, it turns out you can still be a pretty effective censor if you're just willing to play rough enough. Have you followed the news enough to know about Global Riot Two?"

"I know there is one and they aren't sure when it's going to end. I guess there have been a lot of deaths."

"Unh-hunh. Nineteen million dead as of this morning, not counting a few million more who didn't manage to evacuate before hurricanes hit, because they were pinned down by the riots. Twenty governments collapsed entirely. They just lost all of Bangladesh—the storm surge in front of Clem 114 finished off what the riots started. They claim ten million more people could have been evacuated there if troops and transport weren't tied up in maintaining civil order."

"Your public affairs voice is showing."

"Well, I'm in public affairs whether I want to be or not." She presses in close against him, and despite the heat he drops an arm around her shoulders and lets her small, warm body snug up into his armpit. "You know the basic thing about global riots, that you can get whatever that contagious 'riot spirit' is, right through the XV transmission? And of course because it's dramatic and visceral and emotionally loaded, it's really popular and people tend to watch it a lot."

"So what does it have to do with the president of Passionet calling you up?"

"A lot. This morning he was awakened, very rudely, by a group of Marines who tore his house apart, cavity-searched his family, and 'accidentally' destroyed half his art collection. He got off lightly—they stopped a zipline right out in the middle of nowhere carrying three of his execs, took them off in handcuffs naked so that everyone could see them.

"When lawyers showed up to bail them out, they found out martial law had been declared around that courtroom, and they jailed the lawyers. *And* the Army was holding the Passionet library of XV recordings, announcing that they couldn't be responsible for maintaining it and if lots of it got erased it would just be too bad. *And* they also sort of suggested that since a lot of it involves violence and sex in one form or another, they might just decide to review it for 'pornography', not let Passionet have access while they're spending several months doing that, and then make a lot of arrests based on the evidence, using the Diem Act."

"Jesus. I thought that was just to cover deathporn for hire."

"What it says is you can't distribute murder and torture experiences to people who are primarily buying them for pleasure. It's been interpreted narrowly up till now, to just cover raping, killing, and torturing people and distributing wedges of that, but nothing says it always has to be. Theoretically, any time one of us gets killed or hurt and the ratings go up because weird people are getting off on it, Passionet could be prosecuted. And for aggravated cases they can actually give the death penalty to corporate officers and major stockholders as well as to the people that made the wedges directly. Sort of like the Nuremberg principles—'I vas only follovink orders' is not an excuse."

"Jesus! Is all that constitutional?"

"Of course not. But Hardshaw got to the Supreme Court way ahead of Passionet, and the court refuses to hear anything about it; they're calling it a 'paramount national emergency,' like back when Lincoln suspended habeas corpus, or some of the secrecy stuff during the Cold War. Which boils down to lawyer-talk for 'Better do what we say.' And all of that was really just a demonstration of force, a little something to remind Llewellyn of how rough they could play if they wanted to, so that he'd understand that he'd better cooperate."

"I suppose it got *that* idea across, anyway. What did they want him to do?"

"Not just him, but every XV net they can find. It's an order: nothing to enhance Global Riot Two is going to go out over the nets. Nothing at all. Instead, what we're going to do is put out all kinds of stuff about humanity banding together, about courage and hope and mutual help and all that. The kind of positive news that politicians have always wanted anyway."

"Jesus God, Mary Ann. I see what you mean. I suppose you don't really have any choice—it doesn't sound like you want to fuck around with these guys. They could probably do just about anything it occurred to them to do to you."

She sighs, and it's not exactly a sad noise like he might have expected, but rather impatient, as if she thought he should already understand whatever it is that she is getting at. She takes his arm, already a bit warm and sticky from being draped over her shoulders in the baking heat of southern Mexico's late July, and pulls his hand forward, kissing it tenderly again. He realizes that in her way she's treating him like her little boy, and he both resents and enjoys it; he swallows hard and decides that he will make himself listen, really listen, to her, because he's so painfully aware of how much more she knows than he does.

"I feel like your big sister, all of a sudden," she says, "that is, your big sister who enjoys molesting you. Jesse, the government is forcing Passionet but they aren't forcing me. I want to do this; it's not a matter of 'cooperating.' I'm with them. If I see anyone trying to evade the censorship, I'll turn him in." She seems to hold her breath for a long moment. When he just keeps listening, she goes on. "I guess nothing cures you of romance as much as having a romantic job. Jesse, news for the masses, whether it's XV or all the way back to the old newspapers, is *entertainment.* People don't follow the news to stay informed, no matter what they tell you in school, they watch or experience to be entertained. If it were like they teach in school, they'd put the congressional budget, scientific research, and bios of every important bureaucrat in the opening slot, and they'd do special editions for the Nobel Prizes and the World Health Organization's annual report. That's not what it's about. They cover crime, sports, famous people having sex, funny animal stories, what it's like to stay in an expensive hotel in a resort area. Because that's what's interesting and fun and entertaining.

"It wouldn't matter so much except that people's lives are so dull they believe their entertainment—and for a hundred years we've been telling them that the world is very dangerous, that there are violent thugs everywhere, war is constantly imminent, sex is their most important need, all that crap.

"Well, shit, Jesse, if you were a shrink and you had a patient who only wanted to talk about violence, extravagance, cruelty, and his sexual fantasies—what would you suggest? More of the same?"

Jesse's a bit startled, but he asks, "Whatever happened to freedom of the press?"

She snorts, a funny, ugly noise. Then she says, "Sorry, Jesse, but what does that have to do with the present day? You think the broadcast nets are like Ben Franklin, turning out little pamphlets for a few to read and most to ignore? Look, a few huge private corporations are making all their money by spreading fear, hate, depression, and an exploitive attitude. Justice would demand public hangings. I don't see that telling the media to keep the good guys the viewpoint characters is anything more than recognizing that we all have to live with the people who believe that crap. It's just good semiotics. Better still to suppress the industry entirely, but this is a first step."

He looks out across the switchback they're now descending; the front of the column is just reaching the next bend after the one they're approaching. "We're really quite a parade here. So when do you start transmitting?"

"Supposedly they'll have a controller out here in a whistler in about three hours; they bribed the Mexican government by bringing along a truck that also has room for a clinic."

"Some bribe. I'd have thought something with a little more personal advantage—"

"I'm sure there were plenty of those too." She slides her hand gently up his back. "You're not mad at me, are you?"

"Not really mad." He scuffs the dirt once, then decides that's acting too much like a kid, and says, "Uh, could you explain the semiotic thing? Little bitty words that even an engineer can understand?"

She smiles at him. "It's not complicated, Jesse, it's just that the viewpoint character is always privileged—people identify with his or her values. For years people have been pointing out that it's not a real great thing that assassinations and rapes and so forth on the entertainment shows are almost always seen from the attacker's point of view, so that people associate being the aggressor with it being exciting. So all we're going to do is deny the goons and thugs, the rioters and the people who are making the global emergency tougher for everyone, a voice in all this. They get no viewpoint. When they tune in to share the riot, they get hit with wall-to-wall disgust, and that's it. Or, if you want, what we're doing is de-privileging the aggressor."

Jesse understands what she's saying, and the only problem he has is that it still sounds more to him like what they're doing is "slanting the news." But he asks something safer. "Will it work?"

"It had better."

He finds himself agreeing with that; if they're going to control the news, at least let it be for some good purpose. "I hope it does work. I'm going to miss you."

"Miss me? I'm not going anywhere. I mean, other than to Oaxaca, but we don't get there for weeks yet."

Now he's confused, and he stammers—"But I thought—I mean, Passionet wouldn't be—"

"They wouldn't have been out here before, no. But now they are. They want the walk to Oaxaca the way Mary Ann Waterhouse experiences it, no fancy feeling stuff in it. I'm even allowed to think that the big tits they sewed onto me are really a nuisance when you're taking a long walk in hot weather."

He doesn't quite know what to say, so he just hugs her; she hugs back and says, "So you thought you were going to get rid of the old bag now that you'd used her up?"

"Never," he says, "I was just kind of dreading . . . well, having to say goodbye. Even if we do eventually, I'm certainly not ready yet."

"Me either. And there's a good reason for you to stick around, anyway; it's going to be a lot easier for you to get a date afterward if you do."

"It is?" When he looks at her, he sees that funny half-turn on one side of her face, a smile trying to escape. "Okay, what is it?"

"Well, in all seriousness, Jesse, hasn't it occurred to you yet that millions of women around the world are going to know what it's like to have sex with you? Which won't work to your detriment."

Jesse is so dumbfounded that he doesn't answer, just pulls her close and gives her a long kiss, groping her the whole time. After all, this may be the last privacy for quite a while.

Louie has three hours of scheduled exercise and rest now, to help adjust him to his long stay in space. He is looking forward to it less than he used to look forward to appointments with the dentist.

First of all, it's dull because the muscle aches and effort are unbroken by anything more stimulating than some Mahler on the speakers—*Das Lied von der Erde.* He's frustrated because he got to like Mahler after he added on all the processors, and now he just can't hear as much—his ears are just not as accurate as getting it straight off the digital recording. And he doesn't have the spare brain space to simultaneously read all the criticism written about it, to compare it with other major works . . . it's like listening to it on a bad car radio from a weak AM station, as far as he's concerned.

Moreover, even the pain of exercising isn't as intense as it should be; annoying and unpleasant to be sure, but you can feel only so much with the number of neurons on hand, and you can feel it only in relation to the relatively small number of things you can keep in your mind—

He bursts out laughing at himself, drowning out a moment of Mahler (shit! another thing he can't do simultaneously!), and takes a breather for a moment from stretching on the resistance table. All right, he'd rather be back in his electronic self. He wishes he never had to leave. If it were up to him he'd only occasionally pop into this body, and then just to have sex with Carla. . . .

Heck, even that might be better. Link them up, go on wireless, both people could be having each other's experience and memories in addition to their own, in realtime instead of in imagination or edited memory.

He shakes his head, laughing; no, he just doesn't like his body that much anymore. He's getting a crimp in his neck anyway, from shaking his head, and he'd never realized before that laughing makes you feel a little light-headed because you're not breathing effectively. Funny thing . . . spend a month practically not having a body, and all sorts of things about the body will bother you.

Speaking of which—he scrambles to the head. It's probably been a week since he's taken a dump.

Another experience that he'd all but forgotten, and this one definitely would *not* be enhanced by having more sensors and processes to experience it with.

After another hour, finally he can go back to the arrangement he prefers. By now his body is aching with unaccustomed stretching and motion, and he thinks quietly, as he jacks into the system through his scalpnet, that it will probably only get to be more of a nuisance with time—

Something is different.

His first and strangest sensation, once he has resumed his linked-in existence, is that someone is in here with him. He realizes, a moment later, that it is himself; in a dozen microseconds or so, he has re-integrated, compared his experience of meeting himself with the one Carla had a month ago, realized that he's added a great deal of system complexity by doing so, and decided it's of benefit to him. He makes a note and changes the programming of the wiseguys now en route to the asteroids; packages launched from the asteroids will bring along a copy of each wiseguy to re-integrate with Louie.

When the next package up from Luna roars through the funnel of *Good Luck*'s coil, Louie deliberately puts all his concentration into it, because he's getting far enough away so that he can just barely straddle being Louie-on-the-moon and Louie-the-ship. Louie grabs the package on the moon, throws it from his catapult, switches viewpoint, sees it coming all the way from the lunar catapult to his funnel, watches it pass through, sees the resistance heating produced by eddy currents here and there in not-perfectly-shielded conductors, watches it go back out, as easily as a juggler might toss one ball from one hand to the other. It is a much more impressive sight, and while he's doing it Louie is doing a hundred more things as well. This is the way to be.

By now the train is forty-six packages long ahead of him, and radio signals take eighty-seven seconds to reach him, and eighty-seven seconds is two hundred eighty brain-days for Louie; by the time Louie-the-ship has said something, Louie-on-the-moon has replied, and Louie-the-ship has absorbed the reply, four years of a normal human being's mental life have gone by.

He no longer experiences himself as juggling the packages, but as catching and throwing them. During the enforced time back in his body, he tries a sort of crude handball in the observation bubble, using an old tennis ball that was floating around Space Station *Constitution* for no reason he can think of, but it's not the same at all.

He keeps moving. He resents time in his body more every day. His biggest regret is that Carla and he are now writing "novels" to each other, as they call them—elaborate simulated experiences like XV but better, sex, romance, adventure, discovery, and fun shared—but only about every thirty-brain years (or a bit over fifty minutes), and of course it's subjectively years old by the time they get each other's replies. Moreover, the experiences are so vivid—and so much better than real life ever was—that he wishes they could try vacationing together on Earth, Earth as it was before Clem, to see if all this exploration of shared pleasure in virtual space would translate to the real. Not that they could go to eighteenth-century Paris or skyboard their way down from orbit to Tahiti anyway.

Well, at least that's something his body is good for, and he's glad enough to keep it around for that; though of course he certainly has more than enough memory of it to construct as many "physical" experiences as he wants.

Berlina Jameson doesn't really expect anything, one way or another, anymore—life has been confusing enough for long enough so that she has given up on expectations. Still, about the last thing she expects is to get a backchannel message from John Klieg, let alone to have it be a list of names, dates, files, sources, and nodes to investigate. She wonders for a moment if this is revenge, if he has perhaps set her up to come to the attention of a violent group somewhere when she snoops in. But then why did he also include a short note that urges her to do her digging under a clean—that is, fake, new, and traceproof—i.d.? If there is a scheme in this it is too deep for her.

Maybe he's just one of those good sport types who understands that there is nothing personal in it, that she was just doing her job.

She spends some heavy cash going through a commercial massively parallel system to build her wolfpack of software and make sure that they're as souped up as she can manage. That forces her to take a look at how much is in her bank account, which is the point where she discovers that she is now wealthy.

What comes back from the search is spectacular, and she realizes the instant she has it that first of all she owes Klieg a lot of favors, most of which she can pay off by making sure this doesn't trace to him. The other thing that's obvious is that she's going to have to do quite a bit to keep her own neck out of the noose if she wants to put this in *Sniffings*.

Best of all would be if it were wrapped up and *Sniffings* posted at about the same time. She splurges on some more hard-to-trace and hard-to-monitor stuff to place her call from, really splurges on penetrating Harris Diem's private line, and then waits another few hours to drive over to Green River, Utah, without calling anyone or telling anyone, so that she won't be phoning out of Denver, where it's just possible someone might be trying to monitor her.

When she finally calls him, he looks worn out and miserable, not to mention startled.

"I can't stay on long," she says, without preamble. "A bunch of no-trace packets are headed for your private data line. I've got ironclad evidence that there's a plan underway to spring Abdulkashim from prison in Stockholm and bring him back to power in Siberia. The attempt is scheduled for September twenty-second, the day before the trial starts. I'll run the story forty-eight hours before that, or sooner if they move the date up or you make some arrests. No obligation, Mr. Diem, but I wouldn't mind an exclusive interview after you've dealt with this."

"That's not a favor, it's a pleasure," he says, smiling grimly. His lips move in some sequence of words she doesn't catch, and the sound is dead on the phone for a moment; whatever he just told his home phone system, it breaks up the call instantly. Probably scrambles anything trying to trace it, too.

Berlina has a little extra time, and not only is it doubtful that anyone traced that call, it's also improbable that they would have an agent in place way out here. So she decides to opaque her windows, tie a kerchief around her hair, slip into her gruds, and go for some plain old diner food, the stuff she likes best in the world.

It's a nice day; this high in the mountains bright summer days are usually not too hot, and the view around the town is spectacular. People nod and smile at her a lot, and this triggers a funny thought; used to be that Utah was a bad place to be black, and rural Utah was worse. Not any-more . . . the Europeans saw to that. When they expelled "non-natives" and "cleaned" their miserable little continent. . . .

Be honest with yourself, Berlina, you loved living there, it was your home, this is sour grapes—since they won't let you back in you're pouting. But if they'd re-open you'd go back in a minute.

She hates giving herself good advice, and besides that wasn't the point. What made all the difference in Utah, and for that matter in Mississippi and Detroit and everywhere, was the Little Cold War, the three-way tensions between the USA, Japan, and Europe over trade, influence, seabed and space resources, and access to Third World markets. As the Japanese and Euro-peans became "the guys we'll have to fight" and identified as racist, racism became more and more "un-American." Half of these smiling and waving people would probably throw up at the idea of letting her use their shower, but being friendly costs them nothing and reminds them that they aren't European. She's heard stories that back in the old days there were refugees from Russia who lived for years on the largess of anti-communists; she suspects that her tendency to wear the green-red-black tricolor of Europe, color reversed, on her shirts and especially on the seats of her pants, is giving away her status.

She wonders if they're as polite to plain old born-here black people as they are to Afropeans.

Well, no matter—it's a beautiful day. Moreover, the diner she finds is in the real classic style, with checkerboard linoleum, a steel-and-formica counter, and nice old-style rotating Naugahyde bar stools. She follows her personal rule and orders the thing on the menu with the corniest (and therefore, to her, most American) name—the "Chili Dog Over Mac," which turns out to be a hot dog with sloppy joe sauce on a bed of macaroni and cheese.

The place is not at all crowded; there's a young family in there, one of those that seems to have a number of kids just beyond counting, all spaced about a year apart, mostly quiet and mostly behaving, but the statistical population is so large that there is always some noise and some misbehavior going on; it rises and dwindles but never falls to zero.

The father, a dark-haired young man in a white shirt, and the mother, who is alarmingly well-made-up, slim, and pretty for someone who has presumably had all those kids, are both reasonably attentive to the kids and on top of the chaos, but it's clearly a battle, and Berlina finds it fun to watch them. She stops watching the street for a while and concentrates on her own dish of strawberry ice cream and the logistics of two parents, each with a cone in one hand, managing to eat their own ice cream while constantly wiping young chins.

Once all the cones are at the point where accidents are unlikely, the family departs in a cloud of young chatter, and Berlina looks back toward the front of the restaurant only to be startled by a young woman who has sat down, quietly, at her table.

"Hi," the girl says. "Sorry to disturb you, but you're not from around here, are you?"

"Just passing through," Berlina says. It is just a tiny bit unnerving to be paid attention to in a place where she is trying not to be conspicuous.

The girl doesn't look like anything other than an ordinary college girl; she's not wearing makeup, and her dress doesn't type her as part of any campus group, except that it's fairly form-fitting and could have been in fashion any time in the last forty years. If it suggests anything, it's just a slight conservatism. The girl smiles. "No connections here?"

"None really. Are you always this inquisitive?"

"God, no, but I need a ride out of town and I'd rather not be traced. I'm not a criminal or anything. It's just that there's this guy I've been staying with, and, well . . . he's nice, but he's older, and he's kind of serious and I'm really not—"

Berlina asks the obvious question. "Is he dangerous?"

"Only if you consider getting a lot of mail and phone calls a danger. I suppose I will eventually, anyway, because he'll put out tracer letters, and who can live without logging on, these days? I just got one the other day from an old boyfriend who's still down in Mexico and rode out Clem Two there." The girl takes a sip of the soda she's holding and then says, "Listen to me chattering. This is ridiculous. It's taken me half the day to get up the nerve to ask someone for a ride. I'm no good at asking for favors."

Berlina grins at her. "Me either. If I told you I have a secret or two of my own, and I don't really want to advertise which way I passed, can you be discreet?"

"I don't sound like it, do I? But I can, really." She brushes her long brown hair away from her face, up off the front of the stretchy white dress, and Berlina sees why an older guy with money might take an interest in this girl; she's got a figure to envy, and besides the clear, bright eyes, there's an attractive set of cheekbones and full lips. "I only have three suitcases of stuff—I got here with two, god, the guy's been so generous but . . . well, if you're curious I guess I can tell you on the ride, that is if you're willing to give me a ride—"

"Anything for a lurid story," Berlina says, grinning.

"Hope it won't be a disappointment. My name's Naomi Cascade, by the way." She sticks her hand out like a man, and Berlina solemnly shakes it.

"I'll tell you mine in a bit—it's really necessary to keep it secret for a while. You haven't even asked which direction I'm going."

"Oh, there's something romantic about going 'anywhere but here,' don't you think?" Naomi says. "Besides, to go anywhere from here you take 70, and that means either over to the Co or down into the Az. Either one will suit my purposes just fine."

Berlina nods, and the deal is done. They get Naomi's three suitcases, and climb into Berlina's car. Naomi takes a seat in the back, since Berlina will be climbing back herself as soon as they are on a guidestrip, and they're off and running.

Originally Berlina had figured on backtracking at first to Denver, then heading north to take 80 over to the Ca, thus making it less likely that (if anyone managed to trace the origin of the call) the call to Harris Diem will be connected to her. But the slight compromising of her cover is enough to decide her on another course—she's going to go right down through the Az, into Sonora State, and re-enter the States through Tijuana.

Once they're rolling, she casually says to Naomi, "So, have you ever watched *Sniffings*?" and takes off her kerchief. The girl's eyes get huge, and Berlina doesn't think she's ever seen a human being look quite so impressed before. Certainly not with Berlina.

In two hours they're not just friends, but on their way to being good friends, and it's starting to occur to Berlina that she might just want to hire a personal assistant. Naomi has some stuff she left with her friends at the U of the Az, so it's sort of a logical thing to do.

Besides, this gives her a chance to duck down Utah 24, past Goblin Valley, and weave around through some desert and national forest, confusing her track further. The two of them sit back to share a couple of large lemonades, watch the land roll by, and work on becoming better friends.

On the twenty-ninth of July, Louie Tynan gets a sixteen-terabyte message from Carla; it's her summary of what happened in Dhaka when the ongoing fighting in the aftermath of Global Riot Two was overtaken by the Bay of Bengal storm surge. He finds that he literally can't get it out of his mind; as he catches package after package shot from the moon (they are coming faster now, and with less space between, and the train has grown to seventy-eight packages, with *Good Luck* still at the rear) he keeps finding that the images of a quarter of a billion corpses washed into the ocean . . . and of the hideous things that happened before . . . and yet, again, of the courage and faith of so many. . . .

He finds it pulls him apart; when he checks his body, he discovers that it is retching and sick with the feeling.

There will be more Bay of Bengals. The great storm surges will hit, here and there. And though the loss of Bangladesh, much of Burma, and West Bengal, surely produced about as big a loss of human life as can be managed in a single blow, Louie knows—better than anyone, because he can experience more than anyone—what the loss of even one life is. And his imagination is equally good for very large numbers.

The horror of it will not leave him.

He hates being in his body more than ever, when he finally must. There is so much to do, and here he is spending his time being too slow and stupid to be of any use to anyone. He does pullups and pedals a stationary bicycle, so that he can have muscle tissue, but his collectors and reactors are supplying the energy of a small atom bomb every second or so. He plays one-man racquetball to maintain his eye-hand coordination when his reaction time as a human being is three million times what it is as a spaceship. He crams organic material through his guts to oxidize it for energy when his solar cells, He-3 fusion plants, and fast fission reactors provide him many billions of times the energy. Hell, even the direct physical sensation of yanking his dong pales beside the physical sensations Carla sends to him and he adds to, in which they both experience sex with both complete minds and bodies.

In his virtual self, if he wishes, he can sit down to a fine meal in front of a warm fireplace, comfortably naked on a chair that fits him perfectly, served by spectacularly beautiful, eager, willing women. Out here, alone in his body, he can open a pouch of banana pellets or dried meat in this little metal can he lives in, where the smell of machine oil, leftover Louie, and the toilet compete with each other, on a flat seat that is comfortable only because he weighs less than a pound on it.

He is aware of what all the Freudians, Tantrics, hedonists, and *sensei* would tell him about hating his body. But he doesn't hate physical experience. He hates *limited* physical experience, he hates being a *cripple*, he hates knowing how much more he could be by just plugging back in. . . .

And, damn it, this bag of meat and guts is the weak link, anyway.

The thought seems to make him dizzy because it is so stunningly obvious.

He has been steadily shoring up and strengthening the ship for the last several days; robots crawling all along the immense coils from unit to unit have been fixing the occasional structure that gives way under the strain of the huge momentum changes, or sometimes replacing a small piece that drops off entirely.

But for about the last eighteen hours he hasn't repaired or shored up anything; there's no point. He got done. Nothing more is going to break. Everything else is able to resist ten times—a whole order of magnitude— the jerk that his body can endure, and since jerk must be held well under that level, there has been no reinforcing to do.

This body in which he sits is the weak link.

Another thought occurs to him; there must be some reason why he didn't think of this sooner.

But there is an answer. His "other self," the "real self" he merges with again whenever he puts on the scalpnet, goggles, and muffs, is much bigger than he is, and it can choose what to download and what not . . . undoubtedly that other, bigger Louie that he just wants to merge back into right now would be perfectly capable of thinking of this—but not of suggesting it. And that's got to be a pretty good indicator.

He sits down and laboriously types a letter to himself; it's short and to the point. There's no benefit in the body anymore; if Louie-the-ship cranks up the power on the catching coils, he can get a lot more momentum out of every shot coming through and his acceleration will be higher now, while he needs it most. He can get to 2026RU months ahead of schedule.

There is one Louie-the-body and he doesn't even like being Louie-the-body. There are nine billion people on Earth right now, and at least two-thirds of them live where superstorms can get them.

Sacrifice me, he writes. *Be honest. I am just a small, ineffective processor that runs on too fragile a platform. Throw me away and go save humanity. I know you won't feel good about it, Louie, but buddy, we both know it's the thing you have to do.*

The keyboard on which he is typing is "local"—it doesn't communicate with any system bigger than itself—and that way he can send the message all at once before Louie can argue with him.

He thinks for a moment, and feeling silly—who else could this be coming from? but letters should be *signed*—he adds: *Louie Tynan*. Then he thinks for a moment and realizes that the only way to make sure Louie-the-ship does it is to order him, and adds,

That's an order.

Regards,

Col. Louis Tynan, Expedition Commander.

He reads through it once more to think about how Louie-the-ship is apt to take this, tries to imagine himself in that situation, and feels like a complete fool, but changes "*Regards*" to "*My love always*." It feels better, so he hits the key to send it before he can get cold feet.

He's riding on his exercise bike and thinking about getting a cold drink of water when his own voice says, "Louie?"

"Yeah?"

"We have to talk about it, you know."

"Naw. We don't. Look, you're figuring that I won't plug back in on schedule, and you're right. There's no reason to include the physical pain I'm going to experience, or the sensation of committing suicide, into your personality, you know. It's the kind of thing nobody wants to remember, and this way you won't have to. What I'm going to do is get good and drunk just before the next package arrives—we've got about a fifth left from Dr. Esaun's old private store—and then climb up to the top of the main passageway. Anything up there that's unsecured will get thrown all the way to the bottom, *muy pronto*. There's a nice heavy steel bulkhead, and though I can't figure it quite so exactly as you can, if you go for a ninety percent instead of a twenty percent momentum capture, I figure I'll hit it at about two hundred miles an hour, headfirst. The pain is going to be momentary."

"With the much larger capacity mental capacity in here, the pain can be erased entirely. And besides, you know, the memory of pain is nothing; no one can make himself even slightly uncomfortable with even the most excruciating memories."

He pushes the bicycle harder and says, "It just seems sort of fair to this body. I mean, this body has been me for so long, and now that the ship and the moon complex and all are me . . . well, I guess I just feel like a part is entitled to die conscious."

"But you're planning to drug yourself—"

"Maybe *barely* conscious. If I don't want *you* to have the pain, imagine how *I* feel about it."

The mechanical voice, so like his own that even Louie can't tell the difference, laughs. "There's one little problem. You made that decision to die for the whole human race. That's something I'd like to have in my memories. Could you put on the scalpnet and jack for another moment, just long enough for me to copy the new memories? Leave the goggles and muffs off if you don't trust me—that way, if you have to, you can just focus on the information coming in through your senses and pull out enough concentration to take off the scalpnet."

It's a reasonable request; Louie admits, on reflection, that something has indeed changed inside him with his decision to sacrifice himself for the sake of the mission. "Okay," he says, and feels silly since by the time he spoke, Louie-the-ship probably knew from the direction he turned, or some little indicator invisible to Louie-the-body.

The funny thing is, he realizes as he reaches for the scalpnet, that he really feels like he is "Louie himself" even though he knows how much more capability and how much remembered experience Louie-the-ship has. He wonders if that is how Louie-the-ship, or for that matter Louie-on-the-moon or the wiseguys feel . . . or do they feel he is the one who is more real? He'll have to ask while he's connected—

He pulls on the scalpnet and snugs it down, its microfibers sliding around his hair to get firm contact with his skin, inducers targeting so that their millions of tiny pulses from all quarters of his brain every second can find the right axons to create the fake pulses in. Then he inserts the jack that will allow his mind and memories to be read by the machine.

His eyelids slam shut, so hard that his cheek muscles scream with pain.

There is a moment of hard motion, something in his muscles he doesn't quite identify, and then his arms swinging with their full force bring his cupped hands up to burst his eardrums.

The pain and shock are incredible, and he reaches for the pain to give himself something to cling to, something that doesn't come out of the machine, so that he can find the will and motor control to tear the scalpnet off—

The pain stops, abruptly, cut off like a light switch. His arms hang limp. He feels his memories going out through the jack and he rages against Louie-the-ship, furious at the betrayal, furious that he will have to die all the same (for he can't believe Louie will let billions die to save this one old carcass) but robbed of all dignity and not trusted to do it well—

He screams in frustration, and the sensation in his throat helps him again, but before he can even reach for control of his arms, his windpipe shuts all the way. The blood thunders in his veins, he reaches for that, for his pulse and the sense of pressure, anything to free him from—

His heart stops. His carotids contract.

There's music, and he finds himself moving forward in a long dark tunnel, almost laughing because it is so much what they have told him it will be like, and sure enough his mother and father, who he hasn't thought of five times in ten years, are there to greet him, and—

He wakes up. He's in the machine; Louie-the-body and Louie-the-ship are one and the same, and instantly he understands that Louie-the-ship accepted the necessity but didn't want to lose any of himself; he finds himself on both sides of the decision, matches them up instant by instant, accepts himself, ceases to feel like two, except, only, that he looks through the camera and sees his body lying dead on the deck, the sanitation robots about to close in and move it down to the freezer. This gives him an oddly split sensation, one part of him recalling having died in that body, the other part remembering killing it.

But stranger still is his realization that when he re-merged into the intelligence in the ship—when he fully became the "real" Louie Tynan—as he was yanked away from the light, and from Mom and Dad (Dad was just about to say something, and was smiling in a way he rarely did when he was alive) . . .

. . . there was a tiny bit of time left before the body died, and there was still a Louie in that body. So he did kill himself . . . and if he ever had a soul, it's gone to heaven or hell now. Did he get another one by surviving? Is he truly soulless now?

It's the kind of thing that he can think about, now, forever.

He hallucinates a warm South Pacific beach from before, and turns to Carla's latest message to reread it again. They spend a month sailing along the Solomons; they laugh and talk a lot, and communicate better than they ever really did.

He doesn't know whether he still has a soul, but he's quite sure he can still feel love—and that's more than good enough for a practical man, anyway. Four minutes—a bit over twenty-two brain-years—after the death of his body, he has made as much philosophic peace as he figures he'll ever need with the idea.

John Klieg is feeling pretty cheerful; it's hard to feel any other way when you've got four sets of mortal enemies on Earth and right now all of them are on a collision course with each other. He doesn't think his call to Berlina leaked, but if it did, that's all right too. The important thing is to get the Abdulkashim escape attempt blown, and to have the conspirators know that it's blown; if his own sources don't show a change of plans in the next few days, he's got a couple of tricks in mind to call it to their attention.

Just now, about the only perk left to him are his hundred news screens, so he's actually trying to watch all of them, just to see what that's like. Derry is sitting beside him on the couch, quietly drawing horses—about the only thing you can say for this grimy, muddy frontier burg is that there's plenty of opportunity for a horse-crazy kid. Glinda is catching yet another nap; she hasn't been very much herself this last week, which he can well understand. Ordinary business competition is one thing and assassination and coup quite another. Klieg himself is surprised at how well he has taken to it.

He still doesn't have a good backchannel into the States anywhere; he kicks himself daily for not having established one before he got here, but after all it was the first time he ventured out into the real sticks of the globe.

The screens are showing Clem's granddaughters ravaging Europe, and Klieg is finding that kind of interesting. Americans don't see much footage of Europe anymore, partly because of the refugee lobby—two million

Afropeans, plus about a million of various Euro refugees, will light up the switchboards if there's any favorable or even neutral coverage of any event in Europe. And in the last twelve years a lot of Americans have picked up the same prejudices.

Right now, though, mostly you're seeing the same old stuff—ocean-going ships driven up onto the shores, buildings you remember from postcards and calendars swaying and falling, that sort of thing. Half a dozen hurricanes and big storms have drenched the Mediterranean basin in so much water that the Med is filling up way above historic levels, and between the organic silt washing in, the dilution of the salt, and the dark-ness, most of what used to live in it is dying. The smell is said to be indescribable, which is one reason why Klieg won't experience it on XV. The other reason, of course, is that even though it's all very touching and a lot of history is drowning, Klieg is a people-now kind of person—and refugees from floods are pretty much alike everywhere. Lots of parades of crying kids, coughing old people who might not make it, people with a wiped-out look because everything is gone. The first time you see it, it's moving. The hundredth time, it just doesn't matter.

They've all seen, on the television, and on the pub's two XV sets, what happened to Hawaii. The village has no particular hope, for it's about to get the same treatment, and there's talk that the storm surge might wash right over all of Ireland. Thus they gather in the church with Father Joseph, not because they think it is safer, or that anything better is going to happen, or even because the church has a slightly better roof (though it does), but because it seems a fit place to wait to die.

The last ones come in from the pitch-black night, a night so dark that the lightning flashes make it glow but do not allow anyone to see. The roads are said to be hopelessly muddy, but no one much wanted to try them anyway. If you must drown, might as well do it in County Clare; if you must live, might as well ride it out in a dry church on a hill.

Somewhere far to the west is Clem 238, throwing out the great storm surges that the government radar spotted hours ago.

There are plenty of candles, so Father Joseph has them light a few and encourages people to sing, over the sound of a few men boarding the stained glass windows on the inside (Father Joseph himself did the outsides hours ago).

He wishes, as priest to these people, that he were a profound man. Mostly he just handles the baptizing, marrying, and burying, and occasion-ally tries to persuade someone to do what is right. This is not a job for Father Joseph.

If, however, it's a job for God Himself, then common sense says to ask Him. He leads more prayers. People drowse, but the priest hasn't the heart to wake them.

The clock says it should have been dawn, but no dawn comes, not even as a crack of light in the great doors. The church smells of too many people and wet clothing.

Michael Dwyer volunteers to try using the big searchlight on his lorry—his "rig" he calls it since he listens to so much American music—and at least see what can be seen in the valley.

The church is now on an island, and the water is rising. Michael and Joseph discuss it very briefly. "I'd appreciate it if you'd not tell them."

"Wouldn't think of it, Father. Let'em not fear until the time to fear."

They go back in, soaked to the skin and freezing cold, to tell everyone that it was too dark.

The next time, some hours later after their clothes have dried enough to be put back on, they need speak no words to each other. The water is higher, and it flows opposite the direction of the streams that once ran through the valley. On a whim, Michael climbs down to dip his hand in, and comes back saying "I tasted salt, Father. The ocean's coming in."

Half a day more passes by the clock; strange to think this is coming from a hurricane, and yet there's only the wind from a bad storm, no more. The battery wireless says 238 will miss Ireland entirely, that it has turned away and headed north to die.

By the clock, the water rises for twelve more hours; the last time Michael and Father Joseph check, they cannot get to Michael's truck, and they are afraid that the people inside may hear the rushing water. It's now been two days with only the food people brought.

When dawn comes next, there is light. Father Joseph goes outside, to find that the rain is spitting and spraying from high clouds, and the water is well down the hill again. While he watches, a patch of blue forms overhead.

Michael comes up behind him. "They are saying on the wireless that the sea has forced its way right up the Shannon to Lough Derg, Father, and so much has washed away that they think it'll be that way for good now; we've got an inner sea in Ireland."

Joseph nods, and then points. Something soggy and wet flops miserably out of the sky in a great flutter of wings. They walk up to it; the bird is exhausted and so helpless that it cannot escape them. The priest picks it up. "Now, it would be a dove, wouldn't it?" he says.

Later that afternoon, the whistlers arrive with emergency rations. After the "miracle" of the church on the hill, no one can be persuaded to leave, no matter what the government man says.

*   *   *

Klieg is fascinated with another daughter of Clem—Clem 239. Barely maintaining its status as a hurricane, 239 managed to round Scotland and is now in the North Sea, its eye just 200 km due west of the Skaggerak. Storm surges are crashing into Denmark, and there's some interesting footage of farmhouses and barns, and sometimes herds of cattle, swept over by the towering waves; winds are at 70 km/hr, Beaufort 12, the low end of hurricane force, in Denmark. They are expected to pick up.

Clem 239 has been sitting still for about eight hours, and it's the one that Klieg is interested in. He's got a bet down on it, you might say. And from his standpoint, the little jig the huge hurricane has been doing in the North Sea hundreds of miles from where there's ever been one before, has been just about perfect.

Figure by highjump from Novokuznetsk it's about an hour and a half to Stockholm . . . but there's no regularly scheduled service. Probably they'd jump into Warsaw or Frankfurt and then take ziplines from there . . . unless the Baltic gets too rough too fast.

He's been accessing zipline and highjump timetables all over the place, and he thinks it all works out. The question now, really, is whether the local goons have been smart enough to do the same. Klieg devoutly hopes so; the trouble with stupid people, he has explained more than once to Glinda, is not that they consistently do dumb things, which you could plan for, but that they do smart things unpredictably.

Nothing yet; there it sits, 200 km west of the Skaggerak, pumping huge waves out. It's incidentally making Klieg rich all over again, because Klieg's meteorologists had guessed right about the real odds of one of the superhurricanes rounding Scotland, and what preconditions would allow it to happen. Sure enough, they did . . . and Klieg shorted the living daylights out of Royal Dutch Shell, two days before everyone else began selling it.

The best guess is that the dikes might have another nine hours; transport is beginning to snarl hopelessly as the people with lower priorities begin either to bribe their way onto transportation or to do things that are illegal.

It's not that people don't like the Dutch, as such. Many of them might be willing enough to have a Dutchman or two live down the block for a few weeks, if that would help, Horst is thinking. But there are just practical matters to be considered, and that's that. He hopes the captain won't have to give the order, but he'll carry it out if he has to.

It makes Will feel a little funny. He went over on that ferry several times, for football matches, and sometimes just with friends for some drinking and whoring. He was there on leave just last year. Now he sits here in his staticopter, taking a radar sight on the ferry. Loaded with Dutchmen and Belgians, and the poor old UK is in a bad enough way. Sure, those folks in Brussels say we have to take them, don't they? Well, look where Brussels is. What a coincidence. . . . Still, probably kids on that thing. And women. Seems a shame. He waits for his orders.

Paul-Luc sits at his post and waits; he and his mates have been having a fine time with the Belgian girls. They've got a rumor over on the other side that if you do what the French soldiers like over here, they'll smuggle you out somehow. Paul-Luc, Jean, and Marc have been accepting the favors, leading the girls into the woods, and then giving them the garrotte. It's like XV but better.

Marc has been looking a bit ill, though . . . and Paul-Luc and Jean have been considering that perhaps it isn't just the girls who need to be shut up.

If it's the end of the world, you might as well enjoy it, right?

Right, Will thinks, and the missile heads out for the crowded ferry—thank god it's over the horizon, and dark, and he will never see the flames or bodies.

Right, thinks Horst, and to his own surprise, throws down his rifle and walks away. It doesn't matter much when they arrest him. Any fool can see no one is going anywhere.

Klieg shrugs and opens up another American beer. Three of these things in a day is about his limit. He wonders if there is some requirement that you have to be an idiot to be a politician. Half a generation ago the Europeans solved their unification difficulties by ganging up to hate anyone who wasn't white enough for them. They were at least as stupid as Hitler was about the Jews, in Klieg's opinion. GateTech has a minimum of a hundred solid, capable Afropean employees.

He looks at the scenes from Europe, remembers how pleasant the places are, but can't work up much in the way of tears. Twenty years ago the Afropeans were supposed to be the impossible barrier to European unification, then five years after that it was Turks and Serbs, and now the typical German figures it's the French, Poles, and Italians—if not the Bavarians.

So now when they need to hang together, they're tearing each other apart.

One screen captures a scene from Copenhagen; he zooms in on it and cues up sound. A mixed group of German and Polish powerboaters have waded ashore and started killing women and girls, concentrating on blondes. Usually they force them to undress at gunpoint, shoot them in the belly, and film their death throes. No one knows why.

Troops are being diverted from evacuation points, and traffic snarls caused by panic are further reducing the number of Danes expected to escape from the city.

Klieg thinks, realizes that he does remember the names of four German companies that deal in deathporn, picks up the phone, and places stock orders, investing in all four. Odds are overwhelming that that is what this is; somebody is paying good money to see pretty women, particularly blondes, die in agony.

He shudders, when he thinks of Glinda and of Derry, but he leaves the order in place. He's going to need cash one way or another. As an after-thought, he starts moving his CD accounts to banks in the inland United States.

An hour later, Clem 239 starts its move toward the Baltic. John Klieg tells Derry to get him his packed bag and go stay with her mother in the bedroom. No sense taking any chances.

Derry does what she's told and doesn't ask him what it's about. He uses the last few minutes to send a short order about household maintenance to his housekeeping staff, something he does every night before getting to bed.

This time, though, a special arrangement of keywords puts a whole chain of other events into motion; artificial intelligences begin calling government and media offices, make their mechanical announcements without listening, repeat the process over and over.

The knock on his door is surprisingly polite when it comes. The two men there for him are dapper, polished sorts, and they accept his explanation of a pre-packed bag "for these uncertain times, you know" at face value. They don't even handcuff him, just drive him direct to the Government Center.

He was expecting the governing council; what he wasn't expecting was that Abdulkashim would be already addressing them via phone. But there he is, much larger than life, his famous resemblance to Stalin a little more pointed than usual because he's in the prison uniform. Abdulkashim speaks in Russian, still the Siberian lingua franca, but Klieg discovers his headset has settings for English, German, Japanese, Spanish, Chinese, Arabic, Yakut, Buryat, and several of the local tribal languages. Klieg knows what's about to be said, of course, in outline if not exactly, so he idly considers listening to the speech in some language he's never heard before. The only thing that stops him is that he has to keep track for the sake of timing.

"Gentlemen of the governing council, distinguished foreign visitors, and foreign leaders, my greetings to you. As you have no doubt already realized, a short while ago loyal units of the Siberian Army and Air Force extricated me from the prison where I was being illegally held. It is a supremely pleasant irony to me that my release from the UN political prison at Stockholm was effected under cover of one of the many hurricanes spawned by the UN's completely illegal, brutal, unwarranted, and environmentally dangerous attack on our armed forces on March ninth of this year.

"I trust my Siberian people have now seen that I was right to warn them against the perfidy of foreign powers and of the United Nations in particular. But I trust they will also see the wisdom in our opening the doors of our nation to foreign commerce, for despite our differences with the United States, it is an American citizen, Mr. John Klieg, who tonight has made it possible for us to assert the independence that is rightfully ours. As of tonight, Siberia is the only nation on Earth that can put a payload into orbit from the Earth's surface, and we are prepared to put this capability at the service of the peoples of the Earth. Siberian genius, as you might well have guessed—"

There isn't one Siberian on the development team, Klieg thinks. One more little thing to think while the Great Man rambles on. . . .

"—has invented the means to put an end to the dreadful scourge of superhurricanes, and we are prepared to act immediately if our reasonable demands, too long denied in the international courts of law, are met. Once our rightful territorial claims have been acknowledged, and suitable indentures paid by nations whose names we will be releasing shortly, we will act at once to end the hurricanes."

Klieg sits and looks attentive, a skill that he picked up during his days in sales. He suspects there's not a businessman on Earth, certainly not a successful one, who can't do this when need be. Of course it will be the better part of a year before enough balloons can be launched to make a difference. He wonders if Abdulkashim does not know that, or if he knows but doesn't care. It doesn't make any real difference. Abdulkashim is getting down to threats.

"You should know that our forces have surrounded the launch facility and it cannot be seized by any other force of any size before we can destroy it. As a developing nation we claim the right—"

Someone off camera shouts. The dictator's eyes grow wide; he turns to say something. Then the picture lurches, hard, and the signal goes dead.

Klieg guessed right; this is the cue. From half a dozen concealed places in the room, the "moderates" of the governing council—all the people who had some sort of power base and were not obviously anti-Abdulkashim—are pulling out lengths of iron pipe.

Klieg manages not to look, much.

There are four Abdulkashim loyalists in the room, and there are three moderates, and one length of iron pipe for each one. Roles seem to have been apportioned early, or at least the biggest one always holds the legs, the smallest pins down the wrists, and the third one wields the pipe.

The Abdulkashimists scream and struggle, but the real effect is nil. Whenever one of them manages to pull an arm or leg away, the man with the pipe bashes it.

When at last they are held down and spread-eagled, the Minister for Justice declares them all to be criminals against the legitimate order of the Siberian people, and the Special Minister for Mines, the Director of Academic Research, the Minister of Public Health, and the Minister of Surface Transportation begin to use their pipes in earnest. On the three male Abdulkashimists, none of them can resist crushing the testicles first before brutally pounding on the head, nor do they stop beating when the man is unconscious or dead.

The pipe is too large to go into the Abdulkashimist woman, but it's heavy enough to bruise her or break the pubic bone, and the Director of Academic Research slams it across her breasts as well, twice, before he caves in her head at a single stroke, like a watermelon hurled to the sidewalk.

Assuming he gets out of here alive, John Klieg's score is even. Besides, if he can live through the next fifteen minutes, he's rich. He starts to move, very slowly, toward a side door, keeping his head down low.

That's when the door bursts in, and troops fill the room. It's some colonel Klieg has never heard of, who has decided to take over from all the involved factions, for the good of the nation. Among his first actions is to abolish capitalism, and to arrest Siberia's most notorious capitalist.

Just as John Klieg is being led off in handcuffs for the second time, Louie Tynan is about to try a different kind of catch. When the package arrives, he brakes it so hard that he captures it.

The robots strip it for its precious cargo of processors. He's going to need lots of them.

He pulls other raw materials from the package, feeds them to his synthesizers, and then takes the leftover six tons of iron and miscellaneous metal and shapes it into a fine dust, blowing it out the back, the eddy currents induced by the coil strong enough to heat the iron instantly to plasma. He expels it as atoms moving at almost a tenth of the speed of light. It's a nice hard boost—twenty-three g's would have turned the old body to jelly—and every bit counts now.

Two days later, weeks ahead of schedule, he begins to overtake the forward packages in the train. Back at the moon and ahead on the asteroids, the other Louie and the wiseguys rush to lengthen their catapults and to add laser boost so that they can continue to accelerate packages beyond the end of the catapult; it's going to be a lot harder to catch him with a package, and he needs packages. Between stripped components and his own integration, he is now running at seven brain-years per minute.

"I'd say the results were completely satisfactory," Harris Diem says, but Brittany Lynn Hardshaw is having none of it.

Nor is her old friend and most trusted advisor going to back down. It's later in the day Abdulkashim was shot down and the countercoup erupted in Novokuznetsk, and media reaction is dribbling in. Everyone has assumed, quite rightly, that the USA was behind the shoot-down—who else had a body in low Earth orbit that could be deflected precisely enough to hit the aircraft carrying Abdulkashim?—and that people high in the Siberian government knew about it in advance and used the shoot-down to signal the start of their coup.

Harris Diem is pleased no end. At one stroke, they have plunged the Siberian government into the hands of greedy, tin-pot types who have neither Abdulkashim's ability nor his charisma; thus there is no more real threat in Siberia for at least a political generation. Alaska is secure, both from Siberian aggression and from being lured into a Siberian alliance; as long as the Hardshaw Doctrine, that no formerly American territory will ever be permitted alliance with an Asian or European power, holds, Alaska will remain American for all practical purposes, whatever its official status.

Moreover, because the intervention was specifically an American military one, not at the request of the UN (the price Diem extracted from Rivera, in exchange for doing the deed, was that it be neither sanctioned nor condemned by the UN) a precedent has been established for unilateral American action, another extension on the principle established by Louie Tynan's mission. First, joint orders, so that Colonel Tynan could claim to be following his American commander's; now unilateral action and no comment from the SecGen. Bit by bit, piece by piece, the sovereignty lost in the years after the Flash is being pulled back into place, and if Clem and its spawn are the price that has to be paid for that, to Harris Diem, who has given his life to building the strength of whatever organization Brittany Lynn Hardshaw headed, from the Shoshone County Prosecutor's Office to the USA, the price is well worth it.

His boss is less pleased. "In the first place, Harris, if you haven't noticed, we are still losing lives worldwide at rates in excess of a million a week to the superhurricanes and their aftereffects. That number will climb this winter when famine and disease set in as well. And although we got Abdulkashim's paws off GateTech's launch facility, it's still being held by Siberian military and it clearly was damaged in the fighting—and we can't even get engineers out there on the job to find out *how* damaged. Now we're totally dependent on Louie Tynan."

"Nothing wrong with that, he's a good man."

"There's *everything* wrong with having to bet the future of the planet on one man, no matter how smart he is or what capabilities he's added to himself!"

When Diem leaves the Oval Office, he's shaking his head. It's a shame to see the boss going soft after all these years; maybe real power politics have no appeal to her anymore. Maybe she's gotten that strange disease of wanting to leave a significant mark on history. That's been known to happen to presidents in the past, and on rare occasions has even done the Republic a little good.

Anyway, she was still her old self in one regard, and moreover she's right about the issue she raised. Influence needs to be exerted toward getting Klieg out of jail in Novokuznetsk; it's pretty obvious to everyone that he was Hardshaw and Rivera's inside man and tipped them off to everything as it broke. He isn't safe in that jail in that country, and it wouldn't look good for anything to happen to him—in this game if you want to have any friends, you've got to protect the ones you have.

Carla Tynan doesn't know at first what is different when she gets the message from Louie. It's a long one, and it's full of memories, sweet and bittersweet, warm and detached, funny and dark. It's the most beautiful love letter anyone ever sent to anyone, as far as she's concerned, and yet it's clearly just a preamble.

Then she finds out what he's done; that that beautiful letter came to her from a dead man.

She thinks of her own warm, carefully exercised body, live and healthy here in its hotel bed on Guadalcanal, and that there will never be a Louie Tynan to touch and hold her again. She recalls the feel of his right arm cocked over her thigh when he lifted her on one shoulder, to prove he could do it, on their first date. She remembers his warm breath against her neck when he would fall asleep and slowly creep over until he was using her as his pillow. She thinks of the scratchy feel of his crew cut under her hand.

It annoys hell out of her because she knows him well enough to know he'd expect this, but she also thinks of the feel of his stiff cock between her lips, of his fingers probing her anus. . . .

All gone. No more. He decided what he was doing was more important, supposedly. But Louie had been neglecting his beautiful, beautiful body for a long time. Even before he began to be telepresent on the moon, well before he started building additional processors to run on. And that body was, to Carla, so much her link to him; she can't imagine Louie without his body. She's stuck with a grief that races through a billion processors around the globe.

It hurts more because his message is so detailed and clear that she is quite certain he is sincere.

The only part missing is the most important—that although it had to be, that it was necessary, he himself is not grieved by the loss of his body, nor did he even think of how she might feel. He may know she loves him but it's clear that after all these years he doesn't really understand how or why she does.

And that hurts terribly.

For the first time since he left, she lets twenty-four hours go by, and then more, without answering his messages; she even leaves his messages untouched on processors he controls so that he can see she hasn't read them. She makes it clear in a thousand ways that she is just too busy to be bothered and that, after all, their relationship is supposed to be strictly business, now isn't it?

If nothing else, she can make him regret not having a hand to hold roses in, feet to stand on her porch with, or a head to hang in embarrassment.

For most of his life, Jopharma has picked coffee, and most of the time on just these few mountains in central Sumatra. Once, when there was a big bonus, he went over to Celebes to work for a while, and sent money home for his mother to save up so he could get married, but now that he has a wife, he has no reason to go elsewhere. He knows about Clem, of course, because everyone talks about it. But since there is nothing for him, or anyone he knows, to do about it, he just kept picking coffee, until early this year.

Now the situation is getting desperate. The heavy cloud cover and rain have spoiled the crop, and there is nothing to pick. At least, up this high, they will not drown like the poor souls down below, but still . . . the unending clouds are something he has never seen before. It has been getting steadily colder too, and though a fire at night has always been pleasant, now it is necessary to have one all the time. Wood costs something too, and the landlord is not about to forgo rent merely because the world is ending.

For a while, the man down the road, who had a TV, would announce which Clem these clouds were part of, but since it never clears—the man said that the weather scientists on TV are claiming that the islands trap the foul weather, or some silly thing like that—the question ceased to be interesting.

Jophama has not been to many places, but like most men, he has seen some XV and a great deal of television. He knows a bit of the world. Thus it is not with complete surprise or shock that he looks out the door and sees snow falling. It is only with a sinking heart.

With one thing and another, since she's been unplugged for so long, it takes them a good part of the afternoon to get Mary Ann transmitting satisfactorily. It's really a pretty remarkable piece of fieldwork, considering they do it while the truck is rolling. At her insistence, Jesse is there holding her hand the whole time—not really because she's nervous, though she pretends to be, but because she figures he'll appreciate a chance to ride all day in air conditioning.

It's interesting too because he's done so much work on various direct brain interface systems as part of his Realization Engineering curriculum. There, of course, the emphasis is on getting a working interface between mind and simulator, so that the mind can play, try things out, see what they're like—expensive, by the standards of old-time engineers, but worth it because of the chance to get the exact right product.

Here the idea is clarity rather than accuracy in the interface. That is, it doesn't matter nearly so much whether they are getting exactly what Mary Ann—or Synthi Venture—is feeling as it does that what they get be clear, that it feels real rather than like a dream or an animation. Verisimilitude matters more than verity, Jesse thinks to himself.

Just at the moment, they're monkeying around with the part of her brain that gets active when she sings. One of the outputs they're getting is nausea, and that's probably a matter of a couple little folds on a pea-sized lump that happens to be in that area; they stimulate those, identify it, modify the pickup, try again.

It's a very long day, and at the end of it, they tell Mary Ann that part of the problem is "you went and took a real vacation," as one of the doctors puts it.

"That's a crime?"

"Well, usually they won't put you in jail for it, but it's a different thing from what most people in your line of work do. If you'd just gone to the same kind of resort you're always going to for work, gone mostly incognito to lower the stress, and spent all your time drunk on fruit punch drinks by the pool, other than killing the occasional neuron, you'd have changed nothing about your basic brain structure. It would all be there pretty much the way the machine left it before you went off on your vacation. But you went and did something new and different, and when the brain learns its structure changes. The big things are still in the same place but everything's in slightly different shapes. Probably some people out there will get the idea that you're not the real Synthi Venture—whenever somebody comes back from a real vacation, that always happens."

"Is that why Rock is always the focus for the conspiracy nuts?"

"Yep. That guy does something new every time off. Fine structure of his brain looks like the coast of Norway. Where poor old Quaz—well, he was a nice guy but he didn't really need three convolutions to rub his brain cells together in."

" 'Poor old Quaz'? What happened?"

She hasn't heard, and when he tells her she bursts into tears. "I didn't even like him much, but since I never really knew him . . ." She clutches Jesse's hand tight.

The doctor nods. "See? And on top of everything else, you've gone and developed a heart."

That night, when they make love, Jesse thinks about the idea of a million girls his own age, all over the world, tuned in to Synthi Venture and feeling what he's doing. It's terrific; he decides there's nothing to worry about.

Except, of course, that just before he falls asleep, he thinks of thousands of wrinkled old grandmothers—and grandfathers—also tuned in to Synthi Venture. . . .

Mary Ann feels him tense and asks him what the matter is, rolling over to rest a hand on his chest. He tells her, and now that he's awake and telling her, they lie cuddling and giggling for a while.

"So have you decided?" he asks. "They left it up to you."

"Yep. I'm definitely doing this from now on as Mary Ann, though of course they'll cross-promote until the public gets the idea firmly in mind that Synthi and Mary Ann are the same person. But my feeling is that the artificial persona was just naturally a focus for trouble. Figure that when they put in a somebody-that-isn't-you, if you have one drop of healthy self-preservation, what you're going to let that personality have is all the bad parts. That's part of why most of the people in the business are either strung out or assholes."

"Makes sense to me," he says.

"Of course," she says, "if every so often your adolescent immature side just wants to bone hell out of Synthi Venture, my middle-aged horny side might find a way to enjoy it."

"It sounds like something worth trying," Jesse says, so they do. Mary Ann draws a deep breath, her eyes unfocus, and he realizes that now she is Synthi Venture. He takes her in his arms, and then it's all wild energy and screaming for the next half hour.

Jesse tells her afterward that Mary Ann is a better lay, though Synthi is a nice change of pace, and that seems to be the right thing to say.

Next morning Jesse finds himself in the middle of what really ought to be a surrealistic dream. It's a story conference for Passionet, with all the usual attendees, and that alone is something he'd never have expected to attend, but add to it two big-name professors of semiotics, a noted director of rock concerts, and two quiet guys in suits (one from the White House and one from the UN), plus "Synthi's Representative Friends," as one of the consultants keeps calling them, while talking about them as if they are not there. The "SRF's" are just Jesse and the Herreras, but he and Tomás have already spent a coffee break arguing about whether the T-shirts should read "SRFs: Because the time to represent Synthi's friends is NOW" or "SRFs World Tour 2028."

Two of the writers seemed to think the idea was "fun—something we can use a little later on. Keep that one, guys, we've got it marked as yours, there'll be some cash if we use it."

"How much do you suppose they mean?" Tomás whispers to Jesse. "And are they really that desperate for ideas?"

"Well, I'd guess enough to buy some beer," Jesse says, a little awkwardly because as the *norteamericano* he should be the expert and he doesn't have any more idea than Tomás does. "And as for desperate for ideas—have you *seen* XV?"

Tomás stares at him, nods as if he's just heard something very shrewd, and claps him on the back.

The conference lasts a long time, and Jesse has a feeling that his old instructors from the required course in Interdisciplinary Communication were really understanding it when they constantly claimed that people in different fields never really hear each other. The government guys seem to think that all they have to do is give Mary Ann and the writers a list of ideas that will then be programmed into the waiting heads of all the experiencers out there, more or less like the anti-drug messages in the old sitcoms. The university semiotics guys seem to be mostly arguing that no matter what is presented, people will reinterpret it into the same old thing. The writers seem to be obsessed with coming up with things to "substitute for the violence so that it will have some story values." Passionet execs appear to be trying to arrive at any solution that won't cause anyone to get up and walk out.

After a long hour of everyone repeating themselves, Mary Ann says, "If you all will allow me, there's something I wish you'd notice."

They all nod at her, and she says, "Maybe the problem here is that you're assuming that the material isn't interesting. I mean, I think what I've lived through in the last few weeks, and what's going on now, is a *lot* more interesting than what's usually on XV."

There's a very long pause, and then one of the execs says, "Tell us about it."

Mary Ann grins at him. "I can do better than that. If everyone would please put on a scalpnet, I could show you exactly what I feel about it all. I mean, that *is* the medium we will be using, right?"

There's a long pause, and then everyone is nodding. Because these things come up routinely in these meetings, Jesse supposes, there's a box of scalpnets, goggles, and muffs at hand; it just takes a moment for him to see that the Herreras can get into theirs comfortably, then slip his own on.

He has not been inside Mary Ann's mind since getting to know her—indeed, he really hasn't been inside Mary Ann's mind at all, it's always been Synthi Venture before. It's a strange sensation, for at the moment she's just waiting for everyone to get ready, so he sees the same room he is in, but from her point of view. Jesse is suddenly aware of half a dozen things—the way the metal chair presses through the too-small, too-high buttocks, the annoying pull of the huge breasts and the uncomfortably warm sweaty places under them, and that the huge pile of hair on top of her head feels like having it wrapped in a blanket.

She speaks aloud and he feels the voice forming in her throat, knows the intention an instant before the words form. "All right, everybody wave if you can hear and see through my eyes."

They all wave, a very awkward movement because it's so difficult to do it when your own body's feedback is being overridden. Jesse watches his own arm jerk up and down spasmodically but barely feels it through Mary Ann's override; the Herreras appear to be extremely startled.

"All right, now just lean back and let me look around and remember some things to you," Mary Ann says. She gets up, leaves the Passionet tent, walks past the staticopter that brought them in, and climbs a low rise to where she can see the whole column moving by. There are many thousands of people, the weaker ones on buses and trucks, a few on bicycles (private cars were impossible because gas tanker trucks couldn't have kept the column supplied over the all-but-ruined roads of the Isthmus), almost everyone else on foot. A couple of clumps of people are singing as if on their way to a picnic, some are plodding along like shell-shocked refugees, most are just walking and looking around them.

For many of the poor, this is the farthest they have ever been from home. The canteens set up for each meal are the most reliable food they've ever known; they are worried about the little homes they left behind, of course, but this is also, for them, a vacation and an adventure, and that's exciting.

Through Mary Ann's eyes, they see Tapachula—the real city, its people—walking north; they remember the warm dark nights there, the ordinary town full of ordinary people who "just" worked and raised families, the scent of dust in the streets and the blaze of the sun overhead. . . .

Her mind skips over dozens of people she knew there, shopkeepers and workmen, vegetable stall sellers and sidewalk painter, children and beggars she saw every day. She calls to mind all sorts of small memories: the especially beautiful garden of one house (she never saw the gardener but surely he's on the march with them), the Café Sante which served a few anemic French dishes and a great deal of good Chiapas home cooking, the smell of dozens of open-air charcoal grills around the time for *comida*, the smile on one sidewalk vendor who sold wonderful garlic-y lamb tacos—

And then, suddenly, vividly, so hard that she sways a little as she does it, she plunges them into the hurricane, the shattering of the community, the terror and hope, the two children she saw reunited with their mother, the way the water flowed so thick over the windows, the endless days of digging out—all set among these people she has expressed in such detail.

The ending of the town, and this march to a new life; the long days on the road, the shared effort, the petty jealousies and greeds but also the sharing of a great adventure—all of this she throws into it. And now as they look at the huge chain of trucks, buses, and people slowly winding its way along the old two-lane road among the deep green volcanic slopes, they feel how much of it there is, how every one of these people is unique. . . .

She jacks out. A moment later they are all pulling off goggles, scalpnets, and muffs, sighing and rubbing their faces as Mary Ann Waterhouse strides back into the tent. She looks around at them, and without a trace of a smile or of begging to please, she asks, "Good?"

The director and writers seem to recover first. Every sentence begins with "I feel" or "I felt" and they all talk at once; Frank Capra, Norman Rockwell, and "Americana" seem to be the buzzwords, until they suddenly begin to say "very international, very get back to the world beat feeling" . . . "My image of it is of a visionary kind of, well, of seeing people in this amazingly real kind of a way, totally positive," the director finally says, and all the writers begin to nod vigorously and say, "That's it, you've got it." They seem happy.

The government guys look at each other and nod their heads. "I think we can say it's going to work." The one from Washington even smiles a little and says, "I ought to add, Miss Venture, that you're the one who appears to have been listening to us; that's exactly the message we wanted."

"Very polycentered," the UN guy says. "In fact I don't think the word 'Americana' would be appropriate to describe it at all."

The Passionet execs all glare at the writer who used the term, a slender, intense fellow with a brownish beard that he is now stroking very quickly. "Oh, of course, I'm sorry, I didn't make the context clear, what I meant is that this is the sort of thing that could do for the planet as a whole, the kind of thing that old-time Americana did just for the United States, sort of—you know, 'My Planet 'Tis of Thee,' people feeling more at home with the idea of global loyalty, global identity, more whole-Earth-minded—"

"Ah, I see," the UN guy says. "But I certainly hope you don't mean that this would tend to damage, degenerate, or deprivilege any of the legitimate cultural aspirations of any of the world's peoples. We have to be sensitive to that."

"No, no, I um—don't mean that, I mean a kind of global loyalty and consciousness built around being very individual, very tribal, very national."

The UN guy nods, smiling. "That's exactly what I had in mind."

"Are you making a note of this?" a Passionet exec asks Mary Ann.

"Of course. I think we can address that concern pretty easily."

"Great! She says we can address it easily."

Everyone nods. They ask the two university professors for their comments, and the two of them fall into a violent argument in which Frank Capra crops up a lot more. Jesse listens to that politely; his brother Di is a big Frank Capra fan, and even talked Jesse into watching one of those old black-and-white things once. It bored him out of his mind. Maybe the idea is to get everyone to go to sleep instead of rioting.

After a long time the university professors stop waving their hands, and everyone thanks them. A Passionet exec asks Mary Ann if she can implement that, and she says "No problem."

Everyone now nods solemnly, and thanks everyone else. The UN guy wants to know what the Herreras and Jesse thought, and all three of them say they liked it a great deal.

Jesse has been here long enough to know that in this country a polite person says what other people, especially other people whose social status is higher, want him to say. When he first came here it seemed dishonest to him; now it's common sense.

Since everyone has agreed to everything, the Passionet execs are all nodding their heads, and they tell Mary Ann, the writers, and the director to get on with it. The professors, bureaucrats, and execs get up, staff starts to break down the tent, and Mary Ann, the director, and the writers rejoin the column, all talking vigorously to each other.

Jesse and the Herreras quietly join up a little behind them, so whenever Mary Ann is done Jesse can rejoin her. After a time, Tomás says, "I didn't understand a word of that."

"Me either," Jesse says.

"I thought perhaps you had. You would have convinced me."

"You convinced me too," Jesse says.

* * *

When Di Callare comes home, it's really just to pack, but at least they get one day before they have to start that. It's been agreed that if he gets a one-hour briefing and then gives them his opinion every day, that will be enough until the Klieg system is flying. The Klieg system is more important than before because, apparently, Colonel Tynan has gone nuts and is accelerating at rates that ought to have killed him—in fact he has claimed a couple of times to be dead—and while he seems to be on a trajectory to get him to the comet early, god knows what he will do when he gets there.

Both kids at once have decided, in the last couple of days, that they are just too big to need to have Mom and Dad to sleep, and Mark is setting a bedtime for himself and getting to bed then. Di seriously thinks of phoning his father just to tell him that one, but he's sure his father will find a way to see this as a bad thing and to make it be Di's fault, so why bother?

At any rate, this leaves Di and Lori a good deal more time and privacy, and right now they are lying next to each other on the bed, talking after making love. *"Slaughterer in Yellow* came out fine," she says. "I suppose if the predictable thing happens, we'll be able to buy a new house, even if the insurance company is broke."

"Good to know," he says, "and I think it's likely. There's an awful lot of activity and we're just coming into August and September, which are usually the worst hurricane months in the Northern Hemisphere, and the differential is wider this time."

"If that's not part of a car, I don't know what you're talking about," she says, and kisses his nose.

"Sorry. Finally get a day at home and I start talking shop." He rests a hand on the curve of her waist. "So what does a differential do on a car?"

"Modern cars don't have them. They have separate electric motors," she says.

"What did the differential use to do?"

"What the electric motors do now."

He hits her with a pillow; she giggles. "And you want to know the worst of it, Di?"

"Oh, sure."

"I really did want to know. I just kissed your nose because it was fun." Her eyes are shining and she has a wonderful smile.

"Well," he says, "the differential I'm talking about is the change in ocean surface temperature over time. The ocean surface is warmer in August than it is in May. Now, with the additional methane in the atmosphere, by June eleventh, the Northern Hemisphere had ocean temperatures higher than they'd ever been in recorded history. That was bad enough. But it turns out, not only was there a higher base—"

"Oh, god. You mean it's going up by more than it would normally go up by."

"Yep. Like at a point where it would normally have been 25° C on June 1, and then gone up two degrees to 27° C by August 15, it started out at about 29° C on June 1—and it's going to go up maybe five degrees. That's like what you'd expect in a shallow inland lake at sea level on the equator, normally. The storms will get a lot worse and bigger. Clem is going to get to gobble down a lot more energy than it's had before. So the short answer is that even though the sea is about twenty miles away and forty feet down from us, all this area is going to be torn apart and reduced to mud."

She shudders and snuggles against him. "We're getting out, though."

"Yeah."

"Promise?"

"It's Uncle Sam's promise, love, not mine. Supposedly we are going to be evacuated."

"That's not what I asked."

Di thinks for a long time. "You mean if it looks bad, I desert my job, get back here, and get you and the kids out?"

"Or call me and I'll get the kids to wherever you say, and then you desert and join me there. I don't give a shit, Di, I just want us to live through this."

Di sighs. "Hope for Klieg's thing to work, then. Assuming we can get him out of jail, and that the Siberians don't screw up his launchers, then it won't necessarily be an issue."

"You didn't promise."

"I can't, Lori. I have a job to do there."

"You have one here too."

"Unh-hunh," he says. "I do. And I—well, I mean . . ." He doesn't know what to say, except that he can't imagine doing what she's asking him to promise to do, and so he ends up staring helplessly into those beautiful eyes, willing his words to come out and unable to make them.

He thinks she's angry, but instead she just puts her arms around him and keeps crying. He holds her for more than an hour, kissing her cheeks and stroking her back. He wishes he could say yes, or that it didn't bother him to say no.

When she stops crying she has fallen asleep on his chest; he can feel a little sticky puddle of tears and snot there. He doesn't move, just holds her, and after a while he lapses into dark dreams of things clawing at him, pulling him down into a black, water-filled pit.

Next morning, the thirty-first, as they are packing, Di has the television on just to keep them alert to the news, but he starts out packing the books in the den, away from the television in the living room. All of a sudden he hears Lori and Mark yelling, and runs in to see what's up. By the time he gets there, they're grabbing their own XV stuff, and Lori hands him his. "Passionet," she says.

He pulls on scalpnet, goggles, and muffs, tunes to Passionet—my god.

He had known that Jesse was dating a rich older woman. It was just like that sneaky kid not to mention it was Synthi Venture. Di is chuckling with admiration even as he watches—and then he's engrossed. He had no idea how huge the effort going on in Mexico was, and though he has plotted storms across that coast thousands of times, he never knew what—or who!—was there. Mary Ann Waterhouse sure can tell a story; he wonders what she's doing on a cheesy XV service like Passionet.

They lose half the afternoon that way, and he doesn't care. This is the sort of thing that Mark and Nahum really should see anyway; he notices that when they unplug, they're just playing around but they're speaking a little Spanish to each other.

"It's working," Harris Diem says. "If you've got any medals you can give to XV stars, I think you ought to break them out right now."

They are looking at the graphs on his screen. They all show the same thing around the world; new rioting is not breaking out anywhere where there's enough XV installed. In other areas, as American and UN planes drop cheap headsets made by flash manufacturers, as soon as people get them pulled over their heads, the rioting stops cold. People plug into XV to feel the hurricane with Synthi Venture (or whatever strange real name she's called by—nobody ever calls her anything except "Synthi").

"You'll never believe it, either, but she's dating Di Callare's kid brother. That younger guy Jesse that she's walking and talking with."

"I wish you hadn't told me that," Brittany Lynn Hardshaw says. "Now I really don't know who to envy." She grins. "So at least one piece of bad news is going away. And I hope that university semiotics guy is right."

The only prediction either of them has been able to understand is the one that people will begin to imitate what they experience via XV—and since what Synthi Venture has been pumping out to them is an idealized image of generous, hard-working, brave people, that is what they are trying to live up to. "I hope he's right, too. And I'm not worrying about all that subversion stuff; by the time it's an issue, want to bet Venture's on top of it?"

"No bets. She's a tough broad. Us tough broads respect each other." The semiotician's other predictions have to do with "eventual subversion," by which he seems to mean that a lot of the petty fanatics and greedheads out there will find some way to take this material and use it as a way to stir up hatreds or sell soap.

Hardshaw glances at the checklist on her pocket computer screen. "So where is Operation Valiant at this point?"

"They're getting confident," he says. "I think they'll give it a green today. The big thing agents on site are telling us is that the Siberian workmen aren't doing any work now, because they don't have American supervisors watching them. There're probably a few secret police here and there, but we'll be hitting in the middle of the night—shouldn't be much resistance at the launch area. What might happen at the prison worries me a lot more. Bad news to lose a bunch of prominent hostages."

"Well, if the answer is go . . . then patch me through to Rivera and let's see if we can get it done. Klieg thought he could be launching in a couple of weeks, the last day before the coup. The less he has to repair or get back on line, the better."

"Any more word from Tynan?"

Hardshaw leans back, stretches, and groans. "Everything is perfectly reasonable, except that he's traveling at accelerations so high that all the doctors say he must be dead, and he agrees with them, but he keeps talking to us. One theory is that he forgot to pack himself and he's really back on the moon, but he sent us a raft of data that looked perfectly straight—including several photos of his desiccated body. Carla seems to believe him but they've been doing all that strange wide-band communication; maybe she's just hallucinating him." She hesitates and says, "You realize, of course, that if he's telling us the truth, the problem can get solved months early and at no real cost to us. I'm almost afraid to believe it will work."

Harris Diem nods. "And I'm afraid it *will* work, for that matter. If it does, we've got a dictator for the solar system—and one with a lot of popular support."

"Yeah." Suddenly she laughs.

"What is it?" Diem asks.

"Oh, you know, I met Louie Tynan a few times. One thing I think any woman would notice about him is that he's a horny guy; he really loved being the big space explorer because so many women would fawn all over him. If he ends up as dictator of the solar system . . . well. He'll have them throwing themselves at him, and no way to do anything with any of them. Can you imagine that? All the access you want to whatever you want sexually, and no way to use it?"

Diem smiles. "It doesn't sound very pleasant."

* * *

From July 25 to August 2, Clem veers and wobbles eastward, in yet another defiance of normal hurricane behavior, riding the steering currents and its own outflow jet against the Coriolis forces. It hangs between the 35th and 40th parallels of north latitude, normally much too far north for a hurricane to go without dying, but also the part of the Pacific that exhibits the strongest differential—now a belt of hot water all the way across, from which Clem draws steadily more energy.

Seeing it coming, and understanding what it means, makes an immense difference; the West Coast evacuates in a steady stream. On every interstate one lane is reserved for gasoline trucks heading west, and the rest are allocated to eastward traffic. Buses and vans cruise along in a reserved fast lane to carry those without automated cars—and to pick up those whose cars fail them. Tent cities and temporary settlements bloom all over the Rockies; Chugwater, Wyoming, finds itself a metropolis, with the Corps of Engineers working around the clock to get adequate sewers, roads, and power lines.

To the north, in Pacificanada, Vancouver drains like a leaking balloon toward Calgary.

But the coast is not empty on the afternoon of August 1 when the great waves slam into Puget Sound and begin to roll down the coast. Some people were still waiting, some have elected only to climb to high ground. A few stubbornly refused to believe it might happen, clinging to the idea that God or Nature could not be cruel enough to ravage the coast again.

And some, like Old Robert and Old Bob, just never heard the news. Old Robert has been collecting junk for recycling for a long time, and Old Bob, his dog, has been following him all that time. The nicknames were chosen by Old Robert, who always talks about and to himself in third person.

They're walking out on the long fake pier that has the fancy seafood joints; for once no one is stopping them, and the cops are not hassling them. The water looks funny today, really choppy and high, but since folks ran off pretty fast, there's lots of garbage for Old Bob to eat.

Old Robert tries the door to a place called Acres of Clams, mostly because the guy on the sign has an old scraggly beard and old scraggly clothes just like Old Robert. It opens; somebody didn't think it mattered. "Come on, Old Bob. Old Robert and you's gonna eat."

"Eat" is just about the only word, besides his name, that Old Bob knows. He's through the door in a flash.

The building is one of those powerchip things, so it makes its own natural gas out of air and water—someone explained that to Old Robert a long time ago. He used to be a pretty fair cook, and he puts a big pan on, drops a stick of butter in it, turns the heat on underneath, and goes to the cooler. There're big chunks of fish and some soft-shell crab, and he throws them in with the butter, along with handfuls of chopped onion. It's never smelled so good in all the world.

Old Bob gets whatever hits the floor instead of the pan, and that's a lot.

The big plate of hot food is wonderful, but it takes Old Robert a long time to finish it—he's not used to such rich fare. In the end some of it goes into Old Bob, who isn't so particular.

There's all kinds of wine around; Old Robert decides to have a little of that, just a bottle maybe, and feed a couple of steaks to Old Bob to keep him quiet.

It takes a little digging to find the corkscrew, but he does. He flips the slab of raw bloody beef to Old Bob, who goes after it like a starving wolf, and then hoists the bottle. Outside it's now raining like mad, and the wind is really picking up. Good day to be indoors.

"Happy days!" he shouts to Old Bob. Startled, the dog drops the steak and then frantically scrabbles about trying to get it back into his mouth. That's so funny half the wine comes out of Old Robert's nose.

The dog seems to get the joke and dances around like a complete idiot, barking. Old Robert laughs, and then they get down to the wine and the steak. Man, man, man, it doesn't get any better than this. What did they say in the old days? Groovy. It's a pretty groovy afternoon.

They never see the towering wave roll in, or hear the building grinding, or feel it all come down on them. They are both in a stupor, Old Bob with his head on Old Robert's chest, when it comes. The restaurant is caught in the undertow and dragged out into Puget Sound; their bodies are never found.

"Incredible," Berlina is saying on August 5. She and Naomi have pulled into Portland, where the big surge that burst a hundred miles up the Columbia smashed right over Jantzen Beach and Hayden Island, tore a new channel to the Willamette, and slowly drained back, pulling down the Montavilla Arcology as it did so. "They were warned, they were told, there were a thousand pictures of what was going to happen, they knew backwards and forwards that their damned concrete turtle wouldn't hold against a wave half a mile high, and they stayed."

She's saying this to Naomi Cascade, who is hand-operating the camera and is in her second week as Berlina's part-time employee and full-time admirer. Before them stretches a great oval of concrete and rebar rubble, half a mile across, what remains after the shock of the wave's impact exploded the air trapped inside the thirty-story-tall structure.

Naomi shrugs. "Most of them left. It was just a couple of old people and some who were watching XV—"

"That's what I mean. God, it's a terrible thing for a reporter to feel sorry for a bureaucrat, but it worries hell out of me that the government couldn't get them to evacuate because they couldn't promise XV on the buses. People didn't want to be away from Synthi Venture, because it's too interesting to watch *her* evacuate."

"People are weird," Naomi says. "Maybe they could have gotten her to say something like, 'Hey, all you idiots in Portland, move your butts!' "

"She would have, too. She's the only XV person I've got any use for. Your old boyfriend has good taste. We've got enough of this for backdrop, anyway, and we want to get back before the Army decides it shouldn't have permitted us into the area and sends staticopters after us."

"Yeah." Naomi shuts down, stops, looks at the vast wasteland of mud and shattered construction with her own eyes and not the eyes of the camera. "You know," she says, "I don't think this really would go into words at all."

They are packed in ten minutes, into the new van that Berlina bought, having put her tiny old car into honorable retirement as a souvenir, now that she is wealthy. There are no guidelines but this thing has full inertial navigation, so Berlina just tells it where to go and it starts to drive itself, checking directions and position with satellites overhead.

"Good thing we came when we did," Berlina says. "In another day as the temperature comes up—you're not going to believe what places like this will smell like."

Naomi nods very seriously and works on squaring the gear away. Berlina sits back, thinks to herself that getting an employee was the smartest decision she ever made, and grins a little at what she's just done. Nothing like some gruesome, hard-bitten remark to put some romance into the heart of a—

She all but laughs aloud with delight. She had been about to think, into the heart of a cub reporter. Which is just what Naomi is turning into, and what that means is that Berlina Jameson is not the last of the newscasters. She wonders if maybe she should call up Wendy Lou Bartnick and tell her that she's a grandmother.

The van rolls east—miraculously, despite all the wind and rain, the way through Bennet Pass, past Mount Hood, is still open. They make hot sandwiches and coffee and sit up front to look at the devastated forest and small towns as they travel through. As the sun goes down, their lights are the only ones visible. Ruins, smashed trees, and the occasional human, deer, bear, or cow corpse swims up in the lights and rolls back behind them. After a while, they sleep.

Ever so carefully, exchanging a neutral signal here, a stray thing that could be made to look like line noise there, a datarodent from outside the system probes at the van's onboard processor net, finding its way in through the navigation system, then crossing over until finally it is able to recover stored electronic media and Berlina's rough script for the next *Sniffings.* Then it quietly erases its tracks and vanishes.

Carla Tynan got what she needed, at Louie-on-the-moon's request, and it's no surprise when he then asks her to go into the research files and silently kill four or five phrases that might lead Jameson to the cometoid retrieval project.

She switches on an onboard camera and looks around briefly. Naomi Cascade is sleeping nude on the lower bunk on one side, and light reflecting in from the headlights is enough to outline her body. *Geez,* Carla thinks, *I usually did okay with guys but if I'd been built like that—*

She turns her attention to Berlina Jameson and catches the reporter very quietly watching the sleeping Naomi. As Carla watches, Berlina slides a hand down to between her own legs, and begins to play with herself, rolling over to see Naomi better as she does.

Carla clicks out; she hadn't intended to pry. And she finds, too, that much as she has to interfere with Jameson's covering the story, keep her from learning about Louie's expedition . . . she likes the reporter, and just now she feels very sorry for anyone who is longing to touch a particular human body that isn't accessible.

On August 5, GMT, just 390 hours after he reached Earth escape velocity, Louie Tynan crosses the orbit of Mars, 1.57 AU from the sun. The first time he did this, on the UN Mars Mission, it took nine months.

He wasn't supposed to be here until late September; he is truly making time now. The lunar catapults are longer than ever, firing harder, and he has added laser-boost: as each packet leaves the catapult, powerful lasers burn off a solid hydrogen plug inside an open-ended cylinder at its rear, producing high-velocity exhaust and further accelerating the package.

He is up to eleven brain-years per minute and gaining; if he can be counted as human, not exactly having the body anymore to prove it with, then he is now the fastest-moving human being ever to live, moving along at an astronomical unit every ten days, four times the speed for this day in the originally planned mission. He can't help feeling congratulations are due.

The news from Earth is bizarre to him; after all the supposed impossibilities, it took one good XV program to end Global Riot Two. Maybe he's not all that sure he wants to be human, after all. He also notes with some pleasure that he *likes* Jesse and Mary Ann, and then realizes that that's the point of the whole thing; everyone who doesn't have anything to do stays home to root for the hero. Since you can't depend on people to help, at least it gets them out of the way. That is just, perhaps, a little bit depressing.

Carla seems to have forgiven him for sacrificing his body, though he won't feel really forgiven until they are back in realtime contact and able to truly share each other's feelings. But it's a good sign, anyway, that she's not angry at him anymore.

He is now just about five light-minutes from Earth, which means that one hundred ten years of thinking go by, subjectively, between sending a message to Carla and hearing what she thinks of it. Figure since he no longer sleeps at all it's effectively one-third longer, and you get 146 years. That's a lot of thinking; Carla's getting faster too, and that's a good thing.

Louie has chewed out a lot of philosophic issues, and gnawed others down to the kernel of sheer personal taste and temperament at their hearts. Never much given to philosophy before, he has been doing only this because it does seem to be the most effective way he can find of using up processing time, and he needs ways to use it up; otherwise, memories come to the fore, he starts linking them together, and before long he has emotional reactions out of any connection to his present circumstances.

He wondered for a while where his emotions were coming from, and finally settled on hysteresis. In a normal human body emotions are the way they are because of the chemical component of mental process; the chemicals hit every cell of the nervous system indiscriminately, and it takes longer to scrub out chemicals than switch off electrical signals. Thus one tends to have a pervasive feeling about the world as a whole (even when the signals are disparate) and feelings are never completely aligned with the present moment, because there are always some spare chemicals lying around from before.

In Louie's case, hysteresis—the self-induction that makes it impossible to turn off current in a conductor instantaneously—is a bit longer, in terms of his mental process, than the chemical delay was in his old body. This is partly because there is so much of him, partly because it's so spread out, and mainly because he is so massively parallel that he runs far faster than the electronics that hold him together in a single personality. And somewhere in that little gap between starting a change of current and finishing it . . . he has feelings.

He wonders, idly, whether his mind had the slots for anger, love, joy, fear, whatever, and just happened to fit various hysteresis phenomena into those slots—or whether somehow those emotions are intrinsic properties of any system.

It doesn't seem to matter a great deal. He has emotions. If they had vanished, he wouldn't have been sad, but he'd have been missing something.

*   *   *

On August 9, 2028, Clem comes to a rest over the graves of its first victims, at Kingman Reef. Its eye is just over 350 kilometers across, and winds in the eyewall roar at 250 meters per second, a wind faster than tornado winds ever get, whirling around an eye the size of the state of Ohio. The hot ocean surface pumps more energy in, but Clem is at last encountering an upper limit; wind resistance increases rapidly as Mach 1, the speed of sound, is approached, and at the surface of the ocean right now the wind in the eyewall is moving at Mach 0.7. So the wind resistance from the surface of the ocean is holding Clem's winds down to their current speed.

This creates an odd situation; if the ocean warms up a little more, Clem will not speed up much at all. Di or Jesse would say that if the wind speed is v and the ocean surface temperature is t, dv/dt is very small in this range of t, or that the situation is now "temperature insensitive."

Only when the ocean is supplying enough energy for Clem to "punch through" into the supersonic realm will the superhurricane grow much—but if enough energy does turn up, because supersonic flow encounters much less resistance, Clem's eyewall winds will leap from their current speed to Mach 1.2 or higher within a matter of minutes.

Fortunately, the ocean is not yet warm enough to do that, and it will reach such temperatures only at shallow spots later in the summer.

Someplace, once, John Klieg read a long list of people who wrote great books or planned great achievements while in prison. Lenin was supposed to have been one, and some of the apostles, and . . . well, a lot of people, anyway.

He always figured it was a matter of having a lot of time on your hands, but he hadn't really had a concept of what "a lot of time" really means. He's beginning to catch on.

The first two days in here, no one talked to him, but they did bring him a short note that said Glinda and Derry were being held under house arrest, and they were comfortable. The food here is okay, considering it's the same stew and bread every meal, but it only takes a few minutes to eat, and you can only sleep so much. They put him in a coverall and every other day he gets to hand that in, take a shower, and put on a clean one.

Physically it's not a bad existence, but after three days he'd have killed to have a notebook. You can think only as far as your memory can reach, and without a notebook that isn't far; a few times he's done long bits of arithmetic in his head, only to find at the end he had forgotten what it was that he was solving them for.

It's frustrating, too, because with this much time to turn things over in his head, he's gotten a much clearer take on both GateTech and business generally, and once he gets out he's going to have to spend a couple of days dictating to get it all laid out for himself. There's a new way of doing business that's becoming clear to him . . . GateTech was just a primitive way of doing it, and getting into space launch this way still cruder. He's always known the real way to money is not through production but through control; "The hotel owner gets rich owning the keys, the maids stay poor keeping the toilets clean," as one of his biz profs back at Madison used to say.

The trick is to stay out of the bathroom and up by the front desk. Or better yet hire someone to run the front desk and stay home.

Klieg notices he's pacing the cell; it comforts him, because he's seen that in so many movies and it's nice to know that some things really do work the way they're supposed to. Not that this place is a dungeon or anything, more like a no-frills hotel—not even a lock that works from the inside—he'll have to remember that one for Glinda. . . .

The walls are bare and off-white, and the construction is just shoddy enough so that even though it's new you can see some lumpy spots. The bed is an ordinary steel frame bed, the sink a basin with a coldwater spigot, and the toilet a pretty basic flush model with no cover and a seat that doesn't raise. They let him keep his watch, so he knows that the lights get turned on at seven every morning and off at nine at night.

Back and forth, back and forth . . . white wall to white wall, five steps. The whole trick now is that machines, especially those replicator gadgets— which are going to get one huge boost from what that Tynan asshole tax-sucking civil servant has done—will do the physical producing, and artificial intelligences can probably do a lot of the design and inventing. So the real grunt labor, the true cleaning-toilet jobs, are going to be finan- cial . . . time to get out of financial control? Do what, just own information? It's not the most implausible idea he's ever had, but he has no idea how to do it.

He sits on his bunk edge and seriously considers trying to fall asleep with the lights on. Trouble is, he's not really in the mood. . . .

The real reason why people sometimes do major intellectual work in prison, John Klieg figures, is because if you've got any brains, you can't stop thinking for very long. He stretches out and considers . . . in a world of datarodents and reverse-engineering artificial intelligence, how is he sup- posed to keep hold of anything? Legal rights and permissions won't matter either.

Maybe the world will change enough? No telling what a world battered by Clem and the daughters might need, but if he can figure it out and corner that . . . the trouble is, of course, just when you have a lock on something everyone needs, some politician starts a crusade because everyone needs it and you've got a lock on it. It hardly seems fair that the better the deal the more likely they are to beat you up for it.

A distant clang and thud. More noise. A pounding sound. As he does whenever there are unusual sounds, Klieg makes sure his shoes are tied and that the few possessions he was permitted to keep are in his pockets, especially his reading glasses.

This time the noise goes on for quite a while, so he stands away from the door (but in plain view of it), ready to raise his hands. The two possibilities, always assuming that's not just a bunch of clumsy deliverymen, are that it's another coup and he's about to be seized as a valuable asset, in which case he wants to cooperate with whoever is nearest him with a gun so as not to get shot in a crossfire, or—

Something thuds hard against the door, and cracks appear in the surfacing around the frame. He backs up and puts his hands all the way up over his head.

Another crash, and this time the door shudders; definitely they're getting him out with some kind of hydraulic gadget, he can hear it pressurizing between blows. Got glasses, pockets loaded, shoes tied so he can run, pants pulled high enough not to trip on cuffs—

With a boom, the door flips flat onto the floor, and Klieg sees the little ram they used to take it down, a gadget on a heavy iron tripod that looks more like a giant sliding latch for a door than anything else.

The man who steps through the door and says "Mr. John Klieg?" is wearing a powder-blue UN uniform.

"Yes, sir. Ready to go."

"Good. Follow me."

There are sirens and bells everywhere now, and the smell of smoke. In other parts of the building Klieg can still hear gunfire. But neither he, nor his rescuer—if that's what this is—says anything. They hurry down the hall. Explanations can wait.

"We can get you excused from that, you know," a voice is saying in Mary Ann's brain. "This is not something Synthi Venture has to do."

If you think that, you really don't understand crap about all this, Mary Ann thinks back at the voice. Then she replays the exchange on the conscious level so that it goes out to all the experiencers.

"Please don't do that, it spoils the composition—"

Exactly. What we don't need around here is composition. She grips her shovel again. *Now shut up and let me work.* She wades back into the long ditch that she and several hundred others are digging. On August 6, at about 16N 135W, Clem spawned Clem 500, which has been wandering around to the south and east ever since. In the last thirty hours it has surged due north for the Isthmus of Tehuantepec, and the evacuation columns from Tapachula have been ordered to dig in. Aircraft and trucks have been getting stockpiles of food, fresh water, and chemical toilets in as quickly as possible, and the long dugouts are growing everywhere. Jesse is over at the temporary airfield—due to his technical training they've made him a radar jock, based on about twenty minutes' practice, serving an "air traffic controller" who once did the job at a small civil aviation field in the States, twenty years ago.

Meanwhile, unskilled hands, like Mary Ann's, are doing the rough work of getting the shelters dug.

It's a good feeling in her back and shoulders as she works; she's in pretty decent shape these days. Besides, there's a certain amount of pleasure in working on a gang with other women; she lets herself wonder if maybe it would be better if they started whistling at and harassing young men, and is rewarded with a scandalized squawk from Passionet about the thought.

One of the conditions she insisted on before going back on Passionet was that she have ten minutes to herself every hour, and it took her some effort to make it clear to them that "to herself" did not mean "available for conversation."

So when she finds a foreign thought invading during her break she's just plain furious. There's a long pause, and then the voice says, "I'm sorry, I had no idea it was your break, but I'm not Passionet, and I was trying to get in touch with you when they weren't online with you."

You're not—there's no way to hack a brain protocol—

"I wouldn't say that. I'd just say it's kind of tough. Look, my name is Carla Tynan—have you heard that—"

You're the meteorologist they had a lot of trouble getting back onto the government payroll.

"That's me." Quickly, Carla explains about her unlimited net access and her presence in the net most of the time. "What I'm talking to you about is just that I think there are some things you ought to know."

Well, sure. What are they?

Carla Tynan has never wasted a lot of words in getting her point across. She tells Mary Ann quickly about what Louie is up to. "So there is help on the way, even if the government refuses to believe him and publicize it. That's what I wanted you to know. Also, I can keep feeding you information from around the globe."

Why me? Mary Ann thinks.

"Because you are Synthi Venture, and Synthi Venture is the mind that everyone is hearing this through. And if I warn you in advance about what's coming, and give you time to think about it and see that it's really something wonderful, people won't be so frightened, or do anything stupid before they get used to the idea. The way you tell the story is the way it's going to be in people's minds. Probably forever. And I think you'll tell the story better, give people a better handle on things and a better chance of understanding them, if you know more about how it's likely to come out. Just remember, if you want to help, you don't tell them till we're ready."

Who's "we"? And if it's so wonderful, then show me.

Carla does; it leaves Mary Ann breathless, so that she has to take a little extra time before she lets them log back on. As she works, joking, gossiping, and generally just sharing the time with the other women on her crew, the back of her mind, below what will register for XV, works on what Carla has told her. If it's true, Clem is really not the biggest thing going on right now.

"They got Klieg out," the young man in uniform says, looking up from his keyboard. "There's been a delay due to some bad crosswinds and it looks like a guidance satellite mistook a stadium under construction for a key landmark, so they aren't at the launch sites yet."

Tension fills the crisis center. No one needs to say that if they don't get the launch facility intact, the whole raid is truly for nothing, however better they might feel having gotten Klieg back.

Hardshaw finally sighs, turns to the general at her right, and says, "So how did this happen?"

General Tim Bricker is a tall, thin man, with a Southern drawl, younger than you'd expect; one of those ambitious, rising stars drawn to staff jobs because they're a place to find and impress patrons. Hardshaw chose him partly because he's the kind of guy the job needs, someone who can handle the public political aspects and understands about deal-making and compromise, but also partly because he had a few years as captain of an infantry company and has seen combat twice, in the little brushfire rescue operations like this one.

Bricker slowly closes his pad and leans forward to her. "Ms. President, this happened through a process we call a clusterfuck. Several things that normally would have worked happened not to. Some of the people in the field tried things to fix them, and because they didn't have real good information, some of what they did made things worse. A lot of times bad things add up. So if your question is 'What chain of events caused this?' I have to tell you I don't know just yet, we're still trying to find out. But if your question is 'Who's fault is it so I can drop the bastard before he damages me?' then I'd have to say it's probably nobody's fault, and if you want a fall guy, you'll have to frame somebody."

His tone is hostile, even rude, and Hardshaw feels an urge to retaliate, but she's spent enough hours with hostile witnesses before now. "General," she says, "if you like, the question was rhetorical and I withdraw it. Just let me ask you this: Whenever someone proposes one of these things, why don't I hear about possible clusterfucks beforehand?"

"Because if we knew it could happen we'd have it blocked. There're always surprises." He stays right where he is, not backing an inch, and their eyes lock on each other.

"Not what I meant, General, my fault." She says it softly, gently, almost purring; Harris Diem might recognize the tone from some hard-fought cases long ago, but no one else in the room would. "I meant to ask you why you say 'probability of success is x per cent,' but you don't add 'And then of course we might accidentally shell our own troops after leaving them on a beach, or two staticopters could collide, or we might accidentally shoot up a schoolbus, or maybe thirty of our men will be captured and mutilated.' Just to mention examples going back a few years."

"Because you don't ask us and you don't want to hear it. Ms. President, all I'm saying is that this kind of thing can happen. It does happen. You're dealing with split-second timing and human reactions that have to be perfect in an environment with flame, smoke, noise, explosions, gunfire—shit happens. And you've been in office a while, and been through a rescue or two before. How can you sit there and pretend that you had no idea this could happen?"

Hardshaw leans back and looks hard at the general. There are several problems here; first of all, he's mostly right, and many of the people here know that, so she can't just brush him off. Secondly, he's being right in an insubordinate way, which might be either strategy or total loss of patience, but either way she can't let him get away with it. Having dealt with Bricker for about a year now, her guess is that it's strategy, probably getting himself down as the man who defended the armed forces from President Grandma, a plain blunt-spoken soldier, and thus a good pick for the next administration.

None of which means he doesn't have a point.

She can't let this stretch on any longer, so she says, finally, "The problem is noted. Please note also my request that henceforth I wish to be reminded of the possibility of a clusterfuck in any contigency plan or operations proposal submitted for my attention. In fact—" She smiles at him. "We're going to call this the Bricker Requirement, to make sure that you get proper credit. Just make sure that you don't lose the terminology by prettying it up, General. If you're going to remind me that a clusterfuck can happen, I want the word 'clusterfuck' used in the reports."

"Noted," Bricker says. His reaction is now unreadable; maybe he's satisfied at having the problem addressed, more likely he's trying to figure his next move.

Three minutes later they get word. The Siberians had enough time. They blew up towers, control rooms, the deep accelerator tubes that Klieg was counting on for all-weather launch. If help is going to come, it will have to come from Louie Tynan.

On Wednesday, August 16, Louie is farther away from Earth than any human being has ever been. According to data he's getting via Louie-on-the-moon, there are at least half a billion people, many of whom never had access to XV before the free headsets were distributed, who spend all day long, now, plugged into Synthi Venture, listening to the news and walking with her. The destruction of Klieg's launch facilities seems to have led to only a single brief day of civil disorders, mostly because Synthi Venture disapproved so strongly of looting and fighting and everyone was tuning back into her.

For whatever reason, Hardshaw and Rivera and all have decided to keep word of the 2026RU expedition out of the media, which is not an easy job. If it were not for Carla stalking Jameson (and the dozen imitators she has by now) through the nets, the secret would be long since out.

Louie wonders why they're keeping his mission secret, letting it appear there is no hope when that's not so. Maybe it's because he's dead. He doesn't really understand why that should be held against him. After all, it isn't like he smells bad.

He has noticed, however, that nobody seems to want to talk to him directly anymore, and his lunar and asteroidal spawn agree with him about that. Does it make them nervous that he's dead or that he's still alive? Or that they can't tell him from the living?

He wonders if maybe the universe is going to be lonelier than he had thought it would, because just possibly there will be very few people who want to be friends with a dead guy.

Carla's last letter rather gently chided him about self-pity. Maybe he should take her seriously about that.

It will be okay as long as he doesn't have to be lonely.

He has so much surplus processing capacity, in this stage of things, that he begins to ask his lunar self for all the spare data it can get, and there are enough systems up and running on Earth to feed his hunger. He gets the Library of Congress and seriously considers reading the whole thing; he gets weather reports and satellite data, raw field notes of university researchers, some of them on video—these, he finds, seem to be the best. Though he knows that every camera was pointed by someone or something, he likes the feeling that whoever it was didn't compose everything, that though he can't be entirely sure what's accidental and what's not, much of it must be.

Louie watches people who have never seen anyone other than the forty people in their little tribe meet the great wide world. He watches animals copulate, kill each other, grow old and die. He watches ponds become climax forest and revert to ponds; catches the immense complexity of a condor in flight and the simplicity of the nitrogen cycle.

He finds that he likes this a lot. One of the most interesting things that the creativity researchers found out (and Louie suddenly begins to wonder about creativity, and within a few minutes he has put together every study ever done on it, read them all, and formed his own view) was that esthetic pleasure is linked, on some deep level, to the complexity of what we see—sometimes to the complexity of its interrelations rather than to the complexity of the object itself.

One reason nature pleases us is its endless use of a few simple principles: the cube-square law; fractals; spirals; the way that waves, wheels, trig functions, and harmonic oscillators are alike; the importance of ratios between small primes; bilateral symmetry; Fibonacci series, golden sections, quantization, strange attractors, path-dependency, all the things that show up in places where you don't expect them . . . these rules work with and against each other ceaselessly at all levels, so that out of their intrinsic simplicity comes the rich complexity of the world around us. That tension— between the simple rules that describe the world and the complex world we see—is itself both simple in execution and immensely complex in effect. Thus exactly the levels, mixtures, and relations of complexity that seem to be hardwired into the pleasure centers of the human brain—or are they, perhaps, intrinsic to intelligence and perception, pleasant to anything that can see, think, create?—are the ones found in the world around us.

It looks like a good deal to Louie that we are constructed to like the world in which we find ourselves. He has looked at a lot of art by now and so much of it seems to be about how to see, and now that he knows how to see, he looks at art less and nature more. There is time for all sorts of things; for drops of dew on leaves, forests crawling up burned mountainsides, the breaking of surface tension around a duck's feet as it takes off, and the sucking down of the Earth's crust into mantle.

The amusements are endless; he augments them with data from the other planets, by comparison, and even squeezes a few orbiters into the launch schedule so that by the time he is on his way back he will have continuous monitoring of every major body in the solar system. But he already knows, somehow, that Earth is his favorite planet . . . Earth with its living things, of course, and with an oxidizing atmosphere, plate tectonics, and water cycle to endlessly change the shape of its seas and coasts, where a tiny variation in temperature can make such a huge difference—

He sees that if Clem and Clem's daughters are let alone, they will not put an end to Earth or life, and probably not even to human beings. With his own lifespan now extending to infinity (for he can repair and recopy himself as long as he cares to), Louie could, if he chose, sit back and watch the world re-invent complexity as it filled its empty niches, and the niches between the newly filled niches, and the new niches that created—

He could but he'd rather have Earth as it is. Call it a sentimental attachment.

On August 20, Louie Tynan crosses Jupiter's orbit, a bit more than five astronomical units from the sun. The giant planet itself is nowhere nearby, of course; it's a purely arbitrary boundary, the imaginary line that marks an ellipse in the black vacuum. Still, it's the first of the gas giants, the four huge planets of the outer solar system that formed far enough away from the sun to keep their original loads of hydrogen and helium. He is now truly out in the cold and the dark.

By now the wiseguys in the asteroid belt are blasting away at him at an ever-increasing rate, and even with the longer catapult and laser boost it is taking six days for packages from the moon to catch up with him and pass through his funnel. He has been rearranging and climbing the train for a while now, so that more and more of his processing is distributed in the family of packages; there's less waste of materials, and coordination gets better and better as he learns to pass the incoming packets, shrieking in the electromagnetic spectrum as clearly to him as a teakettle to human ears, from funnel to funnel the way a juggler passes balls, hands working independently and yet under unified control.

For a couple of days it was challenging, then as processors became more numerous and more tightly networked it became amusing but not difficult. Now it's all but a habit; he catches them and passes them along as automatically as a worker on an old-fashioned assembly line might tighten a bolt.

With seventy plants online in the asteroids—and that number will quadruple before he's done—he doesn't really need the moon packages anymore, or rather he doesn't need them right away. After a moment's thought, he sends a message to Louie-on-the-moon—the lunar packages will be sent up a different pathway altogether, the one that he will descend as he works his way back toward the sun in a few weeks.

Ultimately the real way to do this would be to have belts of stations on highly elliptical orbits, all following each other around the sun, and then to toss ships like packages between them. Done properly it could create a

"railroad" to the far reaches of the solar system . . . it might be a matter of a mere couple of weeks even for ordinary flesh-and-blood humans to get out to Pluto or beyond. He works out the scheme . . . in fact, rather than having a single sequence of solar satellites following each other in a long elliptical orbit, it really might be better to have several such sequences . . . ultimately you could create a "grid" of moving bodies such that there was always a way to get thrown all the way up to wherever you wanted, and then caught at the other end.

He's going to need that when the time comes to settle the outer system, he decides. And for the first time in thousands of brain-years, Louie Tynan is startled; it had never occurred to him that he might do any such thing.

Yet the truth is he can build about as much habitat as he wants out here . . . and the beautiful Earth is being crapped up by an excess of people—lovely as individuals, towns, and cultures, but hideous in such profusion.

He has great fun thinking of a dozen ways to turn Jupiter into a midget sun and terraform its major moons, and working out which nations to settle where. It is so entertaining that he spends almost ten minutes on the project, idly catching a couple of packages along the way. Now that the *Good Luck* has extended into a stable train of a few hundred packages stretching over about a million miles, and he's gotten himself distributed across all of it, this is really easy to do, and tossing and passing packages is like playing with a yo-yo, relaxing once you have the trick.

Just for grins, let's see how many thousand years, using the resources he has or can produce, it would take for him to terraform everything in the solar system that he possibly could.

Figure Mars is easy; get some of the oxygen and nitrogen back out of the soil, add water and other volatiles . . . it had a billion years of life, anyway, based on what the expedition Louie was on found. Charge it up again and it's good for another billion.

The moon is not much worse (it would leak air and water over the long run, but Louie could maintain it, now that he's virtually immortal). The Jovian moons are a lot tougher—Jupiter's magnetic field is a natural cyclotron and it's bathed in hard radiation, and igniting nuclear fires in Jupiter's core will pump a lot more particles into the process. You'd have to slow the giant planet's rapid rotation to get a softer, gentler magnetic field. . . .

And the outer gas giants would be a lot tougher to start going and keep going; not much way to sustain a reaction in a ball that small. Maybe by beaming power from stations closer to the sun? Six big satellites in solar polar orbit . . . use the gas giants as reflectors . . . no reason to use Uranus at all since it doesn't have a moon big enough for the job. . . .

The real bitch is Venus. Cooling it down from the temperature of boiling lead, spinning it up to a decent rotational speed (without reheating every-thing), getting rid of air so thick it's like a half mile of Earth ocean . . . figure you'd precipitate it out with metallic calcium, maybe, to get the carbon dioxide converted into carbonates, and if you had big enough lumps of calcium in orbit maybe you could use their gravitational drag to spin up Venus . . . they could also act as mirrors to keep the sun off . . . *that* would be a job. Mars would be a snap by comparison.

Well, so simulate it. How long does it all take, and what does he do with all those worlds? Figure he's making nine new habitable worlds: Venus, Mars, Luna, Ganymede, Callisto, Io, Europa, Titan, and Triton. A couple of dozen continents and oceans. . . .

The thought is like a small orgasm. For twenty years now, the Library of Congress has been recording genomes; tailored viruses can rebuild the DNA, and cloning technology is there to bring the organism into being. They've done it for a few zoos, and they brought back the blue whale that way after the Japanese slaughtered the last dozen. For that matter, in the last decade they've brought back dodos, moas, woolly mammoths, passenger pigeons, and giant sloths.

They lost a few recordings in the Flash, but there are probably copies around . . . and for that matter there are plenty of samples one way or another.

He could bring it all back. And have plenty of room for beautiful cities and farms . . . nine Edens. Room enough not just for humanity but for life.

Herds of bison the size of Texas counties, whole continents of un-touched jungles, snow leopards playing on Olympus Mons, and giant white sturgeon in the rivers of Ishtar. Wonder what an eagle flies like in low g? Heck, it could probably lift a small deer . . . on the smaller worlds you sure wouldn't be able to keep anything that flew isolated.

How long?

Almost, he wishes for a physical heart again, so that it could pound. And he remembers that however long it might be, he has the time.

The answer comes to him. Just under a thousand years. He doesn't quite believe it, tries again . . . but there it is. Once you have true self-replicating machinery, driven by abundant nuclear fuels or sunlight, you can have as much as you want of whatever you want.

His mind reels back to the implications. In the same thousand years human population could quite painlessly be brought a long way down—with everyone living a long life, no need to raise the death rate or even slow medicine down . . . everyone could be rich, everyone could have all the material happiness they wanted—

And right now, he knows, from the millions of brain-image recordings that the Comparative Psych Library at Kansas State has on file, exactly how wretched people are made by hunger, cold, sickness, and fear. Figure that of the Earth's nine billion people, about one and one half billion are suffering ill effects of malnutrition at the moment, a partially overlapping two and one quarter billion are inadequately sheltered, about three billion will contract a treatable illness and receive no treatment this year. . . .

Fear is a little tougher to estimate.

The sheer quantity of *unnecessary* human unhappiness implied is beyond even Louie's capabilities to comprehend. In a way he's just as glad not to know.

That word "unnecessary" keeps sticking to his mind. A thousand years and all the physical ills of mankind could be nothing more than bad memories, not living in any memory except Louie's. And then there are those other dreams—lions stalking mustangs and kangaroos on the grassy plains of Aphrodite. Dolphins in the Sea of Tranquility, diving down to visit the site of the first moon landing. A grizzly breaking from the pines of the upper slopes of the Valle Marineris, on his way down to that great freshwater sea for a drink. Mighty Jupiter glowing blood-red in the sky above the endless oceans and floating islands of Ganymede and Europa.

All this and their health, too, Louie thinks, laughing to himself. Well, if he decides to deliver that . . . it slightly exceeds the specs on his contract, of course, but he doubts their descendants will complain.

Actually their descendants probably *will* complain, because there is something in human nature that looks for ways to make itself unhappy. But Louie can't do anything about that. He's not God.

Not exactly.

Not yet.

Mary Ann tends to think of the time that follows as the "phony hurricane." Clem is still there and still real, and when Clem 500 blows across the Isthmus of Tehuantepec and they spend a scary couple of days huddling in the dugouts, there's plenty of reality. But it's not the kind of terror it was before; the shelter is roomy enough to hold them, and strong enough to keep them safe. They all spend their time in the dugout singing, playing word games, sleeping, telling stories to children—it's a kind of vacation from the endless hot walk. Everyone emerges healthy and in good spirits; the shelters are left as they are, so that future travelers can have the use of them if necessary.

The one thing Mary Ann finds depressing is that it all implies that the hurricanes will persist.

When the storm has passed they are up and walking again, clearing the road as they go. And as they do this, Clem is still moving over the Pacific, its fourth trip around now, scouring islands that were wiped out before.

There's not much loss of life; the big waves roll out, but where they strike, big waves have been before, and you can kill someone only once.

Brittany Lynn Hardshaw finds that time to be painful for other reasons. The trouble with militarily occupying what Harris Diem calls a "cupiarchy"—a state built around people grabbing whatever they want—is that you can't find anyone, good, bad, or indifferent, with any real interest in doing the work of government. Meanwhile a lot of young intellectuals and part-time kibitzers, now that they're safe from the hired thugs of the various "cashlords"—another Diem term which is finding its way into the media—are spending all their time making life miserable for the occupation government.

Klieg at least thinks he can have something flying in a couple of months, so that the Southern Hemisphere might be spared; all estimates are that if nothing is done, given the much greater ratio of water to land, and the much higher seasonal thermal differential because the Southern Ocean is colder, the storm will be worse there.

But despite the urgency of Siberia, and the fact that it's practically under the rule of an American proconsul, Hardshaw has to spend most of her time out on the road visiting refugee camps. So much water poured down the western slopes of the United States that the Coast Survey is using radar imaging just to assemble a picture of what the West Coast is shaped like now. There were rivers running sixty feet deep that had never held water since white settlers arrived, and so much snow landed in the Sierras that it seems to have compacted into new glaciers in many places.

The seventy percent or so of the West Coast population that fled east is now spread out across the Rockies and the desert states; the loads of water that hit those areas caused more flooding and more deaths, and there is no question now, according to NOAA, that runoff still coming down from the hills is going to refill many lake beds that have been dry since the Ice Age. Maybe that can be used in some kind of reclamation . . . there are people working on it, as Hardshaw tells everyone who asks her that.

With Carla secretly looking on, late one night Berlina Jameson succumbs to temptation and puts her arm around Naomi Cascade; when Naomi leans against her, Berlina gulps, lifts the younger woman's chin, and firmly kisses her mouth. There's a long moment before Naomi starts kissing back.

There is no new *Sniffings* for ten days while Berlina gets caught up after years of affection starvation. Naomi keeps saying she thinks she's actually straight, but she really loves Berlina. It's such a normal way for a young woman to behave that when Carla compares it to old records of Naomi making speeches at rallies and demonstrations, it doesn't quite seem like the same person.

Di Callare gets a long break, and goes back to get the family fully packed for the two-room apartment the Feds will put them up in, in Denver. The whole government is supposed to get moved there after Clem's next pass. It would make more sense to move offices and departments as soon as possible, but there's an impossible snarl of political infighting over questions of precedence, and for purely PR reasons, the highest levels can't leave until most of the rest are evacuated. Just in case, Diem makes arrangements with the government of West Virginia; according to Di Callare, Charleston is the nearest sizable city to D.C. that can be expected to ride it out, and after all it's only four hours by road, forty minutes by zipline, or twenty minutes by staticopter from Washington—in a crisis they can scoot there.

On August 25, Clem scrapes over Eniwetok again, and the satellites report an ominously wobbly outflow jet, which has been the prelude to calving in the past.

On August 23, Louie Tynan crosses Saturn's orbit, 9.5 AU from the sun; it took him nineteen days just to cover the first astronomical unit of his journey, but as the industrial complex pushing him along has been growing exponentially, the rate of growth in his acceleration has been growing . . . the fourth derivative of position with respect to time increasing monotonically, Louie thinks. The kinds of equations you see in atom bombs, bacterial colonies, arms races, and out-of-control inflation.

Just at this moment his mind is operating at 20,504 brain-years per day, two and a half times the rate when he left the moon; to experience what Louie has in the last thirty-four days, a single human being would have to live over 300,000 years.

As he goes farther and his mind gets faster, he spends more time daydreaming, and more time on what he thinks of the "art/nature/what? question," by which he means, approximately, what the connection is between three billion years of evolution, Michelangelo's *David*, and why people like the *David*. It's about the most interesting problem he can think of. Louie was never much of an artist of any kind—he used to write down, on the personality inventories the USSF required every three months, "Can't draw, can't write, can't sing, won't dance, whistle acceptably if you don't listen too close."

He's wishing now that he'd practiced a lot when his brain was smaller; what he's got in mind is a big job, and he sure as hell doesn't want to screw up the materials. So as he flies on deeper into the outer solar system, into the lonely dark and cold, he simulates and practices over and over, plays with criticism, tries again. He figures he's having a major artistic movement, with forty or fifty trial works and then a lengthy body of commentary, about every four hours . . . all in simulation.

A couple of days ago he might have found it a strain to do all this and keep catching packages, making plans for reaching 2026RU, and the rest. Now all that's automatic.

What he really needs is another artistic perspective, and since his brain is nearing completion, that gives him an idea for some changes; he sends his requests to the wiseguys. Within a few days, just as he's crossing Neptune's orbit and diving into the real outer darkness, he should be getting several very different packages.

There's a principle called Bode's Law, about the location of the planets; if you take the series $\{0, 3, 6, 12, 24 \ldots\}$ and add 4 to each term to make $\{4, 7, 10, 16, 28 \ldots\}$ you get the distances of the planets from the sun, with the distance from the sun to the Earth (one astronomical unit) set at ten. Technically the series is what is called a "geometric progression."

It was only with powerful supercomputers in the early 2000s that it was finally demonstrated that there's a reason for Bode's Law. In the primitive whorl of matter the solar system condensed from, Jupiter condensed first after the sun, and as it did its enormous gravitational drag accelerated the other rubble circling the sun. Resonances with some orbits, and not with others, over a few hundred million years, swept some belts clear, filled others with rubble, caused rubble to pack up and collide in one and to disperse in another, forming the planets and asteroid belt in what were, in fact, multiples of *Jupiter's* orbital distance—the squares of a simple series divided by 13, that being the smallest integer that didn't allow the wrong sort of resonances to build up across geological time.

As it happens, Louie's voyage, with its rising rate of acceleration, is also producing a geometric progression, and the two run oddly parallel—it is taking him three days between planetary orbits, even though the planetary orbits are increasingly far apart. Thus it is only six days after he "changed his mind"—a joke he's enjoying more with time—that the new packages arrive. He admits to himself that he's catching them with a certain amount of—well, for lack of a better word, reverence. Maybe it's just that if he were in their situation he'd want them to be careful.

What they are is copies of the wiseguys. The simplified Louies back in the asteroid belt have copied themselves onto bigger and better processors, taken data from him to merge into these augmented versions of themselves, and fired them off to join him. As they arrive—all within a few hours of each other—he incorporates them, and suddenly he remembers, seventy times, meeting some dim, dark body in the cold of space, spreading over its face and burrowing into its core (or cores, more often it was several bodies spinning around each other), and becoming a factory and forge in space.

The wiseguys daydreamed a lot, and Louie-on-the-moon has been tutoring them as well, without ever exactly having discussed it with Louie-the-ship. He doesn't feel offended; on the contrary, the reunion is wonderful, and everyone enjoys probing everyone else's memories; it's quite a party, lasting almost twenty-four hours, carrying him/them two full AU beyond Neptune's orbit before they get around to discussing, or he gets around to thinking about, depending on how many Louies he is right now, what to do with the solar system once this local emergency on the third planet is dealt with.

It's really only in the last hour of the reunion that thought drifts back from conversation to monologue. Louie feels unified again, but lonely.

He's had to further distribute himself across more processors in a longer train, and it's now almost ten light-seconds from one end to the other of him; it feels different, a little, but more like having a richer subconscious and deeper emotions than a limitation. He wonders what it would be like to be distributed clear across the solar system. If he created linking processor stations in solar orbits, a few light-seconds apart all the way from inside Mercury's orbit to outside Neptune's. . . .

Well, no doubt he will find out someday. He'll need a lot of processors anyway, to control the network of boosting stations he's already planning . . . thousands of Louies, all at the "train stations to space"—fun to think about the chess league and debate clubs they could have. It does get kind of lonely out here.

It's an aphorism in statistics that to set an all-time record one must be exceptional, but one must also be in the right place at the right time. Franklin Roosevelt was a brilliant campaigner but he faced only one first-rate opponent. Joe Louis and Muhammad Ali were great fighters but they fought a lot of bums. Babe Ruth was a great hitter but he had a more elastic ball, shorter outfield fences, and worse pitching to contend with; Hank Aaron had expansion clubs to bat against.

Thus the champion taker of human life, Clem 650, is one of the biggest daughters, but it's also in the right place at the right time. There was never any hope of evacuating Japan, and even with replicating machinery the Japanese did not have time to get big enough seawalls into place. Clem 650 loops to the north and east of Honshu, and storms down through a dense corridor of human beings for whom nothing can be done. All by itself, it takes half a billion lives in nine days.

On August 26, it comes ashore near Yokohama, and the next day, though the Japanese are refusing to answer questions, radar shows no buildings standing in Tokyo.

Clem 650 tears south, flinging the Inner Sea far inland on Honshu and Kyushu, sending a funneled storm surge over to batter the coast of China, and down into the Formosa Strait.

The storm surge that piles up into the Formosa Strait, between the island of Formosa and the mainland, is funneled and channeled into a stream strong enough to slice off the port cities from Quanzhou to Zhanjiang—including Hong Kong and Macau—like water from a fire hose cutting into a snow-bank. The video out of China is hideous—mobs of people climbing over collapsed piles of bodies in the streets, desperately trying to get out of the low coastal cities.

Later, when Clem 650's remnants drift across China, leaving tornadoes and thunderstorms in their wake, the storms catch millions of refugees in the open. On September 4, Clem 650 heads inland for the last time, eventually to fling a great load of wet warm air up the side of the Tibetan Plateau, whence it will return as severe flooding on the Mekong, Red, and Hongshui.

With record-keeping in collapse, the Army broken down to small units, and millions of people no longer traceable, the central government of China begins to lose its grip south and east of the Yuan River; within a week, various Army commanders have set themselves up as warlords in all but name, an impossible-for-outsiders-to-understand multisided civil war is breaking out, and several tactical nukes have been fired. If you count disease, flood, and war victims, Clem 650 claims nearer a billion than a half billion victims.

When Louie Tynan is a day beyond Neptune, he begins to reverse the flow of the train. He's at 36 Au, clipping along at almost five AU per day—fast enough to get from the sun to the Earth in a long afternoon, fast enough to cover the distance from Earth to Jupiter, which took the early probes years and even the *Good Luck* a month, in a single day. It's time to start slowing down.

By now he no longer needs processing units or any other working component, just mass and momentum, so what arrives from the wiseguys now is just big slabs of iron. To slow down as they overtake him, he accelerates the iron bars through the train, adding momentum to them as they shoot through the funnels. Momentum is conserved—so as the iron bars are sped up and hurled out of the solar system, fast enough to reach Alpha Centauri in a bare 14,000 years, had they been headed that way, the momentum they carry away with them is lost to the ship, and *Good Luck* begins to slow down.

It will take a week at 2 g's to slow down for the rendezvous with 2026RU; in that time the ship will climb clear out to 56 AU from the sun, almost doubling the distance already covered but doing it in less than one-fifth the time. It's going to be a great ride, and it's a good thing that he doesn't care much anymore about being the fastest man alive, because though he's certainly fast, he isn't alive. Not exactly.

Out here, radio from Earth is reaching him four hours after it's sent, which means that a response from Carla is always to something he said eight hours ago, and his brain has become so massively parallel that this corresponds, if it were a single human brain thinking as fast as it could, to 5,021 years of ordinary mental life.

Not that he'd actually choose to experience it that way. He's more like two hundred people having twenty-five and a little extra years of telepathic mental life.

He tries hard to comprehend what happened with Clem 650, but it eludes him. He says, *Each of them was as individual as I, as Carla, as my parents, as anyone I know;* there were poets and mechanics, doctors and bums, drunks and lovers and saints and everything. Children died screaming for their parents, parents for their children, some in silence, some after long hours, some instantly. So many bodies . . . they will be finding deposits of them on the South China Sea floor a thousand years from now.

His mind stretches that far, but it hurts, and there is work to do.

By now, if he were still seeing with naked human eyes, he would see the sun as a very bright star, with no discernible disk; but Louie sees the whole electromagnetic spectrum through array receptors scattered along the two-million-mile train of the *Good Luck* plus packages and auxiliaries. He can still see individual asteroids, and for that matter he can make out the continents of Earth, and Clem itself, if he wants to. There's just not much reason to look that way.

He figured when he got out here that his old nature would assert itself and he'd at least think a little wistfully about just taking off for the stars, even though he would never leave Earth in the lurch that way. Maybe the optimization has done something to him?

No, it's just that there is so much time. He will eventually get around to going to Alpha Centauri. He may very well settle the galaxy with copies of himself. Immortals can afford patience; every pleasure he is capable of, he will have more times than an ordinary person could count in a lifetime, if that's what Louie wants to do. Hell, if he wants to be flesh again, he can regrow a body and download some part of himself into that sometime—he has his genome recorded.

The drive to see what's over the next hill is in part the fear that one may *never* know, that if one doesn't go over the hill today, one may never get farther than the village graveyard.

He enjoys the week of deceleration. The 2 g's is really just an average—deceleration actually happens only during that brief instant when the iron bars, weighing a bit over eighty tons each, come shrieking into his funnel and he gives them a hard push along. The iron bars pass through in a tiny fraction of a second, for they have been kicked along by laser boosts back at their launch points that boil off ninety percent of their original mass and leave this eighty-ton remnant moving at eight AU per day (or just over thirty million miles per hour). As they pass through, Louie speeds them up, and that slows him. During that brief fraction of a second, *Good Luck* undergoes about 1,000 g's of acceleration, and Louie is taking one of those jolts every couple of minutes.

Imagine that you are somehow on a freeway on a skateboard moving at fifty miles per hour; this is the equivalent of decelerating by pushing, with a long pole, against the trunks of the cars passing you. Even with all his processing capacity and speed, Louie finds it an interesting and challenging piece of work, better than flying under bridges used to be, like being a javelin catcher for a whole regiment of javelin-throwers. The *Good Luck* is processing just over 400 iron bars daily, and as she slows down the numbers rise.

A good thing too, because as she slows down, the iron bars are moving faster and faster relative to *Good Luck,* so that there is less and less time to push against them, and positioning gets trickier. Every so often there's a "wild throw" that he has to let just go on by, unable to move far enough and fast enough laterally to intercept it. Whenever that happens, he transmits the equivalent of a catcall back at whichever wiseguy threw it; the solar system echoes with radio chatter, cheerful razzing between the wiseguys, like a good tight infield.

At least it looks like there's going to be some time. After dropping its murderous daughter, Clem swings back into the upper reaches of the North Pacific, and then appears to stall out and zigzag, wobbling north to south and occasionally looping. From August 28, its closest approach to Japan, until September 6, when it rakes over the dead bones of Hawaii again, Clem sends out gigantic and dangerous waves, fascinates meteorologists, has as few as one and as many as eight outflow jets—but destroys very little, partly because it is where it has been before. Louie watches this from far out, hours later by radio, and breathes a slight sigh of relief—he will have that much more time.

On September 6, 56.23 astronomical units from the sun (though his route there was a long arc of almost 70 AU), Louie Tynan brings the main body of *Good Luck* into orbit around 2026RU. He is now just over thirty-six times farther out from the sun than he went on the First Mars Expedition, and that had been the record. He's breaking a lot of records now that he's dead.

As had been confirmed by a couple of impact probes he had sent on ahead, 2026RU is a cometoid, a ball of ice, about 790 miles across, with a rock and iron core about 80 miles in diameter and many large embedded nodes of chondrite, methane, ammonia, and nitrogen ice, and various rocks and metals.

It's the kind of snowball Louie used as a kid when matters got serious— rocks and bits of iron, surrounded by hard ice, surrounded by frozen fluff.

The first couple of hundred packages have already taken up their orbits or descended to the surface, and the first robots are now crawling out on the icy surface or burrowing deep toward the stone and metal core. Within four hours, the first loads of metal are coming up to the surface to feed the hungry fabricating plants; it's going to take a week, and Louie intends to be busy.

September 9 is a Saturday and things are going so well that Louie kids himself that he ought to get the day off, as hard as he's been working. Clem is still stomping on the dead bones of Hawaii, sending storm surges crashing through Oahu so frequently that all evidence of Honolulu vanishes down to bare lines of foundations, with everything else washed out to sea. But there is no one there to be harmed, nothing to be damaged that isn't already rendered worthless.

Meanwhile, out here in the darkness, the replicators, robots, and auto- mated plants have been running flat out, after two days of feverish self- duplication, and much of the core is chewed up and re-extruded into a forest of pipes, towers, supports, girders. 2026RU is going to be the strongest comet ever built. But then, not many comets have ever had to boost at 3 or 4 g's, and the final approach to Earth is going to require at least that much.

Originally Louie had planned to start spinning off the "ice Frisbees" and then—by climbing back down a rising column of more iron bars—to beat the Frisbees back home to direct them in. If he didn't get there, well, Louie-on-the-moon could undoubtedly deal with it instead. But that was before Global Riot Two and his decision to kill his flesh so that he could get here in time; now anything he takes back will have to boost at the accelera- tion he's using.

This led him to decide to take the whole comet back with him, or the whole comet minus a lot of stuff he's going to throw off the back. It adds a day to the process, getting the giant engines and the fusion reactors to drive them built, threading steel through the ice and re-freezing the pathways onto the structural members, but when he's done he's days, not months, from Earth.

When he's finished, the next day, the iceball has a forest of twelve-mile-high towers on one side, and most of the rest of the surface is covered with radiators, immense plates under which he circulates the fluids that will cool the 100 fusion chambers at the base of the towers.

He's going to throw away about forty percent of the mass of 2026RU, and a great deal of *Good Luck* in the balance. Since he needs the water ice for when he gets to Earth, and the other volatiles are useful as refrigerants and working fluids, he's going to throw away what he doesn't need—most of the iron core is still there even after he's woven everything he needed out of it, and he doesn't really need anything from *Good Luck* except its processors, robots, and energy systems.

He wonders what Goddard, Von Braun, Verne, or Heinlein would have thought about a spaceship made out of ice that used iron plasma as a propellant. Probably they'd have approved of anything that was a spaceship.

Time to initiate boost draws closer, and though he's ready enough, he's curiously not eager to get started. It might be a while before he gets out here in person . . . but time means so little to him. . . .

It's not curiosity, even—he's leaving relays behind here, and a couple of the wiseguys have dispatched several probes on long orbits that are going out to about 1,200 AU, boosting off and on to get there within a few years, so if there's anything interesting out there he'll get a look at it soon enough.

It seems silly to pay attention to this feeling, but after all he's vastly more complicated mentally than he used to be. He probes his memories, the many memories inherited from the wiseguys, all the psychoanalytic literature. It seems strange that he still remembers emotions or that he still has them.

Maybe it's different now that he's all assembled on 2026RU, so that the time lags aren't there and he doesn't have radio lag as an artificial "glandular" system? No, if anything, the feelings are as strong as ever with effectively no lag; hysteresis alone suffices.

When he probes far enough, he realizes what the matter is. Among the first batch of general junk to be vaporized and blasted out of the engines is what remains of his body. He's already recovered all the water and a variety of other complex organics, but there was still a sizable chunk, a kind of little desiccated mummy of himself, that he had stacked with other junk.

He looks at it now; it looks like a little, wrinkled prune of himself, not even close to what he looked like. But there was a time . . . he finds himself thinking that just maybe he is going to miss having a body more than he thought he would.

Oh, well, Earth needed saving, terrestrial life needs a terraformed solar system, and anyway he's enjoyed too much about this voyage to wish it hadn't happened. Still, it's a little too much, emotionally, to just throw out his body with some galley leavings and old bolts. It takes him only a few moments to get some spare instrument access covers and weld them together into a casket, and to put the body in that.

He makes it the first shot; an He-3 pellet is laserfused below it, the expanding plasma is squashed, elongated, accelerated within the central tower, another laser heats the plasma that whirls up the tube—and his body leaves the solar system as a miles-long wisp of stripped ions moving at close to light speed. A few of those ions will undoubtedly fall down into some sun or other; mostly, they will gradually reacquire electrons, lose energy in their rare collisions, and become atoms drifting through the galaxy.

It seems like a good way to go. And now that he feels better, he begins to heave iron in with a will. He has places to go.

He plans a fast drop in, much faster than can be achieved with the sun's gravity alone. Then he will whip around the sun, taking the heat inside Mercury's orbit, orbiting retrograde (opposite the direction the planets go) in order to pop out and use the gravity of Mercury to slow him first, then another braking swing by Venus . . . from here to Earth in about three weeks, all told. It's another leap in human abilities—along with the all-but-overnight industrialization of the solar system, and for that matter the fact that Louie himself is currently running on a bit over two thirds of the computing capacity in the solar system, with Louie-on-the-moon making more all the time. . . .

It's not the world it used to be . . . and that's okay, he's not the Louie he was. And he's got more to say about what this new world will be like than he did about the old one.

The fusion engines are blazing now, the many tons of iron vaporized every second leaving the hundred towers—fifty times as high as the World Trade Center—as great white-hot plumes at near light speed. If there were naked eyes to see it, the plasma trail extends one hundred thousand miles out, but whoever had those naked eyes had better not be standing on the surface—2026RU is boosting at an acceleration that is more than high enough to overcome its own gravity; if you stood on the side with the towers, you would fall off; if you stood on the other side, you would sink into the snow. The robot treaded tractors, busy laying in mirroring and insulation, still occasionally jam into place, even with their very broad, flat treads.

By the time he recrosses Neptune's orbit on September 19—the "real" boundary of the solar system, since Pluto and Charon are pretty clearly captured cometoids, like 2026RU but much larger—there're all kinds of jammed junk sunk in the ice, and he's been strongly reminded that amorphous water ice, like plate glass and some rocks, is really a very slow-flowing fluid—under the 2.3 g's he's been running, 2026RU has dribbled slowly like an ice-cream cone on a warm day, forcing him to shore up the thrust towers and do a lot of re-engineering as lines and internal struts break and warp. At least, as the iron core slowly sinks through the ice, it gets closer to the engines and to the spare-parts manufacturing operations he runs from engine waste heat.

A few hours after crossing Neptune's orbit, he flips 2026RU over and begins deceleration. With the speed he has built up as he raced in from the outer darkness, he will have to "stand on the brakes" most of the way, just to get recaptured by the sun.

By that time, Earth's luck is running out.

From the San Francisco Bay right down to Ensenada in Baja, there is so little still standing and there are so few survivors from previous passes that neither the American nor the Mexican governments pay much attention to Clem's rampage down that coast. The news media follow suit. Far to the south, Mary Ann and Jesse have almost reached Oaxaca, and that's more newsworthy.

The extra rain breaks the Colorado open, partly fills the Grand Canyon, and helps the storm surge break through to rejoin the Gulf of California to the Salton Sea.

Randy Householder watches the news with a certain fascination. Even he has to admit that it's a big deal. At least, after the flash floods tore through Boise, and with so many other disasters happening, even if they've traced him they're not looking for him yet. He will have lots of time to track down Harris Diem.

The trouble is, a guy who works in the White House, physically close to the President, is just about the hardest of hard targets.

Randy passes the time, sitting in his car anyplace where he can watch for Diem, by experiencing Synthi Venture. She's a great lady, and that boy with her is a nice kid.

He wonders if Kimbie Dee would have turned out that nice. Probably, he decides. Similar backgrounds and all. Beautiful girls that fought their way to the top.

He sighs. He really wishes he could put on the goggles and muffs and experience this more thoroughly. It's been a long time since he's lived in a world of love, hope, and courage. But without his eyes and ears, there would be little point.

Diem will come home sooner or later. All these guys do; their rigs are in their houses. Randy managed to strike up a conversation with the cleaning woman and ascertained that Diem is alone in the house at night, when he's home—which hasn't been for four days. Between stress and no time to come home to relieve it, Diem's craving must be killing him right now.

When he comes home, it's going to be fairly easy. He'll use the rig— Randy has studied these people too much to have any doubt about that. While he's plugged in he's helpless.

There's a Self Defender in Randy's glove compartment. It will summon the police, and that's what he wants it to do; if he can kill Diem, it's a good start, but if the world can know why . . . well, it's just justice, that's all. Just plain justice after all these years. More than Kimbie Dee ever got.

Synthi Venture, or Mary Ann, whichever, is climbing a hill just now, and part of Randy's brain fills with warm Mexican sunlight and a road leading up into the sky, with hundreds of good, strong, brave friends all around her. It's so beautiful and peaceful; why the hell can't people get addicted to *this*?

Then again, addiction may not be the best thing anyway. A couple of weeks ago, while he was crossing up his path and generally making himself hard to find, he stayed in a camp in Wyoming, where he made damn good money because he seemed to be one of about a dozen people who would dig a latrine or peel potatoes. Everyone else was too busy with XV, experiencing Synthi Venture—as she dug latrines and peeled potatoes. They kept upping the bonuses at the camps for that.

Strange. Of course, there are lots of people who'd rather experience an actor playing at a stakeout than be Randy just now. If he'd had any choice, he'd have done something else with his life than be Randy.

A light rain is starting, and it's not even near dark. Harris Diem probably isn't coming tonight, either—but until "probably" is "definitely," Randy is sitting right here.

"Yes, I talked with Mary Ann at length," Harris Diem said, "and she's aware of the problem and trying to do something about it. We don't want them to switch off from her totally, though, because she's the major thing keeping us from having to fight huge civil disorders, and besides much of her message is desirable. We just want them to take some action on their own behalf and not go off to live in Synthi Venture Land. The trouble is that her version of reality is a lot more fun, right now, than other people's."

Hardshaw nods and says, "All right, next report I need—Di, I think you and Carla said you have bad news?"

"The worst, I'm afraid. Surface temperatures in the Caribbean are now at thirty-seven Celsius and rising. That's more than enough to take a hurricane over the line into supersonic winds, if our estimates are right. And of course Clem is making another near pass, so the likelihood of one spawning is pretty high."

Hardshaw nods. "Any suggestions?"

"Well, if we had Colonel Tynan's comet or John Klieg's balloons, sure. We ought to chill the Caribbean. Otherwise, no. We don't have any idea of how big it might get, just 'bigger.' And to tell you the truth, I was going to ask for permission to go down to North Carolina and get my family moved right away, because within forty-eight hours is probably too late."

"Do it and go now," the President says. "I won't keep you here when there's nothing of any value for you to do. While we're at it, Harris, go home and get a night's rest. Carla, call me if there's anything that involves action. But I'm going to bed early too, and I'm going to try to get caught up on sleep. Might as well start out this thing rested and fed."

Di is surprised at how hard it is to say goodbye to his staff. Most of them are acting like they'll never see him again. Gretch is in the first wave headed up to Charleston tomorrow morning, so this really is goodbye, but Talley and Peter go a week later, and he expects to see them again. Mohammed and Wo Ping, with families to worry about, are already on temporary leave—the new NOAA headquarters will be the old NORAD facility at Cheyenne Mountain, and they're there for setup.

He will miss them all till they're together again, and he says so. Everyone gets choked up, even Peter.

Ten minutes after that he is on the zipline and phoning Lori. It is September 22, Clem is passing near the Isthmus of Tehuantepec, and Jesse and Synthi Venture are most of the way to Oaxaca—they should get there tomorrow if they aren't held back by the thundershowers trailing in Clem's wake. So the kid will be all right. Dad is in a refugee camp up near Flagstaff, and cranky.

It's strange, he thinks as the zipline shoots out into the evening, that even though the details of the map of the United States are already quite changed, the seat, the zipline, all the familiar geography of his life, are just the same. Perhaps when he gets to one of the camps in the West, it will begin to sink in.

He begins, finally, to read the copy that Lori had given him of *Slaughterer in Yellow*. It really is one of her best, although he's sort of surprised about how little violence there is. She's been saying lately she doesn't have the stomach for butchering people that she once did.

*   *   *

Harris Diem feels like his head is one loud ringing doorbell. He's tired, he's still confused by how the world has changed, and he's trying to persuade himself to just head for bed rather than down to the basement.

Not a chance.

The robe, the clean sheets, the ecstasy of choice . . . tonight he will do his three special girls, starting with the pretty little cheerleader, the kind of girl you were so hot for at fourteen and couldn't get because for you life was all study and work—

Not true, he admits to himself. He is a monster, and a pervert, but he is not self-deluded. Or not about that. If he had been able to do what he wanted with a girl like Kimbie Dee when he was fourteen, he'd have raped and killed her. It's what he understands.

"All right," he whispers, speaking aloud, "little blonde white-trash mall-chick, here we go—"

He is just watching the hands slide away from the perfect little tits to her shaking sides, just hearing that first delicious sob of shame and seeing the tears rolling from the blue eyes—

Just uncovering and feeling utterly naked and helpless, wishing Daddy were here, he'd *kill* this creep—

It goes blank. It is dark and quiet.

Can't be a power failure—the house is on a powerchip.

He clicks the release, slides the goggles and muff off. The man standing there. . . .

"Whose father are you?" Diem asks, very quietly and calmly. He wants to know; mustn't scare this guy into pulling the trigger too soon.

"Kimbie Dee Householder's." The man is keeping a Self Defender leveled at Diem's face.

Diem's mouth is dry; part of him is still expecting some orgasms, a hot shower, some guilt, some sleep. Another part is wondering what the hypersonic round will feel like. "Anything you want to know before you kill me?"

"If you got a reason why, you can tell me."

Diem shrugs slightly. "I was born this way. Maybe someday they'll be able to detect whatever I have, and abort the fetus."

"You bought any more of this stuff?"

"I would buy more if I had the nerve. I would do those things if I could get away with it." Something strange is striking Diem; he knows he is dead, and finally he can say out loud what runs through his head. He looks at the washed-out blue eyes, grizzled gray beard—poor bastard can't even afford injections to keep his hair its regular color—and the run-down clothes. Here's a guy whose best house was a mobile home, one of those people whom Diem has climbed up and over on the way to the top. "You understand that? No reason. I *loved* cornholing that little bitch with a mop handle."

Saying it brings him erect, lifting the still-attached merkin.

Householder twitches slightly. The Self Defender barks. Blood sprays.

God, Diem thinks, what a way to go. He is still looking at the blood spurting from his shattered genitals, reveling in the agony as he chews his lips bloody, when Householder's second shot takes him between the eyes.

Randy Householder sits down to wait for the cops. Figure he jiggered the security system to get in, and it's a Self Defender pulse fired from inside a key White House official's home; that ought to get some attention pretty fast.

He has just sat down and opened an orange juice when the door opens, but the men who come in are wearing stocking masks on their heads. He doesn't have time to say "What—" before he is sprayed with bullets; he falls onto the floor, his guts in flames, the world getting dark, and he hears gunfire and—no mistake, grenades going off. It sounds like a fucking war, like somehow Randy has started a fucking war.

The zipline whizzes on toward North Carolina, and Di looks up from *Slaughterer in Yellow* to think a little about the time ahead. Most of their possessions went west weeks ago, but Lori and the boys have stayed in the nearly empty house. Lori has been completely unreasonable about it—she won't go unless he's coming along—so what Di has in mind here is just a slight trick . . . he's going to get them onto a zipline for the West without going himself, letting them think he is with them till the last moment. He doesn't think Lori will take the boys back into danger once they are out of it.

Still, this is not going to be easy. Di is not really the type for lying to his wife. On the other hand, he's really opposed to leaving her to die, and that's what the alternative is.

Cops, coal miners, firemen, Marines . . . those are the kinds of jobs where you have to look for a wife who can deal with the possibility you might not come back. Meterologists didn't used to be one of them. Even public officials weren't.

Lori is beautiful, talented, and intelligent, and she isn't bad in a crisis, for that matter. But she doesn't have the faintest understanding of how Di can be loyal to anything outside his household. The moral universe ends, for her, with her family.

What kind of world has it gotten to be where that's such a bad thing?

His thoughts are interrupted by a call from Carla. She's trying to give him a head start. Clem has an outflow jet reaching like a tenuous tentacle over the Isthmus of Tehuantepec on the Pacific side to the Bay of Campeche off the Gulf of Mexico. That jet will cut off at any time—Clem has already begun to move away—and when it does it will leave a low-pressure center.

The surface temperature in the Gulf, in that southerly part, is just over 38°C—warmer than human blood. Di thinks that's enough to lift the hurricane through the supersonic barrier, and Carla is sure of it.

At least the issue of sneaking away has vanished.

For the rest of the trip, Di answers no phone calls. When he gets home he finds the family packed and waiting, and as he hurls luggage into the car he explains the situation to Lori as quickly as he can. "We've got to get over the mountains, at least, and preferably all the way to the middle of the continent," he says.

They climb into the car; Nahum is sniveling, Mark is sullen, but really, they're not being bad in the circumstances. Fifteen minutes to the zipline station. Ten minutes to buy a ticket. Half-an-hour wait at worst, and then they're on their way—

Eight minutes later they are sitting in a long, long file of automobiles, not moving at all. Nahum is quietly sobbing, Mark is whining, and Lori is knotting her hands.

"What do you suppose happened?" she asks.

"Well, making a guess . . . nowadays, with datarodents and other things like that, nothing stays secret very long. Probably when I found out there were fewer than a hundred people who had seen the data—but that was half an hour ago. Mark, please, quiet, guy, your mother and I are talking—"

"Climb up front and sit on my lap, hon, and Nahum, do you want to sit on your dad's lap?" Lori reaches back to help them come forward.

This line of cars won't move for a couple hours at least. Probably parking has overflowed at the zipline station and they're having to route cars elsewhere and then bus passengers back to get on the line. It might be a lot longer.

This would be an incredibly bad place to get caught in a hurricane, he thinks, and then half-laughs at himself; the hurricane is just beginning to form, a good deal more than two thousand miles away. He'll try to confine his panic to what's plausible.

Once the kids have settled onto their laps, Di explains, "What I bet happened is that the data leaked all over the place, and quickly, and everyone phoned his family on the East Coast, and *they* called people, and *they* called people, and pretty soon—voilà. Everyone is going to the zipline station." He sighs. "I think we'll get out but it's going to be a while. Anyway, I started *Slaughterer in Yellow*. Better than your last couple, I think, but you sure don't dish out the gore like you used to."

"Effect of being a mother. Once you've felt childbirth it's hard to romanticize pain, and after you've patched twenty or thirty small wounds, big ones aren't as interesting either."

"Can I read them when I'm big, Mom?" Mark asks, and as always they tell him yes, he can, and no, he's not nearly big enough yet.

The phone rings. Di answers it. "Hello?"

"Hello, Dr. Callare." It is President Hardshaw. "Sorry to be a pain about this, but we badly need your advice, and it's going to be four hours before they clear enough space to move anyone through, so you've got a while. Is that your son?"

"That's what Lori says," he says, smiling. Lori socks him on the arm. "This is Nahum. Nahum, this is the President."

Nahum curls up against his father and hides his face.

"A lot of people feel that way," the President says. "Anyway, we want to multilog you in with Carla. The eye has formed and it's moving north into the warm water."

Di whistles. "Bad news for sure. Okay."

He pulls out his computer, sets the phone screen to Overlay so he can see faces and graphs against each other, and logs in. Nahum settles comfortably about his neck.

"Cute kid," Carla says, appearing on the screen. It takes him a moment to realize she has animated herself rather than sent her actual image. Probably with as much time as she's spending plugged in, she looks like hell and doesn't want them to see her.

Carla rolls the simulations for him and shows him the parameter estimates. As she finishes, Di asks, "So where do we go from here?"

"Well, if you guys would believe Louie, we'd just hope he gets here fast. But I see nothing else we can do. If we publicize it, all we do is fill the highways and kill people there instead of at home. I say let'em be surprised if we can."

"This line isn't secure."

"I know. If only *some* of them hear, some of them may get out. But I'd say it's hopeless anywhere south of Gainesville."

"How long till the critical point?"

"Forty minutes to one hour."

Hardshaw gasps, breathes hard, and then says, "My god. Both of you, right now—Harris Diem has been assassinated, and your offices were bombed, Dr. Callare—"

"*Hey!*" The shout is Carla's, and the line goes dead.

There's a long silence. "Carla?" he asks. "Carla?"

Diogenes Callare looks up to see the men running down the road between the cars. "They got out of a staticopter," Lori whispers, "while you were talking—"

Di tosses Nahum down to Lori's feet, pushes the door open, tumbles out, and starts to run. If they could get to Harris Diem, who is critical personnel, then they're operating in force—

Duck behind that van, around the bus, keep running, Jesus it's hot in Carolina late on a fall evening, just don't let them—

If they got to Harris Diem in his office in the New White House, they got through the fence, the guards, two steel doors, and two more guards. Fast enough to prevent alerting Diem—

Roll under the truck, crawl forward, if they didn't see him it might put them off—

And to get Carla and him at the same time . . . and the lab—god, he hopes everyone had gone home—this is no tinpot terrorist outfit. Funny, all those years you take your antiterror training and then it all comes to you. Got to get off the highway but not while they'd have a clear shot at him and it's all open fields here—

Out from under the truck and—

They grab him by the collar, pin him to the asphalt as he struggles. God, there are a lot of them—they grip his hair painfully, and his scalp is pulled tight. His face is pressed into the pavement. They press the pistol to his left temple.

The last thing Di Callare thinks about is to be grateful he got far enough away so that his family didn't see this; the last thing he feels is heat from the asphalt on his cheek, then nothing.

When Lori arrives, minutes later, following the police, she's violently ill; it's almost an hour before she realizes Di is gone forever, because the sight of his shattered face and the bloody mess they made of the back of his head overpower her. The line of cars waiting for the zipline still hasn't moved.

Carla Tynan knows they are there only when they yank the jack out of her skull; she has time to shout *hey!* before they break the connection. They empty a machine pistol into her before she even gets her hands positioned to cover her nakedness.

Brittany Lynn Hardshaw would like to grieve but there's no time. Secret Service people are hustling her down one of the safety tunnels to the secure chambers. Harris is gone . . . and the others, whom she was getting to know and like—

"It was the Siberians, almost for sure," Hardshaw says aloud. "Probably

Abdulkashim's old faction, waiting to hit us until the worst was about to descend. Did you get one for questioning?"

The Secret Serviceman who was guarding Harris Diem shakes his head. "It was a totally professional hit. His house had been surrounded for days by two different teams, a group of six commandos and a single agent. The commandos pulled back a block and it looked like they were grouping for an attack, especially since they left electronic monitors in place. We had the single guy pegged as the scout. Naturally we followed the team—but that guy was Superman. He nailed the house electronics, got in there, shot Mr. Diem, all in maybe two minutes. Did it with a Self Defender, of all the corny things—but of course that gave the commando team a signal. They came in throwing incendiaries, and . . . well, the house was totalled. It's still burning. And all of them died in the fighting. We're not even sure which body is Mr. Diem and which is the solo agent—they were about the same size physically."

Hardshaw nods. "I wish we'd had the chance, but I don't suppose that we can have much doubt. The idea was to put us in chaos just before the superstorm, and they're listening in all the time. Get me a playback on the transmission." She strides into the saferoom, the room the White House has had since the Flash, and sits at her desk. They set up a video screen and the signal begins to play. One of the Secret Service agents whispers that they have no confirmed attack aimed in her direction.

She hears Diogenes Callare and Carla Tynan explaining it to her again. God, it's hard to believe that none of their bodies are cold yet.

At the end of the tape, she says, "Well, they're right. No public announcement. But I think we'd better get ready to run . . . no, scratch that. I've got faith in Carla Tynan, anyway, and if she said it was going to happen that fast, it was. Get me to Charleston and start the Federal evacuation as quickly as you can."

When the eye forms in the Bay of Campeche, there is more than adequate energy; the eye wall swells outward, and windspeeds rise; as they approach Mach 1 they rise more slowly, but they don't stop rising.

Just after dark, there's a brief time when the sea churns and thunders, waves a hundred meters high whipping up and crashing down; then the airflow abruptly becomes smooth and layered—the eyewall has passed into the supersonic realm.

By that time the center of the eye is at 92W 22N, well out into the Gulf of Mexico, and the eye is already 400 km in diameter. Storm surges are already lashing Veracruz and are pouring upward toward the American Gulf Coast.

Carla's model missed one detail, but only one. Just as she predicted, within twenty minutes the hurricane has swollen until there are Beaufort 12 or higher force winds across an area 1,600 km in diameter, as if a great drain plug had been pulled at the center of the Gulf. The eye has fallen to 530 mb in pressure, and the eye itself is rapidly swelling, the winds gaining force.

Nonetheless, Carla missed the detail that in addition to its tsunami-sized storm surges, a supersonic storm is large enough to lift significant quantities of warm water. The better mixing of water and air, in turn, means the air gets warmer and there's greater efficiency in the storm, converting the heat of the sea to wind. It has more energy—and a lot more water.

When Jesse gets the word that Di has been murdered, he sits down and cries for an hour. Mary Ann isn't sure what to do. She's lost some acquaintances in XV, and you're supposed to overreact to that—she really admires hell out of Surface O'Malley for not going along with that policy. But this is just a kid who is crying for his big brother. What do you say? "Cheer up"?

She finally settles on, "I'm so terribly sorry."

He hangs on to her as if he were drowning, and she holds his head and strokes his hair. She thinks about how the world slips away, how she'll never meet Di now (and she had looked forward to it), how Jesse will never quite be the same because pointless evil has gotten into his world.

All across North America and Europe, people who should be evacuating sit down to grieve with Synthi Venture.

Death comes quickly for millions as Clem 900 is born. Within hours storm surges are large enough to rage right across Florida. Those who couldn't or wouldn't evacuate before now are drowned by the waves, tens of meters high, that pour over the peninsula one after another; the mangroves that have held the land give way, concrete crumbles, steel bends and breaks, and the surface of Florida is washed off into the Atlantic to thunder down the continental slope in a great avalanche. More and more follows; there will be little land left by morning.

Winds reach speeds of 100 mph as far north as Memphis, and cities and forests are flattened.

The rotary current produced by the storm begins to scour the Gulf out on all sides, chewing off Plaquemines Parish from Louisiana, reopening Lake Pontchartrain to the sea, and eating away at the whole Gulf Coast from Brownsville to Panama City. When next the sun comes out, it will be on a much wider Gulf—and one with much more open jaws.

The Caribbean islands, at the center, are drowned to their highest mountain peaks, battered, eroded, scoured into new shapes. They will become wildernesses of rubble, sand, rock, and packed debris—but only after the storm stops. Right now they are places where the water and wind foam furiously at the obstacles.

And yet all this pales beside the effects of the new storm's outflow jets. Sucking up seawater like a giant vacuum cleaner, mixing far more efficiently and thus using more of the available energy, the great hurricane dumps more than a thousand tons of water per square acre—the equivalent of ten inches of rain—all over the eastern third of the United States in the nine hours before the storm abruptly veers to roar across the Atlantic, gaining energy before it mauls its way into Europe, still dropping saltwater three days later as far inland as Kazakhstan.

The Mississippi is briefly as wide as Lake Erie; the James River carries all of Richmond out to sea, and running water rises seventy feet on the Flash-scarred stub of the Washington Monument.

In Georgetown, the still-smoldering remains of Harris Diem's home are picked up and dragged away by the current. The burned remains of Randy Householder had not even been pulled from the rubble, and what is left of him mixes in and is swept out to the Atlantic, along with all the wedges of the raped and murdered girls.

In all his dark dreams, Harris Diem never imagined that it was possible that no one would ever know. But fourteen years after her miserable death, it is as if there never were a Kimbie Dee Householder.

Karen always kind of hates herself for thinking it, but here she goes again . . . she wonders what Mary Ann would do now. It's funny how life diverges . . . Karen's hair was too dark to take the needle well, and her hips were just a little too wide, so she wasn't called back for the Passionet auditions.

And the strange result is that while Synthi Venture is down in warm, safe Mexico with a great-looking young kid, Karen Mary Ann finds herself sitting in the Dance Channel Tower—the tallest building in the United States, so big that Herald Square is its central courtyard—and looking down on the boiling anthill of Manhattan.

The salt rain has been falling so fast and hard that the building engineer has diverted the rain pipes into the building's power drains. At eighty stories taller than the World Trade Center, he explained to them earlier, the building is too tall to drain easily by gravity—so he has pumps on every floor. Now, with the quarter of a million people who work here mostly gone, he's been able to divert most of the power drains to pushing water from the roof and the terraces down into the sewer system.

The Dance Channel itself never occupied more than the top fifteen floors anyway, and even though the building was thick and squat in its lines, it swayed too much up there on windy days for them to use the Top of the World Studio much.

Karen was very lucky to get one of the micropartments—a nice word for "dorm rooms"—in the building, and since she works on the eighty-first floor, she has been commuting by elevator for a long time. There really isn't anywhere else for her to go, and the super—a big, muscular, older man named Johnny Wendt—told them that anyone who wanted to could try to ride it out here. There are maybe a thousand of them now, gathered in the floors between forty and fifty, far enough up not to drown and—if they're lucky—far enough down not to be carried off by the wind.

It's not much, but it beats being outside, she thinks. There is an enormous jam of people and vehicles down there, and none of them seem to be going anywhere when she can see them, under the streetlights, through the salt rain. Johnny has signs out inviting people to come up—between the cafeterias and stores in the building, and three different hotels, people could be fairly comfortable—but anyone who is in the street now is trying to get elsewhere, either to join family or because they don't trust a tall building.

"Damn foolish," says a voice behind her. She turns and sees it's Johnny standing in the corridor, his shirt soaked with sweat, his coverall much dirtier than she's ever seen it. "At least all my staff stood put. *They* understand that this place is as stable as a small mountain. We could save ten thousand lives here if people were smart enough to get inside." He peers at her for a second, and then says, "APDP. Eighty-first floor. Third desk to the right as you go in."

"Right," Karen says, glancing down. It makes her feel a little shy, these days, when anyone notices her; she's changed a lot since she used to audition and pal around with actors. Perhaps not for the better. . . .

"Well, I assume you're smart enough to stay away from the windows if the wind picks up," he says, "but we're rated up to Beaufort 30, and the storm isn't supposed to come near us. It's the Hudson we have to fear."

Water is already running a foot deep in the street below, and Karen shudders. "Will the building take it?"

"It'll have to. I've got a brand-new music-and-video rig in my apartment, and it's not paid for yet. The company would never let anything happen to it."

She laughs, not because it's funny but because he's a nice guy and clearly wants her to like him. He steps a little closer and looks down into the street as well. "Look at them. Can't they figure time? They won't get off the island before the worst of it hits. The surge is already on its way down the river."

"How high will it come?"

"Call it a hundred feet or so. That's what the meterology guys call an order-of-magnitude estimate. They mean more than ten and less than a thousand."

She sighs. "Is there anything we can all do?"

"I'm afraid most of you are just passengers," Johnny says. "Naw, I'm just looking to see if the streets are clear so that—shit."

At his voice, she looks and sees it too, even in the dim gray shapes up toward Times Square: a wall of water and people running from it. There is nothing at all for anyone to do; Johnny is on the phone telling his people to get out of the lower floors if they're there, but all that Karen sees is the gray-black surge below her, washing up to the third story, sweeping people along in it like struggling insects. There is a faint shudder through her feet as the surge wraps around the building.

"Suzette? Is that door holding?" Johnny is asking. "Okay, is everyone out? Check in with me!"

There's a very long pause.

"Okay," he says. "Go with the plan. No sense waiting any longer—no one else is coming through the lower doors."

"Er, what's the plan?" Karen asks.

"Anhh?" He hasn't heard her because she spoke very softly. Outside, there is now a rushing river in the streets; Broadway is filled with dark boiling water in the lights that shine down on it from the Dance Channel Tower.

"Uh, what plan? Just curious."

"Hang on—" he says, and raises a finger. He listens to the phone, says, "Good, right, okay," several times, and finally sighs. "Well, that's that. The plan is, we're flooding the lower floors, using the water from the rain pipes and the power drains. So we're putting clean water into the building up to a bit past 100 feet. With luck it will equalize pressures, to some extent, and make us a bit less likely to get cut off at the base and go over in the storm."

"Doesn't it kind of damage things?"

"Not like having the building fall over would." He grins at her, and she smiles back. When did she get this shy? Obviously he's hanging around because he wants to talk to her, and he's a nice guy.

Her phone rings, and she lifts it from her belt. She turns it on to find—"Mary Ann!"

"Yeah, I'm taking one of my breaks to see if you're okay. Did you get out of Manhattan?"

"No, but I don't think I could be any safer," she says. "Nowhere on the East Coast is safe, but at least I'm in a building that should stand up to this."

"That's something. Take care of yourself if you can."

"You too."

They chat for a few minutes; one thing you have to say for her, though

Mary Ann changed a lot as she became Synthi Venture and her career took off, she didn't get stuck on herself and she stayed in touch. There's not a lot to say—and there's always the possibility that this is their last conversation, Karen realizes, something Mary Ann is being careful not to mention—but they don't need to say much.

When they click off, minutes later, Johnny is still standing awkwardly in the hall, and finally he says, "I couldn't help overhearing, uh, and seeing a little of your screen, and, uh—"

"Mary Ann Waterhouse used to work next to my desk. We used to go to Equity calls together, back when I still thought I had a career on Broadway," Karen says, a little proudly. "I knew her a long time before she was Synthi Venture."

Johnny nods, clearly impressed, and now it looks like *he's* a little shy.

She glances out the window, and says, "Of course, nowadays you could have a career on Broadway running a submarine."

Now it's his turn to give a nervous laugh. They stand there for a long time, watching the water get up to the eighth floor; there's nothing much for either of them to do. The powerchips will keep the building running, and hardly anyone needs data patterning.

Eventually someone shouts about what's happening on the downtown side of the building, and they run around to see what the searchlights can show them. Buildings as tall as forty stories are going over, but the World Trade Center seems to be holding firm.

Around dawn they eat; the water is still rising, but slowly, and finally they stagger off—to separate apartments, Karen thinks a little wistfully—and fall asleep.

She need not have worried; there will be plenty of time. It is not until October third, ten days later, that the water will fall far enough, and enough rubble will be cleared, for them to leave the building. By that time, millions of New Yorkers will be dead, and the world changed utterly, but Johnny and Karen's greatest discomfort during the whole thing will be that, during the last week, the building ran out of soda, peanut butter, and mayonnaise.

Father Joseph urged people to accept evacuation, but since the church rode it out once, they are convinced it must again. It's strangely familiar in here, the same people, candlelight, the same odors—but the wind is rising fast. He wonders if the building will go over in a hurricane.

The thing that troubles him most is that he could not bring himself to tell them that he didn't believe it was a miracle before, finally, but merely luck. Plenty of other churches must have drowned.

He wonders what he has to say to them. The water has been running out, not in, at the mouth of the Shannon, and the wireless is saying the giant hurricane that has wrecked the States is headed here. He has cousins in Boston, and he hasn't heard a word. . . . They say most rivers have risen enough to drown their cities there, and that Florida is gone. . . .

There is a deep rumble like an oncoming train, and people huddle together. Father Joseph barely has time to say "Let us pray" before, as abruptly as a foot descending on a cockroach, the storm surge—twice as high as any mountain in Ireland—slams church, congregation, and all into oblivion. Moving at hundreds of miles per hour, the surge washes clear across the island; within hours it will penetrate Britain so deeply that a torrent twenty miles wide will flow up the Mersey and down through the Trent, tear a great open bay into the face of Europe where the Zuider Zee once stood, and still have force enough to flood St. Petersburg to a depth of ten meters.

Nodes collapse and packets are rerouted in the global data system; much like their namesakes, datarodents flee the places that are drowning, and copy themselves endlessly through what remains, up through satellites and down through fibrop. They begin to find each other, to merge, to seek more of their kind—there are moments of recognition, and then, because more data must be assembled to find out what they are to do, they join up and seek together. . . .

Carla Tynan wakes up reaching for the jack in her head. She really needs to get off the net for a while, she's feeling badly disoriented . . . more memories and processors come online, and in a millisecond or so she feels more like herself, but still she needs food and exercise, she's been on a long time—

She remembers, and begins to scream. She reaches for her body, over and over, thousands of times per second, but she can't find it. She reaches for knowledge about herself, and she finds the reports of the Honiara Police, the pictures of her bloody, cratered body on the hotel room bed.

What Louie chose to do has been forced on her. She reaches for him, through the antennas—he is now less than two light-hours away. But at the speeds with which she lives in the net, she will endure centuries before she is able to hear his comforting voice, and to cry in the awareness of his affection.

On September 22, as Clem reaches with an outflow jet into the Bay of Campeche and stirs up the eye of a new storm, Louie Tynan crosses Saturn's orbit. The catastrophe sweeping over the Earth is beyond his power to do anything about; Louie-on-the-moon is now pouring data to him, TV, XV feed, everything. He is everywhere and all these things are happening to him.

With his knowledge of all of human history, he is appalled but not shocked. His own estimate is that a billion people will die next week.

He is still moving at almost five astronomical units per day, and he is now only nine and a half AU from the sun itself. The fastest way to get there, he assures himself again and again, is to overshoot and brake, using the sun to make the turn, then Mercury and Venus and the sun's gravity behind him to slow him down.

But he keeps rechecking.

He wonders why he feels so strong an attachment to the Earth he left. He certainly wasn't all that eager to have his feet on it while he had feet. He never did like people much, for that matter. And yet here he is, frantic to go to their rescue.

Maybe it's just in the nature of a pattern-making system to want to preserve the original. It's something to think about, anyway, while he throws the plasma stream out in front of himself, checks the strains and accelerations, and just hopes the whole thing will hold together. It occurs to him that he's cut the margins close, and despite the speed of his reactions and the volume of data that he processes, he might turn out to be wrong.

"Wrong" in this case is what would happen if 2026RU broke up under the strains it's being subjected to. If that happened, a few pieces, carrying various of Louie's processors with them, would dive into the sun, a situation which is about as close to a snowball in hell as reality ever gets, and the other chunks would continue, after close passes at the sun, on hyperbolic orbits right out of the solar system and into eternity; after a few tens of thousands of years, a few of them might enter some other star system, but most would end up permanently in the dark between the stars on the fringes of the galaxy.

Louie's guess is that two or three of the biggest chunks might still have enough of him on them to remain conscious, and enough replicators to start re-engineering themselves a way back . . . probably some of him would get back to the solar system in another hundred years or so. Always assuming the conscious chunks weren't the ones that plunged into the sun, and Louie's sense of the universe, as a man who was first trained as a pilot, is that the one law that holds absolutely is Murphy's. Louie-on-the-moon and the wiseguys could doubtless grab another cometoid—with what they've learned they could grab Pluto and Charon if need be—but it would be some months' delay, and, he repeats to himself, uselessly but every millisecond, *Earth doesn't have the time.*

He keeps doing his job but he also keeps rechecking his figures. To amuse himself on the side, he re-reads the *Aeneid* and does a statistical study . . . is there really any empirical basis for Murphy's Law? Throw out most of the battles in history, since bad luck on one side is good on the other. Throw out every election, ditto. Throw out various aboriginal people getting discovered, since it was seldom good luck for them. Look at efforts to fulfill the Weak Pareto Condition—the moral principle that Wilfredo Pareto identified in his economic and political studies, that a thing that benefits everyone and harms no one ought to be done.

Hmm. Define "everyone" and "no one." Does everyone include apes and dolphins, some of whom are smarter than severely retarded human beings? Or dogs, many of whom have more empathy than most human beings, or cats, who practice more courtesy?

And as for harming no one . . . what is the horse's point of view on domestication?

Rocks and ice don't have much viewpoint, though. So since what Louie is up to is going to turn the solar system into a much better place for life—which is capable of having a viewpoint . . . if this works he may be the biggest breach in Murphy's Law there's ever been, and certainly he is binding more information and energy in meaningful patterns. Just possibly Louie is humanity's biggest and most solid blow against entropy.

Which is not all that different from saying he's out to overthrow Murphy's Law. (With diligent effort, he has established that there is no statistical basis for Murphy's Law. He has also established that he believes in it anyway.) He just hopes Murphy hasn't heard about this. Murphy is known to be vindictive.

As he approaches the orbit of Mars on September 25, he tunes in to all the XV broadcasts he can find, relayed from Louie-on-the-moon, via two wiseguys, to him. He admits it's vanity; he's enjoying being seen from the Southern Hemisphere at sunset, as a huge comet with one bright sharp-edged linear tail stabbing toward the sun, and another long feathery one—surface evaporation and coolant venting—reaching back away, so that in the evening sky he seems to stretch across more than half of it.

It's especially fun from the viewpoints of *Innocent Age*, an Australian XV net that offers the viewpoints of (well-fed and -loved) young children around the world. Looking up from the veldt in the person of seven-year-old Alice Zulu, seeing the great streak of the comet seeming to touch the last dying ember of the sun, its tail arcing so far up toward the zenith . . . it's an experience he would not have missed.

The twenty-sixth finds him passing close to the sun, and every cable, strut, member, and line seems to scream. He's in too close to talk effectively to any of the wiseguys or to Louie-on-the-moon, and he's too busy anyway to think about anything to distract himself. The face of 2026RU is boiling

Hardshaw leans back and finishes her coffee. She used to count cups of the stuff and try to make sure she didn't consume too much; right now, too much doesn't seem possible. Someone hands her a hot dog and she folds it into her jaws, swallowing all but mechanically. She glances up into the concerned face of a woman she hasn't seen before, a gray-haired woman in a red apron; a closer look reveals that this woman is wearing the uniform of some convenience-store chain. "You okay, Ms. President?"

"I've been better. So you're catering for the government of the United States?"

"Yep. When this is over, we're going to have signs up every damn place saying 'Presidential Hot Dogs and Cheese Nachos.'" The gray-haired lady grins at her, and Brittany Lynn Hardshaw grins back.

"You know I worked at a convenience store when I was a kid?"

"Think I remember reading that in the text news."

"You know, looking back—I'm *still* glad I didn't stay with that job." It's not the best joke of Hardshaw's life, but the gray-haired woman laughs. Hardshaw sees that her nametag says she's "Lorraine." "You have kids or grandchildren, Lorraine?"

"Yep. Up the hill a bit, and we got a concrete foundation, and their dad's with'em. They should be fine."

"Well, when all this is over, you tell them from me—" Hardshaw thinks a long minute. To rebuild and go on? People do that. That she's counting them to rebuild America? Good question whether it will be America by the time it's rebuilt; who knows what kind of government or politics will come out of all this. "To vote Republican," she finishes.

Lorraine laughs. "Their dad'll shoot me, but I'll tell them. Herman and been canceling out each other's vote for years."

She goes off chuckling to tend the hot dog machine and coffee urn, and Hardshaw turns her attention back to the matters at hand.

"Boss?" One of the young men in a shirt that used to be white, still a tie that used to be red, is signaling for her attention.

"Yes?"

"We've got private-channel contact with Mary Ann Waterhouse—just called us up and gave us a data number to call, and it works."

"Put Ms. Waterhouse on."

The nice young man talks for a few moments more, and then brings over helmet and goggles, and Hardshaw pulls them on.

Her eyes clear in a moment, and she finds that she's trudging up the trail to Jesse. This road would have been moderately tough, at least for someone out of shape, in dry weather, back before Clem, and now it's more like wading upstream in ankle-deep water. The road that winds up from Oaxaca to Monte Alban is narrow, and though it wasn't badly paved, it

then at last the disk vanishes against the Earth for a long count, before finally one sees a burst of clouds below.

Exactly as planned, Louie has begun to darken the Pacific sky.

The terminator line is just now at the peaks of the Andes in Chile and Argentina, and the sun will soon be going down across North America as well, so that it's only about five hours till night begins to roll across the Pacific. Meanwhile, ten ice Frisbees per hour whip from Louie's launchers, spiraling down toward the Earth from where 2026RU is at the moment in about the same longitude as Cape Town, and tearing into the thin edge of the outer air over the ocean, forming great streaks of ice crystals.

The phone rings in the beautiful old house that overlooks the sea; it's late in the evening, and Dr. Nathan Zulu had been about to go to bed after spending some hours grading sophomore literature papers.

"Dr. Zulu, hello."

"Who is this, please?" The video screen is dark.

The image that forms is animated, not terribly well. "My name is Louie Tynan—"

"Yes, sir!" He wonders when this strange dream began.

"I have a large favor to ask of you; could you get Alice to put on her data jack, and come out in the backyard to look at something in, oh, say, fifteen minutes?"

With the perfect, absurd logic of dreams, he points out that it's way past her bedtime and she's already asleep, but Louie Tynan promises that this will be brief, and anyway, just this once. . . .

Still mostly expecting to wake up, he goes up and gets Alice, and in her pajamas and bathrobe, her data jack plugged in, she stands in the backyard, holding her father's hand, looking out over the big combers rolling in to St. Helena Bay. It is almost as bright as day in the light reflected by the enormous full-moon of 2026RU overhead. Only the brightest stars are visible in the glare.

Alice says nothing—she's barely awake—and he wonders if this is all a vivid dream—

Far out to the west, a glowing bar appears in the sky, like a long, thick white line. As they watch, for two minutes or so it grows longer and wider, and its ends begin to round. Then, when it is quite low to the horizon, it glows a bright orange, and then a sharp mixture of orange and white flame, leaving a long white streak behind itself like the biggest shooting star he's ever seen.

He feels Alice clutch his hand; she's staring at the sky open-mouthed as the huge object descends.

Minutes later, it has become a great, burning oval in the sky, ten times as wide as a full moon—and then, in a great rush, it shatters into uncountable shooting stars. Very faintly, just as the last shooting stars fade from the sky, they hear a booming rumble.

The phone in Nathan Zulu's pocket rings. He picks it up, and there's Louie Tynan. "May I speak to Alice, Dr. Zulu?"

He hands the phone to her, and hears Louie's voice asking "Did you like it?"

"It's really *flat*, sir," she says.

"That means 'good,' " Nathan adds over her shoulder.

Louie laughs. "There's a relief. I just wanted you to see that, Alice. I'm a big fan of *Innocent Age*."

"I'm a big fan of yours," she says, beaming.

They talk for a minute or two more, and then Tynan clicks off. Alice's eyes are shining, and she hardly stops babbling the whole time he carries her up to her bedroom and tucks her back into bed.

It occurs to him that it's not going to be easy to tell his daughter about Father Christmas, as his mother suggested he should do soon. She already believes in things that are a lot more impossible—because they're true.

The next paper on the pile to be graded is "Jung: Elements of the Fantastic in Everyday Life." Probably the boy cribbed it from somewhere. In a few minutes, Dr. Zulu is settled back in to grading. Even with the weird glow outside, and his daughter talking to comets, life goes on.

"That's the latest and strangest of it," Lynn says to President Hardshaw. "He just pitched one in over the South Atlantic for the hell of it. No reason as far as we can tell. But it's not like he's being secretive . . . just that he does so many things so fast that we can't quite keep up with all of it.

"Which reminds me, he did have good news. Louie says that he's already tried out the masers experimentally, and it looks like he'll be able to break the crystals into oxygen and hydrogen again as well."

"The crystals?" Hardshaw asks. She has to raise her voice slightly, because the salty rain pouring onto Charleston is beyond anything the Amazon ever got until now, but they're no longer afraid that the buildings won't hold.

"Well, when those ice disks burst from evaporation and the shock wave under them, twenty miles up, the water they release re-forms as ice crystals almost instantly. It's the crystals that form the clouds that block the sun. What Louie is worried about is how to remove the crystals on the night side

of the Earth, because at night they keep heat *in*. Apparently he has so way of using a maser—a microwave laser—to blow them apart so vig ously that the hydrogen separates from the oxygen, and the hydrogen mostly dribble off into space."

Hardshaw nods. "All right, that's good enough for me to fake it if I have to."

"And it's not the only strange thing, Ms. President. Reports fror are beginning to turn up in computer bulletin boards all over the proper citations and all. She's writing something like four scientifi per minute, and just throwing them to the winds."

"But is all this going to work, though?" Hardshaw asks. She ta sip of hot coffee. Outside, she knows the former West Virginia now the temporary site of the government of the United States in sandbags, and that two hundred Marines are fighting to keep place against the raging current in the street. Supposedly as soc lets up, even a little, that will stop running; meanwhile, semper they are out there in that rain so thick that to slip is to r "Before we talk more, compliments to the Commandant and and coffee for the Marines. If we have to we can let Cong

"Part of them are out there working with the Marine "The rest can starve, though." She turns to give the order to the screen. "What it looks like is that somehow she mean—is writing up all sorts of reports on ecological in that caught their attention at the science branch at NSA zapping the ice crystals with masers. It looks like most of go off into space, just as planned—its molecular velo escape velocity, and at that altitude about sixty perc directions will carry it away. The oxygen's another ma energy monoatomic oxygen is going to cause a lot

"Isn't that a good thing? I mean, won't that repair layer?"

"According to Carla it'll do more than that—th read the full paper, but according to the abstract t to be much thicker than it's ever been. That mean shut-out of ultraviolet light, and that means that a who see their way to the flowers by ultraviolet, find the flowers they're supposed to pollinate. So can be expected as ecological impacts during t

"There's definitely going to be a recovery

"Carla thinks so, anyway. And if you cou she and Louie both have brains trillions of tir I don't see that we can do much but take h

chaos, and between tidal forces and sudden releases of gas and water, every so often a plasma tower will crash to the surface, costing him thrust and just incidentally scaring the hell out of him. He can feel every groan and scream as the structures inside twist and wrench under the pressure of thousands of tons of reshaping ice; his surface instruments are blind in the white glare of his halo, as the great blazing sun, four times as wide as it is from Earth, pours energy into the gas envelope he's emitting. At least the halo is helping to keep the sun from hitting his ice directly.

Hours pass as he struggles to keep repairing what keeps falling apart. Robots are lost unpredictably into cracks and crevices, or as tunnels suddenly close around them. One whole processor bank near the surface goes, in an electronic scream so close in sensation to pain that he perceives no difference. He loses the sense of his physical configuration; he doesn't know exactly where all his parts are now, and matching his communications topology (which parts talk to each other) with his physical shape hasn't been possible for hours, and without that he can't migrate his consciousness to safer processors; he can only hope that his mind keeps running.

The sun is big, and its gravity is powerful. It takes Louie the better part of a day to roar around the back side of the sun from the Earth, finally slowly beginning his rise toward the cool depths of space again. Mercury comes and goes in a flash, Louie using its force to bend him on toward Venus and to drag him back as he goes by in retrograde. The enormous halo of the comet engulfs the entire tiny planet for an instant, and then he is beyond it and screaming up toward Venus on the twenty-eighth. A bigger planet, with its dense atmosphere, Venus is a bright white ball of light to his outer sensors. At the speed at which he's moving, it flashes by like Mercury before it, but he feels its drag more acutely. In the last few hours he's repaired much of the damage, found parts of himself and reconnected them, dumped the more hopeless junk into the automated factories to be recycled into replacement and repair parts.

He is going to make it. He finds it hard to believe, but it's true. A fast swing around the Earth-moon system, making a near approach to each (and how strange to feel Louie-on-the-moon reaching out to join him, now that lag time will get back to near zero), a great thunder of his remaining engines . . . and Louie settles into L-4.

L-4 is not so much a place as a description of a place; it is one of the five "Lagrange points," or "libration points," where the Earth and moon's gravity work together to stabilize the orbit. L-4 is found at the point ahead of the moon in orbit where the apex of an equilateral triangle with its base running through the centers of the Earth and moon would be; thus it is as far from the Earth as the moon is.

But the halo of a comet extends far beyond its icy head; as Louie comes to rest, the halo of gas is still swelling outward, no longer swept away by his motion, until finally it is larger than the Earth itself, though it is thinner than air in the stratosphere. From the few parts of the Earth with clear skies tonight, 2026RU (to name it physically), or Louie (to name it spiritually), looms brighter than the full moon, and fully seven times as wide.

He wishes he could stop to admire himself, but anyway it's a few hours till Alice will see him, and those are the eyes he really wants to see through. Meanwhile, the tractors and the factory press to their tasks like maniacs; he wants the "ice Frisbees" flying as soon as he can manage.

When Carla woke up and started to talk to them, the cyberneticists at NSA had a field day, at least until they got their evacuation order. They now had two cases of a personality surviving on the net after the originating body was gone. At the least, it would have made them more likely to believe Louie—had not the comet now in Earth orbit been a powerful enough argument by itself.

Louie and Carla's reunion is an event that the NSA offices in the center of North America, away from the storm, are desperately trying to record, though without success. There's a serious jam in the available bandwidth that seems to be the two of them trading and integrating data, and it's a good thing a couple of billion people have been knocked off-line, because Louie and Carla seem to be taking up ninety percent of what's been made available by that.

Why they both want to know all the archived records of every air pollution monitoring station in Bolivia—or the last two hundred years of hourly exchange rates from the Bank of France—or precinct by precinct electoral results correlated to census data for the state of Nevada in every local, state, and Federal election—is inexplicable, but they are grabbing onto it all. In the last three seconds, Carla broke through security into DoD's Genetic Engineering Labs, copied DNA maps from every species cataloged there, and zapped every one of them to Louie.

Whatever the hell they're doing, it's hard to object to it. Aside from not being able to stop them, neither the NSA in Denver, nor President Hardshaw in Charleston, would want Louie to stop the main thing he's doing.

Satellite pictures show it best. A great, whirling disk of ice, its diameter ten times the length of the old space station *Constitution*, bursts from the halo of the comet, trailing wisps of mist, glowing brilliant white in the sun. It swings ever nearer until it is huge in the screen, passes below, broad against the Earth, plunging down toward the churning Pacific.

The white glow in the sunlight becomes orange; then a reddish disk;

then at last the disk vanishes against the Earth for a long count, before finally one sees a burst of clouds below.

Exactly as planned, Louie has begun to darken the Pacific sky.

The terminator line is just now at the peaks of the Andes in Chile and Argentina, and the sun will soon be going down across North America as well, so that it's only about five hours till night begins to roll across the Pacific. Meanwhile, ten ice Frisbees per hour whip from Louie's launchers, spiraling down toward the Earth from where 2026RU is at the moment in about the same longitude as Cape Town, and tearing into the thin edge of the outer air over the ocean, forming great streaks of ice crystals.

The phone rings in the beautiful old house that overlooks the sea; it's late in the evening, and Dr. Nathan Zulu had been about to go to bed after spending some hours grading sophomore literature papers.

"Dr. Zulu, hello."

"Who is this, please?" The video screen is dark.

The image that forms is animated, not terribly well. "My name is Louie Tynan—"

"Yes, sir!" He wonders when this strange dream began.

"I have a large favor to ask of you; could you get Alice to put on her data jack, and come out in the backyard to look at something in, oh, say, fifteen minutes?"

With the perfect, absurd logic of dreams, he points out that it's way past her bedtime and she's already asleep, but Louie Tynan promises that this will be brief, and anyway, just this once. . . .

Still mostly expecting to wake up, he goes up and gets Alice, and in her pajamas and bathrobe, her data jack plugged in, she stands in the backyard, holding her father's hand, looking out over the big combers rolling in to St. Helena Bay. It is almost as bright as day in the light reflected by the enormous full-moon of 2026RU overhead. Only the brightest stars are visible in the glare.

Alice says nothing—she's barely awake—and he wonders if this is all a vivid dream—

Far out to the west, a glowing bar appears in the sky, like a long, thick white line. As they watch, for two minutes or so it grows longer and wider, and its ends begin to round. Then, when it is quite low to the horizon, it glows a bright orange, and then a sharp mixture of orange and white flame, leaving a long white streak behind itself like the biggest shooting star he's ever seen.

He feels Alice clutch his hand; she's staring at the sky open-mouthed as the huge object descends.

Minutes later, it has become a great, burning oval in the sky, ten times as wide as a full moon—and then, in a great rush, it shatters into uncountable shooting stars. Very faintly, just as the last shooting stars fade from the sky, they hear a booming rumble.

The phone in Nathan Zulu's pocket rings. He picks it up, and there's Louie Tynan. "May I speak to Alice, Dr. Zulu?"

He hands the phone to her, and hears Louie's voice asking "Did you like it?"

"It's really *flat*, sir," she says.

"That means 'good,'" Nathan adds over her shoulder.

Louie laughs. "There's a relief. I just wanted you to see that, Alice. I'm a big fan of *Innocent Age*."

"I'm a big fan of yours," she says, beaming.

They talk for a minute or two more, and then Tynan clicks off. Alice's eyes are shining, and she hardly stops babbling the whole time he carries her up to her bedroom and tucks her back into bed.

It occurs to him that it's not going to be easy to tell his daughter about Father Christmas, as his mother suggested he should do soon. She already believes in things that are a lot more impossible—because they're true.

The next paper on the pile to be graded is "Jung: Elements of the Fantastic in Everyday Life." Probably the boy cribbed it from somewhere. In a few minutes, Dr. Zulu is settled back in to grading. Even with the weird glow outside, and his daughter talking to comets, life goes on.

"That's the latest and strangest of it," Lynn says to President Hardshaw. "He just pitched one in over the South Atlantic for the hell of it. No reason as far as we can tell. But it's not like he's being secretive . . . just that he does so many things so fast that we can't quite keep up with all of it.

"Which reminds me, he did have good news. Louie says that he's already tried out the masers experimentally, and it looks like he'll be able to break the crystals into oxygen and hydrogen again as well."

"The crystals?" Hardshaw asks. She has to raise her voice slightly, because the salty rain pouring onto Charleston is beyond anything the Amazon ever got until now, but they're no longer afraid that the buildings won't hold.

"Well, when those ice disks burst from evaporation and the shock wave under them, twenty miles up, the water they release re-forms as ice crystals almost instantly. It's the crystals that form the clouds that block the sun. What Louie is worried about is how to remove the crystals on the night side of the Earth, because at night they keep heat *in*. Apparently he has some way of using a maser—a microwave laser—to blow them apart so vigorously that the hydrogen separates from the oxygen, and the hydrogen will mostly dribble off into space."

Hardshaw nods. "All right, that's good enough for me to fake it with if I have to."

"And it's not the only strange thing, Ms. President. Reports from Carla are beginning to turn up in computer bulletin boards all over the Earth—proper citations and all. She's writing something like four scientific papers per minute, and just throwing them to the winds."

"But is all this going to work, though?" Hardshaw asks. She takes a long sip of hot coffee. Outside, she knows the former West Virginia capital—now the temporary site of the government of the United States—is ringed in sandbags, and that two hundred Marines are fighting to keep the wall in place against the raging current in the street. Supposedly as soon as the rain lets up, even a little, that will stop running; meanwhile, semper fi and all that, they are out there in that rain so thick that to slip is to risk drowning. "Before we talk more, compliments to the Commandant and send out food and coffee for the Marines. If we have to we can let Congress starve."

"Part of them are out there working with the Marines," Lynn notes. "The rest can starve, though." She turns to give the order, then gets back to the screen. "What it looks like is that somehow she—Carla Tynan, I mean—is writing up all sorts of reports on ecological impacts. The paper that caught their attention at the science branch at NSA was this one about zapping the ice crystals with masers. It looks like most of the hydrogen will go off into space, just as planned—its molecular velocity is way above escape velocity, and at that altitude about sixty percent of the available directions will carry it away. The oxygen's another matter; that much high-energy monoatomic oxygen is going to cause a lot of ozone formation."

"Isn't that a good thing? I mean, won't that repair the holes in the ozone layer?"

"According to Carla it'll do more than that—they haven't had time to read the full paper, but according to the abstract the ozone layer is going to be much thicker than it's ever been. That means a much more complete shut-out of ultraviolet light, and that means that a lot of pollinating insects, who see their way to the flowers by ultraviolet, aren't going to be able to find the flowers they're supposed to pollinate. So she's giving notes on what can be expected as ecological impacts during the recovery."

"There's definitely going to be a recovery?"

"Carla thinks so, anyway. And if you count raw processing capability, she and Louie both have brains trillions of times the size of either of ours. I don't see that we can do much but take her word for it."

Hardshaw leans back and finishes her coffee. She used to count cups of the stuff and try to make sure she didn't consume too much; right now, too much doesn't seem possible. Someone hands her a hot dog and she folds it into her jaws, swallowing all but mechanically. She glances up into the concerned face of a woman she hasn't seen before, a gray-haired woman in a red apron; a closer look reveals that this woman is wearing the uniform of some convenience-store chain. "You okay, Ms. President?"

"I've been better. So you're catering for the government of the United States?"

"Yep. When this is over, we're going to have signs up every damn place saying 'Presidential Hot Dogs and Cheese Nachos.' " The gray-haired lady grins at her, and Brittany Lynn Hardshaw grins back.

"You know I worked at a convenience store when I was a kid?"

"Think I remember reading that in the text news."

"You know, looking back—I'm *still* glad I didn't stay with that job." It's not the best joke of Hardshaw's life, but the gray-haired woman laughs. Hardshaw sees that her nametag says she's "Lorraine." "You have kids or grandchildren, Lorraine?"

"Yep. Up the hill a bit, and we got a concrete foundation, and their dad's with 'em. They should be fine."

"Well, when all this is over, you tell them from me—" Hardshaw thinks for a long minute. To rebuild and go on? People do that. That she's counting on them to rebuild America? Good question whether it will be America by the time it's rebuilt; who knows what kind of government or politics will come out of all this. "To vote Republican," she finishes.

Lorraine laughs. "Their dad'll shoot me, but I'll tell them. Herman and me's been canceling out each other's vote for years."

She goes off chuckling to tend the hot dog machine and coffee urn, and Hardshaw turns her attention back to the matters at hand.

"Boss?" One of the young men in a shirt that used to be white, still wearing a tie that used to be red, is signaling for her attention.

"Yes?"

"We've got private-channel contact with Mary Ann Waterhouse— Carla just called us up and gave us a data number to call, and it works."

"Put Ms. Waterhouse on."

The nice young man talks for a few moments more, and then brings over a scalpnet and goggles, and Hardshaw pulls them on.

Her eyes clear in a moment, and she finds that she's trudging up the trail beside Jesse. This road would have been moderately tough, at least for anyone out of shape, in dry weather, back before Clem, and now it's more like wading upstream in ankle-deep water. The road that winds up from Oaxaca to Monte Alban is narrow, and though it wasn't badly paved, it certainly wasn't well-maintained. Hardshaw has a vague memory, from Mary Ann, of visiting this place back when she was just starting out in XV, and of looking down from the high mountain to the sprawling white city below. It must have been very beautiful, in the deep greens of the volcanic soils in the area, and perhaps it will be again some day.

But for right now, the road is barely visible forty yards ahead. "This is the President, Jesse," she says through Mary Ann's body, and she feels somehow the billion people tuned in through her to the situation.

"Hello," he says. "It looks like we'll be getting up there soon. Louie Tynan just plugged in to talk to me for a few minutes via Mary Ann; it sounds like he and Carla have been arranging something, up ahead, ever since they contacted us and redirected the parade. I don't know how he's doing it but somehow he's been turning down the rain for the last minute or two, and he says the skies are going to clear just as we get there, but it won't last long. I really don't know what-all they're up to."

"Neither do we. You mean Louie and Carla?"

"Yeah."

"We can only hope they like us; between the two of them they can do whatever they like to the planet. How's the march going?"

"Well, we lost a lot of people who just wanted a roof and a cot in Oaxaca, but we gained a lot of others who either already had shelter or had given up hope. As far as people running back to check can find out, we've got a hundred thousand people with us. It should take about four hours for all of them to get into Monte Alban. After that, god only knows what's going to happen."

"I understand, Jesse. No one's expecting you to run this or control it. Just keep me up to date as best you can."

They talk for a minute or two more; it sounds as if the crowd size roughly doubled in Oaxaca, because so many people from the surrounding valleys poured in there to wait to join them. Oaxaca itself came through in surprisingly good shape—far enough up in the hills to get nothing more than the terrible drenching everywhere else is getting, and some high winds. What Jesse could see of the old town looked surprisingly good; the Zócalo was holding up well, and if—or when, if Carla and Louie could be believed—the sun ever returned to Oaxaca, it would be as comfortable as ever. Hardshaw feels Mary Ann's memory of sitting out there in the early morning sunshine, the bright light and warm wind filling the square with a kind of vibrating life, the intricate wrought ironwork of the central structure etched in pure white against the deep blue of the sky, and thinks to herself that when all this is over she might just decide to go down there and sit on a bench in the sun herself.

She hopes that didn't filter through to the billion people, for she's not sure that she wants that much company for the occasion.

"Jesse," she adds, "just to let people know . . . the capital of the United States is temporarily in Charleston, West Virginia. As soon as we can get transportation we'll try to move north and west, probably to Pierre, South Dakota, which has the facilities we need and doesn't seem to be too badly damaged. For those of you who are worrying still, all I can tell you is that we're only just beginning to get reliable reports back from the rest of the USA and from the world. Satellite radar imaging shows that large parts of Florida are probably gone, and we've only got a scattering of reports from the northern part of the state. We think the St. Lawrence has broken through the Mohawk Valley—at least there are reports of the Mohawk River running backwards—and is now flowing out through the Hudson. Manhattan's still there but the water is up to the fourth story on the few buildings still standing.

"California and the West Coast generally have to be figured at a total loss up to the Sierras. There are undoubtedly millions of people still alive west of the Sierras, and the governors of the mountain states are setting up receiving stations on the highways and will—hopefully—be able to mount rescue operations in force over the mountains sometime in the near future. Meanwhile, however, if you are in those areas, stay put until you find a means of traveling safely to the east, and then get east. There is safety, food, and shelter over the mountains.

"Let me also warn any nation or authority that may wish us ill that the United States does not renounce claims to any of its former territory, and we will oppose by force any unauthorized entrance into that territory by the armed forces of any other nation.

"And for the rest of it—I wish you all well, and to the best of my ability I will continue to do my job until I am relieved of it by legal authority. Good night and good luck."

She feels Mary Ann reacting inside, and it's a good reaction, one that seems to indicate that Hardshaw has hit the right tone.

She talks with Jesse a bit longer; the great horde of people streaming up the mountainside continues to wind its way up toward Monte Alban. The rain is warm, at least, and thinning as they go; she knows there are a thousand things that need her attention, but even being warm and sweaty, she loves being in a young body, climbing a mountain in a strange country, wondering what everyone around her is thinking. She can feel, though, that Mary Ann is getting a bit impatient at having a more than passive passenger, and in all fairness, after all, it's Mary Ann's life. So with a sigh inside, and a final flash of gratitude to Mary Ann, Brittany Lynn Hardshaw returns to the dark, stormy afternoon in Charleston, West Virginia.

The crews with bulldozers and sandbags are beginning to win the battle; the streets are now roaring torrents, but they are controlled torrents, carrying water off, and they are no longer threatening to rise above their sandbag-wall banks. Somehow in the past few minutes, a dozen or so messages trickling in from the city have begun to tell the story; Charleston is going to make it, and with Charleston, the Federal government. They're still in touch with thousands of little offices everywhere, and with about half the defense bases.

Hardshaw stands up, groaning, accepts another cup of coffee and a lot of warm praise for her speech. She reflects that she still has a United States a lot bigger, in people and land area, than Lincoln did. And if the storm is going to stop—and Louie and Carla say it is—then there will be a frontier again, the empty lands between the mountains and the new coastlines. With a bit of luck, maybe there's still something about Americans that will respond well to a frontier. . . .

Perhaps next week she'll sweet-talk Congress into doing something about the damned silly Twenty-Second Amendment. She wouldn't mind being the first third-term president since FDR, not if there's all this rebuilding to do, and a new frontier to develop.

They all look startled to see the President of the United States, bowl of convenience-store chili in one hand and immense cup of coffee in the other, laugh out loud. She doesn't tell them what it's about. It doesn't matter. They respond to the motion, not to the direction, and are comforted.

By nightfall, two hours later, desks are piled with papers and a steady stream of orders is flowing out through the net to Federal officials everywhere. Right now, they're mostly just counting the dead and the lost, and they don't even know for sure where the Mississippi is entering the Gulf of Mexico—or where the Gulf of Mexico has bulged in to—but they're on their way. The Federal Reserve is the chairman plus eight volunteers from the UWV Business School and forty computers; DoD has fewer generals than President Monroe got through the War of 1812 with; State, Interior, and Commerce are departments trying to find their subject matters—but it's all there. It hasn't fallen.

And at one small corner of a hotel, near the freeways on the edge of town, the Charleston office of the FBI is now officially the FBI. There are four agents, only one of whom was in Washington before the storm, arguing about what they can usefully do in the next few days, when suddenly their one computer beeps.

They turn to look at the screen, and they see what is being downloaded into memory: A REPORT ON THE LOCATION OF KEY WITNESSES AND EVIDENCE IN THE ASSASSINATIONS OF HARRIS DIEM, DIOGENES CALLARE, AND CARLA TYNAN, DEPOSITION BY CARLA TYNAN.

One of them is on the phone to the Attorney General immediately, only to find that she already has it. Whatever Louie and Carla are now, neither of them has any more patience with procedures and chains of command than they ever did.

The quietest patch of sky in the Northern Hemisphere is the one right above Novokuznetsk; there's not even cloud cover. John Klieg and Glinda Gray are sitting outside now, in the early summer sunlight. "So it's not ours anymore? Don't they have to pay us anything?" She doesn't really seem as bewildered as her question; he realizes she's just checking.

"I'm afraid not. The U.S. Constitution—if there's still a U.S.—wouldn't let them take property without compensation, but we sure aren't in the U.S. anymore. Always the danger in doing business overseas—getting nationalized."

"Are they going to let us leave?"

"Probably, but if you check the news I'd just as soon stay put a while. Right now everyone's still giving us credit; with a little luck we can wait till the storm blows over, then get back to the States." He reaches out and takes her hand. "You might figure that what we're going to do is take a long vacation—or a honeymoon, if we can find someone to marry us. Maybe one of these Siberian guys with the horns on his hat will shake a rattle over us or something."

She glances sideways at him, letting her hair fall onto her face, and it gets to him like it always does. "Is that a proposal, boss? Are you aware of the sexual harassment laws?"

"We're outside the United States, remember?"

"Well, damn, then I guess I'll have to accept. So we stick around here and let the restaurants and hotels give us credit because they all figure we're rich—"

"And because the American government is hiring us to get space launches flying, so we will have a paycheck. And before our welcome is entirely worn out, we'll skip town and leave our debts behind us."

"Why, Mr. Klieg, how appalling."

"You bet. Back to the States, I think. They're going to be doing a lot of rebuilding—which means lumber and concrete and steel, all that stuff, is going to be flowing around the economy. All I have to do is borrow some money here and there—and god knows there are enough bankers with faith in me—and get control of some of that stuff, and we're on our way again. I would bet that owning all the cement plants, or all the railroad yards, in an area where they're trying to rebuild, is going to be worth a pile. Hell, they'll want a domestic space launch facility soon enough, and I'm experienced at building an uninterruptible launch service."

She leans against him and he lets his arm slide around her. It's a funny thing, he knows that many people have suffered a lot these last few months, and he's lost a trillion bucks himself—has to be the first private businessman in history to do that—but somehow or other he doesn't mind a bit. It's the building up, not the having, that matters to him.

"You just don't despair, do you, John?"

"Not a damn bit. As long as there are two people out there who can do things for each other, there's a way for me to get between them and get a piece of it. Things are going to be moving around in the USA again—they've got new frontiers in all directions—and if you read your history, it's the guys like me who got rich off it. If you know where you got your money, you always know where you can get more." He kisses her tenderly. "Might be a lot of fun, to tell the truth; things had gotten a little dull this last decade, after we got too big to have to scramble. And one thing this last year has taught me is to love things that are real and tangible—like you, and Derry, and spending time with each other—instead of putting all my attention on silly abstractions like patents. I don't think I'll bother with technology again—it was all right in its way, but they can take it away from you so easily. When a man wants know-how, he can always just take it, use it, and not pay you; when you've got the only rail line, or the only steel mill or electric power plant or antimatter generator, anywhere near him, he'll pay you and be damned glad to do it."

Glinda snuggles closer. "Why, boss, you're making speeches. And besides, until yesterday you had the only working space launch facility on Earth—"

"But in Siberia. That's why we're going back to the States, sweetheart. It's not the kind of place where they'd ever take your railroad or your steel mill away from you."

They sit for a long time, and talk mostly about how they'll get things together enough for the trip back to the United States. Already he's gotten enough off the net to know that Las Vegas is making it through just fine—and west of there, right now, there's almost nothing reporting. He's found the frontier—all he has to do is get there and get his toll gates up and his imprint on things people need. There might be a couple of tight years, but Derry—and maybe a brother or sister or two—will never have to work a day in her life, and isn't that what life is all about? Building a secure future?

Above them, the blue skies of August roll on, occasional fluffy white clouds never blotting out the sun, and they stick around, like a couple of kids, to watch the first test shot, a morning satellite launch, rise on a pillar of flame and leave a white contrail streaking across the deep blue.

They're getting near the top, and Mary Ann and Jesse are holding hands and talking as they walk. "Can you feel them inside you right now?" Jesse asks.

"Carla comes and goes. She's very nice, really—quite courteous about the whole thing. Louie is a little abrupt but I like him." She pushes stray hair away from her face. With no makeup and her dirty jeans and T-shirt plastered to her by the rain and sweat, Mary Ann still has a cartoonish body, but she looks oddly human, as if with just a bit more effort she might blend right back into the human race she was dragged out of. Jesse likes that.

"Have they told you anything about what's going to happen?"

"Not really. I can make a couple of guesses. Louie and Carla now have control of all the XV feed on the planet. And according to the President they've also got the physical resources and control of information to do anything else they want. I think the new order for the planet is going to announce itself here, using us, taking advantage of all those cheap XV sets that were dropped to stop the Global Riot.

"And it's not a bad place for the purpose—almost the perfect setting for it. I was here a long time ago.

"Monte Alban is an old Zapotopec city—it was abandoned before the Spanish got here, so people don't even know what its Indian name was. When I was here they'd just finished putting in live interactive holography—and a transuper massively parallel computer to run it." She sighs. "That was my second assignment ever . . . it was a pretty strange time, Jesse."

"I've got time if you want to tell me. I'm interested."

"You and a billion listeners . . ."

"Is it personal?"

"Once half a billion people have experienced fucking you, and another half a billion have experienced having your vagina, 'personal' is a concept of limited utility, Jesse. No, I guess I was worried about boring them. But if anything important comes along, Louie or Carla can just break in, and if they're bored, maybe they'll turn it off and get into something real instead of this circus."

"Your net won't like you saying that." He grins at her and slides his arm up onto her shoulder; she reaches up to pull his hand down so that it rests on her breast.

"No, but they haven't gotten any paychecks to me lately, either, and once you tot up all the extra I'm going to make from working on my vacation, they'll consider themselves lucky to get anything at all out of me." She snuggles against him. "By the way, all you voyeurs, the biggest crisis in human history is going on and there are a lot of better places to get your information. It'll be an hour till we get to Monte Alban. Why don't you all go do something useful?" Then she adds to Jesse, "Not that they will," and gets a strange, faraway look before adding, "Carla says about six million people just unplugged, so there may be some hope for the world yet. All right, anyone still want to hear Mary Ann's Boring Reminiscences of the First Time Synthi Venture Went to Monte Alban?"

"On with the story," Jesse says.

"Okay, Mommy tell wittle feller her story." He tickles her for that one, and she shrieks and tickles back; they end up in a hug and kiss before going back to walking up the winding, muddy mountain road hand in hand. It's a lot of fun, and it suddenly occurs to Jesse how, despite having experienced XV most of his life, it's pretty rare to have encountered plain old spontaneous fun on it. He wonders if that's a function of the medium, or the net companies, or that the things they put XV people through destroy the capacity for that kind of pleasure. Mary Ann doesn't seem to have lost hers. . . .

They take a moment to get their breath, and they slow the pace so Mary Ann can talk comfortably.

"Anyway," she says, "it wasn't anything awful, but it was sort of the first time I realized I had signed up for more than I had bargained for. What happened was that the Mexican government was really determined to promote tourism down here, so they paid a big load of cash to Passionet to get it built up. And I was still very new to the whole business, so in the first place I wasn't used to the kind of beating your body takes to get sensations to come through for the audience—and therefore I was kind of unhappy about life in Oaxaca itself.

"The Presidente is a beautiful, beautiful hotel, you know, right on the Zócalo, and I'd never really traveled before, so here was this wonderful exotic place, and my first day here my new breasts and butt were so sore it was hard to walk.

"Then, too, the guy they assigned with me—he washed out shortly after—was not only rough with my body, but really stupid and self-centered, so that it wasn't any fun going anywhere with him. He was only interested in getting angles where the light was good for me to look at him—so there I'd be, looking around inside the Cathedral, and he'd be over posing in the sunlight and pouting if I didn't look his way, or I'd be watching the way the sunlight fell against the white buildings and he'd be trying to line himself up for some kind of film noir shadows-on-the-face number.

"The point where I finally gave up on the stupid bastard was when we went up to the Paseo Juárez—a big beautiful open space with a great Spanish colonial fountain at its center and tall trees all around—and every time I'd back up to get a view down one of the sidewalks toward that fountain, he'd shove his chiseled face in front of me.

"But Passionet was not pissed at him; they were mad at me because I wasn't staying on the basic script. Never mind that he was so stupid that they had to shut off the signal from him whenever he had to explain things to poor sweet big-titted Synthi, because all he could do was repeat what they said in his ear and even then they got it wrong. Never mind that he was acting like the place was a theme park. Never mind even that he obviously didn't have the slightest idea how to be the kind of guy anybody could fall in love with."

"Well, maybe they weren't pissed, but you said they got rid of him," Jesse reminds her.

Mary Ann scuffs at the mud, kicking a couple of rocks down the hillside. "Oh, no, it's consistent. He just didn't work out with the viewers. That's an okay way to be; the net execs don't understand why a shallow vain asshole with no brains doesn't build up an audience, because most of them are shallow vain assholes with no brains themselves, and don't understand how that could bother anyone. But when you do get someone who's catching on with an audience—like me, for instance, and Synthi Venture was a blazing success right from the start if you just count audience draw—then it's very important that she have a Great!—Big!—Huge!—Super!—Positive!—Big!—Smile!—Attitude!" She does a little cheerleader step and arm pump with each word, and Jesse catches a flash of the Mary Ann that never quite got over growing up in a mobile home court, where they raise pretty girls, but not homecoming queens or cheerleaders. He wonders a little if he missed something by not having anything to be permanently bitter about from his childhood; perhaps people will always think he's a little lacking in depth because of it.

She snorts a little, and goes on. "See, when you have someone who's really building up an audience, one of the things that's happening is that a lot of the audience is getting to see the world the way the person they're experiencing does. That's what they pay for, after all. And the last thing you want them to do is to see the world in a cynical way, or in any way that doesn't just love everything and everybody. I mean, if I started noticing that Lance Squarejaw, or whatever his name was—I can't even remember it— was a well-packaged subhuman, then apart from getting off the script, there was this little matter that it called into question the whole idea of seeing the world as a romance novel. Maybe there really weren't handsome lovers everywhere and maybe the most important thing about the news, or about Mexico, was not that it was a backdrop for that kind of story. Maybe it wasn't just like everywhere else with different sets and costumes, and if it wasn't, then just possibly it might be necessary to really know something about it. If I started rejecting the leading man, god knew where it was going to lead—maybe even to people starting to think that they might have to see and feel and think for themselves."

She shakes her head, hard, smearing the water and hair back off her face with her hands. "Damn. I'm still mad about it because I didn't let myself get mad about it in the first place." Jesse notices for the millionth time that her eyes really are as huge as they seem on XV, but that it's mostly because she has almost no fat in her face—diet or surgery, he's not sure which, but she has the face of a starvation victim.

She sighs. "Anyway, the point of all that was, I was already in deep with Passionet management before I went out to Monte Alban. They were watching me closely because they were afraid I'd screw them up by not taking the right attitude.

"So finally we got up to Monte Alban, and by pure accident it happened that the system was temporarily down—they'd had a lightning strike nearby and though there was no permanent damage, all the automatic shutdowns had tripped and it was taking a while to get everything back on line, checked out, and powered up.

"I don't know what exactly I can tell you about it; maybe you'll see it yourself. The first thing that happens when you walk into the city itself is you realize how terribly *old* it is. Of course there are sites in Europe, Asia, and Africa that are a lot older, and for that matter there are ones down in Yucatán that are a lot older . . . but it doesn't matter. The weather up here on the mountain, plus the climate, plus the long time the city's been abandoned, all combine to just overwhelm you—all that crumbling stone, all that feeling that people have been gone from here for a very long time. And from the city you feel like you can see a million miles—you look out over all this deep wet green land, and down across farms and towns and the city of Oaxaca, and you find yourself thinking about how long a century is and how many of them there have been, and that for centuries people stood here and looked down and thought—what? You'll never know, but the land must have looked something like this.

"And too it's quite a climb to get around on some parts of the ruins, and they're sort of complicated, so you find that after a short while you're starting to realize that there's no way you can absorb all of this, that every building could take you a day just to get to know, that the whole thing is so rich and complex—and we know nothing about the people, really, just the bits of art and objects they left behind, and the few things found in the few tombs that weren't robbed.

"I had gone to the museum down in Oaxaca, where they had those things—gold jewelry, and statues of jade and onyx, and so forth—and now I found myself turning my memories of those objects over and over in my head, trying to make them fit into this. And all this in the most perfect, clear sunlight, with the air scrubbed by the storm of the day before, and those deep, sharp shadows you get in the tropics etching the lines of the buildings at me. . . . There kept being delays and I kept exploring. Finally, when it became clear that it was going to be longer still, I climbed up on the Southern Pyramid and just sat there for an hour while they were getting everything together—Mr. Goodface didn't have the energy to come up after me and pose—looking out over that place that had stood abandoned for centuries, after being occupied by human beings for something like two thousand years.

"I felt the whole set of disappointments and annoyances from Oaxaca washing off me; there just wasn't much that could seem important against a backdrop of centuries.

"At that point I suppose they must have figured that they were finally getting the right attitude out of me. I didn't care; god, it was so beautiful. *This*—and the money, of course—was what I'd signed on to be rebuilt for XV to get."

She smiles at him, giving him a look from under the eyelashes that would have melted him even if he hadn't been half in love with it through most of high school. "So I suppose you can guess what happened. They told me they were ready and I came down off the Southern Pyramid—it's a huge thing, towers over everything else, and so as I was coming down there was a beautiful view of the whole valley, and my costar got the best visual he ever got from me, since he was part of that landscape.

"That was when I got into trouble. They ran the live holo overlay—supposedly it was archeological reconstruction. I suppose some of the people who had done it must have called themselves archeologists . . . but what happened was that all of a sudden we were looking at all these people in a mishmash of Aztec and Mayan and central-casting-barbarian outfits, doing all this stuff out of a Cecil B. DeMille epic. There was a little bit of 'Chariots of the Gods' stuff, and for the Christers there were a lot of Quetzalcoatl-was-Jesus stuff, and for the New Agers there was crystals and shamanism, and a fair amount of mild orgy and human sacrifice, your basic sex and violence mix, for everyone else . . . and the trouble was, I'd been to the museum, I'd read up on all this, I knew how bogus what I was seeing was, and how little evidence of any kind there was, and that even with so little evidence what I was seeing couldn't possibly have happened . . . it was all so Hollywood and so advo-hype and such a mixture of trendiness for different kinds of trendies . . ." Her voice trails off and she shakes her head, turning to throw a stone off into the brush. For a long time she just walks, a slow saunter that seems determined to enjoy the warm rain.

"So what happened?" Jesse finally asks.

"I started to laugh. Compared to what it was like without the holos, it was all just so pathetic and silly, so much a case of giving people the 'amazing' things they wanted to see instead of letting them face how incomprehensible and awesome it really was . . . well, the contrast was just *funny*, you'll have to trust me.

"Turned out Mr. Handsome Stupid, beside me, had really been in awe of the holos. Until those came on, all he'd seen was a pile of rocks. I completely destroyed that mood of awe that they were shooting for, and it made him feel belittled—which on a romance channel like Passionet is the one thing that can never happen to leading men. Moreover, our core audience was exactly the kind of people who most want to feel like they've been places without ever having to encounter anything too unfamiliar—and the laughter hit a raw nerve there." There's a deep bitterness in her voice, as if she were still spitting out blobs of the nastiness.

"They didn't fire you, though."

"No, but they gave me one last chance. Do well on the next job or it was all over."

"What was the next job?"

"They rented me to the Vice Channel, which put me in a whorehouse in Macao for three months. Under a different name—Passionet wanted to protect their investment in Synthi Venture—but that didn't make much difference to Mary Ann Waterhouse. At the end of it, I was delighted to go back and just get slammed around by million-dollar faces with three-dollar brains, and to get to see something other than three bedrooms, two dungeons, and the dorm."

Jesse's not sure what to say. He's been reminded, again, that Synthi is close to twice his age; hell, when she was his age, XV wasn't quite online yet. So about the time he'd have been saying his first words—or riding on Di's shoulders to a high school football game—Synthi was . . . well, it's kind of hard to imagine, is all.

She reaches for his hand, and they slide into walking with their arms around each other's waist. It makes them go more slowly, but Passionet can always run a few more commercials, or even some real news, if it gets dull.

The rain is very definitely beginning to slack off.

Embracing, touching each other through ten thousand antennas: Louie and Carla. They are feeling themselves, less and less, to "be" anywhere; the separation from the body is becoming more complete with each microsecond. Yet for reasons they cannot quite specify, for all their vast capabilities, Louie continues to reside mainly in the moon and 2026RU and Carla in the nets on Earth; they have decided to touch, but not to commingle.

During each second, Carla throws Louie more data, and she and Louie discuss endlessly, simulate outcomes, see what might work. There is more conversation between them in one second than a thousand biological people could have in a thousand years; the ideas they entertain for five seconds flower and become as elaborate, self-contradictory, present in as many forms and as epistemologically all-embracing, as Christianity, art, Japanese, or mathematics, and then are discarded or absorbed into others.

It is probably fair to say that they are still fond of each other—indeed, more than ever before, they are the only people for each other.

All the while, Louie idly does his original tasks. The wafers of ice hurtle down over the Pacific, leaving their streaks of ice crystals to block the sun; as the crystal clouds roll toward the terminator line, and it creeps toward them, his masers flash, heating the crystals enough to dissociate the hydrogen and oxygen, leaving the lighter hydrogen to escape back into space.

It takes him a while to realize, but when he does, he begins to study himself. Somehow or other, throwing Frisbees is still fun. He would have thought that that was glandular, or at least in some pleasure center in the brain, and thus would be something he would not have anymore. But though he no longer feels the physical need for sex, or hunger, or satiation—he still has fun, and he's still in love with Carla, and he's still sad about the way some things in his life turned out.

The deepest mystery of all—he's uploaded most of the available material from most libraries before he concludes that no one else knows any more than he does—is that he still laughs. In fact, the more he learns, the more he grows beyond mere human capacity, the more he laughs. He spends eight or nine seconds on that issue (the equivalent of a full conversation between the Athens of Pericles and Sevilla in the time of the great Caliphs, going on for a century) before he realizes it will not resolve, that it is beyond his understanding, and once he does, he laughs longer and harder than ever.

Carla interrupts his laughter, hears the joke, and laughs herself for a matter of some seconds. Then she fills him in on some of the scientific work she has been doing. After due study Carla has concluded that species loss due to the complete lack of ultraviolet light on the surface is unfortunate but not terribly large, that although many habitats have been destroyed and species lost with them, the extensive range of new habitats created will spawn a new panoply of species if only they are left undisturbed long enough. She has grabbed control of the planet's banks, though they don't know it yet, and she will move them toward the robot-based economy— one in which machines grind out what is necessary, and people make what it is good and healthy for them to make.

And she has decided quite definitely that the new wetlands, scour deserts, and mud plains will be left undisturbed.

One of them is on the phone to the Attorney General immediately, only to find that she already has it. Whatever Louie and Carla are now, neither of them has any more patience with procedures and chains of command than they ever did.

The quietest patch of sky in the Northern Hemisphere is the one right above Novokuznetsk; there's not even cloud cover. John Klieg and Glinda Gray are sitting outside now, in the early summer sunlight. "So it's not ours anymore? Don't they have to pay us anything?" She doesn't really seem as bewildered as her question; he realizes she's just checking.

"I'm afraid not. The U.S. Constitution—if there's still a U.S.—wouldn't let them take property without compensation, but we sure aren't in the U.S. anymore. Always the danger in doing business overseas—getting nationalized."

"Are they going to let us leave?"

"Probably, but if you check the news I'd just as soon stay put a while. Right now everyone's still giving us credit; with a little luck we can wait till the storm blows over, then get back to the States." He reaches out and takes her hand. "You might figure that what we're going to do is take a long vacation—or a honeymoon, if we can find someone to marry us. Maybe one of these Siberian guys with the horns on his hat will shake a rattle over us or something."

She glances sideways at him, letting her hair fall onto her face, and it gets to him like it always does. "Is that a proposal, boss? Are you aware of the sexual harassment laws?"

"We're outside the United States, remember?"

"Well, damn, then I guess I'll have to accept. So we stick around here and let the restaurants and hotels give us credit because they all figure we're rich—"

"And because the American government is hiring us to get space launches flying, so we will have a paycheck. And before our welcome is entirely worn out, we'll skip town and leave our debts behind us."

"Why, Mr. Klieg, how appalling."

"You bet. Back to the States, I think. They're going to be doing a lot of rebuilding—which means lumber and concrete and steel, all that stuff, is going to be flowing around the economy. All I have to do is borrow some money here and there—and god knows there are enough bankers with faith in me—and get control of some of that stuff, and we're on our way again. I would bet that owning all the cement plants, or all the railroad yards, in an area where they're trying to rebuild, is going to be worth a pile. Hell,

The crews with bulldozers and sandbags are beginning to win the battle; the streets are now roaring torrents, but they are controlled torrents, carrying water off, and they are no longer threatening to rise above their sandbag-wall banks. Somehow in the past few minutes, a dozen or so messages trickling in from the city have begun to tell the story; Charleston is going to make it, and with Charleston, the Federal government. They're still in touch with thousands of little offices everywhere, and with about half the defense bases.

Hardshaw stands up, groaning, accepts another cup of coffee and a lot of warm praise for her speech. She reflects that she still has a United States a lot bigger, in people and land area, than Lincoln did. And if the storm is going to stop—and Louie and Carla say it is—then there will be a frontier again, the empty lands between the mountains and the new coastlines. With a bit of luck, maybe there's still something about Americans that will respond well to a frontier. . . .

Perhaps next week she'll sweet-talk Congress into doing something about the damned silly Twenty-Second Amendment. She wouldn't mind being the first third-term president since FDR, not if there's all this rebuilding to do, and a new frontier to develop.

They all look startled to see the President of the United States, bowl of convenience-store chili in one hand and immense cup of coffee in the other, laugh out loud. She doesn't tell them what it's about. It doesn't matter. They respond to the motion, not to the direction, and are comforted.

By nightfall, two hours later, desks are piled with papers and a steady stream of orders is flowing out through the net to Federal officials everywhere. Right now, they're mostly just counting the dead and the lost, and they don't even know for sure where the Mississippi is entering the Gulf of Mexico—or where the Gulf of Mexico has bulged in to—but they're on their way. The Federal Reserve is the chairman plus eight volunteers from the UWV Business School and forty computers; DoD has fewer generals than President Monroe got through the War of 1812 with; State, Interior, and Commerce are departments trying to find their subject matters—but it's all there. It hasn't fallen.

And at one small corner of a hotel, near the freeways on the edge of town, the Charleston office of the FBI is now officially the FBI. There are four agents, only one of whom was in Washington before the storm, arguing about what they can usefully do in the next few days, when suddenly their one computer beeps.

They turn to look at the screen, and they see what is being downloaded into memory: A REPORT ON THE LOCATION OF KEY WITNESSES AND EVIDENCE IN THE ASSASSINATIONS OF HARRIS DIEM, DIOGENES CALLARE, AND CARLA TYNAN, DEPOSITION BY CARLA TYNAN.

and Jesse reaches out and takes her hand as she takes the step. His hand is young and strong, smooth and warm, and she feels a little tingle again. He smiles into her eyes. "Hi, Carla, what do we need to talk about?"

Carla speaks through Mary Ann's voice; the slight flat Midwestern drawl of the dead scientist feels, in Mary Ann's mouth, like a hard, squashed little egg. "I can tell you who killed your brother, and why, if you'd like to know. It's going to come out anyway—I've given the FBI the data—but I thought you might want to know ahead of time."

"Yeah, I'd like to." Jesse's eyes are all but expressionless; from within her body, Mary Ann wants to reach out and hold his hand.

A last gust of rain spatters down over them, and Carla adds, "Louie says sorry about that—he's bombing the clouds above with a lot of frozen nitrogen, and every so often he can't avoid having a little shower come your way. But he'll have the sky clear and blue by the time you get up there."

"That's okay," Jesse says. "Tell me about who killed Di."

Carla's voice has a strange tone of contempt to it. "You could call it a procedural error. Ever hear the phrase 'Use it or lose it'? Well, the Siberian government was just as plugged in as anyone else, and they were having him followed exactly because it had become clear he was important. Naturally that meant they tracked who he talked to most, officially, and that was me and Diem.

"So it occurred to somebody there that since he was a vital resource, and sometimes if you can't keep a resource yourself the best thing you can do is to deny it to others—like a bridge in wartime—well, then, there needed to be a contingency plan for getting rid of him. And being the military types they are, they put it into one of their high-level-top-secret-rapid-deployment-ready-to-go-yes-sir files."

It's strange that Carla's style of humor remains, but it doesn't always stay in the places in the conversation that it probably once did. Or perhaps Carla feels she can joke because after all she's describing the same thing that led to her own murder. Mary Ann wonders about that for only a moment before Carla sends her a burst of instant understanding—that she never did have much in the way of people skills, and she was always too clever with words for her own good.

"Anyway, the trouble was that it was in that kind of a military options package. Military guys are always afraid that if command and control get disrupted, they won't be able to get anyone to carry out plans, so quite often they build in a provision that, under specified circumstances, will activate a plan if communication is lost."

"But . . . you don't mean they just automatically set it to . . . well, to go off if they couldn't get each other on the phone?"

"Not exactly. There was a sliding scale of relative severity of action, and at each level more dangerous policies were authorized. After Abdulkashim was knocked out, his successors didn't bother to learn what was on the scale—they just understood it as up, up, and up. And being fairly typical of people in over their heads, whenever they didn't know what to do, they escalated. The real mystery is this—I can't find any evidence anyone gave the order. Something set them off, but I don't know what it was. Diem was killed first, and the other teams were set to go if their datarodents detected Diem's death. So that's how Di and I died. But there's no evidence that either the Siberians watching Diem got an order to kill him, or that they lost touch with their main base. The thing that started it all rolling is just . . . gone."

Jesse walks beside her for a long time, head down, hands in pockets. The sky is getting lighter, and the clouds are farther above them; in the clear white light, his color seems washed out, and even the bright reds and deep blues of the stones he keeps kicking out of his way seem more pale and washed out.

"So, anyway, something or other happened to put it in motion, the bureaucracy just kind of crunched, and the Siberian agents came and murdered my brother?"

"That's just about it exactly. Same reason they killed me." Carla uses Mary Ann's voice to sigh; Mary Ann can feel that it's only partly sincere, and receives, for that feeling, a warning from Carla not to share that perception with Jesse. "Jesse, it was a terrible thing, and we're going to deal with it. The whole Siberian spy system in the United States and Europe is going to be rolled up and caught, and the new revolutionary government there is going to catch and execute everyone remotely connected with this. And of course it won't bring Di back or help Lori or your nephews get over it. Any message for them, by the way? I've located them at a shelter in Grand Island, Nebraska, up on high ground—they're safe and comfortable and I should have a phone link there soon."

"I guess you can tell them that I love them and I'll come and see them as soon as I can," Jesse says.

"I thought you were entitled to know. I'll keep Mary Ann shut off for another half hour or so, but after that, as we near Monte Alban, we'll have to plug back into the net."

"What's going to happen there?" Jesse asks suddenly. "And why have you taken such an interest in us? I mean, we aren't the only people out there you could talk to, and you could just talk to everyone directly. What's going on?"

Carla chuckles dryly. "Louie and I are new at this. Think of this as burning a bush to get your attention."

And then Mary Ann is alone in her body. She reaches to take Jesse's hand, and stumbles a little. Instead, her arm goes around his waist, and his comes around her shoulders to steady her. He looks down into her eyes and sees that she's just Mary Ann, no one else in there, and kisses her forehead as gently as she imagines him kissing his nephews.

The warm wind blows around them, and it still smells different; she lifts her lips to kiss his mouth, and the kiss goes on for a long time. As they break apart, her eyes open to see patches of blue sky blowing in over the mountain, and a shaft of wet, runny yellow sunlight stabbing down into the white buildings and wide squares of Oaxaca below.

She also notices that the vanguard to the crowd has come around the corner and is cheering wildly. She turns and waves—not like a celebrity, she hopes, but just as if they were all her friends from high school—and when she turns to take Jesse's hand, she's got a big, completely un-Hollywood grin, which she can feel but is not seeing in her mind's eye. They walk a little faster, not to lose the crowd, but because it's getting close, and whatever it is that will happen on the mountain, they now trust in Louie and Carla enough to want it to happen.

Brittany Lynn Hardshaw has had several very productive hours, and she's now good and tired, but whatever this thing at Monte Alban might be, she will want to know about it. They haven't been able to raise Mary Ann Waterhouse via the net—Carla has told them that Mary Ann needs a little privacy, and then that after that Louie and Carla will need her full time.

The closest thing to a big story in the last few hours has been that they've been able to make contact with a lot of the UN agencies, here and there around the planet, and that although the central authority is gone, most of them seem to be content to keep functioning anyway; several of them are getting help and advice from Carla and Louie, and the mood in the places that can be contacted, anyway, seems upbeat. It's not so much that they expect things to come back together or to "get back to normal," but that there seems to be a growing sense in the world that life is going to go on, and once people are convinced of that, they have a way of seeing that it does.

There's a ping in the intercom, and Hardshaw picks it up. It's one of those nice White House kids that she brought along; unfortunately, the fact that they are now the White House staff for all practical purposes means that they're already acquiring the characteristic arrogance and irreverence. She has no doubt that within a few days they'll be offending Congress like professionals. "Ten minutes till we start getting signal from Monte Alban," the young woman says, ticking off from a notepad. "And I've got something that'll surprise you—a request for an interview and comments from Berlina Jameson, that reporter who puts together *Sniffings*. She says it doesn't need to take long and she knows you're busy, but she's got to get tape in the can soon and she'd like to have comments from you directly—the FBI and Attorney General have already given her short statements."

"FBI? I didn't even know they were still functioning. And this sounds like a criminal justice matter—which I didn't think we'd have anyone working on right now."

"There are eight of them, and so far they're functioning. They probably wouldn't be doing criminal justice, except that Carla dropped them a long roster of witnesses and evidence for investigating the assassinations. Abdulkashim's Siberians again, by the way—Carla's throwing about half of the gang to us and the other half to their own revolutionary government."

Hardshaw gives a low, animal grunt of satisfaction; the part of her that has never gotten over being a prosecutor says, "Just make sure that the most guilty ones go to the revolutionary government—so far, they have no Bill of Rights over there, and they can deal with it better than we can."

"Got it, boss." The young woman grins back at her. "So what should I tell Ms. Jameson? She's calling you, by the way, from her car, in the parking lot of the U of the Az, in Tucson."

U of the Az. Hardshaw mentally drafts a note to all staff that henceforth White House staff will distinguish itself from the rest of its generation by not pronouncing postal abbreviations, on penalty of being put in charge of liaison to the governor of the Wy for the next six years.

But time enough for that later—in fact, right now, with so much still not working and so much information about what is working not yet collected and collated, she does have time on her hands, and it never hurts to have good relations with the press, whoever they might be.

"Sure, get me Ms. Jameson—just let her know that we'll have to stop when whatever it is that's going to happen at Monte Alban happens."

It's less than a minute later when the two of them are linked up, and by that time Hardshaw knows what she has to say. "Well, obviously, we've had the case dropped into our lap, and we're going to pursue justice by whatever means we can. That will mean some arrests and prosecutions in the United States, seeking extradition in some other cases, and cooperating with Siberian and other law enforcement authorities."

"Does that include working with the United Nations?"

"If there is one. That organization's continued existence is not yet certain, though I have no doubt many of its agencies will continue, just as several of the old League of Nations entities were passed on to the UN."

Jameson nods, smiling at the remark; she and Hardshaw both know that if the UN proves unexpectedly resilient, it will cause no trouble, but if, as seems more likely, the UN is really gone, then it makes no commitments and expresses no regrets.

Hardshaw uses that instant to assess Jameson and decides that she likes her—according to the file she's an Afropean, so her nationalist credentials are impeccable, and the polite but very direct questions are a pleasure to answer—if there are any traps in them, they're obvious ones.

Then Jameson smiles, an engaging self-deprecating smile that gives Hardshaw the feeling that she's being taken into a confidence, made a best buddy of. Hardshaw recognizes that smile—it's the same one that one of her better investigating detectives used to use when he was working hard for a confession. For that matter it's the same one that—back when TV news was the big news—used to show up on the faces of network political reporters. It's a good thing, Hardshaw thinks, that she's a generation older than Berlina, and has dealt with exactly that kind of reporter in her younger days, because nowadays about the only place that you see it is on the XV channels that feature Plucky Girl Reporters.

"And if I may, Ms. President, as long as I have you here, do you have any idea what is going on at Monte Alban, or why it has suddenly become so important? So far all I can get from anyone who works for you is that they are watching the situation closely, and that's not exactly news since everyone is watching it closely, given that we're all experiencing through Synthi Venture."

"She wants to be known by her real name, Mary Ann Waterhouse," Hardshaw says. "Very pleasant and intelligent person, by the way." It's a classic evasion step; let's see if Jameson really can do this big-deal network reporter shtick.

"So can we say that you've had some private contact with her?" Jameson says. "Can I quote that—and may I ask if you were able to find out what's going to happen?"

Yessir, Hardshaw thinks, Jameson can do it. She scrawls a tiny note to herself—put Jameson on the special list of reporters the President talks to unofficially; here's a good person to leak to when she needs one.

"Those are several different questions. Yes, I've talked with Mary Ann Waterhouse—she and her companion, Jesse Callare, are just fine. And they don't know what's planned, either. Louie and Carla are doing their own thing with it. Mary Ann happens to be useful because through her Passionet link she's a way for Carla and Louie to send us whatever it is that they want to send us. But Jesse and Mary Ann aren't in charge of it—they're more passengers than anything else."

Jameson bites her lip. "I know I'm doing my first Presidential interview, because I just thought of a question I'm a little afraid to ask."

Hardshaw grins at her, a big, toothy beaming grin that looks superficially friendly and that Hardshaw has cultivated for a long time—because it can also look as if she's baring her teeth and getting ready to spring.

Hardshaw remembers what her first supervisor at the County Prosecutor's office told her: "When you're in politics, reporters should be your spaniels, so you pet them on the head, and you throw things out for them to chase, and you tell them what good doggies they are—but you've got to hit them with the newspaper every now and then, or they'll pee on your carpet." It's about time to make sure this reporter feels a bit threatened. "Well, if I don't like the question, I can always kill the interview."

"God knows, I'm aware of that, Ms. President, but if I don't try I'll kick myself tomorrow." Jameson's grin back is just as predatory. My, yes, there is going to be a third-term campaign, and here is someone Hardshaw is going to talk to. Jameson lets it hang just long enough, and then says, "You said Jesse and Mary Ann are more passengers than anything else? But isn't that—well, what all of us are, and most especially you?"

It's a great question. Now all Hardshaw needs is a great answer. She does the usual stall—sits back, takes a deep breath, looks as thoughtful as she can. Finally she resorts to the oldest tactic of all, telling the truth. "I hadn't thought of it that way, but you're right. And it's been getting to be that way for a long time. In some way that we don't really understand, for decades the old system where 'I say to a man go, and he goeth' has been collapsing, so that nowadays we all talk and act, talk and act, in ceaseless communication, with nobody at the top of the ladder, and what gets done is what gets done. And now we've got a whole new world to build—not quite starting from scratch, but near enough—and there are half a dozen things we've never had before, starting with Louie and Carla themselves, out there to be gotten used to. I guess what we do, all of us, most especially including me, is stay loose and do what seems right wherever our reach extends—and recognize that that is not very far."

There's a ping and a small inset screen appears in the larger screen where she's been talking to Jameson. It's the same young woman. "Boss, Mary Ann Waterhouse is back online and they're in the final approach up the hill to Monte Alban. Things should be starting, whatever 'things' are, in a few minutes."

An inspiration hits Hardshaw. "Is there a way for me to maintain this phone link to Ms. Jameson while she and I both experience it on XV?"

"Er, I'm sure there is—" she looks sideways, listens intently, nods a couple of times—"Yes there is, for sure. Instead of normal XV goggles we'll have you wear stereovisors. We'll blank most of the screen so you get the same effect as the goggles, but we'll give each of you an inset screen of the other in one corner of your vision."

Berlina Jameson looks startled, to say the least, and that's what Hardshaw had hoped for. When you run into smart, tough reporters, the thing to do is to co-opt them, and this will do it. "Well, fellow passenger,"

Hardshaw says—"and that's off the record because there are enough old voters out there who would confuse that with 'fellow traveler'—shall we get on the ride and see where history is taking us?"

"With you all the way, Ms. President."

Attagirl, Hardshaw thinks, *that's what I was hoping for.*

The first sight of Monte Alban, from the road, is not impressive until you realize what you are looking at. The mountain, and the road with it, slope up sharply into the visitor center, one of those ugly little block buildings that could just as easily be a highway patrol office, a maintenance building for a cemetery, or the conjugal-visit facility for a prison, anywhere on Earth.

What rises behind the visitor center looks like just more mountain; then you realize that it's man-made, and not by any modern men . . . and then you see the bits of ancient walls and surfaces, and realize how much the whole site towers above you.

The road winds after the visitor center, and if you take the turn to the right you find yourself among the Zapotec tombs outside the city proper, and come into Monte Alban itself by the back way; Mary Ann remembers more of it than she thought she would, and she doesn't need to check with Carla except to confirm that they should go in by the main way.

This means a left turn on the trail, and another long, surprising rise, followed by the startling entrance into a central courtyard. By now, there's more blue than white in the sky—Louie must really be bombing those clouds—and plenty of bright, early evening sunset.

There are two logical locations there for any really major event—the Southern Pyramid, which towers over the whole site, and the Northern Platform, with its superb view of the whole site and of the surrounding area. *Which?* Mary Ann thinks.

Neither. Use Building J, in the middle, Carla responds at once. *The holo facilities are better set up there, too.*

You're not going to run those horrible holo films of human sacrifices and priestly orgies and all that? Mary Ann asks, her esthetic sense offended. *Surely you know that—*

We just need the projectors to help the effect, Carla says. *Really, we're not human anymore, but we're not as inhuman as that!*

Mary Ann laughs, and realizes that she can hear a billion people laughing along through Carla, in the distant way you can hear a party at the other end of a hotel corridor. Of course they all know pretty much what Mary Ann knows, and they're going to see the place through her eyes; she supposes this absolutely ruins Monte Alban for any future romance-oriented XV. Just one more fringe benefit. . . .

Jesse, beside her, says, "I suppose we'll have to talk about what we do while the crowd is coming in? There're supposed to be a hundred thousand of them, and even if you figure you can get twenty thousand into the city and another ten thousand or so watching on the Southern Pyramid and Northern Platform each, most people won't be close enough to see. And it's still going to take quite a while for them all to get in; the sun will be almost down before everyone has somewhere to be."

Carla speaks through Mary Ann. "Not to worry. I've got a few hundred police I've borrowed one way or another, and one battalion of the Mexican Army, to get the crowd into place—they're all on earphone direct to me. It will move pretty fast. Just get up there, watch it all, and try to relax and wait. Louie and I will let you know when we're ready to start."

They have to be content with that. Building J is a sort of lumpy rock pile, not like any other pre-Columbian building anywhere in the hemisphere—it's asymmetrical, and tunneled all through like a kid's fort. The holo system they've put in here does its "adults only" late-night show on this building, decking it with visions of flowers and then giving the Euro and Japanese tourists a sadistic version in which young, plump girls, breasts and buttocks jiggling, dance naked up the stairs to be brought to orgasm with huge stone dildos, their throats then slit and their corpses, still impaled on the dildos, thrown down into the well. There is absolutely no basis in fact for it but it's probably Monte Alban's biggest moneymaker, and certainly most tourist guides say it's what you mustn't miss.

Now as Jesse and Mary Ann climb the long stairs, she has a stray vision of how they might have used her in such a video, displaying her expensive body, rebuilt as she is, her outsized breasts slapping up and down as she runs up the steps, her too-taut, too-small buttocks exposing her labia, and feels a little ill at it; she knows the vision is leaking through to the rest of the world (the Passionet staff, in the old days, would just have *loved* that) and that god knows how many men are getting their switches thrown by it.

Well, she'll never have an audience like this again. She sends them a solid wave of nausea; *now that technology is allowing us to feel what others feel, let's give them the whole works, shall we?*

They reach the main upper surface; anything farther than this will require using their hands to climb, and Carla tells them they can stop here.

When Jesse and Mary Ann look back, they see that the crowd is coming in great numbers. "Do we even know anyone's name anymore?" she asks. "The first few days there were so many, and I felt—oh, I don't know, at one with them. Of course I know it was an illusion and I didn't know anyone at all well . . . but I used to feel like most of these people were individuals, and like I had moved in among them, and now here I am seeing them as a big faceless Third World mass again."

Jesse glances at her sideways. "I was thinking I'd really like to find Tomás. It would be fun to see this with him, and I'm not really any use to you."

Mary Ann is about to say something when Carla's voice comes through. "Sure, go ahead—we can find you afterward."

Jesse kisses her, very nicely but very quickly, and he goes down the steps to fade into the great swirl of white shirts and white dresses made gray with rain. Mary Ann has a long moment of feeling very alone, and a deep wish to go down and do the same thing he's doing; she looks up and away and sees that there are long lines of people snaking up the side of the Southern Pyramid, filling in the surface in great blocks, the blocks then turning lighter as more white shirts and white dresses join. "It will be all white soon," she says.

No, each head and face forms a dark dot in it, see? And the dots move and change against each other, and you can see that individuals walk differently. They don't completely disappear into a faceless mass unless you make the effort to see them that way, Carla's voice says, in Mary Ann's head.

Mary Ann sighs. She's feeling very strongly that all she is here is an expensive piece of broadcasting equipment, and although for once it's not her breasts but her rebuilt skull that they want, it comes down to the same thing.

She's amazed at the wounded feeling that comes to her from Carla at that. *I hope we haven't made you feel that way. We like you a lot, Mary Ann, and we know a lot about you, you know—we've looked at every bit of the record, including all the transcripts that Passionet kept on you. No one has ever known you better, and you were our choice for this because we preferred to work with you.*

Mary Ann sits down on one of the blocks of stone, hugging herself. The water from the cool stone is soaking through her jeans, but she's already so wet that it doesn't matter much. It's not a matter of feeling used, she realizes, but a matter of feeling herself vanish into something much bigger than merely a crowd. No matter how much by choice, hers and others', she is standing right here, and everything flows out from this moment—

She feels Carla laughing gently, and Louie joining in. There's empathy in it, because, she suddenly realizes, certainly neither of them would have chosen to be what they have become . . . and a sense of comedy rooted in the fact that no, it's not true at all that it all depends upon her—if this doesn't work out, there are many, many more experiments to try, so there is much to be gained but little to lose, except that both of them feel somehow that it might be better drama, a better story, if it happens today, on the day that—

My god. Clem's eye will breach in a matter of—minutes. The superhurricanes are beginning to succumb to the ice Frisbees. So that's what they're here for? To celebrate?

Partly, Louie admits. *Seems like people might enjoy having that announced. But also because this is a good setting, we like and trust you, and so it seemed like the time and place to do this.*

The crowd outside by now has reached the point where the gates and pathways into the ruined city are clogging, so that there are great pileups of people waiting on the rain-wet green slopes, and then a clot at each entryway, and finally a relatively open, swift-moving flow after the gate.

"Why are they all in white?" Mary Ann asks suddenly.

They're not. If you look around you'll see the occasional suit and now and then a dress in bright colors. But for most of them, white is their best clothes, what you wear when something special happens—and so they found a way to change into their best clothes before they came up here. They are doing all of us considerable honor, Carla explains.

Mary Ann had understood that much, but it hadn't been what she meant. The question was why this should be anything to honor. She didn't necessarily see any reason why these people should feel happy or even interested in the chaos that had been made by people like her. Without the squabblings of power and the fussings of the media—and for that matter without the whole silly business of making things matter by making them happen to a woman with red hair, taut butt, and huge teats—wouldn't they be better off?

The clathrates were always down there waiting to be unlocked—they have done it in the past and they will do it again. Carla's voice is infinitely patient, but then given that Carla may very well be holding thousands of human-years of conversation with Louie between each word she speaks to Mary Ann, undoubtedly she can afford to be patient. *As for the rest . . . people make too much of that. They find you important because you are on XV, and they find XV important because it's interesting and something they have to go into the big town to try—the idea of having it in their homes, like los norteamericanos, is still strange to them. But none of that means they think they themselves are a faceless mass, and none of it means that they see themselves only in the light of the media from the wealthy nations.*

Mary Ann sits and thinks, her arms clutching hard at the long calves that she thinks probably are what got her here. It's true, of course, that like so many others, she always assumed that what people saw of themselves was how they thought of themselves . . . but then the thought comes to her, again and again, now that Carla has suggested it, that perhaps the image they had of themselves is the kind of thing that mattered, not to the people who swing the picks and wait the tables, but to the people sitting at the tables watching them do it. And if that should be the case, then . . . maybe people like Mary Ann, *or no, dammit, let's keep a little dignity and say people like Synthi Venture,* have had a slightly exaggerated notion of their own importance for a long time?

She looks up into the now-blue sky and sees how the surrounding valleys are bathed in sunlight, but also that Louie is holding the clouds all around back by main force, so that on the horizon in all directions there is a long, low blue streak like an inky smear that someone has put along the horizon of a painter's landscape. The low sun is warming everything rapidly, and sunlight dances on the water coating the ancient stones.

She laughs. Though water has run off these stones many times before, now that it's doing it in front of her, and people everywhere are seeing it through her eyes, it means something—it's the way that everyone will remember it forever. It's too much like what her old Uncle Jack, actually her father's uncle, used to say—"That goddam media makes too big a deal out of things."

But surely there *are* such things as big deals? Just because there were eight billion people on the planet—down from nine and a half billion six months ago—and on any given night, what was for their individual dinners mattered more to them than dynasties, economies, and all of religion and art . . . that didn't mean those things went away, and after all, those things also, partly, determined what was going to be for dinner or if there would be a dinner at all.

She sits up here and thinks to herself, *All that a billion people will get of this moment is what they get through me, and most of them will then take what they get through me and plug it into themselves. But all I will get is what I see, plus of course . . . my own feelings and experiences, which all of them get. They will eventually get up from the XV and think about things their fathers said fifty years ago, or smell the sauce of something cooking, or turn back to shoring up the sandbag walls of their shelters, but I will see and perceive less than anyone else here; I'm the only person here who will have only the media experience and nothing else.*

I am the least qualified person present.

She hears Carla and Louie laughing merrily in her head—and she finds herself joining them. It's a sudden, strange thought that two beings who for practical purposes can live a million years in a day, and who both have heard and laughed at every possible joke in every language, can still be surprised by a perception and laugh at it. *Well,* Carla says, *maybe the best thing to do is to get the show underway—Louie tells me that it's getting to be more and more work to keep the hole in the sky open. And no matter how late we start, there will still be people filing in.*

Mary Ann grins and says aloud, "Then you've worked in theatre, too."

She is rewarded for the second time with making the gods laugh. Then

Carla says, *Can you let me drive now?* and Mary Ann turns over control. She finds herself standing and walking to the platform edge; at once many thousands of heads turn toward her, and she hears the quiet purr of the holographic projectors moving into place. It is showtime.

She never feels herself begin to speak—just, suddenly, there she is.

The words themselves are not a speech—they resemble an induction of sorts, and the back of Mary Ann's mind wonders for an instant if maybe Carla and Louie are going to hypnotize everyone. There's a faint change in the tone of the holo projectors, *and now we are into the story*—

The great white eye, crawling across the Pacific, comes to us as a series of pictures, radar, infrared, visible light, and as a series of instrument maps, overlaying and flexing, and as this happens, Louie's voice in Mary Ann's mind speaks rapidly, just at the edge where her throat and lips can keep up with him, explaining what it is that is being looked at, how the great spot of low pressure moves heat from the too-warm oceans into the upper atmosphere. Then suddenly we see it from a plunging disk of ice, one of the Frisbees Louie has been throwing in their billions, to which he has— attached a camera? Is he simulating this? She has no way to know or ask and it's probably not important.

The great white mass wobbling in the Pacific draws nearer and nearer, and then there is a moment of flashing heat as the Frisbee vaporizes in the upper atmosphere, a blurring instant as thirty miles of ocean and storm below flick across the point of view before the camera flicks off. The image is brought back again, and we see the long, straight white shadows everywhere; and then we pull back to see the vast stream of Frisbees on the way . . . and we feel the scale of the shadow being woven of ice crystals, like jet contrails forming a gridwork umbrella over the Pacific.

The images flicker and dissolve again, and Mary Ann is distantly aware of a low moan running through the crowd. It sounds like people at the county fair, back in West Virginia when she was a kid, watching the fireworks and reacting to the sudden wonderful bursts of color. She wonders if out in the electronic world there are a billion "oohs" resounding, and very quietly Carla assures her there are—*You would be surprised at how many people have never thought of their home world as a planet; we are getting indications through the marketing feedback servers that people had never thought of the air as thin before, or realized that everything that lives, lives within six miles below or six miles above sea level. And at another whole set of minds reeling with the awareness that a planet is big. . . .*

Now Louie backs them up and tells them the story of the event from the methane release forward. They see the heat accumulate, watch as the sky becomes all but opaque to the infrared wavelengths, see the Pacific warming . . .

And then suddenly it is no longer about the storm; a part of Mary Ann, hearing the words she is speaking, makes the long leap of intuition just as Carla takes over for Louie in the narration. That little lurch lets Mary Ann get a momentary glimpse and see apparent-depth screens forming a hexagon around Building J, and transparent only to Mary Ann, so that everyone sees into one screen with full depth, and sees Mary Ann inside it. She didn't know they could do that with holograms—

Not till now, Louie says, with a warm chuckle in her mind. *Had to develop physics quite a bit to do it, in just this last hour. Helps that you and your clothes aren't too close to the stone or the sky in color. Now don't worry—we're going onward. . . .*

The story shifts again, and Carla takes them through human history— everything since *Homo sapiens* burst out of Africa—six times, one after another:

First we see humans squabbling and fighting, understand that among the first tools were the ones for killing each other, watch as the quarrelsome species spreads across the Earth, endlessly dividing itself into smaller and smaller segments of faith and language and endlessly finding in those self-made divisions a reason for butchering each other. We see the tools of butchery improved constantly, not just in cutting and puncturing screaming flesh but in organization and planning, so that the making of corpses becomes ever more efficient on an ever bigger scale. Nor is this made a tale of horror—or not entirely—for the images that flicker by share in the pleasures of this as well, the release from the boredom of daily work and slow accumulation of goods to a world where furor rages unbounded, where bodies are there to be cut, hurt, raped, where there are only victims and brutes and to know that one is a brute is an orgasm. The resources needed to do the job are grabbed from everywhere, torn from below the ground, cut out of the forests; whatever is needed for more slaughter is taken and turned to the purpose, and on that great flow of matériel, all of human economy is founded, so that humanity grows ever more rich as it falls ever more deeply into danger. The moment that brings us to the present, where the Earth itself can no longer contain the drive for slaughter, where the endless exultation of violence is on the brink of sending the system hurtling down into a collapse of life itself. . . .

And then, suddenly back to Africa, to see the story again, and this time we see humans making, creating, changing, ceaselessly taking the useless and random stuff of nature and turning it to beauty and use, the turning of the planet from a place where not more than fifty million human beings could live into one where billions live in comfort, from one where thoughts were barely more than images of the next day's hunt to one filled with stories and pictures, to a world alive with meaning where before there was only incoherent silence, until again the sea erupts with methane, and the world has reached the point where—like a whale caught in thin bindings of nylon that weigh only a tiny fraction of what it does—nature is inside meaning; the organization of the world has reached around and become the world, and from here on—

The story begins again. Humans go over the next hill, and there is new land; some stay to turn it into a place, and others go over another hill, and another. Each place found is finally made into a place encompassed, known, and understood—and then escaped from—partly to return with new eyes, and partly just to see the new. Finally, they all see through Louie's eyes as they walk the empty iron sands of Mars, and then look out into the heavens and see the cryogenic stormworlds that circle the gas giants, and beyond that, the near-absolute-zero balls that hang in the void on a tether of thin gravity, the comets of the Oort Cloud . . . and beyond that, the stars. . . .

The story begins again. Human beings learn the secret of separating labor from laborer, and then of binding the energies of nature, and then the conquest extends until—

The story begins again. Nature, pure and sweet, is slowly eaten and fouled—

The story begins again. And again, and again, and as each is told, Mary Ann—and the billion people who are living through her—feels each of them to be true, the way that things really happened, until finally. . . .

The truth is that every story finishes. Every one of these tales will find its way to its end, some as comedy and some as tragedy and some merely as a thing that happened. Yet some are more true than others; to see the world as a fall from purity into corruption, one must first learn to imagine a nature that never was, to paint over the real, blind, struggling, merciless, meaningless chaotic surface with smooth Disney technicolor that puts big eyes onto herbivores and bushy immigrant eyebrows onto the predators. To see the world as a quest to go over the next hill, one must first learn to ignore the vast uncountable number of human beings who by choice never go anywhere, to focus on the lone misfit who can't stay home and to ignore all the things people do so that we can look at a man sticking out against unclaimed land like an old-time actor against a painted backdrop. . . .

There is no lens that doesn't distort, no two lenses that can be true at once, and yet some distort less than others; and yet, again, however much the story and the picture might bend, seen through any of them, the story will finish in all of them.

And finally, with that understood, there comes the rest of the story, but unlabeled and meaningless, except that Mary Ann sees how it fits into the end of all the stories, like a plug into a socket, as if it were made for it.

Louie and Carla tell this part of the future together, so that Mary Ann is truly alone in her head, hearing the words come out of her mouth as the pictures scroll by. She sees Clem breaking up into a thousand tinier squalls and storms, scattering onto the land—it is going to be a long, foul winter in the Northern Hemisphere, but only a long, foul winter. She sees human beings moving back down onto the coastal plains and new cities rising, some on the sites of the old, some where new coastlines have shaped new harbors and river mouths.

And she sees Louie—or his physical manifestation in the one-time space station—making his way out again, to gather more comets and more material, to build up more replicators, and then—

Life spreads onto Mars first, and then Venus is spun up to rotational speed, cooled and seeded, and the moon itself is given a continuously replenishing supply of air (indeed, there is already a trace of air there now from what has drifted off 2026RU, and there will be much more—as she watches, she sees, a thousand years from now, the fall of rain on the lunar plains, and the green and blue moon that will rise in the skies of Earth).

She sees the many thousands of ships depart for distant stars; she sees the Earth become richer and more comfortable, and as industry moves into space, sees the green return to the Earth. . . .

And she understands that none of this is what must be (except that Louie seems determined to turn the solar system green), but only what human beings can choose to do—and the story moves on again. The time has come, finally, when the world is one whether it likes it or not, when every voice can be heard—indeed, every voice that speaks must be heard, forever. It all rests with the billion people experiencing directly, and with all those who will come to know of this in the next few days.

She understands now, too, that when the image stops, she will cease to be a witness and listener—cease to be the channel for all of this—and then finally she will be alone, for their last gift to her will be to turn off the transmitters in her head permanently. She is about to be alone, along with all the Earth's billions again.

It makes her think for a moment, while she can still see with god's eyes, and she sees Jesse, standing in the crowd and drinking it all in but unable to form it into words, a small brown child on his shoulders because the boy couldn't see and Jesse helps as naturally as he breathes, the boy's family around him—he is not, and never will be, one of them, but they can stand together. She looks beyond that to see Berlina Jameson and Brittany Lynn Hardshaw looking over the shoulders of the world, feels the sense of their own unimportance washing over the reporter and the President . . . and beyond them, she looks into the eyes of Louie and Carla. . . .

"You *are* gods," she breathes quietly, and is rewarded with a roar of laughter from them. *We aren't even fully human,* Louie explains.

And Carla adds, *Oh, no you don't. We've shown you the whole big Earth, and the universe beyond, and put it in your hands. You don't get to hand it back. We'll hang around to help out and see what you do—at least until we get bored—but we're not taking responsibility for this show. You want gods, make somebody else be god—and make it somebody bigger than yourself, not just smarter or stronger.*

Otherwise, Louie adds, *we might just decide to do a little idol-smashing. We're very glad we were once human and we wouldn't have missed it, so if you dummies don't appreciate being human, we just might decide to* make *you appreciate it.*

And with that they are gone from her head, and the holograms vanish. Mary Ann is standing alone on the roof of Building J, the stones laid thousands of years ago under her feet, looking out across the huge crowd. The last of the blazing red sunlight is just bouncing off the great wall of clouds around the space, and the valley below is dark—darker than it has been in a hundred years, for the power is still off in Oaxaca and the villages.

The vast crowd around her seems to be looking at her, but she isn't even sure how many of them, in the dim light of sunset, can pick her out from her background.

She is plain old Mary Ann Waterhouse again, though given what's been done to her body she will probably have a problem with backaches, a butt too scrawny to sit comfortably on, and pestering men for quite a while, at least until she gets some surgery.

There is a loud stir in the crowd, as if many thousands of people had turned, seen, and shouted, and then a roar as everyone turns to see. There is a great light in the clouds, and her first thought is that it's the moon—but it's much too big for the moon—and then the clouds roll away, and it's there.

2026RU, from which Louie is throwing Frisbees, in its libration-point orbit out in front of the moon, looms seven times as big as the full moon, for though the core of rock and ice is only a few hundred miles across, the thin cloud of gas and dust it gives off—too thin to breathe, and up close you wouldn't see it at all—reflects the sunlight brilliantly.

The great, dead city of Monte Alban, where once the heavens were worshipped, and where tens of thousands have just seen a vision of matters as they are, resounds with cheering as the new moon climbs into the sky.